Cassiel's Servant

TOR BOOKS BY JACQUELINE CAREY

KUSHIEL'S LEGACY

Kushiel's Dart

Kushiel's Chosen

Kushiel's Avatar

THE SUNDERING

Banewreaker

Godslayer

Miranda and Caliban

Starless

Cassiel's Servant

Jacqueline Carey

TOR PUBLISHING GROUP
NEW YORK

This is a work of fiction. All of the characters, organizations, and events portrayed in this novel are either products of the author's imagination or are used fictitiously.

CASSIEL'S SERVANT

Map by Jennifer Hanover

A Tor Book
Published by Tom Doherty Associates / Tor Publishing Group
120 Broadway
New York, NY 10271

www.tor-forge.com

The Library of Congress Cataloging-in-Publication Data is available upon request.

ISBN 978-1-250-20833-0 (hardcover)
ISBN 978-1-250-20835-4 (ebook)

First Edition: 2023

Printed in the United States of America

0 9 8 7 6 5 4 3 2 1

This book is dedicated in loving memory to my parents,
Robert and Martha Carey.

Innisclan
EIRE
Bryn Gorrydum
ALBA
THREE SISTERS
Morhban
Lusande River
TERRE
Kusheth
Hamarre
Siovale
Euskerria
ARAGONIA

N
W
E
S
THE FLATLANDS
SKALDIA
Azzalle
Rhenus River
Allthing (Selig's Steading)
Troyes-le-Mont
D'ANGE
Camlach
Gunter's Steading
L'Agnace
La Serenissima
CAERDICCA UNITAS
City of Elua
Milazza
Eisande
Marsilikos

Cassiel's Servant

CHAPTER ONE

"They're coming, they're coming!"

It was my younger brother Mahieu who brought the news, bursting into the manor's great room, breathless and flush-cheeked, dried burrs and brittle twigs caught in the shearling cuffs and collar of his oversized winter coat. A swirl of yelping hounds accompanied him.

Everyone looked at me, and my heart kicked inside my chest like a hare thumping an alarm on the frozen ground. For as long as I could remember, I'd been awaiting the moment when my destiny came calling; I'd been expecting it since I turned ten years of age some days ago. Nonetheless, it struck a punch to the gut. From the kitchen came the crashing sound of a piece of crockery falling to the floor and shattering.

Our father set aside the ledger he was reviewing and took the moment in hand. "Jehane, assist your mother; Luc, alert the stables," he instructed my older siblings. "Let us prepare to welcome our guests. Mahieu, how near are they?"

Mahieu dragged his sleeve over his nose before replying, leaving an ignominious trail of snot on the sheepskin. "A quarter hour." Our middle sister Honore, jiggling last-born baby Beatrice in her arms, caught my eye and gave me a grimace of disgust. I wanted to laugh at Mahieu's uncouth manners too, but the laughter that bubbled up from my belly caught in my throat and strangled there.

My entire life was about to change, and I was about to change with it. I swallowed hard, trying to force the lump in my throat down.

"Joscelin." My father's steady voice anchored me. He put his hands on my shoulders in a rare gesture of affection. It heartened me and I stood straighter, lifting my face to meet his gaze. "Today is a proud day."

In Terre d'Ange, noble families that honor tradition pledge a middle son—if they are fortunate enough to have one that survives into childhood—to the Cassiline Brotherhood, the order of austere warrior-priests sworn to serve Cassiel.

I was the middle son of House Verreuil.

We had been on the lookout for an emissary from the Prefect since before my tenth birthday last week, and I'd been veering wildly between exhilaration and apprehension. A noble calling was a blessing, but it meant leaving my childhood home and my entire family to pursue a rigorous path of honor and discipline.

Now I took a deep breath, willing my voice to sound as firm and sure as my father's. It *was* a proud day and I was determined not to let him see that it was a frightening day, too. "Yes, Father."

He gave my shoulders a squeeze and let me go.

My mother emerged from the kitchen, dusting her floury hands on her apron. In many noble households it would be reckoned beneath the dignity of the lady of the manor to bake bread for her family, but in the province of Siovale, we were descended from Blessed Elua's Companion Shemhazai, the divine scholar whose precept was *All Knowledge Is Worth Having*. According to my father, knowledge encompassed matters both homely and heady and no distinction in merit or worth might be drawn between the two, although I had never known him to try his hand at baking bread.

There was a faint furrow etched between my mother's brows. We looked nothing alike—she was slight and dark-haired, while my siblings and I bore the blond and blue-eyed stamp of House Verreuil and our father's lineage. All of her sons and daughters were tall for our respective ages; at ten years, I lacked but two inches of our mother's height. But there were unspoken ways in which we understood each other, she and I, and I could not fail to see the shadow of concern in her expression.

I was grateful when my mother did not voice those worries, only gave me a quick, fierce hug before departing to don attire appropriate for receiving guests. It would have been harder to bear if she'd coddled me.

Some quarter of an hour later, the Cassiline Brothers arrived.

My father and brothers and I awaited them in the courtyard. It was a cold, crisp late-winter day. As Mahieu had reported, there were two of them; one older and one younger. Although it was a momentous occasion in our household, they arrived without fanfare. Both sat easy and attentive in the saddle, clad in the unadorned ash-grey garments of their order. The twin daggers that Cassiline priests bore at all times were hidden by the folds of their heavy winter cloaks, but the hilts of the longswords strapped across their backs protruded over their shoulders, throwing cruciform shadows that stretched westward across the snow-dusted flagstones in the morning sunlight.

Catching sight of us, they nudged their mounts into a collected trot, the sound of well-shod hoofbeats echoing across the courtyard. My father raised a hand in greeting. The Cassilines drew rein and bowed in the saddle with effortless grace, forearms crossed, winter light glinting on their steel vambraces.

My elder brother Luc shot me a glance that might have been envy or pity or both. I ignored him and squared my shoulders.

"Well met, brethren," our father said. "I am the Chevalier Millard Verreuil. I pray you be welcome."

The older Cassiline bowed again, a gesture as natural as breathing. "Our thanks for your hospitality, my lord Verreuil. We would be honored to break bread with you." There was a faint huskiness to his voice. "I am Jacobe Ulric of the Cassiline Brotherhood." He nodded at his companion, who offered another bow. "And this is my student Léon, a cadet of the Third Cohort. I trust you know why we are here?"

"We do," my father affirmed.

Jacobe Ulric's gaze scanned my brothers and me before settling upon me as I stood between them, neither the oldest nor the youngest. "You must be Joscelin."

I stiffened my spine. "Yes, messire."

He smiled ever so slightly. "Very good."

After so long, it didn't seem quite real that this day was finally here. It felt as though I were in a waking dream. There was a flurry of activity as old Henri the ostler hurried out to tend to the horses and we proceeded into the manor to be greeted by my mother and sisters. I was surprised to see that Jacobe Ulric dismounted with some difficulty and walked with a pronounced limp, using the aid of a walking stick that had been lashed to his pack roll.

His student Léon saw me take notice. "It is an old injury," he murmured. "Do not make the mistake of thinking him any less the warrior for it."

I inclined my head in respect. "I will not."

Inside the manor, chaos swirled anew as our guests were divested of their cloaks and ushered to seats by the great fireplace, members of the household bustled in and out of the kitchen and larder, while an indeterminate number of tall, hairy Siovalese hounds milled around in circles, tongues lolling in excitement.

I was accustomed to my father being the calm center at the heart of our home, but this morning it was our visitors. Jacobe Ulric had accepted a seat by the fire and slung his baldric across the back of the chair. His walking stick was propped against it, and he stretched his bad leg toward the warmth of the fireplace, rubbing it absentmindedly. Léon stood beside him, at once attentive and at ease. Although the younger Cassiline had deigned to remove his cloak, he had retained his longsword. His vambraced arms were crossed before him, hands clad in chainmail gauntlets resting lightly on the hilts of the twin daggers at his hips. Like his tutor, he wore his hair bound in a warrior's club at the nape of his neck. He was poised and relaxed, his gaze alert.

That, I thought, was what a Cassiline Brother ought to look like—still and contained, unassuming and deadly.

Blessed Elua willing, I would be one someday, too. The thought made me shiver inside with a mixture of pride and apprehension.

Once the table was laid, we dined together without a great deal of ceremony. If there had been time for a hunt, we might have feted them properly, but the only correspondence we had received regarding their arrival was some months ago. Still, there was good crusty bread warm from the oven, honey and sheep's milk cheese, jams and compotes, a roasted capon and Aragonian ham sliced thin and translucent. I reckoned it was feast enough, and the Cassilines made no complaint of the meal.

Such is not to say it was a *comfortable* meal; it was not. We were strangers to each other, and their purpose, alluded to and yet unspoken, loomed over us.

Upon the conclusion of the meal, Jacobe Ulric set his wooden trencher aside and cleared his throat. He was some ten years older than my father—later, I understood it was more—with black hair greying to iron and an olive hue to his skin that hinted at southeastern heritage. His dark gaze met my father's with the same gravity I had noticed earlier.

"I knew your brother, my lord Verreuil," he said quietly.

The background murmur of whispers and babble among my siblings halted. My father seldom spoke of our uncle.

My father took a slow, deep breath. "Did you fight beside him, maître?" The title of respect meant Jacobe Ulric was a Master mentor within the Brotherhood itself.

"No." Master Jacobe shook his head. "I did not have that honor, but I had the honor of being one of his teachers, and it grieved me deeply to hear that he had been slain in the line of duty." He paused. "I'm sure you received correspondence from the Prefect when his arms were returned to the family, but I am grateful for the opportunity to say the words. Your brother died a noble death."

A muscle in my father's jaw twitched. "I never doubted it."

"I'm named for him, you know," Luc said abruptly. "But I'm the oldest."

"Yes." Master Jacobe's gaze shifted to him, touched with sympathy. "And I do not doubt in turn that you would do your uncle's memory honor, but as the eldest son, that role does not fall to you."

Across the table, my eldest sister pulled a face and mouthed the words to an old adage all of us had heard many times: *First-born son, father's strength; youngest son, mother's comfort.* It went without saying that a middle son was consigned to be dedicated to the Cassiline Brotherhood; it also went without saying that there were no such adages pertaining to the daughters of the old noble houses of Terre d'Ange.

Our mother gave her a stern glance and Jehane composed her expression, putting on an innocent look.

Oh, Elua! I would miss her.

I would miss them all; Father and Mother, all my sisters and brothers, all the household members whose families had served Verreuil for generations and were like family themselves, even the over-excitable hounds and our flocks of daft sheep.

My throat felt tight again.

I will not cry, I thought, fighting the sting of tears. *I will not cry.*

". . . trust you have your brother's weapons in keeping?" Jacobe Ulric was saying to my father.

"Of course." At the head of the table, my father half rose from his seat, then halted. "Joscelin," he said, bringing me back to the moment. "I do believe this task is yours. Kindly fetch them."

I nodded and hurried to obey.

My uncle Luc's blades and armor were stored in a trunk in my parents' bedchamber, wrapped in oilcloth. Once a year on my birthday, my father had opened the lid and shown them to me, explaining that they would be mine one day, but I had never been permitted to handle them. To my knowledge, they had lain untouched since before I was born. The bulky packet on top contained the vambraces and gauntlets, I assumed. The oilcloth was stiff and the twine tied around it fraying with age. I set the parcel carefully aside. Below it were the twin daggers, wrapped in a single packet.

Last was the longsword. I removed it with the reverence instilled in me, though in truth I felt a slight pang of disappointment upon seeing it at close range. The hilt that protruded from the wrappings was plain and tarnished and rusty, the leather binding on the grip brittle and cracking. Save for the sheer length of the parcel, it was not an impressive sight. Nonetheless, I gathered all three parcels with care and made my way back to the hall, struggling with the unwieldy weight of my uncle's weapons and praying I wouldn't drop them. Master Jacobe beckoned to me and I laid my burden on the table, relieved that I'd managed not to embarrass myself.

Somewhat to my surprise, it was the sword that he unwrapped first; very much to all of our surprise, he unsheathed the blade in one swift motion. It made a rasping sound as it slid free of the scabbard, followed by sharp hisses of indrawn breath around the table. I felt myself tense, my palms itching, my fingers curling into fists.

The Cassiline Brothers were elite warriors, trained from youth to serve as guards to the scions of Blessed Elua and his Companions. A great many rumors surrounded their training and discipline, including one that all D'Angelines held to be an article of faith: Cassilines only drew their swords to kill.

"Forgive me." Master Jacobe favored us with his slight smile and set the sword carefully on the table, resting his fingertips on its tarnished length. "I did not mean to cause alarm. I fear that betimes myth outpaces truth."

"So it's *not* true that you only draw your swords to kill?" My brother Luc sounded unwontedly aggrieved by the revelation.

Léon offered a reflexive bow, vambraces crossed. "Our mission is to protect and serve, young lord Verreuil," he said. "In adherence to our oaths, we never seek to end a life save in the most dire of circumstances. But a blade is a blade, and it must be properly maintained to be of service. For that, it must be drawn."

"This is a fine weapon forged by a master craftsman." Ulric tapped one finger on my uncle's sword. "Do not be deceived by its lack of adornment. The balance is impeccable. But it has not been properly maintained."

My father raised his eyebrows a fraction in an expression that Luc, Jehane, and I had tried to emulate on more than one occasion. "I was given to understand that dedicated Cassiline weapons should not be touched by undedicated hands," he said in a neutral tone. "I offer my sincere apologies if I was mistaken."

"You are quite correct, my lord Verreuil," Master Jacobe said. "And I offer *my* apologies on behalf of the Brotherhood. Guidance and dispensation should have been provided and were not."

"It would have been welcome," my mother observed.

"Yes, my lady." He inclined his head to her, folding his hands on the table. "I pray you understand, our numbers have dwindled," he said. "Fewer and fewer of the noble families raise sons taught to cherish the honor to be found in the service of the Cassiline Brotherhood. We are seen as—"

"Old-fashioned," Léon supplied.

"Old-fashioned," Master Jacobe Ulric agreed ruefully.

My father's expression shifted into something more complicated. "Betimes the old virtues are the best virtues."

I felt as though I ought to say something; what that might be, I didn't know. The fire crackled in the great hearth, hounds rooted around beneath the table for fallen crumbs and discarded bones. My brothers and sisters nudged each other and whispered in muted tones. All the adults were still, but they were still in different ways. I counted Léon as an adult; his stillness was one of discipline and training. Jacobe Ulric's stillness was patient and waiting. My father's was a contained and familiar stillness, that of a proud, self-sufficient nobleman around whom his household revolved.

My mother's stillness was unreadable. It had never until that moment occurred to me to wonder at her thoughts, to seek her counsel. Now it was too late.

I looked at my uncle's longsword lying on the table. At some point Léon had unwrapped the vambraces and the daggers, too. All the metal was tarnished and spotted with rust and none of the blades held an edge. The leather buckles of the vambraces were rotted in places and covered with white blooms of mildew.

"Your first task would be to restore these weapons, Joscelin Verreuil," Master Jacobe said. "We will teach you that and much more. But know that we will not force this choice upon you. It is yours to make."

My father stirred, but said nothing.

No one had ever told me this would be presented as a *choice*. With a surge of confused indignation, I scowled at the Cassiline Brother. "Do you mock me? Would you have my family be foresworn?"

He shook his head and there was no mockery in his eyes. "No, young lord. Cassiel's service is infinitely rewarding, but it is demanding, too. You may refuse."

A *choice?*

If Luc had said such a thing to me, I would have known it for a dare. It seemed likely this was a test of sorts. I picked up my uncle's sword and let it rest on my palms, my fingers curling around the dull edges. If the blade had been honed and polished, it would have looked out of place in my boy's hands with their grubby nails. In its neglected condition, it didn't. The rust was superficial, though. The scabbard and the sheaths for the twin daggers were lined with sheep's wool and its grease had kept the worst of the damage at bay. Once one looked past the tarnish and rust, even the vambraces were fairly well preserved in their wrappings. I ran the ball of my thumb along the sword's edge, feeling for nicks.

There was a sound as though I had plucked a harpstring.

Only it wasn't a sound, exactly . . . it was a feeling *like* a sound, vibrating in my bones. The hair on my nape prickled like a hound's hackles when it senses danger and yet my heart ached with the sort of almost painful happiness one can't explain, like when sunlight slanting over the mountains sparkles just so on the waters of Lake Verre.

It was a feeling like a voice calling my name, only the voice wasn't anything human, it was the wind in the pines, it was the roar of the river in flood, it was the thunderous roll of an avalanche.

I opened my eyes, not realizing that I'd closed them until I did. Silence reigned around the great dining table. Emulating Master Jacobe, I set my uncle's sword down carefully on the tabletop.

No, not my uncle's sword.

My sword.

"The choice was made long ago," I said. "I will go with you."

CHAPTER TWO

We rode north that very morning.

My sisters wept and hugged me; my mother gave me a fierce, lingering embrace. I kissed the baby's soft cheek; I had not yet begun to reckon the cost of losing such tenderness and the presence of women in my life. Luc attempted a manly arm-clasp, giving me a rough hug when I fumbled it. In turn, I gave Mahieu an awkward one-armed hug when he stared at his feet, shuffled, and mumbled a farewell.

My father offered me an arm-clasp, too, waiting until I gripped his forearm in a firm exchange. "The next time I see you, you'll be wearing vambraces."

I nodded, not trusting myself to speak. Unless I failed—an unthinkable shame—the next time I saw my family would be in fifteen years.

Fifteen years, half again as long as my entire lifetime.

That, too, was unthinkable, so I did what I reckon any ten-year-old boy would do and avoided thinking about it. Right now, I was embarking on the adventure of a lifetime.

On the first day, we ascended and crossed the high, wind-scoured massif that lay north of Verreuil. I loved travelling in the mountains even in the depths of winter, but I will own, there was a cutting edge to the wind that had even me huddled in my sheepskin coat. We rode in single file, our mounts with their shaggy winter coats plodding, heads held low. Although both Cassilines wore their hooded cloaks pinned tight, they appeared largely untroubled by the cold and the wind, sitting easy and upright in the saddle.

We began our descent from the massif in the late hours of afternoon and made camp on a small plateau. There was a site on the leeward side of the mountains used by hunters in better weather. It had a pair of crude but sturdy lean-tos, one large enough to provide a measure of shelter for the horses.

On Léon's orders, I scrambled to collect deadfalls and tinder while he unpacked their saddlebags and tended to the horses. Master Jacobe built a fire in a stone-ringed pit that looked like it had been there from time out of mind. I sawed at green pine boughs with my boy's hunting knife, dragging them into the lean-to to lay a bed against the cold stone of the plateau, spreading our bedrolls of sheepskin and woolen blankets across them. The sun sank below the horizon, fiery red fading to violet, then darkness. At home, only a day's ride behind me, it would be gilding the waters of Lake Verre.

Here, I had only strangers for company. Ranged around the campfire, we ate a portion of the supplies my mother and sisters had packed for the journey—the crusty bread baked that very morning, wedges of a firm, sharp sheep's milk cheese, and wild boar sausage seasoned with juniper berries.

No one spoke.

I wondered if this were a lesson of sorts or a test, as I had reckoned earlier. I didn't know. I didn't know what to expect, how to behave. I didn't know what was expected of me, or what boundaries I might overstep.

I had questions—was I meant to ask them?

Or was I meant to learn to abide in silence?

In the end, weariness overtook me and rendered the matter moot. My thoughts chased themselves in circles until my mind was exhausted and my eyelids fluttered and closed. Like a dog despairing of catching its tail, I let my chin fall to my chest and began to sink into sleep. I was only vaguely aware of Master Jacobe helping me to my feet, taking me by the elbow and steering me to the lean-to.

Wrapped snug in my bedroll with the scent of fresh pine needles filling my senses, I gave myself over to sleep.

In the morning . . .

In the morning I awoke to the sight of Léon performing the ritual Cassiline morning practice. He moved in a circle, one foot crossing over the other, his vambraces and the twin blades of his daggers glinting in the dim predawn light as he essayed a complicated series of strikes, blows, parries, blocks, and thrusts. One movement flowed into the next as simply and naturally as a stream flowing down the mountainside spilled from crag to crag.

I stared, my mouth agape. It was the most glorious thing I'd ever seen and I wanted it for myself.

"We call it 'telling the hours,'" his mentor murmured beside me, leaning on his walking stick. "You see how Léon moves in a circle, like a shadow around the face of a sundial." I nodded wordlessly. He pointed with his stick. "Note how all his movements focus inward. He is telling the sphere of containing an enemy. Léon!" He raised his voice. "The sphere of defending a ward, if you please."

Léon shifted his focus outward without faltering. There was a different kind of vigilance to this pattern. There were more blocks than strikes and the elaborate footwork contained judicious turns that allowed him to maintain awareness of the imaginary ward in the center of his circle.

Master Jacobe scowled. "Left guard, lad. Keep your left guard up!" Moving almost too quickly for the eye to discern, he plucked one of his daggers from its sheath, flipped it in midair, caught it by the tip, and hurled it overhand. I let out a strangled shout and yanked belatedly at his arm. Léon sucked in a sharp breath and took an ungraceful step backward, jerking his left forearm up to deflect the flung dagger. It clattered against the steel vambrace and fell to the ground.

I let go of Master Jacobe's elbow in a hurry.

He eyed me with the shadow of a smile. "Scared for him, were you?"

"Yes. No." I didn't know the right answer; once again I didn't know what I was meant to do or say. "Would you have hurt him?"

"He damn well would if I weren't quick enough," Léon said mildly. "But that's the nature of the training, young Verreuil, and if you make it to the Third Cohort, the old man will test you, too." His own daggers were sheathed; he approached and proffered the other's hilt-first. "Your weapon, maître."

We broke our fast, packed our gear, and continued onward.

I grew accustomed to the silence, for there were long stretches of it. In between, I garnered bits and pieces about the actual workings of the Cassiline Brotherhood—mostly from Léon, who wasn't adverse to conversation when the route through the mountains was wide enough to ride two abreast.

I had been raised with the understanding that it was only scions of the old noble D'Angeline families who were pledged to the Brotherhood, but that was untrue. Léon was an orphan, pledged by impoverished relatives who couldn't afford an extra mouth to feed. He had been formally adopted by the Prefect of the Cassiline Brotherhood and taken on his surname in the honorific form—Léon nó Rinforte—but he came from a line of untitled farmers from the province of L'Agnace.

"Do you think less of me for it?" Léon inquired upon having divulged his heritage.

"No." The question perplexed me. "Why would I?"

He shrugged. "People do."

"All knowledge is worth having," Master Jacobe said behind us, jogging his mount closer; there was a wry note in his voice as he quoted the proverb. "Léon, you will find that the scions of Shemhazai's line have minds more apt to find equal merit in a farmer and a Duc than many of the descendants of Elua and his Companions. Joscelin . . ." The smile left his voice. "I pray those words hold you in good stead."

I hoped he would say more, but instead he dropped back, leaving me to wonder.

As a scion of Shemhazai, I garnered as much information as my companions were inclined to divulge. I learned that the Cassiline Brotherhood was supported by a royal charter. In exchange, the sitting monarch of Terre d'Ange was guarded at all times by two members of the Brotherhood. The latter fact I had known, for it was the highest honor to which any Cassiline could aspire, and although my father had never said so aloud, I knew in the way that children sense such things that he regretted that his brother had not lived to attain it and hoped that I would succeed in doing so.

I hoped so, too, for the shame of failure was unthinkable. In the small hours of the night, sleeping under winter skies while my childhood home lay ever farther behind me, it seemed a heavy burden for a ten-year-old boy in the company of strangers to bear. But any pangs of fear and loneliness I kept to myself, not wanting to appear weak or timid in their eyes.

I learned that the grounds of the Prefectory contained a particularly fine olive grove, and all the Brothers took part in tending to the harvest and the pressing.

I learned that the Cassiline pledges were divided by age into three cohorts. Initiations and graduations were on the first day of summer. I would be expected to take the Oath of Water and enter the First Cohort, where I would begin my tutelage and training along with other members of my cohort.

"What's the Oath of Water?" I asked Léon. "Why *water*?"

"Because all things yield before it in time and though it may take centuries, water shapes things as it will." Leaning over in the saddle, Léon tapped my brow. "Consider it a pledge of fealty, an expression of your willingness to be shaped into a warrior beyond compare. Do you know the title Cassiel bears?"

"No," I admitted.

"He is called the Perfect Companion," Léon said. "Because alone among Blessed Elua's Companions, Cassiel never forsook his duty to the One God."

Behind us, Master Jacobe cleared his throat. "These are heady matters to discuss on the road," he said mildly. "Let us leave this conversation for the classroom."

Léon inclined his head. "Maître."

So that was as much as I learned of the First Cohort of the Cassiline Brotherhood, of which I would remain a member throughout my twelfth year. In the spring following the thirteenth anniversary of my birth, I would take the Oath of Fire and be inducted into the Second Cohort.

Fire . . .

Well, I could guess at that easily enough; fire refined and purified. Water quenched; fire tempered. That was how weapons were molded and forged. It did not surprise me to learn that those inducted into the Third Cohort took the Oath of Steel. Of that Master Jacobe said nothing and Léon said very little, only enough that I understood it was an oath that they both took very, very seriously. Of the final oath binding one as a full-fledged priest of Cassiel they said nothing at all.

Of steel itself, on the other hand, I learned a great deal.

Villages in the Siovalese mountains were small and scattered. There were no inns catering to travellers nor any markets where one might purchase goods in the midst of winter, but mountain folk are hospitable—at Verreuil, we never turned anyone from our doors—and open to barter in all seasons. At the first village large enough to sustain a smithy, Master Jacobe procured a sack of crumbling sandstone, a flask of crude vinegar, and a pouch of sheep's-wool grease, and set me to the task of restoring my uncle's weapons.

My weapons.

Well-tempered steel is stubborn, reluctant to reveal its luster, yet all the more rewarding when it does so at last. Following Master Jacobe's instructions, I made a paste of sandstone and vinegar in a battered tin plate, applying it and rubbing hard at the residue of rust and tarnish with a burlap sack. I began with the daggers, first the left-hand blade and then the right, working on them in the evenings before night fell and the mornings before we broke camp or bade farewell to our hosts. My mittens grew stiff and soaked; when I set them aside and worked bare-handed, my hands and fingers became stained with a dull reddish patina, dark metal tarnish around and under my nails. My mouth tasted of rust, a taste not unlike that of blood, which I remembered well from a time that Luc and I had quarreled over a wooden toy sword and he'd hit me square in the mouth, knocking out one of my baby teeth.

Bit by bit, the steel revealed itself.

When it did, I coaxed it to a shine with grease, polishing every inch with a scrap of chamois. The repetitive labor was soothing, easing the dull ache of absence inside me.

"The daggers need whetting, maître," I said to Master Jacobe. "Forgive me, but I do not possess that skill."

He examined the blades. "They've need of a blacksmith's grindstone to restore a true edge. We'll see it done at the Prefectory. After that, I daresay you can maintain them yourself." He smiled a smile of unadulterated pride and laid a hand on my shoulder. "Well done, lad."

My heart soared at the praise and for the first time, I essayed a Cassiline bow, inclining my head, bending at the waist, and crossing my ten-year-old-boy's skinny forearms over my chest.

Master Jacobe chuckled, but there was warmth in it. "Just so," he said. "Next, you may begin on the vambraces."

I bowed again, and it felt good and right.

CHAPTER THREE

As we descended at last from the Siovalese mountains, the air became thicker, warmer, and damper.

I missed the heights.

I missed my family, although I did my best not to think on it. I missed fresh-baked bread, my mother and brothers and sisters, my father's stern affection, the warmth of the great hall and the genial chaos of milling hounds.

At the same time, it was my first visit to a city, and I could not help but be excited. The city of Bergeroche spilled down the foothills of the Siovalese mountains along the course of a tumultuous river, broadening at the base where the river slowed and widened. All the streets were paved with cobblestones and bustling with activity. There was a market in the square at the city's center with vendors selling various preserved goods and cellared root vegetables, as well as early spring crops like peas and sallet greens.

Although we arrived in the city with hours of daylight to spare, our mounts were weary from the long journey and our stores were low. In a spate of magnanimity, Master Jacobe determined that we would pass the night in a genteel inn where we might enjoy a hot meal and a decent pallet and our horses would be well tended.

The inn was called the Shepherd's Sweetheart; it is peculiar, sometimes, the details that one recalls.

There was a brief silence that fell as we entered, which did not seem strange to me—I was a lord's son, I was accustomed to people assuming a respectful silence in my father's presence and it seemed to me that a pair of Cassiline Brothers were no less deserving. But I had also learned to listen to different kinds of silences in the past weeks; this one held a certain curiosity, too.

I learned why soon enough.

My younger brother Mahieu loved to build dams in a creek that flowed from a small mountain spring into Lake Verre, endlessly fascinated by the way the patterns of water changed with each branch or twig he placed. I could not help but think of that when the lone woman entered the inn's common room, her presence preceded by the ripples of attention it sent through the place.

I thought nothing of it at first; she was a pretty dark-haired lady, not young but not old, either. She greeted a number of the inn's patrons with a variety of familiar pleasantries—a gracious smile, a pleased nod, a lingering touch. She acknowledged those who struck me as fellow travellers with sidelong glances of warmth and welcome, a hint of merriment and promise lurking in the upturned corners of her mouth. The barkeep poured her a brimming cup of cordial unbidden, and it wasn't until she turned to accept it that I saw the finial of the marque inked at the nape of her neck below her upswept hair and realized that she was a Servant of Naamah.

At ten years of age and pledged to the Cassilines, even *I* knew what that meant.

This is what I understood of the history and founding of Terre d'Ange: A thousand and a half years ago, the One God begat a divine son on a mortal woman and that son was Yeshua ben Yosef, who was revered for his wisdom by the people of his ancestors. But Yeshua and his teachings caused trouble and strife in the Tiberian Empire, and so the Imperator had his soldiers execute him by nailing him to a wooden cross like a criminal, taunting him and piercing his side with a spear. But they did not know that Yeshua was divine. As he hung dying, the woman who loved him best in the world, as much and more as his mother even, knelt at the foot of the cross and wept, covering her eyes with her hair. Her name was Mary of Magdala and my sister Jehane *always* insisted on taking her role when we staged a tableau. Of course, Luc was Yeshua, sagging dramatically on a wooden ladder, his head hanging and arms outflung, while I had to content myself with being a Tiberian soldier poking him in the ribs with a broom handle.

But a thousand and more years ago, Yeshua's dripping blood mingled with the Magdelene's falling tears in the soil, and there Blessed Elua was engendered and nourished in the womb of Earth.

As our own mother explained, the Earth is the Mother of us all, not just the ground upon which we walk. As the sun of the One God in his Heaven shines upon her, she brings forth all things: the wheat we grind into flour, the grapes we press into wine, the grass on which our flocks graze, the trees we hew into timber.

And she brought forth Blessed Elua.

Blessed Elua burst from the womb of Earth fully formed, laughing and singing; but the people of Tiberium reviled him as the scion of an enemy and the people of his ancestors regarded him as an abomination, for his birth seemed unnatural to them.

So Elua wandered the world, exploring it with no plan or purpose, simply rejoicing in its existence.

Our father had a great fondness for maps and he took considerable pleasure in charting Elua's journey for us. "From here to here," he would say, tracing a course with a hovering forefinger on a faded vellum map. "Elua wandered barefoot and alone, leaving a trail of flowers blooming in the wake of his footsteps. And thence to ancient Persis . . ." He would look up at his attentive children with a bright, expectant gaze. "And of course, you know what happened there, do you not?"

There was always a clamor as all of us older children begged to be the one to tell how the King of Persis threw Blessed Elua into prison and the tale of the One God's wayward grandson reaching Heaven at last. And while the One God turned his face away, still grieving for the earthly suffering and death of his rightfully begotten son Yeshua, there were eight members of the angelic hierarchy who were moved by Elua's plight and descended from on high to attend to him.

Those were Elua's Companions, and they were Shemhazai—the ancestor of my family's line—Camael, Azza, Eisheth, Kushiel, Anael, Cassiel, and Naamah.

It was Naamah who beguiled the King of Persis into freeing Blessed Elua from his prison, and there were many adventures that followed until Elua and his Companions found their way to Terre d'Ange, where the people received them with open arms, and they knew that they were home.

Although I was bound for a life of celibacy, I was not above surreptitiously skimming the pleasure-books that Luc found on the high shelves in the library at Verreuil, so I understood to some extent what it meant that Naamah lay with the King of Persis to secure Blessed Elua's freedom or that she lay with strangers on their journey to procure money for food, for Elua was half-mortal and unlike angels, must needs eat. I understood enough.

And there in Terre d'Ange, Elua founded the city that bears his name.

His Companions divided the land amongst themselves into seven provinces and shared their gifts with the people. During their time on mortal soil, they begot a great many children—all save Cassiel, who claimed no province for his own and lay with no woman nor any man.

Those chosen to serve Cassiel followed in his footsteps.

Those who chose to serve Naamah followed in hers.

In the Shepherd's Sweetheart, the dark-haired woman's gaze alighted on our small party, seated at the far end of one of the long tables. Her eyes widened in curiosity at the sight of a pair of Cassiline Brothers. Léon blushed furiously and stared down at his trencher as she crossed toward us, gliding with a practiced elegance that would have turned my older sister green with envy.

Master Jacobe sighed.

"Messires Cassiline." The dark-haired woman lifted her cup in salute. "Welcome to Bergeroche. Pray tell, what brings you?" Her gaze shifted to me. "Are you their ward, young messire?" The curve of her mouth deepened. "A royal heir in disguise, mayhap? You look as though you're on an adventure."

There was only warmth and no unkindness in her teasing, but it angered me nonetheless. I didn't care to be treated like a playacting child and I didn't like the way her presence turned Léon from a dazzling warrior to a blushing youth.

I stood and bowed with cold precision, relishing the thump of my crossed forearms. "I am Joscelin Verreuil, second-born son of my House," I informed her. "And I am pledged to serve Cassiel."

That wasn't true in a strict sense, since nine years of training and a series of vows lay between me and the goal of becoming a Cassiline Brother, but it was true enough and it took the dark-haired woman aback. She looked at me in a brief moment of surprise, lips parted, then gave her head a rueful shake.

"Well then, may Elua bless and keep you, young messire," she said to me. "'Tis a challenging course you've set for yourself." She cocked her head and angled her gaze at Master Jacobe, who returned it impassively. "I daresay *you* understand the full cost of the sacrifice you're asking the boy to make even if he doesn't yet," she mused. "Is that why you begin training them so young?"

He didn't deign to reply, but Léon jerked his chin up, eyes blazing. "It takes a fair bit more skill to become a warrior than a whore!"

This time, she didn't flinch, only looked amused. "Oh, *does* it?"

"My lady." Master Jacobe cleared his throat. "Forgive my students' uncouth behavior. We did not come here to provoke." He grimaced and kneaded his bad knee. "There may be fundamental disagreements of philosophy between the Servants of Naamah and Cassiel, but we are all D'Angelines, are we not?"

There were murmurs of agreement from the dozens of patrons eavesdropping on the entire encounter. I sat down, feeling chastened.

"Ah, old man." The dark-haired woman's tone softened. "Yes, and I hear the admonishment you are too courteous to say aloud. You are right, it was unbecoming of me to bait your young students." She studied him. "Though you're not so old, are you? It's only that your body has known no mercy, no tenderness." Reaching down, she laid a gentle hand upon his knee. "I studied with an adept of Balm House in my younger days. Let me make amends and ease your pain."

I was fairly sure wagers were laid on the outcome of his response.

"No." Politely but firmly, Master Jacobe removed her hand from his knee. "Be assured, my lady, that I do believe your offer was made in good faith. But please understand that it does not accord with *my* faith."

Behind me, I heard the discreet clink of coins being exchanged. Wagers had definitely been laid.

She straightened. "I spoke only of comfort."

A muscle in his jaw twitched. "Nonetheless, it is a luxury I cannot afford."

The dark-haired woman inclined her head, her gaze filled with regret. "As you will, messire."

To that, Master Jacobe made no reply.

When my thoughts chanced across that encounter many years later, I wondered if my mentor truly understood what was offered and refused that evening; and mayhap he did, for he was a man who thought and felt deeply in his own quiet way. I think it is likely, however, that he did not.

As for me, there was no way my ten-year-old self could have known the encounter for a harbinger of events not yet set in motion.

That was likely for the best.

CHAPTER FOUR

I was glad to put the memory of that exchange behind me when we departed Bergeroche the next day.

It was complicated.

It was just, as my father would say in a rare mood, *too damn* complicated. Naamah's service was a matter for adults on a different journey than me, and I didn't want to think about complicated things that lay beyond the grasp of my understanding. All I wanted was to set my feet firmly upon the path of becoming a peerless warrior of the Cassiline Brotherhood.

By the time we crossed the border from the province of Siovale into L'Agnace, not only did my uncle's daggers shine like stars—albeit dull-edged stars—but his vambraces did, too, even the chainmail gauntlets that covered the back of one's hands. I must have tried them on a hundred times, hoping by some miracle that my own forearms and hands would have lengthened and grown enough so that the vambraces didn't hang loose upon them and jut past my elbows.

"Stop fussing," Master Jacobe said after my hundredth or so effort. "Even if they did fit you—and they don't—the leather needs to be replaced before they're suited for wear. Those straps are rotten enough to break as it is." He tapped the oilcloth-wrapped length of the sword. "Start work on this."

It still felt strange to see it laid bare, but I had become increasingly conversant in the language of steel.

Not so long ago, I had dreamt foolish boy-dreams about this blade. Recalling tales of lore, I had imagined it had a history that would only be revealed to me when I accepted my destiny. I had imagined it might be etched with mystical runes or contain a gem of rare value inset in its pommel. I already knew none of those things were true, but I did hold out a vain hope that there was a story behind the blade or at the very least, a tale to be told in the forging of it.

We had made camp for the evening on the verge of the Senescine Forest when I voiced that thought aloud.

Léon laughed. "Do you know the history of *my* weapons?"

"No," I admitted.

He drew his whetstone down the length of one dagger. "Nor do I. So far as I know, there isn't one. I was allowed to choose them from the armory of dedicated weapons when I entered the Third Cohort, and I chose the arms with the heft and balance that suited me best. But I trust you know the story of Cassiel's dagger?"

I nodded.

That, too, was part of the history of Terre d'Ange. When the One God ceased his grieving long enough to turn his attention to the mortal earth, he was dismayed to see that Blessed Elua and his Companions had begotten scores and scores and scores of children who threatened to overrun the earth. And so he sent his arch-herald to summon Elua and his wayward angels home to his throne in Heaven.

Blessed Elua refused the summons. Turning to his boon companion, Elua reached out his hand for Cassiel's dagger and Cassiel gave it to him. Elua smiled and scored his palm with the point. Blood welled and fell to the earth, and where drops of Elua's blood sank into the soil, scarlet anemone flowers bloomed.

"'My grandfather's Heaven is bloodless,'" I murmured, quoting the history that had been taught to me. "'And I am not.' And then Elua called upon our father the One God and our mother the Earth to create a place such as had never existed before, and Blessed Elua and his Companions passed into it through the bright gate without dying, and although we who are mortal-born must pass through the dark gate of death, the true Terre d'Ange-that-lies-beyond awaits us."

Léon and his mentor exchanged a glance.

I felt confused. "Did I make a mistake?"

"No," Master Jacobe said in a gentle tone. "You have retained the lessons you were taught very well, young messire. But not all lessons are true."

I frowned in Léon's direction. "Why did you ask me, then? If what I've been taught isn't true, what *is* the truth?"

He shrugged. "Just wanted you to understand there's no magic in plain steel nor in what we do. Symbols are powerful things." He knocked his knuckles on the flat of the blade he'd been whetting. "But at the end of the day, a dagger's just a dagger and a sword is just a sword. Isn't that so, maître?"

A little silence fell.

It was dusk; deep shadows had settled under the ancient trees of the forest alongside which we had made our camp. Under open skies, the sinking twilight was violet-blue. Not yet replying, Master Jacobe poked at our fire with his walking stick. Sparks rose in a flurry, reflected in his dark eyes.

"Yes," he said at length. "And no." And then he spoke a phrase in a language I didn't recognize.

Like most children of noble houses in Terre d'Ange, I had been tutored in Caerdicci, which is often called the scholar's tongue, from a very early age; living as near as we did to the border, my brothers and sisters and I had also learned a fair amount of Aragonian. But those were languages with common roots and this was like nothing I had heard before. "I'm sorry," I said. "I don't understand."

"It is a line from the Tanakh," Master Jacobe said. "The sacred books of the Yeshuites." He stirred the fire again. "It tells of how when Edom the First Man and Ieva, the Mother of us all, fell from grace and were expelled from the garden of Eden, Adonai—the One God—set one of the *Malakhim*, his angels, to guard the gate with a flaming sword." He regarded me with his ember-lit eyes. "Cassiel was not the only warrior among Elua's Companions, but he is the only one who remained faithful to the One God's commandments. He is the only one whose sword's flame was never extinguished. And that is why a Cassiline's sword is *never* just a sword. It is a covenant."

My skin prickled.

"But it *is* also just a sword," Léon said pragmatically. "Metal is metal, as surely as we're flesh and bone. Nonetheless, that's why we don't draw sword unless we're sure death is Adonai's will."

"How do you know?" I asked.

Léon made a deferential gesture. "That I cannot say. I have not yet completed my training and taken the final oath of binding that would permit me an assignation in which I might encounter such a situation."

"Have you done so, maître?" I asked Master Jacobe.

He withdrew his walking stick from the fire and rested it across his knees, offering his rueful half smile. "No, young lord Verreuil. I was no older than Léon when I sustained this injury. My own mentors in the Brotherhood deemed it better that I become a teacher myself than essay to convince the

peers of Terre d'Ange to hire a lame Cassiline. I cannot say whether that was right or wrong, but it is the path I have travelled."

"You said you taught my uncle," I said. "For as long as I can remember, I've known I was meant to follow in his footsteps, but in truth, I know naught about him. What was he like?" I hesitated, then voiced the question I'd never dared ask my father. "And how . . . how did he die?"

Master Jacobe looked up at the stars in the deepening dusk. "Scrupulous," he said after a long moment. "If I had to choose one word to describe your uncle Luc, that would be it. Luc paid attention to *everything* he was taught. If he made a single misstep, he'd be on the practice grounds from dawn until dusk, telling the hours backward and forward. If he misspoke a single syllable of the Tanakh, he would practice reciting it for it so long one might hear him mumbling it in his sleep."

"But he died protecting his ward, did he not?" I asked. It was what I had always been led to believe.

"Yes and no," he said quietly. "I would that it were that simple. I trust you are aware of Blessed Elua's precept?"

I nodded. "Love as thou wilt."

"It is an admirable goal toward which to aspire," Master Jacobe said. "And one perhaps the divine may achieve. But we are mortal and fallible. It is not uncommon for people, especially peers of the realm, to conjoin their fortunes for reason of dynasty or power or finance." He paused again and I waited out his silence. "Your uncle Luc was assigned a post guarding the wife of a man she did not love. You might say that he died protecting her."

"Might?" I frowned. "You said he died a noble death."

"He did." His gaze settled on me. "Do you know what the *terminus* is, young lord Verreuil?"

I shook my head.

Léon whisked his whetstone down the length of one of his daggers. "It's the last and most dreadful act a Cassiline can be asked to perform," he said in a flat tone. "To take your ward's life and then your own to prevent a fate worse than death."

I couldn't conceive of a fate so dire. Blessed Elua have mercy, 'twas no wonder my father never spoke of his brother's death. A foreboding sense of horror unfolded behind my eyes. "And that's how my uncle died? *Why?*"

"No, no." Master Jacobe held up one hand. "Forgive me, your uncle didn't take his ward's life. But she loved another and her husband was a jealous man." He rubbed his temples. "'Tis a hard thing to explain to a child."

I watched the sparks skirl upward as the fire crackled low. I might be a long way from growing into my uncle's Cassiline gear, but I felt far less a child than I had only a few days ago. "Just tell me, please."

It was a simple enough tragedy, I suppose, remarkable only in the depth and breadth to which it betrayed Blessed Elua's precept. My uncle Luc was hired as an elite guard for the Comte de Sarles' wife during the ostentatious and lengthy celebration of the anniversary of their nuptials. The wife's lover, one Vicomte de Gontier, staged a raid to abduct his married beloved. In the normal course of events, one might suppose that my uncle was simply slain protecting his ward. In truth, the Comtesse had been forewarned and defected to her lover's side.

In a fit of rage, her husband bade my uncle to perform the *terminus.*

My uncle Luc refused. And in the end, it was the Comte's own men who slew him from behind.

An ice-hot fury flared and then settled deep into the marrow of my bones as I listened to Master Jacobe relate the tale. A grievous wrong had been committed against House Verreuil. "I will kill him," I said in a cold, distant voice that didn't sound like it belonged to me. "I will avenge my uncle."

"You will not," he said in a tone that brooked no objection. Something as hard as bedrock surfaced in his gaze. "Do you imagine your father did not have the same desire? Do you imagine the Cassiline Brotherhood would tolerate such a crime? Justice was meted out long ago. The Comte de Sarles was tried, judged, and put to the sword by the Prefect himself." With the aid of his walking stick, he got to his feet. "There is no recourse here for revenge."

"What of the Comte's men?" I demanded. "Those who did his bidding?"

Master Jacobe shook his head. "That matter is long settled, young messire. Your own parents may attest to it. Your path lies in the future, not the past. If you would do honor to your uncle's memory, do so by becoming a Cassiline warrior worthy of his legacy. Do you understand?"

I didn't, not wholly, but he was right. The manner of my uncle Luc's death would have grieved my father thrice over; if he were satisfied that honor and justice had been served, so must I be.

Recognizing the wisdom of my mentor's words, I inclined my head. I would follow in my uncle's footsteps to become a Cassiline Brother worthy of serving the throne, a Cassiline Brother beyond reproach. I would bring honor to House Verreuil and his memory.

That was the goal to which I would dedicate my life.

Or at least, that was my plan.

CHAPTER FIVE

By the time we reached our destination, early signs of summer were unfurling across the earth.

The Prefectory of the Cassiline Brotherhood was a sprawling estate occupying a valley alongside a tributary of the Lusande River. There was a stone keep with a manor house that looked to be many centuries old, but from our vantage atop the foothills surrounding the valley, it was in excellent repair. Long barracks and adjacent stables flanked the manor. It was very much a working estate—there were vegetable and herb gardens, a millhouse with a waterwheel, a chicken coop, a dairy barn and a smithy. Northward was pasturage and hay fields, while the fabled olive grove lay to the west. A row of bee skeps lined a field of lavender not yet in full bloom, and greyish-white sheep dotted hillsides terraced by stone boundaries that had probably been laid before Blessed Elua set foot on the land.

It was also obvious that this was a great deal more than a simple working country estate. The quadrangle enclosed by the manor and barracks was no formal courtyard, but rather a training ground where figures spun and sparred in elaborate circular patterns.

"Home," Léon said with quiet satisfaction. I couldn't claim to share the sentiment.

A brown-clad figure making repairs to the bee skeps spotted us first and raised a hand in greeting. Master Jacobe returned the salute, and the beekeeper relayed the news of our arrival with a sharp whistle, sending a smaller figure in dingy white dashing for the manor. The tower bell sounded as we descended into the valley, riding single file on the narrow path that marked the approach from the south.

There was no ceremony to our reception. A handful of Brothers in sober grey met us in the forecourt, exchanging pleasantries with Master Jacobe and Léon. A lanky young man in the rough-spun brown garb of the Second Cohort directed boys nearer to my age, all wearing the undyed white woolens of the First Cohort, to stable our mounts and unpack our gear, save for the wrapped parcel of my uncle's weaponry.

"Young lord Verreuil." He presented me with my uncle's arms. "I am Jean-Pierre Desmarais, Senior Cadet of the Second Cohort." He nodded toward the manor. "Once you pass through those doors, the rank of your birthright ceases to exist. No rank exists save that of the Brotherhood. Do you understand?"

I kept a firm grip on my unwieldy parcel. "I do."

"Good." Jean-Pierre beckoned to one of the boys of the First Cohort. "Come, let's get you settled."

"Be of good faith," Master Jacobe bade me with a smile and a warm pat on the shoulder. "You'll see us about."

The long journey had accustomed me to a sense of impermanence. It was strange to enter a place knowing that I wouldn't be leaving in the morning. I wondered if I would ever call the Prefectory *home* as Léon had, or if Verreuil would always be home to me. The boy whom Jean-Pierre had chosen to accompany us was named Ezekiel, and he chattered like a magpie as we passed through the entrance hall and down the vaulted corridor that led to the quadrangle. A cacophony of sounds echoed in the passageway—the clash of steel and the clatter of wood, grunts and yelps and the stomp and scuffle of dozens of feet against the worn flagstones.

As we emerged into daylight, I stood transfixed.

Here within the confines of the keep's inner walls, all the nine long years that went into the training of a Cassiline Brother were represented in every stage, from the members of the Third Cohort like Léon at the far end of the quadrangle flowing with deceptive grace and speed through intricate maneuvers to boys around my age in the near end, walking empty-handed through patterns painted on the flagstones with whitewash. Half a dozen youths ranging in height and size occupied the middle section of the quadrangle and performed a variety of arcane exercises with a disparate array of skill.

Their numbers may have been fewer than they once had been, but old-fashioned or no, the discipline of the Cassiline Brotherhood on display was a sight to behold. I yearned to be among them.

Breathing deep of air that smelled of stone, steel, and sweat, I turned to Jean-Pierre. "When do I begin?"

"Soon," he said. "Once you take the Oath of Water, you'll commence your formal training."

"Until then, you'll be shoveling dung and such," Ezekiel added with helpful cheer. "'Course, you'll be shoveling dung afterward, too. Just not every day."

If they had told me I'd do naught but muck out stables day in and out for a year before I could begin training, I'd have readily agreed to it, but we had arrived in a timely manner and the solstice was a mere ten days hence.

We proceeded beneath the open colonnade along the perimeter of the quadrangle to the armory of dedicated weapons. There Jean-Pierre bade me to stow my uncle's arms—*my* arms—in a wooden chest much like the one in which they had resided for so long in my family's home. There were a great many other chests, and I wondered what stories they contained and how many were empty. The barrack of the First Cohort was an austere space lit by narrow windows. Low wooden cots with straw-filled pallets lined the walls; by the look of it, fewer than ten were actually in use.

Jean-Pierre pointed to the furthermost, which had a pile of neatly folded clothing atop it. "Don your whites, cadet-candidate. Supper's at six bells. Ezekiel will show you around the rest of the grounds today and you'll pull kitchen duty after supper." He cast an assessing gaze over me as I tugged at the too-short sleeves of my tunic. "You're tall for your age. Long-limbed. Which hand do you favor?"

"The left," I said, buckling the accompanying belt around my waist.

"Put it behind your back." He spun me around by the shoulders as I obeyed in bewilderment. Almost before I could blink, he'd wound a leather cord around my wrist and lashed it to my belt. Ezekiel grinned at my surprise. "Good. That will help you practice favoring neither."

There are things that you do not know you do not know until you know them, my dear ones.

It was something my mother would say to us in her calm, tranquil way when we balked at our lessons; which, being children, my brothers and sisters and I were wont to do at such times when the weather was particularly fine and the mountains and forests and the lake and streams beckoned for exploration. Like our father, my mother was a descendent of Shemhazai's lineage and valued knowledge in all its forms, but she was more private in her thoughts, tending to vague expressions where our father's observations were keen-edged and clear. It was not a saying to which I had given much consideration except insofar as it meant we must apply ourselves to studying when we would prefer to be at play.

That day, I understood it better.

I did not know what I had not known.

I could not have imagined the extent to which having a hand tied behind my back disrupted my balance, and I could not have imagined the extent to which having my balance disrupted threw my entire being off-kilter. I stumbled in Ezekiel's wake as he led me on a tour of the estate, casting grins over his shoulder in a manner I was beginning to find considerably irritating.

"Not so easy, is it?" he asked me.

If he were my brother Luc I would have punched him even if there'd been hell to pay for it. Instead, I gritted my teeth. "How long?"

Ezekiel cocked his head. "Depends on how fast you learn," he said. "Could be as little as three months, could be at least a year."

I rolled my shoulders, trying to ease the strain. "How long was it for you?"

He grinned again. "One year, six weeks."

It seemed a very, very long time.

We traversed a fair amount of the grounds before the tower bell sounded a single clang to alert us that the supper hour was nigh. Cassiline adepts streamed from every quarter, descending upon the keep. At an actual tally there were not so many of them—I counted twenty-seven cadets plus half a dozen full-fledged brethren—but altogether, it seemed a substantial number. Each cohort was allotted its own long trestle table, while the masters sat at the head of the hall at a U-shaped table.

Ezekiel introduced me, and the boys of the First Cohort rattled off their names in quick succession. Most of them were in their second or third years in training. There was only one other candidate like me, yet to take the formal oath. He was a thickset, black-haired boy named Toulouse Godet, and I could tell by his appraising glare that he was going to regard me as competition.

"From Siovale, eh?" he said. "I s'pose you're from one of those families can trace your line back to Shemhazai without a break."

I shrugged, the movement hampered by my bound arm. "We keep good records. Where are you from?"

"Azzalle," he said. "But I'm of peasant stock. Couldn't even tell you my own great-grandfather's name." He said it as though it were a point of pride, and I had no idea how to respond.

"Don't mind him," Ezekiel said to me in his cheerful manner. "Typical bull-headed Azzallese. He'll settle down once he's sworn to Cassiel's service."

"Or fail out," another cadet muttered, and a few of the others snickered. Toulouse scowled and hunched over his trencher, sopping up mutton drippings with a hunk of bread, his right hand lashed behind his back.

After the evening meal was concluded I was officially inducted into the endless roster of chores that went into running the Prefectory. While a pair of older cadets tended to the great kitchen fireplace and kneaded bread dough to rise overnight, I scoured and sluiced pots one-handed, bracing them awkwardly against a broad oak countertop that was scarred and burned and worn smooth by hundreds of years of usage, until Jean-Pierre came to release me from my duties and bade me take to my bed.

Having been on kitchen duty, I was the last of the cohort to retire for the night. The barracks were cold and dimly lit, a single tallow candle sputtering in a sconce at either end of the row of cots. Deep breathing, faint snores, and the occasional dream-induced whimper were the only sounds to break the silence. My saddlebag had been delivered and stowed at the foot of my cot. I was grateful for my bedroll of warm Siovalese fleece, and doubly grateful when Jean-Pierre untied my left hand, for the other cadets had led me to believe I'd have to sleep with it affixed behind me.

I lay awake in the slow-breathing stillness, feeling alone amidst the sleeping strangers and missing Verreuil. And I thought myself the only one awake until I heard someone stir on the adjacent cot and felt the prickling sensation of another's gaze on me. Dark eyes glimmered in the shadows cast by the low-flickering candles.

"Are you homesick?" Toulouse's voice whispered in the darkness. "Do you miss your mother? Are you going to cry?"

"Yes, of course." I looked over at him. "But no, I'm not going to cry. Are *you?*"

He snorted. "Gods, no. I don't miss anyone or anything."

I thought about that for the length of a few heartbeats and offered an honest answer. "I'm sorry to hear it."

Toulouse rolled over. "To hell with your pity, Siovalese."

In the days leading to the solstice, I kept to myself, concentrated on the chores I was given, and did my best to ignore Toulouse's animosity. I scoured pots, hauled water, mucked stables, and weeded barley fields. Unfortunately, many of these tasks were ones I shared with Toulouse while the oath-pledged members of the First Cohort were at work in the training yard or the classroom. Cadets from every cohort were expected to take part in the duty roster. Even the masters did not exempt themselves from menial labor. My father would have approved of the egalitarian nature of the Prefectory, although as I had noted, it was a notion he was more wont to employ in theory than practice. There did exist a hierarchy of rank and status, however, and every cohort was supervised by a senior member of the cohort above it.

As cadet-candidates, Toulouse and I weren't even on the lowest rung of the ladder. We stood upon the ground beneath the ladder, reaching for somewhat beyond our grasp—reaching with one hand bound behind our backs, too. As frustrating as *that* was, I had to own that mayhap there was more than one kind of wisdom in it, for while it forced us to concentrate on our balance and strengthen our weaker sides, it also rendered us less inclined to scrap through our differences in the manner of boys everywhere. We simply didn't have the energy to waste.

The masters didn't concern themselves with petty disputes and rivalries amongst the younger cadets. I had supposed that dignity would be demanded of us at all times, but the Cassiline Brotherhood had been training peerless warriors for centuries. They understood the need to balance discipline with the wild impulsiveness of boyhood and youth.

And we were middle sons, all of us. We had always known the camaraderie of brotherhood. Over time, I would learn that meant different things in different families. Some were like me, middle sons in the purest sense, the second-born of three; others had two or more younger brothers. Some had sisters, some were born into a family of boys. Most, like me, came from old noble families that held the tradition in high regard—although we were meant to abandon the rank of our birthright upon entering the keep, I soon discovered that everyone knew each other's lineage.

I held my erstwhile travelling companion Léon, who was a farmer's son, in high regard and I attempted to make it clear in word and deed that I was willing to extend the same sense of kinship to Toulouse, but he didn't make it easy.

One day it was likely we would come to blows—afterward, mayhap we might become friends. After I thrashed him, anyway.

Toulouse was ignorant enough to believe that scions of Shemhazai's line were soft because we had a scholarly bent. The estate of Verreuil had been in our family for six hundred years, but my father had earned the title Chevalier fighting against the Skaldic invasion during the Battle of Three Princes. Although my father never spoke of it, I knew that title was a matter of great pride and somber regret for him. Pride, for he acquitted himself with such prowess and valor that the King's own brother knighted him afterward. Regret, for it was at the Battle of Three Princes that the King's son Rolande, the Dauphin of Terre d'Ange, was slain.

At the time, I gave little thought to those events beyond my family's personal history and what impact it held for my life at the Prefectory. I was ten years old, and the next decade of my life was to be circumscribed by the stone walls of the Keep and the green slopes of the valley. Master Jacobe had told me that my path lay in the future, not the past; but here in the Prefectory, the former seemed as distant as the latter. Terre d'Ange enjoyed peace and prosperity across the realm, with no storms gathering on the horizon.

Now it is hard to imagine.

CHAPTER SIX

I awoke in high spirits the day of the summer solstice.

I didn't mind hard work. I was becoming more skilled at navigating chores and simple tasks one-handed and I could ignore Toulouse's surly attitude, but although it hadn't even been a full week, it galled me not to *learn*. I wanted to know how to restore a true edge to the blades I had so painstakingly cleaned and polished, I wanted to know those secrets vouchsafed only to Cassiel's sworn servants, I wanted to know the history, meaning, and purpose behind the patterns of footsteps painted on the flagstones of the training ground, why one placed one's feet just so here and here and here.

It was a long process, that much I knew. Members of the First Cohort weren't even given wooden training weapons until their second year. Every third day, the whitewashed patterns were scrubbed clean and new patterns painted in their place. I wanted to be one of the boys walking the steps. I wanted to begin the journey of the days, months, and years it took to attain the effortless precision of the cadets of the Third Cohort.

A couple more boys had arrived after me, one from the southernmost province of Eisande, one from the City of Elua. While allowing for the vagaries of travel, the Brotherhood did its best to ensure that cadet-candidates spent the minimum amount of time at the Prefectory before being oathsworn. Feeling like a seasoned hand with all of several days' experience under my belt, I did my best to help Jean-Pierre and Ezekiel ensure that the new candidates were made welcome.

There were four of us prepared to take the Oath of Water on the first calendar day of summer. We gathered in the quadrangle facing the assembled Brotherhood, each of us backed by the Cassiline Brother who had escorted us here. The Prefect, Lord Charles Rinforte, faced us, flanked by half a dozen Brothers on either side. Behind them stood the cohorts in order of rank.

It was the first time I'd seen the Prefect himself. He was a tall man with elegant, austere features. At a guess I'd reckon he was in his early sixties though his age was difficult to gauge, ivory-white hair belying the taut bearing of a man half his years. He crossed his forearms and bowed to us.

"Young messires—" he began in a resonant voice.

In the distance, a whistle sounded. Lord Rinforte glanced toward a waving figure atop the southern parapet. The tower bell began to toll, followed by the sound of more whistles and shouting.

"I do believe we have a late arrival," Master Jacobe, standing as my sponsor, murmured behind me.

At a signal, two Third Cohort cadets broke ranks and dashed across the yard to unbar the postern gate, flinging it open. A single horse with two riders came through at a hand gallop, hoofbeats clattering against the flagstones. It tossed its head and snorted, its neck and withers lathered with sweat, as the lead rider reined it to a halt.

The aft rider dismounted with alacrity and offered a Cassiline salute. "Selwyn de Gaunte, Lord Prefect!" he called. "I'm here for the oath-taking."

His escort slumped wearily on the pommel of his saddle and offered an ambiguous grunt.

In all the years I trained at the Prefectory, I never saw a more composed cadet-candidate than Selwyn de Gaunte. For a ten-year-old boy who'd entered the keep like a leaf blown through the gates on a gust of wind, he presented himself with an aplomb that nearly matched the Prefect's own.

Lord Rinforte surveyed him, then glanced at his escort, who responded with a brusque nod. "Very well. Take your place."

The oath-taking was a solemn affair, although I daresay all of us candidates were unsettled by the unexpected late arrival. The Prefect waited in stern silence until we had regained our composure. "Adonai is the Lord and Creator of all that exists," he announced. "His will and His grace flow through all things, and all things yield before it. Adonai so loved the world that he sent his son Yeshua ben Yosef to redeem the sins of humanity with the sacrifice of his death." His gaze alit on each of us in turn. My heart beat faster and I felt a tightness in my chest and weightlessness in my bones all at the same time. "We are D'Angeline and this is our heritage. But there is a lineage of the spirit mightier than the lineage of blood, and that is the first great truth of Cassiel's service. Today you pledge to yield like water before the truth and meaning and honor of Cassiel's service, to yield to Adonai's will and grace as it flows from the heavens through his son Yeshua, his grandson Elua, and to Cassiel the Perfect Companion and to those of us who keep its flame aloft."

He beckoned and a member of the Third Cohort stepped forward with a ewer, passing it ceremoniously.

All of us had been taught what to expect, including the latecomer, Selwyn. I stole a covert sideways peek at him as I extended my cupped hands before me, unbound for the ceremony. His wind-tangled hair, half loose from its braid, was the hue of a ripe apricot and his features in profile were sharp and foxy.

Water spilled over my cupped hands, glistening in the spring sunlight and dampening the flagstones beneath me. "Joscelin Verreuil," the Prefect said in a grave tone. "Drink and take the Oath of Water."

I drank; one by one, all of us drank. We were no longer cadet-candidates but oath-sworn members of the First Cohort of the Cassiline Brotherhood.

I'd hoped that we would be allowed to stay and witness the remainder of the ceremony, as graduating members of each cohort swore in turn the Oath of Fire and the Oath of Steel or became fully fledged Brothers, but such mysteries were not vouchsafed to us. Instead, one of the Brothers escorted us back to the keep.

"I beg your pardon, Brother." Selwyn's voice broke the silence as soon as we exited the passageway. "Whither are we bound? May I be permitted to break my fast and wash the dust from my face?"

"You may call me Master Gerard." The Brother gave him a deceptively mild look. "I will tutor the lot of you in the basic tenets of academia, and those studies commence now."

"I have not eaten."

Master Gerard was unswayed. "You arrived late."

I watched the exchange with fascination. A flush of color dawned on Selwyn's cheekbones. It was the first, though far from the last, time that I saw his temper rise. "We were . . . detained."

"So I noticed," Master Gerard said. "And you arrived unarmed sharing a single mount with Brother Ishmael, bereft of the cadet who accompanied him, by which I can only assume that this journey met with considerable ill fortune. Will you begin to make good on whatever losses were incurred to fetch you here or will you waste the Brotherhood's time wheedling like a child denied his supper?"

Selwyn's head snapped up, his flush deepening; then he caught himself and offered a Cassiline bow in silence.

"Very well," our tutor said drily.

The second story of the Prefectory contained a fine library with scrolls and bound tomes in every tongue known to mankind, including some it was the labor of a lifetime to master. Four studies adjoined the library. The chamber in which the First Cohort took their lessons was the smallest of the lot. If the Brotherhood were operating at anything near its full capacity, it would have been necessary for classes to meet in shifts. As it was, we were cramped on hard wooden pews in the dingy room. At least the five of us newly pledged cadets were given a bit of extra space on the first pew to accommodate our jutting elbows. We struggled to balance slate-boards on our knees while Master Gerard directed the older cadets in various studies they were pursuing before turning his attention to us.

"How many of you know your letters?" he inquired. I raised my hand as did Selwyn and Dumiel d'Aubert, the tall, slender lad from the City of Elua. Toulouse glowered as though the question was intended as an insult, although the fifth of our number, the Eisandine boy Paul, was unperturbed by it. As far as Master Gerard was concerned, it was merely a piece of information. "Then we shall commence at the beginning," he said to the latter two before permitting himself a faint smile. "And you other three may commence writing the alphabet . . . with your less-dominant hand." There were snickers from behind us. I'd hoped we'd be allowed to forgo binding in the classroom, but it wasn't so. "Go on!" He gestured. "Get those wrists behind you and assist each other with the knots."

For the first time, Selwyn looked unnerved. "Is this a jest?"

"It is not," Master Gerard replied calmly. "Which hand do you favor?"

All of us leaned forward to peer toward the far end of the pew where Selwyn was seated. His chin rose. "Neither."

"Neither, is it?" Master Gerard opened a drawer in the large desk at which he sat, and withdrew a length of leather cord. "Well then, come here and turn around and we'll see."

Selwyn obeyed without comment, facing down a roomful of smirking boys as our tutor lashed his wrists together behind his back. Although he tried to conceal his anger and embarrassment, I couldn't help but feel bad for him. Catching his eye, I offered a sympathetic grimace.

That was all it took to ignite a spark of defiance in him. Returning to the pew, Selwyn cocked his head at the cadets to my right. "Move down," he ordered them, squeezing to perch beside me. He smelled like damp spring air and horse sweat. "Give me your slate-board, will you?"

Bemused, I placed it on his knees.

Each board had a chalk stylus, the wooden holder affixed to a hole in the frame with twine. Leaning over, Selwyn grabbed the twine with his mouth and managed to get the stylus between his teeth. Someone breathed an admiring curse as he began scratching out the alphabet. After that there was a beat of silence broken only by the squeak of chalk on slate; then Master Gerard burst into laughter.

"Well done, cadet," he conceded. "Henceforth, you'll alternate arms from day to day until told otherwise."

Selwyn spat out the stylus. "Starting today, maître?"

"Tomorrow." Master Gerard nodded at me. "Today I think it meet that you consider your tone and hope that young Messire Verreuil here remains willing to render you assistance."

It's possible that Selwyn and I would have become friends in time regardless, but our tutor's edict surely hastened the process. This became obvious when the morning's lessons concluded, Master Gerard having ascertained the new cadets' levels of literacy and numeracy and dismissed us to partake of the afternoon meal. I was pleased with my performance in the classroom—my father would have expected nothing less from a scion of House Verreuil—and looking forward to being spared the day's chores in order to begin training in the quadrangle.

I hadn't given thought to the process of *eating*.

Meals at the Prefectory consisted of simple, hearty fare. Later in the summer there would be more of nature's bounty on offer, but today our trenchers held dry-cured sausage, bread, and cheese, accompanied by cold, refreshing well water. Selwyn stared down at his meal, both arms tied behind his back.

Toulouse laughed. "What's the matter, Messire High-and-Mighty?" He made an oinking sound. "Too proud to shove your snout in the trough?"

Selwyn glared at him.

"Peace." I reached over and jabbed Selwyn's sausage with my belt knife, extending it to him. "Eat your bedamned food."

His narrow nostrils flared with indignation. "I'm not hungry."

I waved the sausage under his nose. "You were hungry *hours* ago."

"Awww!" Toulouse was enjoying himself. "Does mama's baby boy need his new best friend to cut his food into itty-bitty pieces for him?"

"I'd rather starve than give you the pleasure," Selwyn said coolly. "You gawping illiterate—"

That was as far as he got before Toulouse launched himself across the table, unbound left arm cocked to deliver a punch. Selwyn managed to evade it and butt Toulouse squarely on the forehead, hard enough to make a cracking sound. Then they were both on the floor and it was all flailing and grunting, Toulouse on top doing his best to pummel Selwyn's face with one fist, the latter squirming violently in an effort to throw him. Everyone else at the table exchanged glances; along the hall, chairs were tilted as older cadets turned to observe. No one seemed inclined to interfere.

I sighed, rose, and hauled Toulouse off Selwyn by the back of his woolen jersey. He thrashed and swore, but we were evenly matched in strength and I had the reach of him. Selwyn bounded to his feet, lowered his head, and charged. I spun Toulouse out of the way and got knocked sprawling for it.

"Enough, enough!" It was Marc Labas, the new cadet commander from the Second Cohort, who interrupted us at last. He was laughing. "At attention, boys."

We may have been newly sworn and as green as grass, but each of us had travelled long weeks and hundreds of leagues across Terre d'Ange to pledge ourselves to the Cassiline Brotherhood. All three of us stood upright and squared our shoulders in response, unable to offer a proper cross-armed salute.

"Good." Our new ranking commander made a shooing gesture. "First Cohort, get out of here. Assemble in the yard."

It was a pleasant surprise to discover that Master Jacobe had been appointed to instruct us in the Cassiline fighting style and that Léon would be assisting him until such time as he was assigned to a patron. The First Cohort assembled in the southernmost end of the quadrangle, Léon working with the second- and third-year cadets while his mentor took charge of the five of us. Master Jacobe assessed our appearance without comment, taking in the bleeding gash that split the bridge of Toulouse's nose, the purple bruise streaks already darkening Selwyn's eye sockets.

"All right, lads." He tapped the flagstones with the butt of his walking stick and pointed to the nearest circle of whitewashed footprints, the least complex pattern of the lot. "It's time to tell the hours. Begin."

Four of us exchanged uncertain looks.

The only one who didn't hesitate was Selwyn, and I cursed myself inwardly for failing to take the same initiative.

He was good.

How good, I didn't realize until I followed in his footsteps, the other three doing likewise behind me. There was a very good reason that the Cassiline Brotherhood spent the entire first year of training on footwork: the footwork was difficult. I knew it was based on circular patterns echoing the journey of a gnomon's shadow across the face of a sundial. I had watched Léon tell the hours scores of times on our journey. Of course I'd attempted to emulate him, thinking I had a sense of it. Léon had even given me a few good-natured pointers.

But there was never time on the road for proper training, and executing this most basic of patterns was a great deal harder than it appeared, even with the steps painted as plain as day on the flagstones. One started at noon and crossed left foot over right to one o'clock of the dial, knees slightly flexed in readiness to absorb any impact or pivot at need. Then it was right foot behind the left to two, right over left again to three, marking the first quarter, and that much was easy enough, but then there was a spin that looked so simple and elegant when the Brothers and the older cadets executed it, stepping out smoothly to four o'clock, left leg crossing behind the right.

That was what was supposed to happen in theory as we moved through the four quarters of the dial. In practice, all of us stumbled over our feet in an effort to trace the pattern without an error, no weapons, not even pretend daggers, to flourish in a futile attempt to disguise our essential incompetence.

All of us except Selwyn, anyway. His form wasn't perfect, but it was good. Despite having both of his hands tied behind his back, he glided through the painted circuit of footprints without a misstep, saluting Master Jacobe with a respectful half bow upon returning to noon.

Our mentor scratched his jaw, looking thoughtful. "You've done this before." It wasn't a question. "You know, lad, over the course of a thousand years, there've been hundreds of cadets dismissed for one failure or another, but very, very few fully oath-sworn Cassilines have ever been cast out of the Brotherhood, and to my knowledge only one had the audacity to diagram the training. Long before I was born, but if I'm not mistaken, he was from Camlach, just like yourself."

Up went Selwyn's chin. "It is not forbidden to study it," he said stiffly. "My father said so. Our liege lord the Duc d'Aiglemort himself presented a very fine copy of the manuscript to our family on the occasion of my birth."

Aiglemort was the sovereign duchy of Camlach, the province founded by

Camael, the undisputed military commander amongst Elua's Companions. I should have guessed that Selwyn was one of Camael's descendants by the way he'd flung himself into a fight. My own father had fought alongside Camaelines in the Battle of Three Princes and he said everyone knew they were mad for warfare.

"—not forbidden, no," Master Jacobe was saying. "Nor is it approved. You may think otherwise at the moment, but I can see that through lack of supervised training, you've acquired a few bad habits and they're already engrained. In some ways it will be more difficult to erase them than if you were beginning with a clean slate." He paused and all of us attended. "Camael is one of the greatest warriors ever forged in Heaven. But it bears remembering that not even he could stand against Cassiel's sword." He thumped his walking stick on the flagstones again. "Think about that as you get back at it, lads."

Under his watchful eye, we walked the first sphere while the sun crawled slowly toward the western horizon until we were aching and dizzy, muscles beginning to stiffen from the relentless rigor of the discipline. By the time the bell rang for the evening meal, no one had the energy to quarrel, let alone fight. Even Selwyn couldn't be bothered to protest the indignity of my holding a bowl of soup to his lips.

There were a great many questions I would have liked to ask him, the foremost being what had befallen his company on their journey to the Prefectory, but his manner was off-putting and I was too bedamned exhausted to press him in the dining hall. All five of us new cadets groaned in relief when Marc Labas gave us permission to return to our barracks and untie each other's wrist-bonds. I collapsed onto my cot and wrapped myself in my sheepskin, squeezing my left hand to restore the flow of blood to my cramped fingers.

A final thought struck me.

I rolled onto my right side to face Selwyn. He'd claimed a cot next to mine, moving what little gear he possessed and displacing the two cadets who had arrived after me as though it were his gods-given right. "Hey," I whispered in the darkness. "You said the Duc gave your family the manuscript when you were born. How did he know your mother would bear a third son?"

"He didn't." His tone was flat. "I *was* the third son. Mother's comfort, isn't that what they call it? That was me until my younger brother was born."

The arithmetic didn't make sense, but my tired wits weren't working properly. "Then how—?"

"One younger brother." Selwyn interrupted me. "Two elder. My oldest brother died when I was seven."

Now I understood. "And you became the middle son."

"Yes." The word was bitter on his tongue. "I became the middle son."

CHAPTER SEVEN

There was nothing in the world I wanted more than to become a Cassiline Brother. And there was nothing in the world that Selwyn de Gaunte wanted less. Were it not for what befell his company on their journey to the Prefectory, I suspect he might have fled before the end of our first year of training.

My home province of Siovale was a rugged place, but a peaceful one. It shared a border with the sovereign nation of Aragonia, a longtime ally of Terre d'Ange. Camlach, the province from which Selwyn hailed, was another matter. It bordered Skaldia, a loose-knit federation of barbarian tribes. When the Skaldi weren't fighting amongst themselves, they were wont to make raiding incursions into Terre d'Ange, looting, killing, and raping.

I had the details from Selwyn himself and those I did not discuss with anyone else, for his shame at surviving the encounter ran deep. But the Prefectory was a small community and everyone knew the gist of the tale within a day. A Skaldic raiding party of a dozen warriors had attacked them just beyond the southernmost pass through the mountains. Third Cohort cadet Stephane Dubois made a stand against the entire party and spent his life purchasing time for Brother Ishmael and Selwyn to escape riding double on a single mount, no possessions or provisions but what they carried.

A Cassiline Brother on the verge of taking his final oath had given his life so that Selwyn might complete his journey. No matter how much he might despise having the choice forced upon him, his sense of honor would not permit him to turn his back on that hard truth any more than it had allowed him to refuse this path. Still, the disparity made us an unlikely pair of boon companions. But not only did we become fast friends at the outset, we remained so throughout our time together at the Prefectory, our friendship growing stronger and deeper as the days turned to months and the months turned to years.

There was always a sense of kinship between us; and always elements that were at odds. Both of us were the scions of Minor Houses with modest holdings, Houses that could nonetheless trace our heritage in a direct line to one of Elua's Companions—but there was a vast difference between the values our families held in the highest regard. And yet Selwyn was a keen scholar when he applied himself in the classroom, while I worked harder than anyone to hone my fighting skills in the training yard.

We were both proud in different ways. I had been taught that the measure of a man's worth was intrinsic to his accomplishments; Selwyn had been raised with the understanding that it was his birthright.

Selwyn was arrogant.

He was arrogant in the most infuriating way because he could nigh always make good on his boasts. Selwyn embodied every tendency toward aristocratic condescension that Toulouse had unfairly ascribed to me. He reckoned anyone with a less venerable pedigree his inferior, an attitude I found galling. Amongst our incoming cadets, only Dumiel d'Aubert, who traced his ancestry to Blessed Elua himself, hailed from a more prestigious lineage—but since he lacked innate skill on the training ground, Selwyn held him in contempt, too. I do not think we would have remained friends if I had not proved a worthy rival. There is no place for false modesty in the company of warriors. Even at a tender age, we understood that one day we would hold our charges' lives in our hands.

It is the very essence of the Brotherhood, expressed in its motto: *In Cassiel's name, I protect and serve.*

I believed it.

And I will believe it to the end of my days with a depth and passion that has led me down paths I could never have imagined. At the time, though, it was simply the bedrock truth of my existence.

In the training yard, we walked the steps endlessly. We walked the circle of foundation hour after hour after hour. We walked it forward and backward. We walked it with one arm tied behind our backs until Master Jacobe reckoned our minds and bodies had been sufficiently retrained from reliance on the side we favored; then, in fact, we spent another three days with our less-dominant arms bound behind us, so that our bodies might be reset with the precise balance of a banker's scales.

In fact, were it not that Selwyn was born with the trait of favoring neither side, I would have held a place in the annals of the Prefectory for the shortest amount of time endured training one-handed. As it was, six weeks felt like an eternity, and having both arms free changed my understanding of what it meant to walk the most basic sphere of telling the hours, which thus must be done again.

And again.

And again and again and again.

Of course, we did a great deal more than train in the yard. As chores went, one of my favorite places was the smithy. Although we were expected to maintain our weapons as we had been taught, before any of us might be trained to use the great grindstone to hone our blades, we must learn every aspect of what made the smithy function, from firewood to forge and bellows to barrel. I had always taken pleasure in seeing how things worked, a trait that Master Smith Alphonse spotted early in me. There was an aqueduct and an ingenious system of clay pipes that conveyed water from the millhouse wheel alongside the river to the smithy, including a trough that released a steady trickle of water on the grindstone. It was prone to blockages that required an agile mind and body and nimble young fingers to probe, find, and release, and I had the knack of it. This led in turn to performing similar tasks for the Master Miller, and spending time on the riverbank piqued my interest in the fishing weir, which put me in mind of the countless hours my brothers and I had spent building dams and stringing nets in the mountain streams.

What I knew, I taught to Selwyn, and as a result, we were paired together more often than not in doing chores. Sometimes it meant that one or both of us skipped a round of the more traditional first-year labor of mucking, scouring, or weeding, which incited a degree of envy in some members of our cohort—which I would venture to say was undeserved, as we were forever getting our fingers pinched or limbs nigh-broken by jammed cogs, or drenched by broken pipes.

I learned from Selwyn, too. My family was isolated in our Siovalese mountain estate. My father was an avid philosopher and historian, but he had little interest in the political intrigues of the present day. He had fought for his country and if he were called upon again, he would do so without hesitation, but he had no desire to attain power or status beyond that which was his birthright. Such grasping ambition was reckoned vulgar in House Verreuil.

It was different in Selwyn's family. I knew, of course, that Ganelon de la Courcel was the King of Terre d'Ange and that his son and the erstwhile heir to the throne, Rolande, had been slain in the Battle of Three Princes.

I was distantly aware that this was but one, albeit mayhap the most grave, of tragedies and accidents that had befallen House Courcel, and that King Ganelon's current heir was his only grandchild, the Dauphine Ysandre, who was a mere six years of age when I took my first oath.

These things I knew because serving the royal family was the highest honor that could be bestowed on a Cassiline Brother, one that was reserved for brethren who had proved their worth serving less exalted charges. My father may have disdained political intrigue, but service with honor was another matter and I knew it grieved him that fate deprived his brother Luc of the chance to serve House Courcel. My determination to attain that goal was unwavering.

Our studies in the classroom covered the history and governance of Terre d'Ange in broad strokes, but the Cassiline Brotherhood's interest in the descendants of Blessed Elua and his Companions wasn't political.

It was spiritual.

Elua's Companions did not fall from grace for the sin of loving Blessed Elua, in whose veins flowed the blood of Yeshua ben Yosef mingled with the divine ichor of the One God, Adonai, the Lord of Lords.

No; their fall lay in loving the world itself, in all its mortal frailty and moral failings, more than its Creator. It lay in the fact that upon reaching Terre d'Ange and calling it home, they became enamored of humankind, showering upon us those gifts they brought with them from the celestial realm—gifts of knowledge, healing, and husbandry, but also gifts of pride and desire and belligerence.

Only Blessed Elua offered nothing but himself; the true essence of himself, which is the essence of love.

And yet because Blessed Elua was not Heaven-born but begotten in the womb of the Earth herself, one aspect of his love was carnal. And it is because of his own love for the world of soil and blood into which he was born that Blessed Elua chose not to heed his grandfather Adonai's command to take his rightful place in Heaven, but travelled through the bright gate through which only the divine may pass to create a world past the dark gate of mortal death that is the Terre d'Ange-that-lies-beyond.

One day that will change.

That is the deepest, truest belief of the Cassiline Brotherhood—for Cassiel was ever there beside Blessed Elua, guarding and protecting him.

Cassiel never fell.

Cassiel never failed in his duty.

And one day, Blessed Elua and his Companions will leave the Terre d'Ange-that-lies-beyond, passing through the bright gate, passing over mountain, stream, and forest, lavender field, sheep meadow, and olive grove, to take their place in the heavens. Until that day, Cassiel will ever remain at Elua's side, steadfast and unwavering in his obedience to the One God's commandments, his sword ever ablaze with divine fire.

It is in Cassiel's name that we keep the One God's faith—Cassiel's splendid, shining, glorious example.

These were heady and arcane matters for a ten-year-old's mind to compass, and I do not pretend that I grasped them fully for many years. It is true as I have said that this understanding formed the bedrock of my existence.

In Cassiel's name, I protect and serve.

But it was Selwyn who led me down the path of speculating about whom we might serve and how and why. Camlach had never been known for its political intrigues, but there were subtle changes afoot. The Camaeline warlords who guarded our eastern border grew restless at their lack of status on the realm's greater stage. No one questioned Ganelon de la Courcel's right to the throne, but he was a man past his prime. He hadn't even fought in the last great battle, but had delegated command to his son Prince Rolande, who had been slain in the process of leading a charge against the Skaldi.

And now King Ganelon's heir was his six-year-old granddaughter.

If D'Angelines were ever faithful in word and deed to the precept of Blessed Elua, none of us would wed for aught less than love. But in truth, we are subject to all the frailties and failings of humanity. For peers of the realm in particular, there are significant stakes to be gained or lost and the institution of marriage rests upon material and dynastic considerations that sometimes supersede the considerations of the heart.

According to Selwyn, speculation regarding Ysandre de la Courcel's prospective husband began the instant her father was slain at the Battle of the Three Princes. Later, I might laugh at the youthful naivete of that belief—the groundwork for that speculation was laid long before Ysandre was even conceived.

Nonetheless, it was a revelation to me at the time; and Selwyn had a grasp of the players involved that would have impressed my sister Jehane, who had a fondness for history and gossip alike and at times bemoaned the remoteness of Verreuil.

Selwyn knew that Prince Rolande's first betrothed died under suspicious circumstances in a hunting accident; he knew her name and lineage. He knew that Rolande's bride was rumored to have contributed to her predecessor's death, and that she in turn was rumored to have been poisoned. He knew it was rumored that various figures, including the King's brother, son-in-law, and nephew were positioning themselves as prospects for the throne—or angling to field a contestant for the Dauphine's hand who might then rule over a child bride as Prince-Consort. He knew what foreign powers were reputed to be in the hunt for a claim to D'Angeline soil: Aragonia, the Republic of La Serenissima, distant Khebbel-im-Akkad, even the stubborn little island nation of Alba.

It would be a form of arrogance to claim I thought such considerations beneath my regard. I liked to listen to Selwyn speculate, even if these matters had but the most distant of bearings on our lives.

And one day that might change. We could yet aspire to serve the throne.

Summer passed in a blaze of sun-gilded glory and an abundance of training and hard work. We shook the fruit of the trees in the olive grove into nets spread below the branches. We scythed and threshed barley, we rolled hay into bales and stored it for the winter. We gathered slabs of dripping honeycomb, wrestled sheep to be sheared, packed cheese molds, smoked ham and sausage and trout.

One thing none of us in the First Cohort were allowed to do was attend the weekly market that took place in the nearby town of Rive-de-Lusande, for that was a privilege reserved for members of the Second and Third Cohorts.

To hear them talk, one would think there was no place on earth more exciting than the town square of Rive-de-Lusande on a market day in high season, and within the parameters of life at the Prefectory, I daresay it was true. There were farmers and craftsfolk of every ilk selling their wares, there were companies of Tsingani passing through on their way to and from the great horse fairs, there were wandering Mendacant storytellers from Eisande spinning extravagant tales in their multicolored robes. There was a puppet show that only cost a single copper centime, and a falconer who would let you feed one of his birds a gobbet of meat for the same price. In the evening when the light softened into summer's long lavender twilight, hanging oil lamps strung around the square were lit and there was music and dancing.

And of course, there were Servants of Naamah.

Matters of desire were discussed in hushed tones in the Cassiline Brotherhood—mostly by cadets in the older cohorts, but those of us in the

First Cohort stretched our ears when they spoke of it. Every one of us entering the Brotherhood understood that we were pledging ourselves to a lifetime of celibacy, but our understanding of what that meant changed as we gazed down the road from boyhood toward youth.

I thought it noble. Alone among Blessed Elua's Companions, Cassiel possessed a singularity, a clarity, a purity of purpose.

Cassiel *shone.*

I saw it behind my eyes when we trained; I saw that bright, fixed point, the still center of Cassiel's existence around which every movement of defense and offense which we were taught revolved.

There was desire.

And there was abnegation.

These were things that as a child, I understood in my bones and flesh without the ability to voice in an articulate manner. But I felt them. I understood the ways in which opposing forces were necessary to create heat and friction, to hone and temper an edge, to create a spark. There was something in it as deep and profoundly satisfying as the perfect execution of a crossed-forearm Cassiline bow.

"You're an odd one," Selwyn observed when I attempted to explain my thoughts.

Summer turned to autumn; the autumn days began to grow shorter and shorter. By that time, all of us had our routines down. We knew what was expected of us, taking turns at the various rounds of chores to be executed in accordance with our rank. All the cohorts took turns in the training yard. While the older cadets progressed apace and sparred in pairs and groups, we first-years followed increasingly elaborate patterns of footprints on the flagstones, shivering in our white woolens and huffing out frost.

Sometimes I was lonely.

I missed my family. So would anyone, I assumed; although the longer my time at the Prefectory, the more I learned that was not necessarily true. I did, though.

My first Longest Night at the Prefectory brought it home to me. Every province in Terre d'Ange celebrates the winter solstice, the seasonal axis around which lengthening days of sunlight return.

According to Dumiel d'Aubert, in the City of Elua the Longest Night was a wildly extravagant affair. The Royal Palace was lit up like a bonfire with candelabra ablaze in every window, as was every private home in the City.

The cobblestone streets were packed with revelers bearing torches, creating an endless river of light as they sang and danced their way from inn to inn. It was a night of licentiousness and revelry in a nation known for such things, and nowhere more so than in the Court of Night-Blooming Flowers—which, Dumiel informed us haughtily, only provincial rubes called by its full name; even children raised in the City were sophisticated enough to call it the Night Court. Amongst us cadets, the Night Court was spoken of in *extra*-hushed tones, for it was where the most elite members of the Servants of Naamah in the entire realm plied their trade, offering all manner of carnal pleasure in exchange for coin and patron-gifts.

It was a world that was fascinating by virtue of being both foreign and forbidden, and we listened to Dumiel d'Aubert's tales with avid interest, learning that there were a total of thirteen Houses in the Night Court, each of them catering to a specific desire, the significance and nuances of which evaded us at that age.

On the Longest Night, the Night Court closed its accounting ledgers to hold a vast and opulent masquerade during which adepts took lovers of their own choosing, giving and exchanging pleasure freely. It was a time of license everywhere, not just in the villages and towns and cities. In Verreuil, it was our family's tradition to have a great feast. We festooned the hall with holly and evergreen fir boughs and stoked a roaring blaze in the fireplace. My mother and sisters and the kitchen staff baked for three days in a row; my father and Luc and I hunted game. Deer were butchered, geese were slaughtered and hung by the neck to age in the courtyard. Casks of brandy and barrels of wine were breached.

It was different at the Prefectory.

In the Cassiline Brotherhood, we held Elua's vigil on the Longest Night. It was a pledge that we made in solidarity with Cassiel's unwavering faith, a pledge we made to Blessed Elua, his Companions, and their descendants. There are no temples to Cassiel; not here nor anywhere. Insofar as Cassiel possesses a temple, it is built of the flesh and bone and sinew of those of us who serve him. Our bodies are Cassiel's temples and the One God is the architect. On the Longest Night, we offered our vigil in worship, kneeling in silence before an ancient, moss-streaked effigy of Blessed Elua that resides in a grotto alongside the river, his bare feet sunk into the earth, his eyes lowered in serene contemplation.

While the seasons turned upon their axes, while darkness attained its apex and ceded way to light, while warmth and joy and revelry abounded across the frostbitten land, the Cassiline Brotherhood maintained a fixed point around which all these things might revolve, as bright and remote as the stars in the night sky.

It was a proud place in which to abide.

But sometimes it was a lonely one, too. The ties that bound us were bonds of the spirit; there was no place in Cassiel's service for bonds of the heart.

Or at least so they told us.

CHAPTER EIGHT

A year and more passed.

There were only three aspiring cadets who came to take the Oath of Water. One wouldn't think a mere year's difference would be so pronounced at such a tender age, but it surprised me how much younger the incoming cadets appeared; the taut delicacy of their sinews, the fragile stems of their necks, the bony knobs of their joints.

By contrast, those of us who had been at the Prefectory for a year and turned eleven were hale, hardened, and rambunctious.

Myself, I was content to leave the new cadets to their own devices—all I cared about was the fact that my own incoming class was allowed to begin training with wooden practice weapons. Although I craved the sensation of leather-wrapped hilts and the heft of steel against the palms of my hands, there was somewhat nonetheless satisfying about the weight and density of the well-worn wooden daggers and swords with which we learned to execute the strikes and blows and parries that accompanied the footwork we had painstakingly studied for so many endless hours.

As we grew and learned, the scales of our abilities tipped to and fro. We sparred and argued and fought in the training yard and outside it, something that the Brothers and the older cohorts tolerated with amused patience. I was accustomed to being the tallest of my peers until Dumiel sprouted like a weed, growing half a foot in the space of months, and gained reach on me. But he was lanky with it—"colt's years" they call that age when boys' limbs grow long and ungainly, all protruding elbows and knees. Even so, I was stronger than Dumiel, though not so strong as Toulouse, who remained thickset and broad-shouldered. But I was quicker than both, though not so quick as Selwyn, who was quicker than everyone save Paul, the Eisandine boy, whose reflexes were as swift as a skylark on the wing.

By all the gods, we knew each other well in those days, almost as familiar with each other's bodies as our own.

As we entered our third year at the Prefectory, it was a matter of contention who would receive the honor of being the leader of the First Cohort. I thought it would be me. In all honesty, I thought it *should* be me. I was the most well-rounded fighter of our lot. I had the most drive and passion, and I continued to train harder than anyone.

"You're not a leader, Joscelin," Master Jacobe said to me in a private discussion after announcing his decision to appoint Toulouse as the head cadet of the First Cohort. His tone wasn't unkind, but it was blunt. "Not yet, at any rate."

I bristled. "And *Toulouse* is? Forgive me, but is that what the Brotherhood considers leadership, maître? Chivvying and bullying at every turn?"

"There are lessons to be learned by bearing the weight of responsibility, and we gauge those decisions accordingly." He leaned on his walking stick and raised his brows at me. "Do you question our judgment?"

I lowered my gaze. "No."

It wasn't entirely true, but in hindsight I saw the factors in play, the ways in which our teachers sought to utilize our strengths and weaknesses to best complement each other. For all that he was thin-skinned and prickly in matters of perceived slights, it transpired that Toulouse was a stalwart leader and a good mentor to the young cadets joining us in our final year in the First Cohort.

And then, of course, everything changed again. At thirteen years of age, we took the Oath of Fire.

There had been attrition in the years preceding us. Since I'd entered the Brotherhood, two members of the Third Cohort had been dismissed for failure to attain sufficient mastery on the training ground; another had been dismissed under a cloud of hushed rumors regarding a liaison with a young woman at a neighboring estate.

At thirteen, I was not insensible to such matters.

The Cassiline Brotherhood is a discipline. Celibacy is not a choice we make unwittingly nor out of despite for the pleasures of the flesh. I think, mayhap, that is one of the greatest misconceptions regarding the Order. I do not know now to what extent I may speak to those intentions with integrity, but I know what I understood as a boy in the Cassiline Brotherhood. We were *steel.* We took the Oath of Water and learned to yield and bend; and then we took the Oath of Fire. Upon being initiated into the Second Cohort, we stood upon the quadrangle and held our hands above a flame until our callus-hardened palms blistered, pledging to commit ourselves, our lives and bodies and souls, to be hammered and forged in accordance with Adonai's will.

"There will be times in the years to come when it seems an unbearable burden," Master Frédéric, who taught the Second Cohort in the classroom, warned us. He was of Namarrese descent, which was unusual in the Cassiline Brotherhood, and one of the youngest of the masters, possessing a calm and unflappable demeanor suited to tutoring boys throughout their most tumultuous ages at the Prefectory. "I tell you that it is not. Abnegation of desire is the grindstone on which your will is honed. It is not an easy path, but it is the only path by which you may attain the patience and discipline of the perfect warrior, focused solely on the imperative to protect your charge at any cost."

There was some grumbling from the older cadets in the Second Cohort, who had heard a version of this talk many times, but most of it was good-natured.

And then there was Selwyn.

"Your pardon, maître?" Sounding deceptively polite, he raised a hand for permission to make an inquiry. "Does that disclude the warrior brethren of the great Boeotian army in ancient Hellas?"

Master Frédéric paused. "Boeotia."

"Its members consisted of sworn lovers, before the days when Blessed Elua walked the earth," Selwyn said.

I should have held my tongue, but I didn't. "The ancient Hellene philosopher Platon believed they were less likely to disgrace themselves on the battlefield in the eyes of their beloved." I knew this because my father sometimes read Platon's works to us on long winter nights; Selwyn, I assumed, knew about the Boeotian army because Camaelines were taught to reach for a sword-hilt with one hand and a tome of military strategy the moment they slid out of their mothers' wombs.

"Yes, I'm aware of the stories regarding the Boeotian army." Master Frédéric pondered his response before continuing. "Young messires, you're neither the first nor the last cadets to raise this point. I assuredly do not deny the divine force of love. But consider that love a blade that cuts both ways. A man may acquit himself with valor in battle to avoid appearing a coward in the eyes of his beloved." He looked grave. "Or a man may make impulsive and dangerous decisions out of a desire to appear a hero in the eyes of his beloved."

There was a little silence, into which one of the older cadets murmured, "You're speaking of Prince Rolande."

"No." The master's tone was firm. "I do not presume to know the details of the Dauphin's death, let alone his heart and mind. But I tell you this." He rapped his knuckles on the lectern at which he stood. "You are not training to become mere soldiers. What is the precept of the Cassiline Brotherhood?"

All of us, to a boy, offered a reflexive salute, steel clanking as our crossed forearms thumped across our chests. Those of us entering the Second Cohort had only just been granted the right to wear our arms and daggers, but we responded in unison. "In Cassiel's name, we protect and serve."

"Indeed." Master Frédéric nodded. "In Cassiel's name, in accordance with Cassiel's example and Adonai's will. We stand as living reminders of the promise of the grace and protection that Cassiel extended to Blessed Elua in the name of the Lord." He held up a finger. "Upon being given an assignation, you will serve *one* patron with a purity and singlemindedness of purpose. Nothing, including mortal love and the desires of the flesh—and perhaps most especially mortal love, for I believe there can be no greater distraction—must distract you from your duty. Do I make myself clear?"

I found myself nodding in agreement.

Later, Selwyn made fun of me.

There was an attic space beneath the gable of the millhouse that we considered our private hideaway. I'd been the one to discover it. Based on decades' worth of tallow smudge marks and the splintered planks of one wall that had been used as a target for dagger throwing, it had served as a hideaway for generations of cadets before us, but none of our other peers had found it. As an added bonus, at least from a boy's point of view, it was a partially open space with a large central beam and wide-spaced rafters providing ample opportunity for dangerous crossings and the possibility of falling and breaking one's neck. The attic was used to store spare cogs and chains and bits of ironware. The Master Miller doubtless knew of its existence, but so long as we didn't abuse the privilege, he'd been content to turn a blind eye while Selwyn and I squirreled away threadbare blankets and the butt-ends of candles and occasionally took a good hour longer than we ought in the process of unjamming the waterwheel.

On the afternoon following Master Frédéric's lecture on celibacy, Selwyn balanced barefoot on the trestle, presenting his left side to the throwing wall. "Yes, maître," he mocked me. "Of course, maître, I'm a good little cadet who always does what he's told. I've *no* desire to know what it feels like to be a proper man."

"That's not fair," I protested. Selwyn drew his right-hand dagger and threw it with his leading arm. The point failed to lodge and it clattered to the floor. "And you'll get more leverage throwing across body if you haven't got a straight shot."

He leaped over the gap between the trestle and the outer floorboards and glared at me. "I'd die for *you*, you know."

I eyed him in return. "I never asked you to."

"Doesn't matter." Selwyn flung himself onto one of the worn blankets and folded his arms behind his head. "I would. You'd do the same for me, wouldn't you?"

I got to my feet and retrieved his dagger, tossed it by the hilt, and grabbed the tip, pivoting to throw it cross-body. It stuck in the scarred planks with a satisfying *thunk*. I yanked it free. "What's your point?"

"You would," he continued as though I hadn't spoken. "Or for your family or any of your brothers-in-arms, or Terre d'Ange itself. But are you willing to die on behalf of a total stranger? Are you? Even if your death serves no purpose?" He gave me a sideways glance through errant locks of hair that had slipped loose from the Cassiline club knotted at the nape of his neck. It gave his sharp features a stealthy look, like a fox peering through a gap in a hedgerow. "Look at what happened to your uncle."

My hand tightened on the hilt of the dagger I'd retrieved. "Don't speak of him. If it hadn't been for mortal love, he would never have been betrayed."

"No." Still seated, Selwyn pulled on his boots. "You're wrong. It wasn't love that betrayed him, it was jealousy. If love had been allowed to run its course, your uncle would still be alive."

"You can't know that," I said.

"I can speculate on the obvious." He rose. "My dagger?" I flung it in irritation, the point lodging between his feet. He plucked it loose. "Fight me."

"It's too hot." We weren't supposed to spar without our mentor's supervision, but of course, everyone did. From time out of mind, cadets in the Cassiline Brotherhood had issued those two simple words of challenge to each other.

"*Fight me*," Selwyn repeated. Taking a step backward onto one of the rafters, he struck a defensive pose known as Hanging Tree Snake. Leading with his left shoulder, he planted his feet with his left-hand dagger held low, his right-hand dagger high, arm undulating in a sinuous beckoning motion meant to draw the eye.

I sighed.

It *was* hot; hot and dusty, ever-present bits of chaff floating in the beams of sunlight that found their way through chinks in the roof and walls. But to turn down a challenge from a fellow cadet was reckoned cowardice, and the galling truth was that no matter how hard I trained, I never managed to beat Selwyn in an impromptu bout. No one did.

I crossed my forearms and bowed. "Fine."

None of us had ever actually seen a snake hanging from a tree, but according to Master Jacobe, it was a good pose to lure an attacker into one's circle. Even knowing the gambit was a trick and it was Selwyn's left hand I needed to watch, I couldn't help but find the motion of his right arm distracting as I ventured onto the rafter. Still, I was ready when he feinted high and jabbed low, uncrossing my arms in a sweeping parry with so much force it sent both of his daggers flying.

"Win to—" Before I could claim victory, Selwyn simply lowered his head and tackled me around the waist. I let out a holler as I fell, then a sharp grunt as my left arm was nearly yanked out of its socket. We dangled above the second story below us, Selwyn with one arm crooked around the rafter, the other hand clamped like a manacle to my wrist under the leading edge of my vambrace. "Have you taken leave of your wits?" I shouted at him, swinging my legs in a vain effort to generate enough momentum to gain purchase on the rafter. Beneath us, the waterwheel creaked placidly, emptying its buckets into the sluice system. "Pull me up, you bloody arsehole!"

"Say it." Selwyn's grip on my wrist was white-knuckled and trembling, but his gaze was intent.

"Say *what*?"

"Say that you'd die for me."

"Name of Elua!" I was furious at him. "I never said I wouldn't. Pull me up!"

"*Say it*."

I gritted my teeth. "Of course I'd die for you, you bedamned lunatic. Now *pull me up*."

He levered himself to sprawl atop the rafter and hauled on my wrist until I was able to wrap my legs around the timber and pull myself up after him. Straddling the beam, we dangled our feet over the drop, both of us breathing hard, and regarded each other.

"Care to tell me what that was all about?" I asked.

Selwyn picked at a splinter on the beam. "Sometimes I envy you. You're so damn *sure*."

Ah, I thought; it was a topic we had discussed before. "I know." I kept my tone gentle. "And I know you're angry. It's not your fault. You weren't raised knowing the Brotherhood was your destiny, and you're having a hard time accepting the sacrifices it requires. But Selwyn . . . I just don't understand how nearly getting us both killed helps anything."

"It doesn't, I guess. I'm in a foul mood." He looked away. "I had a letter from home. The Duc d'Aiglemort's made Telys an offer of two-fold honor."

I knew that his older brother Telys, the former middle son raised to enter the Cassiline Brotherhood, had gone instead to foster with House d'Aiglemort after the course of his life was altered. An offer of two-fold honor meant that the Duc had found him worthy of formal adoption, entitled henceforth to include "nó d'Aiglemort" in his name. "I trust he accepted it?"

Selwyn nodded. "In two years' time, he'll be patrolling the border with the Duc's son Isidore, maybe even Prince Baudoin de Trevalion. And I'll still be spinning around in circles in the training yard."

There was nothing I could say to him that I hadn't already said, so I didn't bother trying, just glanced over at the ladder leading to the floor below. "We'd best go before the Master Miller loses patience."

"All right." Selwyn stood. "I'm sorry. I didn't mean to scare you."

"You didn't *scare* me." I was offended. "You made me angry, you thrice-cursed idiot."

"Sure." He shot me one last sidelong look, accompanied by a crooked smile. "If you say so."

Such was the nature of our friendship. If it seemed overwrought at times, we were young and foolhardy, our heads filled with lofty ideas and our hearts with high emotions. We were bursting at the seams with life and vitality. We lived close to the blade and held the notion of death more lightly than we ought.

We told each other everything in those days.

CHAPTER NINE

In the late summer of our first year as cadets in the Second Cohort, we were permitted to attend the market in Rive-de-Lusande.

Summer in Terre d'Ange was a heady time and in that particular year it was marked by the return of the acclaimed poetess Thelesis de Mornay from exile on the windswept green isle of Alba to whence she had fled in her younger days upon being pressured by her family to wed against her wishes. Her most famous poem, *The Exile's Lament*, was on everyone's lips that year. At the Prefectory, we heard it first from Dumiel d'Aubert, who was smugly pleased to inform us after receiving a letter from home of his own—we were allowed to correspond with our families through the Royal Post thrice a year—that Thelesis de Mornay had been appointed the King's Poet.

One might suppose poetry had little to do with politics. In Terre d'Ange, one would be mistaken.

One might also suppose that politics ought to play no role in matters of love, but as my uncle's tragic fate proved, our reality did not always reflect our ideals. In accordance with Blessed Elua's precept, D'Angelines set no boundaries on love and desire beyond the age of consent, and the very notion of consensuality was a sacred tenet. But when an inheritance lay at stake, legal and familial negotiations became tricky. Nonetheless, it was unusual indeed for any D'Angeline to willingly undergo exile without substantial gain. Yet I do not think that *The Exile's Lament* could ever have held such an achingly poignant expression of love for Terre d'Ange itself were it not written from the perspective of one severed from their homeland.

Betimes I miss the sweet summer warmth and innocence of my youth.

During our time in the Second Cohort, all of us grew in different ways—betimes by leaps and bounds, betimes by inches. We sought the admiration of our mentors and our peers; we sought to set good examples for the young cadets who succeeded us.

We told the hours day after day, mastering increasingly complex patterns.

In our second year in the Second Cohort, we began practicing with wooden swords; in our third year, with unhoned steel.

We wore our vambraces and daggers during every waking hour, trying to perfect the effortless-seeming balance of alertness and stillness that the full-fledged Brothers and the older cadets had attained.

We grew our hair long like the mighty warrior-priest Shamson in the Tanakh, the sacred writings of the Habiru folk. As a symbol of our covenant with Adonai, we pledged never to cut our locks, binding them instead at the napes of our necks.

We knelt in prayerful meditation, training our minds to be as calm and reflective as the surface of Lake Verre on a windless day, training our bodies to ignore heat and cold and thirst and hunger.

We laughed with the particular strain of humor that manifests when one spends the entirety of one's youth training for the prospect of death. One of our favorite pastimes was expounding on the broad category of inaptly named poses, strikes, and parries. The Reaper's Scythe was a sweeping sword lunge which anyone who ever wielded an actual scythe in an actual field of grain found an absurd comparison. There was a vertical defensive sword pose called Laundress's Paddle, a maneuver that bore no semblance whatsoever to churning a vat of laundry. One category fell under the description of exercises that looked or sounded impressive despite serving no real purpose beyond mere intimidation. The Hawk Stoops was a two-fisted dagger strike that garnered an especial amount of ridicule for exposing one to an opponent from the offset. Its inverse, Flinging Open Shutters, was actually an effective maneuver known affectionately as "*Surprise!*"

During the fallow months, we hoarded our meager funds in anticipation of summer's bounty. We were permitted an allowance of up to five copper centimes a month if our families chose to forgo a portion of our wages; I myself received a half measure, an amount that House Verreuil had deemed appropriate to the circumstances in accordance with tradition. Those of us with coin to spare spent it on cakes and tarts and other sweet treats that were never served at the Prefectory.

When the long, gilded days of summer returned we sauntered down the cobbled streets of the village, mindful of every envious glance cast our way by boys our age. The lively tributary running through the valley in which the Prefectory lay joined the Lusande River proper some league and a half north, where the river was spanned by an old Tiberian bridge. The stone archways were large enough to allow trade vessels of considerable size to pass beneath its span. Venturing across the bridge was like stepping into a different world. After being immersed in the discipline of the Brotherhood for the better part of a year, all of us had half forgotten what it was like to be among ordinary people going about their ordinary lives; hauling produce and other goods to and from the market, hailing neighbors, exchanging pleasantries and gossip, laughing and jesting and flirting as ordinary people do.

We were not ordinary, though.

We were Cassiline Brothers.

Even though we were only cadets, the divide existed. It was amicable and respectful, but undeniably present. Villagers hailed the older cadets, members of the Third Cohort in their dove-grey garb, with good cheer. Those old enough to have seen this cycle play out season after season smiled indulgently to see the youngest among us, this year's inductees into the Second Cohort, giddy at having exchanged their novice's white woolens for our journeyman's brown attire, bright-eyed, keen, and atwitter with excitement at being permitted a measure of license to explore our surroundings.

And then there were the bolder young men and women of the village who eyed us in a different way.

It was often the girls who were the boldest. This may in part have been due to the fact that boys and men were more intimidated by our training, but it was also true that D'Angeline women are notoriously immodest. According to Master Frédéric, it was because they had been misled into taking the pleasures of the flesh for the exaltation of the spirit. As a Cassiline, I have found that there is somewhat in human nature that cannot help but view others' decisions, if they are inimical to one's own desires, as a personal challenge. It was a jarring notion to encounter; nonetheless, thirteen was a well-considered age for our first such exposure. We were still boys, not yet men; old enough to know that our bodies were changing in irrevocable ways, young enough to be shy with it.

But I remember the first time a pretty girl smiled at me just so. She had honey-blonde hair, blue eyes, and fair skin with a sprinkling of freckles, and she carried a parasol in the summer. I was thirteen when she first caught my eye, strolling through the market square and giggling with her friends; I was fourteen a year later when she approached the Cassiline stall with an exceptionally ripe peach in hand and offered me a bite in exchange for a spoonful of the Prefectory's famed lavender honey. As I recall, I stammered some awkward reply, all too aware that the older cadets were watching.

All of us struggled with celibacy in our own ways. In one sense, I was fortunate that my proclivities favored women, for it was more difficult for boys growing into manhood to be surrounded by objects of desire day in and day out. But in another sense, it made fleeting glimpses of that which was forbidden all the more alluring. Boys' bodies were a known quantity as familiar as my own. Girls' bodies were mysteries.

I do remember Selwyn jabbing me in the ribs with a sharp elbow as the girl bit into her peach, nectar dribbling down her chin.

"She likes you," he said under his breath, smiling as he did. "And she thinks you're older than you are."

I flushed. "So? She's just being nice. It matters naught."

He shrugged and offered up an all-too-familiar reply. "If you say so."

I *did* say so, and I did so adamantly. I understood desire, at least a little bit. It is another misconception to believe that the Cassiline Brotherhood is dedicated to repressing desire; I daresay we discussed it with more candor than one might suppose. None of us were exempt from carnal urges. Our gangly young bodies quickened with the urge toward life, muscles and sinews strung taut, yearning to bolt after pleasure like colts bursting from stall to paddock. In the small hours of the night, desire's deep-rooted tendrils found cracks in our resolve. I do not think there is any cadet in the long history of the Brotherhood who did not awaken more than once to the damp and guilty pleasure of having spilled their seed in sleep.

Sleep was one thing; wakefulness was another. Different mentors offered different methods for coping with the thorny issue of the desires of the flesh.

Me, I built walls.

In doing so, I thought about those ancient Tiberian craftsmen who built the bridge across the Lusande River. Say what one will about the Tiberian Empire, bent as it was on conquest and assimilation in the days before Blessed Elua even walked the earth, but the skill of their engineers was surpassingly excellent. As a child of Shemhazai's lineage, I could not help but admire it. They hewed and cast blocks of stone and sank pilings deep into the riverbed, laying strong pillars. Upon those pillars they constructed arches. Weight, pressure, and precision—these elements combined to create structures capable of bearing a tremendous load and enduring for centuries.

A bridge wasn't a suitable image for my purposes, so I built a temple in my mind. It was a pavilion with seven arched sides, one for each of Elua's Companions save Cassiel, representing a primary attribute of every Companion: knowledge, pride, valor, desire, growth, healing, redemption. Blessed Elua's spirit of divine love needed no single place of worship for it was present in every aspect of Terre d'Ange—in the soil, in the vine, in the lavender and the honeycomb, in the sun and wind and rivers and streams. And in my mind's inner eye, the temple itself *was* Cassiel, open to the world yet unswayed by it, adamant and enduring, a symbol of protection and the promise of grace. It was a place in which I could stand and embody Cassiel in all of his fierce and bright-burning devotion.

That was the haven I built within myself, a private space where my own little spark of divine fire burned.

Oftentimes, though, we were simply boys, eager to experience the simple pleasures that were permitted us.

In that, I was no different. We always paid to watch the puppet show that took place in the square on market days. Although Rive-de-Lusande lacked a permanent playhouse, travelling troupes of dramatic players performed at least once a month during clement weather in the town's old Tiberian stadium. Mendacants in their flowing, rainbow-hued robes came and went as the whim took them and spun tales for our enjoyment. According to legend, there was a kernel of truth in every lie they uttered and the seed of a lie in every word of truth. Although they were sworn to Eisheth's service and charged no fee for the entertainment they provided, it was reckoned bad luck not to toss a coin in a Mendacant's bowl.

Riders for the Royal Post brought news of what transpired in the world beyond the Lusande Valley. Some of them were even Cassiline Brothers. The notion that passionate dedication and peerless skill might go in and out of style seemed ridiculous to me, and yet it was true. King Ganelon de la Courcel preserved the tradition of maintaining two Cassiline bodyguards on duty at all times, but our order was considered old-fashioned, and there were fewer and fewer peers willing to pay the tithe for our services.

The Crown, however, was always willing to pay a generous stipend for skilled couriers. Although it was a dull post for a Cassiline, there was a certain glamour to traversing the realm. Royal Post riders, Cassiline or otherwise, were always treated with grave respect at the Prefectory and conducted themselves accordingly. In the wineshops of the village, those couriers not sworn to Cassiel's service were less apt to be diplomatic, and affected casual poses with propped elbows, eyes glinting, awaiting an audience willing to spend good coin to fill their tankards before divulging their spiciest bits of news. We listened outside the windows of taverns and wineshops, speculating in hushed whispers.

The popularity of *The Exile's Lament* continued unabated; in part due to the love of Terre d'Ange which the ode expressed with such sublime simplicity, and in part due to the mysterious circumstances surrounding her flight. In and of itself, the King's Poet's story might have been the sort of tale that made my older sisters swoon while Luc and I gagged in mockery, but it was notable for the fact that it was *Alba* to which Thelesis had fled, and that she had done so successfully. The island nation of Alba was small, but fierce. A thousand years ago, its tribes united to drive back the armies of the Tiberian Empire itself. Alba lay to the west of Terre d'Ange, and at its narrowest part—the Straits—only seven or eight leagues away.

Those watery leagues, however, were ruled over by the Master of the Straits, who controlled the waters and the winds alike and seldom allowed passage between Terre d'Ange and Alba. Thus it was a matter of note that Thelesis de Mornay had won passage from the Master of the Straits—both for her outbound flight and her heartbroken return after the young man whom she wished to wed took his own life.

We stored up these tales like squirrels gathering nuts, tales to be told and retold during the long, dark nights to come, little dreaming that they had aught to do with us. Our lives were bounded by training, labor, and study.

We planted, we weeded, we harvested; we sheared sheep and baled wool, we scythed the grain we sowed and threshed it. We laid canvas around the trunks of olive trees, their leaves silver-green in the late-summer heat, and shook loose a hail of ripe olives. We loaded the press and turned the screws until green-gold fruity oil trickled from the spout. We pulled honeycomb dripping from the skeps, fishing out the dead bees, licking our sweet-sticky fingers.

We scrubbed, scoured, and swept; we chopped and hauled wood and stoked ovens and forges, we mucked, raked, and baked.

In the winter months when the ground lay fallow and frostbitten underfoot, we spent more time in the classroom. There we complained about the shortage of braziers and blew upon our chilled fingers as we studied the writings of all the great Hellene, Tiberian, and Habiru scholars, seeking to master their disparate tongues, and in some cases even unfamiliar alphabets. This in truth I relished, for as a child of Shemhazai's line, studying was an act of prayer unto itself.

And no matter what the season, when no one was looking, we sidled up to each other and muttered, "Fight me."

It's a wonder more Cassiline cadets didn't do each other grievous bodily harm, although I'm sure our mentors kept a closer eye on us than we realized. I was good; in the training yard, I will say without false modesty that I was the best of my class. By the time I turned fifteen years of age, I could easily outmatch anyone in my cohort except Selwyn, and in the training yard, I could usually defeat him, too.

Away from the training yard, it was another matter.

Outside the bounds of formal discipline, Selwyn tapped into a deep vein of ruthlessness that never failed to rock me back on my heels at some point in our impromptu sparring matches—and it was in those moments that he gained the advantage of me.

When I gaze back at those days, that final year in the Second Cohort marked the last of my youthful innocence. I was fifteen years of age, but as Selwyn had observed, I looked older. No matter what stage of our growth, I had always been tall and broad-shouldered for my age, but in other ways, no swifter to mature than my classmates. That summer was the first time any of us dared venture into the Trysting Mews, another rite of passage in the Cassiline Brotherhood that was only discussed in hushed whispers, as though every cadet to come before us hadn't done the same.

Every D'Angeline village has a quarter dedicated to carnal pleasure. In the City of Elua, it was called Night's Doorstep, for it lay at the base of Mont Nuit, the hill upon which all Thirteen Houses of the Night Court resided. In Rive-de-Lusande, the Trysting Mews was a neighborhood of cobblestone streets that surrounded a temple dedicated to Naamah. There were hidden alleys and niches and archways tucked away at unexpected angles, opening to reveal concealed paths that led to intimate gardens with soft beds of grass surrounded by fragrant flowers.

At fifteen years of age, we would dare each other to race through the Trysting Mews. The tradition had been passed down from generations of Naamah's Servants, too, for they were apt to treat our impromptu ritual as a spectator sport, leaning on their elbows on the second-story balustrades above us, watching with amusement as we dashed through the streets, our hearts racing and skin prickling with the thrill of the forbidden. The adepts laughed and sang ditties that were mocking and affectionate in equal measure, lamplight striking shadows along the elegant lines of their cheekbones as the waning daylight gave way to dusk.

I remember those songs, still.

"Hey, boy, pretty boy, let down your long fair hair, oh!"

"Hey, boy, pretty boy, I'll make a man of you, oh!"

And I remember, too, Selwyn's sharp elbow in my ribs, his sideways glance. "Are you *never* tempted, oh fair-haired boy?"

I closed my eyes against the world and stood fast in the temple I had built in my mind. "No."

In that moment, it was true.

CHAPTER TEN

At sixteen years of age, I swore the Oath of Steel.

Water.

Fire.

Steel.

These were the unspoken languages we had spent six years learning. We had learned to flow like water; the substance of our bodies and souls had been heated and quenched, beaten and tempered. Now we were prepared to be honed. All five of us took the oath together in the quadrangle. We were the first class in a generation to have entered the Third Cohort without losing a single member to injury, inability, or moral failure.

It was an unremarkable morning, the skies overcast and grey; and yet fitting in its way, for it was the first time our class donned the grey.

Six years ago, we'd stood where this year's incoming class stood, looking just as young and spindly and stunned as they did, uncertain how to navigate their surroundings with one wrist lashed behind their back.

Three years since we swore the Oath of Fire; now, the palms of our hands were so deeply callused it would take more than a few heartbeats to raise a blister over an open flame.

Today, steel.

It was an especial blessing to have the opportunity to swear on an ancestral blade. Knowing that I pledged my oath alongside Selwyn, whose uncle's arms had been seized by Skaldi raiders, and even Toulouse, whose family had no history of service to the Brotherhood, I was grateful for that which was given to me. Some of the ancestral blades in our overall cohort had names: Thunderstroke, Veinslitter, Rue-the-Day; oddly enough, for reasons lost in the mists of time, Dumiel's sword was called Blanche. My uncle's sword was nameless. It was simply, as Master Jacobe had told me from the beginning, a well-forged blade. All of the elegance it possessed was in its materials and craftsmanship. It was perfectly balanced; suitable for the Cassiline two-handed sword-fighting style, of a length and heft that allowed it to be wielded single-handed at need. After countless hours in the smithy, it was polished until it shone like a mirror and was honed to an exquisite edge.

And on the first day of summer, the year that I'd turned sixteen, I closed my fist around the blade of my sword and gave my oath.

Steel bit as hard and deep as you let it. Every class entering the Third Cohort had heard at least one tale of a cadet so vain and foolish that he clutched his sword hard enough to sever tendons in his fingers. At the same time, it was reckoned bad luck if you *didn't* bleed upon swearing the Oath of Steel.

I clenched my hand hard enough to bleed, not so deep as to threaten sinew. I had to squeeze to cut through the layers of callus. I vowed to offer my body, the whole of my body, unto Cassiel's service. Blood welled from the palm of my hand to trickle down the inside of my wrist, warm scarlet tendrils forking along the length of my forearm. I swore to remain chaste, I swore to always hold my oath in the highest honor. I tightened my grip and said the words I had uttered before, aware that they were setting me upon an irrevocable path.

"In Cassiel's name, I protect and serve."

I had taken another step on my journey.

I do wonder, sometimes, if I would have changed anything had I known exactly how long and extraordinarily challenging that journey would become. Mayhap; yet at every twist and turning it took, I cannot imagine one that didn't lead me back to the same crossroads I would encounter over and over again in my lifetime.

For a surety, I cannot imagine making a different choice at those eternal crossroads, although betimes it took me longer than it ought to make it.

In those times, however, my classmates and I wondered a great deal about what fate held in store for us. A post at the Palace remained the most prestigious assignation a Cassiline Brother might receive; in particular, a position as one of the King's personal guards. But the young Dauphine Ysandre had turned thirteen years of age—too young for the marriage bed, but old enough that protocol suggested she be attended by bodyguards rather than nursemaids.

I didn't care about politics. I truly didn't. Toulouse continued to make jibes at my expense for the attitude of aristocratic condescension he ascribed to me based on my heritage, but many of his assumptions were false. By the same token, Selwyn was apt to needle me for what he considered unacceptable apathy about the intrigues and machinations of the realm.

In a way, they were both right, and if it transpired that they were both utterly wrong, too, it was nothing anyone could have suspected at the time.

So we exchanged news and gossip, paying more and more attention to the posts—or lack thereof—that the members of the Third Cohort were receiving upon completing nine long years of training. Some of us, like Dumiel and Selwyn, came from families that wouldn't hesitate to pull strings to procure a good posting for their sons; others, like Paul and Toulouse, hadn't been born into families with that sort of clout. House Verreuil, of course, wielded no influence since my father would have found the very notion unspeakably vulgar, and I would have expected nothing less.

For those seeking a less conventional glimpse into the future, there were always Tsingani fortunetellers. The Tsingani had no fixed community of place in Terre d'Ange, but travelled in family-based troupes called *kumpania*. Being horse-breeders of considerable renown, they followed the trade routes to horse fairs across the nation, passing through Rive-de-Lusande at least twice a year. Their culture was a closed and private one, and like the Yeshuite folk, they seldom intermarried with D'Angelines, but they were a regular fixture at markets and it was known that Tsingani women had the gift of seeing the future.

It is a true gift, of that I have no doubt—whether it is always used in good faith is another matter, for the Tsingani also had a reputation for concocting schemes to part the gullible from their monies.

It was one such scheme that Toulouse fell prey to. He was always short of coin, but those who can least afford a loss are often the easiest to dupe.

Seven of us from the Third Cohort were attending the town market on the day that Toulouse discovered he was the object of a gambit. I cannot recall the exact details, only that after falling into discussion with a fortuneteller's nephew, he paid hard-earned coin for a magic casket that, upon being buried and exhumed under a specific set of circumstances, was purported to turn copper into silver and silver into gold.

Ordinarily, the Tsingani *kumpania* would have pulled up stakes and been long gone by the time the deception was revealed. In this instance, their departure was delayed by unexpected cases of colic in their herd, which resulted in Toulouse pelting through the village in hot pursuit of the fortuneteller's nephew, roaring in fury at the deception perpetrated upon him.

It was late in the day and Selwyn had vanished, but Paul and I doubled over in laughter until Arion d'Isle, who was the First Cadet of the Third Cohort, gave us genial swats upside the head.

"All right, all right! He's your boy, go catch him before anything turns ugly," he said, making a shooing gesture. "Keep the peace, eh?"

We crossed our forearms and bowed.

It was near enough to dusk that the lamplighters were out with their torches, looking bemused as Paul and I charged past them, following the sound of Toulouse's outrage into the Trysting Mews. Laughter filtered down from above as we encountered a crossroads, cocking our heads to listen.

"Oh hey, boys, pretty boys, have you lost your brother? He went that-away!" someone sang out.

Another voice chimed in. "No, no, he went that-away!"

Paul and I exchanged glances. "You go this way," he said, pointing toward the north. "I'll go south."

I nodded and set out at a hard run.

By sheer happenstance, I took the right angle. I saw the Tsingano boy first, racing atop the garden walls, his soft-soled boots slapping the stones. He saw me below and flinched, his dark eyes glinting as they widened. I ran at the garden wall and vaulted atop it, moss lodging under my fingernails, intercepting him. I was extra-aware of the vambraces on my forearms, the twin daggers on my belt. This was the first time anyone had ever looked upon me with fear.

I did not like the feeling. But I didn't dislike it, either.

The Tsingano fortuneteller's nephew was young; my age at most, mayhap younger. His gaze slid back and forth, darting below and to either side, finding himself trapped. His lower lip trembled as he whispered, "Please, Messire Cassiline? I'm sorry. I'll give him his money back, just don't let him hurt me."

In the swiftly closing distance, Toulouse bellowed. Somewhere below us on the other side of the wall were the murmurs and whispered exchanges of lovers trysting.

I sighed. "Go," I said to the Tsingano boy with all the gentleness I could muster. I didn't believe his sincerity, but I didn't doubt that his fear was genuine. "I will deal with him. Only tell your folk that there's more risk than merit in duping members of the Cassiline Brotherhood. Agreed?"

"Agreed," he promised fervently, taking to his heels and darting away.

I braced myself and waited for Toulouse while the Tsingano's footfalls receded in the distance.

I didn't have long to wait. Toulouse lowered his head like a bull ready to charge, short of breath, fingers twitching over his hilts, dark sweat-damp curls that would never stay properly bound falling over his brow. His jaw was clenched and I could smell that he was angry. "Get. Out. Of my way!"

I shook my head. "No. Stand down, brother."

He glowered at me. "I will *not*."

I planted my feet and spread my arms wide, empty-handed, daggers untouched at my hips. "Come, then. *Fight me*."

As the saying goes, there are battles of which the poets sing; this was most assuredly not one of them. Toulouse tackled me in an unexpected diving lunge. We toppled from the garden wall and hit the grounds of the Trysting Mews. It was a hard fall in the soft gloaming light; I grunted as my weight struck the grass, driving the breath from my lungs. Toulouse huffed and gasped as he landed scowling atop me.

Whispered curses, giggles, and laughter; we *had* interrupted a lovers' tryst.

It was the honey-blonde-haired girl who had smiled at me years ago whom I first recognized, which is a piece of irony. Disengaging from her partner, she cocked her head as she regarded Toulouse and me sprawling bruised and combative upon the green sward of the garden. She laughed at the spectacle, and her laughter was like the sound of bells, at once lighter and wiser than any of us boys understood. The charming spray of freckles across her nose was silvery-dim in the waning light, and she was utterly unembarrassed as she tugged her garments back into place. She ran her fingers through her lover's unbound hair before sauntering into the narrow cobblestone streets, blowing a farewell kiss. "You know where to find me, pretty boy!"

It was Selwyn.

I knew it; I should have known it from the outset. We lived so closely together in the barracks of the Prefectory, we knew every physical detail about each other. But I had not seen him this way.

Toulouse and I scrambled to our feet, all thoughts of the Tsingano forgotten.

"You—" I said stupidly, gesturing.

Toulouse simply said his name, reminding us that he had been in intermittent command of our cohort. "*Selwyn*."

He grimaced and pulled up his breeches, yanking the laces tight. "What?"

"*Selwyn!*"

"*What?*"

The three of us faced each other; there was a tension here I didn't fully comprehend. Later, I would understand it better; now, I simply looked back and forth between the two of them, feeling bewildered and shocked. "Why?"

Selwyn glared at me. "Do you jest? What do you mean, *why*?" He gestured all around the garden. "Why *not*? Are we not deserving of mortal love? That's the question we ought to be asking ourselves."

Standing fast in the temple of my mind, I shook my head. "No. No, it's not. We're agents of the divine, Selwyn. We stand in the gap between this world and the next. And it is a higher calling, one that demands—"

He interrupted me. "The kind of self-sacrificing nobility that you're oh, so very good at espousing?"

That stung. "That's not what I said."

"No, but it's what you meant." Selwyn shrugged, twining his hair and knotting it at the nape of his neck. "Let's get on with it, shall we? Do you intend to tattle, Joscelin? Carry tales to the masters?"

Despite an uneasy prickling sensation between my shoulder blades, I squared them. I disapproved to the marrow of my bones, but I was no telltale. "No, and you ought to know me better than to think it."

Ignoring me, he turned to Toulouse. "And you?"

Toulouse held out one hand. "Cross my palm with silver," he said in a laconic tone. "Make up for what I lost to that lying Tsingano bastard and I'll keep my mouth shut, de Gaunte. Deal?"

Selwyn nodded. "Deal."

Snatching the coins Selwyn shook into his hand, Toulouse counted them with grim satisfaction before stalking away.

"Well?" Selwyn said when he'd gone, folding his arms across his chest. "Aren't you going to give me a stern talking-to?"

I watched the lacy shadows of flowering vines shift on the garden wall. "You asked me if I were willing to die for you, once. That, I understood. But I never expected you to ask me to lie for you."

To that, Selwyn had no response.

CHAPTER ELEVEN

Afterward, nothing was the same.

On the surface, nothing had changed. Summer gave way to autumn; once we'd shaken loose the last of the olives for the final pressing of the season, there were no more market days, only chores and training.

It was my second year in the Third Cohort and there was nothing I could not execute with precision. I even practiced the *terminus*, mindful of the fact that my uncle had died for refusing to perform it. I thought of his death every time I set the edge of one very finely honed dagger to my throat, feeling my pulse throbbing beneath it.

Selwyn and I did not discuss the incident in the Trysting Mews.

I tried once or twice, but he didn't want to talk about it. And the more time that passed, the more a distance between us grew. I had seen him with a woman. I had seen him with his hair unbound. All that was left between us was the challenge.

"Fight me."

And we did fight; we sparred in the training yard, where the forms were strictly observed. The masters judged us on points of precision, skill, and execution. A bout would be called against anyone who broke form. I understood why. It was all part of training until the forms were so deeply engrained in muscle, sinew, and bone that we could execute them without thinking. Selwyn understood it, too. He'd begun studying them almost from the moment his eldest brother had died. But he hated being told what to do, and in the yard I defeated him more often than not.

We fought impromptu bouts everywhere and elsewhere on the grounds of the Prefectory, where he fought with such wild abandon and utter disregard for the rules, I was afraid one of us would lose a limb or even our lives.

"You don't fight fair," I complained once when he pulled off an unexpected counterstrike that didn't exist in the Cassiline forms.

"There's no such thing as *fair* in a real fight," he retorted. "Only winning or dying. And even if we do live to have a chance to defend a ward, it's not going to be against another Brother. The Brotherhood would terminate every single contract out there before they'd allow that to happen. You're never going to draw sword against another Cassiline in earnest, Joscelin. Only an opponent with different training, unexpected moves. I'm doing you a favor."

"An opponent with a hell of a lot less training," I said. "And inferior moves."

Selwyn grinned. "Mine aren't, oh pretty boy. Want me to teach you this one?"

"No." I sighed and admitted the truth. "Yes."

In the quiet months of midwinter, Master Jacobe summoned me to his chambers.

The masters at the Prefectory had their own quarters in a sprawling westward wing on the main floor. The rooms were simple and plain, but there was a luxury in the mere existence of privacy, something none of us cadets were afforded. His chambers had their own fireplace, a tidy blaze lit beneath a soot-blackened brick chimney. It was seven years since Master Jacobe had come to fetch me from Verreuil; seven years that he'd been my primary mentor. I'd been a boy, and he'd been a warrior aging out of his prime—an injured warrior with skills to teach and a fighting potential that would never be realized in this lifetime.

He invited me to sit and poured us both a cup of a warm tea of hyssop leaves, dried linden flowers, and honey. I sipped it, trying not to tense. "You're troubled," he observed. "And you have been for some time. Do you wish to tell me why?"

I shook my head. "No."

"All right." Master Jacobe's gaze sharpened. "Cassiel is known as the Perfect Companion. What does that mean to *you*?"

"Purity." The word came out of my mouth unthinking.

He nodded. "And what does *that* mean?"

I thought about it, turning the question over and over in my mind as though it were a child's wooden puzzle box. In the end, it was a puzzle I couldn't assemble. "I don't know, maître," I admitted.

Master Jacobe leaned back in his chair, considering me. Fragrant wisps of steam rose from the unglazed earthenware cup of tea cradled in my palm, and the fire in the grate crackled. "You're a very proficient fighter," he said at length. "But you know that, too. And yet I sense that you're failing in a manner I can't quite identify. You're disciplined and determined. You're loyal to your friends—or at least to Selwyn de Gaunte—mayhap to the point of fault."

I said nothing.

"I'm not asking you to tell tales," Master Jacobe said shrewdly. "Although I suspect you've tales to tell, I remember what it was like to be your age. But I will issue you a challenge, young Messire Verreuil. You'll be entering your final year in the Third Cohort this spring, and I mean to appoint you as the First Cadet. I trust that you're willing to accept that responsibility?"

I took a deep breath and set my shoulders. "Of course."

He raised his grizzled brows. "Do not underestimate the weight of it. And I suggest that you use this time to consider what purity means to you."

It was a notion that I would return to over and over. *Purity.* What did it mean in truth? Ultimately for me purity was a fixity of purpose—only that purpose was nothing I could possibly have imagined in those days.

In some ways, it feels so very long ago; in others, not at all.

Spring gave way to summer in all of its abundance. All of us took another step on the ladder of the Cassiline Brotherhood's hierarchy and a new class of cadets took the Oath of Water, looking younger, more wide-eyed, spindly-limbed, and knobby-kneed than I remembered any of us ever had. Although Toulouse was angry that he hadn't been appointed First Cadet in our final year of training, he didn't protest the masters' decision, nor did anyone else. Selwyn was merely amused by the decision. I took my duties seriously, mindful of the gravity that Léon had brought to his role when I had first entered the Brotherhood, doing my best to emulate him and set a good example for all the younger cadets.

If life within the boundaries of the Prefectory was ordered and stable, elsewhere in the realm, uncertainty was rising.

When I received my thrice-annual letters from home, they were usually from my sisters Jehane and Honore, chockful of details about the family; gossip, potential romances, petty squabbles, which of the hounds was whelping. There was always a loving message from our mother and my father's more formal greetings. Sometimes an affectionate scrawl from my older brother Luc or my younger brother Mahieu. Nothing from my youngest sister Beatrice, but she had only been a baby when I left. It was disconcerting to think that she was a half-grown girl now, almost the age that Mahieu had been when I entered the Cassiline Brotherhood.

The letters that Selwyn received were very, very different.

The province of Camlach wasn't known for political intrigue, but the Skaldi were making tentative forays across the border. Once again, the burden of defending the three Great Passes in the Camaeline Mountains fell on Camlach's forces. It was a burden Camael's martial-minded descendants were willing to bear, but there were rumblings of an alliance seeking greater power in return.

In the sovereign duchy of Aiglemort, Selwyn's family's liege lord the Duc had died of a septic wound. His son Isidore had been sworn in as the new Duc d'Aiglemort. He was young and ambitious and reputed to be one of the greatest warriors in the history of Camlach, which was saying something.

And Selwyn's older brother Telys, the former middle son who had been intended for the Brotherhood, was riding at the young Duc's side.

"Sharing in the battle and glory," Selwyn said bitterly. "While we spin in circles honing our skills for a day that will likely never come."

"You're awfully eager for a chance to die," I observed, knee-deep in the river, showing my new apprentice how to make repairs to the fishing net strung across the weir without removing the whole affair. Clemente was a sweet-faced First Cohort cadet with a good mind for the way things worked, and he was small enough to reach or squirm into the tight spaces in the mill I could no longer reach.

"And you're awfully eager to avoid one." On the riverbank, he leaned back on his elbows. "Did you know in Camlach it's considered good luck to bed a member of the Royal Guard the night before a battle?"

My apprentice Clemente dropped the rope he was holding, shocked to hear such a thing said aloud. I remembered the guilty thrill of hearing the older cadets speculate about carnal matters. But if their curiosity was prurient, they spoke out of innocence.

Knowing what Selwyn had done, I felt unclean. "Somehow I suspect that particular superstition originated with the Royal Guard," I said dryly. "How do the commonfolk feel about it?"

In a flash, Selwyn was on his feet, hands on his dagger hilts, a flush of anger on his cheekbones. "Do you accuse us of *rape*? You're such an obedient little cadet, you don't even know if your cock works, who are you to accuse us of *heresy*?"

I was angry, too. Clemente looked back and forth between us, his mouth agape. I wanted to fight Selwyn right there and then, but I'd removed my vambraces and dagger belt to keep them dry. I had kept my training sword in its shoulder harness, but it was forbidden to draw even a nondedicated sword outside the training yard unless it was to kill. I was half-soaked in the middle of the river demonstrating a tricky repair job—and I always sought to set a good example for the younger cadets. "Heresy, no, of course not," I said, forcing a light tone. "Merely that the rumor was convenient . . . 'twas a poor jest, no mind." I changed the topic, luring Selwyn with one he couldn't resist. "Do you think that d'Aiglemort's bid for the Dauphine's hand will succeed? Or will Parliament rebel and appoint Prince Baudoin de Trevalion the King's heir?"

True to form, Selwyn snapped up my bait like a hungry trout and launched into a lengthy monologue. He paced the riverbank, thinking aloud, periodically glancing my way to make sure I was listening.

I was, albeit with half an ear, most of my attention bent toward Clemente and the net. I knew Selwyn well enough that even over the river's rush I could hear the faint shift in the tone of his voice before he looked at me, and I was ready with an attentive expression, nodding in encouragement or furrowing my brow in concern.

The truth is that were it not for Selwyn, I'd have known nothing of Baudoin de Trevalion beyond his lineage and the fact that he was the heir to Trevalion, the sovereign duchy of the province of Azzalle. According to Selwyn, Baudoin had a reputation for being valiant and a bit wild. He had fostered at House d'Aiglemort for a time, and now he and his personal cadre, the Glory-Seekers, were riding with Isidore d'Aiglemort and the Allies of Camlach.

Baudoin, however, wasn't angling for the Dauphine's hand in marriage, for his mother was the King's sister. D'Angelines may place no limits on love, but marital law prohibits first cousins from wedding.

And as the King's nephew, Prince Baudoin was angling for the throne itself.

My apprentice Clemente tied the final knot in the broken mesh and gave me a questioning look, beaming when I nodded my approval. Elua have mercy, betimes I enjoyed his company more than Selwyn's. We slogged out of the river together, me on the downriver side lest the current take him. A couple of times it nearly did, but he fought to keep his footing, grabbing at reeds to anchor himself; eleven years old and already imbued with Cassiline discipline and determination.

On the riverbank, Selwyn was still holding forth. ". . . and *now* there are rumors that Baudoin's taken up with Melisande Shahrizai."

I clambered up the bank and extended a hand to Clemente, hauling him up after me. "Who's she?"

Selwyn squinted at me. "House Shahrizai? Not-sovereign-but-would-like-to-be duchy in Kusheth?"

"Yes, I'm aware." That was partially true; I could have located the duchy on a map, but I'd had no knowledge of their political ambitions. I knew little about the province of Kusheth. Alone amongst Elua's Companions, Kushiel made me uneasy. Before becoming one of the Misguided—for that is what we call those mighty angels who turned their back on Adonai, save for Cassiel—Kushiel was a punisher of the damned. According to D'Angeline lore, he administered pain like a blessing, and the sinners in his charge found in it a divine grace so transcendent that it lies beyond redemption. And I could not help but think that it too was a convenient piece of lore, for it was known that the scions of Kushiel's line took pleasure in administering pain and punishment. Dumiel told us in whispers that there was an entire House in the Night Court dedicated to serving such desires, which I found to be an appalling notion. I put the thought aside and sat on the grass, doing my best to wring out my breeches below the knee. "I mean, why is it significant that Prince Baudoin has taken up with this woman?"

"It might not be." He shrugged. "After all, she *is* reputed to be the most beautiful woman in Terre d'Ange."

I wrung out my sleeves, Clemente copying me. "Is she?"

"Who can say?" Selwyn flung himself down on the grass beside us. "Doubtless she's quite beautiful, but it's hardly possible for any one person to have seen *all* the women in Terre d'Ange."

Smiling despite myself, I inched my wool socks over my still-damp feet. "That's very logical of you."

"The interesting thing," he continued as though I hadn't spoken. "The *interesting* thing is that Melisande Shahrizai leaves a trail of dead husbands behind her."

That got my attention. "Mayhap Prince Baudoin needs a pair of Cassilines to guard him."

Selwyn shook his head. "From what I've heard, he wouldn't stand for it. Thinks we're stuffy, old-fashioned, purely ornamental. Anyway, Baudoin's mother disapproves of House Shahrizai and she *is* the King's sister, so I think it unlikely he's going to become husband number three."

Having donned my boots and buckled my vambraces in place, I rose and settled my dagger belt around my waist. It sat low and snug on my hips, tough ox-hide worn and oiled to suppleness. The sheaths were hung at a slight angle so the leather-wrapped hilts of my daggers, sweat-darkened and faintly shiny with use, presented themselves for my cross-armed grasp. I brushed my fingertips over their plain steel pommels. "Well, I'd welcome a chance to show this Prince Baudoin exactly how *ornamental* a Cassiline is."

He grinned his foxy grin. "You and me both. Doubt we'll get the chance, though." He glanced toward the keep, his grin giving way to a grimace. "The way placements keep dwindling, we're probably for the Royal Post."

Clemente was stretching his eyes and ears again, and I didn't think it seemly for an eleven-year-old boy to overhear so much adult discussion. "We should be going," I said, raising my brows a fraction at Selwyn. "Unless you've something further to say about this Melisande Shahrizai?"

"No." He heeded my unspoken admonition and got to his feet; then couldn't resist one last comment. "Anyway, I doubt she's a serious player in the game. After all, she's just a woman."

CHAPTER TWELVE

One hears of prisoners scratching on their cell walls with a sharp stone to mark the passage of days. At the Prefectory, cadets in their final year in the Third Cohort marked the days remaining between the Longest Night and the vernal equinox with hashmarks drawn in chalk on the barracks wall. The five of us took turns ceremoniously rubbing out a mark at the beginning of every day.

It wasn't that the Prefectory felt like a prison. It had been our home for almost half of our lives. We had been molded, forged, and tempered within the walls of its keep. We had tended to the grounds and the valley thrived on our labor. Even in the depths of winter when frost glistened on the fields, the bees slept in their skeps, the olive trees were dormant and the sheep grew shaggy and unkempt, I took pride in the tidy efficiency of the Prefectory, in the smell of clean straw in the stables, the polished gleam of our cooking pots, the well-stocked cellar and larder.

And yet . . .

We were eighteen years old, highly trained, and restless. We had been taught to channel our energy into a watchful stillness, but we were eager to do so toward a specific end, and not simply to hone our discipline. Once, the senior cadets might have the chance to accompany a Brother on the journey to escort an incoming pledge to the Prefectory, but since the cadet escorting Selwyn had been slain, the Brotherhood had determined that only full-fledged Brothers travelling in pairs would undertake those ventures.

By mid-April, there were a mere sixty-some hashmarks on the wall. With just over two months until we became full-fledged Cassiline Brothers, I would have said it was inconceivable that any of us would do anything to jeopardize that future.

I should have known better.

The weather in Terre d'Ange in April was unpredictable. Generally it was mild and pleasant—according to Paul, it got downright hot in the southern province of Eisande—but betimes the spring rains were torrential and the wind whipped itself into gales capable of toppling trees and flattening young crops.

I was surveying the damage to the wheat field after one such a windstorm when Clemente approached at a jog, skinny limbs pumping. "The Master Miller is asking for you," he said, only slightly short of breath. "The pully hook on the sluice gate is cracked bad."

"Is it still holding?" I asked him.

"For now, maybe not long. And he daren't open the sluice," he said.

The sluice gate controlled the flow of water to the aqueduct that led to the smithy and the assemblage of clay pipes and a wooden trough that released a steady trickle onto the grindstone. Without it, half the work in the smithy would be forced to a halt—and if the cracked hook gave way, the damage would be ten times harder to repair.

I glanced at the sun to gauge the time. For all of yesterday's raging winds and roiling skies, today it was warm, sunny, and calm and the sky was a vivid cerulean with nary a wisp of a cloud in sight. "Let's go."

It was a mercy that it was the hook and not the pully itself that had cracked. The Master Miller nodded at it. "I'd have gotten it replaced already if I knew where you lads stashed all the spare bits and bobs over the years."

"We organized them!" I protested; it was true, although it was also to make space for Selwyn's and my hideout. "Everything's in the attic, maître."

"Yes, and these old knees aren't meant for climbing ladders anymore," he said. "Go, take Clemente with you and show him where to find things."

I crossed my forearms and bowed, and Clemente followed suit beside me. His bow wasn't totally reflexive yet, but it would become so. I could see the fervor in him, the will to train the hardest, to be the best, to dedicate heart and soul and body to Cassiel's service. I was fortunate to have him as an apprentice.

It felt like summer had come early as we climbed the ladder to the upper story; the air warm, the steady splash and churn of the waterwheel, dust motes sparkling in the shafts of sunlight that found their way through cracks between the planks.

If it hadn't been for the sound of the waterwheel . . .

It wasn't that loud, just loud enough that Selwyn and I had always counted on it to mask the thump and clatter of our more vigorous duels along the walkway and beams. Well, it did a fine job of masking sound, all right. If it hadn't, they might have heard us coming up the ladder from the upper story to the attic. If it hadn't, I might have heard *them.*

I caught sight of movement out of the corner of my eye at the same time that they saw me. I blinked and froze. For the space of several heartbeats, no one moved except Clemente clambering off the ladder to join me. Belatedly, I moved to block his view. Too late. Clemente had seen. His eyes were so wide the whites showed all around them. He began backing away from me.

I reached for him. "Clemente, *wait.*"

He turned and dashed for the ladder, scrambling down it with an eleven-year-old's agility and speed.

"Elua's Balls, man," Toulouse's voice said behind me, thick with anger and despair. "*Stop him!*"

"It's too late." Beneath the sound of water splashing, I could hear Clemente shouting for the Master Miller. Mayhap I wasn't lucky in apprentices after all. I'd seen so much of my younger self in him, I hadn't expected him to be a telltale.

Then again, I'd never imagined I'd witness one of my brethren break his vows and hold my tongue.

If Selwyn had broken his vows in the Trysting Mews, he'd shattered them in the attic. The image was emblazoned behind my eyes—Selwyn on hands and knees, head lowered, his hair loose and hanging around his face; Toulouse behind him, his hands gripping Selwyn's hips hard. Elua have mercy, for a fleeting moment I thought that they must be wrestling. But wrestling is not an art we study, and no one has wrestled naked in earnest since the ancient Hellenes.

I turned to face Toulouse as he approached me on the walkway. He had donned his grey woolens, but his olive skin was oily with sweat and he stank of fear. "You could tell them the boy was imagining things," he said. "That he mistook what he saw. You're older. You're respected. They'll believe your word over his."

"No," I said. "I won't do that."

Toulouse studied my face for a moment, his thick shoulders tensing. I saw his gaze flick toward the nearest space between the trestle beams and realized with mild astonishment that he was contemplating murder.

"I wouldn't," Selwyn said coolly from the opposite walkway. "Even if you manage to push Joscelin off the ledge, which I doubt, he's likely to survive the fall with a broken bone or two. But more significantly, I've got a dagger aimed square between your shoulder blades lest you think to attempt it."

Showing his palms in a gesture of surrender, Toulouse turned toward him. Selwyn had put on his pants and his dagger belt, but he was barefoot and shirtless. His lean torso was winter-pale and sweat ran down it in rivulets, strands of unbound reddish-blond hair clinging to his skin. He held the tip of one dagger in his left hand, his right hand resting on the hilt of the other, and his expression was serene. "You know," Toulouse said. "I quite loathe you."

Selwyn's expression never changed. "And yet."

I looked away. "I need a hook."

I had no qualms whatsoever about turning my back on Toulouse, because I had no doubt whatsoever that Selwyn would plant a dagger in him if he so much as twitched in my direction. I heard a muttered exchange, the words unintelligible beneath the sound of the waterwheel, then the faint creak of the ladder. By the time I found an iron hook of suitable size, Toulouse was gone.

Selwyn was still there. I brushed past him, heading for the ladder. "I have to get this to the Master Miller." He said nothing, only gave me a Cassiline bow that made something inside my chest twist with a sick feeling.

Downstairs on the main floor, Clemente was nowhere to be found. The Master Miller gave me a complicated look of disapproval and pity. "I sent the boy away," he said to me. "He was quite upset. Do you wish to speak to the matter?"

"No, maître," I murmured. "I'm quite upset myself."

"You know that I have to report this." It wasn't a question.

"Yes."

"Good," he said. "Because silence would be a lie. Now help me replace that hook."

It was an awkward job requiring sheer strength to manually hoist the sluice gate far enough to garner enough slack in the chain to swap out the cracked hook for the whole one. For the time it took, I thought about nothing except the task at hand, which was a blessing. It was a blessing that didn't last long. Selwyn was waiting for me outside the mill. At least he'd put on all his clothes and his hair was pulled back into a loose braid, an acknowledgment of something that had been true for many months: He was no longer entitled to call himself a Cassiline.

Ignoring him, I set out for the wheat field I'd been surveying for damage.

Selwyn fell in beside me. I waited for him to speak, but he was prepared to outwait me. "*Why?*" I said at length. "And why Toulouse? You don't even *like* him!"

He sighed. "Betimes like's got nothing to do with it, Verreuil. But that's something you'll never understand, isn't it?"

I rounded on him. "Oh, don't go trying to turn this on me! You do know you're going to be expelled for this, don't you? And you *do* remember that a man died so that you might live to take your place here?"

"*Do you think I could ever forget it?*" he shouted, eyes glittering with tears of rage and frustration. "Elua have mercy, I think about it *every day*."

Even though I was furious at him, I made my voice gentle. "So . . . why, Selwyn?"

He dragged his inner sleeve across his eyes, heedless of the straps and buckles securing his vambrace. "Oh, well, I wanted to know what it felt like. Pretty good, as it happens, especially when someone wants you so badly they don't even care that they despise you."

I folded my arms.

Selwyn dropped his and looked me straight in the eye. "I should never have agreed to this fate. Joscelin, if I took my final vow and became a full-fledged Cassiline Brother, how many times during the course of my lifetime do you suppose I'd have the chance to fight in defense of D'Angeline lives? Mayhap once or twice, thrice at most; mayhap never."

I smiled wryly. "Some people would consider 'never' to be good fortune."

"I'm not 'some people,' and neither are you," he said. "But you're so damned rigid, Elua help you if you're ever tempted to break *your* vows."

I lowered my crossed arms and rested my hands on my dagger hilts. "Fight me."

"*Now?*"

"Fight me," I repeated.

Although we were in an open field, there was no one to see us. All the cadets were fanned out across the grounds to take stock of the wind damage. Selwyn drew his daggers in a flash of steel and came at me fast and hard, but I was expecting it. Already in motion, I feinted right and spun left, catching him wrong-footed and forcing a graceless parry. In all our bouts, I'd never felt such perfect focus. I channeled all my anger, frustration, and sense of betrayal into that focus, moving with tremendous speed and precision. My vision was sharp and clear, my blood was singing in my veins like a high note ringing in my ears. I pressed Selwyn harder, thinking that for once, at least,

I would defeat him outside the quadrangle. Retreating from my onslaught, he stumbled backward . . .

. . . and drew his sword.

I froze. With a certain gentleness, Selwyn took a step forward and rested the tip of his sword on my breastbone. "I win."

"No." I found my voice. "You can't. Drawing your sword . . . it's *forbidden*."

"Shall I kill you to keep a vow when I've already broken others?" He reached over his shoulder to sheath his sword in one smooth motion. "I mean to ride with the Allies of Camlach. I'll see all the battle my Camaeline heart craves, and I can do more good there. Fight to guard the passes, fight to protect entire villages, the whole province . . . hell, the realm itself. No one's life will have been sacrificed in vain for my training."

I pressed the heel of one hand between my eyebrows, where a knot of pain was forming. "Did you mean to get caught?"

"No." Selwyn paused. "I don't know. Not by you, anyway. You were working on the northwest slope today, I didn't think you'd be anywhere near the mill."

"What about Toulouse?" I asked. "Did you mean to ruin his life, too?"

He scoffed. "He's a grown man, he took his chances. I didn't force him to break his vows."

"Look, I'm not fond of him," I said. "But his stipend supports his family in Azzalle."

"I know," he said. "And there are plenty of ways for someone trained by the Brotherhood to make money. He can apply for the Royal Post, take a private job as a bodyguard, hire out as a mercenary guard for a trading caravan."

I had no response.

Selwyn tilted his head and contemplated the cloudless azure sky. "Do you know why I always beat you when we duel outside the training yard?"

"Yes," I said. "You cheat."

"No," he said. "It's because I'm willing to get hurt."

I waited. "That's all?"

He shrugged. "It's what it comes down to. You're good, Joscelin, maybe the best in a generation on some level. But to be *the best*, you have to learn to fight without fear. Fear of being wounded, fear of dying . . . fear of breaking the rules."

The muscles in my jaw tightened. "I'm not afraid of being wounded or dying. And don't mistake respect for fear."

"Why not?" Selwyn said. "The edge of a blade can't tell the difference between the two." He glanced in the direction of the keep. "I expect I'll be summoned before the Prefect soon. I hope I have the chance to say farewell."

Once again, I said nothing. He hesitated for a moment as though on the verge of saying something further, then departed, trudging across the field with an unaccustomed heaviness to his step. Selwyn could feign blithe disregard as much as he liked, but I could tell this was weighing on him.

It was too late to change course, though. Late that afternoon I was in the Third Cohort's classroom sketching a diagram of the damaged field on a bit of foolscap when a first-year cadet in the cohort came to deliver the message that the Prefect wished to see me.

Lord Rinforte's chambers were spacious and austere. The stone walls were unadorned and there were no carpets or furs on the floor. Despite the heat of the day, it was chilly, but there were only long-dead grey ashes in the fireplace. In the Brotherhood we trained to endure heat and cold, but it was said in half jest that the Prefect was impervious to both. Seated at an ornately carved walnut writing desk that looked centuries old, he beckoned me in and gestured at the chair opposite him.

"So, Messire Verreuil." He propped his elbows on the table, resting palm over fist. "I trust you know why you're here."

"Yes, my lord," I said.

His gaze bored into me. "Say it aloud in your own words."

I swallowed hard. Even though I had no intention of holding back, let alone lying, I'd expected to be questioned. Saying the words aloud this way somehow felt like a betrayal on my part, but I could no more disobey the Prefect than I could lie. "Because my apprentice and I witnessed two of my fellow cadets having carnal relations."

"And those cadets were . . . ?" he pressed me.

Lord Rinforte already knew the answer, but I understood why he was ordering me to say it aloud. Closing my eyes, I raised the seven-sided temple I'd built in my mind. *Purity.* My temple was Cassiel, a flaming sword of faith raised in praise to the heavens. I let Cassiel's fixity of purpose and divine grace flow through me, anchoring me in knowledge that there was redemption in truth. "Toulouse Godet," I said. "And Selwyn de Gaunte."

A wave of relief mingled with guilt washed over me once I spoke Selwyn's name. The Prefect gave a nod of approval. "Well done. You may leave." As I headed for the door, he called me back. "Oh, Messire Verreuil! They'll be departing at first light. You might have a chance to say farewell to your friend in the front courtyard if you happen to find yourself rising before dawn."

I bowed. "Thank you, my lord."

It was a kindness that the Prefect had offered me, but I wasn't sure it was a gift I wanted to accept. I was angry, and with nowhere to go, the anger I'd channeled into fighting was trapped behind a dam now. Dinner was a hushed affair. The rumors were flying, but no one dared talk about it with various masters in earshot at the head table. Toulouse and Selwyn were nowhere to be seen; I assumed they were sequestered somewhere. The remaining members of my class, Dumiel and Paul, mimed silent questions at me. I shook my head and ignored them, concentrating on eating a leg of roasted chicken that tasted of ashes in my mouth.

In the barracks, it was impossible to ignore them. The moment the door was closed for the night, all the cadets in the Third Cohort raised their voices in an unsubtle chorus, demanding to know if the rumors were true.

It was better to get it over with. "Yes."

And then they wanted to know if I'd known.

"No."

And then with furtive glances all around, daring each other, they dropped their voices to a whisper and asked if Selwyn and I had ever . . . ?

"No," I said. "I would never break my vows." I'd already stretched them beyond comfort by keeping my silence. "I know Selwyn could be infuriating. But I have two brothers I miss very much. From the moment he arrived, he filled an empty space in my heart. Right now I'd like to throttle him, but I'm going to miss him like a brother." I gave a wry half smile. "A moody, unpredictable brother I could depend on beyond all reason."

It shamed everyone into silence. Dumiel shooed the younger members of our cohort to their cots, and then it was just the three of us senior cadets. Toulouse's and Selwyn's cots sat empty and bare. All their modest belongings had been taken away.

"I know what you're feeling," Paul Hyères said presently. "I know the two of you never got along, but Toulouse was a good friend to me. I'll miss him, too."

"I know," I said. "I'm sorry."

Afterward we slept; or at least everyone else slept. I tossed and turned, wrestling with my conscience, wrestling with my anger, wrestling with a sense of betrayal. I tried to remember what our parting words would be if our paths never crossed again. I couldn't even recall the last thing I'd said to Selwyn, but I remembered his. He'd said he hoped that we'd have the chance to say farewell.

Not saying goodbye would gnaw at me for the rest of my life.

So I gathered up my bedroll, donned my arms, and made my way along the colonnade that flanked the barracks. It was strange to see a place of hustle and bustle sitting empty, silent, and dark. I slipped across the dim quadrangle, crossing over whitewash footwork patterns, and unbarred the postern gate. I couldn't bar it behind me, but I reckoned the Prefect had given me tacit approval.

The temperature had fallen considerably from the day's heat; not so low that the dew on the flagstones would turn to frost, but enough that I was glad to wrap myself in my sheepskin while I maintained my vigil. The sky had remained clear, its black expanse spangled with stars and a bright waning crescent moon.

There's an art to keeping the dagger hilts from digging into one's belly and the sword harness into one's back when sleeping in arms. That, too, was a skill for which we'd trained. With my conscience as easy as it was like to get for some time, I drifted into a light doze seated on the cold, damp flagstones and leaning against the outer wall of the keep.

I awoke to hoofbeats.

They rode through the postern gate; just the two of them, although I heard the thunk of the gate being barred behind them. I rose and dropped my sheepskin. The sky was a steely grey; light enough to make out faces, dark enough that the fading pinpricks of the stars were still visible.

Toulouse heeled his mount toward me, drawing rein to lean over in the saddle and spit at the ground before my feet. "Go to hell, Verreuil."

"I'm sorry." I meant it. "I never wanted this to happen."

"Tell me," he said. "What would you have done if your apprentice hadn't been there?"

"I can't know for sure," I said. "But honestly, I hope I would have done the right thing and not looked the other way."

Toulouse nodded as though I'd confirmed his suspicions. "You're going to face temptation someday," he said. "Pray that you bend rather than break." With that he gave a mocking Cassiline bow in Selwyn's direction. Selwyn raised one hand in salute, and watched him ride away before approaching me.

"I wasn't sure you'd be here," he said.

"Neither was I," I said. "But here I am."

"I'm glad." He smiled wryly. "I'll miss you."

"I'll miss you, too," I said. "You arrogant, vainglorious, blathering fool."

Selwyn drew his braid over one shoulder and smoothed it. "That's Lord Vainglorious Fool to you now that I'm no longer a Cassiline cadet." His expression turned somber. "Take care of yourself, Joscelin. And remember what I said about fear."

"I will," I said. "But I want you to remember something, too."

"What?"

"The only one of Elua's Companions capable of defeating Camael was Cassiel," I said. "Because Cassiel's sword was never extinguished."

"You aren't Cassiel," Selwyn said with a certain gentleness. "And your sword is plain steel."

"Nonetheless." I bowed. "In Cassiel's name, I protect and serve."

"Nonetheless," he echoed, offering a courtly bow from the saddle. "Farewell, my brother."

I straightened. "Farewell."

I stood and watched him go. In the east, orange and rose hues crept into the grey sky. Color washed slowly back into the world, turning the grass and the leaves myriad shades of green. I watched until Selwyn was a dwindling figure in the distance, his hair the color of ripe apricots a bright receding point.

Then he was gone.

Retrieving my bedroll, I went to bang on the postern gate and return to the keep.

CHAPTER THIRTEEN

The following two months were the most uncomfortable I'd ever known.

It wasn't the first time that a cadet had been expelled for breaking his vow of celibacy, but it was the first time *two* cadets had been expelled for breaking their vows *together*—not to mention being caught mid-deed. So the rumors and speculation continued in whispers in the dining hall and louder tones in the barracks long after the incident ought to be put behind us.

For my part, I ignored the gossip, kept my head down, and worked and trained harder than ever. Although I continued to help maintain the Prefectory's waterwheel, grindstone, mills, and other equipment, after teaching Clemente all the duties I'd performed at his age, I dismissed him as my apprentice. I held no grudge against him for doing the right thing—far from it—but it lay unspoken between us, creating a profound discomfort that no longer made me a fit mentor for him. I read in the library. I wrote long letters to home, although I touched only briefly on the whole business of the expulsion. I wished I could take joy in the steady erasure of the chalk hashmarks on the wall leading to the summer solstice.

When I wasn't training or doing chores, I spent a great deal of time kneeling in contemplation in the grotto where Blessed Elua's effigy stood, his rough-hewn stone features calm and peaceful beneath emerald streaks of moss. We let it grow freely, for Elua loved all living things. Flowers sprang up in his footprints; he would have delighted in the moss. Sometimes I knelt for hours, until I moved past the pain and stiffness to find a small point of perfect stillness in which to dwell. There was no pain there, no abiding sense of loss, anger, and betrayal.

There was only me.

There was only duty, honor, loyalty, and faith.

My sword was plain steel, but I would make myself a conduit for the flames of Cassiel's divine grace.

A week or so before the ceremony, word reached us that the Allies of Camlach had won the most decisive victory against the Skaldi since the Battle of Three Princes, pushing them deep into the mountains. Selwyn's hero Isidore d'Aiglemort had led the charge, accompanied by the dashing Prince Baudoin and his honor guard. I couldn't help but calculate whether Selwyn could have reached them in time to take part in the charge, concluding that it was unlikely unless he changed horses every other day, which he didn't have the funds to do.

Of course, he might be able to persuade a horse-trader to extend him credit. Or he might steal a fresh mount. It didn't matter, and even if our paths did cross again, we would both be very different people. Still, I wondered.

By the night before the solstice, gossip had given way to an atmosphere of barely suppressed excitement. I should have been exhilarated.

I wasn't.

It wasn't a surprise when Master Jacobe summoned me to his quarters that evening. I'd been half expecting it since the day Selwyn was banished. Master Jacobe had known me the longest; he had been the one to escort me to the Prefectory, and he had served as my primary mentor here.

Although I'd been there before, I was struck by how cozy Master Jacobe's rooms were in contrast to the Prefect's austere quarters. Despite the evening light that lingered on the verge of the longest day of the year, there were candles lit, casting flickering shadows on the tapestries that hung on the walls. His writing desk was plain pine, but it was strewn with curios—an astrolabe, a jade carving of a dragon from faraway Ch'in, a large seashell.

Fragrant curls of steam from the hyssop tea Master Jacobe had served before rose from two cups. He beckoned for me to sit. I did so, trying not to show that my stomach was in knots while he sipped his tea. "Tomorrow is an important day," he said eventually. "And yet you take no joy in it. Why?"

"I don't know, maître," I admitted.

"You feel responsible for your friends' expulsion," he said. "That's understandable. But you're not. And you need to pull yourself together, stop trying to escape into contemplation, and start living in the present."

I squared my shoulders, knowing he was right. "Yes, maître."

Master Jacobe leaned back in his chair. Unlike the Prefect's it was a comfortable shape and padded with brocade cushions, albeit worn and shabby ones. We had a similar pair in Verreuil that were often covered in dog hair. "I'm going to tell you something you ordinarily wouldn't learn until tomorrow, messire. Tomorrow, you will become a full-fledged Cassiline Brother, entitled to wear the mandilion over your greys, to wear your ancestral blades at all times. However . . ." He raised one cautionary finger. "You face a journeyman year before you take your final vow and become not just a warrior, but a true priest of the Cassiline Brotherhood."

I was confused. "Forgive me, but what's the difference? And why is this not explained to us before we graduate?"

"As to the latter," he said, "it's primarily tradition. One last test to see how you adapt to surprise and change after nine years of certainty and order. But it's not a hard and fast protocol, and I reckon you're already dealing with enough surprise and change. Tomorrow Lord Rinforte will ask how you wish to spend your journeyman year, given the options. I wanted to discuss them with you."

"What are they?" I asked.

"We don't have a placement for you." Master Jacobe's tone was blunt. "Nor for Paul. Only Dumiel, and I suspect his family pulled some strings."

I was disappointed, but not surprised. "When do you expect a placement to open? And what are my choices in the meantime?"

"There's no telling when," he said. "But unless we receive new requests from patrons with sufficient status and coin to be reckoned worthy and capable of retaining a Cassiline Brother, it won't be until a Brother retires, or Adonai forfend, is grievously wounded or killed."

I rested my chin on one hand. "And until then I do . . . what? Ride for the Royal Post?"

"You certainly could," he said. "Or you could take the year to wander the country, learn a new trade if you wished. Or you could stay here at the Prefectory and assist with training the cadets."

"What do you counsel?" I asked.

He shook his head. "It is for you to decide."

"Would any option allow me to visit home?" I suspected I knew the answer, but I had to ask.

"No," Master Jacobe said gently. "Not yet."

It might have made a difference. I understood that the Cassiline proscription against visiting home prior to age twenty-five was one way of fixing our identities as Cassiline Brothers before all else, but I still missed my family. I considered my options. For all his egalitarian talk, my father would be secretly mortified that his son was riding for the Royal Post like any commoner capable of sitting a horse. A year of wandering had its appeal, but there wasn't anywhere in particular I wanted to go, and after nine solid years of training, I wasn't eager to dive into the grueling process of mastering a new trade.

What I wanted was a posting, and if one were to open, the news would break here at the Prefectory. Any option that had me on the road could put me weeks or months away, and the posting filled before I even heard word of it.

"I'll stay here," I said.

Master Jacobe smiled. "Good. I'm in need of a strong right hand. You've got innate skills, but you've trained hard to develop them, and people who have worked hard at a skill make the best teachers."

Sensing a dismissal, I rose, then paused. "Maître? You never explained the difference between a Cassiline warrior and a Cassiline priest."

He set down his teacup. "As a warrior, offering up your body in defense of one of the descendants of Elua and his Companions *is* an act of worship; but that is between you and Cassiel. As a priest, you may offer absolution. You may hear their sins and misdeeds, and if you gauge that their atonement is sincere, you may offer it up to Cassiel and he will make them pure."

Purity.

"Thank you, maître." I bowed. "I am grateful for your kindness."

It rained the next morning. Not the kind of gentle summer rain that coaxes the damp, rich scent of soil from the earth, but great, lashing torrents that blew across the quadrangle in grey curtains to soak our clothing and plaster our hair to our heads. Paul, Dumiel, and I stood at the front of the Third Cohort, at ease with hands on hilts, gazing unflinching before us. The burden of speculation had fallen on all three of us. No matter what, our class would go down in the history of the Brotherhood as the only class to lose two cadets so close to graduation. Many cadets, especially the younger ranks of the Third Cohort, found it impossible to believe those of us who remained weren't complicit. Regaining their respect in a mentoring role would be a challenge.

One by one, the ranks peeled away behind us; First Cohort cadet-candidates shivering in the rain with one arm lashed behind their backs taking the Oath of Water, incoming Second Cohort members taking the Oath of Fire, outgoing cadets taking the Oath of Steel to join the Third Cohort.

And then there were only the three of us, rainwater streaming down our faces and beading on our eyelashes. Lord Rinforte came before us, disregarding the downpour with remarkable thoroughness.

"Congratulations," he said. "Messire Verreuil, step forward." I obeyed. "Draw and present your sword."

I drew my uncle's blade, feeling a frisson at the forbidden act, and offered it lying on the palms of my hands.

The Prefect touched fingertips to the flat of the blade and closed his eyes. Rain ran in rivulets down the creases that lined his patrician features. "In Cassiel's name, I reconsecrate this blade unto his service. May you wield it only in the direst need, and may you wield it with valor, loyalty, and faith. Do you so pledge, Joscelin Verreuil?"

"I do," I said.

He withdrew his fingertips. "Sheathe your blade. Henceforth, you will not draw it in combat save to kill." He turned to Master Jacobe, who had a damp length of grey wool draped over one arm. "Your coat."

Master Jacobe unfolded and proffered it. The mandilion coat was the final item of Cassiline attire, signifying that the wearer was a full-fledged Brother. It was sleeveless for full range of shoulder motion, fell below the knee, and was tailored in such a way that it offered easy access to one's dagger hilts—according to rumor, the cut and draping was a secret passed down from Master Tailor to Master Tailor. It was the same grey wool as our regular garments, only heavier, so rich in lanolin that it wasn't sodden despite the downpour.

I slipped my arms through the armholes, and Master Jacobe settled the coat over my shoulders. It felt good. Even with my emotions as knotted as they were, I felt the same surge of *rightness* that I'd felt the very first time I'd essayed a Cassiline bow.

The ritual was repeated twice more, and then it was done.

We were Cassiline Brothers.

The Prefect ordered us to await his summons in the keep's library, generously allowing us to return to the barracks first to scrub dry or change into clean attire. I imagined for his part that once out of sight, he simply scared away the waterdrops by sheer force of will.

I was the last one summoned. "Brother Jacobe tells me he's spoken to you," Lord Rinforte said without preamble. "And you've made your decision."

"Yes," I said firmly.

"Good." He dipped a pen in an inkwell and scribbled something on a piece of parchment. "I think you'll prosper here."

I hesitated despite the clear dismissal. "My lord . . . I'm honored, of course, but what I truly want is a posting."

He glanced up. "What you *all* want is a posting, preferably at the Royal Palace. At your age, that's not going to happen, Messire Verreuil. There are dozens of Brothers with seniority between you and the Palace, Brothers in their thirties and forties in the prime of their fighting skills, seasoned in service. Do you understand?"

"I do," I said. "But Dumiel—"

"Yes," he interrupted me. "Dumiel d'Aubert is receiving a posting because of his family connections. That is true. It was a very specific request we had no reason to decline for a posting he is likely to find excruciatingly boring. If your family is capable of procuring the same for you, they're welcome to do so."

"I'm sorry, my lord," I said. "I understand."

He returned to his inkwell, and this time I took my leave.

The next morning, my classmates took their leave and went their separate ways. We parted amicably enough—I'd never had a quarrel with either of them—but I didn't expect any of us would stay in touch. Though it wasn't our fault, we all carried a sense of guilt regarding the expulsion of Selwyn and Toulouse.

I moved my modest belongings to the Waypost, an outbuilding just northwest of the great keep. A handful of Brothers were in residence there, rotating at any given time as assignments became available, assisting in training and the running of the Prefectory in the meanwhile. I'd always supposed the building was named half in jest because it served as a post along the way offering hospitality to couriers, but it occurred to me that it was a post along the way of my journeyman year, too.

Master Jacobe assigned me to training the Second Cohort. Being new to the role, I was met with a subtle degree of disrespect, cadets whispering behind their hands or rolling their eyes when I spoke. I nipped that in the bud on the first day, raising my voice loud enough to rattle their skulls. "Enough!" My boys fell silent, eyeing me sidelong. "Good." I unbuckled my baldric and laid my scabbard on the flagstones, then my dagger belt atop it. I'd seen them train long enough to know who was good and who only thought they were. I picked one of the former and two of the latter and stepped into the center of the nearest whitewashed ring. "Let's get this over with. You, you, and you. Do your best to force me out of the circle."

One glanced at my neatly stacked weapons. "But you're—"

"Older?" I suggested. "Taller, stronger, better trained?"

He folded his arms. "I was going to say 'unarmed.'"

Unsurprisingly, he was one of the ones I'd identified as good. His defiance reminded me of Selwyn, and I had to suppress a grin. "Try me."

It didn't take long to dispatch all four of them.

I retrieved my arms while they grumbled and nursed their bruises. "I want the lot of you running laps around the perimeter," I said, nodding at the walls. "Run until you think you're going to spew, then run until you do." Groaning, they began unbuckling belts and vambraces. "No." I halted them. "You're Cassilines. Run in armor."

They did, despising every second of it and griping about me under their breath; but now they were muttering about how strict and unfair I was.

It was a start.

After a while their grudging respect gave way to genuine admiration. Master Jacobe was right, I was good at teaching, and I enjoyed it. The only aspect that made me uncomfortable was accompanying my cadets to the village market, where they begged and wheedled in time-honored fashion to be allowed to explore. Every time, it evoked a vivid memory of the Trysting Mews; tumbling from the wall in the jasmine-scented twilight, the white flash of Selwyn's buttocks as he pulled up his breeches. I allowed it, for it would have been unfair to punish them for another's misdeeds, but I forbade them to set foot in the Trysting Mews or to have anything to do with the Tsingani.

If that idiot Toulouse hadn't been so gullible in the first place, mayhap the whole business could have been avoided.

As I settled into my new role, it surprised me to discover how much news reached the ears of the journeymen. Couriers travelling near the Prefectory frequently met with the Prefect or various Masters, then passed the night in the Waypost regaling us with tales of their exploits, distant doings, and the intrigue swirling around the Crown. I wished Selwyn were there to hear the news, though unless I missed my guess, he was surely in the thick of it by now. The City of Elua had thrown a great triumphal parade for his idols Isidore d'Aiglemort and Baudoin de Trevalion, who had ridden through the streets of the City, heads held high as though they already wore the crown.

Two heads, I thought; one crown. That alliance wasn't going to last forever.

The long blazing days of summer gave way to crisp, cool, shorter days. Scents of autumn hung in the air—dry, fallen leaves, acorns, ripe apples. But it was also the grand finale of harvest season. The markets closed for the winter. My cadets grew restless and bored as the ground froze and the nights lengthened toward the Longest Night, and I conceived a game into which they might channel their adolescent energy and passions.

The Prefectory grounds bordered the Senescine Forest, a vast tract of deep woodlands that covered a large swathe of Terre d'Ange. The territory belonged to the Crown, but the Cassiline Brotherhood had leave to hunt and forage within it. I took a day's leave from my duties in the training yard and persuaded my fellow journeyman Brother Bernarde to assist me in my first endeavor.

It was inspired by the games my brothers and I used to play in the forests of Verreuil, and by Selwyn and his ruthless approach outside the yard. Bernarde and I established a fortress on a bend in a creek that cut fast and deep through the forest, water so clear one could see layers of brown leaves shining at the bottom of the creek bed. We gathered thick branches, pounding them in place to mark the corners of our makeshift edifice. I laid traps and pitfalls, staged strategic opportunities. I put Bernarde to digging a pit along one obvious approach while I scoured the surrounding area. I tied trip lines, rigged makeshift ladders and bridges, shinnied up trunks to secure lengths of rope long enough to swing from tree to tree.

Never in my nine years at the Prefectory had I seen cadets tackle a training exercise with such sheer exhilaration. The raiders charged through the woods, whooping until they began encountering my traps and their war cries turned to curses; the defenders sent forth a scouting party. After a victory was declared, the cadets trooped back to the keep, flushed and elated, talking over each other as they recounted the details of their adventures. It made me smile; and it made me wonder if it would have made a difference if Selwyn had had an outlet that allowed him to run wild within the framework of the Prefectory's rules.

Probably not.

Master Jacobe didn't entirely approve; nor, according to him, did Lord Rinforte. But as the game continued and evolved throughout the long winter months, they saw the merit in the excitement and keen focus that the Second Cohort carried into their conventional exercises in the quadrangle.

I was proud of my cadets, proud to receive the approval of my mentors, proud of beginning to grow into a good mentor myself.

I was also deeply unhappy.

I was lonely. And as much as I sought purpose in the noble pursuit of teaching cadets, I was eager for my journey to continue beyond the walls of the

Prefectory. I was a warrior by trade, yet untested by battle. I yearned to put my own training to use; to protect and serve my ward like a true Cassiline. Though it be hubris, there was a part of me that dreamed of a heroic calling.

I couldn't imagine the irony with which I would one day regard those dreams.

CHAPTER FOURTEEN

Two events jolted me out of my melancholy.

The first was a courier, a Cassiline Brother some five years older than me, passing through the Prefectory with news of significant happenings in the realm. There is gossip and then there is news—this was definitely the latter. Prince Baudoin de Trevalion, the King's nephew, widely considered a possible contestant for the throne, had been convicted of treason and executed.

It seemed that Prince Baudoin and his royal mother, who was known as the Lioness of Azzalle for good reason, had indeed been conspiring. There had been a coup in Alba, that mysterious green island across the Straits, and the rightful heir had fled into exile. Lyonette de Trevalion had been corresponding with the usurpers using messenger birds. In exchange for their aid in putting Baudoin on the throne, she offered to reciprocate with D'Angeline forces to assist in capturing the Alban heir and his allies and demolishing any chance of insurrection.

What struck me the most was that it was Duc Isidore d'Aiglemort—his foster-brother, comrade in arms, and boon companion—who made the formal accusation of treason. In considering the notion that two heads couldn't wear one crown, I hadn't expected the other to roll, so to speak, in such a manner.

It was interesting to note that it was Baudoin's erstwhile paramour, renowned beauty Melisande Shahrizai, who actually provided proof of House Trevalion's treason in the form of letters from the Lioness of Azzalle to her son. According to rumor, it was likely out of spite after a lover's spat with Baudoin or to punish the Lioness for refusing to allow a marriage between their Houses. Whatever the provocation, it was certainly an extreme response.

The news reminded me that while I was playing children's games—albeit violent and bloodthirsty games—in the woods with adolescent boys, the world was moving on apace. Something shifted inside me, opening a crack in the dam I'd built to wall off the anger, hurt, and betrayal that I'd felt since Selwyn and Toulouse were expelled, the persistent sense of being left behind that I'd tried to ignore since graduating from the Third Cohort.

All in all, it made me think.

The second event was the summer solstice. It seemed impossible that a year had passed. Betimes it had felt as though the days crawled while the weeks sped by; betimes it felt as though the days sped by in a flash while the weeks and months crawled. Nonetheless, it was upon us. My senior cadets would be taking the Oath of Steel and moving onward; a new class would be taking the Oath of Fire and joining us, eager to take part in the Second Cohort's notorious games.

And I would be . . . what?

I'd had an idea what to expect at every step along the way. Léon and Master Jacobe had prepared me for entry into the First Cohort on our long journey from Verreuil; afterward, whispers regarding the details of the oaths that followed filtered down through the ranks of cadets.

No one ever spoke of a journeyman year and a final oath to follow.

There were four of us ready to take the final oath, the others a year or two older than me. It seemed my own remaining classmates were unable to leave their situations to be here for the solstice, as must have happened to these three in prior years. I was grateful this was a step I wouldn't have to delay.

I fell asleep in my shared bedchamber in the Waypost only to be shaken awake in the dead of night by a figure in a hooded white robe. "Wake up." The figure held a small oil lamp on a chain in one hand, and a second white robe in the other. It thrust the garment at me. Beneath its hood, lamplight glinted on the curve of a gold mask. "Remove all attire and don this, then follow me. Leave everything behind, even your arms."

I obeyed.

The four of us journeymen gathered outside the Waypost, each of us with a hooded guide and a couple more for good measure. They drew our hoods low over our faces so we couldn't see past our own feet and led us to the Blessed Elua's grotto.

"Kneel," one of the hooded guides said in an implacable tone that suggested it might be the Prefect himself. "Pray. Pass this night keeping Elua's vigil. We will return before the break of dawn."

As trials go, this was one for which I was well suited. I sat back on my heels and bowed my head, palms resting on my thighs. It was overcast and the starless night sky as black as pitch, but it didn't feel like rain. The air had that particular soft warmth that feels exactly like the temperature of one's skin, and the dividing line between the two became blurred, the edges of one's being fraying into the world.

It felt strange to be naked under my robe, too. Vulgar jests regarding Cassiline modesty notwithstanding, we no more bathed or swam in clothing than we regularly slept in full arms and armor. But we didn't go about naked under loose-fitting attire, feeling the tender kiss of summer night air against our skin, the damp grass beneath our knees and the tops of our bare feet. Pray, we had been told; I'd spent so many hours in contemplation in this grotto praying for wisdom, guidance, and patience, I hardly knew what was left.

So I simply offered my entire being in prayer, breathing slow and deep.

There are experiences that are impossible to describe. This was one. I had the strangest sensation of spiraling inward and outward at the same time, as though my center was a fixed point between heaven and earth. At times I heard sounds—some of them, I think, were real, the rustling, scraping, and faint thuds of the masters making preparations for the next step in the ritual. Other sounds were different. There was a rhythmic sound like waves that might have been nothing more than the blood beating in my ears; but then there was a high sustained note like a plucked harpstring. A clarion blast followed like a call to arms, then a sound like a distant choir chanting.

Behind my closed eyes, I saw an image of Cassiel approaching, limned in brightness. His face was like the sun, hair streaming like rays. Flames ran like water down the length of the sword he held upright in a two-handed grip, streamed from his outspread wings. His lips moved, shaping words I could not see for the brightness, but as he lowered his blade to touch the tip to my breast, I heard them clear as day.

Protect and serve, Cassiline.

Something burst inside me at the touch, a blossom unfurling fiery petals inside the confines of my chest. I wasn't sure if I was waking or sleeping, whether this vision was real or imagined or somewhere in between.

"Joscelin." A hand touched my shoulder and I jolted into full wakefulness. "As you are the youngest, you shall be last to undertake the ritual. Keep your gaze and your mind fixed on Blessed Elua."

Again, I obeyed. Behind me there were whispers and the long hiss of an indrawn breath, followed by the sound of a single drum beaten slowly. Another joined in, then another and another until it was impossible to say exactly how many drums were in the chorus. The pace quickened like a pulse, building to a crescendo, then slowing. This happened twice more, only the third time, the crescendo continued to build for a longer time. Words were spoken afterward, though I couldn't make them out over the drums, which had resumed their slow, steady heartbeat.

Twice again this pattern was repeated, then it was my turn. I rose at a masked figure's command and faced the final ritual.

A broad wooden walkway that led to the grotto had been removed and three stone troughs were nestled in the earth before me. My hooded guide pointed at each in turn from nearest to farthest. "Water," he murmured. "Fire. Steel."

I nodded.

My guide withdrew, passing around the troughs. Obviously I was meant to cross them. They weren't long, but they were broad. The first trough was filled with water, glinting like tarnished pewter in the lamplight. The second was filled with oil that had been set ablaze, ghostly blue flames flickering under the dark charcoal-grey sky. But it was the third trough that had drawn involuntary gasps, for it was lined with sword blades. Beyond it six masked figures faced each other in two lines, tapping out a slow double-beat on handheld drums; a seventh awaited with crossed daggers. The other initiates watched in silence, clad once more in their greys, all of them standing with obvious discomfort.

The longer I waited, the harder this would become. I walked slowly and deliberately through the trough of water, letting the hem of my white robe soak up as much water as possible. Then I passed swiftly through the trough of fire, hoisting my hem so that it didn't touch the oil. Heat roared from the blue flames licking at my knees, but the wet fabric of my robe didn't ignite. Only my feet were wreathed in ghostly blue. I stamped out the flames and rubbed my feet in a patch of dirt, heedless of any blisters.

That left steel.

There were six blades fixed in slots in the trough—old training swords by the look of them, damaged in some way but strong enough to take an edge and hold a man's weight. I looked past the trough, but my fellow initiates had their features schooled to impassivity, and there was no telling what lay under those gold masks.

The blades were perpendicular to me and spaced around a foot apart.

I chose to disperse my weight over two side-by-side blades, spreading my arms wide for balance. The drumbeat began to quicken, urging me to make haste. I ignored it, testing a blade before I put my weight on it. A step leading with the heel was out of the question. I would have guessed that a perfectly flat-footed step would be the safest, but the blade's edge pressed with the least force when I led with the ball of my foot, toes gripping the blade harder than a miser clutching his purse, curled the tender arch, and gently lowered my heel.

One step, one blade; two steps, two blades. The drums beat faster and faster, my blood roared in my veins. It was the same sense I'd had when I'd drawn my uncle's sword for the first time, a wild, shivering brilliance as though every element of the world was calling my name at once. A voiceless shout of exuberance filled me in answer, my eyes and heart and soul flame-dazzled. In that moment, I couldn't have said whether I'd cut my feet to the bone or was walking on air.

And then my naked, questing toes touched down on dew-damp grass. I shifted my other foot forward one last cautious step and the drums fell silent.

Several masked Brothers removed my robe, handed me my garments and arms. I donned them piece by piece, feeling like a warrior girding himself for battle. They examined my feet without comment. I peeked at them myself before pulling on my socks. There were deep vertical creases in my soles, but the skin was unbroken. I didn't know if that was significant, as it seemed everyone else had sustained injuries, or I simply had a heretofore undiscovered talent for walking on swords, a skill that would only prove useful if I forsook my vows to become a travelling Mendacant.

The seventh masked figure, whom I was sure by now was Lord Rinforte, beckoned when I'd finished dressing. He held a small clay bottle in his other hand. "Journeyman, you have spent a year living in the world as a Cassiline Brother. Here at the edge of dawn, you have passed through water, fire, and steel to reaffirm your oaths and the vows attendant on them. Now you cross the final threshold." Dipping into the clay bottle, he smeared a thumbprint of perfumed oil on my brow. "With oil from the Holy Land where Adonai's son Yeshua ben Yosef was born and died and rose, where Blessed Elua burst forth singing from the earth, I anoint thee," he said formally. "Be thou welcome to the Priesthood of Cassiel."

I bowed with crossed forearms and the Prefect of the Cassiline Brotherhood returned my bow.

It was done.

I was a priest.

In the days following the final ritual, a sense of calm settled over me. I wouldn't say I'd attained true patience, that deep pool of perfect stillness some Brothers are said to attain in prayer. But I did attain a measure of grace. It smoothed life's rougher edges and gave me the patience to endure. A spate of excitement shook the Prefectory when we learned that the Palace requested six additional Cassilines to guard the King and the Dauphine around the clock. I didn't expect to be assigned to the Palace—as the Prefect had flat-out told me, there were too many Brothers in their prime with at least a decade of seniority. But in some instances, those Brothers would be transferred from a lesser posting, which would then be given to a junior brother.

I thought surely one of those would be mine.

I was wrong.

My newfound calm helped me through the disappointment. I held tight to the faith that Cassiel's plan for me would be revealed in time.

The golden days of high summer were still lingering when I began turning my attention toward plans for our war games. The newcomers wouldn't know what to expect since my boys kept the details secret, but I wanted to spring a surprise or two on my veterans. I also wanted to implement some measures to ensure they didn't get *too* wild. Last year's participants in my woodland battles had taken to calling themselves the Dirty Tricksters. I had a feeling that wasn't sitting well with the masters, so it didn't surprise me when Master Jacobe sent for me.

But this time, there was no hyssop tea on the table in front of the fireplace. This time, there was a small oak cask and a pair of simple earthenware cups.

"Sit down." Master Jacobe looked troubled. "Have you ever had distilled spirits?"

I shook my head. "No."

"There aren't many times I recommend spirits," he said. "Too distracting. But there are times." He filled both cups, handing one to me. "Apple brandy. Let the heat of your hands warm it."

I cradled the cup in my palms. Beneath the sharp notes of intoxicating spirits, the amber liquid smelled like a sun-warmed orchard. "What is it, maître? Is this about the games?"

"No," he said. "Drink."

It felt as warm as it smelled going down my throat, blossoming in my belly to spread warmth through my veins. I even found myself relaxing a fraction, a tight band across my shoulders easing. Opposite me, Master Jacobe downed the contents of his cup in a single swallow. His expression as he set it back down was grave. All warmth fled and a cold trickle of dread tingled at the back of my neck.

"Maître?" I whispered.

He didn't mince words. "Selwyn de Gaunte is dead."

I heard the words, but they didn't make sense to me. They were just a jumble of sound with no pattern. "I'm sorry," I said. "What?"

Master Jacobe refilled my cup. "Selwyn is dead."

The words settled into a pattern that my mind shied away from recognizing. I gulped my second cup of brandy and began coughing.

Selwyn was dead.

Selwyn.

Dead.

I got my coughing under control and then my breathing, and asked a single word. "How?"

"I don't know if this will bring you any consolation," he murmured. "I find that it does. Selwyn was killed defending the Duc d'Aiglemort from an assassination attempt. His brother Telys de Gaunte sent a letter notifying the Prefect as a matter of courtesy. Telys wanted to be sure you knew." Master Jacobe gave a faint, rueful smile. "It seems Selwyn spoke of you often."

"Does he say *how*?" I don't know why I needed to picture it, but I did.

"There was an attempted coup amongst the Allies of Camlach," Master Jacobe said. "Isidore d'Aiglemort hadn't counted on losing Prince Baudoin's honor guard. When the Glory-Seekers were ordered to return to Trevalion in disgrace, it left d'Aiglemort scrambling to replace them. An opposing faction of the Allies of Camlach thought to take advantage of the momentary lapse. D'Aiglemort's rivals tried to overthrow him, claiming he was guilty of treason by virtue of association. It was an obvious gambit for the sovereignty of Camlach."

"And Selwyn was killed in the attack," I said dully.

"According to his brother, Selwyn was killed *holding off* the attack," he said. "The ambush took place in the dining hall. The attackers had the advantage of surprise and numbers and they held the doors. But they didn't count on a Cassiline-trained warrior defending the Duc while others secured his retreat."

I could envision Selwyn in full dervish mode taking on a score of men. "I thought Isidore d'Aiglemort was supposed to be a great swordsman."

"He is," Master Jacobe said. "Which means he retreated out of prudence and cares naught for shows of bravado. As to what that portends for the realm, I can't say, but . . ." He continued to speak and I tried to follow his words, but my world had been upended and I couldn't stop picturing Selwyn's final hour on earth. I'd wager ducats to ducks—our nanny used to say that all the time, ducats to ducks—that when it came to actually defending his liege with his life, Selwyn depended on nine years of Cassiline training rather than any of the showy tricks he liked to improvise.

Belatedly, I realized that Master Jacobe had fallen silent and was gazing at me with sympathy and regret. "Forgive me, maître," I said. "The news took me by surprise."

"That's why I wanted to tell you myself." He paused, searching for words. "Selwyn de Gaunte was never going to make a good Cassiline Brother. If you think there's somewhat you could have done differently, you're mistaken. Some people are like shooting stars, blazing bright and burning out swiftly. A lifetime of discipline was never going to suit that one. And yet if he hadn't been a trained Cassiline, it is quite possible Isidore d'Aiglemort wouldn't have survived the ambush."

"I know. If Selwyn could have chosen his death, he would have chosen this one. But that doesn't make him any less dead." I pushed my earthenware cup away a few polite inches. "Thank you, maître. If you don't mind, I'd like to be alone now."

"Ah." Master Jacobe held up one finger, indicating I should wait. "I have another piece of news, far better news. Lord Rinforte is assigning you a posting."

I looked blankly at him.

My world had already been turned on its head this evening. I could feel grief lapping at the foundations of my heart like a rising tide and I was braced for a crashing wave of it to follow. But this . . . this was unexpected. My emotions were in turmoil and I wasn't sure I'd heard correctly. Just the thought of it set off that joyful chorus in my heart; and yet I was so far from ready for happiness that it almost hurt.

"Did you say a posting, maître?" I asked carefully.

"Before you get your hopes up, it's *not* the Palace," he said, refilling my cup and pushing it back to me. "It's a very . . . unconventional request. The Prefect considered long and hard before choosing to grant it."

"Why?" I asked. "Who's the patron?"

"Anafiel Delaunay." Master Jacobe watched to see if I'd react to the name, but I didn't recognize it. "One of your countrymen, I'm told—a Siovalese lord from a Minor House."

I cocked my head. "I'm not saying he's an imposter, but I've never heard of a House Delaunay. Is that what makes this an unconventional request?"

"No." He took a deep breath. "Anafiel Delaunay has two wards he adopted into his household in the City of Elua. Both are pledged to Naamah's service. That's who you would be guarding."

"*What?*" The word cracked from my lips with unexpected force. I wrenched my voice into a semblance of calm. "I'm sorry, forgive me. But Naamah's service goes against everything the Brotherhood stands for. Why does Lord Rinforte deem these two worthy of a Cassiline guard?"

"That I do not know," Master Jacobe said. "Only that the Prefect does nothing without a reason."

I stared into my brandy. "What happens if I refuse this posting?"

He hesitated. "I cannot say for certain. You loved Selwyn like a brother and his death has shaken you. Under those circumstances, I think the Prefect would be inclined to forgive you for the lapse in your vow of obedience. But I do not think he will offer you another posting anytime soon, if ever."

It hadn't occurred to me that refusing an undesirable posting was a transgression of such magnitude. Looking up from my brandy, I gave him a sharp glance to determine how serious he was.

Very.

Servants of Naamah; professional courtesans—but members of a noble household, not a pleasure house. Why would they require a bodyguard with the skill and prestige of a Cassiline Brother? To impress patrons? That hardly seemed a sufficient motive for the Prefect to grant this Anafiel Delaunay's request. Everything about the situation felt wrong. Selwyn would have laughed himself sick if he'd been alive to hear it: Joscelin Verreuil, first among cadets, dancing attendance on a pair of Naamah's Servants.

Elua have mercy, I wish he *were* alive to make fun of me, because I was drowning in still waters here and I didn't see any other way forward. At least the posting would take me on an adventure beyond the Prefectory's borders.

Exactly how far, I couldn't have suspected.

I hoisted my cup in a silent toast to Selwyn, quaffed it, and slammed it onto the table. "I'll take it."

CHAPTER FIFTEEN

I left for the City of Elua a day later.

My boys were disappointed, which I will admit was somewhat gratifying. I met with the journeyman, Brother Benoit, who would be taking over the Second Cohort's day-to-day weapons training, and bequeathed him all my notes for plans and pitfalls.

I packed my bedroll and sheepskin coat, a clean set of greys, extra socks and small breeches. My travel kit contained basic necessities like a tinderbox, a water flask, a pouch of sheep's-wool grease, a whetstone, a curry brush, and a hoof-pick.

I made sure my horse was in fine fettle. Aristotle—all the horses in my father's stable were named after ancient philosophers or historians—was seventeen years old and not as spry as he'd been ten years ago, but there's a hardy strain in the horses we breed in the mountains. I gave him a thorough currying and double-checked his hooves for stones or cracks or loose shoes, finding him sound.

I oiled and polished my tack and gear. In the smithy, I used the great grindstone to achieve the sharpest possible edge on my blades, then honed them even finer whetting them by hand.

The quartermaster in charge of supplies provided me with a leather satchel of grain and a sack containing flatbread, sausage, cheese, and apples. He also gave me a purse with sufficient funds to lodge in reputable inns I would encounter after emerging from the relative wilderness of the Senescine Forest.

In the library, Master Gerard unrolled a great map of the realm, parchment scraped thin in places where borders had been drawn and redrawn over the years, and pointed out the best route from the Prefectory as well as a smaller map of the streets of the City of Elua itself for me to commit to memory.

For the second time in all my years at the Prefectory, Lord Rinforte summoned me to his austere quarters, where he presented me with a sealed letter of introduction for my new patron, and bade me be mindful of my vows and my duty to Cassiel. He expressed his pride in me and extended formal well wishes.

Clearly dismissed, I nonetheless lingered. "My lord Prefect, is there aught you can tell me about this assignment? It seems an unusual one for the Brotherhood to accept."

He propped his chin on his fist. "Trust that I have reasons, which I'm not at liberty to reveal at the moment, and that this is not a frivolous assignment. Your charges may be Servants of Naamah, but there has been an attack on one of their lives."

Now I was more curious than ever. "Why? A jealous lover?"

"Your patron will provide whatever details he deems necessary and appropriate," Lord Rinforte said. "Cassiel's blessings upon your journey."

This time, I inclined my head in acknowledgment and took my leave.

That evening's meal in the dining hall was no different from any other. A few of the senior Brothers, including Master Jacobe, stopped by the table I shared with other junior and journeyman Brothers to clap me on the shoulder one last time. In the Waypost cottage, my bunkmates retrieved a jug of perry cider from its hiding place and we all downed half a tankard in the traditional farewell toast, pouring out a few drops in tribute to those before us who were slain in the service of duty. I thought of my uncle, of course; but I thought of Selwyn, too. It was hard to believe he was truly gone. I couldn't stop imagining the look of sheer glee on his face when he heard that the yearned-for assignment I'd received at last was guarding a pair of high-priced courtesans.

In the morning, the Master Cook sent over the parting gift of a generous wedge of egg custard pie with ham and leeks neatly wrapped in a parcel of grape leaves, which would see me comfortably through the day.

And that was it.

No last words, no ceremony of leave-taking, no final salute. The quadrangle was vacant save for a couple of senior cadets from the Third Cohort practicing with unsharpened training swords. The sound of their blades clashing rang with unusual precision in the near-empty yard. They paused in their match to bow to a full-fledged Brother, and one of them ran to open the postern gate for me.

I rode along the path to the main approach. I'd ridden this way many times—our gaming grounds were in a southeastern portion of the Senescine—but today was different. I was *leaving.* Once I plunged into the dark green depths of the forest, there would be no turning back when the sun began to sink low on the horizon, no sturdy stone walls, no comforting buzz of the dining hall, no familiar snores of slumbering bunkmates. There was only me and Aristotle, and I was grateful for his company.

The quality of the light changed as I rode deeper into the Senescine. There were easier ways to traverse the realm, old Tiberian roads—kept in fine fettle, I might add, by Siovalese engineers—that ran the width and breadth of Terre d'Ange, with no more than a day's ride between towns. However, there were no direct routes on decent roads leading to or from the Prefectory. Although pathways in the Senescine were little more than an often-changing labyrinth of deer tracks, it was a far shorter route, provided one didn't get lost.

By midday, the forest canopy was so thick that one couldn't even call the sunlight dappled anymore, and so high overhead that I felt dwarfed by it. There was almost no undergrowth in that shade, only a carpet of pine needles and oak leaves, tall trunks reaching straight into the sky. Here and there, there were chinks in the canopy just large enough to allow a narrow ray of light to stream through, as though Adonai's outstretched hand were reaching down from the heavens.

I made camp that night alongside a spring burbling from mossy rocks. It was tiny, but the water was cold and there was enough of it to quench our thirst. After tending to Aristotle, I ate the last of the egg custard and a chunk of sausage. When dusk fell and the fingers of streaming light withdrew, I built a small campfire. Although I didn't need it for warmth, it felt good to raise a light against the darkness. I fell asleep propped against my bedroll.

The next day I did it again.

And again.

Once in the heart of the woods I scared off a poacher; otherwise, I saw no one for days on end. Although the pathways were narrow and lightly trodden, they either followed or led to water. I subsisted on my traveller's provender and paused to allow Aristotle to graze at any grassy clearings we encountered. There weren't many in those dense woods, but there were places where lightning had struck and the ensuing fire had cleared a glade. The grazing was meager, but it was enough to augment our supply of oats.

I held a compass in my thoughts, its needle pointing true north, so that I might orient and reorient myself with every twist and turn of my journey. It was a trick of sorts that I'd adopted after our father showed us a compass and took it apart and put it back together so that we might understand its inner workings. For a long time afterward, I thought it was a trick everyone could do. Then again, I also assumed that everyone's father could dismantle and reassemble a compass on a whim.

At any rate, we didn't get lost. Day after day passed in an evergreen haze. I kept Aristotle to a brisk walk; a slow jog when he was feeling spirited. It wasn't a pace likely to impress nobles of Great Houses who raced horses for sport, but it could be maintained for days on end and ate up the leagues with deceptive speed.

I spent a good deal of time speculating about this purported Siovalese nobleman, Anafiel Delaunay, who would be my patron. All I knew for certain was that there was no House Delaunay in Siovale. That didn't mean that the man was lying—there were a number of ways one could belong to the peerage without being a member of a dynastic House. But it was unusual in these circumstances. Fashionable or not, having a Cassiline guard was a symbol of elite status. The Brotherhood only accepted clients of a certain stature with sufficient funds to afford the hiring fee. So for some reason, this man Delaunay had either a lineage or a political appointment that commanded respect, and he was wealthy.

And he had two wards whom he had apparently raised to prostitute themselves in Naamah's name.

That was where my mind balked. Even though I was sure Delaunay would have observed legal regulations regarding the age of consent, it just felt *wrong* that children should be taught from the tenderest years to become courtesans.

At the time it failed to occur to me, trained from childhood to be a warrior, that there was a certain irony in the sentiment.

But I did wonder who would want to kill a courtesan and why? A jealous lover was still the only thing I could think of; not that that wasn't plenty of motive. My uncle Luc had received his first posting—and been slain—because of a husband's jealousy. Ignominious death aside, it was one thing to be hired to protect and serve a Comte's wife, and quite another to be hired to protect and serve a pair of expensive prostitutes. At least I was assuming they were expensive. One of them had been attacked, so whatever the threat, it was real.

Beyond that, although it didn't stop me from trying, there was nothing I might surmise before reaching the City of Elua.

After some two weeks, the woods began thinning a bit. There were more poachers clad in forest green and rusty brown, melting into the trees. There were swineherds illegally grazing pigs in the oak groves, hurrying their droves away at the sight of a Cassiline Brother on the paths. On my final full day in the Senescine, I passed a royal courier and a few legitimate travellers on the pathways.

The woods grew increasingly sparser. My path converged with a larger, more travelled path into which any number of small tributaries like mine led, and I saw more and more travellers along the way.

It was my first time encountering strangers as a full-fledged Cassiline, except for market days in Rive-de-Lusande, which didn't count. The estates and the village adjoining the Prefectory were the only places on the face of the earth where seeing a Cassiline Brother in full greys, arms, and armor was an everyday occurrence.

Passersby looked askance at me. Some of the looks were respectful, accompanied by a quick head bob or raised hand of salute. Some were wary, as though I might burst into violence at any moment. I thought that humorous since one will hardly find a more disciplined warrior than a Cassiline Brother. But whatever the response, it served to remind me that I was *other.* I was a warrior and a priest sworn to Cassiel's service.

Late in the day, the ever-widening path opened onto a clearing and an area known as King's Lane, lined with vendors who held royal permits to do business on the verge of the Senescine. Master Gerarde had told me to be on the lookout for a fellow named Pascale, who had a long history of good-faith dealings with Cassilines passing through the King's Lane and a reputation for being an excellent horse-trader.

As it transpired, Pascale spotted me first and hailed me with a sharp two-fingered whistle and a shout. "Hey, Cassiline!"

Ignoring a fresh wave of stares, I kneed Aristotle over to him. "Pascale?"

"The one and only. You need a new mount?" He gestured at a picket line of four horses, all healthy and sound looking. "Let's talk horse-trading."

I patted my horse's neck. "This old fellow's pretty solid yet, I just need to restock my supplies and find a place to camp or lodge."

Pascale cast a critical eye over my mount and me. "All right," he said grudgingly. "I suppose you're right. I can sell you fodder." He nodded at a tall, regal-looking woman across the way. "Madame Tremaine makes excellent savory hand pies, and if she found out I failed to recommend them to you, I'd be in trouble."

I laughed. "I'll pick up a few."

"My thanks." He smiled back at me. The crinkles at the corners of his eyes looked as though he'd spent much of his life smiling. "Are you bound for the City?"

"The City of Elua, yes," I said.

"Folks in the region usually just call it *the* City," he said. "As though there were no other city in the world. Any mind, you'll find it an easy journey from here on out. Plenty of inns along the way. I trust you've a list of reputable ones where a Cassiline can hoist a cup without some damn fool deciding he wants to have a go?"

"I do," I said. "Does that happen often?"

Pascale shrugged. "Often enough. Men can be stupid, and drink makes them stupider. Look, there's a decent inn about two hours' ride from here, you could probably make it by sundown. Or if it's not too humble, you can lodge with my family for the evening. Nothing fancy, but it's clean, and you're guaranteed a hot meal cooked fresh, not congealed slop that's been on the hob for days."

I leaned over in the saddle to clasp his forearm. "Sounds good to me."

It was a happy decision. Pascale's family were the sort of folk who made one feel instantaneously welcome as a guest and like a veritable member of the family within ten minutes of passing through their door. They had five children, three girls and two boys, the youngest of whom solemnly dragged me around the farm to see the animals in their charge, chickens and ducks and goats. I was pleased to see that the oldest son—I didn't catch all their names—was giving Aristotle a thorough currying, even rubbing a special grease to prevent cracking on his hooves.

After a supper of roasted chicken and herbs, the children retired to bed while Pascale, his wife Amelie, and I talked for a while. I was hoping to no avail that they knew something about this Anafiel Delaunay; they were hoping, equally to no avail, that the Brotherhood possessed inside knowledge regarding the political situation. "It seems we're of no use to each other," I said ruefully.

"Ah, well." Pascale handed me a lit taper in a candlestick holder. "Good company needs no excuse. See yourself to bed."

Feeling replete, I slept soundly. Pascale and Amelie did indeed keep an immaculate house. My cot was nothing more than a spare pallet, but it was free of ticks and mites and smelled of the fresh hay with which it was stuffed. Although I quite liked the deep, calm solitude of the forest, it was nice not to have things crawling on me while I slept.

In the morning, I enjoyed a hearty breakfast, said my farewells to Pascale and his family, and struck out for the City.

It was an uneventful journey. All of the inns that Master Gerard had recommended save one were still operating, and I found a suitable replacement for the establishment that had burned. People continued to look askance at me, gazes drifting from my vambraces and daggers to the cruciform hilt jutting over my shoulder, but no one was drunk or foolish enough to try to pick a fight.

The roads grew wider, the distance between hamlets and towns shorter. The closer I got to the City, the more I felt a sense of urgency. I found myself unintentionally pushing Aristotle's pace and backing off, only to discover we had sped up again a few moments later.

At last, the white walls of the City of Elua came into view.

It was a beautiful city, encircled by white walls, divided by the Aviline River. On the west side was a wide harbor bustling with trade ships and barges. On the east side of the river, the Royal Palace dominated the view, its pristine walls and soaring towers and spires echoing the gleaming white of the outer city walls. The Palace was surrounded by gardens, which gave way to an expanse of splendid homes. Beyond that, a more modest residential area sprawled, homes and establishments growing smaller and closer together the farther they were situated from the Palace.

Here and there were temples to Blessed Elua and his Companions—all save Cassiel, to whom no temple exists save the bodies of those of us who serve him. And in the background, rising as though in gentle mockery, was Mont Nuit where the Thirteen Houses of the Night Court were located.

All of this I saw from a slope on the western side leading to one of the great bridges that spans the Aviline. A pair of City Guardsmen were stationed at either end of the bridge wearing tunics, breeches, and short cloaks of cobalt blue and silver, the colors of House Courcel. They questioned all travellers entering or leaving the eastern side of the City, which I was glad to see in terms of security. Even I was questioned despite my Cassiline gear. I showed them the sealed letter of introduction and was waved through.

Up close, the City of Elua wasn't as pristine as it appeared from afar, which I daresay is true of many things. Still, even if the streetsweepers couldn't keep up with the sheer volume of horse dung, fruit peels, rotting cabbage leaves, and the like, the City was majestic and more than a bit overwhelming.

It was early afternoon, early enough that I thought Anafiel Delaunay might yet receive a caller before sunset. Mysterious patron or not, I wanted to make a good impression, so I took lodgings at one of the finest inns in the City, paying extra for a hot bath. Before I scrubbed away layers of road grime alleviated only by bathing in cold creeks or filmy, tepid, much-used water for weeks on end, I purchased a bit of parchment and the loan of a pen and ink from the innkeeper—she could procure anything for a price—and drafted a request for an audience. For another copper centime, the innkeeper's nephew delivered the request. He was back in less than an hour with the response that Lord Delaunay would be delighted to meet with me at my earliest convenience. The nephew assured me gravely that for a small token payment, since I was a stranger to the City and unfamiliar with its streets, he could rearrange his remaining schedule to escort me to Delaunay's residence.

I laughed and reminded him that I'd found my way to the inn without any difficulty. He looked a bit crestfallen, but had the good grace to point me in the right direction.

Anafiel Delaunay's townhouse was located on the Rue des Rossignols, which I found without difficulty. Somewhat to my surprise—I don't know what I'd expected, mayhap a bawdy house on every corner—it was a pleasant neighborhood that spoke of genteel wealth. Elegant, but not ostentatious; exactly the kind of homes that a lord or lady who spent the majority of their time on a country estate in a distant province might maintain in the realm's sovereign city.

From the street, Delaunay's home appeared much like those surrounding it: quiet, modest, and gracious. The property was encompassed by pale grey stone walls, patches of brown autumn-withered trumpet vines clinging to them. There was a wrought-iron gate that opened wide enough to accommodate a carriage, and beyond it was a small courtyard with a chestnut tree growing in its center. There were stables to one side and servants' quarters to the other, and the townhouse itself, also latticed with dying vines, was two stories tall.

I sat in the saddle—although it would have been an easy walk, it felt too casual to arrive on foot—and contemplated the estate for a moment.

This was my new home.

This was my foreseeable future. Once I passed through that gate, a new chapter of my life began. If I'd had any idea what that would entail, my courage might have faltered; luckily—or unluckily—I was blissfully ignorant.

I kneed Aristotle forward, leaned over in the saddle, and rang the brass visitor's bell. A stable lad came running before the last echo faded. He curled his fingers around the iron bars of the gate and gazed at me with a teenage boy's awe. "Messire Cassiline!" he breathed before I could introduce myself. "His lordship's expecting you." Fumbling with the latch, he swung open the gate. "May I take your horse and escort you to the house?"

I rode through the gate and waited for him to close it, dismounted, and handed him the reins. "By all means."

CHAPTER SIXTEEN

Anafiel Delaunay was not one to keep guests waiting unnecessarily. I was greeted at the entrance by his mistress of household, Yolanthe, who managed to convey a nature simultaneously warm and welcoming and full of bustling efficiency. She bade me sit in the parlor and enjoy a cool cup of water while she notified the master of the house that I had arrived.

I looked around as I sipped my water—refreshingly cold and scented with a faint, delightful fragrance I later learned was orange blossom—and saw nothing to indicate this was a bawdy house. It was a light, airy space. There were slightly worn Akkadian carpets on the floor, shelves containing a fortune's worth of bound books, tapestries on the wall—it could have been any gentleman scholar's home.

I wondered if there was a chance I'd been mistaken, and hoped so.

Yolanthe returned before I'd taken more than a few sips. "His lordship will see you now, Messire Cassiline."

"Joscelin." I set down my water as I rose. "I'd be pleased if you'd call me Joscelin."

"Then I'd be pleased to do so," she said with a smile. "Now, come with me."

Delaunay's library was located on the ground floor, lit by tall, narrow windows. If I'd thought he had a fortune's worth of books on display in the parlor, there were two fortunes' worth of bound books, manuscripts, and scrolls in his library, along with instruments such as a spyglass, a compass, and an astrolabe, which made me think that whatever else was true, he was surely of Shemhazai's lineage.

"Joscelin Verreuil." The nobleman behind a rather cluttered desk rose and extended his hand. He had auburn hair, that old patrician beauty with regal cheekbones and a strong, straight nose. Ink-stained scholar's fingers, but a soldier's firm grip clasped my forearm. "Well met. I'm Anafiel Delaunay."

I returned his clasp. "Well met, my lord."

He motioned for me to sit, doing the same. "You must have some questions. Ask."

I hesitated, then shook my head. "That seems inappropriate, my lord. The Prefect deemed your request worthy, and I have accepted this posting. Nothing else is necessary."

"All right." Delaunay steepled his fingers. "Ask me something unnecessary."

"As you will." I began with one of the simpler questions weighing on me. "Lord Rinforte tells me you're from Siovale, but there's no House Delaunay in Siovale. What *is* your heritage?"

"Ah." He nodded. "Yes, of course, as a descendent of Shemhazai, you would wonder. You're right, there's no House Delaunay. It's a family name on my mother's side. I was disinherited many years ago when my family and I had, let us say, a falling-out."

"Why?" I asked bluntly.

Delaunay regarded me. He had grey eyes and a knack of looking clear into you. "The details, I think, will remain unnecessary information for now. But suffice to say that's why I'm not entitled to use the name of the House into which I was born."

"Was it a fair decision?" I asked. "Disinheriting you?"

He looked surprised. "You know, it's been so long, I'm almost never asked. No, in my opinion, it wasn't fair. But before you ask, no, there is no recourse in this matter. Now. What else?"

"I understand one of your wards was attacked," I said. "Tell me about it."

"Alcuin was returning home from an assignation," he said. "Sometimes patrons reveal secrets in the bedchamber. The attack was an attempt to silence him." His jaw tensed. "Alcuin took a grievous wound, but he survived because his guard Guy died giving him time to escape. You might have known . . ." He shook his head. "No, you're too young. But Guy trained in the Cassiline Brotherhood before being expelled at fourteen. What else?"

Fourteen? Adonai have mercy, the man didn't even make it through the Second Cohort. I was sorry for his death, but no wonder he wasn't up to the task. I took a deep breath and asked a harder question. "You spoke of assignations. Lord Rinforte said that your wards, the wards I'm to guard, are Servants of Naamah. Is it true?"

"Yes," he said. "Does that trouble you?"

I couldn't lie. "Yes, my lord. Forgive me, but it does."

Delaunay laughed. "Elua's Balls, man! I wouldn't trust a Cassiline who *was* comfortable guarding one of Naamah's Servants."

"So why engage one?" I asked out of genuine curiosity.

"Because you're the best," he said simply. "And there are times when my wards have taken assignations that have proved . . . dangerous."

"Why?"

"There are forces at work that I'm not at liberty to divulge," he said. "But you will be pleased to know that since I sent my request, Alcuin has completed his marque and chosen to leave Naamah's service. I will of course ask you to guard him under this roof and on any excursions he chooses to take—unless they conflict with guarding Phèdre, in which case I will decide—but there will be no further assignations as a Servant of Naamah for Alcuin."

"Alcuin," I murmured. "So he chose to leave Naamah's service after the attack, and you just let him go?"

"Of course."

"But the girl, Phèdre, she chooses to remain in Naamah's service?" I was on the verge of offending him, but I had to ask it.

"Yes." Delaunay furrowed his brow in thought. "I don't suppose you've heard the term *anguissette*?" I shook my head. "An *anguissette* is one who has been chosen by Kushiel to experience pleasure in pain and submission," he said. I must have looked as skeptical as I felt, for he smiled wryly. "I know, but believe me, 'tis true. And Phèdre takes a great deal of pleasure in Naamah's service."

"As you trained her to do," I observed.

He was silent for a moment. "I understand that Naamah's service is antithetical to the beliefs of the Cassiline Brotherhood," he said at length. "I expected it. You accepted this posting in full knowledge of my wards' trade. But if you cannot commit wholeheartedly to guarding them, I will ask you to take your leave."

I sat up straighter in the chair. "I am wholeheartedly committed, my lord. You pressed me to ask uncomfortable questions, and I did. That doesn't mean I won't lay down my life for your wards."

"Fair enough." Delaunay picked up an apple from his desk, tossing and catching it in one hand. "My turn to test you. Cut this in half for me, will you?" He tossed and caught it, admiring its sheen, before adding, "Mid-air."

It was an old trick. My daggers flashed out of their sheaths as the apple hurtled at my face, cutting the fruit in half with a horizontal slashing stroke, quartering it for good measure with a vertical slice before the halves could separate. I dried my blades, sheathed them, and retrieved the near-perfect apple quarters, arranging them neatly on his desk. "I hope you don't mind, I took the liberty of cutting it in quarters, my lord."

Anafiel Delaunay laughed. "Ah, so there is a little vanity lurking in there, my prickly Adonis!" Rising, he drew a sword from its scabbard on an arms-stand in the corner. "Shall we cross steel, then? Your daggers against my blade?"

I daresay I looked incredulous. "My lord?"

"A man died on my watch," he said. "I need to be sure you're as good as a fully trained Cassiline is reputed to be." With that, he moved with deceptive ease into a duelist's lunge, the tip of his blade jabbing toward my stomach.

I reacted without thinking, only noting that Delaunay favored his left side and that the blade was a cavalry sword, not suited for dueling in close quarters. I sidestepped to my left, deflected Delaunay's blade to his right with one vambrace, pivoted sharply and caught him wrong-footed from behind. I pinned my right forearm across his throat and planted the tip of my left dagger just below the hinge of his jaw. "Does this suffice, my lord?"

"Yes, rather." He coughed and I lowered my arm. Returning to his desk, Delaunay picked up a chunk of apple, blew away floor lint, and took a bite. "I think we'll get on fine."

I wasn't so sure about that, but it didn't matter. My job was to protect my patron's wards, not to like him.

A maidservant knocked lightly on the library door, poking her head in when Delaunay bade her enter. "Mademoiselle Phèdre is returned from the marquist," she said. "Shall I fetch her or ask her to wait?"

"I will see her, please," he said. Taking it as a dismissal, I rose to leave. "No, no, stay," he said to me. "Did you bring your gear?" I shook my head. "That's fine, we'll have it fetched." He nodded toward the southwestern corner of his library. "Stand at attention. This begins now."

I obeyed without thinking, having been taught to follow orders all my life; indeed, there was a certain comfort in it. I stood with my feet firmly planted, hands resting lightly on the opposite dagger hilts. The maidservant returned to announce Phèdre, my first official charge as a Cassiline Brother.

Phèdre nó Delaunay entered the library, and in that moment, I had the strangest sensation. It must be that a drifting cloud occluding the sun passed onward, for a sudden burst of brilliance lit the room. It illuminated Phèdre's face, making her appear to shine with glory inside and out, piercing my heart with inexplicable longing.

I blinked.

And then it passed; a trick of the light faded or another cloud drifted across the sun, leaving behind a very beautiful and rather petulant-looking young woman. "You sent for me, my lord?"

"Yes," he said. "Phèdre . . . before I speak further, I would ask you somewhat. You have an idea that there is a purpose in what I do, and if I have not revealed it to you, 'tis only because I seek to offer you as much protection as ignorance allows. But I am reminded how very slight that protection is. What you do is dangerous, my dear. So I ask again, is it still your will to pursue Naamah's service?"

Her response was quick and eager. "My lord, you know it is."

"Very well." He glanced at me; sun-blinded, she hadn't noticed my quiet presence in the corner behind her. "However, I am not minded to take the same risk twice. Henceforth, your safety will be assured by a new companion. I have arranged that you will be guarded by a member of the Cassiline Brotherhood."

There was a pause, then, "My lord will have his jest."

"No." Delaunay looked amused. "It is no jest."

"Do you mean to set some dried-up old stick of a Cassiline Brother to trail after me?" she asked indignantly. "On an *assignation*? You would set a crochety, sixty-year-old celibate to ward a Servant of Naamah . . . an *anguissette*, no less? Name of Elua, I'd rather you brought back Miqueth!"

I had no idea who Miqueth might be; a prior guard, I supposed. Hopefully he had survived his tenure in this rather singular household. At least I would be better prepared were actual danger to manifest.

Delaunay merely raised his eyebrows at Phèdre's tirade. "King Ganelon de la Courcel is attended at all times by two members of the Cassiline Brotherhood. I would have thought you'd be honored by it."

"Guy was trained by Cassiline Brothers," she shot back at him. "And look what happened to him! What makes you think I'd be any safer with another one?"

I gritted my teeth, irritated by her flippant manner. Never mind attackers, I was at risk of being irritated to death by my own ward-to-be. Half-trained or not, a man had died protecting her fellow Servant of Naamah; another stood willing to do the same. Even if she wasn't yet aware of my presence, there was no reason to be so dismissive, not to mention insulting the entire Cassiline Brotherhood.

"Peace upon him, but if this man Guy was expelled at fourteen, he'd only just begun the weapons training of a Cassiline Brother," I said, the words coming unbidden.

Phèdre whirled and stared at me, lips parted in surprise.

I will own, even in a sullen mood, Phèdre nó Delaunay was stunning. Her skin was fair and creamy, so fine it appeared poreless. Her luxuriant dark hair was held in a black mesh caul, subtle highlights glinting through the netting. Her features were impossibly delicate, only strong, graceful brows and full lips saving them from outright fragility.

But her eyes . . .

Her eyes were large, dark, and a bit wide set, framed in long, thick eyelashes that curled just so. They put me in mind of forest pools, dark and shimmering, fallen leaves and rich brown loam under clear spring water. But the extraordinary thing was the vivid scarlet mote on the iris of her left eye, floating like a rose petal on that forest pool. I'd known people with flecks of color in their eyes; this was well beyond the ordinary. It was strange and haunting.

I bowed to her, straightened, and met that unnerving gaze. There was an unsettling feeling in the pit of my stomach, and I didn't like it. "Phèdre nó Delaunay, I am Joscelin Verreuil of the Cassiline Brotherhood. It is my privilege to attend."

"Joscelin is sure that what happened to Alcuin and Guy would never occur to someone under his warding," Delaunay said in a calm tone. "I have measured my blade against his daggers, and I am satisfied that it is true."

She turned and cocked her head at him. "He bested you with daggers alone?"

Delaunay merely nodded at me. I bowed again, forearms crossed. "In Cassiel's name, I protect and serve."

Phèdre took a seat uninvited. "My lord, at least he is pretty enough to be an adept of Cereus House wearing fancy dress. If you will, then so be it. Is there an offer for an assignation to entertain?"

I bristled silently at being compared to an adept of the Night Court. Delaunay's mouth twitched with repressed amusement, but he answered seriously. "Offers aplenty if you wish them, Phèdre. But there is a matter I would have you attend first."

She inclined her head in mock obedience, bent on baiting at least one of us. "In Kushiel's name, I—"

"Enough." Delaunay raised his hand to silence her, but his glance took in me as well, and it brooked no insubordination. "Phèdre, you of all people should know better than to mock the service of Elua's Companions. Joscelin, we discussed this. Your Prefect has gauged this matter worthy of your order's attendance. You stand in danger of breaking your vows if you question his judgment."

I bowed. "As my lord bids."

Phèdre sighed. "Yes, my lord. What's the offer?"

"The Duc L'Envers is due to return in a fortnight's time," he said. "I would have you request of Lord Childric d'Essoms that he send word to Barquiel L'Envers that I desire a meeting with him."

I did my best to follow the conversation as they discussed the details of which patron's influence would grant them access to the Duc L'Envers. All I knew about him was that he was the Dauphine's uncle on her mother's side and that he had been a diplomatic liaison in Khebbel-im-Akkad for many years. The other names I knew not at all, but it was slowly dawning on me that the primary business of Anafiel Delaunay's wards wasn't prostitution at all. It was espionage.

In the end, I gleaned that my first official assignment would be to accompany Phèdre this very evening to call unexpectedly upon Childric D'Essoms, a regular patron, and ask him to arrange a meeting between Anafiel Delaunay and the Duc L'Envers.

It was all very convoluted.

I was grateful when Delaunay dismissed her, bidding me stay. "Forgive the lack of a warm welcome," he said when we were alone. I'd not said a word, but I daresay my expression didn't fully hide my unease. "And please know it's no reflection on you. Phèdre simply doesn't want a minder."

"And Alcuin?" I asked. "Shall you be introducing me to him as well?"

He smiled. "Oh, I think Alcuin's demeanor will prove a refreshing contrast. You'll find him in the inner courtyard, I'll leave you to make acquaintance."

I was given a bedchamber on the second floor of the main house itself, closest to the stairs so that I might serve as the first line of defense against any would-be intruders. It contained a generous cot with a soft pallet, a clothing trunk, and a washstand with clean linens, a ball of soap, and tooth powder. Yolanthe assured me that Aristotle was stabled and well cared for and that my gear would be brought to my room once it arrived. At my request, she escorted me to the inner courtyard and introduced me to Alcuin.

I'd never met anyone like Alcuin nó Delaunay. He was seated at a mosaic tile table beneath the latticed shadows of a trellis, poring over a scroll weighted by a stone at both ends. His hair was loose and *white,* falling forward to curtain his face; not the white hair of old age, not a very pale blond, but white like snow, like an ermine's winter coat.

"Joscelin!" He leapt to his feet and clasped my arm, beaming as though we were already the best of friends. "Well met!"

I returned his clasp, slightly bemused. "Well met."

"Can you sit for a moment?" he asked eagerly, clearing a space at the table. "I'd love to hear about the Cassiline Brotherhood. Guy never talked about it. Do you really begin training as children?"

Seeing no reason not to indulge his curiosity so long as I didn't divulge any of the rituals we held sacred in the Brotherhood, I sat in the chair opposite his. "Well, I was ten years old when the Brotherhood came for me . . ."

Alcuin listened, enthralled, as I sketched the bare bones of a picture of life at the Prefectory. His beauty had the same unearthly quality as Phèdre's, with fair skin to match his white hair, and dark eyes; an indeterminate deep purple hue that I was later informed had been dubbed "pansies at midnight." But it was his unabashed enthusiasm that I found most disconcerting.

"It's quite like our training when you think about it," he mused after I'd finished.

I did my best to conceal a surge of annoyance. A Servant of Naamah's training couldn't possibly be more different from a Cassiline's. We were night and day. "No," I said. "It's nothing whatsoever like it."

"You don't think so?" Alcuin cocked his head, hair falling over one shoulder in a milky river. "We begin training at ten, too. Not Naamah's arts, but the foundation on which they're built. Poise. Grace. Elocution. That's our footwork, Joscelin. We don't ply our trade until we've passed the age of consent, just as you Cassilines don't begin training with edged steel until after your sixteenth birthday."

"It's not the same," I insisted. "You're trained to, to desecrate your body for a stranger's pleasure. We're trained to—"

"Be judgmental?" he asked gently. Coming from anyone else I'd met, it would feel like an unkind cut, but there was only kindness and patience in

Alcuin's gaze. "I can see that your faith is deeply rooted. I only ask you to consider that ours is, too."

"And yet I'm told you left Naamah's service," I said. "Why?"

Alcuin tugged up the hem of the loose white shirt that he wore tucked into fawn breeches to reveal an angry red scar slashing across his pale torso. "Let us say that I found it becoming too dangerous for my taste."

"Naamah's service or the espionage?" I inquired.

He looked startled, then laughed. "You're a quick study. Both, I suppose. I pledged myself to Naamah's service for good reasons, not necessarily the right reasons. For that, I've made my atonement." Tucking in his shirt, he changed the subject. "You know, I always wanted to learn to wield a sword properly, but my studies never allowed time for it."

I followed his lead. "I can teach you the basics."

Alcuin lit up. "Truly?"

"Of course." I glanced around the courtyard. "This is a good space for it. I'll be doing my daily routine—telling the hours, we call it—every morning. Join me anytime you like."

"I will," he promised. "Thank you!"

Such was my introduction to Anafiel Delaunay's household, and his wards for whom I had pledged to lay down my life.

At least one of them appreciated it. 'Twas a pity about the other.

CHAPTER SEVENTEEN

That first evening was my first time escorting Phèdre to visit a patron, even if it wasn't an official assignation. It was a quiet carriage ride to the Palace, which was fine with me. My thoughts shied away from the nature of this outing like a pair of skittish horses balking in their traces, and in the close confines of the carriage, I couldn't help but be acutely aware of Phèdre's presence.

I was impressed that Childric d'Essoms was well connected enough to have a suite of rooms in the Palace—and, to be honest, that the Palace Guards on duty recognized Phèdre and waved us through without hesitation.

It seemed that Anafiel Delaunay's spies moved in rarified circles.

At d'Essoms' quarters, however, we were only admitted as far as the antechamber by a cautious servant and bade to wait. Phèdre appeared calm and composed in the face of the snub, but I could sense that she was on edge and it made my skin prickle. I kept my attention focused on potential threats.

Lord d'Essoms entered shortly, a pair of men-at-arms attending him. He had handsome, hawkish features emphasized by a tightly drawn-back braid of black hair. "Phèdre." He regarded her with curiosity. "What are you doing here?" Her only response was to sink into a low, wordless curtsy. He made an impatient gesture. "Come, I've no time for games. What brings you here? Is it Delaunay?"

"Yes, my lord." Phèdre straightened, all the poise and grace of which Alcuin had spoken on display. "May I speak with you in private?"

"Yes, I suppose you may." D'Essoms' gaze flicked toward me, taking in my greys and my blades, and I saw him signal unobtrusively to his men. "Come with me."

His men fell in behind Phèdre, cutting off my route and making it clear that I wasn't welcome to attend. I cleared my throat. "My lord." I bowed as d'Essoms looked back at me. "I have sworn an oath."

"Oaths." D'Essoms' lip curled; whatever that meant to him, it was nothing good. "Fine. Accompany her if you must."

In his parlor, he took a seat, drumming his fingers impatiently on the arms of his chair, his men flanking him. Phèdre knelt before him, skirts tucked and eyes downcast. Although she continued to appear calm and collected, I was standing near enough to see that at close range, she was trembling slightly. My pulse quickened in reluctant sympathy. "My lord d'Essoms," she said. "My lord Delaunay sends me to beg a boon."

"A boon? Delaunay?" His brows rose to full arch. "What does he want?"

She clasped her hands together in her lap. "He desires a meeting with Duc Barquiel L'Envers. He asks that you act as go-between in this matter."

D'Essoms' face changed. "How does . . . ?" he began, puzzled, but only for the space of a few heartbeats. "You."

His speed lunging out of the chair took me by surprise. I'd been keeping half an eye on his men, reckoning he wouldn't stoop to dirty his own hands. I was wrong. I didn't understand what had passed between them or why this request was a betrayal, but it was personal. Although I'd thought myself on high alert, there was a naïve part of me that truly didn't believe that such a scene would ever occur in the chambers of the Palace itself. Before I could react, d'Essoms had his knee in Phèdre's back and a dagger at her throat. "All this time, you've played me false," d'Essoms hissed in her ear. "Well, there's no contract between us now, Phèdre nó Delaunay, and no word you may speak to bind me from acting."

That, too, was something I would not understand until later—every Servant of Naamah catering to patrons with what they quaintly call "the sharper pleasures" has a *signale*, a word they may use at any time to call a halt to the game when it threatens to go beyond the limits of their comfort.

At the time, I merely swallowed a raging tide of fury to voice my own response. "There is one." I bowed, my daggers flashing free of their sheaths. "*Cassiel.*"

This sort of close-quarters fighting was well suited for the Cassiline style. Swords are awkward to wield in a tight space. D'Essoms' men rushed me from both sides with blades half drawn; what in Elua's name they were thinking, I cannot say. I didn't know if they meant to attempt to subdue, harm, or kill me. All I knew was that Childric d'Essoms had put a blade to my ward's throat, and I was *furious* at myself for allowing it to happen. It was a relief to put that fury into action. I had both his men spinning away like a pair of child's tops before d'Essoms ever rose to face me.

There was a thin red line etched on Phèdre's throat, a few drops of blood trickling from it. I saw red; red as blood, red as a rose petal. D'Essoms came for me, but I was ready. Sparing a quick glance to make sure his men hadn't regained their footing, I whirled as he charged, disarming him with the quick flick of one dagger, scoring a shallow gash on his palm as his dagger went flying.

It was done; I found stillness.

"I protect and serve." I bowed and sheathed my daggers. "Phèdre nó Delaunay was speaking."

"All right." D'Essoms sank back into his chair, entirely unperturbed by the entire exchange. He waved his scored hand at his men, who scrambled to their feet. The predatory curiosity in his gaze intensified. "First an *anguissette,* now this. He's as real as you are, isn't he?" he asked Phèdre. "Anafiel Delaunay is serious indeed, if he's contracted a Cassiline Brother as your companion. What makes you suppose I serve Barquiel L'Envers?"

"My lord, you spoke of it." She touched her throat, gauging the trickle of blood. "The night you . . . the night you took up the poker."

I caught my breath sharply. I was doing my best not to pass judgment out of hand, truly, but my mind recoiled from the thought of what one might do with a *poker* in the name of pleasure. Merciful Adonai, what manner of perversions went on under the very rooftops of the Royal Palace?

Meanwhile, d'Essoms was staring open-mouthed at Phèdre. "You *heard* that?"

Still kneeling, she gazed up at him. "My lord d'Essoms, you have known from the first that Anafiel Delaunay fished with interesting bait. Did you suppose Kushiel's Dart had no barbs?"

He gave a short laugh. "Barbs, yes. I've known from the first that yours were sunk in me. But these barbs you speak of are Delaunay's crafting, and not Kushiel's."

She shook her head. "Delaunay taught me to listen. But what I am, I was born."

D'Essoms sighed and gestured at a chair. "For Elua's sake, Phèdre, if you would petition me on behalf of a peer, do it seated." She obeyed and I moved to stand at her shoulder. "Now, what does Anafiel Delaunay want with Barquiel L'Envers, and why on earth should the Duc listen to what he has to say?"

"What my lord Delaunay wants, I could not say," Phèdre said. "He holds my marque, and I do as he bids; he does not explain himself to me. I know only what he offers."

"Which is?"

She held his gaze. "Delaunay knows who killed the Duc's sister."

Childric d'Essoms sat unmoving. "Why does he not take it to the King?"

"There is no proof."

"Then why should the Duc L'Envers believe him?"

"Because it is true, my lord," Phèdre said. "By the same token by which I know you serve Barquiel L'Envers, I swear it is true."

"You?" he asked.

"No, but by the same token," she said.

"The white-haired boy." D'Essoms moved restlessly and I tensed, but he was merely shifting as he thought aloud. "My Duc and your lord have been enemies a long time. Why would Delaunay . . . ?" I saw an answer come to him. He bit it off unspoken, his gaze flicking toward me. That was fine with me, I wanted no part of their intrigues. "Delaunay." He uttered it like a curse. "Very well. Duc Barquiel would have my head if I didn't bring him word of this. Tell Delaunay that I will accede to his request. And unless I am mistaken, the Duc will wish to hear what he has to say."

"Yes, my lord," she said, bowing her head. "Thank you."

"Don't thank me." D'Essoms rose smoothly; I tensed again, but Phèdre gave me a subtle shake of the head. He approached and stroked her cheek with his knuckles, ignoring me. "You will have a great deal to answer for, should I choose to see you again, Phèdre nó Delaunay," he said, the dark promise of pleasure and pain in his voice.

"Yes, my lord." She shuddered at his touch, turned her head to kiss his knuckles.

I felt queasy; I hadn't even realized I'd drawn a few inches of steel on both daggers until Childric d'Essoms gave me an amused look. He grabbed the back of Phèdre's neck and gave her a hard, contemptuous shake. "Know what it is you serve, Cassiline," he said to me. "You'll need a strong stomach to be companion to an *anguissette*." I bowed, schooling my face to impassivity. "Tell Delaunay he will hear word," d'Essoms said to us. "Now get out of my sight."

I couldn't oblige him quickly enough. I was mortified by my failure and furious with revulsion atop it. The moment the door to d'Essoms' quarters closed behind us, I turned on Phèdre. "You call *that* service to Elua and his Companions? It's bad enough, what most of your kind do in Naamah's name, but that—"

"No," she hissed, grabbing my arm. A pair of passing courtiers glanced at us. "I call *that* service to Anafiel Delaunay, who owns my marque. If it's that offensive to you, then I suggest you take it up with your Prefect. But whatever you do, do not blather it about the halls of the Palace!"

My jaw clenched tight, but I didn't want to make an even bigger scene. "Come on," I said, yanking my arm free of her grip and striding down the arched marble hallway. I could hear her footsteps hurrying after me, and I slowed my pace, inwardly cursing my impatience and carelessness. I'd been thrown off-kilter from the moment I'd entered Delaunay's household. I didn't deserve the honor of calling myself a Cassiline Brother.

Behind me, a woman's melodious voice called out. "Phèdre!"

I turned, then froze for the space of a heartbeat. I'd been hammered over the head with extraordinary beauty today; this woman's was the final blow. Another patron, no doubt. Even as I returned to Phèdre's side, I saw her reach out to stroke the bleeding scratch on Phèdre's throat with one finger, and the deliberate sensuousness and idle cruelty of the gesture made my blood run cold.

I thought to myself, *This woman is far more dangerous than Childric d'Essoms.*

But she gave no cause for offense when I arrived, beyond seeming startled by my presence. "You?" she asked Phèdre. "The Cassiline serves you?"

I bowed and replied on her behalf, since Phèdre was apparently dumbstruck. "I protect and serve."

The woman laughed, genuine laughter, until it rang through the high-vaulted halls of the Palace. At length she regained her composure and dabbed at her eyes with a lace kerchief. "Oh, Anafiel Delaunay, you priceless man."

I had no idea what courtly intrigues or bedchamber rivalries were at play here, so I simply stood at attention and ignored her, which wasn't easy. There were a thousand poems or more dedicated to her beauty for good reason, though many of them contain lines to the effect that one could no more describe it than one could paint a nightingale's song, sing a sunrise, or breathe a color. Her features were perfectly symmetrical, her skin ivory and flawless. Raven's-wing-black hair, so black it had a blue sheen, framed her face in ripples. Sapphire-blue eyes, garnet lips.

But those were only physical features, and the overall impact was so much more than the sum of her parts. Her beauty was a dark blade honed to a glinting blue edge, and she knew how to use it to deadly effect.

Now she turned it on me, standing close enough that I could smell the warm, spicy scent she wore, cupping my cheek. "It seems the Cassiline Brotherhood has been robbing the Night Court's cradle." I stared past her, feeling my face flush with anger and embarrassment. She drew her forefinger down my chest and smiled up at me. "Lucky brethren."

I breathed hard through my nose, ignoring the line of heat her touch kindled. No one had ever dared do such a thing to me. If she'd been a man, I'd have struck her.

Abandoning me, she turned back to Phèdre, eyes sparkling. "Well, then! Please give my regards to your young friend Alcuin, and my everlasting admiration to Delaunay."

Phèdre nodded.

It is customary for D'Angelines to exchange the kiss of greeting and ofttimes a kiss of parting, too. It wasn't a social nicety we observed in the Brotherhood, but I recalled my parents exchanging kisses with peers on those rare occasions we had visitors or cause to visit a nearby estate.

This kiss was . . . nothing like that.

I fixed my gaze on the distance while it lasted, only turning to Phèdre once the woman had rejoined her entourage and departed. "Who was that?"

She collected herself with an effort, looking slightly dazed. "Um. Yes. That was the Lady Melisande Shahrizai."

I remembered the name. "The one who testified against House Trevalion." I gazed after her, then gave myself a shake. I had to face Anafiel Delaunay and confess my failure to him. I'd failed at my first posting almost before it began, and my gut twisted at the very thought of it. "Are you ready to leave?"

Delaunay was waiting for us in his parlor, Alcuin was sitting cross-legged on a low couch and watching him pace. "Well?" he asked as we entered. "Will he do it?"

It was rude to interrupt him, terribly rude, but the need to confess was urgent and overwhelming. "My lord." I unbuckled my baldric and took a knee, proffering the hilt of my sheathed sword over my forearm. "I have failed in your service. Forgive me. I am unworthy of wielding my uncle's blade."

He looked at me in surprise. "What in Elua's name are you talking about? Phèdre looks fine."

"Show him," I said to her.

"This?" With a line of blood crusting on her throat, Phèdre actually laughed. "From Childric d'Essoms, this is no more than a love-scratch, my lord," she said to Delaunay. "And 'twas Joscelin kept him from giving me worse."

He raised his eyebrows at her. "D'Essoms grew violent toward you?"

"Yes, a bit, when he learned that I had betrayed his patronage to you." She shrugged. "But Joscelin—"

I interrupted again. "Childric d'Essoms laid a blade against her throat and drew blood. I failed to guard her. Then in my anger, I let her out of my sight."

"Melisande," Phèdre said as though the name were explanation enough. "She sends her greetings. Joscelin didn't fail you. D'Essoms took him by surprise, that's all."

"I've not drawn a blade against anyone outside the Prefectory," I murmured, still kneeling. "I was unready. I'm unworthy."

"An untried Cassiline," Delaunay muttered. "I should have anticipated the like. Well, lad, I have measured your skill, and if you succeed this well against Childric d'Essoms unready and untried on the proving-ground of D'Angeline intrigue, I am not displeased." I wasn't sure I'd heard right; my head came up sharply and I proffered my hilt once more. Delaunay shook his head. "To fail and persevere is a harder test than any you will meet in the training yard. Keep your sword, I can't afford its loss." He turned his attention back to Phèdre. "Now, what of the Duc L'Envers?"

"D'Essoms was convinced." She unclasped her cloak and sat, looking for all the world like she hadn't just been held at dagger-point by a wrathful patron, and kissed with unnerving thoroughness by a dangerously beautiful woman. "He will convey your request to Barquiel L'Envers and word of his response in return."

"Good." A measure of tension left Delaunay. I rose silently, feeling more awkward than I ever had in my life, and slung my baldric over my shoulder. It caught Delaunay's eye. "You're dismissed," he said, nodding with absent courtesy. "Both of you."

"My lord," Phèdre began. "Now that—"

"No." He cut her off. "No assignations, not until I have met with Barquiel L'Envers. I'd rather have you keep out of sight for now. We need time to see how this shakes out."

She sighed. "As you will, my lord."

I'd seen enough to know that was my second reprieve of the evening.

CHAPTER EIGHTEEN

After a tumultuous beginning, the following several days in Delaunay's household were relatively tranquil.

Alcuin hadn't been feigning an interest in learning swordplay. He showed up the next morning and watched me tell the hours. I kept to the simpler patterns and forms, and when I'd finished, I invited him to join me in the most primary element of all, walking the first circle. Sharing the details of the Cassiline discipline with an outsider might have met with disapproval at the Prefectory, but as Selwyn had noted, it wasn't forbidden, and I reckoned Alcuin's intentions were innocent. For me it was a reverie of sorts; for him, not having had this rhythm engrained in his flesh and bone since childhood, it wasn't exactly an escape.

"Do Cassiline cadets *really* spend an entire year walking in a circle?" he asked after some twenty minutes.

I smiled. "We do."

He paused to wipe sweat from his brow; although the fall air was chilly, the courtyard was warmed by the morning sun. "I hope you're not thinking to spend ten years training me like a Cassiline Brother. I just want to learn the rudiments."

"These are the rudiments," I said, then laughed at his expression of dismay. "Don't worry, we'll get some training swords and move onward."

I had been wanting to pay a visit to a smithy that Master Jacobe had recommended to discuss the maintenance of my own blades. Since my services weren't required elsewhere, I went that afternoon, accompanied by Alcuin. The smithy was located downwind along the Aviline River, and I found the smith to be a knowledgeable and obliging fellow. As I'd hoped, he had an array of wooden weaponry, ranging from barrel staves hacked into the crude semblance of a cutlass to ceremonial gilded and bejeweled swords and daggers.

Alcuin pored over them with delight, as well as the steel weaponry. I helped him find a training blade that suited him in terms of weight and length, and then spoke to the smith about commissioning an actual sword similar in size and balance. For all his delicate-seeming grace, like any other young man eager to invest in his first blade, Alcuin wanted to carry an imposing longsword. I managed to talk him into a narrow gentleman's short-sword more appropriate for close-quarters fighting and everyday courtly attire.

In turn, Alcuin showed me his favorite places starting with Elua's Oak in the very center of the City, a majestic, ancient tree said to have grown from an acorn planted by Blessed Elua himself. We watched trade ships loading and unloading along the docks. We wandered past ornate edifices that housed social clubs—not just for peers of the realm, but for all manner of explorers, academics, and poets, too. We strolled an area of the Royal Gardens open to all citizens of Terre d'Ange, where Alcuin pointed out a courtyard with a great marble fountain where music students from a nearby conservatory came to play for tossed coins.

It was pleasant spending time with Alcuin. I'd never had any acquaintances outside my family's household and the Brotherhood. I wasn't sure how to respond to an overture of simple friendship that wouldn't result in the two of us facing each other with dagger hilts in clutched fists, saying, "Fight me!"

I suspect Alcuin sensed this and did his best to put me at ease in a subtle manner. He kept up a light line of patter, sharing interesting bits of history and lore regarding the City, its playhouses and inns and taverns. He pointed out Mont Nuit in the northeast, a single long road winding up it. The Thirteen Houses of the Court of Night-Blooming Flowers were located on Mont Nuit. Even at a distance, one could see that these were very large, very wealthy private estates.

"Phèdre came from Cereus House," he told me. "Delaunay bought her marque, and she's been with us since."

As I understood it, the marque referred both to the tattoo on a Servant of Naamah's back and the debt-bond it represented. The completion of the tattoo symbolized the fulfillment of that debt. "Why her? She seems . . ." I let the words trail off because I had absolutely no idea what I thought of Phèdre nó Delaunay. "I don't know. Something."

Alcuin laughed. "You'll have to figure that out on your own. The most useful thing I can tell you about Phèdre is that she's a paradox. As to why Delaunay bought her marque, he recognized the scarlet mote in her eye as the mark of an *anguissette*—Kushiel's Dart, they call it."

"Why didn't the Night Court recognize it?" A certain morbid curiosity drove me. "And why would Delaunay seek out an . . . an *anguissette*?"

Alcuin was silent for a moment. "He didn't seek Phèdre out," he said. "The Dowayne of Cereus House approached him. And the Dowayne didn't recognize the mark of Kushiel's Dart because it's rare and because the Night Court has lost a good deal of its own lore as well as respect over the past hundred years or so."

"I'm sorry," I said. "I'm just trying to—"

He waved away my attempt at apology. "It's all right. Delaunay bought Phèdre's marque because she possesses a unique gift that attracts a very specific clientele. But it's a double-edged gift that may be as much a bane as blessing. And sometimes I worry that she needs protection from her own worst impulses more than her clientele."

"Good to know," I said.

"She won't take a patron against Delaunay's express orders," he added helpfully. "So you needn't worry about that. But she's apt to try his patience. If you find she's missing when you're meant to be on duty, she's probably run off to see her friend Hyacinthe. There's an inn in Night's Doorstep where you're likely to find them. He tells fortunes there, calls himself the Prince of Travellers."

I was startled. "He's a *Tsingano*?"

"Half," Alcuin said. "His mother is Tsingani, I think she's a laundress. Why?"

"No reason." I thought of that summer night in Rive-de-Lusande, racing atop the walls of the Trysting Mews after the Tsingano boy, grappling with Toulouse and falling onto the grass, Selwyn, and the girl. "I had a friend of sorts who was played for a fool by one of the Tsingani, that's all."

Alcuin shrugged. "Well, Hyacinthe claims his mother has the gift of sight, and he inherited it from her." He grinned at my dubious expression. "He also claims his father was the King of the Tsingani if that makes it more believable."

It didn't.

"What about you?" I asked him. "Did Delaunay buy your marque from the Night Court, too?"

"No." He paused and glanced down the cobbled street as we rounded the corner onto Rue des Rossignols. "You might be surprised to learn that Skaldic is my milk-tongue." His faint smile didn't reach his eyes. "I was born in a village near the Camaelines. Back when Prince Rolande was alive and men under his command patrolled the border. One of them got me on my mother and abandoned her."

"But Eisheth's gift . . . ?" It was a boon that Eisheth had bequeathed to the women of Terre d'Ange, that they might not bear children until they lit a candle in prayer to Eisheth to open the gates of their womb. "Was your mother Skaldic?"

"No," he said. "My wetnurse. I think it most likely my mother fell for a soldier's sweet persuasion and lit a candle at the behest of a man who never intended to build a life or raise a family with her."

It seemed outrageous to me. "Why would a man do such a thing?"

"Men do a great many cruel and foolish things exercising power for no good reason," Alcuin said quietly. "I only know that Prince Rolande provided for my mother after he learned it had happened on his watch. And six years later, after the Battle of the Three Princes when the Skaldi returned to raiding over the mountains and my village burned, Anafiel Delaunay came for me."

"Why?" I felt like a child constantly asking why, but in some ways, I had been reborn into a different world and I was trying to make sense of its newness. What place was there for a lone Cassiline warrior in this close-knit and deadly world of grievances, intrigues, and love affairs?

"I'll tell you what I know of our lord Delaunay," he said. "Before he was disowned, he was a famous poet; likely to be the next King's Poet, they say. But he wrote a poem accusing Prince Rolande's bride, Princess Isabel L'Envers, of murdering her rival. It brought the wrath of the Crown down upon him."

"Is that why his family disinherited him?" I asked.

"I imagine so. It's why every known copy of his works was gathered, burned, and declared forbidden. But all that matters to me is that my lord Delaunay felt compelled to uphold Prince Rolande's honor even after his death." Turning his head, he revealed the unfinished finial of the marque tattooed on the nape of his neck. "And I felt compelled by honor to complete my marque so that there would be no debt between us. One more appointment with the marquist and it's finished." He tugged the collar of his brocade frock coat back in place. "I'm hoping Delaunay will tell me more once it's done and we face each other as equals."

"Have you spoken to him about it?" I inquired.

A flush touched Alcuin's cheeks. "No. There are a number of things on my mind that I'm hoping to discuss with him."

"Ah." If I understood the implications of what Alcuin was saying, this conversation wasn't going anywhere I was comfortable following. Clearing my throat, I retreated into the safe familiarity of the mentor's role. "Tell me, do you favor the right hand or the left?"

For coming to it late—at least by Cassiline standards—Alcuin was a quick study. He and Phèdre had been trained by a tumbling master. He could bend his back into a full arch and walk on his hands if he chose, and there was a deceptive amount of strength and control in his wrists and forearms.

While the master of the household was awaiting a response to whatever gambit it was that he'd set in play, we fell into a casual routine. Alcuin watched me tell the hours in the morning, allowing me to complete my training ritual in peace. Afterward, or later in the afternoon, he and I would practice with wooden swords. Phèdre mostly kept to herself—according to Alcuin, both of them were researching a specific arena of Alban history on Delaunay's behalf—but she did venture into the courtyard garden to watch Alcuin and me at practice.

I have no idea what she was thinking at such times, or anytime, for that matter. We'd not exchanged more than a few strained pleasantries since that first evening. I wasn't trying to avoid her, Elua knows I'd be a poor excuse for a Cassiline Brother if I failed to know my ward's whereabouts at all times, but I wasn't trying to get any closer than I needed to. As long as she continued to resent my presence, I was content to do my job at as safe a distance as possible.

That didn't last long.

Nothing in particular happened that afternoon. Delaunay came into the garden and spoke to Phèdre while Alcuin and I were practicing; he stayed a few minutes watching us after she departed. He left looking pensive and returned less than an hour later, looking thunderously angry.

"Messire Verreuil!" There may have been thunder on his brow, but there was ice in his voice. "Have you seen your other charge lately?"

I bowed. "My lord—"

"*Have you?*"

Elua have mercy, I *was* a poor excuse for a Cassiline Brother. I kept my head bowed in humiliation. "No."

"My lord," Alcuin interrupted. "I'm sorry, it was my—"

"No." Delaunay held up one hand. "Alcuin . . ." He paused a moment, wrestling with his next words. "Yes, more diligence on your part would be helpful. We'll discuss this further. Messire Verreuil, I'm told your other charge strolled through the front gate almost an hour ago. Kindly retrieve her."

I bowed again. "My lord."

"The Cockerel," Alcuin murmured to me. "It's in Night's Doorstep, the coachman knows where."

In the front courtyard, the horses were already hitched to Delaunay's carriage and the coachman was waiting. I swung into the driver's seat beside him and bade him take us to the Cockerel. He was a cheerful, good-natured fellow, but he kept a wary eye out as he drove the team from wide thoroughfares into an increasingly complicated maze of narrow cobbled streets lined with shops and taverns.

"Do you fear another attack?" I asked him.

"Not exactly," he said. "'Twasn't me driving when it happened, the patron sent his own conveyance for Messire Alcuin. But this neighborhood's bad enough on its own." He pointed. "And this is as far as I can take you by coach. You'll find the Cockerel around the corner, just follow the sound of fiddling."

It wasn't as easy as it sounded, since every establishment on the block appeared to be a tavern with a fiddler playing somewhere on the premises. Dusk was beginning to fall and the lamplighters were out with their long tapers. Revelers were crowded into salons, leaning on porch railings, spilling into the streets, hoisting tankards and mugs, gambling, laughing, and drinking. At least they made way for me without hesitation, clearing a path at the sight of my greys and the sword strapped across my back.

And then I rounded the corner and found the street blocked by an open carriage whose coachman had dared the labyrinth.

Alcuin had told me that it was fashionable among daring young lords and ladies to frequent Night's Doorstep, but I hadn't fully believed him until I saw a fine gilt-trimmed open carriage containing a party of such peers, accompanied by several beautiful young tumblers and musicians clad in garments of gold and green that I would later learn were the colors of Eglantine House.

Whether or not they had stopped a-purpose or their way was blocked was unclear; either way, it didn't appear to matter to them. The gentlemen had drawn swords to keep the crowd at bay while the tumblers staged an impromptu performance right there in the streets, and a flautist and a singer played and sang perched on the back of the carriage, creating beautiful harmonies in startling contrast to bawdy lyrics.

It was the flautist who spotted me first, playing a lively skirl of notes before pointing at me. The singer threw back her head and laughed, then began singing an even bawdier song featuring the step-by-step seduction of a naïve young Cassiline Brother. I offered a brusque bow and began attempting to push past them in the direction of an inn with a wooden sign painted with a black rooster hanging from its eaves. These revelers were having none of it. The young lords with their gentleman's swords circled behind me. The singer launched into another verse, one that made the tops of my ears burn.

I was under threat of nothing more than embarrassment, which was hardly sufficient cause to draw steel, but nothing in my training had prepared me for this. The tumblers were absurd and merciless in their harassment; people around us were cheering and clapping, stamping out a beat.

One of the tumblers tossed the other in an aerial somersault, dropping to one knee and catching her on his shoulders directly in front of me. Gold and green ribbons were braided into her shining chestnut locks. "Well met, pretty boy," she said with a wink, her rising cleavage practically under my nose.

I took a step backward; the male tumbler tossed her skyward. I had time for one quick searching glance at my goal before he stood on his hands, wrapped his ankles around my neck, and dangled, grinning between my calves at the uproarious crowd. I pried his ankles loose, and no sooner had he rolled and bounded away, but the female tumbler leapt at me, wrapping her legs around my waist and looping her arms about my neck.

"Naamah will have her reckoning with you one day," she whispered into my ear, her breath smelling strongly of wine.

I angled my head away from her in helpless fury, wishing I dared butt her in the smooth forehead. "Fine. Now leave me be, if you please."

She grabbed my face in both hands and planted a kiss on my lips, the unwelcome intimacy shocking me. "You'll see."

All around me was a cacophony of shouting, singing, music, laughing, clapping, stamping. Behind me, one of the tumblers snatched a hank of my hair, tugging it loose from its club knotted at my neck. I didn't know whether to advance or retreat; but no, retreat wasn't an option. Gritting my teeth with frustration, I braced for the next onslaught, trying to figure out how to extricate myself from the chaos without bloodshed or violence. The fraying ends of my temper were ready to snap in earnest.

There was a slight surge as someone squirmed through the crowd from the direction of the Cockerel.

Once again, I had the strangest sensation as Phèdre nó Delaunay squeezed past packed bodies and half stumbled, laughing, into the clear space. For the blink of an eye a stray angle of light—a lantern hanging from the nearby veranda, the lamplighters with their torches—made her face blaze with incandescent mirth.

And then, again, there was merely a disheveled beautiful young woman, bright-eyed with amusement. A disgruntled nobleman grabbed her by the wrist in an effort to tug her away. "Joscelin!" she called out, raising her arm. "Protect and serve?"

That was all I needed.

The sound of my daggers singing free of their sheaths as I rose from my bow was the sweetest sound I've heard since my mother sang me to sleep as a babe. I took two steps toward the rowdy swordsmen, who roared with laughter as they beat a hasty retreat to their carriage. One of the noblewomen in their party offered me an impertinent curtsey.

Phèdre had the decency to look sheepish when I glared at her. "I suppose my lord Delaunay sent you?"

"You're to return with me." I jerked my chin toward the corner and the waiting carriage. "Forthwith."

Over by the Cockerel, a young man standing on an empty barrel leapt down, landing with a flourish. In a press of humanity where the brocades and silks of nobles intertwined with homespun broadcloth and fustian, he managed to stand out like a peacock, dressed in an outrageous version of courtier's attire with a blue brocade doublet, saffron slashes, and scarlet hose, of all things. He had black hair that hung in tousled ringlets and the warm brown skin of the Tsingani, all the better with which to highlight a very white, irritatingly merry grin.

Hyacinthe, I surmised.

"Come when you can," he said to Phèdre, kissing her in farewell. "You know I miss you!"

"I will," she promised, kissing him in return.

It was another silent carriage ride. I had nothing to say; I was angry at her cavalier disobedience when there was genuine danger involved, but I was angrier at myself for allowing it to happen.

Back at Delaunay's townhouse, I fairly marched her into his study, expecting that he'd give her a good dressing-down. But he was immersed in a letter and merely glanced up at our arrival. "It's come," he said to Phèdre. "The Duc L'Envers will see me in two days' time."

A measure of tension eased within her. "Good news, my lord."

"Yes." He looked back at the letter, then up again, something implacable surfacing in his gaze. "Phèdre. I will warn you one last time. If you leave these walls without permission, I *will* sell your marque. Do you understand?"

"Yes, my lord." Phèdre's voice was even, but I was near enough to feel her trembling. It wasn't with half-suppressed excitement this time.

"Good. You may go." Delaunay waited until she curtsied and departed before eyeing me. "What in the seven hells happened to you, lad?"

I faced him without flinching, painfully aware of my failure. A loose hank of hair fell over my face and carmine from the tumbler's kiss had left a greasy smear on my lips. I'd never been so insulted and furious in my life. Let Delaunay dismiss me; I'd sooner ride for the Royal Post than chase after a spoiled, capricious child of a courtesan only to be treated as an object of mockery by japing mountebanks.

No one in this entire city had an ounce of respect for Cassiel's service. Preempting his order, I reached to unsling my baldric. "My lord, I have failed—"

"Enough, please." Anafiel Delaunay sounded genuinely weary. "I don't want your apologies, Cassiline. Never mind the details. I'm sure this is a trial for you. If you fail again, do better. But if you offer to resign your post again, consider yourself dismissed *and* foresworn." He paused to let his words sink in; I absorbed them like a slap to the face. I was wrong, Delaunay did respect the Cassiline Brotherhood—it was my own behavior that was unworthy of my vows. He watched me wrestle with that revelation and acknowledge it with a reluctant nod. I would not tender my sword a third time. "Good. It pleases me that you've struck up a friendship with Alcuin," he added. "Just don't let it distract you from doing your duty toward both your charges. Because between the two of them, there's only one drawn to risk like a moth to the flame. And I need to know I can trust you not to abandon her."

Stung, I bowed. "My lord."

"Joscelin." He called me back as I turned to leave, his expression sober. "Be patient with Phèdre."

It was a considerable request to make when I was still half-ready to throttle her, but he had reminded me of my oath. All I could do was bow. "Yes, my lord."

CHAPTER NINETEEN

I was patient.

I was fairly over-brimming with patience by the time we were summoned to an audience with Duc Barquiel L'Envers. Delaunay had fully intended on going alone, so there was a to-do when the Duc's Captain of the Guard insisted that Alcuin accompany him, which in turn led to Phèdre insisting on doing the same. With both of them in attendance, I would be expected to be on duty, too.

The Captain of the Guard, clad in light chainmail under a dark purple tunic with the L'Envers insignia worked in gold, watched the entire proceedings with bewilderment. In the end, all four of us journeyed to one of the Duc's manors in the countryside of Namarre, accompanied by a score of the Duc's men. Some of them wore burnouses wrapped around their heads and faces and carried unfamiliar scimitars, and I suspected they were from faraway Khebbel-im-Akkad, where the Duc had been posted; and now it was said that the Duc's daughter had wed the heir to the Akkadian throne.

Once we'd cleared the City walls, it was less than two hours' journey. We'd not be enjoying the Duc's hospitality overnight, which was fine with me. I was confident I could handle half a dozen footpads—a score of trained warriors in their own keep was another matter.

Duc Barquiel L'Envers kept us waiting in his receiving room, which was filled with carpets and tapestries so ornate they put Delaunay's to shame and low cushioned furniture carved of a dark, polished wood. When he entered, we all bowed and he sat on a chair markedly higher than the others.

He was dressed in the Akkadian style with a purple burnouse wrapped around his face, flowing robes knotted at the waist over a pair of loose breeches. As he made a show of unwrapping his scarf to reveal cropped blond hair and a strip of suntanned skin, and the violet eyes of House L'Envers, I thought to myself, *This is a man who likes to make an impression, but he is no less dangerous for it.*

"Well, well," the Duc drawled. "Anafiel Delaunay. Have you come at last to make amends for your sins against my House?"

Delaunay stepped forward and offered another crisp bow, a soldier's salute rather than a courtier's. "Your grace, I've come to put matters in the past where they belong."

And then they were off, the two of them, a pair of coursing hounds sniffing and snapping and snarling at each other as they chased down the blame for past wrongs as though it were a fox on the run. I did my best to follow, but it was a twisty trail and I'd missed all save this final stretch of it. The gist of my understanding was that Delaunay and L'Envers had been feuding for nigh unto twenty years, ever since Delaunay wrote a poem accusing the Duc's sister Isabel L'Envers of arranging to kill Prince Rolande's first betrothed in a staged hunting accident. Whether or not that was true, I've no idea. After wedding Prince Rolande and giving birth to Ysandre, Isabel L'Envers herself died of a suspected poisoning.

Barquiel L'Envers wanted to know who murdered his sister, and in the course of Naamah's service and espionage, Alcuin had procured that information on Delaunay's behalf. The names meant little to me outside genealogy charts—they were Caerdicci names, Dominic and Thérèse Stregazza, but descendants of House Courcel by way of Prince Benedicte, the King's full brother.

And if anything were to happen to the Dauphine Ysandre, by right of succession Prince Benedicte was second in line for the throne.

It was enough to make one's head boggle.

With King Ganelon aging and Ysandre of age and unwed, the throne of Terre d'Ange was a prize at the center of a maze, and contestants who'd lain in wait for years were on the move.

So Barquiel L'Envers got the information he wanted. What Anafiel Delaunay received in exchange, none of us knew. When the conversation turned toward it, we were dismissed like common staff to the kitchen, where bustling household servants gave us bowls of stew and chunks of day-old bread more likely meant for the men-at-arms than the Duc's table. But it was hearty fare and I ate with good appetite, part of my attention scanning for nonexistent threats, part listening to Alcuin and Phèdre speculate in hushed whispers, trying to piece together the puzzle.

Insofar as I could tell without knowing Delaunay's actual birthright, he had no angle on the throne. Yet one way or another, it mattered very much to him who stood to claim the throne of Terre d'Ange. *Why?* Even Selwyn, who followed royal intrigue as though it were a tourney, hadn't been aware of a disinherited Siovalese lord in the mix. And what in the world allowed a disgraced poet to seek a boon of the Cassiline Brotherhood?

None of it made sense, and I disliked the feeling that knowledge was deliberately being withheld from me.

"Who is he?" I was frustrated by my own ignorance. "There's no House Delaunay . . . so who *is* he to move in these circles? Who is he that the Prefect of the Cassiline Brotherhood grants his requests? What does he want?"

Alcuin and Phèdre glanced at each other. "Delaunay doesn't tell us that which he reckons might get us killed," she said wryly. "But if you think he might confide in you, by all means, ask him."

"Maybe I will," I said.

Alcuin laughed. "Good luck, Cassiline."

I nearly did, too. It was during an evening not long after our audience with the Duc L'Envers; a nasty evening outside, sleet beating against the costly glass windowpanes behind the shutters, but a cozy evening inside with a blaze in the library fireplace and the heavy velvet drapes drawn against drafts. It was my wont in the evenings to let the master of the household know that everyone had retired for the night before I did so myself. That night, he invited me to join him for a tankard of barley tea with honey. I did so with awkward gratitude, sipping the hot, sweet tea.

"'Tis a cold night to be alone with one's thoughts," I ventured at length. When mentoring the Second Cohort, I found at times that cadets with somewhat weighty on their minds merely needed an invitation to talk.

Anafiel Delaunay gave me an amused sidelong look that reminded me of Selwyn. He had no intention of taking my gambit. "I'm accustomed to it. But sometimes it's pleasant to share the silence."

I hoisted my tankard. "Cheers, my lord."

He hoisted his. "Messire Cassiline."

The silence that stretched between us was a comfortable one, and I chose not to break it. I don't know what Delaunay's thoughts were on that cold night. He was a complicated man, even more so than I knew at the time. And to be honest, I wasn't sure where his loyalties lay. I had assumed they were with the Crown, else I couldn't imagine the Prefect would have appointed me to serve him. And yet by all accounts it was the King himself who had Delaunay's poetry declared forbidden.

So who *did* Anafiel Delaunay serve in the quest for the throne?

That was the crux of the matter, and it was possible that one could be killed for possessing that knowledge. I let the moment pass and chose to enjoy the companionable silence instead.

Two days later, Alcuin finished his marque and the tone of the household shifted in the wake of it. Phèdre accompanied him to the appointment with the marquist, so I was in attendance on the both of them. Although Master Teilhard was the most highly regarded artist of his generation, his shop was modest. There was a low table for clients next to a stand filled with pots of ink, needled tappers, and small mallets; a seating area for guests; and an array of pillar-shaped candles burning in glass globes and costly mirrors arranged just so, that the marquist might work upon his canvas of human skin without casting shadows.

Other than the three of us, there was no one present but the marquist and his apprentice. Alcuin stripped to the waist and lay facedown on the table. The lines of ink that began at the base of his spine and swirled up its length were pale green and silvery grey, echoing the form of a birch tree. It was subtle and lovely and very well suited to Alcuin, who pulled his white hair to the side so that the marquist might complete the crown of leaves that would form the finial of his marque.

It was also an awkwardly intimate situation. I looked away from the sight of the inked tappers repeatedly piercing Alcuin's pale skin under the marquist's expert mallet; at the walls, at the mirrors, even at Phèdre, who was watching the proceedings with a combination of fondness and envy.

So much vulnerability on display made me uncomfortable.

That evening the household was slow to retire. In the parlor where I could keep an eye out for anyone coming or going, I watched Alcuin descend from upstairs to enter Delaunay's library, then rose as Phèdre followed him a moment later. I was debating whether to follow the both of them and inquire whether anything else was required of me that night when I realized that Phèdre had frozen outside the door to Delaunay's library, listening, the door ajar and her hand on the knob.

As I watched, she averted her head, then very carefully—Delaunay's wards could be as silent as ghosts when they chose—closed the door. Backing away from the hallway, she retreated upstairs. Cassiline Brothers aren't trained in stealth and eavesdropping, but we're taught to be unobtrusive, and Phèdre never knew I was there. I followed in her footsteps. The door to Delaunay's library was thick oak wood polished to a fine gleam and one couldn't hear so much as a whisper of conversation through it.

Upstairs, all was quiet. The oil lamps in their hanging sconces were lit, washbasins and ewers filled, clean linens laid out, chamber pots emptied, embers in the braziers banked to last the cold autumn night. The door to Phèdre's suite of rooms was firmly shut, closing her in with all her satins and silks and velvets, whatever fripperies, perfumes, and unguents were part of a courtesan's accoutrements. I stood indecisively in the hallway, unsure whether to return to my post or retire.

It was there that Yolanthe, carrying a tray with a flask of cordial and two stemmed goblets, found me lingering. "You may consider the household abed for the evening, Messire Cassiline," she said kindly.

I thanked her and retired.

I wasn't so naïve that I failed to understand what had transpired. I'd known that Alcuin's feelings—and Phèdre's, too—for Delaunay were anything but filial. The notion wasn't as unfamiliar as one might imagine. It was common for junior cadets to idolize the most gifted senior cadets or develop strong feelings for their mentors; but in the Cassiline Brotherhood the bond between mentor and mentee was sacred.

In one sense, it felt to me as though Anafiel Delaunay were violating that trust; in another, I did a disservice to Alcuin if I considered him less than a grown man sure of his own heart and entitled to his own choices.

At any rate, it was no business of mine. This was a far different world from the one in which I'd grown to young manhood. Relationships that would be grounds for dismissal in the Cassiline Brotherhood were the stuff of poets' verses in the world beyond the walls of the Prefectory.

If there was aught out of place here, it was me.

In the morning, Alcuin had a soft, secret smile he took care not to turn in Phèdre's direction, and insofar as it was possible for a singularly complicated man, Anafiel Delaunay appeared quietly happy. It was as difficult to begrudge them that happiness as it was to condone it.

As for Phèdre . . .

If one of Delaunay's peers hadn't brought news that afternoon that freed her to return to Naamah's service, I daresay she might have attempted to slip away again. I wasn't in attendance at the meeting with Delaunay's old friend Gaspar Trevalion, the Comte de Fourcay, but afterward I was given to understand that Duc Barquiel L'Envers had acted on the information that Delaunay had provided him and whatever threat the Stregazza family posed to the throne had been eliminated.

So the route from the city-state of Milazza to the D'Angeline crown was blocked. The King's brother Prince Benedicte wouldn't make a play without allies. What that meant for the realm was any number of things; what it meant for Anafiel Delaunay's household was that the immediate danger of retribution had passed, and much to her genuine delight, Phèdre was allowed to accept assignations once more.

It surprised me that Phèdre's unhesitating first choice of patron was Childric d'Essoms; in her own way, she felt she owed him a debt of honor. Exactly how that was repaid by . . . well, I cannot say in truth. I didn't know the details of what transpired between Phèdre nó Delaunay and her patrons in the bedchamber or wherever such dalliances occurred. It was a small mercy, for even in those early days I found what knowledge I did possess difficult to endure. I was never one to find pleasure in another's suffering. Over time I came to understand it better, to apprehend that this was an art that involved an exchange of pleasure and pain, of power and consent, that could be at once excruciating and exquisite.

But no matter how long or often I heard it throughout my life, it was never a tune that called to me.

I was grateful that d'Essoms chose to receive Phèdre at his townhouse and not the quarters in the Palace where he'd drawn a knife and gotten the drop on me. Even so, the memory was painfully fresh and it was hard to maintain a stoic façade when Lord d'Essoms grabbed Phèdre roughly by the upper arm, hauling her stumbling in his wake past the doors of his receiving room.

There, I waited.

I cannot say how long. We arrived after sundown and departed before dawn, so there were no daylit shadows or starry skies to mark the passage of the hours. Whether it was out of spite or simply the custom of the household, no offer of hospitality was extended to me, so I simply stood at attention, feeling rather like a piece of misplaced furniture. If the household had been awake, the maidservant would have had to dust around me.

When one of d'Essoms' liveried servants escorted Phèdre back to the receiving room at last, I was shocked by her appearance. The visible damage was confined to a split and swollen upper lip, but beneath the velvet cloak—a near-black crimson hue called *sangoire*—she clutched around her, I could tell she was moving stiffly and with pain.

"Name of Elua!" I reached her in two strides, scooping her into my arms.

"Joscelin!" Against all likelihood, there was a note of irritation in Phèdre's voice. "Put me down! I can walk."

"Not while I'm attending you," I muttered, uncomfortably aware of the warmth and weight of her in my arms. I jerked my chin at the liveried servant, who opened the door with alacrity, and swept out of the chamber, the folds of Phèdre's cloak trailing behind us like dark scarlet wings.

I daresay Phèdre was either more exhausted or hurt than she wanted to admit. She didn't protest as I carried her into d'Essoms' courtyard, where Delaunay's carriage was awaiting us, nor when I lowered her gently into the seat. But when I examined her face by light of the carriage lantern, she flinched away.

"Idiot!" She glared at me. "This is what I *do*!"

I ordered the coach driver homeward and climbed into the carriage opposite Phèdre. I could feel the muscles in my jaw tensing. "Yes, well, if this is your calling, I would that I knew what sin I'd committed to be forced to bear witness to it," I retorted, unable to fully suppress a note of bitterness in my tone. Knowing what the future held for us, Adonai himself must have laughed at the hubris of *that* outrage.

Phèdre gave me an unreadable look, then winced as the carriage set out with a jolt. "I didn't ask to have you here."

Folding my arms, I leaned back against the carriage seat and regarded her. "And you call me an idiot."

CHAPTER TWENTY

Anguissettes heal fast.

It was a good thing, too. I didn't know the extent of Phèdre's injuries, but the discreet Yeshuite doctor who attended the household shook his head in disapproval; not, I suspect, for the first time.

During Phèdre's convalescence, I spent a good deal of time telling the hours by myself in the courtyard. Alcuin continued to join me for lessons in the afternoon, but more and more of his time was spent with Delaunay. When I wasn't keeping up my training, I was grateful to have access to Delaunay's library.

Master Jacobe had warned me that tedium was one of the worst aspects of being a Cassiline Brother with an official posting. With all the self-confidence of youth, I'd been sure nothing could shake my vigilance. After that first incident with d'Essoms, that may have been true when I was on active duty, but it was another matter to be confined to quarters by circumstance with no specific duties or chores to occupy the hours.

It almost, almost made me sympathize with the unexpected rebellious streak that made Phèdre try Delaunay's patience.

I saw a different side of her some days into her convalescence when Thelesis de Mornay, the King's Poet, came in person to invite Phèdre to attend a performance of a play written by an acquaintance.

It was my first time meeting Thelesis de Mornay—although she'd visited before, I'd not been introduced. Just the mention of her name conjured memories. I'd been thirteen during the summer in which Thelesis was named the King's Poet and *The Exile's Lament* was on everyone's lips in the market square of Rive-de-Lusande. Although I didn't have the pleasure of hearing Thelesis recite until much later, even her ordinary speaking voice had a gorgeous timbre. It had a burnished quality, like an instrument lovingly tended to.

I suspected there were few people in the world whom Phèdre nó Delaunay loved in a simple, direct, and uncomplicated manner. Thelesis was one of them. I watched Phèdre light up with unalloyed pleasure at the invitation, and I liked her a little better for seeing the amount of respect and admiration she had for the King's Poet.

A little, anyway.

My presence wasn't required—Thelesis de Mornay was under the King's own protection and it would have been an insult to insist that his mantle didn't suffice—but when I suggested to Delaunay that I might take a discreet stroll that evening, he was appreciative of the implied offer. Nothing happened that evening from a bodyguarding standpoint. Based on the cheers coming from the playhouse, the night was a resounding success. I rather wished I could have seen it as it was performed in the classical Hellene style with full-face masks. Our father had a collection of work by ancient Hellene playwrights and he often read them aloud to us during the long winter nights. Much to our guilty delight, he occasionally forgot from year to year which plays were bawdier or bloodier than he deemed appropriate for a youthful audience.

The play was indeed a success. It had caught the eye of the Minister of Culture and a debut at the Royal Theatre was scheduled two days hence. An invitation for Anafiel Delaunay arrived by courier.

I was half hoping he might ask me to attend as his man-at-arms, but that evening Phèdre had her first assignation since her injuries had healed. And so I found myself cooling my heels in another receiving room in another suite of rooms at the Palace.

Lord Rogier Clavel was only the second of Phèdre's patrons that I'd met. He was cordial and cheerful, nothing like d'Essoms. I'd overheard Phèdre describe him as being almost too sweet-natured for his own desires.

I daresay Lord Clavel's pleasant disposition made him all the easier to manipulate. Within the parameters of the contract, the length of an assignation was at the patron's discretion; thus, it was quite some time before I asked the maidservant if it were possible to make a tactful inquiry regarding our return to Rue des Rossignols. The price she extorted for the favor was a small exchange of flirtatious banter which I attempted so very awkwardly that she burst into laughter and took pity on me.

When the maidservant returned, all traces of laughter were gone. "His lordship is sound asleep," she reported somberly. "Mademoiselle nó Delaunay is not with him."

I took a slow, deep breath. "I need to know where she is."

She hesitated. "I can't—"

My hands tightened into fists, the leather straps of my vambraces creaking. *"I need to know where she is."*

Whatever she heard in my voice, it brooked no argument. She hurried back into Rogier Clavel's inner quarters and returned in short order with his lordship. He wore a luxurious robe of maroon silk brocade and a sleepy expression. "Ah, right," he said upon seeing me. "Forgive me. You're to meet Phèdre outside the entrance to the west wing of the Palace. I'll send word to my driver."

I bowed. "My lord, I am oath-bound to attend Phèdre nó Delaunay. Can you tell me her whereabouts?"

Clavel shrugged. "Precisely, no. She inquired about a manner in which she might depart my quarters unseen and I directed her to one of the service passageways. Beyond that, discretion prevailed, though I understand it is a matter of calling upon a potential patron; one who might find the presence of a glowering Cassiline Brother off-putting."

I closed my eyes briefly. "When did she leave?"

"Oh . . ." Lord Clavel glanced around. "No more than half an hour gone, I think." He paused. "Messire Cassiline, go meet Phèdre at the carriage," he said in a gentle manner. "I'm not sure you understand the discretion your own post requires. If you go storming about the Palace in search of your charge, you're only going to make a scene and mayhap place her in greater danger than whatever foolhardy risk she's taken."

I didn't like it, but he was right. Even if I could tear down the Palace walls with my bare hands—and I felt angry enough to do so—it would only tip Phèdre's hand that she was up to . . . well, whatever in the name of Blessed Elua and all his Companions she was up to. I surely didn't know.

If I had known what she'd witnessed after leaving Clavel's quarters, I might have behaved differently when at last Phèdre emerged from the western entrance to the Palace into the courtyard drive where I was waiting with the coach driver. But I didn't know. I'd had too long to think while waiting and it had stoked my ire rather than cooling it. Dabbling in intrigue was one thing; actively preventing me from doing my job was an affront to my entire life's training and everything I held dear.

I greeted Phèdre with a glare. "I will *not* have my vows compromised because you—"

"Joscelin." There was a note of exhaustion in her voice. "Your order is vowed to protect Elua's scions, yes?"

I wasn't sure what she was trying to say. "You know it is. Why?"

She climbed into the carriage. "Because what I've just seen might endanger House Courcel itself," she murmured in a barely audible tone. "Please don't ask me what that is, because I very much need to collect my wits. And if you've an ounce of sense, you won't mention this to my lord Delaunay or he'll have both our hides for it."

I didn't reply; I needed to collect my wits, too. I offered an ambiguous bow and rapped on the coachman's seat, then settled in for another uncomfortable trip through the streets of the City of Elua. Delaunay returned long after the rest of the household had retired, so I didn't have to decide whether to tell him until later. I slept poorly. My conscience impelled me to honesty, but common sense suggested that Phèdre was correct in implying that complete candor would only result in an unhappy outcome.

Did I trust her?

It was an interesting question. I didn't know the answer. Nothing in my training had prepared me to deal with charges engaged in Naamah's service *and* espionage. Although I struggled with Alcuin's and Delaunay's newfound happiness together, I was grateful that the former had chosen to pursue the role of a gentleman scholar rather than a Servant of Naamah.

Betimes Phèdre's polish and sophistication made her seem older than her years. She'd been moving in these rarified circles ever since her parents sold her into indentured servitude in Cereus House at four years of age—Alcuin told me the details in confidence.

At other times, her impulsive tendencies and reckless disregard for her safety made her seem younger than her age.

I daresay the matter was on Phèdre's mind too, for she came to watch me telling the hours that morning even though the day was cold. She stood shivering, wrapped in a fur-lined velvet coat, while I moved through the quadrants and carved circles within circles, my daggers working in tandem, my breath coming in frosty puffs. It would have been courteous of me to cut my exercise short.

Since I was feeling more put-upon than courteous, I completed my final circuit before sheathing my blades and approaching her. She wore one of her unreadable expressions; a difficult look to describe, as though she were listening to a distant strain of music. The cold had brought a touch of rosy pink to her cheeks and the scarlet mote in her left eye was vivid in the grey morning light.

Phèdre waited for me to speak.

I held her gaze intently. "Do you swear to me that what you ask in no way dishonors my vows?"

She nodded. "I swear it."

"Then I'll say nothing . . . this once." I held up one warning finger. "But only if you also swear not to deceive me while you're under my protection. No matter how I feel about it, I'd never do aught to keep you from honoring your pledge to Naamah. By the same token, I ask you to respect my pledge to Cassiel."

"I swear it," Phèdre repeated, hugging herself against the cold. "Shall we go inside now?"

I bowed. "My lady."

Indoors, we adjourned to the library. Delaunay was still abed, but Alcuin had a fire blazing in the hearth and was poring over a long table strewn with scrolls and bound manuscripts.

Phèdre glanced at his research. "Do you think to solve the mystery of him?"

"Why not?" Alcuin said. "No one else has."

Not for the first time, I was marveling at the depth and breadth of Delaunay's archives. "Do you mean our lordship? One thing's certain, this is a Siovalese nobleman's library, he's got everything in here but the Lost Book of Raziel." I peered at the weighted scrolls on the table. "Does Delaunay actually read Yeshuite script?"

"Probably," Phèdre said. "So it's true that all Siovalese treasure learning?"

"Oh, yes." I smiled at a memory. "There was an old Aragonian philosopher who would trek across the mountains every spring, when the cherry trees were blooming, to visit with my father. They'd spend seven days debating whether man's destiny was irrevocable, then he'd turn around and go back to Aragonia. I wonder if they ever settled it."

"How long since you've been home?" Alcuin inquired.

I squared my shoulders, realizing that I'd overstepped the bounds of professionalism. "My home is where duty bids me."

Phèdre rolled her eyes. "Oh, don't be such a damned Cassiline. So I take it that despite being a fellow Siovalese nobleman, you weren't able to pry any further information from his lordship?"

"No," I admitted. "My oldest sister would know; she once traced the lineage of every Major and Minor House of Shemhazai's descendants." I glanced at Alcuin and answered his question. "Eleven years since I've seen my family. We swear our final vow at twenty. I'm allowed to visit home at twenty-five if the Prefect gauges that I've served well in my first five years."

Alcuin whistled.

"I told you it was a harsh service," Phèdre said to him. "What about you? What can you add to the mystery of Anafiel Delaunay these days?" There was an edge to her voice. He looked at her with his grave, pansy-dark gaze and said nothing. "You *do* know. He told you." She shoved irritably at the nearest book. "Damn you, Alcuin! We always promised we'd share whatever we learned."

"That was before I knew." He moved one of the more delicate scrolls out of her reach. "Phèdre, I'm sorry. I don't know the whole of his story, only what I need to aid him in his research, and I promised not to tell you until your marque was made. You're near to it, aren't you?"

"Will you see?" she asked coldly.

The words meant nothing to me; like so many customs in the realm of Naamah's service, they were foreign to my experience. Later, though, I learned it was the formal phrase uttered by those who entered Naamah's service to the bearer of their marque upon its completion. The ritual of observation was an acknowledgment that all debts between them were settled.

Those were the words that Phèdre had overheard Alcuin saying to Delaunay; his response changed matters between them irrevocably.

Alcuin flushed, but he stood his ground. "You told him how I felt, Phèdre. He might never have let it happen otherwise."

With a sigh, she flung herself on the couch. "I know, I know."

It was an uncomfortable conversation for an involuntary participant. I made a studious effort to avoid eavesdropping, but it was nigh impossible in such close quarters. When Alcuin sat beside Phèdre on the couch and wrapped his arms around her, I departed with a silent bow.

Any hopes that the remainder of the morning would prove tranquil were dashed when I encountered Delaunay emerging from the parlor. He looked a bit disheveled, but in good spirits and none the worse for wear after a late night.

"Messire Cassiline!" he hailed me. "We've an unexpected caller this morning. Lady Melisande Shahrizai comes bearing a rather unconventional offer, and I'd have you in attendance to hear it."

I inclined my head. "My lord. May I inquire what an *unconventional* offer might be?"

He gave a rueful chuckle. "Well you might. But it's no more likely to offend your sensibilities than any assignation Phèdre might accept, it's only that the offer is for the Longest Night." I must have looked blank, for he added, "In the Night Court, adepts don't traditionally accept offers for the Longest Night."

"Oh."

Delaunay regarded me curiously. "How do Cassiline Brothers celebrate the Longest Night?"

"We keep Blessed Elua's vigil throughout the night," I said.

"Not Cassiel's?" he asked.

I crossed my forearms. "We *are* Cassiel's vigil, my lord."

It took him aback; I could almost see the thoughts moving behind his eyes like clouds scudding across an autumn moon. "Mayhap you are," he mused. "Mayhap you are."

I expected to find Melisande Shahrizai with an entourage, but her attendants were awaiting their mistress in the receiving room. Her ladyship was seated in Delaunay's parlor drinking barley tea and chatting with Yolanthe, which surprised me. She and Delaunay were friends of long standing, so it wasn't strange that she would know the members of his household; she just hadn't struck me as the type to make small talk with the servants.

I knew very, very little about Melisande Shahrizai. When all was said and done, I'm not sure anyone did, even those like Delaunay who had known her for many years.

She acknowledged me with a courteous nod and carried on her conversation with Yolanthe concerning a recipe for custard tarts. Shortly thereafter, Delaunay returned and Yolanthe discreetly departed as he and Melisande struck up a lively conversation regarding various bits of news and gossip. I stood quietly at attention, once again doing my best not to eavesdrop. It was easier to do when the discussion had no bearing on my circumstances. Interesting to note, Delaunay was looser and more relaxed than usual in Melisande's presence. They had been lovers once, parted amicably, and remained friends ever since, and it was obvious that there was genuine affection between them.

A few moments later, Phèdre arrived, looking rather unkempt and exceedingly flustered. "My lord, my lady." She curtsied and sat, hands folded.

"Phèdre." Melisande said her name, her voice like stroking velvet. I could see Phèdre's color rise at the mere sound of it. "I've made Anafiel an offer he deems acceptable. The Duc de Morhban is visiting the City and he's holding a masquerade on the Longest Night. His is the sovereign duchy in Kusheth and I'm minded to make a statement on behalf of House Shahrizai. A genuine *anguissette* would be just the thing. Are you contracted for the Longest Night?"

The tension between them was as taut as a drawn bowstring. I'm sure that Melisande was perfectly well aware that it wasn't customary for adepts to take a patron on the Longest Night and was simply toying with Phèdre for her own amusement.

Looking downward, Phèdre shook her head. "No, my lady," she murmured. "I am not contracted for the Longest Night."

"Well, then." Melisande smiled. "Do you accept?"

Based on the quick glance Phèdre gave her under downswept lashes, she was equally well aware that she was being toyed with. "Yes."

"Good."

And with that one simple exchange, even I in my naivete could sense that a threshold had been crossed and a long game of consent and submission was playing out between the two of them.

Melisande turned to me. "A long, dull vigil for you, I fear, my young Cassiline."

Her tone was perfectly pleasant, nothing to suggest mockery; but there was a gleam of mirth in her midnight-blue eyes that said otherwise. It was obvious that she enjoyed toying with people, and I did not enjoy being toyed with. I bowed, expressionless. "I protect and serve."

She arched her brows. "Oh, I'm sure you protect well enough, but I'd ask for a more courteous service were you to attend me, Cassiline."

Clenching my teeth, I bowed again and said nothing.

Delaunay cleared his throat. "The Longest Night, then." He raised a cup of tea in salute to Melisande. "You don't do anything by halves, do you?"

She saluted him in return. "No."

Phèdre closed her eyes and shuddered in anticipation of unknowable pleasure. This year the Longest Night would be a long one indeed, and there was no part of me that looked forward to it.

CHAPTER TWENTY-ONE

The days leading up to the Longest Night were filled with endless discussion of politics and couture.

I'd never heard the word "couture" prior to serving in Delaunay's household. In Verreuil, fine clothing meant costly fabrics and luxurious furs; the style in which garments were sewn and adorned would be reckoned old-fashioned. In the City of Elua, the design and fabrication of clothing was a high art. There were houses of couture that had longer pedigrees than many of the noble houses in the realm.

Phèdre fretted for days about what to wear to this assignation, driving all of us half-mad, until Melisande sent a message that she would be providing all clothing and adornment necessary for Phèdre's attendance at the Duc de Morhban's Midwinter Masque.

It was another means of control. I still struggled to accept Phèdre's nature as an *anguissette*. Having involuntarily witnessed the deep, languorous pleasure she experienced in the aftermath of an assignation, I didn't doubt it. I just didn't understand it. According to Delaunay, the crimson mote in her left eye was the prick of Kushiel's Dart, marking her as his chosen.

But *why?*

Why in the world would Kushiel, once the punisher of Heaven, choose such a frivolous person to work his will on earth? Not only was the question unanswered, it seemed to be unasked, which struck me as peculiar. I didn't raise it, either, since I might as well ask why Cassiel—or at least the Cassiline Brotherhood—had sent me to protect and serve such a frivolous person. Although in my case, it was likely politics of some sort—mayhap Delaunay was owed a boon by the Brotherhood for some past favor in the days before he was disinherited. I simply couldn't imagine what purpose Kushiel had for Phèdre.

Politics, though . . . politics, politics, politics.

Discussion and speculation were endless; betimes in the open, betimes behind closed doors. When I was privy, I listened to them with half an ear and engaged in the calming practice of whetting my blades by hand. In the back of my mind, I saw my father's expression of polite disapproval. But one topic that was of great interest to me was talk of a Skaldic warlord uniting the tribes under a single banner.

Waldemar Selig, he was called. In the Skaldic tongue it meant Waldemar the Blessed. Raiders crossing the border into Terre d'Ange were growing ever bolder, and they shouted his name in battle.

It brought home the blow of Selwyn's death all over again. I wished he were here. After he'd picked himself up—because he would have thrown himself laughing on the floor all over again if he'd seen me serving in Delaunay's household—he would have delivered some shrewd speculation of his own regarding the situation in Skaldia. His information wouldn't rely on parlor gossip, either. Selwyn grew up in the shadow of the Camaeline Mountains, scion of a house that protected our border for centuries. There was knowledge bred in the bone, rooted in experience, that couldn't be conveyed in a courier's missive. I wondered what he might have learned of this Waldemar Selig after returning to Camlach.

I hadn't spoken of Selwyn since leaving the Prefectory; not even to Alcuin, whom I'd come to consider a friend. It might have been different if Alcuin hadn't become absorbed in his relationship with Delaunay so shortly after my arrival. We still had regular training sessions and were easy enough in each other's company, but he spent more and more time in the library poring over manuscripts referencing the Master of the Straits.

So I said nothing, carrying my grief at Selwyn's death like a rock in the pit of my stomach. I missed him. I would have given a great deal just to see his foxy sidelong glance of amusement at my situation.

But Selwyn was gone forever, slain defending his liege. It was precisely the death he would have chosen for himself; for the thousandth time, I just wished he hadn't been so gods-bedamned eager to choose it.

A black carriage with the gold interlocked-keys insignia of House Shahrizai on the door panels arrived the evening of the Longest Night, drawn by four white horses with prettily arched necks. There hadn't been any snow yet, but it was cold enough that hoarfrost sparkled on the cobbled stones of the front courtyard and the driver's breath came in plumes.

Wrapped in her *sangoire* cloak, Phèdre shivered as I helped her into the carriage; whether from the cold or anticipation, I couldn't say. She was halfway elsewhere in her thoughts, listening to that distant strain of music only she could hear. In the early gloaming light, the crimson mote in her eye seemed to float, a tantalizing fruit hanging out of grasp.

It was a small carriage with two facing seats; we could not help but sit so close that our knees were touching.

Phèdre didn't notice.

I did.

Even so, I can't say it was a relief to arrive at Melisande's villa on the outskirts of the City. It was a secluded, charming little estate; however, the Duc de Morhban's masque was taking place at his own manor, and I would not be in attendance. I misliked this arrangement. If aught were to happen at the masque, there would be naught I could do. I couldn't very well protect and serve if I wasn't there. I spoke to Delaunay and proposed that if I weren't allowed to attend the masquerade, I could at least maintain my vigil at de Morhban's estate.

This, Delaunay refused outright. This was a private affair hosted by the sovereign Duc of Kusheth on the Longest Night, and my presence was not welcome. It would be an afront to House de Morhban. In the end I capitulated, not because I agreed, but because defying Delaunay meant breaking my vow of obedience.

Melisande Shahrizai received us herself at her villa wearing a long coat of black-and-gold brocade, her hair braided into a crown. I was braced for more of her veiled teasing—Elua have mercy, Selwyn would have found a kindred spirit in this woman—but she was all solemn courtesy on the Longest Night, introducing me to her Captain of the Guard.

"There is a temple of Elua in the garden if you wish to pass your vigil there, Messire Cassiline," she said to me.

I bowed. "My lady."

Her Captain of the Guard saluted me. "Come with me, messire."

Like most temples dedicated to Blessed Elua, this one had four pillars open to the skies. The effigy was carved of marble with fine veins of green, and Elua's expression was serene and unknowable.

I knelt before it.

My breathing slowed, my heartbeat followed suit. It was cold, but I too was mountain-born and bred and I had been taught methods of enduring stillness and cold. Mayhap I should have been contemplating weighty matters such as the return of Blessed Elua and the Misguided from Terre d'Ange-that-lies-beyond, but it was a relief to simply be in Elua's presence and contemplate the love that Cassiel bore him, a love so pure that he followed Elua into exile. To this day, Cassiel with his bright-burning sword holds the gate for their return into Adonai's fold, no matter how many centuries it may take.

I breathed.

Slower and slower, until it seemed that I was a single fixed point on the earth around which the heavens revolved. The stars overhead rotated degree by degree between one breath and another. Not until the eastern horizon began to pale did I stir. My breath came in a short, sharp flash, jolting my heart into a normal rhythm.

Phèdre.

Her name shot through my thoughts like an arrow, and I was on my feet with daggers drawn in a blink. It wasn't the first time I'd feared for Phèdre's safety while she was with a patron, but this was different. I may not have been fond of her, but one doesn't have to like a person to stop them from running blindly toward the edge of a cliff.

I had a feeling that Melisande Shahrizai was Phèdre's cliff. If so, she'd already plunged over that edge.

"Your ward is fine," a voice behind me said. I whirled to see the Captain of the Guard. "She is resting, and will join you shortly. I've come to escort you."

I waited in the dining hall, a modest, sunlit room designed to entertain no more than a dozen guests. No doubt the lady of the manor had more opulent holdings elsewhere, but this suited her purpose. Despite the Captain's assurance, a sense of foreboding plagued me. I didn't want to know what dark pleasures took place in the chambers behind the villa's sunny façade.

When Phèdre entered at last, I rose with relieved alacrity. She was moving cautiously and avoided meeting my eye, and her expression was more languid and dreamy than usual, but she had suffered no visible harm. Bowing, I resumed my seat opposite her. Unobtrusive servants poured water and offered figs and dates imported at Elua knows what cost from warmer climes. Phèdre drank deep of the water and continued to avoid my gaze.

It wasn't long before Melisande Shahrizai, immaculately dressed and coiffed, came to bid Phèdre farewell. In one hand, she held a drawstring purse, and somewhat I couldn't see in the other. "*Joie* in the year to come, Messire Cassiline," she said pleasantly to me.

I bowed.

"This is for Naamah's honor." She tossed the purse to me. "You may want to hold it for safekeeping."

I caught it out of reflex and I'd be hard put to say which startled me more—the jangling heft of the bag or Melisande tossing it so casually. I tucked it into an inner pocket of my mandilion and bowed again.

"And this . . ." Turning to Phèdre, Melisande tied a black velvet cord around her throat, evocative of the leashes noblewomen use to keep their pretty pets close at hand—except that a single large diamond hung from it. Phèdre closed her eyes briefly as the jewel nestled in the hollow of her throat, her pulse beating beneath it. With her head bowed, now I could see the razor-fine beginnings of bloody traceries etched into her skin. "This is for remembrance, and not for Naamah."

Phèdre touched the diamond and said nothing, everything about her demeanor suggesting submission and obedience.

But Melisande wasn't done yet. With a laugh, she turned and beckoned to a servant hovering in the background, a frothy bundle of fabric in his arms. He came forward with a bow and deposited the torn and wadded mass of sparkling gauze in Phèdre's arms. Her head came up sharply; more sharply than she intended, gaze filled with wariness and wonder. "I've no need of rags," Melisande said lightly to her. "But I *am* curious to see what an *anguissette* trained by Anafiel Delaunay will do of her own accord."

Diamonds.

Those were *diamonds* studding the remnants of a garment wrought of sheer gauze material, not bits of glass. They were tiny in comparison to the teardrop-shaped diamond on the velvet leash, but there were dozens of them, enough to make her marque and more.

Phèdre drew a slow, long breath, turning her head to meet Melisande's gaze, her words scarce audible. "My lady."

Melisande laughed again, kissed her on the lips, and departed.

Once she'd gone, I stared at Phèdre in a state of disbelief.

She stared back at me, looking every bit as stunned as I felt, her arms full of diamonds and possibilities.

CHAPTER TWENTY-TWO

Elua knows what passed between the two of them, but Melisande's villa was over an hour's ride from the City center, and Phèdre spent the first half of it gazing silently out the unshuttered window of the carriage door. As usual, I kept my own mouth closed. There were a great many thoughts running through my mind, most involving the ramifications for my own situation.

I had been assigned to guard two Servants of Naamah in debt-bondage to Anafiel Delaunay. One had earned his freedom and left Naamah's service before I even arrived; now Phèdre.

Did she *want* her freedom?

What would she do with it?

If she chose to leave Delaunay's household, she would be free to dismiss my services on her behalf. If he offered her the choice to stay and she took it, I suppose as master of the household decisions regarding the safety of the household remained his purview, and it would be up to Delaunay to determine if my service would continue.

Did *I* want that?

I was ill suited to this posting. And yet when I thought about leaving it, somewhat inside me balked. I had a purse filled with what felt like at least a minor lord's ransom in gold, sitting across from a vulnerable young woman clutching a second small fortune's worth of diamond-studded netting. We were in the middle of the countryside in a patron's coach with an unfamiliar driver. It was unlikely that harm would befall us. A lone coachman wouldn't be fool enough to try, and from my understanding no one in their right mind would cross House Shahrizai without very, very good reason. Nonetheless, here I was, all that stood between Phèdre and danger.

"I said it."

The words were spoken in such a low tone, I wasn't sure I'd heard them; but no, Phèdre had torn her gaze from the window to look at me. "You said what?" I asked her.

"My *signale*." There was a degree of wry self-awareness in her voice that I hadn't suspected existed. She must have known that Alcuin had told me what the term meant. "I said it."

I responded without thinking. "So you lost."

She narrowed her eyes. "Why do you put it thus?"

My palms were hot and itchy. I rubbed them on my knees and answered with a question. "Am I wrong?"

Phèdre looked away. "No. Forgive me, I've a good deal on my mind."

I inclined my head in respect. "As you will. But remember that one may lose a battle, yet win a war."

She looked back at me, unreadable. "I'll try."

Clearing my throat, I nodded at the twinkling mass of gauze netting in her lap. "And that's . . ."

A faint flicker of amusement crossed her face. "It was a gown."

My cheeks felt hot. "Ah."

Many conversations took place in hushed tones behind closed doors after we returned from Melisande Shahrizai's villa. To what they pertained, I couldn't say; not me, for a surety. What did pertain to me was that Phèdre and Delaunay came to the mutual decision that after her marque was completed, she would remain in his household.

That meant I might stay, too. My lord Delaunay didn't presume it. He summoned me for a private talk in his library that evening and asked me outright if I would stay with Phèdre as my sole ward.

I bowed politely. "My lord, that decision is not mine to make."

"No, I suppose not," Delaunay said. "You accepted this post, you're oath-sworn, and I'd wager you'd sooner chop off your own hand than break your vows. Is that so?"

I bowed, stiffly. "The choice has not presented itself."

It startled a laugh from him. "Fair enough, messire. Permit me, then, to rephrase my initial question. If the choice were yours to make, would you remain in this post?"

I opened my mouth to reply, then closed it, frowning in thought. Behind his desk, Delaunay watched me shrewdly as I pondered. "What would you have me say, my lord?" I asked him, holding out upturned hands. "I am Cassiel's Servant and I serve at the Prefect's behest. That is all that matters."

It wasn't the answer Delaunay wanted to hear, but it was the truth. He contemplated it, then gave me a brusque nod. "So you'll stay?"

"Yes, my lord." I bowed a third time. "I will stay."

Two days later I found myself regretting that I hadn't taken advantage of the implicit offer. At the least I should have told Delaunay that I would happily consider another posting if a more suitable one were available. It may have been the best for everyone concerned. But no, I stood obdurate in my Cassiline discipline, and now here I was accompanying Phèdre to Night's Doorstep.

She'd determined to accept no assignations until her marque—the actual ink limned onto her body—was officially completed. An appointment with the marquist was scheduled to take place as soon as Delaunay's gem merchant was able to find buyers for the diamonds stripped from the ravaged garment. In the meantime, Phèdre was impatient, restless, and bored. Since she was technically indentured to Delaunay until her marque was finished, she obeyed the letter of the law and acquired his permission to venture out to spend time with her friend Hyacinthe. And since Delaunay was canny enough to know she'd slip out without it, he granted it freely and bade me attend and guard her.

To my pleasant surprise, Phèdre chose to venture into Night's Doorstep on horseback rather than by carriage. I didn't like closed spaces. It was easier to fight in the open, and it felt good to journey through the City free of the confines of a carriage.

Everywhere we went, people hailed Phèdre, recognizing her famed beauty and her infamous *sangoire* cloak; and it was beginning to seem that a genuine old-fashioned Cassiline guard was going to become this year's most sought-after new accessory in certain quarters, a notion I found both offensive and amusing. She rode bare-headed, hood down, eyes sparkling in the cold air. I marveled at how it lifted folks' spirits to see one of the City's most famous courtesans riding down the frost-rimed cobbled streets.

Although our excursion took place in the afternoon, Night's Doorstep was as exuberantly raucous in sunlight as it was at nightfall. Although I had taken Phèdre's friend Hyacinthe for little more than a fraud and a mountebank, he wasn't afraid to turn his hand to hard work. We found him inspecting a battered carriage he had purchased for the livery service he was establishing. When he spotted Phèdre dismounting and handing her reins to one of his crew of young hostlers, he grinned with delight, caught her in his arms, and spun her around. "Phèdre! Did you see it? I bought a nobleman's carriage for a song."

Dismounting, I leaned against the wall. The hostlers gave me a wide berth, but they treated my stalwart horse Aristotle with professional care. I nodded at the carriage Hyacinthe was boasting about. "Then you paid a verse too many, Tsingano. Stripping all that fancy gilt trim won't cover the cost of repairing those wheels."

"Happily, Messire Cassiline, I also know a cartwright who will work for a song," Hyacinthe said mildly, turning back to Phèdre. "Did Delaunay let you out of your cage for the day? Can I buy you a jug?"

She jingled the purse knotted at her belt. "My treat. Come, Joscelin," she added to me. "Cassiel will forgive you for setting foot in an inn if you stick to water."

It was on the tip of my tongue to retort that I'd supped and slept in plenty of inns on my way to the City and that I'd drunk brandy poured by the hand of my own Cassiline mentor himself. Fortunately, I recognized the fact that I'd sound like a pitiable twelve-year-old braggart if I did, so I didn't.

The innkeeper at the Cockerel greeted Phèdre with warmth, and she curtsied prettily and kissed his cheek. He and Hyacinthe clasped arms, slapped backs, and referenced some long-running joke between them before he ushered us to their favorite table in the back of the establishment, sparing an annoyed look for me.

Phèdre and Hyacinthe bent their heads together, murmuring in low tones. Once again, I was forced to try not to eavesdrop, but I gathered that she was telling him that after the Longest Night with Melisande, she had more than enough to make her marque. Given the very large diamond hanging at her throat sending stray scintillations throughout the room, it was likely evident. Despite flashing a gem of such value in a public place, Phèdre had the audacity to ask me to buy a jug of wine for Hyacinthe's crew and deliver it on her behalf, eyes wide and sincere.

I stared at her with incredulity, wondering if she truly thought I was too dense to realize she was trying to get rid of me. "No."

"Please?" A delicate, disingenuous furrow formed between her perfect winged brows. If she were anyone else, I might have poked it. "I'll stay right here, I promise. No one would let harm come to me in the Cockerel and it's naught against your vows, just . . . some things I suspect you'd rather not hear."

Oh, she knew. She was counting on my Cassiline modesty to impel me to make a tactful exit. I folded my arms and glared long enough to make my point before snatching the silver coin she'd laid on the table.

Hyacinthe's crew was a lively bunch ranging from boys of eleven or twelve—First Cohort, I couldn't help but think—to young men around my age. They laughed and jested and toasted to Phèdre's health, and there was nothing untoward in it. "Your lot seems fond of her," I said to Emile, Hyacinthe's second-in-command.

"Oh, aye!" He hoisted his mug. "She's a delight."

That wasn't the word I would have chosen. "How so?"

Emile lowered his mug and looked me up and down. "Well, I wouldn't care to be her personal guard, but I surely wouldn't wear my disapproval on my sleeve. She's beautiful, she's kind, she doesn't put on airs, and my best mate lights up like a candle when he sees her. That's enough for me."

Chastened, I bowed and bade them enjoy the wine.

Upon returning to the Cockerel, I found that Phèdre and Hyacinthe had concluded their conversation and moved on to laughing and teasing and exchanging kisses. I paused and gave them a moment before slapping a few coppers of change on the table, making them jump like unrepentant children caught in a moment of mischief. Name of Elua, Hyacinthe well nigh did light up like a candle; and she did, too.

I wondered what it felt like.

At least the outing passed without incident. I wasn't comfortable in the labyrinthine streets and licentious atmosphere of Night's Doorstep, but I could recognize that they protected their own in this neighborhood; and for whatever reason, they most definitely considered Phèdre one of theirs.

It took a few days for Delaunay to conclude a satisfactory deal with the gem merchant. Although she attempted to contain it, Phèdre's impatience was nigh palpable—and I wasn't so petty that I didn't sympathize with her frustration. I'd considered her a songbird warbling happily in its gilded cage, and her occasional escapes mere acts of childish rebellion. I was only just beginning to realize that her yearning to be free of debt-bondage—to belong to no one but herself—was genuine.

Exactly how that accorded with a desire to be bound in restraints, tormented, and brought to a point of utter submission, I had no idea.

"I told you Phèdre was a paradox," Alcuin said mildly when I broached the topic at the end of an afternoon training session. "Look, I'm finally getting some respectable calluses." He showed me his palms, then regarded them. "Most of my patrons would have hated that."

A worm of discomfort wriggled inside me every time he referenced his service to Naamah. "Only most?"

"Mm-hmm." Alcuin smiled at a memory. "Mierette nó Orchis wouldn't have minded a bit. She's an adept of Orchis House," he added. "A friend bought her a night with me as a natality gift."

"Why was she different?" I asked.

"Well, you know what Orchis House is like . . ." He paused, realizing I didn't. "Their motto is *Joy in Laughter.* In Orchis House, they say Naamah laid with the King of Persis for a lark, and they're dedicated to bringing mirth, merriment, and joy into the world. I was taught to receive pleasure as well as give it, but one night with Mierette nó Orchis taught me to find joy in it."

I ran my thumb over the edge of my left dagger, feeling for invisible nicks. "Do you think Phèdre finds joy in it?"

"Yes." Alcuin's response was immediate and sure. "But it's far too dark and bloody a joy for me to covet."

I couldn't imagine why anyone would.

As soon as Phèdre had the coin in hand, she sent word to the marquist Master Teilhard's atelier, where he promptly cancelled all the following day's appointments that he might complete her marque.

We rode astride that day, too; another cold, sparkling day, vendors on every corner selling chestnuts roasted on their braziers. Having witnessed my discomfort during the completion of Alcuin's marque, Master Teilhard had done me the kindness of hanging velvet drapes in the doorway between the waiting chamber and his artist's studio with all its needles, tappers, and inks. I was grateful to be spared the sight of Phèdre sighing with pleasure as the tapper sounded rhythmically and droplets of blood bloomed on the surface of her flawless skin.

Well, flawless if the marks that Melisande Shahrizai left on her were healed, anyway. I'd only caught a glimpse of that damage.

The whole of the shop was heated for the comfort of its clientele, and it was drowsily warm in the waiting chamber. I could hear Phèdre and Master Teilhard discussing the final details and embellishments of her marque. Reckoning this was going to be a long session, I allowed myself the luxury of sitting and stretching my legs, tracing various Cassiline circles and forms in my memory.

It was an agreeable reverie, broken when the bell that hung from the entrance jangled violently as a man burst through the door.

I met him on my feet, daggers drawn.

Seeing my greys and twin daggers, he stopped in his tracks, panting. "You're the Cassiline, Delaunay's Cassiline . . . Yes, sorry. I have an urgent message, I need to speak to Phèdre nó Delaunay."

"Why?" I asked.

He closed his eyes briefly, struggling to control his breath. "I can't say, not to you. Please. I need to speak to her."

The drapes behind me rustled as Master Teilhard's apprentice came to see what the commotion was. "What passes?"

I jerked my chin at the fellow. "He says he has an urgent message for her ladyship."

"One moment." The apprentice vanished behind the curtain.

The would-be messenger eyed my daggers nervously. He was young, hair in a sailor's queue, clothing plain but of good quality. "You can sheathe those, Cassiline. I'm Admiral Rousse's man and I'm here in good faith."

I said nothing.

The apprentice parted the curtains. "Her ladyship will see you."

I stepped aside to let the fellow pass, then fell in behind him, daggers still drawn. I could see his shoulders were tight with fear. He stumbled across the threshold into the studio, where Phèdre was seated on the marquist's bed, fully dressed save for her cloak, an unexpectedly stern expression on her face.

"Call off your Cassiline hound," the sailor said with a grimace. "I've an urgent message for Lord Delaunay."

I placed myself between them.

"Who are you?" Phèdre asked him. "Who sent you and why are you here?"

"Aelric Leithe of the Mahariel," he said. "Oath-sworn to Royal Admiral Quintilius Rousse. I'm here under the Comte de Brijou's standard. I was meant to deliver a message to both of them, Delaunay and the Comte. It's meant for the Dauphine's ears."

"Why should I believe you?" she inquired.

"Elua's Balls! There's a password, right? Never thought I'd need it." The sailor pressed the heels of his hands to his temples as though to squeeze out the words. "Ah . . . I swear it on the King's signet, his only born."

I glanced over my shoulder at Phèdre.

She nodded slightly, and there was fear dawning behind her eyes. "Very well," she said to the fellow. "So why are you here?"

"I was set to meet with the Comte first, but men were watching the manor," he said. "So I went to your lord Delaunay's and there were men there, too. Watching the townhouse, waiting for a messenger. They shouldn't have been expecting me, someone slipped up somewhere. But I saw you and your Cassiline leave and followed you here."

Time slowed.

My heartbeat thudded in my chest, pulsed in my ears. It felt like I was underwater. Somewhere in the distance, the sailor was delivering Admiral Rousse's message. The syllables stretched out long and slow, getting tangled in the echo of the words he'd spoken earlier; words that were gaining momentum as they ricocheted inside the confines of my skull, sounding a note of imminent danger.

Men were watching the manor.

When the Black Boar rules in Alba, Elder Brother will accede.

. . . *I went to your lord Delaunay's and there were men there, too, watching the townhouse* . . .

Time sped up, converging to a single point. I took a sharp flash of breath as Phèdre gave the messenger a coin. He accepted it with a bow, pressing a fist to his brow, and took to his heels.

Phèdre looked at me, and I forced out the words. "*The house.*"

For the first time, I bolted and left Phèdre on her own; I daresay I was astride and riding hell-for-leather down the street before she managed to scramble into her *sangoire* cloak and out the door of the marquist's. But horses in Siovale are bred more for hardiness than speed, and she caught up to me in the next block. Citizens dove out of the way as we careened recklessly toward the townhouse.

I drew rein and scanned the grounds. There were no signs of would-be attackers, but the vines on the walls were torn loose in places and the entrance gate was ajar. In the courtyard, the stable lad Denys was nowhere to be seen, and there were blood smears on the cobblestone drive.

"No!" The word burst from my lips in a shout. "Ah, Cassiel, *no*!"

Every nerve in my body afire, I dismounted and raced into the townhouse with daggers drawn. Late. I was too late.

Dead.

All dead.

Everyone was dead: Delaunay's men-at-arms, all the household staff, the parlor maids, the cook and apprentices. The housekeeper Yolanthe had been slain, her apron covering her face as though her murderer were ashamed of his deed. There were splashes of blood on the walls, bloody footprints on the Akkadian carpets.

We found Anafiel Delaunay in the library.

I knelt beside him and felt for a pulse, already knowing I'd find none. He'd taken at least a dozen blows, almost any of which might have killed him. He'd fought hard, blood drying on the sword still clutched in his hand; but he was dead. I looked up at Phèdre and shook my head. Her face was ghost-white with shock.

A scrabbling sound came from the far corner of the unlit library, and beneath a pile of overturned furniture and precious books, I saw a swatch of shimmering white hair.

Alcuin.

Dashing toward the sound, I dropped my daggers and began frantically shifting items. Alcuin's dark gaze met mine as I uncovered his face, flooded with pain. He'd been stabbed in the gut and the entire front of his fine white cambric shirt was soaked with blood, spreading even as I gently removed the last volumes. I winced at the sight of it, placing both hands on his belly. I could feel the blood pulsing from his body.

"Water," he whispered. "Please."

Phèdre knelt beside him and took his hand. "Get it," she murmured to me. I hesitated only for an instant. My instincts told me to continue trying to stop the flow of blood; but there was no stanching it, only prolonging Alcuin's suffering.

In the kitchen I found a ewer of fresh well water, and a sponge in the cupboard where bandages, salves, and liniments were kept. Alcuin was still alive, Phèdre holding his hand tenderly, tears running heedless down her cheeks. I dipped the sponge into the ewer and squeezed a trickle into his mouth.

Alcuin swallowed with an effort, his eyes glassy. "Too many . . ."

Keeping my voice calm and steady, I asked a single question. "Who?"

It was a struggle, but his vision sharpened. "D'Angelines," he said to me. "Soldiers. No crest. I killed two."

"You?" Phèdre stroked his hair, dampening it with tears. "Oh, Alcuin!"

"Rousse," he whispered to her. "Get him word."

"Quintilius Rousse?" She glanced at me. "It was his messenger found us.

He said the house was being watched." Alcuin murmured somewhat too low for me to hear, and she nodded. "Yes, there was a password . . . the King's ring, no . . . the King's signet, his only born."

Alcuin hissed out a gasp and I realized, impossibly, that he was trying to laugh as he lay dying. "Not a ring . . . *cygnet*, swan. Courcel. Rolande's daughter." When he coughed, blood came to his lips. "Delaunay is oath-sworn to guard her."

At last, this pattern of espionage was beginning to make sense to me. "Anafiel Delaunay stood as oath-sworn protector of Ysandre de la Courcel."

He nodded faintly, licking his blood-frothed lips. "He swore it for Rolande's sake." I gave him more water, wiped his face with the sponge. "Rousse?"

I didn't understand the question, but Phèdre did. "When the Black Boar rules in Alba, Elder Brother will accede," she whispered, squeezing his hand. "Alcuin, don't go! I *need* you! What are we to do?"

I had known that Delaunay's wards were involved in intrigue; I hadn't known they were neck-deep in the scramble for the throne with the waters closing fast overhead.

"Tell Thelesis." Alcuin's voice was down to a hoarse whisper. "She knows about Alba. Trust Rousse. Trevalion. Not the King, Ganelon's slipping. It's the Dauphine." His fading gaze drifted, searching for someone who wasn't there. "He kept his promise," he murmured to himself, and fell still. I thought he was gone, but he clenched Phèdre's hand hard, once, and called out her name.

And then Alcuin was still forever.

Respectful of Phèdre's grief, I waited as long as I dared, my own eyes stinging with tears I'd no time to shed as a rising drumbeat of urgency beat faster and faster in my chest. "Phèdre." No response. "My lady Phèdre! We have to leave. Now." I might as well have been shouting into a void. "*Phèdre!*"

Nothing.

I pulled her away from Alcuin, lifted her to her feet. Her tear-streaked face was blank and unseeing. When I shook her by the shoulders, she was limp, head lolling like a broken doll. "Elua curse you, Phèdre, listen to me!" Gritting my teeth, I slapped her across the face. Her head rose, gaze clearing slightly. "We have to leave," I repeated. "Do you understand? The men who killed them are professionals. They took their dead with them and left no witness alive. And as soon as they find out that sailor delivered his message to you, they'll be back." I squeezed her shoulders. "We have to get Rousse's message to the Dauphine. Do you understand?"

"Yes!" Phèdre pulled away from me, covering her face with both hands for a moment. "Yes, I understand." She lowered her hands. "Thelesis. If the Dauphine won't receive us, we go to the King's Poet. She's involved in this and she'll have the Dauphine's ear. Thelesis will see me."

"Good." I caught her wrist. "Let's go."

A Cassiline bodyguard may have been gaining cachet in certain circles and Phèdre in her infamous *sangoire* cloak celebrated in the streets of the City, but neither held sway at the upper echelons of the Palace.

Ysandre de la Courcel's guards turned us away.

So did Thelesis de Mornay's household staff, and that Phèdre hadn't anticipated. It seemed the King's Poet was engaged in reading verses to the King himself and not to be disturbed at the task. Phèdre nigh pleaded to be allowed to await Thelesis in her suite, but the doorman was adamant, for it was by the King's own orders.

The door was closed in our faces.

I was out of my depth; I'd no idea who to trust in the City of Elua. For the first time in many years, I began thinking as Joscelin Verreuil of Siovale, son of Lord Millard and Lady Ges, wondering if there were any Siovalese peers whom my father would have trusted wintering in the vicinity. Unfortunately, I could think of none. We relish our cold, snowy winters in the mountains of Siovale.

"Phèdre? What is it?"

I reached for my hilts unthinking at the unmistakable sound of Melisande Shahrizai's voice, but there was sincere concern in it.

Phèdre lifted her head as though tugged by an invisible leash, tears streaking her face. "Delaunay," she whispered. "Alcuin. All of them."

"*What?*"

I would swear in Cassiel's name that Melisande's shock was genuine; she caught her breath in a ragged gasp, the blood draining from her features.

Phèdre nodded, wordless.

Regaining a measure of composure, Melisande glanced at both of us. "You're in search of the King's Guard, then?"

"No—" I began.

"Yes, my lady," Phèdre said over me. "Do you know where they're quartered?"

I hastily shut my mouth, abruptly realizing that although Phèdre appeared to be at Melisande's beck and call, subservient to her every whim, she didn't fully trust her.

"I can do better than that." Melisande turned to an attendant in Shahrizai livery standing behind her. "Summon the Captain of the King's Guard to my quarters; the Captain, not some underling. Tell him it's urgent." He bowed and set out at a trot. Melisande turned back to Phèdre. "Come, let's get you somewhere safe. They'll be here in a moment."

House Shahrizai's quarters at the Palace were expansive and luxurious, that much I remember. The primary suite contained its own dining hall with intricate tapestries hanging on the walls and a long marble-topped table.

Melisande invited us to sit and poured two glasses of cordial from a crystal decanter. "Drink," she said to both of us. "It will do you good."

I had precious little experience with spirits. This was sweet and herbaceous and it burned enough to make me cough upon swallowing, but it warmed me from within. Still, I refused a second glass, asking instead if I might have hot barley tea. The servants in House Shahrizai must have been prepared to meet any need at a moment's notice, for I had my tea, sweetened with a good deal of honey, in less time than it would take to put a kettle on the hob.

Melisande poured a second glass of cordial for Phèdre unasked, her worried gaze searching the latter's. "Do you wish to speak of what happened?"

"No." Cupping her hands around the cordial, Phèdre shivered violently. "My lady, I don't know."

Feeling dizzy from the cordial, I took a deep drink of tea, trying to clear my head and follow Phèdre's lead.

"We were . . . Joscelin and I were at the marquist's shop," she was saying. "Making the final arrangements for my marque. Master Teilhard had made changes to the finial that I needed to approve. It was . . . I don't know, I'm not sure how long we were there."

Something was wrong.

I had that underwater feeling again, only this time I was sinking. Phèdre was withholding the full truth from Melisande Shahrizai and I needed to protect my ward. "Three quarters of an hour." It was hard to concentrate on speaking. "Mayhap a bit longer. When we arrived back at the townhouse . . ." I cleared my throat, sipped my tea. My hand was shaking so hard the cup rattled against the saucer when I set it down. "There were signs of battle all over the house and grounds, and no one left alive."

Those were the last words I spoke.

Sinking, sinking . . . my field of vision diminished to a shrinking circle.

"Oh, Anafiel," Melisande murmured, and there was profound sorrow and regret in her voice.

Thud.

I felt the blow as my face struck the marble table. All dark, my vision had gone dark, I was sinking and the world was fading around me.

Gone.

CHAPTER TWENTY-THREE

I awoke to the sound of someone retching.

My head felt thick and achy and I was queasy, too. Resolutely pushing those feelings aside, I took stock of my situation.

There was prickly straw beneath me, woolen blankets thrown over me, canvas lashed taut some feet above me. Wooden clapboard slats, hoofbeats and a jolting motion—I was in a cart. I dragged myself to a seated position, taking stock. Daggers, vambraces . . . my uncle's sword, the sword I'd pledged to Cassiel, gone.

All gone.

I'd gone from a scene of slaughter straight into a trap, I'd been drugged, abducted, and—

Phèdre.

That's whom I'd heard retching. She was sitting in a corner of the cart, watching me, eyes glimmering with fear in the dim light. She was alive. Unharmed . . . alas, that I doubted. But alive.

"Where . . ." My mouth was dry and my tongue swollen. I forced myself to swallow. "Where are we?"

"I don't know," she whispered.

"Melisande." I remembered; her face was the last thing I'd seen. "Melisande Shahrizai."

Phèdre closed her eyes. "Yes."

I didn't want to ask, but I had to. Whatever Melisande had done to her in their last encounter, Phèdre had given her *signale.* I suspected this time it had been worse. But for as much as I'd striven to avoid political intrigue in my life, I was neck-deep in it now. "Did you give her Rousse's message?" I asked her gently.

"No." She shook her head, wrapping her arms around her knees and shivering uncontrollably. "No. No. No."

Elua have mercy, it was too much to bear. I drew her into clean straw and the warmth of the woolen blankets, enfolding her in them, but the violent shaking continued unabated, her entire body shuddering. I wrapped my arms around her until it abated, then shifted away before the moment became uncomfortable. Her eyes were open and her gaze a bit more alert. "Do you know what's befallen us?"

She shook her head. Melisande's diamond no longer hung from her throat and her *sangoire* cloak was gone, stolen along with my weapons.

"Well, let's see what we might find out." I blew on my hands to warm them, then banged on the clapboard wall. "Heya!" I shouted. "You outside, stop the cart!" Hoofbeats paused and voices muttered. I pounded the boards with the heel of my hand hard enough to make them shudder. "Let us out!"

A resounding blow struck the wall from outside. I snatched my hands back as another blow struck the canvas from above, what felt like a quarterstaff hitting my right shoulder with a heavy thud. I rolled out of the way of a second blow.

"You in the cart, keep it down!" a man's voice said. "Or we'll beat you like badgers in a sack. Understood?"

Crouching low under the canvas, I tried to gauge where he was. "I'm Joscelin Verreuil, oath-sworn Cassiline Brother, son of Lord Chevalier Millard Verreuil, and you're holding me against my will," I called to him. "Do you know that what you're doing is both heresy and a crime punishable by death?"

Another heavy blow struck the canvas near me. "Shut up, Cassiline, or I aim for the girl."

Before I could respond, Phèdre caught my arm. "Don't make it worse," she murmured. "There are at least a dozen trained, armed, and mounted soldiers out there. If you're going to play the hero, let's pick a moment when you're not outnumbered and trapped like a . . . like a badger in a sack."

I frowned. "How do you reckon the odds? Did you see them?"

"Listen." She tipped her head toward one side of the cart. "Saddlehorses; they've a lighter step than the pair drawing the cart. Armor creaking. Four before and four aft, two on either side, and I've heard at least two riding scout. If they're under Melisande's orders, likely they're d'Aiglemort's men."

"D'Aiglemort?" I couldn't follow her thinking. "What's he got to do with this?"

"I don't know." Phèdre huddled deeper into the blankets. "But whatever it is, they're in it together. They brought down House Trevalion, and it was his men who killed Delaunay and Alcuin. Isidore d'Aiglemort's bid for Ysandre's hand failed. One way or another, I think he means to have the throne."

I felt a chill that owed naught to the cold. "And to think I once thought you a simple Servant of Naamah."

"Did you learn so little of what we were about in Delaunay's household?" Her voice was bitter with irony. "Better if I'd stayed in the Night Court and gone to Valerian House to be a whipping-toy. Then Melisande Shahrizai wouldn't have had me to use as a hunting dog to flush out Delaunay's allies."

"Is that what happened?" I asked, then caught myself. "Phèdre, you couldn't have known. And I know you loved him dearly, but Anafiel Delaunay should have known, and he should never have used bond-servants thusly. It's not your fault."

"Blame doesn't matter," she said. "Whether or not the fault is mine, I was the cause. My lord Delaunay is dead, and Alcuin, who never harmed a soul in his life. Everyone, everyone who served in the household. All of them lying there in their own blood. I caused it."

"Phèdre—"

"It's getting darker," she said over my words. "Mayhap they'll make camp come nightfall. We've been going north, I think. It's gotten colder since we left the City."

"As far as Camlach, do you reckon?" It was a grim thought, but there was a measure of hope in it. If these were d'Aiglemort's men, Selwyn de Gaunte gave his life for their liege lord; and insofar as I knew, Selwyn's brother was still a member of d'Aiglemort's elite personal cadre. Mayhap these men would listen to me.

Or mayhap not, so I said nothing for now.

"It may be," Phèdre said. "But they ordered us to be silent, not still. That means they fear detection. They'll be wary until they've left L'Agnace and crossed the border into Camlach."

I wouldn't have followed the signs to that conclusion, because I wouldn't have recognized them in the first place. "Delaunay taught you well."

"Not well enough." Phèdre was too tired to sound bitter. Her eyelids drifted slowly closed, her breathing lengthening. From time to time, she shivered in her sleep, and it wasn't from the cold.

I let her be.

Wherever we were and wherever we were bound, my duty was to protect her at all costs. My patron Anafiel Delaunay, slain. My friend Alcuin. The entire household, slain. The temple I'd built for myself as Cassiel's Servant was crumbling all around me, and Phèdre nó Delaunay was the last pillar standing.

Even disheveled, with shadows under her eyes, straw in her hair, and the faint smell of bile lingering beneath the canvas, she was impossibly beautiful. Blessed Elua knows what Melisande had done to her; I'd caught that glimpse of the marks left on her after the Longest Night. Melisande Shahrizai liked to play with knives.

But this time Phèdre didn't give her *signale.*

It would be a piece of irony if she was right and Isidore d'Aiglemort—the liege lord Selwyn died to protect—was plotting to gain the throne by any means. Or mayhap it wasn't; mayhap Selwyn would have approved and reckoned the sacrifice worthwhile if it put the throne in Camaeline hands.

I would never know for sure; I did know there was a painful irony in his description of Melisande Shahrizai. I'd more or less disregarded it, having no interest in delving deeper into Selwyn's political speculations. Now I remembered his words.

Anyway, I doubt she's a serious player in the game. After all, she's just a woman.

Just a woman.

There are disadvantages to being raised among boys and men whose worth is measured by their fighting skills. We're not taught to recognize different kinds of strength nor that the deadliest weapons are not necessarily made of steel.

The jolting of the cart was rhythmic. There was nothing I could do at the moment save rest and regain my strength so that I might take advantage of the first opportunity to escape or seek rescue.

So I slept fitfully, my dreams streaked with blood, until the cart lurched to a halt. Opening my eyes, I saw only darkness. I crouched in readiness as the rear gate was unlatched and lowered.

Torchlight blinded me. "Come out," a man's voice said. "You first, girl. Come out slowly."

Awake, Phèdre gave me an inquiring glance; I responded with a faint nod. Keeping a blanket wrapped around her, she scooted forward to exit the cart. Shading my eyes, I sought to peer past the flames. There were indeed at least a dozen men there, and although they wore no House insignias, they had the demeanor and bearing of professional soldiers.

"All right, Cassiline," the voice said. "Nice and easy."

I obeyed, keeping my empty hands in sight. There were half a dozen men arrayed before me, swords drawn. Still blinking in the sudden glare of torchlight, I looked for Phèdre and spotted her by a campfire, drinking from a waterskin. Our captors were handling her none too gently, but to my relief, at the moment they seemed intent on the job, not violence.

"Come on, Cassiline." The man I took to be the leader of our captors poked me from behind with the point of his sword. I clenched my empty hands, palms itching for the feel of a hilt. "Here, give him a drink," he called, and one of the others tossed him the waterskin.

It smelled of water, leather, and faintly of sweat. If Phèdre gauged it safe to drink, I reckoned I'd sooner trust her than perish from thirst. I drank, then lowered the waterskin and looked the leader in the eye, keeping my tone calm and even. "In the name of the Prefect of the Cassiline Brotherhood, I demand to know who you are and why you've done this to us."

The soldiers arrayed before me laughed.

"In the name of the Prefect of the Cassiline Brotherhood," their leader echoed me in a mincing tone, then punched me hard in the head with one gauntleted fist. Even though I'd seen it coming, it made me stagger. "Inside the borders of Camlach, the only order we obey is the order of steel."

Fury rose in me like a tide. "Then give me mine and try its mettle!"

His men banged their swords and yelled encouragement; unfortunately, he wasn't careless enough to be goaded into taking unnecessary risks. "I'd like to, boy," he said to me with genuine regret. "You're angry enough to go for my head and that would be an entertaining challenge, but my orders are to keep you alive." He jerked his chin at Phèdre. "You need to use the latrine, girl? My man Vincente here will escort you."

Phèdre closed her eyes briefly with a look of utter humiliation.

"Please don't," I murmured to the leader. "She's lost everything; please leave her this shred of dignity."

"Sorry, no." He shook his head, then rolled his eyes and beckoned his man Vincente over. "Be a gentleman and turn your back on the lady while she's pissing."

I took covert stock of our situation while she concluded her bodily necessities. Clearly, we'd crossed the border into Camlach. The turf was frozen hard underfoot and our torches and campfire were lonely lights under the night sky. So it seemed we were in the wilderness, not far past the border, no idea where we were bound or why. If I were to find a way out of this, it had best be sooner rather than later. The further we ventured into Camlach, the deeper we went into what I could only consider enemy territory.

Six men escorted me to the latrine, keeping a wary distance from me, weapons drawn. Although my bladder was nigh bursting, I addressed them in a low tone. "Listen, I don't know what all this is about, but I know you're the Duc d'Aiglemort's men. Selwyn de Gaunte was my friend, his brother Telys can vouch for me."

They exchanged glances. "Selwyn de Gaunte was man enough to leave your precious Brotherhood to fight for his liege lord," one said. "While you stayed to waste all that training serving as bodyguard to a pampered plaything."

Yesterday, I might have acknowledged a small measure of truth in his words; today, nothing could be farther from it. "And yet here I am. If the Duc wishes to see us, we would be honored to accept an invitation."

"It's no business of yours what the Duc wants, Cassiline." He pointed at me. "Your only concern is your ward. If you want to keep her safe, shut up and do as you're told."

I inclined my head, my blood running cold.

Back at the campfire, we were given bowls of what tasted like small game meat stewed with tubers. I ate slowly, sitting shoulder to shoulder beside Phèdre and taking stock of the situation. A total of fifteen men, all fully armed save the cart driver. Their mounts were haltered and tethered, cropping at the frosty grass. There was no avenue to escape; but we were headed farther away from any hope of assistance or safety.

When you can do nothing else, sow chaos.

It was Master Jacobe who said those words, probably Selwyn's favorite piece of counsel throughout the whole of our training. I thought of them now as the leader approached with a silver flask that was most surely not a waterskin.

"You're to drink some," he said to me.

I looked mildly at him and said, "No."

It wasn't the answer the leader expected. He paused in perplexity, unsure he'd heard aright, and I launched myself to deliver a hard chop to his throat. He staggered and dropped the flask, struggling to draw breath.

A sword; all I needed was a sword. I spun, ducked, and dove, avoiding their blades, landing blows where I could. Targeting the slowest of the guards, I managed a sweeping leg strike against the back of his knees that sent him lurching forward, his sword falling from his hand. It clattered to the frozen ground, almost within reach—

"'Ware your swords, you idiots!" The leader had regained his breath. Now he roared into the fray, kicking away the loose sword. "Don't let him get armed!" His men regrouped to surround me, the one who'd dropped his blade abashedly retrieving it, grimacing and favoring one leg.

I'd hurt a few of them rather badly, and I could see the rank hatred in their eyes. So much for chaos.

The leader nodded at his men.

They pressed closer, swords keeping me at bay. Someone struck me from behind with a pommel atop my head, driving me to my knees. My skull was splitting with pain, my eyes watering. I could barely make out the figure cursing and drawing his sword back to run me through for the misery I'd caused him.

Through my hazy vision, I realized he was fully intent on killing me and no one was stopping him. I struggled to get my feet under me, but to my shame and rising terror, my body wouldn't obey me.

"*Stop!*"

The word rang out in a fierce clarion call, battering my ears like wings. Our captors gawped and I squinted in an effort to confirm that the sound had in fact come from Phèdre nó Delaunay.

Limned by firelight, she fixed the leader with an implacable look of determination. "If this man dies, you'll be accountable to Melisande Shahrizai. Sooner or later, one way or another. Do you want to take that chance?"

He hesitated, then bade the man to stand down and called for the flask. "Hold him." Two of his men wrenched my arms behind me. Another dragged my aching head backward and pinched my nostrils shut. I tried not to give them the satisfaction of struggling, but it was hard when I choked on the fiery liquid. I tried not to give them the satisfaction of seeing my despair. I failed at that, too.

The world went sideways and my face struck the frozen ground. "Tie his arms behind him," said a voice that was already fading, fading into a murky darkness pierced with shards of pain. "He'll be less trouble that way."

And then there was only the pain-shattered dark.

CHAPTER TWENTY-FOUR

How many days were we confined in that cart, drugged into compliance? Given the distance we traversed, it was quite some days; mayhap weeks.

If there were any small mercy on that journey, d'Aiglemort's men made no further overt threats of harm. So long as Phèdre and I remained obedient or unconscious, they were happy to treat us as unwelcome cargo they were eager to dispose of.

In the early days, I was incapacitated by the blow to the head. I suspect there was bleeding under my skull, for during those brief moments when I wasn't immersed in a drug-induced sleep, firelight dazzled my eyes and made my head swim. I was a miserable excuse of a human, let alone a Cassiline Brother. I did my best to care for Phèdre during those occasional interviews of lucidity, although I daresay she took better care of me.

It was utterly humiliating.

It wasn't false modesty on my part. People reckon us prudish for our beliefs and our chastity, but those are as much a part of our armor as our blades and vambraces. Growing up in the Prefectory, we were well versed in the ways in which the human body is vulnerable. No one completed their training without sustaining a myriad of cuts, bruises, and scrapes, and at least one broken bone.

This was different. It was my ward tending to me, tucking blankets around me while I slept in our straw nest, my ward who held the waterskin for me when I was too weak to lift my head.

My ward, whom I had failed.

Not only that, I owed her my life. I had thought myself the last thing standing between Phèdre nó Delaunay and grave danger. As it transpired, Phèdre was the last thing standing between me and death. I was grateful for it, truly; I was grateful for her courage, and I was grateful to be granted a chance to redeem myself. But I couldn't imagine anything more humiliating for a Cassiline.

In that, I was very, very wrong.

After an endless stretch of darkness streaked with flames, steel, and strange faces, there came a day when a measure of clarity returned to my wits. That night, d'Aiglemort's men didn't dose us with the dreaded flask. Phèdre and I stared at each other in silent surmise. After they chivvied us into the wagon and locked the rear gate, we speculated in whispers until our captors beat the canvas above us.

By the following day, I was alert enough to perceive that based on the angle of the wagon, the jolts and bumps, the pauses accompanied by grunts and curses, and the sound of boulders shifting, we were descending in mountainous terrain.

And then we stopped.

Based on the light penetrating worn or ill-tied spots on the canvas, it was only midday. As far as I could recall in my blurred patches of memory, our captors had never made camp in broad daylight before.

The rear gate of the wagon crashed open onto the unmistakable glare of sunlight on snow beneath open skies. "Out with you!"

Glancing at Phèdre, I touched my chest and pointed to the rear of the wagon; she nodded in agreement. Shielding my eyes against the blinding whiteness, I exited carefully, wobbling and unsteady. My arms were numb, wrists still lashed together behind my back, and my legs felt like they belonged to someone else. We were on a snowy plain, a mountain range behind us. Phèdre stumbled out of the wagon, and I moved instinctively to place myself between her and d'Aiglemort's men before realizing there were an additional eight men I'd never seen.

They were heavily muscled, fully armed, fur-clad warriors atop shaggy mountain-bred horses. One man with yellow-blond hair, luxuriant mustaches, and a bronze circlet around his brow tossed a greasy leather sack bulging with coins to the leader of d'Aiglemort's men, saying somewhat in a guttural tongue.

Skaldi. Elua have mercy, we had crossed the snow-filled passes of the Camaeline Mountains. They were *Skaldi*.

It made no sense. Our lead captor laughed and called for one of his men to fetch our things. "I think it's safe to untie the Cassiline," he added wryly, and I felt someone cut loose the leather thong that bound my wrists.

Blood returned to my hands in a painful rush. I squeezed them rhythmically, willing function to return. His man returned with a bundle from which the hilt of my sword protruded, tossing it on the ground. The two leaders exchanged a few more words in that guttural tongue, and then d'Aiglemort's men turned and departed, the empty cart clattering behind them.

Beside me, Phèdre looked incongruous, shivering in filthy finery, unkempt hair strewn with straw. Her face was stark white with shock.

"What is it?" I asked in bewilderment. "Have you any idea what just happened?"

"Yes." She turned her face to mine, dark eyes stretched wide with terror and disbelief. "They've just sold us to the Skaldi."

I moved like lightning—or at least I tried to, but my legs wouldn't work properly and my feet slid in the snow as I strained to reach the pack. The Skaldi shouted and cheered, thinking it great sport. One spurred his mount to intercept me, forcing me to dodge; as I did, another thundered past with a short spear, plucking the pack up with the tip. I veered in his direction, hoping to yank him from the saddle, but with a grin, he flicked his spear and tossed the pack to another Skaldi. I spun around, floundering in the snow, already tiring, already knowing I'd lost, poked by blades from every side, unable to stop trying, while the Skaldi leader watched with amusement, white teeth smiling broadly beneath his flowing yellow mustaches, and I didn't know if they'd kill me the moment I stopped trying, so I kept trying and trying . . .

Phèdre called out with desperate insistence—only this time the words she spoke were foreign.

Skaldic.

Phèdre nó Delaunay spoke fluent Skaldic. The Skaldi leader raised his brows and gestured for his men to stand down before replying in the same tongue. I stood gaping and dumbstruck as he rode over and spoke to Phèdre, laughing heartily at her response. She knelt in the snow, and he called one of his men over with a heavy wolfskin garment. She wrapped it around her and pinned it with stiff fingers. He spoke to her again, extending one arm, and hauled her into the saddle behind him.

The Skaldi leader wheeled his mount, bringing it nearer to me. I could see the leather-wrapped hilt of his sword, no more than three steps and a quick lunge away, but his men were keeping a close eye on me, waiting for my attempt. They weren't watching Phèdre, though, and the Skaldi's hilt was inches from her grasp.

Phèdre read my expression. "Joscelin, don't," she said in a low tone. "They paid too much to kill us out of hand. Skaldi value their slaves."

"No." I clenched my teeth to keep them from chattering. "I failed you with Melisande Shahrizai and I failed you with d'Aiglemort's men, but I swear, Phèdre, I won't fail you here! Don't ask me to betray my oath." I lowered my voice, too. "The Skaldi's sword is in your reach. Get it to me, and I swear I'll get us out of here."

She gazed at me over the Skaldi's shoulder. "I've lived in servitude all my life. I'm not willing to die for your oath." She spoke to the Skaldi leader in his own tongue. He gave a good-natured shrug and shouted to his men.

They closed in on me.

I do not remember that fight. I shouldn't have fought—I could barely stand. I should have heeded my ward and stood down.

I didn't.

A red haze of fury clouded my vision. I remember launching into motion, pivoting and spinning, sheer momentum keeping me on my feet. I don't remember getting my numb, clumsy hands on a short spear, but Phèdre told me later that I kept the Skaldi at bay for quite a while before several brought me down from behind. All I remember is coming to my senses facedown in the snow with someone's knee in my back, my body aching with so many bone-deep bruises I wasn't sure where I hurt most.

Skaldic words were exchanged. They yanked me to my feet and tied my hands together, this time in the front, and affixed a long line to a cantle strap on one of their mounts. Phèdre was expressionless; Phèdre, wrapped in furs, clinging to the barbarian in the saddle before her.

Phèdre, who spoke fluent Skaldic.

The Skaldi leader gave a command and our party set out. I floundered in their wake, doing my best to keep up. My grey woolens were stiff with ice, the leather soles of my boots frozen and slippery. My breath came in ragged gasps, the cold searing my throat and lungs, and my heart was pounding as though to burst from my chest.

The Cassiline Brotherhood trains cadets to build stamina and endurance. When all else fails—strength, speed, skill, strategy—sheer endurance remains.

I concentrated on staying alive. The Skaldi raider towing me behind him didn't pause when I fell; more than once, he veered off the return path with a gleeful whoop, the others roaring with laughter as I was dragged face-first through deep snow, trying desperately to get my feet underneath me.

Once or twice, Phèdre glanced back at me.

My ward, the last standing pillar of my temple. I'd spent my entire life training for this moment; to uphold Cassiel's honor, to maintain the light between the worlds, to represent the gate from Terre d'Ange-that-Lies-Beyond to Heaven that was the true home from whence all of Elua's Companions came.

I should have saved my ward or died trying. I'd done neither; not only that, I owed her my own life twice over. And then she'd opened her mouth and spoken in Skaldic like it was her native tongue, which couldn't be true. She'd been a child, a young one, when her parents sold her to Cereus House, or at least so Alcuin had told me.

Why, then?

There was no good reason for a courtesan in the City of Elua to speak Skaldic, only dangerous ones. And the galling thing was that no matter what the truth, I was *still* Phèdre nó Delaunay's oath-sworn protector. Like Blessed Elua, Cassiel cared nothing for lands and thrones. Even if Phèdre were a traitor to the Crown, she remained my ward. My duty was clear—nigh impossible, but clear. If I could manage to stay alive long enough, there might come a chance to free her; to get her away safely.

Too bad I loathed her at the moment.

Leagues and hours passed; mercifully, the Skaldi were wary of the pitfalls of riding over icy terrain, and I was able to keep pace at a dull plod during that final stretch, my feet like lead blocks at the bottom of my legs.

Dusk was falling when I caught my first glimpse of the lights of the steading, as the Skaldi call their small tribal villages, across the snow. The mere thought of the golden warmth of firelight nigh made me weep with gratitude. The leader began singing in a loud, rousing voice, his men banging weapons on buckle shields.

The grounds of the steading were well trodden and packed firm. We passed cozy cottages, crofts, and stables on the way to the great hall that dominated the center of the steading, light and laughter spilling from it. When our captors drew rein and dismounted before the main entrance and the thick-hewn wooden doors were flung wide in welcome, I fell to my knees in pure exhaustion, my head hanging low. My hair had come loose to hang in rime-hard daggers and my fingers were a greyish blue, cut and scraped knuckles dark with frozen blood.

Black red, *sangoire.*

"Joscelin?" Phèdre's hands cupped my face gently. Her hands felt warm against my icy skin. She looked concerned. Not for herself; me. Phèdre in a barbarian's fur cloak, Phèdre with her fluent Skaldic.

Betrayed or betrayer?

I would die to save her.

I hated her.

Pulling away, I spat at her.

Before she had a chance to react, the Skaldi leader reached for her, tucking her under one arm and spinning her away from me with casual possessiveness. He called out to a handful of young warriors who hadn't accompanied the expedition. They descended upon me with rowdy good cheer and yanked me upright, dragging me away from the hall. I resisted and I sought to reason with them, in both attempts to no avail. I didn't speak their tongue. I was frozen to the bone, battered, and exhausted, with no more fight in me than a day-old kitten. They hauled me around the corner to a wooden pen against the southeast wall. Eyes reflected the torchlight; a great many eyes. The Skaldi heaved me inside. Furry shapes slid past me in the flame-streaked darkness.

Dogs.

I was in a dog kennel, my chin planted on frozen mire and dog piss. One of the Skaldi cursed at the dogs, beating them back with a stick, while others held me pinned, jerked my head back, and clamped a steel manacle around my throat, chaining it to a stake. Laughing, they departed, taking the torchlight and leaving me in the company of a pack of hunting dogs.

The dogs continued to circle, none of them tethered. At Verreuil our hounds would be clamoring and belling at having a stranger thrown into their midst, but this breed was eerily quiet. If there was going to be a confrontation, it would happen now. Letting my eyes adjust to the faint moonlight, I moved slowly to a sitting position, wrapping the chain's slack around my wrists.

The dogs weren't as tall as our long-legged Siovalese hounds, but they had powerful forward-leaning shoulders and jaws that looked capable of taking down a deer. One sniffed at me, wrinkled its jaw, and growled low in its throat. I hummed tunelessly for a while, then extended the backs of my bound hands. It sniffed me again, lost interest, and trotted away, curling up in a pile of straw with nose on tail.

I'd passed one test. The dogs were content to ignore me so long as I remained still. I took stock of the situation as best I could by moonlight.

No food scraps, but there was a wooden tub that I reckoned held water if it wasn't solid ice. Moving carefully and staying low, I made my way to the tub. The water held a sheet of ice I gauged to be a couple of inches thick atop it. I'd have cracked it in a trice if I'd had my weapons—even one good blow from a gauntleted fist would have made quick work of it.

But I was unarmed, exhausted, and aching in every part; I lacked even the strength to saw through the leather thongs still tying my wrists together. Looking around, I spotted the well-gnawed remnants of what looked like a deer's legbone. Once I'd retrieved it, a few dogs crowded around in curiosity. Placing the legbone across my lap, I sat cross-legged and hummed without purpose.

Finding neither threat nor reward, at length they wandered away. I hoisted the legbone in my bound hands and brought it crashing down, cracking the surface of the ice. The dogs weren't overly concerned. Amongst the Skaldi, likely they were accustomed to humans making loud sounds. The water was black and so cold it would have stung my cupped hands if they weren't utterly numb. I drank as fast as I dared, feeling it blossom in my belly like an icy flower. Several curious dogs circled back to investigate, either drinking or wandering away.

Now that death by thirst wasn't an imminent threat, there was a strong possibility that I'd die of exposure. There was a lean-to along one wall, near enough that my chain would reach if I dared. It was a low shanty; no side walls, but a slanted roof to keep out the elements, and thick piles of straw along the rear wall. I crawled across the frozen ground, awkward with my bound hands, clutching the legbone and trying to avoid frost-rimed piles of dog feces. I got as far as the threshold before collapsing.

If I could reach the straw . . .

If I could only reach the straw . . .

A blunt snout poked me in the pit of my left arm. I opened my bleary eyes with an effort. A Skaldic hound stared back at me. Its coat in the dim light appeared silvery grey. It had pricked ears and worried human-looking furrows on its brow. "Hey, there," I whispered. Oddly, I was beginning to feel warmer and relaxed, almost as though I were back in my childhood home, snuggled under fleecy sheepskin.

A voice in the back of my thoughts screamed at me that meant I was dying.

But it felt so good and I'd fought so long and so hard; even if I'd failed, I deserved this moment of warmth, of peace, just one moment to close my eyes and rest . . .

Another poke from a dog's snout, this time harder. I forced my eyelids open to meet its intent gaze. It stared at me for a long moment before trotting away and curling up in the straw at the back of the lean-to.

I dragged myself, my chains, and the splintered legbone to the straw, falling on my face. Turning my cheek, I simply lay there and breathed until I could summon the strength to burrow deeper into the straw. The dog that had poked me rose and stretched with a luxuriant yawn, then moved to lie curled with its back against me. Two more came over with casual indifference, lying pressed close. Warmth, real warmth, emanated from their furry bodies. I knew because it *hurt*. It must have taken at least half an hour for my body to begin thawing. I had gone beyond shaking; now, I shuddered violently. My extremities were the worst, hands and feet burning in agony as the blood returned. It is no exaggeration to say that those dogs saved my life. Had they not treated me like an injured pup, I would have perished in the small hours of the deep Skaldic winter night.

Bit by bit, my shuddering diminished to an occasional tremble. Brought as low as I thought possible, I slept at last.

CHAPTER TWENTY-FIVE

Come morning, I was still alive.

At first, upon waking in the dog pen, I wasn't sure. The past days—weeks?—felt like a fever dream. Everything came in flashes; Delaunay slain, his household slaughtered, Alcuin dying, a swatch of moonlight hair and blood spreading on white cambric.

So much blood.

Torch-streaked darkness, the glint of a metal flask; cart beneath, canvas above, jolting through a nightmare. The blinding-white glare of sunlight on the Skaldic snow. Fighting and losing, fighting and losing, running, running, running, desperately trying to keep my feet under me . . .

And Phèdre nó Delaunay's voice ringing out in clear, fluent Skaldic.

The sun creeping toward the eastern horizon cast a pale orange hue over the kennel. There wasn't much more to it—packed snow with frozen patches of yellow urine, piles of feces, fence, lean-to, straw, and dogs. By daylight, the dogs' coats ranged from white and gray to tan and charcoal. The one who had nudged me out of dying had charcoal-colored ears and mask-like markings on her face. None of them were inclined to move yet this morning. Likely at some point they'd be given table scraps from last night's feast, and I had to be ready when that moment came. The pack may have been amenable to a strange human sleeping alongside them, but fighting for food scraps was a different matter.

I took stock.

My hands were the worst of it, blistered and red from the cold, itching and hurting at the same time. All of the knuckles of both hands were bruised and bloody, the heels of my palms scraped sore. The leather thong tying my wrists together was cutting into my chafed, swollen flesh.

Hands first, then. I examined the chain attached to the manacle around my throat until I found a link with a rough joining. Bracing the chain with my feet, I pulled it taut and sawed the thong back and forth across it while the dogs looked on with mild indifference. It took a long time, but the thong parted just minutes before a kitchen boy rounded the corner lugging a bucket of scraps, sending the placid dogs into a frenzy. Crouched in the shadow of the lean-to and watching the dogs snarl and snap over greasy bones, raw offal, and the butt-ends of trenchers, I weighed the merits of entering the fray against the yawning ache of hunger in the pit of my belly. The kitchen boy glanced at me, then away. Reaching into the bucket, he came up with a gravy-soaked chunk of bread and tossed it in my direction.

I caught it clumsily with my damaged hands and scuttled into the shelter of the lean-to to examine my prize. The bread was dense and dark, smelling of rye. It had held roasted meat, gravy, and fat drippings.

It was the most glorious thing I'd ever seen.

My canine protector sidled up to remind me that I owed her, and I dared feed her a bit of bread on the flat of my hand. After she accepted her tribute, she trotted away and I fell upon the bread.

The crust was hard, but the interior was spongy and soaked with meat juices and rendered fat. I inhaled deeply, reveling in the aroma. My mouth was parched all over again and I longed to quench my thirst at the water tub, where the kitchen boy was reaching through the crude wooden fence to break the ice with a hatchet—but no, too many dogs were eyeing me with unhealthy interest. The only safe place to store food was in my belly, so I gobbled it as quickly as possible, pausing after every bite in order to generate enough saliva to swallow.

Once I was done, I drank long draughts at the water tub, then returned to the straw to sleep and heal.

During the following days in the kennel, I was at least half-mad. I was frozen and furious, ravaged by hunger and deprivation, captive in a foreign land where I couldn't speak the tongue or make myself understood. I had been forcibly separated from my ward, who appeared to be in league with the Skaldi.

If she *was*, I might as well perform the *terminus* and kill both of us.

If she *wasn't* . . . Elua have mercy on us.

From time to time, Skaldi warriors—thanes, I later learned they were called—would stop by the dog pen to taunt me and poke at me with long spears. I would endure it until somewhat inside of me snapped, loosing my rage, and I would fight back in vain, lunging and spinning on unsteady legs, grabbing at their weapons until they laughed so uproariously that humiliation brought me back to myself.

On the third or fourth day, escorted by a pair of solicitous thanes, Phèdre came to see me.

She looked . . . fine.

Her filthy gown had been exchanged for a clean and well-tended dress of rough-spun wool, her hair was combed and braided, and she had a healthy glow suggesting she'd been basking in the heat of the great hall, warming the Skaldi leader's bed, and eating and drinking her fill while I fought for scraps in the dog pen. The injustice of it was beyond bearing. A red haze of rage filled me. I scrabbled in the snow with my bare hands as one of the thanes unlatched the gate. "Joscelin." She stooped to meet me where I crouched in my chains, murmuring in D'Angeline. "I need to talk to you."

I responded by hurling a fetid handful of snow at her. "Traitor! Treacherous daughter of a whore! Leave me alone!"

Phèdre dodged the worst of it, wiping her face. "Listen to me, Cassiline. Do you want to know the face of treachery? Isidore d'Aiglemort is paying the Skaldi to raid Camaeline villages. How's that for treachery?"

The words penetrated my haze and I paused in the process of digging up another handful of snow. "Why would he do that?"

"I don't know," she said. "But it's allowed the Allies of Camlach to rally around his flag and build up his own armies."

A shiver that owed nothing to the frigid air trickled down my spine, rational thought penetrating my awareness as I began to realize the implication of what she was telling me. "You really think d'Aiglemort means to overthrow the Crown?"

"Yes." Reaching out, Phèdre took my cold, cracked hands in hers. At close range I could see she was far from fine. There were haunted circles beneath her eyes and urgency in her gaze. "Joscelin, I can't make it through these lands. You can. Gunter has set no guard on me, no chain. I can steal out of the great hall tonight, I can free you, find you a weapon, clothing, a tinderbox." She squeezed my hands. "You have a chance to reach the City, to deliver Admiral Rousse's message to the King's Poet and let them know what d'Aiglemort is doing."

I stared blankly at her. "What about you?"

"It doesn't matter!" she said grimly. "Gunter means to bring me to the Allthing and give me to Waldemar Selig. I'll learn what I can and do what I may. But *you* have a chance to escape!"

I felt sick. Gunter must be the leader's name, I'd heard the thanes speak it. And I'd heard the name Waldemar Selig, too. Waldemar the Blessed, the Skaldic warlord who sought to unite the tribes. Selig must be Gunter's liege lord. Was Duc Isidore d'Aiglemort truly paying them to raid D'Angeline villages over the mountainous border? If it were true, it was a horrifying notion.

If it were true, Phèdre nó Delaunay was no traitor.

If it were true, Phèdre had been betrayed as profoundly and deeply as I had. I may be suffering greater physical deprivation, but she'd been forced into sexual servitude to a Skaldi clan lord. I had no illusions on that score, and there was a part of me that would almost rather know Phèdre was a traitor than confront the violation she was forced to endure. I had crossed water, fire, and steel to become a Cassiline Brother. She was my ward. This was the purpose for which I'd trained my entire life.

I couldn't leave her.

There was a clarion ringing in my ears, a brightness bursting inside my skull. "No." I shook my head. "Phèdre . . . if you're no traitor, I can't leave you. My oath is to Cassiel, not the Crown."

"Cassiel bade you protect the Crown!" she hissed, lowering her tone when the thanes glanced over. "Joscelin, if you would serve me, do this thing. Please!"

"You don't know." I pressed the heels of my hands to my eyes, hearing the despair in my voice. "You don't understand, Phèdre. It has naught to do with crowns and thrones. Cassiel betrayed God because God himself forgot the duty of love and abandoned Elua ben Yeshua to the whims of fate. To damnation and beyond, Cassiel is the Perfect Companion, and if you're true, Phèdre, I can't abandon you. I *can't*."

"Joscelin." She tugged my hands down gently, her gaze intent. "Joscelin, I am begging you with all that's in me to do this. Can you not obey?"

Feeling miserable, I shook my head again. "Do you know what we in Cassiel's service call Elua and his Companions? The Misguided. Ask me anything but this. Cassiel cared naught for lands and kings. I can't abandon you."

In the pause that followed, I avoided meeting her gaze. Phèdre didn't understand the purpose and sanctity of my vows any more than I did hers; but in the end, we had nothing here except each other.

"All right." There was a sharp edge to her voice. "Then if you would serve as my Companion, do so. You merit naught chained in the kennel like a dog."

That brought my head up sharply and I glared at her. Crouching in a dog pen strewn with frozen waste, wearing a wolfskin cloak like it was ermine and snowflakes glistening in her hair like diamonds, she might have been a woodland princess in a Skaldic fairy tale. "How may I serve, my lady Phèdre, O slave of the Skaldi?"

Ignoring my tone, she continued. "First, you will learn to be a good slave. Make yourself useful. Cut wood, haul water, whatever is needful. Gunter has half a mind to kill you as a waste of food. Second, you will learn to speak Skaldic." She held up a hand to forestall any protest. "If you would be my Companion, serve your new lord, win his trust, and make yourself a gift worthy of a prince. Because if you don't, Gunter will give me to Waldemar Selig anyway and kill you for sport."

I bowed my head. "I understand."

"Do you?" Phèdre asked fiercely. "Joscelin, I swear to you, if you do this for me and live, I will make my escape with you. I'll cross the snows on foot if we must, I'll do whatever you say. But now we have to stay alive. Will you obey?"

Closing my eyes behind the knotted, frozen daggers of my hair, I nodded. "Yes."

"Good." She spoke to the thanes in Skaldic—it was still unnerving hearing those guttural words emerge from her lips—then to me in our shared native tongue upon their reply. "You'll need to prove yourself, but they're allowing you a chance, so listen well. The word for 'I' is 'Ek' . . ."

Thus began the first of many lessons.

I was descended from the divine scholar Shemhazai himself and I grasped the rudiments of the language fairly quickly during the following days. I couldn't hold a conversation, but I could manage a few simple phrases. The thanes who attended Phèdre seemed fond of her, but it was clear they answered to Gunter. In snippets of conversation, she laid out our situation in as much detail as she'd gleaned. Our captors were members of the Marsi tribe, and would be travelling to a pan-tribal meeting called the Allthing, where Waldemar Selig planned to unite the tribes of Skaldia under his own banner. We were the gifts Gunter meant to present Waldemar Selig in a bid for favor—a highly trained D'Angeline warrior-priest and one of the most famous courtesans in the City of Elua.

I couldn't fathom the notion that the Skaldi thought it reasonable that I would turn traitor to my nation to fight beside them. In time, I learned that it wasn't uncommon in their culture for captured warriors from one tribe to be adopted upon giving an oath of fealty to their new chieftain. Right now, Phèdre warned me at our second lesson, the Skaldi still weren't convinced I was worth the time and effort.

It shocked me to catch a glimpse of myself through their eyes—a furious, snarling feral creature stripped of all dignity, devoid of language, clawing at the snow and fighting dogs for scraps. Generations upon generations of Cassiline Brothers, including my own uncle, would have gazed upon me with regret and profound disappointment.

I would do better.

I *had* to do better.

Treating my captors with respect was hard, for they had done nothing to earn it and everything to provoke the worst in me. I spent that afternoon kneeling in contemplation, breathing long and slow. My heartbeat slowed and I found a point of stillness where the cold was held at bay. There, I realized my own pride stood in my way. As cadets, we'd all been quick to boast that we in Cassiel's service would gladly give our lives to protect a ward.

No one had ever warned us it might be harder to live.

But live I did. My chain allowed for limited movement, so I practiced various close-range fighting maneuvers. After Phèdre smuggled out a worn wool jerkin and rags to wrap around my bare hands and my feet in my ice-stiff boots, I felt a little warmer and considerably more human. It surprised me to learn that these gifts were due to the kindness that the women of Gunter's steading had extended to Phèdre. I suspected the occasional generosity of the kitchen lad was due to her, too. Once a pair of housecarls—so they called their domestic servants—even heaved a poorly cured bearskin into the pen. I claimed it even though it stank to the heavens, for it provided a great deal of warmth, but the dogs stole it and began tearing it to shreds. I wanted that godsbedamned rancid bearskin enough to contest for possession and was badly bitten for my trouble. All I could do was watch grudgingly as the dogs chewed it to bits. I'd earned my place among them, and my status wasn't high enough to merit a bearskin.

After that incident, I concentrated harder on interacting with the dogs like a human, not a fellow pack member; holding back scraps and doling them out to reward simple commands like we taught the hounds at Verreuil.

It was inevitable that upon hearing reports that I'd been acting like a civilized human being, Gunter came to inspect me.

I'd not seen him since the day we were sold into captivity, but I remembered him well—hale and hearty, long half-matted blond hair and beard, a confident air of command. At closer range, he was near my own height, and there was a glint of shrewdness in his grey eyes. And there nestled in the hollow of his brawny throat was Phèdre's diamond, scintillating under the wintry skies.

That diamond, that gods-bedamned diamond from gods-bedamned Melisande Shahrizai. I took a sharp breath at the sight of it.

Mistaking my reaction—there was no way he could have known how I loathed that thing—Gunter laughed and fondled the diamond. "She is a very good bed-slave," he said in Skaldic, speaking slowly and carefully so I might understand. He raised his eyebrows at me. "Very, very good. Are all your women so?"

I kept my expression stoic. "No."

"Hmm." He pondered that for a moment, then beckoned to the housecarl accompanying him. Reaching into the scrap bucket, he drew out what looked to be an entire roasted chicken leg. "Good boy."

My mouth watered at the sight of it, the tips of my fingers curling in anticipation of making a grab for the prize.

No.

No, this was a test of my self-control. I inclined my head in acknowledgment, then stood motionless in the at-ease position. Gunter laughed and tossed the chicken leg toward me. I snatched it midair and gave him a crisp Cassiline bow in response, ignoring the dogs skirling around my legs. Gunter laughed again and left.

I sat cross-legged in the snow, picking at my prize and sharing bits with the pack, wondering if I'd passed his test.

I had.

Gunter returned the following day with several of his thanes, bringing Phèdre, too. The men were in high spirits, drunk and rowdy, passing a waterskin back and forth between them, rivulets of mead running down their beards. Only Phèdre was sober and quiet, a hothouse flower amongst barbarians.

"D'Angeline!" Gunter shouted at me. "Hey! What have you learned? Has my bed-slave taught you to speak like a man?"

I bowed. Phèdre and I had discussed this conversation. "I am at my lord's service."

"So the wolf-cub does more than growl." He laughed. "A-ha, but what will you do if I set you loose?"

I bowed again. "I will do as my lord commands."

"Will you?" Gunter looked skeptical. "Well, there is water—" Thinking out loud, the clan lord began speaking too swiftly for me to follow, rattling off what sounded like a list of chores, then somewhat unintelligible about housecarls and someone called Hedwig, whom Phèdre had named as one of the more kind-hearted Skaldi women . . . and then Gunter was fixing me with a canny look, barraging me with questions I couldn't understand, one after another. Helpless, I looked to Phèdre for assistance.

"He wants your word that you won't try to escape or attack the steading," she said.

"Tell him this," I said. "If he keeps you safe, I'll serve and protect this steading as though it were my own. I'll do aught that he asks save turn against my own people. Unless it's d'Aiglemort's men," I added. "Tell him I swear it on my oath."

She repeated my words in Skaldic, slowly enough that I was able to keep pace and nod in confirmation. They had another exchange in which Gunter scratched thoughtfully at his beard, posing questions to which Phèdre replied with steady assurance. At length Gunter gave a good-natured shrug.

"She says you have been tamed," he said to me. "So, I give you one night to say goodbye to your new friends here, then we will see if you are a useful carl."

For a third time, I bowed; this time dropping to sit in a meditative pose. "I will wait for my lord's command."

Gunter eyed me, then gave Phèdre a questioning look. "Is he going to sit there all night long?"

"I don't know." From the sound of it, she didn't particularly care. "He might."

The Skaldi clan leader found this uproariously funny as he and his drunken thanes shepherded Phèdre back to the great hall, leaving me sitting on the filthy snow-packed ground of the kennel.

I watched them go the whole while. For all the times I'd been beaten into submission, I'd never known what it truly felt like to want to kill a man.

CHAPTER TWENTY-SIX

It was warm in the hall.

By all that was sacred, it was *warm* in the hall. It was a big open space built of massive soot-darkened logs and beams. The hearth was large enough for a tall man to stand inside it, and it held a roaring fire of enormous logs that gave off so much heat that all I wanted to do was curl up beside it and sleep for a week. The odors inside the hall washed over me in waves. It had been so cold in the dog pen I could barely smell; here was smoke and soot and food cooking, stale ale and a sweet, sticky mead the Skaldi favored, the smell of unwashed humanity.

It was glorious.

Phèdre had accompanied the thanes who came to remove the collar around my neck and free me; whether watching to be sure they kept their word or I kept mine, I couldn't say. In the hall, she returned to an area in the northeastern corner where women of the steading gathered to card and spin wool, weave and sew, knit and mend and the like. They looked me up and down in candid appraisal.

I was hoping to be given a morsel of food, or at the least, dry rags to wrap around my frozen hands and feet, but after an exchange with Gunter, one of his thanes—Thorvil—poked me in the back with the point of a dagger. "Today you fetch water."

It was some seven hundred steps on the snow-trodden path from the kitchen door to the stream that ran through the dark fir woods surrounding the steading. The stream ran fast and deep enough that it didn't freeze solid, only formed a thick skin of ice. It would have been simple to break with a stout stick—or my elk bone—but Thorvil shook his head.

"No stick," he said, cleaning beneath his nails. "No weapons."

His overt surveillance almost made me laugh. If I'd wanted to escape, one man with a dagger was no obstacle. Since I didn't, I managed to crack the ice with the water buckets, dip, and fill them. Seven hundred steps was nothing; seven hundred return steps with a yoke and full buckets was more arduous, my boots with their ice-slick soles slipping on every step up the slight incline. Once was challenging; by the third time, I was sweating under my ragged greys, the sweat freezing on my skin before it could evaporate. Cold air seared my lungs, and my hands and feet, which had never regained proper feeling, turned into icy lumps. I reminded myself that it was considerably better than being dragged behind a Skaldi raider's horse.

I made a dozen trips, refilling the cisterns in the kitchen and hall. It was strange to see Phèdre at ease amongst the Skaldi women. They were tall, strong-boned folk, mostly fair-haired with skin ruddy and chapped by cold air, sunshine, and chores. By contrast, with her dark locks of hair and skin caressed by a lifetime of costly lotions and unguents, Phèdre looked every bit as delicate as I was beginning to suspect she wasn't.

Gunter had been gone on a hunting party that day, returning with a good-sized hart, occasion for a feast. Before getting roaring drunk, he had his thanes chain me by the ankle to a massive stone bench near the hearth.

In that moment, I couldn't have cared less that I was in chains. Being close to the fireplace was glorious. There was even a bed of dried rushes rustling beneath me, and all I wanted to do was curl up and sleep until the warmth of the hearth melted the ice lingering in the marrow of my bones. But I needed to maintain my semblance of civilization, so instead I sat upright and cross-legged in the rushes.

From time to time, women of the steading paused in passing to offer a surreptitious kindness—a tankard of water, a trencher of bread and venison. I ate and drank as though I weren't parched and starving.

Gunter took note when Hedwig, the daughter of the steading's previous leader, slipped me a leather pouch of bear-grease for my hands. When he scowled at her, she planted her fists on her hips and glared back at him. Sitting beside Gunter, Phèdre ducked her head to hide a faint smile. Still scowling, he grabbed a handful of her hair and gave her a hard warning shake. My chain stirred as every muscle in my body tensed at once, fury spiking me, ready to lunge. With Gunter's hand still entangled in her hair, Phèdre flashed a silent *no* at me. It was nothing more than a slight widening of the eyes, but I understood and kept my temper in check. She slipped out of Gunter's grasp with a light touch to his wrist and a subtle twist of her neck, a movement so fluid and easy it seemed spontaneous. Having spent my life in physical training, I could tell it wasn't. Tilting her head, she gave Gunter a look of exaggerated innocence so blatantly false, he burst into laughter. "Oh, fine," he said. "Let them give the wolf-cub salve for his wounds. I won. I am the bigger man." He nudged her. "Tonight I will show you again just how big. You like that, eh?" The look of utter despair and self-loathing that crossed Phèdre's face was so fleeting, I might have imagined it. I blinked and it was gone, replaced by her distant look as she withdrew into herself.

Gunter took her to bed that night.

It was late; except for a sleepy pair on guard duty, all the thanes had either passed out in the hall or stumbled home to dwellings of their own. Gunter took Phèdre by the arm and steered her before him toward his bedchamber.

The great hall was sturdy and well built, any chinks between the logs plastered with clay to keep out the wind. But there were gaps where the interior doors weren't hung plumb and sound carried throughout the hall, in which there was precious little in the way of privacy in the first place.

I heard them.

I heard them that night, and many others, too, but the first was the hardest to bear. A cowardly part of me wished I'd never seen that fleeting expression. Elua have mercy, it had been simpler to believe her a traitor; it had been easier to regard her as a spoilt little courtesan playing at being a spy. Catching a glimpse of the deep anguish behind the façade was a dagger blow to the heart.

Gunter was grunting loudly and rhythmically, the sound only slightly muffled by the bedchamber door. It was loud enough that one of his thanes roused with a grumble and threw an empty tankard in that direction before slumping back to snore on the rush-strewn floor. All I could picture was Gunter grunting and thrusting atop her, Melisande's diamond winking mockingly at his throat.

I could hear Phèdre, too.

I rolled over in the rushes and vomited bile. *Kushiel's Dart*. I hadn't given it the credence it deserved, and gifts from the gods were double-edged. If there were any blessing in it, this was surely the curse. I pulled my knees to my chest and clapped my hands over my ears, trying not to hear.

"Poor boy." A woolen blanket settled over me, scratchy but warm. Opening my eyes, I saw Hedwig. "Gunter's not a bad man," she said in the emberlit dimness. "He has a good heart. He won't harm her."

A bitter laugh escaped me. "But he *is*."

"Is he?" she asked gently.

"Yes." I didn't know the Skaldic for what I wanted to say, for the word I needed to speak aloud. "He's *raping* her."

Hedwig was silent for a moment; she may not have understood my actual D'Angeline words, but she grasped my meaning. "Gunter bought her," she said in Skaldic. "She belongs to him. You, too. I am sorry. But if you want to live, remember it."

There were many things I wished I could say to her, foremost among them that no matter how licentious D'Angeline behavior appeared to the foreign eye—indeed, to the Cassiline eye, too—consensuality was a sacred tenet in Terre d'Ange. To violate it was a serious crime and an act of heresy. All D'Angelines hold this as an absolute article of faith, Cassiel's Servants as surely as Naamah's. It mattered naught if Phèdre found pleasure against her will in it.

But even if I'd possessed the vocabulary for such a conversation, it wouldn't have changed anything. So I simply nodded in acquiescence, pulled the blanket over my head, curled tight, and slept.

In the morning, Phèdre avoided my gaze whenever I passed through the hall carrying buckets of water or armloads of firewood. One of the women—Thurid, the shy one—was attempting to teach her to spin wool, repressing giggles. Apparently Phèdre's general domestic incompetence was a source of amusement to the Skaldi women. It surprised me that they bore her no resentment for it.

For my part, soul-sick though I was, at least my body felt considerably better. Cold water and a hard chunk of rye bread rinsed the bile from my mouth and filled my belly. My tattered clothing had unfrozen and steamed almost dry, and even an uneasy night's sleep had done me a world of good. I performed every task given me with steady obedience. If Gunter thought to diminish me with menial chores, he was mistaken. I'd spent ten years of my life doing chores as a cadet, and we'd been taught to take pride in honest labor.

Later in the day, I noted that Phèdre had abandoned her futile efforts at domesticity and was seated at a low table, scribbling on it with a burnt twig while Hedwig and another woman sat opposite her and sang a duet in Skaldic. Curious, I settled a bundle of firewood on my shoulder and drifted close enough to see that the entire surface of the table was covered by lines of verse and musical notations.

The Skaldi women paused at my approach; Phèdre blew on the tiny ember at the end of the twig, then continued to scribble. Now I felt awkward and miserable, unable to unhear what I'd heard and acutely reminded that Phèdre was still silently furious at me for refusing to leave her, as furious as I'd been when I thought her a traitor.

I cleared my throat. "What are you doing?"

"Translating Skaldic women's songs," she said without looking at me.

"Why?"

She did look at me then, and there was a bleak amusement far too old for her years in her gaze. "Do you have to ask, O scion of Shemhazai? Because no one else has ever bothered to do so." I opened my mouth, then closed it, making a prudent retreat before the thane overseeing my labors today took notice. He was an ill-tempered fellow named Evrard and I was doing my best to give him no cause for complaint.

I'd always considered Alcuin the scholar in Delaunay's household, mayhap because he'd left Naamah's service, mayhap because I came to know him as a friend. Phèdre was Delaunay's student, too, but the things that held her interest were patrons, fêtes, gowns, and baubles. I'd reckoned her a reluctant scholar at best. And mayhap she had been. I surely wasn't the same Joscelin Verreuil who had reluctantly deigned to accept a post guarding a frippery-minded young courtesan. When I looked back at that man, I saw a condescending prig certain in the knowledge that he was the best cadet of his generation, annoyed at every turn by being oath-sworn to protect a ward he didn't deem worthy of a Cassiline Brother's service.

Since that time, I'd found myself thrust into the cogs of a conspiracy in motion and spit out in shards; betrayed, abducted, stripped of my ancestral arms, defeated, beaten into submission, chained, starved, and humiliated.

Who was I now?

Who was she now?

Alive, at least. Mayhap that was the only answer that mattered right now; and the best we could hope for was survival. So I continued to do every chore assigned to me with unobtrusive alacrity.

Gunter's thanes didn't cease their vigilance, though they did relax it as long as I kept my head down and did what I was told. I had a vain hope that I'd be able to fade into the background as an obedient housecarl and plan a well-thought-out escape before Gunter's steading rode for the Allthing.

I hadn't reckoned on the women. The more I played the well-behaved housecarl, the bolder they grew; especially Ailsa, who was tall and pretty and unwed, with ruddy gold hair the hue of sunrise. She took every opportunity to saunter past me, giving me significant looks out of the corner of one eye. Upon one such occasion, Phèdre informed me in all sincerity that the whole of the Manni tribe would welcome me as one of their own if I found a tribeswoman willing to take me as her husband. There was a glint of genuine mischief in her eyes, and I swear in Cassiel's name, it gladdened my heart to see it.

The next time Gunter and his thanes went on a hunting party, the women of the steading conspired to bathe me. A small bathing chamber held a wooden tub half-filled with water heated in the kitchen hearth, as well as a brazier for extra warmth and a three-legged stool. Thurid, the quiet one, brought a well-mended, sturdy woolen jerkin and breeches that had belonged to her brother. It pained me nonetheless to strip off my filthy, tattered greys. With my arms stolen—at least until I found a way to retrieve them—they were my last outward connection to the Brotherhood.

Phèdre was sympathetic, understanding what that meant to me. "I'll wash and mend them with my own hands if I have to, Joscelin."

I laughed, surprising myself. My Skaldic had improved enough to tease her in response. "Thank you, but I have heard of your sewing."

"*I* will mend them," Ailsa promised slyly, gathering up my greys. "It is good to be kind to strangers."

The tub had to be emptied and filled a second time before I was clean. Using a coarse rag and a lump of lye soap, I sat with my knees drawn tight to my chest and scrubbed my body, scouring away layers of grime, lines of scum where frozen sweat had melted and refrozen. I dunked my entire head and lathered my greasy, matted hair before clambering into the tub a second time. This time, I took stock of my myriad injuries, cautiously wiping away crusts of drying blood.

The women of the steading giggled a great deal and took every occasion to peek at me, curious about D'Angeline men. I didn't think I was so different in appearance from Skaldi men save for the absence of facial hair—even at that, one of the young thanes who doted on Phèdre was known as Harald the Beardless—but it seemed there were rumors that D'Angeline men and women alike possessed unique organs of pleasure. I was fairly sure it wasn't true. I'd seen enough Skaldi men pissing outdoors to know their phalluses were no different in appearance than any man's.

When I was clean and clothed, my boots steaming dry beside the brazier, Phèdre shooed away the other women and tended to my hair herself with a wooden comb Hedwig had loaned her. Unsurprisingly, she had a deft touch. I sat on the floor while she coaxed out the tangled mats and knots. When at last my hair was clean and sleek and only slightly damp, she plaited it into a long braid. It was a moment of blissful luxury and I almost wished it would never end, but end, it must. When I emerged from the bathing chamber, the Skaldi women raised eyebrows, whispered, and giggled amongst themselves. I did my best to ignore them, especially Ailsa—the surly thane Evrard was pursuing her. Phèdre had told the women of the steading that I was vowed to chastity, but I knew that to a woman they found the notion absurd and unbelievable. Their frank sensual appraisal made me uncomfortable, reminding me of Naamah's Servants calling down from their balconies in the Trysting Mews.

Hey boy, pretty boy, let down your long fair hair, oh!

It brought me back to that night when I'd given chase to a Tsingani trickster and found Selwyn with a girl in one of the gardens, and thoughts of Selwyn always tapped into a deep well of grief. Those were things that happened to the Joscelin who had been, not the Joscelin I was now.

Despite everything, it was glorious to be warm and clean and dry. Even the endless grind of outdoor tasks was easier to bear in the absence of the bone-deep chill I'd endured. Gunter continued to tolerate me, although he never forgot to ensure I was chained to the great stone bench every evening.

I studied the patterns of the steading. The best time to attempt an escape would be in the small hours of the night under clear skies lit by a bright moon, when Gunter and his thanes were sleeping off their drink. As much as I desperately longed to reclaim my Cassiline arms, I could make do with any weapon. We would need provisions, horses, warmer attire if we were to survive the journey. So I observed and plotted and regained my strength, waiting for an opportunity that never presented itself.

Playing a waiting game, it could have been easy to lose sight of the direness of our situation for a day or two at a time. That changed when Gunter led a raid across the mountains into D'Angeline territory. Gunter was no fool, and shrewd in his ambitious way. He took harsh measures when he deemed them necessary—such as trying to break my spirit—but he wasn't an innately cruel man, and he had a name for being a sensible leader who listened to his people. I don't think he staged the raid out of spite toward his D'Angeline captives. It was simply what steadings near the border of Camlach did for sport and spoils—and now at the behest of Isidore d'Aiglemort, whose very name made my blood boil with righteous fury.

The steading roused hours before dawn, Gunter and his thanes laughing and jesting as they armed for the raid. It was like being dashed in the face with a bucket of ice water. I felt sick and angry to the point of shaking while watching them, knowing where they were bound and why, knowing that innocent D'Angeline blood would be spilled, knowing it likely my countrywomen would be violated by the Skaldic right of conquest. And there was *nothing* I could do save look at Phèdre and see the same pale horror on her face. If I'd had any lingering doubts whether or not she was a traitor to our nation, that put an end to them.

"I ride into battle, little dove!" Gunter shouted, emptying a tankard of ale and striding toward Phèdre, heedless as she flinched away from him. "Kiss me for luck!"

I moved without thought, stepping between them and sweeping his arms apart and down. "Allow her one piece of pride, my lord."

He narrowed his eyes at me, thinking. I kept my face calm and utterly expressionless, crossed forearms resting low at ease. He'd seen me fight and lose, but he'd never seen me in single combat. I could defeat him and he knew it; but I'd never leave the hall alive if I did. As it was, I was walking the dagger's edge, praying that my words touched some vein of human decency in him, that the self-control I was maintaining would suffice for him to ignore one small gesture of disobedience. In the end, I think he relented out of expedience more than anything, giving me a brief nod and a warning look before shoving me aside to rally his men. "We ride!"

I stole a glance at Phèdre once they'd gone, leaving only a few thanes to remain as guards. She looked deeply relieved and there were tears of gratitude in her dark eyes as she met my gaze and mouthed the words *Thank you.*

Ah, Elua; her face, the look in her eyes. Knowing how profoundly precious that last ounce of dignity was to her. That was the first chisel stroke, the first crack in my heart. Tendrils of an emotion I didn't recognize crept into the breach in my innermost sanctum, delicate and inexorable.

If I'd known what it meant, I would have been scared out of my wits. I was Cassiel's Servant and there was no room in my heart for aught else.

Or at least so I believed.

It was a long, tense day in the steading waiting for the raiding party to return. I'd given thought to attempting an escape in their absence, but Gunter had been clever enough to assign a close guard on Phèdre, knowing I wouldn't dare make a move that would jeopardize her life. One was a stalwart older fellow named Knud who had shown her a measure of kindness, but I'd no doubt either thane would do whatever Gunter deemed necessary. Edvard the Sharptongued—I'd learned that was his nickname—had been assigned to guard me, something neither of us welcomed. He was one of those men with a grievance against the entire world. Since he'd chosen to believe that I was the reason Ailsa had refused his suit, he was quick with a harsh word and a sharp prod. The women of the steading were quieter than I suspect was their wont; they, at least, had enough compassion to refrain from anticipatory celebration.

All that changed when the raiding party returned, trampling their shadows before them, loud and rollicking, blowing through the doors of the great hall already half-drunk on victory and ale. They hadn't taken prisoners, which was a mercy of sorts. The spoils I helped unload were all foodstuff—sacks of grain, dried root vegetables and fruits. It looked as though it was a small farming village they raided, though there must have been Allies of Camlach nearby, for I caught excited chatter about a proper battle with two thanes and quite a few more D'Angelines killed. Beyond that, I closed my ears. I didn't want to hear, didn't want to know. There was nothing I could do about it.

Unless I abandoned Phèdre to her fate and made my way to Terre d'Ange to report that Isidore d'Aiglemort was paying the Skaldi to raid along the border; but I *couldn't*. I was Cassiel's Servant, and my vows were more than mere words. My vows were who I was, a warrior-priest, steel hammered and tempered in the forge of the Cassiline Brotherhood. Cassiel turned his back on Heaven itself, accepting the possibility of eternal damnation in the eyes of Adonai, the father of us all, to serve as Blessed Elua's Perfect Companion. And if I were damned by the peers of the realm for my choice, so be it.

No tender feelings were spared that night. I was chained beside the hearth while the Skaldi drank, feasted, and sang victory songs and laments that sounded much alike, for Skaldi slain in battle were said to join the table in the great hall of their gods in the afterlife. They were still roistering when Gunter rose with a decisive shout, calling for Phèdre. He flung her over his shoulder and carted her off to the bedchamber to rousing cheers of approval and encouragements. I lay in my bed of reeds with my arms wrapped around my ears, waiting for the rest of the clan to pass out or retire. I slept fitfully when they did, waking to the lightest of footfalls approaching.

It was Phèdre, disheveled, shivering, and barefoot, clad in a shapeless woolen tunic that dragged to her knees. Her dark eyes shimmered with tears in the dull red glow of the banked hearth. "I couldn't stay there."

"I know." I folded back my ragged blanket to make space for her. She curled up against me, burying her face against my chest, and I put my arm around her.

It ought to have felt shocking.

It didn't.

It felt like coming home. I felt her shuddering ease and her breathing slow, tense muscles relaxing. There was an ethereal quality to Phèdre's beauty, but beneath it she was flesh and blood. I could feel her heart beating near my own. For a fleeting moment, the rest of the world fell away and I was at peace.

Then Phèdre broke it. "Joscelin, you have to leave."

"I *can't*." I kept my voice low, but I couldn't hide the anguish in it. "I can't leave you here."

"Damn your Cassiel to hell, then!" she hissed.

I stroked her hair ever so lightly. "He believed he was, you know. So I've been taught all my life, but I never understood it until now."

"I know." She sighed, closing her eyes, and I don't think she was speaking only of Cassiel. "I know."

Now I lay awake in the ember-lit dimness with Phèdre nó Delaunay in my arms, trying to forge a place of safety in that circle, trying to banish the images of the raiding party returning triumphant, of Gunter throwing Phèdre over his shoulder. I couldn't help but think about those Allies of Camlach outnumbered and slain by the Skaldi, and the horrifying depth of Isidore d'Aiglemort's betrayal of his own people.

"How can d'Aiglemort bear it?" I whispered aloud. "He's sending D'Angelines to die at Skaldi hands."

"For every ten that die, a hundred more will flock to his banner." She gazed at the hearth. "And he can blame Camlach's losses on the King's refusal to grant him more troops. He's building an empire, though I'm not sure exactly how. It puzzles me that Gunter doesn't fear him."

"Why should he?" I asked. "D'Aiglemort pays him."

Phèdre shook her head against my chest. "No, it's more than that. Gunter knows somewhat that d'Aiglemort—they call him Kilberhaar, silver hair—doesn't. He laughs about it, but he won't tell me. I think it's to do with Waldemar Selig. One of Delaunay's allies said it a year ago, the Skaldi have found a leader who thinks."

I shivered. "Elua have mercy."

After that we both fell silent. There was too much to say and at the same time nothing to say, and there was far less risk in silence. Quietude eased into sleep cocooned in warmth, comfort, and the illusion of safety.

The young woman Thurid woke us near dawn with a light tug on Phèdre's sleeve, eyes wide and alarmed at our audacity. "You must go," she whispered to Phèdre. "They'll be waking soon."

Phèdre nodded and sat up, broken bits of rushes tangled in her hair. In the middle of the night, both of us soul-racked, it had only seemed natural to find comfort in each other. Now, in the grey light, she looked at me with surprise. I felt the skin on my face grow warm as I flushed in response. Drunken thanes were beginning to stir; there was no time to speak. She gave my hand a grateful squeeze before slipping back to Gunter's bedchamber.

That was the second crack in my heart.

CHAPTER TWENTY-SEVEN

Skaldic winter nights are long and the days short. There were no more raids for now and fewer hunting parties; 'twas the time of year when Gunter and his thanes spent most of their time in the great hall, eating and drinking supplies laid up for the winter, singing and boasting and telling tales.

Many of the tales they told were of Waldemar Selig, who had his own personal mythology. They claimed that after his mother died giving birth to Waldemar, he was nursed by a great white wolf; that he was impervious to poisons and blades. Others told of how he roamed the land in disguise in his youth, rewarding those who offered him hospitality with gold, issuing challenges to those who shunned him. The litany went on and on, the glory of Waldemar Selig's deeds increasing with each telling. I couldn't always follow the entire thread of conversation—there was one escapade involving owls and wizards—but enough to see the pattern of adulation forming around the man. It was frightening. Not because I believed the tales were true, for they struck me as a blend of old Hellene myths and Skaldic folklore, but because Gunter and his thanes believed them to be true.

That meant Waldemar Selig wasn't just a leader who thought, he was a leader who inspired—and that was a dangerous thing. Duc Isidore d'Aiglemort was a leader who inspired and Selwyn was dead because of it. He was a leader who thought, too; but if he thought he had the upper hand in his dealings with this Waldemar Selig, he might find himself mistaken.

I was alone with my thoughts during the days after the raid. Having taken a grave risk, Phèdre wasn't minded to press her luck. Most of the communication between us was silent, consisting of glances and gestures. I learned to read her expressions, subtle as they often were, like a sailor studying the horizon. If there was more in it than our mutual reliance, it was not a thought I was willing to contemplate.

Adding to my tension, Ailsa continued to make her interest in me blatant, convinced that my status would rise from slave to a carl to a thane and thus a worthy husband; which in turn stoked Evrard the Sharptongued's jealousy. I'd done my best to explain in my halting Skaldic that I was sworn to celibacy, and Phèdre explained it to the women of the steading with considerably more clarity. The simple fact of the matter was that no one believed either of us. It was outside their ken; presumably a jest or a protective ruse. At any rate, Evrard went out of his way to torment me with childish pranks—pushes, taunts, jabs. I did my best to ignore him, all too well aware that I stood on dangerous ground.

It even worked, for a while.

I was hauling an armload of firewood when Ailsa caught my eye, winked, and hoisted her breasts in her kirtle to display her cleavage. I blushed and averted my gaze, not seeing Evrard, who deftly tripped me.

I toppled headlong, branches scattering everywhere as I slapped my palms on the floor to break my fall. Evrard laughed uproariously; and that, I could have endured. I knelt and gathered spilled kindling, keeping my head bowed. It wasn't enough. Evrard grabbed my braid in one hand and yanked. "Look at him," he said to the hall at large. "What man has such hair on his head and none on his chin? What man blushes like a maid? No man, I say, but a woman!"

My shoulders tensed, but I held still, closing my eyes and waiting for Evrard the Sharptongued to weary of this game. Gunter was watching idly from a great chair near the fire. Phèdre was seated on the stone bench to which I was chained at night, eyes downcast, playing a borrowed lute. The thanes were doubled over laughing. Encouraged, Evrard gave my braid a contemptuous flick. "He's pretty enough to be a woman, eh? Maybe we ought to have a look," he suggested, beckoning to a few companions. My muscles locked in protest. "What do you say, lads? Let's strip the wolf-cub and see if he's a bitch after all!"

Phèdre's lute strings fell silent.

Evrard and two others tackled me at once, attempting to pin me to the floor, but I lunged into a forward roll, grabbing a sturdy length of branch as I rose and spun, kicking a second branch and grabbing it midair. Evrard and his companions spread out in front of me.

The circle of self-defense wasn't one we studied in great depth at the Prefectory, for our primary objective was to protect our wards, not ourselves. But study it we did, for betimes it was necessary. I crossed my improvised staves and waited while more thanes joined the fray to encircle me. There was no way I was going to win this fight, and there was no way I was going down without fighting, so I chose to fight solely on the defensive in the hopes that Gunter would appreciate my restraint.

By the same token, his thanes were wary of inflicting too much damage without explicit permission. So I fought in place, no more than two steps in any direction from my center point, blocking and parrying as I pivoted from vector to vector. I inflicted a good dozen or more solid whacks, sending thanes staggering in every direction until they closed ranks in a concerted effort, bringing me down with a hail of blows.

I thrashed in a vain effort to escape the pounding fists, a boot in my side, the hands yanking at the drawstring of my rough-spun breeches. Their jeering faces swam in my vision and white-hot fury rose in me.

"*Enough!*" Gunter's roar nearly rattled the rafters; he'd grown bored. His thanes withdrew. I rose with as much dignity as I could muster, dropping my staves and offering a precise Cassiline bow. He drummed his fingers on the arm of his chair, looking thoughtful. "So you claim injury of this man, eh, Sharptongue?" he asked Evrard.

Evrard was quick to air his grievances. "Gunter, this carl, this *slave* of yours has made this steading a cuckoo's nest. Look!" He pointed at Ailsa. "Look how he woos our women under our very noses!"

"If there's wooing being done, look to yon vixen," Hedwig called out, evoking laughter that made Evrard flush with anger.

Propping his chin on his fist, Gunter regarded me. "What do you say, D'Angeline?"

I straightened my garments and met his gaze. "My lord, he questions my manhood. I beg your leave to answer with steel."

It was a risky response, but it made Gunter chuckle. "So we've not drawn the wolf-cub's teeth, eh?" He raised his brows at Evrard. "Well, Sharptongue, I do believe he's challenged you to the holmgang."

I'd no idea what that meant, but Evrard's angry flush deepened. "Gunter, he's a housecarl at best. I will not stand for the shame of fighting a slave."

"Maybe he is a carl, maybe not," Gunter said. "When Waldemar Selig was captured by the Vandalii, he defeated their champions one by one until they made him their leader. Do you say Waldemar Selig is a carl?"

"Waldemar Selig is a warrior, not a D'Angeline fancy-boy," Evrard spat. "Do you mock me?"

"Oh, I do not think any man will mock you for fighting the wolf-cub," Gunter said dismissively, glancing around the hall at his bruised thanes. "Will you?" It was more command than question, and his men nodded in grudging acquiescence while Evrard the Sharptongued glowered. Gunter grinned and slammed his fist down. "So be it! Tomorrow we have the holmgang!"

Once the matter was announced, the thanes waxed enthusiastic about the upcoming contest and began placing wagers on the outcome. I gathered up the spilled firewood and went quietly about my chores. Amused by my ignorance, no one was willing to explain to me what the holmgang entailed, so I'd be walking into the situation blind. I reckoned that didn't matter as long as it was a reasonably fair fight.

I found out soon enough, for the following day was bright and clear and the folk of the steading were minded to make a holiday of it. A large swathe of snow was trampled flat and an immense hide was brought forth. They stretched it on the flattened ground, hammering stakes to affix it in place. Next came hazel rods placed a few paces from each corner to mark a precise square around the hide.

Gunter arrived in high spirits, with Phèdre in tow. I took a chance and approached him, offering a respectful bow. "My lord, if I may ask, what is the manner of this fight?"

"What, you the challenger, and not knowing?" He found it amusing, but he gestured at the snowy field. "It is the holmgang. One sword to each man and three shields if you can find the loan of them. The first to spill blood or force the other into the hazel field wins." In one smooth motion, he drew his sword and offered me the hilt. I stared into his shrewd grey eyes in surprise. "You defended yourself like a warrior, D'Angeline, and for that I lend you my second-best blade. But you must go begging for shields."

My hand closed around the hilt without thinking and a shudder went through me.

A sword.

There was only one reason a Cassiline Brother drew his sword, and that was to kill. I shook my head and reversed the blade, returning it hilt-first. "My lord, my oath forbids me. I may only draw my sword to kill. Give me my daggers and arm-shields."

Gunter gave me a cheerful clap on the shoulder. "It is the holmgang, wolf-cub. You should kill him if you can, or he will challenge you again and again.

Anyway, I have a bet on you." With that he wandered away to shout at one of the men placing hazel rods, leaving me holding his second-best sword.

I looked at Phèdre in helpless dismay.

There was a faint furrow between her brows; she knew what this meant to me. "He will kill you if he can, Cassiline," she said in D'Angeline. "And leave me utterly alone and unprotected. But I cannot tell you what to choose."

Her guard Knud sidled over to us. "Here." He handed me a shield. "Take this, lad. There's no honor in forcing a slave to fight unguarded." I accepted it with thanks, and he nodded and escorted Phèdre to Gunter's side.

I took up the sword-hilt and slid my arm into the battered wooden buckler. I essayed a few moves, testing the heft and range and balance of both weapons. The sword-hilt felt hot against my left palm; whether due to the warmth of Gunter's grip on it or my own nerves and imagination, I couldn't say.

A sword.

But it wasn't a blade dedicated to Cassiel's service. A sword, but not *my* sword. I'd sworn no oath upon this blade. This was more akin to training with serviceable practice arms at the Prefectory—except Evrard the Sharptongued would kill me if he could. I watched him jest and boast with his companions. There weren't as many taking his side as I'd expected—his sharp tongue had earned detractors—but he was Skaldi and I wasn't. He had plenty of supporters, including thanes standing at the ready with a second and third shield.

This didn't have to be a fight to the death. All I had to do was spill first blood or force Evrard off the hide.

"Last bets!" Gunter shouted, having determined that the placing of the hazel rods was acceptable. "No? Let the holmgang begin! First blow to he who accepted the challenge!" That meant Evrard was to have the first strike. He stepped onto the hide, testing its surface. I stepped onto the opposite end to meet him. One glance at his face told me I was fooling myself if I thought this was anything less than a fight to the death.

So be it.

Evrard the Sharptongued took a deep, deep breath, letting it out in a growl that grew to a deafening roar before he charged me, leading with his shield, sword arm raised to deliver a hammer strike of a blow.

It would have been easy to dodge. One quick pivot and I could land a blow from behind; if it spilled blood onto the hide, the fight was over. That wasn't as simple as it sounded. Evrard wore a heavy fur vest over his woolens, wide strips of thick leather around his wrists and forearms, tall boots, a leather harness with heavy buckles. It would be difficult to strike hard enough to spill blood without killing him. And like as not, I'd be despised by the Skaldi for attacking from behind like a coward.

All of these things flashed through my mind as I awaited Sharptongue's approach, and I chose to stand my ground and take his blow. It was a clear, sunny day and his blade glinted against the blue sky as it descended.

I took the blow on Knud's shield, which splintered into pieces. I cast the remnants aside and took up Gunter's sword in a two-handed grip, angling it across my body. Evrard paused just long enough to confirm that no one was offering a replacement for my shield, then snarled and launched a second attack. This one I parried smoothly, sending his sword low and outward, then putting my strength into a backstroke that broke his shield. That was the moment when Evrard the Sharptongued began to realize he ought to be afraid. "Shield!" he shouted, backing away from me. "Shield!"

I waited patiently as one of the thanes handed him a new shield and he settled it on his arm. This time, I feinted left. I hadn't taken the offensive until now and it caught Evrard unprepared. He swung in a wild blow I evaded with ease, stepping inside his guard. He got his buckler up in time to block my straightforward thrust, but my blade stuck in the cracked wood. I yanked it from his grasp, withdrawing my sword and snapping the shield with one quick stomp.

Evrard backed away from me, groping blindly behind him. "Shield."

I waited.

Time was a fixed point around which the world revolved, and I stood in the center of it, waiting, waiting. Beyond the hazel rods, Phèdre was watching, her dark eyes glimmering with concern.

I smiled a bit.

It was Evrard's third and final shield. He attacked without hesitation, but I was already in motion. Sidestepping his blade, I spun to gain momentum and split his last shield in twain, splinters flying.

"No," he whispered, voice trembling with rage and humiliation. He took a step backward, then another. One foot was off the hide; if I understood rightly, one more step and he would forfeit the fight. "Please."

He will kill you if he can.

If Evrard backed down, there would be no need for bloodshed of any kind; but I'd fought with drawn sword. Even if it wasn't a dedicated blade, there had to be a reckoning in accordance with my oath. I set my shoulders and angled my blade. "I will not be foresworn, Skaldi. Step off the hide or die."

He chose to die.

It was a wholly unnecessary choice born out of rancid pride. With one last roar, Evrard launched a wild berserker's attack on me. I parried, pivoted, and struck in return, an angled blow across his midriff.

It was a death blow. Evrard the Sharptongued crumpled in a pool of his own blood, open eyes fixed on the blue skies in empty fury. After a long moment of silence, Gunter proclaimed my victory. Ignoring him, I knelt on the hide beside Evrard's still-seeping body and laid my bloody sword before me. "May Adonai have mercy on your soul," I murmured. "This I pray in Cassiel's name."

Rising, I cleaned the blood from the blade with a handful of snow, wiping it dry with the hem of my tunic. Approaching Gunter, I presented it to him hilt-first. "Thank you for allowing me to defend my honor, my lord," I said to him in my slow, careful Skaldic. "I am sorry for the death of your thane."

"Sharptongue brought it on himself, eh?" Gunter slung one meaty arm over my shoulders. "How is it if you take his place, wolf-cub?"

I wasn't sure I'd heard him aright. "My lord?"

He grinned. "I'm minded to take a risk on you, D'Angeline. If I give you back your weapons, does your oath still bind you? Do you swear to protect and serve me? Give your life for mine?"

It was a hard thing to do. I had never expected to find my own vows twisted and used against me. But Evrard Sharptongue, lying dead a few yards away, had found it so hard to swallow his pride that he'd sooner die than take a single step backward. I needed to do whatever was necessary to protect Phèdre. I glanced at her, my resolve hardening. "I swear it. So long as you keep my lady Phèdre safe."

"Good!" Gunter gave my shoulders a hearty squeeze. "Give him a cheer, eh?" he called to his thanes. "The boy's proved himself a man today!"

CHAPTER TWENTY-EIGHT

In the course of a single day, I'd gone from a slave to a trusted thane.

First of all, Gunter returned my weapons and vambraces to me. I would call him foolish to give his trust unstinting, but the truth was, he had my measure. I'd sworn on my oath to serve and protect him, and I was bound to do so as long as he kept Phèdre safe on his terms. Trusting or not, he was clever enough to make certain that there was always someone other than me keeping watch over her.

No longer was I chained beside the hearth at night, but given a pallet in the long, narrow bedchamber that served to house some half a dozen thanes within the steading's great hall.

No one particularly mourned the loss of Evrard the Sharptongued, which troubled me simply because his death had been so unnecessary. But it was done and the modest spoils of his possessions were bestowed upon me. I kept a blanket, a fur cloak, and a few useful accoutrements like a tinderbox and waterskin, donating the rest, including his arms, to the general stores of the steading. I did so because my own steel was infinitely superior to the quality the Skaldi used, but it won me some goodwill, too.

Now the steading began preparing to attend the Allthing. In winter weather, Waldemar Selig's steading lay a week's journey away. Gunter would be bringing a score of thanes, including me, and Hedwig and three other women of her choosing. There was an old Skaldic lay about how Brunhild the Doughty won the right in a wrestling match for women to speak at the Allthing. And of course he would bring Phèdre. It wasn't officially common knowledge that he meant to present the both of us as a gift to Selig, but it was widely assumed to be true. I looked for opportunities to escape with her before we departed Gunter's steading and found none. I would have taken it if I'd found one; especially if I could have found a way without spilling blood and most especially the blood of Gunter, to whom I was honor-bound. And Gunter would likely swear with genuine indignation that he *had* kept Phèdre safe. The Skaldi regarded bed-rights acquired by conquest to be the natural order of things.

Not a crime.

Not heresy.

But it *was* those things; it was a profound violation of the body and of an essential sacred tenet of D'Angeline belief.

At any rate, no such opportunity presented itself and the extent to which I was willing to bend a vow based on false premises went untested. Instead, an old priest came from another steading to read the omens for Gunter's venture. He led us to a winter-bare oak grove and mumbled over some carved bones he cast before announcing that the omens were favorable. Across the grove, I caught Phèdre with her head cocked, gazing distractedly at a raven on a nearby branch, and I wondered what in the world was going through her thoughts. Betimes it was nigh impossible to tell.

The following day, our company departed Gunter's steading. If we hadn't been headed farther from Terre d'Ange and deeper into enemy territory—as well as an uncertain future—I might actually have enjoyed the journey despite all its hardships. The surface of the snow had melted during a few days of false spring then refrozen into a hard crust, so we progressed with care, mindful of injury to the horses' legs. Mountain bred and born as I was, now that I was riding astride in warm attire rather than being dragged behind a horse in frozen rags, I couldn't help but appreciate the scenery of winter in Skaldia.

As soon as the first hint of purple touched the distant crags, we made camp for the evening, usually along the verge of forests of pine and spruce where we were able to gather sufficient wood for a large campfire. Our fare consisted of dried meat and pottage, bland but sustaining. At night we slept under crude tents of cured hide, four to a tent except for Gunter and Phèdre.

I had no chance to speak to her on that journey. Gunter kept her close, and I daresay she was too cold and weary to protest.

We arrived at Waldemar Selig's steading, where the Allthing was taking place, on the eighth day of our journey. Selig had scouts posted around the outer perimeter of the steading and we were still in what appeared to be untrammeled forest when Knud, who had a reputation for being a skilled tracker, drew rein and pointed silently before us. As though he'd invoked them into being, three figures clad in hooded white wolfskin cloaks burst from the snow brandishing Skaldic short spears.

I'd no idea who or what they were. I kneed my mount sideways to block the path and executed a vaulting dismount and roll, coming to my feet with crossed daggers drawn. The scouts looked human and startled behind the empty eyeholes of their wolfskin masks.

Behind me, Gunter was laughing uproariously. "So you would defend me, eh, wolf-cub? I'd rather you not do so at the cost of the Blessed's hospitality!" He nodded affably at the disgruntled scouts. "Well met, brothers. I am Gunter Arnlaugson of the Marsi, summoned to attend the Allthing."

"What is this fighting thing you've brought here, Gunter Arnlaugson?" the leader of the scouts asked in a sour tone. "Surely he's no Marsi, unless the maids of your steading have been straying across the D'Angeline border." Another caught sight of Phèdre and tugged his companion's sleeve.

Gunter moved his mount to shield her from view. "What I have brought, I will reveal only to Waldemar Selig himself," he said. "But they are loyal to me." He gave me a significant look. "Eh, wolf-cub?"

I bowed and sheathed my daggers, keeping my expression neutral. "I protect and serve, my lord."

"You'll answer for them, then," the leader said to Gunter with a shrug. "We'll lead you down."

Waldemar Selig's steading was situated in a bowl-shaped valley on the eastern side of a lake, the ridges ringed with forests. Even under ordinary circumstances, it was an impressive settlement by Skaldic standards. The great hall was at least thrice the size of Gunter's and there were two lesser halls almost as large. With the Allthing taking place, massive encampments representing a multitude of tribes sprawled all over the basin. We followed our guides through the snow-packed aisles of tents. Everyone we passed deferred to Selig's scouts—the White Brethren, I learned they were called—but there were whispers in our wake.

D'Angeline . . .

It made me shudder to hear it. There was no love lost between our countries, and a single misstep this deep in enemy territory could be deadly.

The lead scout paused amidst a swathe of unoccupied space. "You will find lodging there," he said, pointing at one of the lesser halls. "You may bring two thanes. Your headwoman and two female companions may lodge in the women's hall. The rest of the steading will make camp here, where you may draw one armload of wood a day from the common pile. Your horses you must tend yourselves."

Gunter wasn't pleased at being assigned to one of the lesser halls. "I wish to see Waldemar Selig," he said. "I have much of import to tell him."

It did not impress the White Brethren. "You may tell him at the Allthing where all may hear it," the leader said. "But the Blessed will receive tribute this evening. The doors to the great hall open when the sun stands two fingers above the horizon."

"Thank you for your courtesy, brother." There was an ironic edge to Gunter's tone. I saw the White Brethren take heed of it, reminded that Gunter was the leader of a steading in his own right and no mere thane. They took their leave, mayhap to bury themselves in the snow and ambush other new arrivals. Gunter spoke quietly to Hedwig, who nodded and looked at Phèdre with sorrow. Phèdre closed her eyes briefly and Gunter cleared his throat. "Well, then. You will stay with me, wolf-cub; you and Brede. The rest of you do what is needful and we will meet here when the sun is two fingers high, eh?"

I didn't like this arrangement; we would be in separate halls, neither of which lay under Gunter's command. I didn't know how the women's hall was staffed or guarded, but there was no way Gunter could ensure that Phèdre would be protected within it. "My lord, my oath is based on my lady's safety," I reminded him.

"She will be safe, wolf-cub," Gunter said quietly, and there was a trace of sympathy in his gaze. "She goes to a King, and you with her."

There it was, then.

I'd known, we'd both known. Phèdre and I were Gunter's property. He'd paid good coin, probably stolen D'Angeline coin, to purchase us from the gods-bedamned traitors that the thrice-cursed queen of traitors Melisande Shahrizai had handed us over to. He'd bought us as a gamble, a gift worthy of a King, to impress Waldemar Selig. If he'd grown fond of Phèdre along the way, he might feel a twinge of regret.

Or mayhap he'd simply miss having a bed-slave whose skills were worthy of diamonds by the armful. I glanced at Phèdre; she returned my gaze with a wry look that almost made me laugh for the sheer absurdity of it.

We dismounted and set out for our respective halls, leaving the others to establish a campsite. The layout of the lesser hall was much the same as Gunter's, but the steading leaders and thanes granted lodging within came from various tribes, not all of them friendly with each other. They were drinking, singing, gambling, and arm wrestling just as the thanes were wont to do at Gunter's steading, but there was an underlying tension that suggested any argument could turn into a fight to the death on a moment's notice. I did my best to be unobtrusive, keeping my head low and the patchy fur hood of Evrard's cloak drawn around my face to shadow my features.

There were housecarls and serving maids scurrying everywhere, bringing out trays of roasted meats, trenchers of dark rye bread, great pitchers of mead and ale. Hungry after a week's journey with scant provisions, I welcomed hot, fortifying food. I'd learned all too well that one's fate could change in a heartbeat. Whatever lay before us, at least I'd face it with a full belly.

A large group of Skaldi assembled outside the doors to Waldemar Selig's great hall, tribe members in loose federation while the members of individual steadings gathered in tighter knots. The women emerged from their hall to join the men, and I was relieved to see Phèdre had taken no harm in my absence.

The temperature lowered as the sun sank toward the horizon. When it hovered two fingers above the mountains, the doors to Selig's great hall were flung open wide, a blast of song and firelight bursting forth.

I'd gleaned from what Gunter had gathered that representatives from several of the largest, most powerful tribes had already arrived; tonight another steading from the Marsi tribe would be offering tribute, as well as steadings from two other tribes. There was a good deal of showmanship on display that night. Waldemar Selig sat in a thronelike wooden chair before the enormous hearth, backlit by flames. While groups from other steadings jockeyed for position to offer first tribute, Gunter held us back. He wanted his tribute—his two D'Angeline slaves—to leave the final and lasting impression.

At last it was our turn. We had the misfortunate of following a steading from the Manni tribe, who had brought a full dozen flawless white wolf pelts; a generous gift, for the white wolves of the North were notoriously difficult to hunt in addition to being Waldemar Selig's totem animal.

While we'd waited, the throng had been too thick to get a look at Selig. All I'd been able to note was that he had a deep, confident voice and he was deliberate about giving his full attention to every clan leader to approach him. Gunter ordered me to remain behind with Phèdre and the other women as Waldemar Selig greeted him. A D'Angeline would have knelt before his King, but Selig wasn't a King—at least not yet—and Gunter was Skaldi. He stood proudly before the man who would be King, thanes from the steading arrayed on either side of him. I concentrated hard on the conversation. My spoken Skaldic was still halting and limited, but I understood a fair bit more.

"Gunter Arnlaugson of the Marsi, well met, brother," Waldemar Selig said warmly. "It gladdens my heart to see you. Your steading wins glory for Skaldia on the western border."

"We come to the Allthing in good faith to pledge our loyalty to the great Waldemar Selig." Gunter made an expansive gesture. "My thanes' spears are keen for your enemies' blood. Our headwoman Hedwig Arildsdottir and her women keep the hearth alight for our triumphant return."

"Be welcome among us, folk of Gunter Arnlaugson's steading," Selig said in his deep voice, his gaze sliding past the assembled thanes. He was looking. He'd heard the rumors.

"We bring tribute, too, Blessed." Gunter stepped to one side, and his thanes laid hands on Phèdre and me, propelling us forward. "Two D'Angeline slaves purchased with gold won by Skaldi blood. I give them to you, warlord."

Waldemar Selig was a clever, thoughtful man; but he was a man nonetheless. His gaze rested intently on Phèdre. She'd been bathed and groomed and given a gown of snow-white wool in the women's hall, setting her off against the dark interior. Her beauty caught the light as vividly as the diamond still tied around Gunter's brawny throat. She sank into a deep curtsey that I recognized from long-ago lessons in court etiquette as a child in Verreuil. It was no mere social courtesy, nor any obeisance I'd seen her offer a patron. This was a formal acknowledgment of a monarch.

It intrigued Selig, even if he didn't know its precise meaning. I could tell, I was close enough to observe and he'd paid me no heed yet. There was a flash of interest in his eyes, but he leaned back in his thronelike chair with a casual air. "So you bring me two more mouths to feed, eh, Gunter?"

Gunter flushed, but he hadn't drunk nearly enough to let himself be baited. "She is trained to serve Kings, my lord."

The gathered Skaldi murmured, noting his choice of words. Selig raised his eyebrows. "And the lad?"

"A lord's son," Gunter replied. "A warrior-priest sworn to serve the girl. As long as you keep her safe, he'll guard your life like hers depends on it." He jerked his chin at the White Brethren arrayed on either side of Selig. "Ask them."

"Is it so?" Waldemar Selig asked his wolfskin-draped thanes. They muttered and argued amongst each other. He eyed Phèdre again; he still hadn't cast so much as a glance in my direction. "Is it so?"

I doubt he'd expected Phèdre to reply in fluent Skaldi any more than I had. She curtsied again. "Yes, my lord. Joscelin Verreuil is a lord's son and a member of the Cassiline Brotherhood. In Terre d'Ange, the King himself does not stir without two Cassiline Brothers to attend him."

I bowed again.

Waldemar raised his brows slightly at Phèdre. He was handsome in the Skaldic manner, with even features, a strong jaw, and a proud nose. His long brown hair and beard weren't as unkempt as most Skaldi men, bound at the brow by a gold fillet, his beard plaited into two points twined with gold wire. "You speak our tongue," he mused. "And you are trained to serve Kings. What does it mean?" He searched her face. "If I wished to tempt my enemy to foolishness, I would send one such as you. How is it that you claim you came to be a slave?"

My blood ran cold. It wasn't a thought that had occurred to me, but Waldemar Selig's logic couldn't be faulted.

Phèdre held his gaze without flinching, that slight furrow of concentration between her brows as she weighed her response. In the end she chose the truth stripped down to its bare essence. "My lord, I knew too much."

It was a truth that spoke to Waldemar Selig, and he gave a nod of understanding. "That can happen if one is trained to serve Kings." His wording was a deliberate echo of Gunter's, evoking another wave of murmuring from the crowd. He ignored them, turning his attention to me at last. "And what of you? How do you come before me?"

It felt like being caught in the glare of the great Menekhetan lighthouse of lore. The acute focus of Selig's hazel-green eyes was unnerving. I had just enough presence of mind to gamble, turning to Phèdre and addressing her in D'Angeline. "Tell him I'm oath-sworn to guard your life," I said, hoping no one from Gunter's steading would insist I demonstrate the Skaldic I'd learned. "Tell him that it's a matter of honor."

She nodded and turned to Selig. He held up a hand to forestall her. "I speak a little of your tongue," he said to me in halting D'Angeline. "You must speak a little of mine to hear my question." He switched then to near-fluent Caerdicci. "Do you speak the scholar's tongue, D'Angeline?"

I considered lying, but the savvy glint in Waldemar Selig's eye told me he knew full well that a D'Angeline lord's son would have studied the writing of ancient Caerdicci and Hellene historians and philosophers. This was indeed a leader who thought, and a leader clever enough to know his enemy. "Yes, my lord."

"And do you swear what Gunter Arnlaugson has promised?" Selig inquired. "Do you swear to guard my life as your own, Joss-lin Ver-ai?"

I bowed, offering the only answer I could. "I swear it on the safety of my lady Phèdre nó Delaunay."

"Faydra," he mused; as with my name, his pronunciation was close enough and I had no desire to correct him. He glanced at her. "That is your name?"

She curtsied. "Yes, my lord."

"Faydra, you will teach me D'Angeline," Waldemar Selig informed her in Caerdicci. "I wish you learn more. Josslin, we will see what kind of warrior you are." He made a specific beckoning gesture to one of his White Brethren.

With a resounding battle-cry, the thane lunged at Selig, his short spear extended for a mortal thrust. To this day, I've no idea if that White Brother would have pulled his blow or not, but I think not. Selig wanted every man and woman in that hall to know *this* was the level of absolute faith he required from his thanes; and that he was Waldemar the Blessed, proof against steel.

Those were thoughts that came to me later. Then, I slid between Selig and the thane, drawing my daggers. I caught the spear haft just below the sharp head and redirected his thrust upward, landing a solid straightforward kick to the belly that drove the air from his lungs and sent him tumbling to the floor. I grabbed his spear as he went down, sheathed my daggers, and bowed, then presented the spear to Waldemar Selig.

He rose to accept it, then slung a brotherly arm over Gunter's shoulders. "You've given me a mighty gift, Gunter of the Marsi!"

That night Waldemar Selig feasted the leaders of all the steadings in the great hall. After ascertaining D'Angeline protocol, he had me serve as his bodyguard, standing at ease behind him at the long table. He ordered Phèdre to serve mead throughout the night, which she did with grace. I knew Naamah's Servants were trained in all manner of services and niceties, of course, but it was quite something else to see them on display in a hall full of half-drunken barbarians banging their tankards on the table. Selig's chieftains may not have noticed those subtle niceties—where in Elua's name Phèdre acquired a square of linen to hold beneath the heavy mead jug, I couldn't begin to guess—but Selig did.

There was no talk of any war plans; whatever serious discussion was to be held would occur at the Allthing proper tomorrow. But there was a good deal of boasting and arguing that threatened to teeter over into violence, and finally did when members of rival tribes drew blades to fight over some ancient blood-feud. Skaldi cheered and cleared space for the men to duel, and Gunter shouted out a wager.

Before the fight could commence, Waldemar Selig slammed his tankard down, commanding silence. "Are you men or dogs to quarrel over a dry bone?" he asked in a challenging tone. "I have a rule in my household. Any man who bears a grudge, let him bring it to *me*. Any man who would settle it by right of arms, let him take up his cause with *me*." He appraised them. "Is that your wish?" The men muttered denials. "No? Good. Then make peace and behave as brethren."

I thought the matter settled when the two men clasped wrists and grasped shoulders, declaring mutual regret.

In that, I was mistaken.

"Well done." Waldemar Selig rose, using his looming presence to dominate the space. "You are here because you have learned to lead among your own folk. But if you would truly be leaders of men, you must learn to unite, not divide. Divided we are nothing but dog-packs squabbling in the kennel yard. United, we are a mighty people!" His chieftains cheered, but he wasn't finished. "You." He pointed at Gunter. "Gunter Arnlaugson of the Marsi, did I hear you cry out a wager?"

"It was the heat of the moment, Blessed," he protested. "Surely you've placed many a wager to pass the time on a long winter's eve."

"If a man wagers on a dogfight, how does his hunting pack fare in the spring?" Selig sat opposite Gunter, planting his elbow on the table and rolling up the right sleeve of his jerkin to reveal an exceedingly muscular arm. "A wager is a wager and you are a guest in my hall. Tell me, what will you wager?" He nodded at Melisande's diamond nestled in Gunter's beard. "That stone which shines so prettily around your neck? A D'Angeline trifle, is it not?"

A brief look of dismay crossed Gunter's face, but his recovery was swift and brash. "Do you admire it, Blessed?" He wrestled the cord over his head and held the diamond dangling from one fist. "Then it is yours!"

"Ah, no." Waldemar Selig smiled. "I would win it as honestly as your respect, Gunter. If it's a wager you want, try your luck against my arm."

The Skaldi roared in approval. Backed into a corner, Gunter reacted with good humor. Displaying the diamond to the hall at large, he sat opposite Selig and placed the diamond between them. He rolled up his own sleeve and the two of them clasped hands and began attempting to force the other's arm down. It was an impressive show of brute strength and it went on for quite some time, until both were red-faced and straining, tendons in their necks standing taut, muscles and veins bulging. But Selig was just a bit stronger and a good deal more patient, and he was a warrior in his prime with some ten years' experience over Gunter.

The White Brethren cheered the loudest when Selig forced Gunter's arm to the table. Gunter laughed and shook out his hand before picking up Melisande's diamond and passing it ceremoniously to his warlord.

Now it was Waldemar Selig who held the cord of that thrice-cursed diamond, contemplating it as it dangled. "Never let it be said that we are cruel masters," he said. "Let the D'Angelines keep their baubles! Who fears a race trained to servitude?" He raised his voice in a shout. "Faydra!"

She set down the mead jug and approached, kneeling gracefully, keeping her expression serene. "My lord."

Selig eased the cord over her bowed head, settling it so the diamond hung between the upper swell of her breasts. It was a masterful display of power and possession, and it made me sick with helpless fury. "See how the D'Angeline kneels to receive with gratitude what is hers by right," he said to the chieftains. Grabbing a handful of Phèdre's hair, he yanked her head upright. "See it and know it for an omen." I averted my gaze while the Skaldi banged their tankards. "Look well at our future!"

CHAPTER TWENTY-NINE

The Allthing met the next day.

I hoped that Selig's pleasure in using his two new D'Angeline slaves as symbols of our inferiority would extend to having one or both of us attend him, but he was too savvy for that. The Allthing was a revered Skaldic tradition and there was no way he was going to allow a D'Angeline presence there.

Instead, Phèdre and I were confined together in a small storeroom in the great hall, the door barred firmly shut while the Skaldi crammed together in the main chamber. At least it was an opportunity for the first time in a long while for the two of us to speak in private; or at least so I thought until Phèdre began pressing her ear to the wall, trying in vain to decipher the muffled conversation taking place beyond it.

I paced the storeroom, assessing its contents—sacks of grain, barrels of ale, nothing of use at the moment. I tested the door several times to confirm it was well and truly barred. Phèdre cocked her head at the ceiling, studying the rafters.

"How bad was it?" I asked her.

"Be quiet," she murmured, looking from the barrels to the rough-hewn rafters overhead. "Joscelin!" She scrambled atop a barrel. "Get over here and help me."

I eyed her dubiously, rolling a second barrel in place. "Are you mad?"

"The Skaldi are planning somewhat." Standing on her toes, she reached upward, gauging the distance. "If we do manage to escape and reach Ysandre de la Courcel, do you really want to tell her that the Skaldi have some dire plan, but so sorry, we couldn't hear it? Hoist up another, we need to get higher."

"You *are* mad," I grumbled, but I did as she asked and wrestled barrels.

Hoisting them into tiers was no easy feat, and three high was as tall as we dared go lest our efforts topple the whole thing.

Standing on the uppermost barrel, Phèdre stretched for the rafters, nowhere near within reach yet, then knelt. "Remember those Eglantine tumblers? Lift me onto your shoulders and boost me to the rafter, so I can hear the Allthing."

I looked up at the rafters, realizing just how precarious and risky this attempt was. "Phèdre . . . you can't."

"Yes," she said softly, extending her hand. "I can. What I can't do is lift you. But this is what I was trained to do, Joscelin. Let me do it."

Cursing myself for a fool under my breath, I took Phèdre's hand and scrambled atop the top barrel. Glancing at the white woolen gown she yet wore, I shrugged out of my mended grey mandilion. "At least take my coat." I eased it onto her and closed the fasteners, uncomfortably aware of her nearness. "It's filthy up there, no need to tell them where you've been."

She nodded gravely and I dropped to one knee before my heart could crack for a third time, afraid it might shatter into pieces if it did. Phèdre stepped carefully onto my shoulders. I grasped her ankles and rose, feeling her weight sway as she reached upward. "Joscelin," she whispered. "Lift my feet."

Praying silently, I tightened my grip around her ankles and hoisted her overhead. For a few heartbeats, she swayed alarmingly; and then her weight vanished as she secured a grip on the rafter and swung herself astride it. Glancing down at me, she put one finger to her lips, then pointed and began inching forward.

Name of Elua, I hadn't expected her to actually crawl above the gods-bedamned meeting space.

There was nothing I could do but wait, and it was one of the longest waits of my life. I descended from the barrels and paced the little storeroom, listening to the rise and fall of half-heard discussion. It was an exercise in futility, for as much as my grasp of the Skaldic tongue had improved, it wouldn't have been enough to follow what sounded to be lengthy and detailed speeches of crowd-pleasing oratory. It seemed as though it went on for hours, and mayhap it did, before at last I caught sight of Phèdre wriggling backward atop the high rafter, trying not to snag her skirts on the coarse splinters.

I scrambled back atop the highest barrel. "Get down!" I hissed, reaching for her. She lowered herself to dangle from the rafter until my hands closed around her ankles. "Let go, I've got you."

Releasing her grip, Phèdre slid through my arms as I eased her carefully down until I had her by the waist. She shuddered and clung to me, pressing her face against my chest, slowing her breath. "They mean to invade," she whispered, looking up at me with shock and tears in her eyes. "They mean to take the entire realm and that cursed d'Aiglemort's given them a way to do it. Joscelin, this goes far beyond border raids. We have to find a way to warn them."

"We will." I cupped her face in my hands, brushed away her tears. "I swear to you, Phèdre, I'll get us out of here." I could see her draw strength from my certainty, even though both of us knew the odds weren't good. In the main chamber, sounds of the Allthing shifted in tone.

"The barrels," Phèdre said in alarm, and I let her go. The two of us scrambled to return the barrels to their original formation.

When we finished, the Allthing had yet to conclude. Phèdre had made her retreat when the talk turned from invasion to individual grievances, and there were a great many grievances to be aired and settled. We had time upon finishing to work the worst of the grime out of her gown and my coat.

I glanced at her from time to time and caught her doing the same. It was hard to believe she'd done what I'd just witnessed. "You know," I said to her, "when I was assigned to attend you, I nearly thought it was a punishment of some sort. I thought you were nothing but an expensive plaything for the descendants of the Misguided."

"Oh, I was," she said bitterly, tugging on the diamond that hung below her throat. "I still am. If I weren't, you and I wouldn't be here, and Alcuin and my lord Delaunay would still be alive."

"No." I shook my head. "You weren't part of Melisande's plan. You just got in the way of it."

"I let it happen." There was a savage note of self-loathing in her voice. "I let her use me, I let her mislead me. Tonight Waldemar Selig will use me as he sees fit. And Elua help me, I'll welcome it when he does. While I eat my heart out with anguish, I'll prove to him a thousand times over exactly how debauched and yielding a D'Angeline whore can be, and I'll thank him for it when he's done."

Phèdre's mask slipped so very seldom, my heart ached to see what lay beneath it. "Then do it, and live!" I said fiercely to her. "And when Selig crosses onto D'Angeline soil and I'm there to plant ten inches of steel in his guts, I'll thank *him* for the pleasure of it." She stared at me for a moment, brows quirked, then burst into unexpected laughter. Recognizing the relative absurdity of my boast, I offered a rueful smile of acknowledgment as the White Brethren unbarred the door to release us.

There was yet another feast to mark the conclusion of the Allthing that night. It pleased Selig to show off his new acquisitions. I was once again ordered to stand guard at his shoulder, serving as a living example of a D'Angeline warrior beaten and molded into compliance. Let the Skaldi think whatever they liked, my only concern was keeping Phèdre alive and whole. Selig had her seated beside him; it seemed he'd determined that it was a greater show of power to treat her as a prize than a common maidservant. Waldemar the Blessed, proof against steel, had no fear of enemy captives. He wasn't as crudely possessive as Gunter, but he made a point of demonstrating his control over Phèdre in subtle ways, feeding her morsels from his own plate and the like. Whatever she thought about it wasn't evident in her expression. Her mask was firmly in place.

I'd expected Selig to make another long evening of it, but he rose after the third round of songs, bidding the tribesfolk to enjoy his hospitality. He dismissed me for the night, then turned to a pair of his ever-present White Brethren and nodded at Phèdre. "Bring her to my room."

There was nothing I could do save stand at attention and let them pass. The bawdy jokes and laughter had already begun; somewhere in the hall, Gunter was bellowing out a humorous and unnecessarily detailed lament for all the lascivious pleasures lost to him. Flanked by White Brethren, Phèdre ignored the jeers. She walked with her head high and the Skaldi fell silent as she passed.

I saw the dirty elbows of her gown and smiled a little.

No one bade me what to do in Selig's absence. It was assumed that I'd simply drink until I passed out or staggered home like any thane. Instead I explored the great hall to the extent I dared without jeopardizing the Skaldis' trust. There were four White Brethren on duty at all hours and they kept a careful watch on me as I wandered. Eventually I gave up and found a quiet corner to sleep.

For a mercy, Waldemar Selig's bedchamber was far enough from the main hall that any sounds that might emanate from it were faint. But in the morning, Selig had a sated air of pleasure, while there were shadows under Phèdre's eyes and she kept her gaze averted. Ascertaining as best I could that Selig hadn't injured her, I didn't press the matter, leaving her as much dignity as grace allowed.

The tribes were making ready to return to their own steadings, packing up supplies and tents, giving their mounts a good feed and watering before departing. Selig spent the morning touring the encampment, ordering me to accompany him along with a half dozen of the White Brethren. I paused before responding, disliking the idea of leaving Phèdre unattended in uncertain circumstances.

"She is *mine*. No one in my hall will lay a finger on her." Waldemar Selig raised his brows. "Do you question it?"

I gritted my teeth, bowed my head, and lied. "No, my lord."

If Phèdre had stayed put, he probably would have been right, but Selig hadn't realized he needed to order her thusly. He'd determined that she was exactly what I'd believed, nothing more than a plaything for the wealthy. It never occurred to him that Phèdre wouldn't simply stay where he left her. Of course, it also wouldn't have occurred to him that she'd crawl onto a beam over a twenty-foot drop to eavesdrop on the Allthing.

I knew, and I should have been warier of her impulsive streak. But I hadn't fully reckoned on her sentimentality. There were folk from Gunter's steading, even a couple of thanes, who had been kind to her after their own fashion, and she had spent many long hours with Hedwig and the women listening to their songs; those hearth-songs of the mothers, wives, and daughters of Skaldi warriors left behind when their men went raiding.

Waldemar Selig took his time visiting the various steadings' encampments, taking time to share a word of fellowship or a jest with every chieftain. Some of them he drew out of earshot for private discussions. There was no hiding the fact that the Skaldi were setting forth to prepare for war, but Selig was careful to ensure I heard no details.

As Gunter's steading had been one of the last to arrive, our encampment was farther along the frozen lakeshore and one of the last that Selig headed toward. The sound of the fracas coming from a Gambrivii camp ahead of us was unsurprising—even in good fellowship, the Skaldi were always ready for a brawl.

And then I saw that Phèdre was at the center of it.

I'd been scared before, but not like this. A pile of Gambrivii tribe thanes were kicking and pounding a fellow on the blood-spattered snow; another thane had pinned Phèdre's arms from behind and was pressing against her.

All the fury I repressed every bedamned minute of the day burst forth in a single shout. "*Phèdre!*"

I vaulted from the saddle without thinking and drew my sword.

I killed the first two Gambrivii to draw steel. The one holding Phèdre loosed her to draw his own blade and charge me. I moved smoothly out of the way, scoring his side as he passed. The Gambrivii regrouped to encircle and close in upon me. I fought in a tight circle of my own, defending the four quadrants with sword and vambraces. Somewhere a deep Skaldic voice was roaring orders I ignored, too busy fighting for my life to decipher the words. A short spear jabbed at me. I angled away from it, shifting into a forward thrust.

It never landed.

I'd been taught by and trained with some of the finest swordsmen in the world. I was one of them. And I'd never in my life seen anyone fight with the natural ability and brute grace of Waldemar Selig. He waded into the fray as fearlessly as though he truly was proof against steel, using his shoulders to shove the Gambrivii aside. "D'Angeline, I ordered you to *stop*!" he shouted. Sweeping my blade aside in an effortless parry, he stepped completely inside my guard and brought the pommel of his sword crashing against my left temple.

It felt like I'd been hit by a mallet. For the second time since I'd been abducted, I fell to my knees, my sword slipping from my grip, black spots clouding my vision.

Waldemar Selig regarded me with disgust before turning to the White Brethren. "Kill him."

"*No!*" Phèdre flung herself to her knees before him, hands clasped, a frantic note in her voice. "My lord, please, let him live! He was only honoring his vow to protect me, I swear. Please. I will do anything, anything you wish, in exchange for his life."

"You will do it anyway," Selig said impassively.

She said nothing and I couldn't see her face, but from her silence and the set of her shoulders I knew that a trace of that unexpected adamance showed in it.

What Selig might have said in response to it, I don't know. He was spared the need by Knud, kind, homely Knud from Gunter's steading. He was the one the Gambrivii had been beating. Now he limped over to nudge the body of a fallen thane with the toe of one boot, nodding at his undone breeches and his exposed phallus, pale and shriveled. "Found this useless prick trying to get atop the lass, Lord Selig," he said. "It's true, the lad's oath-bound to protect her. Gunter used it to keep 'em tame."

Still on my knees, I fought to remain conscious.

Waldemar Selig regarded the Gambrivii tribesmen with a thunderous scowl. "Who spoke against this?" he asked them. "No one? Would you let a man steal my horse? My sword? No?" Reaching down, he grabbed a handful of Phèdre's hair and gave it an ungentle shake. "This woman is as much my property."

I tried to protest, but the blurred world was sliding sideways, and the last I remember is my cheek striking the snow.

CHAPTER THIRTY

I woke up in chains.

I was alone in an empty woodcutter's hut, my head splitting with pain. My weapons and vambraces were gone. There were manacles around my wrists and ankles, a chain connecting them, and a longer chain attached to an iron ring on a stake driven into the floor of the hut. I sat upright too quickly and set my head to swimming anew.

Phèdre.

I scrambled to my feet, her name shooting through my thoughts like a meteor; then wobbled at having risen too fast. Blessed Elua have mercy, after all the careless abuse she'd endured, my ward had nigh been violated in public; were it not for Knud, it would have been worse. And I would have been too late.

Instead I'd drawn my sword to kill.

A wave of furious self-loathing broke over me. And what in Elua's blessed name had Phèdre been thinking? She'd taken a needless risk trusting Selig's mantle to protect her amidst a vast camp of barbarian warriors. Nonetheless, I should have waited. One command from Selig would have put an end to the fracas without further violence. But no, two men were dead because Phèdre was impulsive and I acted without thinking. I shouldn't have drawn to kill. It was a violation of my vows. I could have defended her with daggers alone. I could blame it on extreme provocation, I could say I'd lost my wits in battle-rage. It didn't change the truth. No one had to die. I'd *wanted* them dead. And then Waldemar Selig took me down with all the careless ease of a man swatting a fly. Now I was in disgrace, chained in isolation amidst the rubble of broken vows, any goodwill I'd accumulated squandered, and Phèdre in a more vulnerable and precarious position than ever. And I'd put her there.

Gunter had been clever enough to realize that ensuring Phèdre's safety was a means of keeping me in line; tame, as he liked to say. Selig, twice as clever and a good deal more dangerous, had realized that keeping me alive was a means of controlling Phèdre. Not only had I failed at every turn to safeguard her, but I'd become nothing more than a liability, a weapon to be wielded against her.

I broke.

My soul was a blown-out candle. I dropped back to my knees, lowering my head. Here I was again, alone in chains, my head aching, my battered body stiff with a bone-deep cold that would only get worse. I'd failed too many times. I'd failed Phèdre, failed myself, I'd failed House Verreuil, I'd failed the Cassiline Brotherhood. I'd failed Cassiel himself, Blessed Elua and his Companions, Adonai the Creator. Better I should have died at birth than bring such an abundance of shame upon all that I held dear.

For the first time, I envied Selwyn the manner of his death. Too soon, too young, yes; but he'd *chosen* it. He'd never known the bitter taste of defeat. He'd died victorious, albeit in defense of the traitor d'Aiglemort. I'd chosen nothing. From the moment that Melisande Shahrizai betrayed us, I'd reacted out of blind fury. I'd been defeated at every turn, beaten into unconsciousness so many times my skull must surely be dented.

And it had accomplished nothing.

Now there was nothing I could even attempt to do.

There was a certain peace in succumbing to total despair. I looked at my red, cold-blistered hands wrapped in rags. They'd never had a chance to heal fully from my imprisonment in the dog pen. Empty hands, useless hands. I'd slain three men with these hands. I'd mourned the first death for its sheer unnecessariness, but at least Evrard the Sharptongued was an armed man determined to fight to the death. Not this time. I'd gone straight for my sword and killed at least two Gambrivii out of hand. And as a result, I was foresworn, more useless than ever, chained in exile, my very living, breathing existence nothing more than a threat to keep Phèdre compliant.

Unless . . . unless I didn't exist.

The thought rolled over me like a great, dark wave, dragging me under to quiet depths. It was peaceful there.

It didn't feel like making a choice, but rather setting down a burden too heavy to carry. I'd tried; Blessed Elua knew I'd tried, but all my decisions had been bad ones. Dying quietly was the best thing I could do. The trail of bloodshed and broken vows that stretched behind me would end. It meant breaking my utmost vow, the one that mattered a thousandfold more than any other, and abandoning my ward.

But in a sense, it was the only way I could see to keep it.

I didn't make any grand, dramatic gestures. It would have been difficult even if I'd wanted to. The hut held nothing but a pile of straw and a blanket and, just beyond my reach, a small brazier eking out a trickle of warmth. There was nothing I could use to take my own life, but it didn't matter. My body was ready to accept its demise.

Like a racehorse ridden too hard, too fast, too long, I'd stumbled to my knees before reaching the finishing line, my heart bursting. Now I was ready to stretch my neck in the sand and die.

Outside the hut, there was ongoing bustle as the camps departed for their respective steadings. One of Selig's thanes brought me a wooden bowl full of cold pottage. Still nauseated from the blow to my head, I found it easy to eschew eating. By the next day, I settled into a strange feeling of calm. All the ever-present harm dealt to my body, the exposure and privation, the beatings and dragging, the multitude of bruises and cuts in various stages of healing; all of that began to fall away. All of the hurts to my spirit, the defeat and humiliation, the brief glimmers of hope squashed, the broken pride, the devastating futility—all of those began to fall away, too.

On the third morning, the thane who came to retrieve yesterday's bowl took notice of the fact that it was untouched. He spoke gruffly to me, but his words came from far away, too far to make sense of them. I was glad when he left. I don't know to whom he reported, but I was surprised out of my downward-spiraling reverie by the appearance of Harald the Beardless of Gunter's steading, who had always been kind to Phèdre and reasonably decent to me.

"Hey, man." Harald had brought a low wooden stool, slinging it on the frozen ground and taking a seat. "I hear you're not eating. Why?"

I licked my parched lips, forming words with difficulty. "Why are you here?"

He braced his elbows on his knees. "Every steading left a go-between. Gunter chose me. Why are you not eating?" I shook my head; there was no point in attempting to explain it. Lowering his voice, he leaned forward. "You're not doing her any good, you know."

I met Harald's gaze. He had earnest blue eyes and shaggy blond locks, and his beard was finally coming in, a thick bronze scruff that hid the lingering traces of soft adolescence in his features. "I couldn't keep her safe from Gunter," I said to him. "Nor from Waldemar Selig. All I can do is stop making things worse."

"But—"

I cut him off. "And what do you think will happen to Phèdre when Selig tires of her? Will he gift her to some foreign prince? Or throw her like a bone for his thanes to fight over?"

Harald flushed. "I would bid for her hand myself!"

"And would you set her free if she did not come willing to your bed?" I inquired.

He averted his gaze, his flush deepening. "She would be my wife," he muttered. "It is more than Gunter or Waldemar Selig offered, and she went willing to their beds."

"That is a lie you are telling yourself." I let my eyes close. "Now go away."

It was a blessed relief to be left in peace. I drifted in the tranquil depths between being and not-being, kneeling with crossed forearms as though I were keeping Elua's vigil on the Longest Night. There was a piece of hide tacked above the open doorway of the hut. I watched the shadows lengthen around it, dimming to twilight and then to black.

Blackness.

Emptiness.

Peace.

When the sun rose, I saw the shadow of booted feet passing the hut, but no one brought food. I reckoned that after speaking with Harald the Not-so-Beardless, Waldemar Selig or one of his lieutenants had determined that it was best for all concerned to allow me to choose this path for myself.

I was wrong.

Later that day, the hide was flung back and sunlight illuminated the hut. I cracked open my eyes to see two figures standing in the doorway—the slight one was Phèdre, and the tall one Selig. All I could do was blink at them. Phèdre darted forward and knelt before me, peering at my haggard face. "You idiot!" she hissed in D'Angeline. "What are you doing?"

It was like being dashed in the face with a bucket of ice water, and I stared blankly at her for a moment. "I dishonored my vow." The words emerged in a cracked whisper. "I drew to kill."

"Blessed Elua, that's all?" She sat back on her heels, looking disgusted, then turned to Selig. "He grieves for his wrongdoing," she said to him in Skaldic. "He is atoning."

It was true, and if it were far from the whole truth, it was one that Waldemar Selig understood. "Tell him to live," he said to her. "I have paid weregild for the lives of the men he killed. And I wish him to teach me his manner of fighting." Turning to me, he repeated his words in Caerdicci.

It startled a wild laugh out of me. "My lord, you bested me with ease," I replied in Caerdicci. "Why would you want to learn what I know?"

Selig shrugged. "You didn't expect to battle me. You have given me your pledge. And you did not expect me to step inside your guard. Another time, it might be different."

I turned to Phèdre, shaking my head. "I can't teach him to fight like a Cassiline," I said in D'Angeline. "It's just not possible without years of training. I've failed you too many times. I've dishonored my vow. Better I should die."

I'd expected a measure of understanding, a measure of sympathy.

I got neither.

Phèdre's eyes blazed with righteous fury and the air around her grew taut and shivery, edged with the acrid scent of forge-hot bronze. "How many times do you need to discover your humanity, Joscelin?" she demanded. "You're not Cassiel reborn, but you are vowed to me and I've never needed your service more!" I stared at her, wondering how in the world Selig, leaning idly against a wall, didn't sense what I did. Phèdre grabbed my shoulders with a surprisingly hard grip and shook me. "Do you remember what Delaunay said? 'To fail and persevere is a harder test than any you will meet in the training yard. Keep your sword, I can't afford its loss.'"

Another desperate laugh escaped me. "I can't, Phèdre. I just can't do it any longer." I addressed Selig in Caerdicci. "I'm sorry, my lord. I'm not worthy of living."

Before I could say anything further, Phèdre erupted in seething rage. Swearing in every tongue she knew—which included one I didn't even recognize—she shoved me so hard I toppled sideways in my chains, then stood over me and planted her fists on her hips. "Elua curse you if that's all the courage you've got!" She narrowed those lustrous, dart-pricked eyes at me. "If I live through this, I swear to you, I'm writing a letter to your Prefect and telling him how Blessed Elua was better served by a courtesan of the Night Court than a Cassiline Brother!"

It stung hard.

It stung because it was true, it stung because it pricked the Cassiline pride I'd thought gone and buried. It stung because after all we'd been through, I'd given up, while Phèdre stood before me radiant in her anger; improbably stubborn and resilient, challenging my courage and honor. And most of all it stung because that was the third and final chisel-strike to my heart, bursting it into shards, the broken temple of my soul lying in its rubble. A bone-deep truth I'd been trying to deny had grown too immense to ignore.

Blessed Elua have mercy, I loved her.

I was also furious at her. "You will *not*!"

"Then stop me." She brushed bits of straw from her skirts. "Protect and serve, Cassiline."

"It's hard, Phèdre," I said quietly. "Elua help me, but it's hard."

"I know," she whispered.

Whatever Waldemar Selig had understood of our exchange, it didn't trouble him. He called to one of his thanes, who entered the hut carrying a wooden bowl of steaming broth. "Eat," Selig said to me in D'Angeline. "Live." With an effort, I opened hands half-frozen into discolored claws, accepting the bowl. They took their leave, Phèdre glancing back at me just once. The warmth of the bowl eased my hands. I lowered my head and took a sip, saliva flooding my mouth at the taste. My body reluctantly began to awaken from its torpor, forcing me to confront my revelation.

Love.

It was a terrifying word. There were plenty of cadets like Selwyn who were expelled from the Prefectory before reaching their journeyman year, but in all of the Brotherhood's recorded history, I couldn't recall an incident in which a fully sworn Cassiline warrior-priest violated his oath for the sake of romantic love.

Not that I intended to, of course. One could love from afar, and if ever there were occasion that called for discreet grace and understanding, this surely was it.

First and foremost, I needed to keep myself alive and regain strength and health. It was the second time I'd been down this path, and this time my body was slower to heal; especially my fingers, which continued to blister and ache, although at least it was an excuse to avoid training sessions with Waldemar Selig. As much as I longed to have my blades restored, I will own, there was a part of me still in shock over how handily he'd been able to defeat me, and I was reluctant to confront it.

After discovering how dangerously low I'd sunk, Phèdre managed to visit me every day. It would have been wildly uncomfortable if she'd known how I felt, but I concealed it. There was no way in Adonai's creation that I would add the weight of my feelings to the burden she already carried. There was always a thane on guard with her, so we were careful never to speak of strategy, even in D'Angeline, but merely of familiar innocuous things that evoked memories of comfort. Although she didn't say it outright, I had the impression that her position in Selig's steading was resented by the others.

I wondered, often, what she was feeling. Fear and quiet, constant fury, I think; toward me, mostly frustration with a touch of concern. I had no one but myself to blame for it. From the beginning of our misadventure, I'd picked my battles foolishly.

No more.

Waldemar Selig grew sufficiently impatient at my delay to summon a healer, Lodur the One-Eyed, who was a priest of their god Odhinn the All-Father. This fellow was nothing like the priest who'd mumbled over bones in the oak grove at Gunter's steading. He was an odd bird, white-haired and wild, bare-chested save for a wolfskin vest, with a patch over one eye. His good eye was a pale, icy blue and he brought the scent of fir trees and clean snow with him. Selig looked thoughtful. I think that one-eyed old priest may have been the only person he truly respected.

"Let's see 'em, boy," Lodur said, squatting before me. His skin was tan and weathered by the elements. He examined my cracked, suppurating hands and wrists. "Ah, I've one of my mother's recipes will do for that." He fished around in a leather satchel and withdrew a stoppered jar of balm. It stank of rancid grease and pungent herbs as he slathered it on me.

"Lord Selig wishes that you become well enough to teach him your manner of fighting," Phèdre informed me in Caerdicci.

I inclined my head. Even if it was a futile effort, I meant to do my best. "I look forward to it, my lord. To teach the Cassiline style, I will require my arms; or at least a wooden training sword and daggers."

"The Skaldi do not train with wooden toys," Selig said. "I sent your arms to my smith to duplicate their design." He addressed Lodur the One-Eyed in the Skaldic tongue. "Are you done, old master?"

"Oh, nearly." Lodur drew a number of improbably clean linen strips from his satchel and began wrapping my balm-smeared hands and wrists. "He'll heal quickly now. These D'Angelines, they've gods' blood in their veins. It's old and faint, but even a trace of it's a powerful thing, Waldemar Berundson."

It was the only time I heard anyone refer to him by his patronymic birth-name, and I suspect no one else would have dared. A whiff of the ordinary ran contrary to the supernatural mythos of Waldemar the Blessed, who frowned in response, hearing a warning in Lodur's words. "Old and powerful, and corrupted by generations of softness. Their gods will bow their heads to the All-Father, and we will claim the magic of their blood for our own descendants and infuse it with red-blooded Skaldi vigor."

The old priest gave Selig a wintry one-eyed glance. "May it be as you say, young Waldemar. I have lived too long to strong-arm the gods."

I flexed my hands in their clean bandages, already feeling a measure of ease. I wasn't entirely sure what had transpired between the two, having guessed at a number of unfamiliar Skaldic words, but it heartened me to see Waldemar Selig discomfited.

Lodur spoke the truth; I healed quickly. I've no idea what was in that balm, but it drew out the poisons. My blisters began to shrink, the cracked fissures to close. Within three days, my hands and wrists had healed enough that I could wield a blade without doing further harm to myself.

It was such a relief to have my chains struck and my arms returned, I was nigh light-hearted. Having spent my journeyman year as a mentor to the Second Cohort, I knew that I was a tolerably good teacher. While I had no intention of training an enemy warlord in the true intricacies of the Cassiline technique, I needed to make the semblance of a genuine effort before he grew bored. Over recent days, I'd put a lot of thought into how I might break down the Cassiline style to its simplest essence.

I began by using a long branch to draw a circle in the packed snow of the semi-secluded glade that Selig had chosen, marking the quadrants and adding the steps of the first pattern. I walked through it empty-handed at a moderate pace.

Waldemar Selig wasn't pleased. "What is this?" he asked me, making a dismissive twirling gesture. "It's not fighting."

He'd brought Phèdre with him, as well as a pair of White Brethren. The latter looked suspicious, while Phèdre was concealing a faint spark of amusement. "It is the Cassiline way of training, my lord," she said to him.

Selig eyed me dubiously, and I bowed. "It is true, my lord. We begin at ten years of age, but we do not train with weapons until our thirteenth year."

"I killed a grown man when I was twelve." He tested the heft of his new Cassiline-style longsword. "Show me the fighting."

I sighed. Already knowing he wouldn't find it to his liking, I ignored a frisson of wrongness and drew my sword, setting my feet and angling my blade. "As my lord wishes. This is a two-handed parry we call Splitting Lightning—"

"You call it a name?" Selig interrupted me. "Why do you call it a name?"

I halted my demonstration. "Well . . . because it has one, I suppose. Some of the names may sound a trifle foolish, but it makes them easier to remember."

"Remember?" He sounded genuinely bewildered. "There is no time to remember the name of a thing in the middle of a battle."

"Not for my lord, no," I said. "But those of us who were not born great warriors must train for many years to earn the gifts with which you have been blessed. This is the manner of that training, which you have asked me to teach you."

At least that pleased him, and Blessed Elua knew it was true. Selig *was* that good, and he had far too much experience to unlearn and start anew. He grew increasingly impatient with the notion that one must practice these movements and forms until repetition was second nature. For Selig, fighting truly was first nature to him. By the end of our third session, he'd come to the conclusion that this was a waste of time.

"You tried, Josslin Verai," he said to me, clapping one heavy hand on my shoulder. "You are good at what you do. But it is not what I do."

"True, my lord," I agreed. "It is not what you do. But I have made a good-faith effort to teach it to you."

Selig chuckled. "You think I should trust you because of it. No. Let us see if you can continue to be reasonable." He called to his thanes to take me back to the hut to be manacled and chained.

I tried not to be overly disappointed. At least I'd managed to be obedient and keep my temper. If I could remain patient longer, Selig might relent and give me a second chance to serve as one of his thanes. According to what Phèdre had gleaned eavesdropping on the Allthing, the Skaldi were waiting until summer to invade, when it would be feasible to supply an entire army on the march. I could afford to bide my time and earn my way back into Selig's good graces. But it sounded as though there was renewed activity around the steading, which didn't bode well. Since nothing was certain, I occupied myself by exercising to the extent that my chains allowed, as well as working to loosen the stake to which they were attached. It was a good thing I did.

"Look," I said to Phèdre upon her next visit, nudging the wobbling stake. "What's happening out there?"

"Kolbjorn of the Manni is here," she said. I didn't know what that betokened, but the tremor in her voice brought my head up sharply. "Joscelin, he brought a letter from the south. It was routed through Caerdicca Unitas." She wrapped her arms around herself. "I saw the seal. It was from Melisande."

It shocked me into silence for a moment. "What did it say?"

Phèdre shook her head. "I didn't have a chance to see it. But I know she assured him d'Aiglemort doesn't suspect anything."

"Do you think that's true?" I asked.

"I don't know," she admitted. "It might be true, or it might be that she's playing Selig into d'Aiglemort's hands." Although we were speaking in D'Angeline and the White Brother on guard stood outside the hut, she lowered her voice. "Either way, the Crown falls and Melisande stands to gain. Joscelin, could you kill a man with your bare hands?"

I stared at her. "Why do you ask?"

She told me.

In honor of this Kolbjorn's visit, Selig had planned a great hunting excursion on the morrow. Phèdre was proposing that we attempt an escape while a good portion of the steading was afield. It was reasonably simple, wildly foolhardy, and it commenced with me killing a man in cold blood.

I paced as far as my chains would permit, trying to sort out my thoughts. "You're asking me to deliberately betray my vows," I said without looking at her. "To attack and kill unprovoked goes against all the tenets I've sworn to honor. What you're asking . . . Phèdre, it's murder."

Her voice was soft. "I know."

There were many things I might have said, theological and practical arguments to be parsed, but in the end it would have changed nothing. The matter lay between us. Phèdre knew exactly what she was asking me, and by the determined set of her slender shoulders, she was prepared to bear the weight of it.

I could do no less.

I met her gaze and nodded. "I will do what you ask."

CHAPTER THIRTY-ONE

Aside from the part wherein I killed a man, the majority of our plans rested on Phèdre's shoulders. It was difficult for me to accept, but the truth was that every action I'd undertaken had been impulsive and ended badly. It was her restraint that had kept us both alive, including pleading for my life on more than one occasion. Now she had a plan and a driving sense of urgency. Anafiel Delaunay had trained his pupils in observation and analysis, and I'd learned at last to appreciate the merits of it.

It was time I let myself trust her.

Once it was decided, I felt a sense of clarity and purpose. I worked at the iron stake until it was fully loose, then replaced it carefully. I ate every scrap of food brought to me and drank deep from the water bucket, preparing my body for the hardship that lay ahead. I took light exercise, just enough to keep my body limber in the cold, and slept as long and as deeply as possible.

In the morning, I could hear the hunting party assembling, then departing to cheers and fanfare and hunting horns. That was the sign I was listening for. Phèdre would visit as soon as she could after the party's departure, escorted by one of the White Brethren left behind to guard her. I wiggled the stake loose and tested the length of the chain between my manacled wrists. It would be easier if my wrists and ankles weren't bound together, but there was enough slack to do what was necessary.

It would depend on the element of surprise, though. That's what made it murder.

Inside the dark hut, I knelt and prayed. "Cassiel, forgive me for what I am about to do," I whispered. "I do not ask for grace on my behalf, but for the sake of my ward. Let me be damned, so long as I don't fail her again."

Something stirred in my soul, a sullen glow like banked embers buried below cold, dead ashes. I rose and bowed, then took a stance beside the hide covering the doorway, drew my chains taut, and bided my time. It wasn't long before I saw the shadow of feet approaching. The hide was drawn back and Phèdre entered, backlit and blinking against the dimness of the hut. She spotted me and nodded, stepping smoothly to one side. The diamond hanging from her throat caught a ray of sunlight and scintillated like a star. The White Brother on escort duty followed her inside the hut.

I had a length of chain around his throat before the hide flap closed. Partially protected by his wolfskin hood, he fought back, digging in his heels, hands dragging at my arms while he fought to draw breath and call for aid. I kneed him ruthlessly in the back. Letting go of the chain as he crumpled, I grabbed his head in both hands and gave it a sharp twist. The thane's neck broke with a loud crack, and I lowered him to the floor.

Phèdre removed the brooch pinning her cloak. "Give me your hands." I held them out, and she made short work of the clasps on the manacles. "Thank you, Hyacinthe," she murmured, dropping to her knees to unlock the shackles on my ankles while I rubbed my stiff, chafed wrists. Sitting on her heels, Phèdre looked up at me. "We need to strip him."

I nodded. "Let's do it."

Stripping a dead body is an unpleasant and unwieldy task, but we worked swiftly together. I donned the White Brother's attire in place of the threadbare rags of my Cassiline greys.

"Let me see you." Phèdre beckoned for me to sit on the stool. She unbound my hair from its single braid and shook it out, then grabbed a handful of dirty ashes from the brazier, rubbing it into my hair and face. Fingers flying, she twined a handful of small braids hanging on either side of my face to shadow my features. Satisfied with her handiwork, she held out the thane's white wolf-pelt. "Here."

Sliding the wolfskin over my shoulders, I knotted the forelegs as the White Brethren did and drew the hood over my head, empty eye sockets hanging low over my brow. I felt foolish, but Phèdre assured me I looked the part.

"The great hall will be the worst of it," she said. "I couldn't bring a satchel without arousing suspicion, but we need more clothing and a tinderbox, and Melisande's letter is there. We can get the rest of the stores from the lesser hall, there are fewer folk about."

"I need my arms," I said.

She frowned. "They're not Skaldi weapons. Take Trygve's."

So that was the name of the man I'd just murdered.

"I need my vambraces," I said. "I'm not trained to fight with a shield, you saw as much in the holmgang." I paused, lowering my voice. "They were bequeathed to me by my uncle, and his uncle before him, Phèdre. Let me keep that much."

"All right." She wasn't going to waste time arguing. "Take Trygve's for now, it will look strange if you don't have them. Keep your head down and look sullen. If anyone speaks, shake your head. If they persist . . ." She switched to Skaldic. "Say 'Selig's orders. He's making camp.'"

"Selig's orders. He's making camp," I repeated.

She made me repeat it several times, correcting my accent until it was good enough to pass for a native speaker. "Oh, and treat me like dirt," she added. "Are we ready?"

"One moment." We had moved the White Brother's—Trygve's—body into the deepest shadows of the hut. I knelt beside him and murmured the Cassiline prayer for the dead, then rose and buckled his sword belt in place. I slung his round shield over my shoulder. "Let's go."

It was bright enough outside that I was grateful for the wolfskin hood shadowing my eyes. Gripping Phèdre's upper arm hard, I steered her toward the lesser hall. One of the housecarls approached, touching his forelock in a gesture of respect for one of the White Brethren. "How may I serve you?" he inquired.

This, I hadn't expected. I felt Phèdre tense beneath my grip, and gave her arm a rough shake. "Tell him."

She cleared her throat. "My lord Selig has decided to make camp with Kolbjorn and a few thanes. He's sent for a skin of mead, two sacks of pottage, and a cookpot. Bring them to the stable. Trygve will ride to meet them."

"Only one skin of mead?" the housecarl inquired.

"Three!" I growled. Giving Phèdre's arm another hard shake, I turned away as though impatient, towing her in my wake. Behind us, I heard the housecarl calling for assistance with supplies.

My grip on Phèdre's arm was hard enough to leave bruises, but I didn't dare drop my pretense. When we reached the doors of the great hall, I yanked her before me, shoving her with enough force that she stumbled. Gathering herself, she straightened and glared at me. I glared back at her.

It was enough to get us through the open hall to Selig's bedchamber unheeded. There, Phèdre pointed to a cupboard she'd unlocked earlier. I retrieved my arms, buckled my vambraces in place, and exchanged Trygve's sword belt for my own, daggers settling neatly into their sheaths. I donned my baldric, concealing the scabbard under the wolfskin. Phèdre tangled my long hair around the hilt of my sword to hide it. My blades needed tending. I couldn't find materials with which to properly clean them, but I found a whetstone and a leather pouch of bear-grease, as well as a tinderbox, while Phèdre withdrew woolen breeches and tunics, stuffing them into a pair of saddlebags.

She fetched Melisande's letter from the topmost shelf and showed it to me before stowing it in a bag. It was written on thick vellum, the broken wax seal imprinted with the distinctive House Shahrizai emblem of three intertwined keys.

"You're sure it's her?" I whispered.

"It's signed," she murmured in reply. "And I know her handwriting."

There was somewhat disturbingly intimate about the comment. I hadn't given thought to how this cruel twist to Melisande's betrayal had affected Phèdre. Whatever lay between them, it was powerful.

But there was no time for that now. I grabbed the saddlebags. "Are you ready?"

Phèdre nodded; then froze. "No. Wait. Melisande's letter."

I hoisted one of the bags. "It's in here."

"I know." She grabbed it from my hand and rummaged frantically for the letter. "I wasn't thinking. Selig has no idea that we know his plan to betray d'Aiglemort. If we take Melisande's letter, we tip our hand. He'll alter his plans accordingly, and any advantage will be lost. We'll have to forgo proof." Finding the letter, she stood on her toes to replace it on the top shelf of the cupboard. "All right. Let's go."

The good fortune that had won us clear passage upon entering the great hall failed us upon departure. A woman I'd never laid eyes on emerged from the kitchen to intercept us; more specifically, to intercept *me*. "Where are you going now?" she demanded. "Trygve, you promised!"

So she was sweet on the man I'd just killed, which meant she'd see through my disguise in a few more steps. I lowered my head and continued to drag Phèdre toward the door. "Selig's orders."

Looking dubious, the woman kept advancing. "*I* never heard anything about it!"

Phèdre shook my hand from her arm and stepped between us. "And why would you?" she asked, her words dripping with disdain. "Does Lord Selig send for *you* when he desires pleasure? Does he send for any woman in his steading?" She cast a contemptuous glance around the hall and the Skaldi gaping in surprise. "No, he does not. Waldemar Selig is worthy of the title King and he sends for the only woman here worthy of pleasing a King." Her voice rose. "And if it is his pleasure to make camp and send for me to join him, anyone who would remain in his favor would be well advised not to question it!"

With that, she turned sharply and headed for the doors. I gave a disgusted shrug and followed her. Outside, Phèdre hurried in the direction of the stables. "Not so fast," I murmured to her. The carls tending the stables—which weren't much more than long rows of rough lean-tos in a large paddock—had scrambled to prepare for our departure. One came running at the sight of my White Brethren garb.

"The stores were sent, and we're saddling your horse, sir," he said respectfully. "Is it true Waldemar Selig is making camp this evening?"

"Selig's orders," I said.

"Lord Selig has sent for me," Phèdre announced in a haughty tone. "You will have my mount saddled as well." The carl looked at me to confirm permission. I gave a brusque nod, and he shouted to his stable lads. "And fodder for the horses," Phèdre added, turning toward me. "How many did Lord Selig say? A dozen?"

"Fodder for a dozen," I agreed.

I couldn't help but think that any moment now, our deception would be revealed; but no, the carls were eager to please one of the White Brethren, who were an extension of Waldemar Selig himself. They fetched the shaggy pony Phèdre had been given to ride on occasion, swiftly saddling it and loading packs of supplies on both mounts. I had to lash Selig's saddlebags in place atop them before swinging astride my—or Trygve's—horse. Once I'd done so, I realized that I'd no idea which way the hunt had gone. I snapped my fingers at Phèdre. She nudged her pony alongside mine, leaning forward to pat its neck. "Ride to the north end of the lake and up the mountain trail," she murmured in barely audible D'Angeline.

I gathered my reins. "Let's go."

We rode past a number of small encampments on our way to the shore of the big lake. Some of the visiting Manni tribe thanes called out cheerful obscenities along with accompanying gestures. I laughed in response and returned the gestures in kind.

At the far northern end of the lake, a trail made by mounted men and their hunting dogs led into the forests sloping along the basin. We followed it upward, grateful for the trampled snow. Both of us had our ears cocked for the sound of Selig's hunters ahead of us, but there were only the ordinary sounds of nature.

I drew rein atop the basin's rim. Phèdre gazed down at the steading far below us, the blue bowl of the lake. It was a wonder it wasn't frozen solid in this cold, it must be fed by hot springs. I blew on my icy fingers, marveling that we'd escaped Selig's steading with such relative ease. But I had no illusions; pursuit was inevitable, and the worst likely yet to come. "So. How shall we do this?"

"We'll follow the trail until we're out of sight of the steading. Then we head west." Phèdre shivered, wrapping her fur cloak tighter. "Joscelin, this is as far as my plan went. Thanks to Selig's maps, I know where we are, and I know where home lies." All the hauteur she'd summoned was gone, replaced by vulnerability. "How we get from here to there alive, I've no idea. All I know is that we'd best get as far as possible before they find us gone." Tears shimmered in her eyes. "And I didn't even think to get us a tent!"

"You found us a way out," I said. She'd had to be brave a long time, but I needed her to keep the spark of her courage alight. "I'll find us a way home. Remember, I was raised in the mountains."

It heartened her. "Lead onward."

We rode some distance along the hunter's trail before veering left toward the west. Some fifty yards into the unbroken snow, I dismounted and handed my mount's reins to Phèdre while I snapped a long-needled pine branch loose from its trunk. Wading back through our trail on foot, I used the branch to smooth over our tracks, erasing the sign of our passage. It cost us time, but if it worked, it would buy us more than it cost.

Upon returning to Phèdre and the waiting horses, I tossed the pine branch into the woods. "All right. Let's put some distance between us."

I'd forgotten one thing; indeed, both of us had. Selig had his White Brethren in their winter camouflage lurking around the outskirts of his territory. It was all a part of Waldemar the Blessed's mythos. So it came as a surprise when a pair of White Brethren burst from a hidden bunker in the seemingly untouched snow before us, short spears cocked for a throw. They checked at the sight of my white wolf-pelt.

"Well met, brother," one of them hailed me uncertainly, lowering his spear and trying to peer at my face under its wolf mask hood. "Where are you bound?"

My heart ached, but there was no going back and only one way forward. "Forgive me," I whispered, digging heels into my mount's flanks and drawing my sword as we charged. I rode down one White Brother before he even knew what was happening, one swift slice across the throat. The other scrambled backward, spear cocked. His gaze flickered with uncertainty as he sought to choose his target—me or my mount.

He chose me.

I dropped low on my horse's neck, clinging like a trick rider as the White Brother flung his spear at my heart. It passed harmlessly overhead and I swung back. He set his buckler and drew his sword, and it took me a few strokes to batter through his defenses. Arterial blood sprayed like a crimson fountain. Feeling sick at the carnage I'd wrought, I looked at Phèdre and saw my expression echoed in hers.

"It had to be done," she said softly.

I nodded and dismounted, wiping my blade clean with a bit of rag. One of the White Brethren—the fellow I'd slain first—wore crude fur mittens, one hand still clutching his unused spear. I eased the blood-spattered mittens from his hands and gave them to Phèdre. "Don't argue, just put them on."

She obeyed, and we set out again. Behind us, I heard the cacophonous calls of crows discovering the bodies.

It was hard going from there on out. At least it appeared that we were well and truly in uninhabited territory beyond the perimeter of the White Brethren, which was to the good, although I remained on high alert. We pressed the horses as hard as we dared, but the snow was so deep at times that it was chest-high on Phèdre's shaggy pony. We stopped at a narrow, fast-running stream to water the horses, taking care not to let them drink too much of the icy water. I emptied a couple of meadskins and refilled them from the stream. Phèdre made a face at our midday meal of dry pottage oats and cold water, but she didn't complain. From time to time, I dismounted to break a trail on foot to spare my mount. It got my blood moving and helped allay the biting cold. When I saw Phèdre shivering in the saddle, her lips tinged blue, I ordered her to take a turn.

"I can't," she said through chattering teeth. "I'm too cold."

"You can," I said ruthlessly. "You have to. I didn't just kill three men in cold blood to have you fail me now."

A spark of outrage flashed in her eyes. "*Me* fail *you*? Elua have mercy, but you can be an arrogant bastard!"

She did it, though, dismounting stiffly and breaking a path in snow so deep she could barely flounder through it, her hardy pony in tow. I bade her remount once her color looked better, and she admitted she was warmer for the exertion. When the dark trunks of pines were silhouetted against the red skies of sunset, I called for a halt to make camp. I tramped down snow and gathered dead wood for a campfire and a windbreak, tearing loose green boughs to serve as a layer of bedding between our bodies and the frozen ground. Everything I did, I explained to Phèdre. She listened attentively, hauling wood for the fire, watering the horses, melting snow in our cooking pot, and stirring in the oats for pottage while I tended to our mounts and made two pair of makeshift hobbles from scavenged bits of leather lacings and trim. I didn't say aloud that I was deliberately teaching her everything I could to survive the Skaldi winter because they were tools she'd need if anything were to happen to me. I didn't need to. She knew.

When I'd finished, I spread a woolen cloak over the green pine boughs. Feeling self-conscious, I drew my sword and began giving it a more thorough cleaning and whetting. "We . . . we should sleep close for warmth."

Phèdre glanced at me with weary amusement. "After all that we've been through, that embarrasses you?"

I concentrated on my sword. "It does if I think on it, Phèdre. I've not much left of my vows to hold on to."

"I'm sorry." The contrition in her voice sounded sincere; abandoning the slow-bubbling pottage she was tending, she came to sit beside me, wrapping both mittened hands around my right arm. "Truly, Joscelin. I am sorry." I didn't wish to discuss it further, but I squeezed her hand in gratitude. We sat side by side, watching the fire crackling the dark wood, casting twisted branch-shadows on the snow before she broke the silence. "I tried to kill Selig last night."

I drew a sharp involuntary breath. "Why? They'd have killed you for it!"

"I know." Phèdre gazed at the fire, her face cameo-perfect in profile. "But it would have been better that way. The Skaldi won't unite under anyone else, he's the one holding the alliance of the tribes together." She did look at me, then. "And you wouldn't have had to betray your vow."

"What happened?" I asked quietly.

She shrugged. "He woke up. Maybe it's true, maybe he really is proof against harm. Anyway, he woke up. I was lucky he didn't know what I was about."

"Phèdre nó Delaunay . . ." I didn't know whether to laugh or cry; the sound that emerged was an unintelligible mix of the two. Of course she tried to kill him, and if she'd succeeded, she would have gone to her fate with her head held high. Alcuin had been right, she was nothing if not a paradox.

"Plaything of the wealthy. Blessed Elua have mercy, you put me to shame." I rubbed my eyes with the heel of my free hand. "I wish I'd have known Delaunay better, to have created such an unlikely pupil."

"I do, too." Pulling off one oversized mitten, Phèdre reached up to pluck a twig from my hair, easing her fingers through the tangles. "But in all fairness, when I first met you, I thought you were—"

"A dried-up old stick of a Cassiline Brother." I smiled. "I remember."

"No." She gave my hair a sharp tug, but she was smiling, too. "That was before I met you. When I did, I thought you were a smug, self-satisfied young prig of a Cassiline Brother."

That drew a genuine laugh from me. "You were right. I was."

"No." She shook her head. "I was wrong. The man I thought you were would have given up and died of humiliation in Gunter's kennel. You kept fighting and stayed true to yourself. And kept me alive thus far."

I nudged an errant branch deeper into the fire. "You did as much for yourself, and for me, too. Trust me, I've no illusions on that score. But I swear, I will do whatever is needful to get you alive and whole to Ysandre de la Courcel. If I'm to be damned for what I've done, I'll be damned in full and not by halves."

"I know. I know you will." She took a deep breath. "We should eat."

"Eat and sleep. We need all the strength we can muster." I got up to fetch the pottage, and we took turns sharing our only spoon, hot food warming us from the inside out. When we'd finished, I packed the pot with snow and nestled it in the embers to melt overnight.

"Did I tell you I hit one of those Gambrivii louts with a cooking pot?" Phèdre asked, shivering under her cloak.

"No." I glanced at her to see if she was jesting and I piled every bit of clothing I could find onto the pine-bough bed. "Did you really?"

"Mm-hmm." She snuggled into the heap of wool and fur, drawing it back for me. "For all the good it did."

It really was a wonder we were both alive.

I eased cautiously into bed and Phèdre slid into my arms without the slightest hesitation, pressing against me. I tightened my arms around her and she pressed harder, burying her face against my shoulder. The sheer trust with which she sought comfort in my nearness made my heart ache.

"Sleep," I whispered against her hair. "They won't find us tonight. Sleep."

CHAPTER THIRTY-TWO

I loved winter in the Siovalese mountains of my childhood, but winter in Skaldia was challenging.

The second day was much like the first, a lone Cassiline Brother and one of the most famous courtesans in the entire realm of Terre d'Ange trudging endlessly on horseback and on foot across a stark, snowy landscape.

I taught Phèdre more wilderness skills along the way—how to wrap her face and head in wool like a burnouse, how to pick a trail through a dense thicket, how to recognize mounds where fallen branches deep under snow might trap an ankle or fetlock. I taught her to examine her extremities for signs of frostbite. I taught her how to tend to the horses—watering, feeding, and currying them, cleaning their hooves of hard-packed ice and snow. I gave her Trygve's dagger to carry and showed her how to use it.

Waldemar Selig would send trackers after us, of that I was sure. Whether or not they would find us was uncertain. We had a day's lead on them, but they had the advantage of knowing the territory, and all the stubborn resilience in the world wasn't going to transform Phèdre into a hardy, self-sufficient traveller overnight.

Balancing our need for urgent progress with constant vigilance was exhausting—and Selig's trackers weren't the only danger. On the second evening a wolf pack spotted us as we were setting up camp for the night and prowled around the perimeter while I tried frantically to get a sizeable fire going, my hands cold and shaking. The wolves continued to circle while Phèdre stood guard with Trygve's dagger until I managed to ignite a large branch. Torch alight, I ran after them, yelling and waving.

The wolves made a prudent withdrawal. I built the fire high, hoping the blaze and my shouting didn't draw the attention of any trackers in distant earshot. I couldn't afford *not* to take the risk, but it made me uneasy. I'd have stood watch all night if I could have; it simply wasn't humanly feasible to go without sleep and maintain anything near the level of exertion I was putting forth. So we huddled for warmth and slept in shifts.

Sometimes in the small hours when the night sky was a vast dome of stars above us, we spoke in whispers, conversations we wouldn't have had in daylight. I asked her somewhat I'd wondered about since our abduction. "Phèdre, why did Melisande Shahrizai let us live?"

She twined one of my Skaldi braids around her finger. "I asked her that at one point while she was . . . well. When it was obvious that I wasn't going to give my *signale*. She said she'd no more kill me than she'd destroy a priceless fresco or a vase."

"Lucky you," I observed wryly. "Why me?"

Phèdre gave the diamond pendant a tug. "Oh, I'm sure she means to reclaim me. Letting you live improves the odds of my survival."

"That was a miscalculation on her part." I couldn't keep a touch of bitterness from my tone.

"And yet here we are." She placed a hand on my chest and gazed up at me. "Joscelin, I think you and I are only just beginning to discover what we are."

"And what am I, if not a Cassiline Brother?" I asked.

She smiled. "*The* Cassiline. Cassiel's Chosen."

"I think that's yet to be determined," I said ruefully. "And what are you?"

"According to that old priest Lodur, a weapon thrown by the gods," she mused. "Albeit a small one."

"A dart is a small weapon," I said.

"Yes." The starlight was bright enough that even through the branches of our lean-to, the crimson mote in Phèdre's eye was visible. "It is."

Misfortune struck on the third day. Phèdre had studied many a map, including one in Selig's possession, but distances were crudely reckoned and there were no major landmarks between Selig's steading and the three Great Passes of the Camaeline Mountains. There were steadings, though, and Phèdre had memorized the order of their location in relation to the westward trajectory of our journey.

"Raskogr's steading lies there." We had dismounted atop a snowy ridge to get our bearings, and she pointed north. Beyond the nearest mountain peak, trickles of smoke rose into the blue sky, visible from a distance. "We need to bear south and follow this ridge."

Even knowing mountains, all it takes is one misstep.

I felt the snow crumble under me the moment I took that step. Nothing to grab, nothing to brace myself against—the ground beneath me was a sliding vertical sheet of snow, carrying me a good thirty yards down the ridge face before petering out. I collected myself with disgust, looking up to see Phèdre's terrified face. Seeing me alive and unharmed, her expression eased. She pointed to a spot halfway up the face where the hilt of my sword protruded from the snow. I patted my daggers to make sure they were in place and began climbing. It was slow, hard going and the snow kept giving way beneath me, erasing my progress.

When I finally reached the summit and regained solid ground, all I could do was lie on my back, exhausted. Phèdre brought me a waterskin and I took a deep gulp before forcing myself to my feet. "We have to keep going."

She nodded. "At least the horses are rested."

My laughter turned to coughing in my cold-seared throat.

The lost time was on both of our minds that evening. We'd been lucky, in a sense; the wolves had fled my torch, I'd survived the landslide of snow, the weather had favored us. But today had served to remind me that our luck wouldn't hold forever, and the dangers we faced from the elements were as grave as an enemy's steel. That night at the campsite, I fetched Trygve's round hide-covered buckler from our packs. It was an awkward item to port and I'd debated leaving it behind a number of times. In the end I kept it lest I need to disguise myself as a Skaldi thane again.

I brought it to Phèdre and showed her how to wield it. "Listen to me. If—or when—they catch up to us, play along with whatever I say. If you have the chance to get away, take it. You know enough to survive on your own as long as the supplies hold out. But if there's no chance, use the shield to protect yourself. And I will do what I can."

"Protect and serve," she whispered. "Oh, Joscelin!"

The conviction in her voice made me feel whole; a Cassiline. I turned my head so she wouldn't see the tears in my eyes. "Go to sleep," I murmured. "I'll take the first watch."

As though to prove my worst fears, around midmorning of the following day, the wind shifted to the north. A snowstorm descended upon us in icy gusts and veils of snow so dense they blocked out the world. When that happened, we were forced to halt, hunching over in the saddle, and wait for a brief glimpse of the passage ahead, lest we blunder into a tree or plunge unwitting over a drop-off. Elua only knows what manner of curses I shouted at Phèdre, willing her to keep moving. I could see her movements slowing and her pauses becoming more frequent, and I was terrified that at some point she would simply crumple and let icy death claim her.

I underestimated her.

"Joscelin!" she called. I turned back. In the middle of a gods-bedamned snowstorm, she'd unwound her woolen wrappings and was bare-headed. Ice rimed her eyelashes, turned her hair to frozen locks. She pointed with one mittened hand. "They're coming."

I couldn't hear anything over the howling storm; and then a faint call in the distance. "How many?"

Phèdre held still, listening. She shook her head. "I can't tell for sure. Six. Maybe eight."

I set my gaze ahead of us. "Ride!"

It was a desperate gambit, and I knew it within minutes. I trusted Phèdre—she had keen ears and Anafiel Delaunay had trained his pupils in the skill of isolating, identifying, and analyzing the sounds surrounding them. But even I could hear the Skaldic war-chants rising as our pursuers spread out to encircle us. It was an urgent, bloodthirsty pounding rhythm intended to panic its prey. As we emerged into a clearing where a tall promontory of rock offered some shelter from the north wind, Phèdre shook her head at me.

There was nowhere to run. My horse was done in, head hanging low as lather froze on its neck. It was time.

"We will make a stand, Phèdre." My voice sounded clear, sure, and very far away. Dismounting, I unlashed the buckler. "Take this and guard yourself as best you may." She descended stiffly from her weary pony and accepted the shield, settling it in place and putting her back against the promontory.

I had a plan. It was a lousy excuse for a plan, but it was the only way I could think to gain even a small element of surprise, and I didn't dare hesitate for fear my nerve or my heart would break. Drawing my sword, I strode into the center of the snow-swirling clearing. The Skaldic war-chant fell silent. Seven mounted figures emerged through the wintry veils, ranged in a semicircle. Angling my sword across my body, I turned slowly. Faces hidden beneath overhanging hoods, the Skaldi waited to see what I would do.

I flung my sword down and clasped my hands above my head. "In Selig's name, I surrender!"

They laughed.

A gust kicked up snow-devils, obscuring my vision. When it cleared,

I saw that four of the thanes had dismounted to circle around me; three armed with swords, one with an axe. Two more waited astride, while another mounted thane rode toward Phèdre.

That was a problem. All I could do was what I could do now, in this moment. A sense of clarity suffused me.

This moment.

This moment was all there was.

My sword lying in the snow at my feet, I waited with my hands clasped high until the first thane to reach me poked my chest with the tip of his sword, trying to gauge the situation, the others closing in to tighten the circle around me.

Now.

I swatted the thane's blade away with one sweep of my vambraced right arm and drew my twin daggers; already turning, already tracing the circular patterns drilled deep into my flesh and bones since I was ten years old.

A low jab to the first thane's upper thigh elicited a furious roar. I was already in motion and he was already dead although he didn't know it; I'd nicked the big artery. Step, pivot, sidestep. The Skaldi took a few paces back to regroup, leaving me a sliver of time to sheathe my daggers and sweep my sword from the snow, taking out a thane behind me with a backward thrust before setting my guard.

Phèdre.

I heard the thane's voice before I could make them out through the snow. "D'Angeline!" he shouted. "Let be! I have the girl!"

On the heels of his command came Phèdre's voice pitched to carry over the wind with fierce urgency. "Joscelin! Don't listen to him!"

I couldn't have if I'd tried. One of the mounted Skaldi who'd hung back was charging, a battle-axe in hand. I dodged and whirled, switching to a one-handed grip. Drawing my left-hand dagger, I flung it hard. It stuck square between his fur-clad shoulders, deep enough that he slumped lifeless over in the saddle. By the promontory, Phèdre was struggling with the thane. Alive, then, Elua be thanked. I'd halved the odds against me, but there were still three other Skaldi to contend with. Or there were until one yelled and pointed at the promontory. Blinking snowmelt from my eyes, I tried to make sense of what I saw, which was Phèdre still gripping the shield and a man-sized bundle of hide and fur prone on the ground at her feet.

She'd killed him. For the space of a heartbeat, no one moved; and then the last mounted thane heeled his horse in Phèdre's direction, drawing a short throwing spear.

Lightning crackled in my veins. My temple had fallen; my temple stood. What was broken could be rebuilt.

I was Cassiel's Servant and I had *drawn my sword.*

I don't remember killing the last two thanes afoot, only my blade shining and crimson-splashed as it cut through the snowstorm. I do remember vaulting astride the nearest horse, lashing it in a desperate attempt to intercept the last Skaldi thane. Too far, I was too far away. His spear arm jerked forward in a hard, unerring cast. I heard wood splintering, I saw Phèdre scrambling backward while the thane drew his sword. My borrowed mount stumbled, pushed too hard. Its forelegs buckled and it fell heavily to the frozen ground, throwing me from the saddle in the process.

A Skaldi warrior, a dark figure wreathed by snow, held a sword high overhead. A much smaller figure stood in its shadow. My sword-hilt was clutched in my left hand. His stance shifted in preparation for a killing blow. I let go my hilt, grabbed the sword-blade by the tip, propped myself on one arm, whispered a plea, and hurled it.

The sword turned end over end as it flew across the snow-wraithed yards separating us. His killing blow never landed, his sword slipping from his fingers. All I could do was stare, open-mouthed, as he slowly turned to reveal the tip of my blade protruding a bloodstained handspan from his chest. When he sank to his knees, I let go a breath I hadn't known I was holding.

Dragging myself upright, I limped over to Phèdre. The last Skaldi tracker lay facedown, my hilt and a length of steel sticking out of his back. I had to brace my foot on his back to draw it free. "Do you know what the odds of making that throw were?" I asked hoarsely, regarding the blade. "We don't even train for it. It's not done."

She looked at the thane she had killed and I saw it was Harald the Beardless from Gunter's steading, the one who had stayed after the Allthing, the one who doted on her. "Do you know he gave me his cloak?" she murmured. "He never even asked for it back."

"I know." My head ached, but I suspected that wasn't the worst of my injuries. I pressed one hand gingerly against my lower left side. There was a slash through my leather jerkin. It was beginning to hurt like hell, and I could feel warm blood seeping beneath my hand. It was only going to stiffen and get worse. "I'm sorry. But we have to keep moving. Take . . . take anything we can use." Withdrawing my hand, I wiped it discreetly on my breeches. "Food, water, fodder, blankets. We'll take whatever mounts are freshest."

"I hate leaving them to the wolves," she said wistfully.

"They might find their way to the nearest steading," I said, knowing it was unlikely.

A note of stubbornness entered her voice. "I'm keeping my pony."

It drew a tired smile from me, though in fairness her shaggy pony was hardier than the taller mounts. "All right. We'll use him as a packhorse."

We made quick work of collecting useful stores and gear, gathering as much as the horses could safely tolerate. The one that had fallen and thrown me had broken a foreleg and had to be put down for mercy's sake. I did the deed after retrieving the dagger I'd thrown, making it as swift and painless as possible. At least the storm abated to occasional squalls while we stripped the dead and set out anew.

It had always been Phèdre's plan to make for the Danrau River and follow it all the way to the Camaeline Mountains, though we couldn't be sure when we might reach the river. We came across it that afternoon, a broad, swift-moving river cutting a grey path across the snowy landscape. I had to assume that there would be more pursuers, and it was my idea to travel along the shallow verge for some distance, leaving no tracks. It was hard going. We had to be sure our mounts picked their way with care and didn't lose their footing. I used a long, sturdy branch to break the surface ice when necessary so the horses' legs weren't cut by its sharp edges.

When the wind began to kick up again, we departed from the river. I wished we'd done it sooner, for the intensifying wind bore a second storm on its wings. It hit full force when I went back to cover our trail leading from the river. Mayhap I shouldn't have bothered, for the storm likely erased all traces of our passage. But I couldn't know for certain; the Skaldi were highly skilled hunters accustomed to tracking prey in the worst of winter's weather.

I hadn't reckoned on my own exhaustion nor the extent to which my injuries had drained my strength, though. I could barely make out my own tracks to sweep them away as I staggered back to Phèdre. She was on foot, huddled with the horses, one small snow-covered lump shivering among three large ones.

She took one look at me. "Get in the saddle. I'll lead."

I didn't argue.

That portion of our journey is a white blur. If Phèdre hadn't found the reserves to keep going, we likely wouldn't have survived the night, for I had none left. I rode hunched against the pelting snow, fighting to retain consciousness and remain astride. During brief moments of visibility, we saw only rocky terrain dotted with thin trees, nowhere to take shelter from the wind and make a campsite. Phèdre pointed to the south, altering our trajectory slightly and trudging forward. Icy whirling whiteness was my world. I kept my gaze fixed between my mount's bobbing ears, following blindly. At some point, I began to pray—a prayer without rites or vows, a wordless plea from the heart. I envisioned Cassiel with his flaming sword aloft, holding the gateway. In my vision, I knelt and bowed my head. Cassiel lowered his flaming sword and the tip touched the center of my brow, sending a burst of golden light through me, warming me outward from my innermost soul.

"Joscelin!" It was Phèdre's voice, muffled by the snow. "There's a cave! Give me a torch!"

Dismounting was hard. My joints were locked with cold and my body had stiffened as much as I'd feared. I nearly crumpled when I sought to put my weight on that first foot to strike the ground, and only saved myself by hauling on the stirrup strap. At least my mount was too weary to react to my ungainly scramble. The Skaldi trackers had carried torches wrapped tightly in pitch-soaked rags and we'd taken as many as we could port. Phèdre fetched one and went to explore once we'd managed to get it alight.

She returned with her eyes full of gratitude and relief. "It's huge! And it's empty."

It was true. A broad tunnel led into a vast stone arena. A firepit stained with old soot and a smoke-hole above it suggested it had been used for human habitation. The dark stillness and absence of old bones or other detritus suggested no one had inhabited it for a very long time. Stripping off her mittens, Phèdre unloaded her pony's packs and dragged them to the far wall, where she'd left the burning torch wedged in a crevice.

"Unpack our gear," she said. "I'll get a proper fire going and see to the horses."

"You can't—" I began.

"Yes, I can." Suiting deeds to words, she lit a second torch from the first and plunged back into the storm.

Entirely on her own, Phèdre nó Delaunay managed to find sufficient wood to build a fire that would last throughout the evening, including a deadfall that served to barricade the horses in the cave's entry. While I sorted through our things and piled furs and blankets into a cozy heap, she put on a kettle of snow to melt and tended to the horses, unsaddling them. All three were spent, heads hanging low while ice-melt dripped from their hides, but they ate and drank when fed and watered. Wavering on her feet, Phèdre refilled the cookpot with snow and stirred in a handful of pottage oats before collapsing beside me. I handed her a strip of dried venison, also courtesy of our pursuers' stores. We ate in silence, tired beyond words, letting the nourishing warmth restore us.

When we had scraped the cookpot clean, she hauled it outside to refill with snow, nestling it in the embers before fetching a few things from our packs, including the one meadskin I hadn't refilled with water. "We're going to clean you up a bit."

I nodded.

I'd no idea how I'd taken those wounds; the battle had taken place so swiftly that the sequence wasn't fixed in my memory, only a series of vivid images. At any rate, I'd a gouge near the back of my skull that I assured Phèdre looked worse than it was, head wounds bleeding as they do, and a shallow cut across my right cheekbone. Her touch was deft and gentle as she cleaned my injuries with warm water and unsoiled rags, then doused them thoroughly with mead. "I wondered why you kept one skin," she said. "That was clever."

"Not really." I winced as she dabbed at my cut cheek. "I thought you might need it. The Skaldi drink it for warmth."

"Do they?" She squeezed a stream of mead into her mouth. "It's not bad." Sitting on her heels, she regarded me. "So. Tell me how bad the wounds you're hiding are?"

I grimaced. "Is it that obvious?"

"Yes. Don't be an idiot." Her voice softened. "I know. But you have to let me see."

Wordlessly, I unlaced my leather jerkin and the woolen tunic beneath it, easing them over my head.

Phèdre caught her breath and I looked at my naked torso. It was a mass of bruises; fresh bruises blossoming dark violet over layers of healing bruises fading to a jaundiced yellow. A handspan above my left hip was the deep gash that had left my jerkin soaked and stiff with blood.

This one *did* feel as bad as it looked.

"Joscelin." She gave me an apologetic look. "It needs to be sewn."

"By you?" I'd heard tales of Phèdre's poor sewing skills in Gunter's steading. I held out one hand. "Give me that meadskin." I tilted it and drank deep, coughed, and drank more. It was sweet on the tongue and warm in the belly. "I took a sewing kit from one of Selig's men. It's in my saddlebag."

It hurt.

It hurt a whole gods-bedamned lot, because the wound was deep, the needle was crudely wrought, and the waxed twine thread was thick-spun. I took a gulp of mead before each stitch, while Phèdre winced every time she had to pinch my gaping flesh together and shove a large needle through it. When it was done at last, she slathered it with salve, then stretched out beside me on the furs in pure exhaustion, unwinding the last of her woolen head wrappings and shaking her ice-melt-wet hair out to dry in the warmth.

I handed her the meadskin. "You did a good job. Throughout all of it. Phèdre . . ."

"Shh." Propping herself on one elbow, she laid her fingers over my lips. "I don't want to talk about it. Any of it."

And then she kissed me.

It was tender and gentle, and every nerve in my aching, battered body came to life beneath it. Phèdre drew back, those grave, lustrous, god-marked eyes asking a soft question. *Will you?* She knew what a deep and solemn choice it was for me. In a thousand years, I never thought my answer would be yes, but my vows had been pared to the marrow. If damnation was the price of love, so be it. Here and now, in this moment, it was worth the cost. I slid my arms around her and returned her kiss in answer, my lips parting beneath hers as I broke my oath. The tip of her tongue touched mine, a strange shock of intimacy that sent blood surging to every part of me.

Phèdre laughed aloud with sheer unalloyed delight, eyes now sparkling brighter than that gods-bedamned diamond.

I drew her back down to me.

We had prayed to the gods and the gods had answered our prayers; now they held us cupped in the palm of their hands. We kissed until the unfamiliar intimacy of it melted into molten-gold pleasure and a deep connection that I hadn't known was possible. Breath of my breath. I truly hadn't understood why D'Angelines beyond the Prefectory walls considered lovemaking a sacrament.

It was.

The fire crackled, filling the cavern with its red-gold warmth. Our mounts dozed in the shelter of the tunnel, stamping the occasional hoof. Phèdre unlaced her kirtle, baring her shoulders. I traced the line of her slender throat, the lines of her collarbones, so delicate and precise. I eased the kirtle over her head, pausing to kiss every part of her as it was revealed, for every part was a revelation. The thorny black lines of her briar rose marque, accented with red petals like teardrops of blood, stood out starkly against her creamy skin, rising from the base of her spine to entwine its length, incomplete at the top.

I knew women's bodies only from a distance; I hadn't anticipated the contrasts between languid grace and lithe strength with which Phèdre's body was filled. I wondered at the softness of her skin, the heft and feel of her breasts in my rough palms. Glancing up, I saw tears in her eyes and for a heartbeat, I feared I'd done somewhat to hurt her, but she shook her head urgently and pulled me closer. I brushed my thumbs over her nipples, marveling at the way they grew hard, darkening to a rosier pink as the surrounding areolae drew taut. My phallus, already hard and straining against my breeches, twitched at the mere sight. She unlaced my breeches; I pulled off my boots and yanked the breeches free, leaving us both naked.

Phèdre had trained in Naamah's arts from a very young age, but I think it is only a true master of an art who can make utter simplicity shine. That night she offered no artistry, no flourishes—only herself. She touched my body with reverence, kissing the uninjured parts; and then my eyes stung with tears, for no one had ever touched me with such love before. When I stroked the supple length of her inner thigh, she parted her legs and guided my hand. I didn't know she would be so warm and wet inside. I circled Naamah's pearl with one fingertip. I didn't know it would throb with pleasure that made Phèdre writhe.

When I braced myself over her and entered her, it felt holy. Her hands on my hips, urging me. Her body as it arched beneath me, legs wrapped around me; holy. Her face at the moment of climax, wreathed in firelight; holy.

I lifted my head and she pulled it down fiercely, burying her face against my shoulder, hands drawing me deeper inside her.

Our temple.

My hips rocked rhythmically, driving me to spend inside her. I couldn't help but cry out in amazement at the end.

I would have stayed in that transcendent moment forever if I could have, but it was fleeting by its very nature. I was a Cassiline Brother. Even as my vows had shattered one by one, I drew strength from the shards. Cassiel bestowed many graces upon his servants, but mortal love was not one of them. I rose from our bed and walked some few steps away, bowing my head in thought.

"We've dreamed today," Phèdre said softly from behind me. "Joscelin, we're still dreaming. We'll wake from it tomorrow."

I turned to face her. "I'm Cassiel's Servant. No matter how I've broken my vows, I cannot be otherwise. And I need to draw on the strength of that if we're to survive this journey. Can you understand?"

"Yes, of course. Do you think I'd have survived this long if I weren't Naamah's Servant and Kushiel's Chosen?" She shook her head. "You're bleeding again."

"Oh." I returned to sit beside her on the makeshift bed while she rummaged through our things for any piece of cloth clean enough to use for a bandage. "I thought . . ." I stopped and cleared my throat. "So it's not only pain that pleases you, then? I didn't know."

"No." She gave me a sidelong smile. "Did you think that? I answer to Naamah's arts, not just Kushiel's rod."

I touched the diamond hanging from her throat. "But the latter calls louder."

"Yes." Phèdre shifted to clutch the diamond, yanking it so hard that the knot on its velvet cord broke. "Blessed Elua, I'd be free of it if I could!" she said in disgust and hurled the necklace. It soared in a scintillating firelit arc across the cavern, landing with a clink in the darkness beyond.

I gazed after it for a moment before speaking. "Phèdre. We've nothing else of value to our names."

"No," she said stubbornly. "I'd rather starve."

"Would you?" I asked. "Because you made me choose life over pride."

Phèdre sighed. "All right. Fetch it back, and I will wear it and remember. If we need to buy our lives with it, so be it." Her tone turned to one of grim determination. "And if we don't, I will wear it until the day I throw it on the ground at Melisande Shahrizai's feet. And then she will have the answer to her question: It is Kushiel's Dart throws truer than Kushiel's line!"

I rose and retrieved the diamond pendant from the darkness beyond the firelight, returning to kneel and tie it around Phèdre's throat. What exactly lay between her and Melisande, I didn't understand—nor was it for me to understand. But I knew that a part of what that diamond represented, ironically, was freedom. I traced the lines of her marque with one finger. "I'm sorry you had to leave it unfinished," I said softly. "It's beautiful, you know. Like you." She turned to glance up at me. I shrugged wryly. "If I've fallen from Cassiel's grace, at least I know it took a courtesan worthy of Kings to do it."

"Ah, Joscelin . . ." She left the thought unspoken, taking my face in her hands and kissing my brow. "Go to sleep, my Perfect Companion. We've a long way to go and you've a lot of healing to do." I lay down and she heaped blankets atop us both. "I'll tell you a story if you like . . . Do they tell Naamah's temptation of Cassiel in the Brotherhood?" I shook my head and she smiled. "Here's how they tell it in Cereus House . . ."

I've no idea how the story ended, but I fell asleep smiling, too, enfolded in warmth and love.

CHAPTER THIRTY-THREE

In the morning, the campfire had burned low and the cavern was chilly. I stoked the fire just enough to melt snow for drinking water and provide a measure of heat while Phèdre and I scrambled into our clothing and packed the horses, our teeth chattering. Outside it appeared that the storm had passed, leaving the skies an empty grey.

We didn't discuss what had transpired between us; not out of awkwardness, merely the exigency of our journey. But before we set forth, I caught a glimpse of silvery lines that stopped me in my tracks etched above the entryway to the cavern.

"Phèdre!" I pointed.

It was Blessed Elua's sigil, a lily and eight stars representing his Companions, shimmering like veins of silver against the dark grey rock. It meant that they had sheltered here crossing the Skaldic wilderness in search of a home—in search of Terre d'Ange, where they were welcomed with open arms and the ichor of their blood was written in the veins of their descendants.

We stared at the sigil and then at each other, both of us wide-eyed with wonder. "You know what this means," I said. "They took shelter here. Blessed Elua, Cassiel, Naamah . . . all the Companions. They were here."

"They were here." Phèdre echoed my words as though they were a prayer. "Joscelin, let's go home."

I tugged my wolf-pelt in place. "Home."

In the following days, I thought often about that night. It was only in the secret places of my heart that I dared wonder: If the gods themselves condoned our joining, was there a measure of grace in it? Of hope? Or was I truly damned for eternity for a single night of soul-shattering joy? For even if I never spoke of it again, I could never forget. Although it lay sealed behind us by Elua's blessing, it was an absurdly pleasurable distraction from the things which attempted to kill us as we travelled toward the Camaeline Mountains; things which included first and foremost the weather, more wolves, and once, a bear we disturbed from its winter sleep in a cavern we'd thought empty. It lumbered after us, gaunt and massive, one last swipe nearly taking down the pony as we floundered away through the snow.

For a mercy, our attackers did not include further human pursuers. Between the markings on Selig's maps and her own well-trained powers of observation, Phèdre was adept at spotting signs of human habitation or activity in the distance, and we were able to steer clear of any steadings or hunting parties.

Given our circumstances, we made good speed, but Waldemar Selig had not been idle. Our pursuers had been forced to track us across the wilderness through which we'd fled. According to Phèdre, Harald the Beardless had traded places with one of Selig's personal thanes to accompany the trackers, for he had some vision of restoring the honor of Gunter's steading by securing her return.

That meant it was likely Selig had sent riders carrying word of our flight to the steadings between us and the border. And likely there was a bounty on our heads. Phèdre didn't think he'd discovered the extent of her knowledge regarding the planned invasion—most importantly, the timing of it and Melisande's role in the plot—but he knew she'd heard enough to at least warn Terre d'Ange about it. And she had embarrassed him in the eyes of the tribes.

Me, I suspected Selig simply wanted dead. He'd wasted time and supplies on me, and I'd responded by escaping, stealing his stores, and killing a number of his men. It was most expedient to dispatch me. Phèdre was another matter. Selig would want to reclaim her. She hadn't outlived her usefulness as a bed-slave and status symbol to the would-be King of Skaldia. It was possible that he meant to display her at his side as living proof that no one could escape Waldemar the Blessed. It was also possible that he intended to bestow her upon a favored clan leader like Kolbjorn of the Manni.

Or worse.

If Phèdre was reclaimed, Selig might choose to punish her for embarrassing him, and those possibilities ran from bad to unthinkable. I thought about my uncle, slain for refusing to perform the *terminus* at his patron's order. I would have refused, too; but these were very different circumstances.

I asked Phèdre indirectly the night we first made camp within sight of the Camaeline Mountain range. "If it were to come to it—"

"I know what it's called." Her head was bowed over a saddlebag strap she was attempting to sew. Better the leather than my flesh, although it was healing clean.

"Then you know what I'm asking," I said quietly.

She nodded. "Yes."

"Yes?"

"Do you think I'm a coward?" she asked. "I know Selig. He's furious. And I'm terrified of what he would do if he got me back."

"So am I," I said. "And no, I don't think you're a coward. I think you might be the bravest person I've ever met."

"And I think you're an utter marvel." Phèdre smiled. "Did you ever imagine we'd be saying such things to each other?"

"No," I admitted. "Never."

That was all we spoke of the matter, and it was enough. The following day, we reached the verge of the mountains and travelled some leagues toward the southeasternmost pass, hoping against hope to find it unguarded. I suppose I'd known all along it was a vain hope. If I were Selig, I'd have dispatched parties to guard all of the Great Passes—or alert any border camps already posted there—immediately. When we saw the signs of woodsmoke in the distance, I reconnoitered on foot.

Sure enough, when I'd climbed high enough to find a safe vantage point, I saw a Skaldi encampment spread along the base of the path leading to the pass. Selig's men were doing the sorts of things all soldiers consigned to a dull post enjoyed—drinking, singing, dicing, and fighting with each other—but the scouts posted along the perimeter kept a sharp eye on the horizon in all directions. I went back to retrieve Phèdre and our horses, detouring from my ascent to break a trail our mounts could traverse. Drop-reining the horses out of sight, we scrambled up an escarpment to lie flat on our bellies and survey the distant camp.

"Those are Marsi tribesmen," Phèdre murmured. The Skaldi didn't have heraldry as we knew it, but there were accoutrements specific to each tribe. "Gunter and his men might be among them."

"No love lost there," I said. "I count two score. You?"

"The same." She gave me an uncertain, questioning look.

"Not a chance," I said with regret. "There are too many of them and they're on open ground, Phèdre. I'd be slaughtered." I turned my head to gaze upward at the snow-covered mountain peaks towering above us. "We have to break a trail to go around them."

"No." There was a note of profound exhaustion in her voice. "Joscelin, I can't."

I wanted to hold her close, to protect her from this endless nightmare, but anything reassuring I said would have been a lie. "We have to," I said in my gentlest tone. "It's the only way."

Phèdre took a moment to gaze at the distant forces arrayed against us. "Then let's go, and may Elua have mercy on us."

There are a number of good reasons why no one attempts to cross the Camaeline range save through one of the Great Passes—jagged crags and promontories, sheer cliff faces, hidden crevasses, crumbling ledges of snow, wind, pelting snow and ice. At least there were neither bears nor wolves, and most importantly, no humans pursuing us from behind or waiting in hiding for us. There was only the cold and snow and treacherous footing. All the elements that had nigh killed us on the horizontal outset of our journey were now vertical.

We lost Phèdre's mount on the first day of our ascent. We had to forge trails on foot to find secure passage for the horses. She was taking a turn leading the way—gods be thanked she wasn't riding—when it happened.

It was much like what had befallen me atop the ridgeway, one misstep and a sheet of snow sliding loose into a small avalanche. Only this time it was no smooth, steep slope, but a long plunge onto crags in a gulch far below.

I got to the edge first and blocked Phèdre's view. "Don't look."

"Is he . . . ?"

"Yes, the fall killed him." I angled my body as she sought to peer around me. If it wasn't true yet, it would be very shortly. "We have to keep moving."

She drew a sharp breath. "Our supplies!"

I shook my head. "There's no way to retrieve them. We've at least enough left for two more days. If we don't live that long, it won't matter how many supplies we have."

The ascent was one long white blur of snow, ice, and rock. I think it unlikely that either of us would have survived that trek alone, but as long as Phèdre drew breath, I wasn't giving up. And as long as she drew breath, she was determined to continue, drawing on that deep inner well of stubbornness.

Paradox.

Another time upon attaining such a summit, I might have shouted aloud with sheer joy at beholding the Camaeline Mountains in their glory. We'd been graced with a clear day and azure skies above the majestic ocean of ice and stone, lower peaks casting angled blue shadows on the white snow. Despite everything, it made my mountain-born heart soar. Phèdre gave me a fond, wry look and trudged past me in search of a viable downward route.

Our supplies ran short after the summit. We were out of pottage and could barely scrape together enough fodder to keep the horses alive. I boiled the last of our dried meat to make a broth. Our fires were small and parsimonious, built with sticks I'd gathered before we passed the treeline on our ascent. I assured Phèdre that one could survive for days on end without food so long as one had water. It was true, though not undergoing this level of exertion or privation.

While the descent was a great deal easier in terms of exertion, it required a significant amount of concentration—and even then, accidents happen. My horse's left foreleg plunged through a pocket of snow and was wedged in a crevasse beneath. It thrashed in panic, breaking its pastern bone in the process. Once again, I had to put a horse down. This time, I asked Phèdre to bring the cooking pot before I cut the big vein on the side of its neck.

She did, though she looked ill. "You're not—"

"One of Duc L'Envers men told me that the Akkadians make blood-tea when they're caught out in the desert," I said, holding the pot in place. "They can live on it for days without killing the horses if they only take a small amount of blood. But this one is dead already, Phèdre."

She aided me without comment. My horse folded its knees, sinking peacefully to the snow. That night we drank blood-tea.

The farther we descended, the easier it became to pick our way down, leading Phèdre's sure-footed pony. Winter's grip had loosened and game was stirring. I wished I had a bow, but the animals in the wilds of the borderlands had no fear of humans, and I was able to dispatch a good-sized hare and a couple of burrowing grouse with a thrown dagger. It made me grateful for all those hours in the millhouse loft throwing daggers with Selwyn.

It was strange to think I hadn't spoken about Selwyn to Phèdre; indeed, strange that outside the bonds of this horrific shared experience and one night of profound intimacy, we knew very little of each other save for our misleading first impressions. There was no opportunity to converse during our time at Gunter's and Selig's steading. Throughout our flight, time and breath were short enough that talking was reserved for matters of necessity. When we reached the eastern foothills of the Camaelines, I didn't dare breathe a sigh of relief—with the sparsely inhabited border, it was impossible to tell the precise moment we crossed into Camlach and set foot on D'Angeline soil—but I did let myself begin to hope.

Too soon.

We didn't let our guard down, not exactly; we spent the latter part of the day continuing eastward and deeper into Camlach so that we might cut a wide berth around the southern pass where the Skaldi may have posted lookouts. We made enough progress that I reckoned it safe to build a modest campfire in a secluded pine grove. I was wrong. We were roasting frozen chunks of hare on green-wood branches. With the fire crackling and the meat sizzling, it drowned out the sound of the scouting party's approach. Phèdre heard them first, her chin raising sharply at the faint jingle of metal and creak of leather. That was all the time we had before they burst into the grove, firelight gleaming on polished chainmail shirts. I sprang to my feet, kicking snow onto the campfire.

Too late.

I crossed my forearms, bowed, and reached for my daggers. Phèdre flung herself at my legs, knocking them from beneath me. "They're Allies of Camlach," she whispered, covering my mouth with one mittened hand. "Follow my lead."

I gave a slight nod of acquiescence. I saw it, now. The chainmail, the attire, the fine-cut D'Angeline features. And yes, a gods-bedamned banner of the Allies of Camlach bearing a burning sword on a sable field. Below it was a smaller banner with the insignia of an unfamiliar Minor House.

Their leader nudged his mount closer into the circle of light cast by our half-extinguished fire. "Identify yourselves!"

"My lord!" Phèdre sounded sincerely concerned. "I'm sorry, we meant no harm. Do we trespass here?"

He regarded her. "No, lass. You've the right to passage, but it's not safe this near the border." Dismounting, he set one hand on his sword-hilt. "Who are you and where are you bound?"

My heart sank at the question, but Phèdre spun a tale faster than I could decide whether a lie or the truth would better serve us. "Suriah of Trefail, my lord, and my brother Jareth. Our village was destroyed by Skaldi raiders a few days ago." She lowered her voice. "My brother took a blow to the head and I hid him in the granary. Once it was over, we took some gear from those won't need it any longer, and we're bound for the City of Elua. Was that wrong?"

"No, not wrong." The lead scout's expression was unreadable. "So you thought we were Skaldi?"

"You might have been." Phèdre glanced at me, and I averted my gaze. "We didn't know, my lord. My brother got scared."

I nodded in dumb agreement.

The leader looked us up and down, taking in our exhausted, ragged condition, our Skaldic attire, my Cassiline weapons, and Phèdre's beauty only half-hidden by wolfskin. "There's nothing for you in the City. Winter's been hard, and it's fever-stricken. You'll ride with us to Bois-le-Garde. Don't worry, the Marquis will see you're well taken care of. We never turn away Camaeline refugees." He beckoned to one of the other scouts. "Brys, ride ahead and tell the castellan we're coming. Be sure to give him the details."

He stressed that last sentence, which meant one thing for certain—he meant to take us into custody. And if his liege was a member of the Allies of Camlach, that meant we were dead or imprisoned before we could reveal Isidore d'Aiglemort's traitorous alliance with Waldemar Selig, let alone Melisande Shahrizai's involvement.

I'd followed Phèdre's lead; I had to trust that she would follow mine. The designated rider was already setting his mount's course for home. But I was already drawing my left-hand dagger, pinning the scout leader's sword arm, and setting the dagger's keen edge against his throat. He tensed in protest and I pressed the edge hard enough against his skin to draw a faint line of blood. "Everyone dismount!" I ordered. "Now!"

If their leader had countermanded me, they might not have obeyed; but I'd caught him by surprise and he remained silent while his men looked questioning at each other before dismounting.

"Two horses," I said to Phèdre, who was already working frantically to stow our gear and load the pony. "Scatter the rest." Working with speed and precision, she lashed the reins of the nearest horses to a tree and drove the rest away, dodging around the motionless unmounted scouts, shouting and slapping hindquarters. I held my breath until she finished, watching for the slightest twitch of a threatening overture. "Phè—" I caught myself. "Suriah, mount up."

"You won't get away," the leader said bitterly. Now that the initial shock of mortal fear had eased, he was growing angry and risk-prone. "We'll come after you."

"Our kin in Marsilikos will protect us!" Phèdre retorted with so much righteous indignation that I nearly believed we had kin in the city of Marsilikos. "You've no right to detain free D'Angelines!"

"Quiet!" I hissed at her. "Suriah, get out of here!"

Phèdre paused just long enough to look at me with a question in her eyes. I saw it and gave a slight nod. We'd grown adept at communicating without words. Yes, I meant *go now*; yes, I would follow and catch up with her.

Wrestling her fractious stolen mount under control, Phèdre plunged into the dark woods surrounding us, trailing her Skaldi pony. We heard branches cracking and twigs snapping in the wake of her flight.

As soon as it faded, the leader tensed in my grip. His men were beginning to exchange glances and shift.

"Stop." I moved the tip of my dagger to the scout leader's chin, lifting it until the length of his blood-streaked throat was exposed. "One move from any of you and I shove this into his brain pan."

One of them moved anyway, looking to get past the periphery of my vision.

I applied pressure, forcing the leader onto his toes. "Is that what you want? Think about who's next, then, because I can plant a dagger in your eye at twenty paces."

"You can't kill all of us!" someone called.

"I know," I said with regret. "But I can try. And you'll be unpleasantly surprised by the number I will kill or maim before you stop me. That's why I'm offering you the opportunity to choose." I paused. "The ironic thing is, I don't want to harm any of you, I just want to join my sister and keep travelling. All you have to do is hold still for a few more minutes and I'll be on my way."

"You're no Camaeline," the leader muttered. "No Camaeline would disgrace his honor by taking a fellow D'Angeline hostage."

There were plenty of retorts I could have made, all of them true, none of them wise. I kept my mouth shut and waited. Over the past months, I'd had an unfortunate number of lessons in the art of gauging the tension of an opponent, or a group of opponents, and knowing when it was tight enough to snap. I cut it close, backing toward the second horse that Phèdre had secured, my hostage serving as a shield. Mounting and making a getaway would be my greatest moment of vulnerability. I needed to do it fast, for the scattered horses were already returning. Lowering my knife hand, I spun and hurled the leader over my shoulder in an old Hellene wrestling throw.

The suddenness of it startled the scouting party just long enough for me to fling myself astride my new mount. Clinging low and tight over its withers, I heeled my horse hard and sent us pelting after Phèdre's trail.

I caught up to Phèdre in less than a mile, the sounds of pursuit audible behind us. "Where to?"

She pointed. "South. We'll try to reach Eisheth's Way by morning."

I nodded. "Ride like hell."

The skies were clear, but it was the dark of the moon and only stars were in sight, casting a weak silvery light over the snow and rocks and trees. We paused periodically to breathe the horses and Phèdre attempted to gauge our location in relationship to the stars, correcting the angle of our course.

Eisheth's Way is one of the old Tiberian roads built in the days of empire, before the tribes in the tiny nation of Alba united to overthrow their conquerors. My father, in a jesting mood, declared that Terre d'Ange toasted their retreat with wine, thanked them for the roads, bridges, and aqueducts, then went back to preparing for the arrival of Blessed Elua and his Companions.

Sunrise found us staggering onto that fine example of Tiberian engineering, which lay bleak and empty in either direction. Our horses were blown, sides heaving. I was half-dead of exhaustion, and I knew Phèdre must be, too. That hardy Skaldi pony of hers was in the best shape of the lot of us. There was no stream of travellers into which we might merge and vanish, only a long, straight paved road and an angry party of Camaeline soldiers in pursuit of us.

"A side road." It took an effort for Phèdre to get the words out. "Any road leading west. And pray they press on toward Marsilikos."

With no stream anywhere in sight, we watered the horses with the last of our waterskins and continued plodding southward. Within an hour's time, I'd come to the reluctant decision that we needed to turn the horses loose and continue on foot over rough terrain; and then I saw the western side road with a faded wooden signpost bearing Elua's sigil.

I pointed. "There."

Phèdre cocked her head and listened as she did every time we paused. This time her eyes widened. She didn't bother to tally our pursuers, just heeled her mount and spoke a single word. "Ride!"

This would be our last flight on horseback. My thoughts were spinning like a weathervane, trying to gauge the precise moment and location when we ought to depart from the narrow roadway while avoiding observation. I daresay Phèdre was, too; until, veering around a sharp turn, we nearly ran down a mule-drawn wagon. Our horses balked at passing it, while the mules showed their strong teeth, braying in protest.

The wagon was constructed to serve as storage, living quarters, and conveyance like a Tsingani wagon, only without the ornate, colorful adornment, and I realized belatedly that a Yeshuite prayer-scroll case was affixed to the rear doors. Onesuch hangs at the door of the study in the Prefectory dedicated to Habiru studies.

"B'vakashah, father!" I called, spoken words trickling back to me. "Please! We mean no harm."

Reining in his team, the driver regarded us with a quizzical look. "What do you want?"

I offered a Cassiline bow from the saddle. "Barukh hatah Adonai, father. Forgive our intrusion."

"Barukh hatah Yeshua a'Maschiach, lo ha'lam," he responded automatically, continuing to study me. "You are a follower of the Apostate, I think."

I bowed again. The double doors at the back of the wagon were cracked open to reveal heavy hanging curtains and a pair of excited girlish faces peering through the parting. "Yes. Joscelin Verreuil of the Cassiline Brotherhood."

The Yeshuite raised his eyebrows. "Indeed. And who is chasing you so hard?"

"Men who are apostate even from the teachings of Blessed Elua, fruit of Yeshua ben Yosef's line," I said. "Stand aside and we will go, father."

He wasn't ready to budge yet. "And why do they chase you?"

"To kill us, most likely, by the time they catch us," Phèdre said with strained courtesy. "Messire—"

He interrupted her. "Your horses, I think, will not go much further."

She gritted her teeth. "Yes, messire, but—"

"Shelter us," I said abruptly to the man. "Please, father. The men pursuing us won't think to look in the heart of a Yeshuite family. They believe we're rebels, mayhap spies on behalf of Skaldia. I swear to you, it's not true. We're free D'Angelines, escaped from captivity, and we bear information on which the fate of our realm hinges."

It was a gamble; Phèdre looked at me in shock. But for once my instincts were good and true. The Yeshuite gave a slow nod, then called out to his wife within the wagon. "How do you say, Danele?"

A woman with kind eyes and a shrewd face opened the aft curtains fully, shooing away her daughters. She looked both of us over, her expression softening. "He is one of the Apostate's own, Taavi. Let them in."

I bowed a third time, this time in gratitude.

"Girls!" Danele said. "Make room!"

CHAPTER THIRTY-FOUR

Coming upon the Yeshuite family was a huge piece of luck.

Taavi was a weaver, his wife a dyer, and their wagon was filled with skeins of wool and bolts of fabric. The family was relocating from a village in Camlach, where the small Yeshuite community had been blamed for an outbreak of fever. He assured us that it was a false rumor spread by those who bore unwarranted resentment toward Yeshuites. The fever was real, but it was a courier for the Royal Post who brought it there.

His wife Danele set about rearranging the interior of the wagon to accommodate us, working with pragmatic efficiency while her daughters giggled and helped, no idea of the gravity of the situation.

The last thing we did was turn the horses loose. Taavi and Danele's girls had conceived an immediate fondness for Phèdre's shaggy pony and begged their father to keep it. To my surprise—and Phèdre's delight—he acquiesced. "A little truth seasons a lie like salt," he observed. "You have freed your horses. We will say we found the pony wandering if they ask. If they find us."

"They will," Phèdre murmured.

She was right.

We hadn't been back on the road long before she heard the hoofbeats. "Less than a dozen and closing fast!"

Danele ushered us both into the hiding space she'd created behind bolts of fine-woven cloth. We crouched low in the darkness behind our concealing bulwark of fabric, breathing in the scents of dye and lanolin from the unspun wool. I heard the approaching hoofbeats slow as they spotted the wagon. Phèdre was trembling, and I knew she was thinking that if this were the end of our run, not only were we doomed to fail, we'd made this kind, lovely family accessories to our perceived transgressions.

She leaned against me and I put my arms around her, whispering in her ear. "Shh, it's all right. Just breathe."

Outside, the riders were questioning Taavi. He responded with polite bemusement; no, they weren't bound for the City of Elua, they were bound for L'Arène where they had distant kin. Yes, they found the pony wandering loose on Eisheth's Way; no, they hadn't seen any other travellers today. Yes, of course the Allies of Camlach were welcome to look inside the wagon.

The curtains were drawn back and one of the scouts took a cursory glance, seeing only Danele and the girls shrinking modestly away from his gaze amidst the supplies of a weaver's household.

"Just a family," he reported wearily.

"They can't be far ahead." That was the leader's voice. "If they've loosed the horses, they're on foot. Let's go."

I let out a slow sigh of relief and felt Phèdre relax in my arms, burying her face against my throat. We were safe, we were warm, we were alive. Adonai had not forgotten the wayward descendants of his bastard grandson. By the time Danele whispered to us that we ought to stay hidden for a while lest the riders return, Phèdre had already fallen asleep and I was well on my way.

Sleep is a vastly underrated blessing. I slept like the peaceful dead, surfacing briefly to soft murmurs and occasional giggles before sinking back into the depths. Those were comforting sounds, reminding me of my childhood, playing games of hide-and-hunt with my brothers and sisters. Danele woke us before sunset, shifting a couple bolts of fabric. "You're safe for now, those men doubled back and passed us a few hours ago." Her brows creased; I don't think she'd fully taken stock of our filthy, exhausted appearance. "We've made camp for the evening. I'll heat extra water."

After the long months of being enslaved, beaten, abused, and struggling merely to survive, I'd forgotten such a thing as human kindness existed. That first evening, Danele gave us a full kettle of warm water and a bit of soap to share, and I was so grateful for it that I had to splash water on my face to hide the sting of tears. They asked us no questions about our circumstances and that was a kindness, too, even if it was in part from a desire to protect the girls—Maia and Rena were their names—from knowledge they were too young to bear.

There are commonalities between Yeshuites and the Cassiline Brotherhood, for both acknowledge descent from Adonai and follow His commandments. However, Yeshuites revere Yeshua as the Mashiach, the Anointed

One, whose death granted salvation to all peoples. Cassilines revere Yeshua as the son of Adonai and the father of Blessed Elua, not as the savior of mankind.

Taavi and Danele told their girls that I was a very special knight, sworn to protect and serve his lady with honor and a pure and faithful heart. They were just old enough to see it as a chaste fairy tale, and decided Phèdre must be a princess in disguise. She laughed at the notion and assured them she was a regular commoner. To the girls' delight, she braided their hair into intricate coronets, and when they became fascinated with Melisande's diamond pendant, she gave it to them to play with.

Danele paled at the sight of her young daughters playing a game of catch with the pendant. "That *is* just a bauble, is it not?"

A funny expression crossed Phèdre's face. "Ah . . . not exactly."

Danele shook her head and made the Yeshuite sign of the cross, then went about her business.

That night Taavi invited me to linger beside the campfire. I sat quietly, working on the nicked edges of a dagger with a whetstone, waiting for him to speak. "She serves Naamah," he said eventually.

I didn't look up. "Yes."

"One of Lilit's demon brood," he mused, referencing the writings of ancient Habiru mystics and prophets regarding Naamah. Not so long ago, I might have agreed without thinking, but my understanding of Naamah's service had deepened in ways I didn't yet comprehend. "Does she know you're in love with her?"

My shoulders tensed. "No."

"I didn't think so." He rose. "One way or another, a difficult path lies before you. I wish you luck, my friend."

Not long afterward, we parted ways at a crossroads where the narrow road we travelled intersected with a thoroughfare that led to the City of Elua and one that circumvented the capital and headed toward the province of Eisande and smaller cities such as L'Arène.

If Taavi had his way, they'd have made a detour and taken us to the City gates, but Phèdre and I refused his offer. There might be fever yet lingering in the City; moreover, we were uncertain of the reception awaiting us and unwilling to expose their family to either danger. So I retrieved my white wolfskin pelt from one of the girls, who was wearing it while chasing her sister around the wagon, and offered my final thanks. Phèdre, impulsive as ever, sought to give them Melisande's diamond, an extravagant offer they declined in polite wonder.

"You're stuck with that thing," I informed her. Watching the girls hugging our Skaldi pony, I turned to Taavi. "But I think there is one gift you may accept, father."

We left them heading southwest to L'Arène, pony in tow, while we proceeded on foot toward the white walls of the City, slightly stunned by the realization that safety and the end of what seemed an endless journey were almost in sight.

On the heels of that realization came the urgent awareness that the City was fraught with pitfalls, and we didn't have a plan to navigate them. We'd been gone for months. As far as Taavi and Danele knew, King Ganelon de Courcel remained on the throne and the Dauphine Ysandre was yet unwed; but the public face of the Crown didn't necessarily represent the political maneuvering behind the scenes.

Trust Rousse, Alcuin had told us as life slipped away from him; that was Royal Admiral Quintilius Rousse. Gaspar Trevalion, a longtime friend and ally of Delaunay's. Thelesis de Mornay, the King's Poet. Trust the Dauphine, not the King.

The problem was access. Since it was a cryptic message from Quintilius Rousse that had set events in motion, Phèdre reckoned he was posted with the Royal Navy near the Straits. Gaspar Trevalion had a small estate in the vicinity of the City where he might or might not be in residence; either way, she'd no idea where it was located. Ysandre might grant us an audience—we had the clandestine passphrase, after all—and Phèdre was certain that Thelesis de Mornay would trust and aid us without hesitation. But we didn't know how far and wide the strands of Melisande and d'Aiglemort's web of intrigue had been cast.

If we attempted the Palace, *anyone* we encountered could be an enemy.

"I have an idea," Phèdre announced as we trudged toward the capital. "But you're not going to like it."

"What is it?"

"Hyacinthe."

"You're right, I don't like it." I adjusted the waterskin over my shoulder as the road slanted up a rise. "Isn't there someone else you can turn to? A friend of Delaunay's?"

She shook her head. "Not without risk. We aren't talking a simple favor,

Joscelin. Whomever we approach will hold our lives in their hands. I trust Hyacinthe with mine. No one else."

"The Prince of Travellers," I observed with irony. "How much gold do you suppose your life is worth?"

She slapped my face so hard it shocked me into silence. I stared at Phèdre and she glared at me, eyes glittering. "Tsingano or not, Hyacinthe has been a friend to me when no one else was, and never asked a centime for it," she said with icy precision. "When Baudoin de Trevalion was executed, it was Hyacinthe who gave me money to make an offering in his memory at the temples."

"But Prince Baudoin—"

"I know," she interrupted me. "He sought to overthrow the Crown. Still, I had cause to grieve for him in my own way. Did you know I was Melisande's farewell gift to Baudoin before she betrayed him?"

"No," I murmured. "I'm sorry."

She sighed. "If you've a better idea, say it. But I won't have you speak against Hyacinthe."

The tops of the white walls glinted in the distance. "I can approach the Captain of the King's Cassiline Guard. He'd receive any member of the Brotherhood, and he's oath-sworn and may be trusted."

"Are you sure, Joscelin?" Phèdre asked earnestly. "Sure beyond doubt? Because you disappeared from the City with your ward, a notorious Servant of Naamah and plaything of the wealthy, leaving behind the slaughtered household of Anafiel Delaunay. Who knows what poison's been spread in our absence? Are you *sure* of your welcome by the Cassiline Brotherhood?"

The implication hit me like a second blow; it had never occurred to me that my honor as a Cassiline Brother would be impugned. "No one would dare suggest such a thing," I said. "And even if they did, no Cassiline would believe it."

"No?" Phèdre looked at me with sympathy. "But I thought of it, and if I could, others will have done so, too. As for believing, which is easier to credit, a simple lie or a complicated truth? We need someone we can trust to be our go-between."

I weighed the matter. Ultimately, she was right. We needed a go-between we could trust, and there was no one I trusted with the absolute surety she placed on her friendship with Hyacinthe. "Your way, then," I said. "And pray your trust isn't misplaced."

She nodded. "It's not."

I was worried about the City Guard at the gates, for they were stopping and questioning all travellers seeking entrance. There was indeed yet fever in the waning days of what became known as the Bitterest Winter, though my primary concern was that if the Allies of Camlach had influence among the guard, they might have gotten word to be on the lookout for us. But no, our luck held. A pair of guards asked us where we were from and why we were bound for the City of Elua. Phèdre gavc false names and cobbled together a plausible story of fleeing Skaldi raiders to seek posts with our kin in the City. They asked a few questions about our health and bade us stick out our tongues for inspection. Satisfied, they waved us onward.

For Phèdre, this was home, the only true home she'd ever known. I didn't have her deep, abiding connection to the City, but I saw the wonder of it written on her face. I had to remind her to keep her hood drawn close to hide her features.

I understood it, though. The City was the pinnacle of D'Angeline achievement; not just the Palace and the multitude of grand manors, but the boulevards and parks and gardens, the Court of Night-Blooming Flowers, the theaters and performers, salons and artists, ateliers with their couterieres and marquists, temples and priests and priestesses. It was Blessed Elua's city, the central square sporting a thousand-year-old oak tree that grew from an acorn planted by Elua himself. It belonged to every D'Angeline descended from Blessed Elua and his Companions—even Cassiel's Servants, for while Cassiel was pure and chaste and sired no children of his blood, we are the descendants of his spirit.

Twilight was falling when we reached Night's Doorstep. The street-lamps had just been lit and revelers in their silks and brocades, fewer than before, were venturing into the streets of the district. At Phèdre's suggestion, we made for Hyacinthe's livery stable, and I drew my sword as we entered, adding to the list of sins for which I had to atone.

Between the naked blade and my wild, ragged appearance, it nigh terrified them into pissing themselves. Both of them cowered, and one squeaked aloud.

"Do you work for Hyacinthe?" Phèdre asked, and they nodded. "You." She pointed at the one who hadn't squeaked. "I need you to find him and bid him come here. Privately, and as quickly as possible. Your friend's life depends on it. Tell Hyacinthe that an old friend needs his help. If he asks who, tell him we used to eat tarts under the bridge at Tertius' Crossing. Have you got that?"

He nodded again, rapidly. "Old friend, tarts, Tertius' Crossing. Yes."

"Good," she said. "If you breathe a word of this or anyone overhears you, your friend will die. Do you understand?"

He gave me a sidelong glance, nodding so fast his forelock flopped. "Yes! I swear it!"

"Good," she repeated. "And if we don't kill you, Hyacinthe will if you make a mistake here. Now go!"

The lad bolted from the livery stable like a hare sprung from a trap, the sound of his pelting feet trailing away. The other attendant was white-faced with fear. Taking pity on him, I sheathed my sword. "You're safe if he keeps his word," I said. "Just don't think of following him."

This one shook his head frantically. "No, messire!"

It was a peculiar coincidence that Phèdre and I were trained alike in the art of patience. She had been trained to wait on a patron's desires and could kneel motionless in the subservient *abeyante* posture for hours. I'd learned it on the training square of the Prefectory, learning and repeating a single step in the Cassiline fighting style ten thousand times over before being taught the next. From vastly different circumstances she and I had been thrown together and cast into the vagaries of fate, challenged to the depths of our beings.

And now all we could do was wait.

There were footsteps approaching the doors to the livery stable. I looked instinctively toward Phèdre, having come to have considerable faith in her keen sense of hearing. She nodded and held up two fingers. Reaching over my shoulder, I drew my sword. Two dark figures entered, the smaller one the stable lad we'd dispatched.

The other was Hyacinthe, his expression strained with disbelief and hope so intense it hurt. *"Phèdre?"*

She flung herself into his arms with a gulping sob, crying unabashedly. All the tears she hadn't allowed herself to shed for Delaunay, for Alcuin; all the hardship, abuse, and suffering she had endured. Hyacinthe held her tightly like she was the most precious thing in the world, his head bowed over hers. Trying not to disturb their reunion, I kept my gaze on the two terrified apprentices.

It wasn't long before Phèdre collected herself. We'd become adept at dealing with a sense of urgency.

"All right?" Hyacinthe asked, turning to his assistants when she wiped her eyes and nodded. "Listen to me, you two," he said to them, fishing in the purse hanging from his belt. He held up a couple of silver coins. "What you saw tonight never happened. Understand?" He gave a coin to each. "You did well. Take these and keep your mouths shut. Don't even talk to each other about it." His dark eyes flashed in a glint of lamplight. "If you do, I swear I'll call the *dromonde* upon you and curse you so you wish you'd never been born. Understand?"

Between his threat and my sword, they swore trembling promises, taking to their heels when Hyacinthe dismissed them.

For the first time, he took stock of me and realized who I was, a note of surprise in his voice. "*Cassiline?*"

I sheathed my blade and bowed. "Prince of Travellers."

"Blessed Elua, I thought Cassilines never drew their sword except . . ." Hyacinthe let his words trail off. "Never mind. I'll take you to the old house," he said to Phèdre. "Both of you. You were right to be cautious. It's not safe for you to be seen."

She closed her eyes. "Do they think . . . ?"

"Yes," Hyacinthe said in a gentle tone. "I'm afraid so. You were tried and convicted in absentia for the murder of Anafiel Delaunay and his entire household."

So much for a joyous homecoming.

CHAPTER THIRTY-FIVE

It wasn't Hyacinthe's fault that I disliked him.

I knew little of Tsingani culture, none of it good. They were a private folk with their own language and traditions. It was said that they were doomed to follow the Lungo Drom, the Long Road, for failing to recognize Blessed Elua and his Companions when they passed through Bhodistan.

And I knew of the *dromonde*, the gift of sight. Once I'd asked Phèdre if she truly believed Hyacinthe possessed it and she said he did, but speaking the *dromonde* was considered women's business and forbidden for a man. Hyacinthe's mother had spoken the *dromonde*, too. She had passed away during the Bitterest Winter, leaving him a small home on Rue Coupole where he had grown up watching her take in laundry and tell fortunes.

Hyacinthe took us there now, stoking the woodstove and heating water, sending the most trusted member of his crew to fetch food and drink from the Cockerel and putting out the word that he was entertaining in private that evening. When his second-in-command returned, he put a jug of red wine and plates of roasted squab trussed with rosemary sprigs in front of us. "Tell me."

Phèdre and I told our tale in turns, both of us tearing off famished bites while the other spoke. He listened intently without interruption until she described the Duc d'Aiglemort's treachery and Waldemar Selig's plans to conquer Terre d'Ange.

"D'Aiglemort? He wouldn't." Hyacinthe looked sick. "He couldn't!"

I raised my brows.

"Oh, he thinks to pull it off." Phèdre took a long draught of wine. "But he has no idea what he's facing, what kind of numbers Selig can muster. Hyacinthe, we need to speak to the Dauphine, or someone who can reach her."

"I'm thinking," he said. "If anyone knows you've set foot in the City, your lives are forfeit."

"Why?" I asked. "I still don't understand. Why would they think we did it? What possible gain could there be?"

"I can tell you the popular theory." Hyacinthe regarded the contents of his wine cup. "Phèdre, rumor has it that Barquiel L'Envers paid a fabulous sum for you to betray Delaunay—and you, your oath, Cassiline—and admit his Akkadian Guard into the townhouse. They say it was to settle the old score for Isabel's fate. There's no proof, of course."

Phèdre was pale. "I would never—"

"I know," he said. "I knew it for a lie and I told anyone who would listen. There were a few peers who spoke on your behalf—Gaspar Trevalion, Cecilie Laveau-Perrin. And the Prefect of the Cassiline Brotherhood sent a letter protesting the order's innocence," he added. "But Parliament wanted a conviction and the courts obliged."

"Melisande?" Phèdre asked.

Hyacinthe shook his head. "If she was behind it, she kept her hand well hidden."

"She would." There was a bitter note in Phèdre's voice, and she fingered that gods-bedamned diamond at her throat. "She played that card at Baudoin's trial, she's too canny to play it twice. It would look suspicious."

He met my gaze briefly and both of us exchanged slight shrugs. It was a relief to know that I wasn't the only person who didn't understand that relationship. After we'd stripped the squab to their bones, he cleared our plates and sat at the table, propping his chin on one fist. "All I have is at your disposal, Phèdre. Poets and players go everywhere, I can get word through them to whomever you wish. The problem is that not a one of them can be trusted to keep their silence."

She looked at me. "What about the Cassiline Brotherhood?"

Only a few hours ago, I'd been outraged by the notion that anyone would impugn the honor of a Cassiline Brother. Even with a trail of broken vows behind me, I'd trusted that the Brotherhood would grant me a means of atonement, for through extreme adversity, I'd kept the one vow that mattered most: I had protected my ward. Now, I wasn't so sure. "You say the Prefect sent a letter attesting to the order's innocence?" I asked Hyacinthe, who nodded. "I don't know," I admitted reluctantly. "Lord Rinforte wrote rather than testifying in person, and he wrote on the Brotherhood's behalf, not mine . . . if we're to contact him, best I go myself."

"No." Phèdre pressed her temples. "It's too uncertain and it would take days. There's got to be a better way. Hyacinthe, can you get word to Thelesis de Mornay?"

"Absolutely." He flashed a white grin. "A love letter, perhaps? A message from an admirer? Nothing easier. The only problem is that I can't guarantee it will arrive with its seal intact."

There were those two delicate furrows between Phèdre's eyebrows. "That's all right. Do you have paper and ink? I'll couch the real information in Cruithne. If any of your poets can read Pictish, I'll eat this table."

While we waited, she penned a note of admiration in D'Angeline, adding a postscript in transliterated Cruithne. "Cruithne," I murmured. "You speak Cruithne."

She flashed me an impish look. "I like surprising you. How does this sound? 'The last student of he who might have been the King's Poet awaits at the home of the Prince of Travellers, begging for your aid in the name of the King's cygnet, his only born.'"

"Suitably cryptic," I said.

"It will do and then some." Hyacinthe held out his hand. "Leave it unsigned. There's a gathering at the Lute and Mask tonight. I'll see this delivered to Thelesis de Mornay by noon tomorrow if I have to bribe half of Night's Doorstep to do it."

I watched him go, his satin-lined velvet cape swirling about him. There was substance beneath his mountebank's flare. "You were right to trust him," I admitted to Phèdre. "I was wrong."

"Well, and you were right about Taavi and Danele," she said. "I wanted to throttle you when you asked total strangers for help. But you were right."

"They were good people." I smiled at the memory of their kindness. "If there's naught else to be done—"

"Go, get some sleep," she said. "No one knows we're here, and Hyacinthe has a couple of crew on lookout just in case."

Of course, she wanted time alone with her oldest and dearest friend. They'd been eating stolen tarts beneath a bridge since I was a ten-year-old cadet in the First Cohort. They doted on each other.

Of course.

My smile twisted wryly. "I'll leave you alone, then. I'm sure you want a chance to talk with him."

"Joscelin . . ." Phèdre was seldom at a loss for words, but she groped for them now. "Joscelin, whatever happens to us . . . you did it. You kept your vow to protect and serve. You brought me home safe." She met my gaze, the scarlet mote in her left eye crimson in the lamplight. Kushiel's Dart, a small weapon cast by the gods. "Thank you."

I gave a Cassiline bow, leaving her to await Hyacinthe's return.

A part of me wished that Phèdre hadn't been so quick to accept my tactful withdrawal, for there was no way I could sleep while she waited alone and untended. But the roots of their relationship were deep and enduring, and they deserved a moment of privacy. If it ate at my heart, I had only myself to blame. I had chosen of my own will to break my oath. What had passed between Phèdre and me in the cavern was a sacrament, but it was many leagues away in the snowbound past, and there it would remain. I was Cassiel's Servant and my job was what it had always been: to protect and serve my ward.

That was true regardless of how I felt about her. So I lay awake and restless until Hyacinthe returned, reporting the results of his excursion in a low murmur. I couldn't make out the words, but his tone sounded reassuringly self-satisfied.

In the morning while we awaited word from the King's Poet, a young Tsingano woman arrived at Hyacinthe's behest to clean and cook and help render us presentable. I bathed and donned a dove-grey doublet and breeches and began working at the shaggy mane of braids and tangles that was my hair.

"Let me." Phèdre took over my efforts as she had in Gunter's steading so long ago. She had bathed twice before donning a blue velvet gown that didn't fit too poorly. Her gentle touch was soothing, and unless I imagined it, she was lingering over the task. I definitely felt her hands go still when she took stock of my weapons and vambraces stacked upon the kitchen table. "You're not . . . ?"

I shook my head, feeling my hair spill through her fingers. "I may have kept you alive, but I've broken my vows nonetheless. I've no right to bear Cassiline arms."

She didn't argue, just tweaked a lock of my hair in silent disagreement. "Do you want it in a single braid, then?"

"No." I gathered it myself, winding and binding it into a Cassiline club at the nape of my neck. "As a priest, I've still the right to this much."

We piled an assortment of worn and filthy hide, fur, and woolens together. Hyacinthe wrinkled his nose. "We should burn these."

"No, leave them," Phèdre said in alarm. "They're the only proof we've got. Blessed Elua, the smell alone will testify to our story!" I laughed, and she gave me a sidelong smile. Hyacinthe shook his head in bewilderment; survivors' humor can be impossible to understand from the outside. He peered out the window onto the street for the dozenth time that morning. This time, he tensed visibly.

"There's a carriage drawing up to the doorstep," he said tersely. "Get in the back, there's an exit out the postern gate. If it's not de Mornay, I'll hold them off as long as I can."

I swept my gear from the table, ushering Phèdre into the scullery where a passage led to the rear of the house. We heard the front door open. Hyacinthe offered a courteous greeting, and a woman's voice, faint but deep and rich, replied.

"Blessed Elua," Phèdre whispered with tears in her eyes. "It's her."

She pushed past me and I followed quickly as she stumbled into the kitchen, where the King's Poet was drawing back the hood of her cloak, revealing plain features lit by an inner beauty. There was grief mingled with gladness in Thelesis de Mornay's gaze. She embraced Phèdre without hesitation, murmuring words of condolence in her ear.

Nodding, Phèdre collected herself and wiped her eyes. "Thelesis, we need to speak to the Dauphine. Or Gaspar Trevalion, Admiral Rousse . . . whomever you trust. The Skaldi are planning to invade, they've a leader, and the Duc d'Aiglemort plans betrayal—"

"Shh." Thelesis gave her shoulders a quick squeeze. "I got your message, Phèdre. I knew you were no traitor. I'm here to take you directly to an audience with Ysandre de la Courcel. Are you ready?"

It was exactly what we wanted, but the suddenness of it was disorienting. Phèdre had suspected there might be rumors, but neither of us had anticipated finding ourselves tried and convicted for murder in our absence. I saw a flicker of panic in Phèdre's eyes, and stepped forward to take my place at her side. "She will not go alone," I said with calm certitude. "In Cassiel's name, I will bear witness to this."

"And I." Hyacinthe bowed. "I have lost Phèdre nó Delaunay once already, my lady, and protested too little. I will not make that mistake again. And mayhap my small gift of the *dromonde* will be of service in this matter."

Thelesis de Mornay fixed her intent gaze on him. "I pray it might, Tsingano."

Travelling through the streets of the City in a closed carriage felt unsettlingly familiar; less so the fact that we spent our passage spilling out the relevant details of our travails to the King's Poet. Thelesis listened with rising horror at the tale we bore, pausing us on occasion when she suffered from a coughing fit. She had contracted the fever and survived, but it had left her with a weakness in her lungs.

Her driver brought the carriage to a seldom-used side entrance where a cadre of guards in the midnight-blue livery of House Courcel met us. "They're members of the Dauphine's personal guard," Thelesis told us. "They may be trusted."

The guards took our weapons. I felt a pang handing over the bundle of my Cassiline arms and armor. Hyacinthe gave them the ornate dagger he wore on his hip, and a smaller, plain dagger stashed in his left boot. Phèdre bore no weapons, but they confiscated the pack that held those Skaldic items we'd retained, including Trygve's dagger. When Phèdre protested that the pack contained the only proofs of our story, Thelesis asserted that she would take custody of it, and the Dauphine's guards deferred to her.

They led us to a private audience room where the Dauphine herself awaited us, seated in a high-backed chair.

It was the first time I'd seen Ysandre de la Courcel. She was tall and slender with fair skin, light blonde hair, and eyes the violet hue of House L'Envers courtesy of her maternal lineage. She looked at once younger than one would expect, yet older than her years. Her expression was unreadable.

"Your highness." Thelesis curtsied deeply. "From the bottom of my heart, I thank you for granting this audience."

"We appreciate your service to the Crown, King's Poet," Ysandre responded in a neutral tone. "Who do you bring before us?"

"Phèdre nó Delaunay. Joscelin Verreuil of the Cassiline Brotherhood. And . . ." Thelesis hesitated, unsure how to introduce Hyacinthe.

He stepped forward and bowed. "Hyacinthe, son of Anasztaizia, of Manoj's *kumpania*."

"I see." Ysandre de la Courcel's gaze settled on Phèdre, and there was barely banked fury blazing in it. "You. You, to whom Anafiel Delaunay, my oath-sworn protector, gave his very name—stand convicted of killing him. How do you plead to *that, anguissette*?"

The nape of my neck prickled.

Phèdre was *angry*. Her spine stiffened and her shoulders squared. "In the name of the King's cygnet, his only born, I bring you a message, your highness. When the Black Boar rules in Alba, Elder Brother will accede."

Her words seemed to echo in the chamber. The Dauphine's expression turned bemused. "Yes, I know. Quintilius Rousse sent another messenger. Is that all you have to say?"

"No, but it was the message I was charged to deliver." Phèdre took a deep breath. "I swear on all that is holy, I am innocent of the death of Anafiel Delaunay and his household. Joscelin Verreuil of the Cassiline Brotherhood is innocent, too." I bowed in acknowledgment. "You have been betrayed, your highness," Phèdre continued. "Duc Isidore d'Aiglemort conspires with the Skaldi warlord Waldemar Selig to gain the throne. Joscelin and I were betrayed and sold into slavery. All these past months, we've been slaves in Skaldic steadings. They plan to invade. And they plan to betray d'Aiglemort. And unless they're stopped, they *will* succeed."

Ysandre de la Courcel had gone as still and pale as a marble statue, only her eyes alive and blazing. "You charge Isidore d'Aiglemort, hero of the realm, leader of the Allies of Camlach, with this terrible crime?"

"Not alone." Phèdre held her gaze unflinching. "I also charge Lady Melisande Shahrizai of Kusheth. It was her word that betrayed Delaunay, and is her word, in her own writing, that assures Waldemar Selig of the Skaldi that his plan will succeed."

"She speaks the truth," I added.

Ysandre whispered to one of her guards, turning back to us when he departed. "Tell me what you claim to have witnessed."

Together, Phèdre and I told the whole of the story, beginning with the Longest Night through the slaughter at Delaunay's, Melisande's false offer of sanctuary, her betrayal, and our time amongst the Skaldi. When we had finished, Thelesis spilled the satchel of worn Skaldic pelts and Trygve's dagger on the marble floor, while Hyacinthe confirmed the condition in which he found us.

After hearing us out, the Dauphine contemplated our dubious spoils. "And that is all you have to offer as proof? A wild tale and a heap of stinking hides?"

"Summon Melisande Shahrizai, then, and let her be questioned!" I challenged her. "I swear by my oath that everything we've told you is true."

The guard the Dauphine had spoken to reappeared, shaking his head at her inquiring glance. "It seems the Lady Shahrizai is not in residence," Ysandre informed us. Her speculative gaze returned to Phèdre. "But if what you say is true, why would she let you live? No member of House Shahrizai is a fool, and that one least of all."

Phèdre flushed and stumbled for a reply; I didn't know what to say. Thelesis offered an old Eisandine adage, saying, "If you catch the speaking salmon in your shrimp net, cast him back," while Hyacinthe offered a far more impudent response, saying, "The answer, your highness, is worth a thousand ducats and would take some time to give."

"Ah." The Dauphine's brows rose ever so slightly.

"Your highness." I bowed. "Phèdre bears the sign of Kushiel's Dart. For a scion of Kushiel's line to kill one marked by Kushiel himself would surely bring a curse upon their House. Nor is it lucky to murder a priest. Melisande Shahrizai did not have us slain, but she disposed of us in a manner that made our survival unlikely. I daresay she never dreamed we would escape without recapture. No one in their right mind would have dreamt it," I added. "That we stand before you is a testament to Blessed Elua's grace."

"So you say." She sat unmoved. "Is there aught else?"

Thelesis de Mornay stepped forward. "They have my word, your highness. I knew Anafiel Delaunay. I knew him well. He trusted his pupils with his life."

"Did he trust them with his secrets?" Ysandre inquired. "Did Phèdre nó Delaunay know he was my oath-sworn protector?"

Thelesis looked uncertainly at Phèdre. I already knew the answer was no; it was Melisande who told her.

"No," Phèdre murmured, bowing her head. My nape prickled again. "No, my lady, he did not. But you would have been better served if he had." Her head rose; her words emerged sharp and precise. "Anafiel Delaunay taught me and used me and kept me in ignorance, thinking to protect me. And if he hadn't, mayhap he would not have died, for I might have guessed Melisande Shahrizai's game if I knew what was at stake. I was the only one close enough to see it. But I didn't and now he's dead." I touched her arm unobtrusively, as though we were slaves again in Gunter's steading, warning her not to press too hard. Instead, Phèdre's tone shifted, lightening with relief. "The Palace Guard! Your highness, question the guard."

Of course. I could have slapped my forehead. "Your highness! We sought an audience with you and then with the King's Poet on the day of Delaunay's murder. They turned us away, but surely one of them would remember a Cassiline Brother and an *anguisette* in a *sangoire* cloak."

Ysandre de la Courcel frowned, but she didn't refuse, turning to the guard she'd sent in search of Melisande. "Go. Be discreet." Looking back at us, something in her regal mien cracked, the fear beneath it surfacing. "Ah, Elua! You're telling the truth, aren't you?"

Phèdre knelt, gazing up at the Dauphine. "Yes, my lady," she said quietly. "I am sorry. It is true."

The weight of it settled on Ysandre's shoulders. I watched her accept the bitter truth and delve within for some hidden depths of resolve. It occurred to me, not for the first time, that the Cassiline Brotherhood failed to teach its cadets to understand the ways in which women are strong. "And my uncle the Duc L'Envers?" she inquired. "Rumors implied his involvement in your disappearance."

Phèdre shook her head, rising gracefully. "To the best of my knowledge, Barquiel L'Envers had naught to do with it. He and Delaunay had settled the score between them."

The Dauphine wasn't finished. "Is it true that my uncle had Dominic Stregazza killed?"

I'd never fully understood—nor had I wanted to—the complicated web of intrigue into which I'd unwittingly been ensnared, but it was Phèdre's forte. "I believe it to be true," she said now. "The name of your mother's murderer was the coin Delaunay paid for a truce between him and the Duc. He reckoned it worthwhile to protect you from the same fate, your highness."

"And you gathered this information for him?" Ysandre asked.

"I had a companion. Both of us gathered information for Delaunay." Phèdre paused to wipe her eyes. "His name was Alcuin nó Delaunay. It was Alcuin who garnered proof of the Stregazzas' guilt. He died with my lord Delaunay."

"You weep for them," Ysandre observed. "I wish I had known Anafiel Delaunay better. I wish there had been time." She rose. "Come with me."

I hadn't realized that we were in the King's quarters until she led us to his bedchamber. A pair of Cassiline Brothers stood guard on either side of the door. I wouldn't call them elderly—trained warriors may be fighting-fit into their fifties—but their stern, disciplined demeanor reminded me of Phèdre's initial perception of Cassiline Brothers. Despite the club knotted at my nape, neither of them recognized me as a fellow Brother without my greys and weapons, and I took care not to meet their gazes. They bowed to the Dauphine in acknowledgment and opened the doors for us.

Ganelon de la Courcel, King of Terre d'Ange, lay on a canopied bed, his face fallen into deep lines. He appeared motionless, and for a long moment, I daresay all of us thought he had passed away. Then his breast rose and fell shallowly with a slow intake of breath.

"So lies my grandfather the King," Ysandre murmured, twisting a heavy gold signet ring on her right hand. "So lies the leader of our fair realm." She stepped back abruptly, forcing us to scramble in an undignified attempt at observing royal protocol. "He suffered a second stroke in this Bitterest Winter. I have been ruling in his name." She closed the doors and the Cassiline Brothers took up their posts, hands crossed to rest on dagger hilts in our at-ease posture. "Thus far, the peerage has endured my pretense. But if we stand upon the brink of war . . ." She paused. "I do not know how long I can last before the reins of control are wrested from my hands. I do not even know if it is a mercy or a curse that my grandfather lives still." She shook her head. "How long can this last? I do not know."

Behind us, Hyacinthe gave a ragged gasp and staggered, leaning against the corridor wall and fumbling at the collar of his doublet.

"Hyacinthe!" Phèdre was beside him in an instant, but he waved her away, doubling over. His brown skin had gone ashen-grey.

With one long indrawn breath, he straightened. "Three days." His voice was faint and husky, but it resonated with an eerie certitude. "The King will die in three days, your highness." He offered Thelesis de Mornay an exhausted nod. "You did bid me to use the *dromonde*, my lady."

It was Ysandre who responded curtly, leveling her gaze at him. "Do you claim the gift of prophecy, son of Anasztaizia?"

"I claim the *dromonde*, though I lack my mother's skill at it." Hyacinthe rubbed his temples. "Your highness, when Blessed Elua was weary, he sought sanctuary among the Tsingani in Bhodistan and we turned him away with jeers and stones. In our pride, we predicted that he and his Companions would be cursed to wander the earth and call no place home. It is unwise to curse the son of Earth's womb. The fate we decreed became our own, cast out and forced to walk the Long Road. In her cruel mercy, the Mother-of-All granted us the *dromonde* to part the veils of time, that next time we might see truer."

Whether or not Ysandre believed him was impossible to determine. "You will say nothing of this," she said to the Cassiline Brothers. "I bid you by your oaths." Both of them bowed in obedience. I wondered if either one had ever broken a vow.

We followed the Dauphine back to the audience room, where her guard had returned with a Palace Guardsman. He looked once at Phèdre, gaze lingering on her features, then gave me a quick up-and-down glance. "Those are the ones," he said with certainty. "Her in that dark red cloak, him in Cassiline grey. They asked to see the King's Poet, but I thought—"

"Thank you." Ysandre inclined her head. "You have done us a service. Understand that this is a matter of utmost secrecy, and to speak of it is treason and punishable by death."

Swallowing hard, the guardsman bowed and withdrew.

Ysandre paced the chamber, thinking aloud. "Elua have mercy. Who do I trust? What do I do?" Remembering our presence, she paused and switched to a more formal manner of address. "Forgive us our ingratitude. You have done us a mighty service and endured great hardship to do so. We are grateful, I assure you in the name of the Crown, and will see that your names are cleared forthwith. You will be reinstated as heroes. You have my word upon it."

A sense of relief suffused me.

"No." It was Phèdre who spoke, brows furrowed again. "Your highness, you can't. Isidore d'Aiglemort is your most imminent threat. He has an army at his command, assembled and at the ready. You have one advantage: He isn't aware that you know him for a traitor. If you reveal it now, you force his hand. Gather those peers you trust and seek their counsel. If you do not marshal your strength, he will strike—and he may win. If he doesn't, it will lay Terre d'Ange bare for the Skaldi to plunder at will."

"Then you will still be named a murderess, Phèdre nó Delaunay," the Dauphine observed. "And your companion with you."

"So be it," Phèdre said. "Hyacinthe and Lady de Mornay are safe, there was no rumor of their involvement. Joscelin . . . ?"

I bowed to her with deep sincerity, then turned to the Dauphine. "I am already condemned. I have broken every vow but one to bring us here alive, your highness. I do not fear the judgment of Terre d'Ange when a greater judgment awaits me."

Ysandre inclined her head in understanding. "Know that I am grieved by this necessity. However, you are too valuable to dispatch into a safe exile. Thelesis, you have my complete trust as always. In my grandfather's name, I place the rest of you under the custody of the throne." Out of slavery, into custody; there was a certain irony to it. I caught Phèdre's eye and knew she was thinking the same thing.

CHAPTER THIRTY-SIX

We spent the following days in a state of suspended anxiety, waiting to see if Hyacinthe had spoken the *dromonde* truly.

Although we were in the Crown's custody, Phèdre and I weren't actually confined—we just didn't dare show our faces in public. Thelesis de Mornay resumed her duties as the King's Poet, which were reduced at the moment to reading to his majesty's unconscious figure in her rich, soothing voice. Ysandre permitted Hyacinthe to return to Night's Doorstep with a promise that he was at her beck and call. A generous suite of rooms fit for visiting royalty was allotted to Phèdre and me. We were attended by two maidservants whom Ysandre trusted, and members of her personal guard rotated to ward our quarters day and night.

I might have taken offense at the notion were I not so thoroughly exhausted. One of the first things Ysandre did was to send her personal Eisandine chirurgeon to examine us.

"Your own handiwork?" he inquired wryly as I removed my tunic to reveal the coarse stitches straggling the length of the half-healed wound in my side.

"Mine," Phèdre admitted. "I'm a poor seamstress." There was an impish note in her voice, and I cocked an eyebrow at her. The night of Elua's cavern was a sacrament we had implicitly promised never to discuss. She merely gave me one of her most sparkling looks in return, breaking my heart anew.

"You likely cracked any number of ribs, too." The chirurgeon probed delicately, fingers tracing the bone beneath the flesh. "But those are healing clean. You're lucky you didn't pierce a lung."

After washing the wound with spirits that stung like hell, he applied a poultice to draw out any lingering poisons, then prescribed saltwater baths for me, extensive rest, and a rich diet for both of us to recover from the deprivation our bodies had endured.

Three days after Hyacinthe spoke the *dromonde*, Ganelon de la Courcel, King of Terre d'Ange, passed quietly into death.

As my weapons and vambraces had not been restored to me, I was in the middle of telling the hours empty-handed for the first time since our return when the mourning bells rang. Thelesis de Mornay came to confirm the news shortly thereafter. Word went out across the realm. The coronation was to be a hasty affair. Ysandre was young, untried, and unwed, and she needed to act swiftly to assert her authority. D'Aiglemort and a number of other Camaeline peers were quick to send word they were unable to attend due to increased Skaldi activity on the border.

It was a lie; or if not entirely so, it was predicated upon treachery. Isidore d'Aiglemort was conspiring with the Skaldi to step up their raiding. I wondered how many innocent villagers and townsfolk had been killed in the process—and I thought about the fact that Selwyn *died* preserving d'Aiglemort's life.

At least I'd never know if he'd have reckoned it worthwhile had he known what the Duc d'Aiglemort intended. There was a certain mercy in that, for I wasn't entirely sure. Selwyn had a prickly sense of honor, but he was a staunch supporter of the Allies of Camlach and he'd idolized d'Aiglemort. If nothing else, I liked to think Selwyn would have been clever enough to see the flaw in his idol's plan, which rested on the assumption that Waldemar Selig could be trusted to keep his bargain.

Then again, I'd first heard the name Melisande Shahrizai from Selwyn during one of his speculative monologues on the political intrigue swirling around the throne. It was when Prince Baudoin had first taken up with her. Selwyn had dismissed her as an insignificant player in the game.

After all, she's just a woman.

If he'd said that to me now, I'd have fallen down laughing.

I suspect Melisande, among other things, weighed heavily on Phèdre's mind during those days of inaction. It was a somber time as it was, all the guards wearing black armbands in a show of mourning. I thought much about my own sins, tallying my failures, shortcomings, and broken vows. My day of reckoning was coming, for I'd be called to account by the Cassiline Brotherhood. One could debate whether love could ever truly be a sin, but it was my deeds for which I would be judged. I'd have said that Phèdre had no cause for penitence. The deaths of Delaunay, Alcuin, and the entire household weighed heaviest, and that was no fault of hers in any way. There was the loathing she bore for her own body's betrayal, but that, too, was no fault of hers. It made my heart ache for her, and most especially for the last one—and to that I couldn't speak. I knew who could, though.

"You give Elua and Naamah their due," I said to her. "But it's Kushiel who marked you as his chosen, and it is Kushiel's will you challenge when you despise what you are. If you challenge the will of the gods, you will break. I know, I was on the verge before you drew me back." She listened intently to me. "You have a need for penance," I said. "Beg leave to attend the temple of Kushiel. They will accept your atonement."

She nodded. "I will."

I do not pretend to any deep comprehension of what takes place at Kushiel's temple, but I understood the mortal need for atonement in a way I couldn't have before. Only the Prefect of the Cassiline Brotherhood—or Cassiel himself—could shrive me of my sins. For the rest of Terre d'Ange, there was Kushiel's mercy. Ysandre granted leave for a discreet visit to the temple, where Blessed Elua knows Kushiel's priests and priestesses hold all manner of secrets behind their anonymous bronze masks. Phèdre returned with a renewed lightness of spirit and a soft, languid smile.

Shortly thereafter, Ysandre issued a formal public announcement that on the heels of the coronation, she would be retiring to one of the Courcel estates to mourn for a fortnight. Privately, we were informed that she was summoning a council of trusted peers and our attendance was required.

The location Ysandre had chosen was a luxurious hunting lodge that her grandfather the King was wont to use for retreats. It was a good choice, a logical place for a young Queen to retire to for a brief time to mourn her loss and prepare to shoulder the burden of ruling the realm. Ysandre was somewhat of a mystery. For the entirety of her life, everyone had wondered whom she would wed. No one had wondered how she would rule, but they were going to find out very shortly.

The lodge was less than a day's ride from the City. We rode in covered carriages painted with the colors of House Courcel, with ornately carved panels bearing the swan insignia. Members of the Queen's Guard rode alongside the royal entourage. I was uneasy at being unarmed. I'd rather have my weapons back than half a dozen guardsmen, but Ysandre deemed it wiser that I should appear unarmed before the council, since to their knowledge I was a convicted murderer.

The inner circle that Ysandre had assembled was discouragingly small. There was Thelesis, of course—and the influence of poets in Terre d'Ange was never to be underestimated, but she held no direct powers.

Other lords and ladies represented a majority of the provinces. I'd never met the Comte Tibault de Toluard from Siovale, but my father had spoken well of him. Barquiel L'Envers I remembered well. From what I'd seen, I neither liked nor trusted him, but he was Ysandre's uncle and the sovereign Duc of Namarre.

Comte Percy de Somerville represented L'Agnace; more importantly, he held the title of Royal Commander. Gaspar Trevalion, Comte de Fourcay, was a longtime trusted friend of Delaunay's and represented Azzalle.

Duchese Roxanne de Mereliot, often called the Lady of Marsilikos, represented the sovereign duchy of Eisande. There was one other prominent personage in attendance: Lord Charles Rinforte, Prefect of the Cassiline Brotherhood.

No one had warned me, and my heart stopped and stuttered at the sight of him. He was well into his seventies now and his white hair had the yellowish tinge of old ivory, but he wore it tightly bound in a club and his carriage was as upright as ever, his eyes as sharp and hawkish as ever.

Elua have mercy, I hadn't expected my reckoning with the Brotherhood to happen this way, but mayhap it was for the best.

The seven peers rose to offer deep bows and curtseys when Queen Ysandre entered the room with her unlikely entourage. They rose at her bidding, and Gaspar Trevalion's voice rang out in joyful surprise.

"Phèdre!" Heedless of protocol, he crossed the room to embrace her. "Blessed Elua, you're alive!"

"Delaunay's *anguissette,*" Barquiel L'Envers drawled as he approached us. "And the Cassiline. Did you not enjoy my largesse in the Khalif's court? I'm told I sent you to Khebbel-im-Akkad after paying you to betray your master."

I stepped between them. "Your grace, it is not a matter for jesting."

He looked me up and down. "You've grown some spurs, lad. Ysandre, I damned well hope you brought them here to clear my name."

"It is one reason," she replied. "Though I fear it is the least of them."

I bowed to her, then turned to the Prefect. "Lord Rinforte, before we progress, allow me to confess that I am in violation of my sworn vows." Kneeling at his feet, I bowed my head and crossed my forearms. "I remand myself to your justice."

"You stand condemned of betraying the household you swore to protect and serve, Joscelin Verreuil." The Prefect's tone was grim. "That is no mere *violation*, young Brother."

"Of that, he is innocent." Ysandre raised her voice with impatience, reminding us all that she was the Queen. "My lord Rinforte, the integrity of your order is unbreached. Believe me when I tell you that I wish it were not so, for the truth is far worse. Hear their story for yourselves."

Once again, Phèdre and I told our story.

It was received with a moment of silence, broken by Barquiel L'Envers lounging at his leisure on a couch. He raised his brows at his royal niece. "Sure you don't expect us to believe this ludicrous confabulation, Ysandre."

"Not on their word alone," she said calmly. "The Palace Guard confirms they sought an audience on the night of Anafiel Delaunay's murder. My own chirurgeon examined them and attests that their condition was consistent with the privation they describe, down to the weals on Joscelin Verreuil's wrists where he was bound in chains."

"And yet these things may have other causes and other explanations," Tibault de Toluard mused with Siovalese logic.

"They may," Ysandre acknowledged. "Yet the most damning piece of evidence in their conviction was their absence. Here they stand before us."

"Is there no other evidence that we might consider?" Roxanne de Mereliot inquired.

Phèdre glanced at Ysandre for permission, curtsying to the Lady of Marsilikos at the Queen's nod. "Yes, your grace. You may send word to the Comte de Bois-le-Garde of Camlach, whose men came upon us in the borderlands. Or you may venture into Skaldia if you wish," she added with a sidelong look at L'Envers. "I can sketch a map to Gunter Arnlaugson's steading. You're welcome to ask him about the two D'Angeline slaves he bought from Camaeline soldiers."

"And whether it's true or false, either way we show our hand to d'Aiglemort, if we're not killed outright for our troubles." Barquiel L'Envers scratched his close-cropped hair. "Delaunay taught you well. It's a pretty trap if you've laid it. If it's not, Elua help us all."

"Elua help us, indeed," Gaspar Trevalion murmured. "I've known Phèdre nó Delaunay since she was a child. There is no way she would be party to Anafiel's death. And as for the Cassiline . . . look at him, Barquiel. He wears his honesty on his face. I do not know you," he said to Hyacinthe, "but I see no gain in this for you."

Hyacinthe bowed without his usual Prince of Travellers flourish. "I've known Phèdre longer than anyone, including Anafiel Delaunay. I saw her the night they returned to the City. She does not lie."

The Comte de Toluard cut to the heart of the matter. "But why would Isidore d'Aiglemort desire Delaunay's death?"

Ysandre flushed, but her chin rose. "Because I asked Anafiel Delaunay's aid in a certain matter which d'Aiglemort may have believed dangerous to his plans."

"No." Barquiel L'Envers sat upright. "Oh, no. You can't mean to abide by it!"

"I can, and I do!" she retorted.

I had no idea what they were talking about; at a glance around the chamber, I suspected that was true of most of us. Thelesis de Mornay and Gaspar Trevalion were the only ones following the exchange. The rest of us appeared bewildered—except for Phèdre, who had that vague look of abstraction like someone listening to a strain of music no one else could hear that meant Elua-knows-what was going on in her head.

Meanwhile, the newly crowned Queen and her uncle continued to argue. "Ysandre, if there's any measure of truth to this tale, I can arrange a union with a Prince of the royal House of Aragon who will bring two thousand spears to your aid!"

I think they'd have quarreled for hours, but Gaspar Trevalion interrupted. "The Lioness of Azzalle came a great deal closer to overthrowing the Crown than anyone realized," he observed. "If she'd succeeded in bringing the army of Maelcon the Usurper across the Straits, they would have swept across the realm like a scythe."

Now I wished I'd paid more attention to Selwyn's speculations. They were speaking of Alba, where succession was matrilineal. The rightful heir was the Cruarch's nephew, his sister's son. It was the Cruarch's son, Maelcon the Usurper, who instigated an uprising and claimed the throne for himself.

The Royal Commander, Percy de Somerville, was shaking his head. "They'd have found us unprepared, but it wouldn't work. It's been tried. The Master of the Straits left no vessel afloat."

A memory tickled at my thoughts; Alcuin in Delaunay's study, poring over every reference he could find to the Master of the Straits.

I'd never known *why*.

"No one can say why the Master of the Straits chooses as he does," de Toluard mused. "He granted Lady de Mornay passage for the price of a song. He let the old Cruarch cross, and no one knew why. Who can say what might have happened had he let the Usurper's army cross?" He paused, frowning. "But it came to naught because their conspiracy was betrayed by

Isidore d'Aiglemort and Melisande Shahrizai. My lady Ysandre, what have you to do with that fateful island of Alba, and what has it to do with the death of Anafiel Delaunay de Montrève?"

Montrève?

Ysandre held her chin high. "At the age of sixteen, I was promised to the Cruarch's heir, his sister-son Drustan mab Necthana."

"Delaunay!" Phèdre returned from wherever her thoughts had led her, eyes wide with understanding. "Ah, Elua, that message from Quintilius Rousse, the Master of the Straits . . . you're seeking passage for the Pictish Prince, aren't you? But why turn to Delaunay?"

"Anafiel Delaunay de Montrève." Ysandre smiled faintly. "You never even knew his proper name, did you?"

"I know he loved your father Prince Roland, your majesty," Phèdre said quietly. "And I know he was oath-sworn to protect you."

The Queen nodded. "His father the Comte de Montrève disowned him for it. My grandfather didn't like him, but he knew the strength of his oath and discretion. He wanted to learn if there was any merit left in an alliance with a deposed heir. I wanted somewhat else." She took a deep breath. "Drustan mab Necthana."

"The *blue boy*?" Barquiel L'Envers gave a short, disbelieving laugh. "You really want to wed the blue boy?"

"I want to wed the rightful heir to the Kingdom of Alba, to whom I am betrothed!" she shot back at him. "Yes, uncle. And it is to that end that Anafiel Delaunay was working, and it is to prevent it that he was killed."

Lord Rinforte frowned, his brows drawing together over the stern prow of his nose. "But what has this to do with the Skaldi and the Duc d'Aiglemort?"

"Nothing," Ysandre said, "or everything."

My knees were growing stiff and sore from kneeling on the marble floor; Elua knows, I'd been driven to them far too many times in the past months. No one but Hyacinthe noticed or cared when I rose from my penitent pose. He caught my eye and we exchanged faint, rueful shrugs, both of us in well over our heads. I daresay the Tsingano knew all manner of secrets and gossip regarding the lords and ladies at play in Night's Doorstep—it was his stock in trade—but that was far from being privy to watching the gears of monarchy at work.

Queen Ysandre paced the chamber, hands clasped behind her back. "All of my life, I've been nothing but a pawn in this game of alliance by marriage," she announced. "I have been courted, besuitored, and feted by D'Angeline lords who saw nothing in me save a path to the throne. The Cruithne did not come for power. They came following a dream, a vision of a black boar and a silver swan, so strong it swayed the Master of the Straits to grant them passage."

I saw Phèdre mouthing words to herself, and wondered for neither the first nor last time what was going through her mercurial mind.

"Drustan mab Necthana does not desire leadership of Terre d'Ange," the Queen continued. "We spoke of it in broken tongues; a dream of the two of us grown, ruling our kingdoms in tandem. A romantic dream of youth, but there was truth in it. I saw somewhat in him I could love, and he in me. When he spoke of Alba, his eyes lit like stars." She cleared her throat. "I am not prepared to abandon this alliance for mere political expediency."

There at last was the crux of the matter.

Love as thou wilt, Blessed Elua bade us; but Elua was immortal and cared naught for crowns or thrones. Love ran roughshod over whatever stood in its way, including my own vow of celibacy. And love and marriage did not always run in tandem when there was a matter of succession at stake, even here in Terre d'Ange.

"You are the Queen, my dear," Roxanne de Mereliot was saying. "You may not have the luxury of choosing."

"The House of Aragon—" L'Envers began.

The Lady of Marsilikos cut him off. "Aragonia will send aid regardless if Terre d'Ange is invaded by the Skaldi. But the most immediate danger to the throne lies within our own borders." She looked sympathetically at Ysandre. "The simplest solution, my dear, is for you to wed Isidore d'Aiglemort."

There was an outraged protest from Percy de Somerville, but in its wake came grudging murmurs of agreement as the assembled peers began convincing themselves that making would-be traitor Isidore d'Aiglemort the Prince-Consort of the realm was the best, most logical way to bind his loyalty and consolidate D'Angeline forces.

It was a pleasant fiction if one hadn't actually seen Waldemar Selig uniting the tribes of Skaldi under one banner.

"No." Phèdre whispered the word with an urgency that halted the discussion. "That would *not* be the end of it. The Skaldi threat is ten times more dire than anything d'Aiglemort could muster. And then there is Melisande, who has a secret correspondence with the warlord Waldemar Selig. Joscelin and I have seen the Skaldi. If they know themselves betrayed, not even the full loyalty of the Allies of Camlach can save us."

"Then we will take Melisande Shahrizai into custody," Lord Rinforte said brusquely. "It is a simple enough matter."

I damn near laughed out loud at that; Phèdre actually did, though it was a humorless laugh. "My lord, there are no simple matters when it comes to Melisande Shahrizai. Do you think it a coincidence that she is in Kusheth and not the City for the coronation? I wouldn't wager on it."

"But why?" Tibault de Toluard inquired. "Why would she betray the realm? What stakes are worth such risk?"

Phèdre touched the diamond at her throat. "Two realms lie at stake, my lord, not just one. But when you come to it, it is the game and not the stakes. The Shahrizai have played the Game of Houses since Elua's footsteps echoed across the land, and Melisande plays it better than anyone." She regarded the peers. "She has made her mistake. I am the proof of it and this slight advantage we bear is its sole outcome. Do not count on her to make another. If you take the Duc d'Aiglemort to be our greatest foe, I fear it will be our undoing."

"And yet we cannot ignore a province in revolt," de Somerville observed.

"Nor can we know for certain that Camlach is in rebellion," Barquiel L'Envers retorted. "Establishing the truth of this confabulation is our first order of business."

The ensuing conversation was lengthy, but in the end one conclusion was reached and I understood the players better. It harkened back to Prince Baudoin and his mother's betrayal. While they had been condemned to death for sedition, the Prince's father and sister were exiled for their lesser role. House Trevalion, the sovereign duchy of Azzalle, was currently under the aegis of Percy de Somerville's son Ghislain. The essence of the plan was to rescind the sentence of exile, effect a marriage between Ghislain and Baudoin's sister, Bernadette de Trevalion, and dispatch the remainder of Baudoin's Glory-Seekers to feign loyalty to the Allies of Camlach and spy on our behalf. The Prefect agreed that members of the Cassiline Brotherhood would serve as couriers to spread the truth once it was confirmed.

It seemed gods-bedamned complicated to me when they could simply take Phèdre's and my word for it, but at least it was forward motion.

"Well, Ysandre," L'Envers said. "What of your blue boy? How do matters stand in fair Alba?"

The young Queen nodded at Gaspar, whose reply sounded as weary as I felt. "Drustan mab Necthana escaped the bloodbath," he said. "Along with his mother, sisters, and a small band of warriors, he fought his way to western Alba and took refuge among the Dalriada."

I had no idea who the Dalriada were.

"Yes, I'm aware of this." There was a sarcastic bite to L'Envers' voice. "As is much of the realm, as was Ganelon. Which is why he was inclined to break their betrothal, which, of course, was never made public in the first place. Is this the extent of your vast intelligence for which Anafiel Delaunay was slain?"

"No." Despite the lingering effects of the fever, Thelesis had a poet's command of tone. "Delaunay was in contact with Quintilius Rousse. Admiral Rousse carried a request to the Master of the Straits, pleading with him to grant passage to Drustan mab Necthana and his people."

"I take it he refused?" de Toluard inquired politely.

"He answered thusly," Thelesis replied. "*When the Black Boar rules in Alba, Elder Brother will accede.* That was the message Rousse sent to Delaunay."

Barquiel L'Envers rolled his eyes. "A message which makes no sense."

The Queen's Poet shook her head. "Not true. The folk of Alba and Eire are divided into four peoples: the folk of the Red Bull, from whom Maelcon the Usurper descends on his mother's side; the folk of the White Mare, whom the Dalriada follow; the folk of the Golden Hind to the south; and the folk of the Black Boar, to whom Drustan was born. The Master of the Straits is saying that he will grant our request if Prince Drustan can reclaim Alba."

"As he would, no doubt, if Blessed Elua were to return from Terre d'Ange-that-lies-beyond to ask a boon." L'Envers shrugged. "'Tis a moot point."

"Do not discount the Cullach Gorrym," Phèdre said aloud in a wondering manner. "Hyacinthe! Do you remember? Your mother spoke the *dromonde* to me once. *Do not discount the Cullach Gorrym.*"

"I remember." He frowned. "It didn't make any sense."

"It does now," she said. "The Cullach Gorrym are the Black Boar. It means Prince Drustan."

Queen Ysandre fixed her intent gaze on Hyacinthe. "You say your mother had this gift, too?"

"Yes, your majesty," he said. "Her gift was greater than mine."

"What do you see now?" she asked.

Hyacinthe stared into the distance, his black eyes blank and empty. "I see a ship," he said eventually. "Nothing more. When paths branch in many ways, I cannot see far. It is only the straight road I see clearly, your majesty. Like your grandfather's."

"Ganelon was on his deathbed," Percy de Somerville said. "Anyone could have foretold his passing."

"The Tsingano foretold the day of it." Ysandre looked thoughtful. "If the Dalriada knew of the Master of the Straits' pledge, they might aid Drustan in regaining the throne of Alba. Anafiel Delaunay would have gone if he'd not been killed. 'Tis a pity, for he spoke Cruithne, as did his young pupil Alcuin. And there is no one else I trust who does." She glanced apologetically at Thelesis. "I do not speak of you, Queen's Poet; I trust you with my life. But I have spoken with the chirurgeons, and you would not survive this journey."

"So they tell me," Thelesis murmured. "But Anafiel Delaunay had two pupils, your majesty."

I'd been lulled into quietude during the lengthy discussion. Until that moment, my own path was short and clear: Cassiel willing, I would be doing whatever penance and atonement the Brotherhood deemed sufficient. Now, my heartbeat began to quicken. It seemed mayhap Cassiel was not yet finished with this servant.

Meanwhile, Phèdre had grown very still. "What are you saying?"

Thelesis drew a deep, careful breath. "Phèdre nó Delaunay, I'm saying *you* could take Anafiel's place as the Queen's ambassador."

"My lady, I'm an *anguissette,* not an ambassador!" she protested. "I'm trained to serve Naamah, not the Crown!"

"Oh, please," Barquiel L'Envers said laconically. "Any pupil of Anafiel Delaunay's is considerably more than a Servant of Naamah, little *anguissette.* You're the only whore I know of to double-cross a Skaldic warleader and survive to warn a nation."

"My lord!" Her voice shook. "What I did to survive, I hope never to do again. I do not have the strength to live through it twice."

"The Cruithne are not the Skaldi," Ysandre observed. "And you would be under the protection of Admiral Rousse and his men. Phèdre, I'm grateful for what you've done. Never think it is not so. We would not ask this of you were it not so urgent."

I rose and bowed to the Queen; almost everyone in the salon looked as startled as though a piece of furniture had stood up on its rear legs. Only Phèdre gazed up at me with hope and trust, and it was to her alone that I spoke. "Phèdre, we've survived worse adventures. I'll go with you. I have sworn it. To protect and serve!"

It was enough to kindle that spark of hope into a flame . . .

. . . which was immediately doused by the Prefect's steely voice. "Brother

Joscelin! We are glad that your innocence has been established in the matter of Anafiel Delaunay's death. But you have confessed yourself in violation of your vows and remanded yourself to our justice. For the salvation of your soul, you must atone and be shriven. Only those who strive to be the Perfect Companion are fit to serve the scions of Elua."

It was a stinging rebuke, albeit a deserved one. "My lord Prefect." I bowed to him. "I am still sworn to the household of Anafiel Delaunay. If there is salvation to be found for me, it lies in honoring that oath."

"You are relieved of your oath to Delaunay's household," Lord Rinforte announced. "I decree it so."

It was an unexpected blow and I braced myself as though he'd struck me. "My lord Prefect, please. No."

There was distaste in his expression. "What transgressions *have* you committed, Brother Joscelin?"

Elua have mercy, I could scarce remember; but the first was the one that mattered the most to me. "I failed to safeguard my ward from harm," I said quietly. "I've slain in anger. I've committed murder. And I've . . ." I glanced at Phèdre, who averted her gaze, a memory hovering like a kiss at the corner of her mouth. No. I would not confess that a sin. "I've drawn my sword with no intention of using it."

The Prefect shook his head, looking profoundly disappointed. "These are grave sins, Brother Joscelin. I cannot allow it. Another will go in your stead."

I stood, thinking.

It was a simple choice. Lord Rinforte was harsh, but correct in his edict. I could atone and be shriven and remain a member of the Cassiline Brotherhood. Or I could abjure the Brotherhood, accept damnation, and continue to serve as Phèdre's protector as she ventured to the westernmost end of the earth on a mission for the Crown.

Turning to Queen Ysandre, I bowed. "Your majesty, will you accept my sword in your service as the oath-sworn protector of Phèdre nó Delaunay?"

"Do it and be damned, young Brother," the Prefect warned me grimly. "Cassiel's vows bind for a lifetime and beyond!"

The Queen was silent for a moment, weighing the gravity of the situation, before she gave me a regal nod. "We accept your service," she said, then turned to the Prefect. "My lord Rinforte, we grieve to cross your wishes. But we must follow the precept of Blessed Elua in such matters, and not the will of the Cassiline Brotherhood. By Elua's teaching, this man is free to choose his own course."

"There will be a reckoning on the Misguided," Lord Rinforte muttered. "So be it. Is that your will, Joscelin Verreuil?"

I met his hawk-eyed glare. "It is."

He bowed to me with Cassiline precision, then made a two-fisted gesture akin to breaking a thing in twain. "Joscelin Verreuil of the Cassiline Brotherhood, I declare you anathema."

CHAPTER THIRTY-SEVEN

It was done.

I felt at once a deep grief and an inexplicable lightness. After formally accepting my sword into her service, Ysandre turned to Phèdre. "And do you, Phèdre nó Delaunay, accept this charge to take up your lord's duty and carry my words to Prince Drustan mab Necthana of the Cruithne?"

She stood and curtsied. "Yes, your majesty. I will go."

"Good." Ysandre's tone was firm, but there was relief in it, too. "Then we must find a way to get you safely to Quintilius Rousse."

"Where is the Royal Admiral?" Phèdre inquired.

"Kusheth."

Kusheth, the province of Kushiel's scions; the province to which Melisande Shahrizai had retreated for the moment. House Shahrizai had at least half a dozen estates there, but it was a large province. The odds of us crossing paths were long, but I wasn't inclined to bet against the improbable.

"Your majesty." Hyacinthe spoke up for the first time in hours, a gleam in his black eyes. "I have an idea. Are you familiar with the routes of Tsingani *kumpanias*?"

Queen Ysandre leaned forward. "Tell me."

Hyacinthe described the manner in which the *kumpanias* travelled the length and breadth of Terre d'Ange to trade at horse fairs, abjuring the primary roads for their own trails marked by secret Tsingani signs. An annual spring horse fair would be taking place in Kusheth, where the Tsingani gathered to vie over the most promising winter foals and yearlings. It cast me back to market days in Rive-de-Lusande when a passing *kumpania* paused to barter, tell fortunes, and scheme to exploit the gullible—to chasing Toulouse atop the walls in the balmy twilight; falling upon Selwyn with a girl in the garden, breeches around his ankles and his long hair loose. That was what Naamah's Servants meant when they leant over their balconies in the Trysting Mews and sang to us.

> *Hey, boy, pretty boy, let down your long fair hair, oh!*
> *Hey, boy, pretty boy, I'll make a man of you, oh!*

I'd just made the single most difficult choice of my lifetime, but no one was paying attention to me. It was to be expected; the fate of the realm was at stake. The council was listening to Hyacinthe's plan to travel in disguise and join a *kumpania* willing to accept good coin to take us to Pointe d'Oest, where Quintilius Rousse and his fleet were anchored. It was a ludicrous plan, which also made it a rather good one. We had to assume that word of Phèdre's and my escape had reached d'Aiglemort. Selig would have sent a message and although we may have outpaced it, the Allies of Camlach scouting party could likely confirm that we'd survived the passage and were on D'Angeline soil.

Whatever semblance we took, there was no disguising the crimson mote in Phèdre's eye. But they would be searching for a courtesan and a Cassiline, not a party of Tsingani; there was no reason anyone would think to search a *kumpania*. Hyacinthe was sure that with her dark hair and eyes, Phèdre could pass as his cousin, a D'Angeline by-blow with Tsingani blood in her veins. As for me, he claimed he had the perfect guise in mind if he could obtain it, somewhat no one could expect from a Cassiline Brother.

Out of the corner of my eye, I saw the muscles of Lord Rinforte's jaw twitch every time anyone referred to me as "the Cassiline." Fair enough; and yet it felt as though he was twisting the knife. In a quiet act of acknowledgment, I untied the leather thong holding my hair in a tidy Cassiline club and shook it out, letting it fall loose and shining.

The Prefect's grimace deepened. Phèdre was the only other person to notice, her eyes widening in surprise.

I kept my expression neutral. I hadn't done it out of defiance, nor did I intend it to be a declaration of anything save my own independence. I wasn't going to answer the siren's call from the balconies. The edicts of the Brotherhood no longer bound me, but there was only one of Naamah's Servants who could tempt me, and what had passed between us was sacred in its own right.

At any rate, as far-fetched as Hyacinthe's plan was, no one could conceive of a better one. All the members of the Queen's Council swore a binding oath of secrecy and loyalty before departing for their various destinations.

Phèdre and I were to remain at the hunting lodge, kept under wraps while Hyacinthe and Thelesis returned to the City to get everything in readiness for our journey. They stayed that evening, though, as did Gaspar Trevalion, and we had the first chance to talk in a more leisurely manner. Gaspar took the opportunity to offer Phèdre his deep and sincere condolences at the loss of Delaunay and Alcuin—the former he'd counted among the dearest of friends, the latter a rare jewel. Alcuin was that, I thought. I'd never truly gotten to know Anafiel Delaunay; enough to respect him, also enough to despise him a bit for using his pupils to trawl for information while keeping them overly much in the dark.

Thelesis inquired gently if Phèdre had aught to call her own since Delaunay's home and all it contained had been seized by the courts.

"Just this." Phèdre flicked Melisande's diamond with one finger. "Which it seems I'm damned to wear until the day I can throw it at her feet. But I lost little to the courts. Nearly all that I had went to Master Teilhard to finish my marque." She cast a rueful look over her shoulder. "A pity he wasn't able to do so."

Gaspar Trevalion squeezed her hands. "I swear on the memory of Anafiel Delaunay, so long as I live, you'll not want for aught, Phèdre. And when this matter is done, I will see your name cleared." He glanced at me. "You, too."

"It seems to me that we might claim a considerable reward from the Queen for this service, yes?" Hyacinthe suggested. He grinned at my expression of disdain. "If you're going to travel amongst the Tsingani, you might as well start thinking like one."

I scowled at him.

"Better than thinking like one of the White Brethren," Phèdre said to me in Skaldic. Hearing her address me in our slave-tongue startled the scowl off my face. The shimmer of a smile in her eyes told me that was exactly what she'd intended.

I raised my eyebrows at her. "And will you teach me to speak Cruithne as you did Skaldic?"

"I don't know," she teased me. "Do I have to have you chained in a kennel to make a willing pupil of you?"

I laughed and shook my head. It was strange to feel my hair stir and shift, utterly unbound. I'd braid it later, but there was still a sense of freedom in wearing it loose. "I think I've learned the merits—and the dangers—of paying heed to your words, Phèdre nó Delaunay. Your lord would be proud of you."

"Mayhap." She met my gaze, her expression soft and deep. "Thank you."

I looked away, almost wishing my memories weren't so vivid. "Well, I couldn't leave you to suffer the guardianship of some dried-up old stick of a Cassiline, could I? And the Brothers would despair of you, Tsingano," I added to Hyacinthe. "At least I might hope to survive our companionship without being driven mad."

Hyacinthe grinned. "You've come a long way since Phèdre had to rescue you from Eglantine tumblers, Cassiline. I hope we face nothing worse together."

I bowed. "Blessed Elua grant that it's so."

We were some days waiting. I didn't care for being cooped up in secrecy, especially unarmed. My blades and vambraces were dedicated to Cassiel's service, but the actual weapons belonged to House Verreuil. Ysandre had promised to see about restoring them, but she had enough on her plate that I didn't press the matter. If they weren't restored to me I'd require a visit to a very skilled smith to acquire replacements, a thought that gave me a pang. I couldn't even imagine trying to explain it to my father.

In the meanwhile, I continued to tell the hours empty-handed and take as much exercise as I might in the confines of the hunting lodge, feeling my body regain strength and resilience with every passing day. At Phèdre's request, Queen Ysandre had every volume referencing Alba and the Master of the Straits that could be found in the Royal Library sent for her to study.

I borrowed paper, pen, and ink from her to write a letter to my family at home in the mountains of Siovale. It was a difficult chore. I didn't even know if word of my disappearance and conviction in absentia had reached them. I should have asked the Prefect if he'd sent word to my family, though I supposed it wouldn't matter either way. Even though I'd not seen them in over a decade, I knew they would never believe me guilty of such a heinous crime, but they would surely be worried to pieces over my disappearance. For the sake of secrecy, I didn't dare include any details. All I could do was assure them that I was alive and well, and advise them to contact the Siovalese member of our council, Comte Tibault de Toluard.

After debating the matter with myself for at least a full day, I chose not to reveal that I'd been declared anathema by the Cassiline Brotherhood. I daresay my mother would understand, but it hurt too much to envision the hurt and disappointment in my father's sober mien. Either they would learn it from the Comte or the Brotherhood, or Elua willing, I would tell them myself in person.

While we waited, Ysandre extended a kind gesture to Phèdre that meant more than I think the young Queen could have known—or mayhap she did understand in her own way. The two of them were of an age; one born into the strictures and constraints of a hereditary ancestry, the other sold into a gilded cage of indentured servitude as a small child. Having learned from Thelesis de Mornay that the near entirety of Phèdre's earnings had gone to Master Teilhard to complete her marque, the symbol of both her covenant with Naamah and her freedom from debt-bondage, the Queen brought the elderly marquist to the hunting lodge to finish his work.

It brought Phèdre a tremendous amount of peace. Whatever befell us, her marque was complete. The finial was visible, the tip of a rose unfurling crimson petals like a lover's kiss at the nape of her neck. The black thorny lines of the stem were in stark contrast against her creamy skin. The effect was bold. It was exquisitely wrought, but there was nothing dainty or delicate about its appearance. The marquist's title was earned, for surely he was a master of his craft to see the fierce determination simmering beneath all the pretty manners and graces of the Court of Night-Blooming Flowers.

I would have liked to see it whole.

That was a dangerous thing to think, but I couldn't help it. When I closed my eyes, I could still trace its unfinished lines on her skin.

The day after the marquist departed, Hyacinthe returned. He brought mounts and pack-mules laden with plenty of stores. And he brought clothing. His own attire was gaudy enough, but now it would be topped with a vivid saffron cape that was apparently the traditional Tsingani travelling color. He'd brought one lined with maroon silk for Phèdre, as well as a colorful headscarf and a blue gown with layers of flouncy skirts, the velvet nap worn shiny in places. It would suffice, especially if she drew the hood close enough to shadow her features and no one was searching at close range for an *anguissette* with a scarlet mote in her eye.

"I thought about giving you an eye patch," Hyacinthe teased her. "'Twould be a rakish look for you."

"Yes, and draw all the more attention for it. I thank you kindly for refraining," she said wryly. "What of Joscelin?"

I was wondering, too.

"Aha." Hyacinthe unfolded a voluminous grey cloak. "As for you, Cassiline . . ." He shook out the cloak to reveal a satin lining in a wild array of shimmering colors, all the hues of the rainbow. Phèdre's eyes sparkled with mirth as she tried to cover an involuntary giggle. "You know what this is?"

I did.

"It's a Mendacant's robe," she said. "I saw one once."

I'd seen Mendacants many times in Rive-de-Lusande; wandering Eisandine fabulists sworn to share Eisheth's joyful gift of story with the world. The riotous color of their robes represented the intertwining of truth and fable.

"It was Thelesis' idea, hers and the Lady of Marsilikos'." Hyacinthe handed the cloak to me. "There's no way you could pass as having Tsingani blood, Cassiline. But this will explain your presence." He paused. "Can you lie?"

I swung the cloak over my shoulders, then gave it a theatrical swirl to reveal the lining. "I'll learn."

"You can start with these." Ysandre de la Courcel entered our quarters unannounced, accompanied by two Cassiline guards. Both of them wore dour looks, especially the one carrying an armload of leather and gleaming steel. It was my gear—my sword, my daggers, my vambraces. "It's my understanding that these arms belong to the family and not the Brotherhood," she said. "You offered me your sword, Joscelin Verreuil, and this is the sword I accepted. You will bear it in my service." She smiled, the hint of a dimple showing. "'Tis up to you to conceive a tale of why a travelling Mendacant bears Cassiline arms."

I bowed to her with profound gratitude, then accepted the bundle. "Thank you, your majesty."

"You've done well," Ysandre said to Hyacinthe. "Phèdre . . ." She presented her with a weighty gold signet ring strung on a long, sturdy chain. It bore the swan crest of House Courcel. "This is my father's ring, the one upon which your lord Delaunay swore his oath." She held up her right hand. "I wear my grandfather's now. If Admiral Rousse doubts you, show him the ring. And when you gain the distant shore of Alba, give it to Drustan mab Necthana. He will know it, for I've worn it since my father's death."

"Yes, your majesty." Phèdre curtsied, then lifted the chain over her head, hiding the ring in her bodice.

I checked my weapons and found that they'd been lovingly tended by a skilled smithy—edges ground and whetted to a razor keenness, all chinks and nicks smoothed, thoroughly cleaned and polished. My vambraces were mirror-bright, and even the leather straps were clean and oiled.

I donned each piece with a sense of ceremony. Anathema or not, these were *my* arms. They had belonged to House Verreuil of Siovale and had since before I was born. I knew them, the heft and balance and reach, the cool slither of chain mail over the backs of my hands, the hilts against my palms as welcome and familiar as a mother's embrace. I had to remove my Mendacant's cloak to don my baldric and scabbard; back on, its flowing folds concealed everything but the hilt of my longsword protruding over my right shoulder.

"Very good, then." Ysandre stood tall, chin lifted with resolve and hope. "Go forth, and may Blessed Elua be with you all."

CHAPTER THIRTY-EIGHT

We set out through the Senescine Forest, a course which retraced the final leg of my journey from the Prefectory, searching for Tsingani indicators—*chaidrov,* Hyacinthe called them—at every crossroads. I was at home in the forest and reasonably comfortable that we were safe travelling across the province of L'Agnace, where Percy de Somerville's influence held sway. It is a bountiful province, for Anael's gift to humankind was husbandry and he taught his children and their descendants to respect, care for, and tend to the Earth that gave birth to Blessed Elua himself.

While we sojourned through the forest, Phèdre was absorbed in reading Prince Rolande de la Courcel's diary, a gift that Ysandre had given her. It detailed his early manhood and his lifelong romance with Anafiel Delaunay, whom he'd met at the University of Tiberium as a passionate young poet with a knack for biting satire. It gave Phèdre a glimpse of the man she'd known so well in his complicated adulthood as the very different young man he'd been. She even grew adept at reading on horseback when our pace was slow.

Hyacinthe was a noisy travelling companion. He carried a timbale of thin-scraped hide soaked and shrunk taut over a wooden frame with metal cymbals, drumming merry tunes to pass the time. I cannot say I was easy in his company. I understood the logic of drawing attention as a means of appearing not to have the slightest fear of drawing attention. But he was *so* loud with his music, his gaudy attire, flashing his smile and doffing the velvet cap he wore atop his luxuriant black ringlets at passing strangers.

There was a great deal that lay unsaid between Hyacinthe and me, and we circled warily around it. What I truly wondered about was his intentions toward Phèdre. It was my understanding that certain things were taboo in Tsingani culture. It was clear that he adored Phèdre—as she adored him—

but it was forbidden for a Tsingani man to have relations with an indentured servant. Now that her marque was fully inked, Phèdre was entirely free of the bonds of debt-servitude.

"What about Tsingani women?" I asked.

Hyacinthe laughed wryly. "No such edict exists, simply because it's unthinkable. Tsingani men are protective of their women's virtue. Any Tsingani woman consorting with one of the *gadje* would be outcast."

"Like your mother," I observed. "Hyacinthe . . . is your grandfather truly the King of the Tsingani?"

He didn't answer right away, jogging his mount ahead. I caught up with him, Phèdre trailing some distance on the empty path behind us, Rolande's diary in her hands. "Honestly?" he said. "I have no idea."

It was my turn to be silent.

"My mother told me her father Manoj was the king of our folk, and he cast her out after she fell in love and gave her virtue to a D'Angeline nobleman," Hyacinthe said. "There is no place in our culture for an unwed woman who has lost her virtue. My mother spoke the *dromonde* truly and she taught me to see and speak it, even though that is forbidden, too. I have no cause to disbelieve her."

"And yet you cannot be sure," I said.

He nodded. "Just so. But I've longed all my life to learn the truth and meet my mother's people. She didn't like to speak of it." Changing the subject, he eyed me. "So tell me, have you conceived a plan to entertain folk as a wandering Mendacant?"

I smiled. "Oh, I've a trick or two that might serve."

He snorted. "I'll believe it when I see it."

That night we made camp in a pleasant clearing. There had been a spring thaw and with clear skies and mild temperatures, we didn't even need to erect a shelter. After the horses and mules had been tended and we had eaten, I rose to stand before the campfire. I'd discovered that my Mendacant's robe contained a multitude of hidden pockets where items could be concealed. Those were of little use to me since I had no training in sleight-of-hand, but the robe also concealed hidden inner sleeves into which wooden rods were sewn in place to manipulate the edges of the cloak.

"Behold!" I flung the cloak wide open with both hands, using the hidden rods to make it flare skyward like wings. "Hear this humble Mendacant's tale . . ." It wasn't a very good tale, to be honest; I hadn't yet begun to polish my story in which a Cassiline Brother bequeathed his arms to a Mendacant who saved his life by spinning a very long tale to distract his enemies. I sketched the rudiments of it, finishing with, "And thus instead of tales, this Mendacant spins . . . *knives*!"

One final flourish of the cape, and I gave a Cassiline bow, straightening with daggers drawn. The blades flashed in the firelight as I flipped them in the air, catching them by thc hilt. It was a skill I hadn't used since Selwyn and I taught ourselves in the millhouse loft; I'd had to test myself surreptitiously to make sure I remembered how to juggle the blades, but my hands had retained the memory. I started slowly, one rotation per throw, then began to increase the pace, faster and faster, adding another rotation and another until my daggers were spinning like stars. Hyacinthe whistled through his teeth and brought out his timbale, tapping and rattling it to my ever-increasing rhythm. Phèdre laughed with surprised delight, clapping as I gave the daggers a last toss and caught them with crossed arms to deliver a closing bow.

"Not bad, Cassiline!" Hyacinthe said.

"Wherever did you learn to do that?" Phèdre's eyes were still sparkling. "Surely it's not an official part of your training!"

Carefully removing my Mendacant's cloak, I reclined on my sheepskin bedroll and propped myself on my elbows. "No, it's somewhat my friend Selwyn and I figured out at the Prefectory. We saw a pair of jongleurs throwing knives in the market square one summer."

Hyacinthe raised his brows. "You do know that's done with unedged knives?"

I shrugged.

"You've not spoken of your friend Selwyn before," Phèdre observed. "What's he like?"

"Canny." It was the first word that came to mind. "Rebellious, unpredictable. He loved fighting and political intrigue."

"Doesn't sound like Cassiline material," Hyacinthe said.

"He wasn't."

"Where is he now?" Phèdre asked softly.

"Dead," I murmured. "He was cast out of the Prefectory for violating his vow of chastity."

"With *you*?" Hyacinthe asked in mild astonishment.

"No," I said. "It was with another cadet. Village girls, too. Selwyn hated the Brotherhood. He wasn't supposed to have been pledged to it, he only became the middle son when the eldest of two others died in an accident."

"I'm sorry, Joscelin," Phèdre said in a quiet tone.

"It's funny," Hyacinthe mused. "I suppose I always thought of Cassiline Brothers as interchangeable, coins stamped by the same die. Consistent, efficient, deadly, and dour. I wouldn't have imagined you as a barefoot boy juggling daggers for fun."

"I'll tell you what's *funny*." I rubbed my face. "Selwyn was from Camlach. Isidore d'Aiglemort was his liege lord. When the Brotherhood expelled Selwyn, he went to join the Allies of Camlach. He was slain defending d'Aiglemort."

Phèdre took a slow breath, a series of emotions reflected in her gaze. "He must have been good."

I don't know why it was the exact right thing for her to say, but it cut through everything that didn't matter. "He was," I said. "Before Waldemar Selig, he's the only warrior to ever best me with a sword."

"Really?"

I nodded. "Selwyn fought dirty. Not in the training yard where the masters could see, only when no one was watching." *Fight me.* I smiled at the memory. "According to him, I needed to learn to expect anything."

"Did you?" Hyacinthe inquired.

"No," I said. "Not until Skaldia."

We let the matter lie, then; neither Phèdre nor I were inclined to invoke those memories, and Hyacinthe knew enough to leave be. I lay beneath the stars thinking that it hadn't been all that bad to talk about Selwyn. I'd let the pain of his death fester for far too long. There was healing in remembering the good times. And I'd made Phèdre laugh with unexpected joy tonight, which was enough to send me into sleep smiling.

Our continuing path led us deeper into the Senescine, following the *chaidrov*—a broken branch or twig, a sign scratched in bark—that Hyacinthe spotted at various crossroads. It was every bit as swift and considerably safer than it would have been to travel the main roads and skirt the forest. When the dense forest began to thin and the pathways to widen, we knew that we must be near the border of Kusheth.

The sense of ease that the deep cover of ancient trees had afforded me lessened as we followed the Tsingani markers to emerge into open skies and fields traversed by winding country lanes.

There was no reason to believe anyone was searching for us in Kusheth; not unless one of the Queen's Council had betrayed us, and they had been chosen with extreme care. Outside of that circle, no one knew Ysandre fully intended to keep her pledge to Drustan mab Necthana, especially since the heir to Alba had become an exile in his own country. Nonetheless, large portions of Kusheth were House Shahrizai territory, and we had to reckon on the probability that word of our escape from Skaldia, either via Selig, d'Aiglemort, or both, had reached Melisande Shahrizai. And while Melisande also had no reason to suspect our presence in Kusheth, any rumor or sighting of one bearing the mark of Kushiel's Dart would surely reach the ears of House Shahrizai sooner than later.

According to Phèdre, House Shahrizai was clannish and secretive. She thought it likely that others were involved in Melisande's schemes, but she didn't know the other individual Shahrizai well enough to suspect which ones. If she was right, it didn't matter as far as we were concerned so long as we crossed Kusheth undetected. The real problem lay at the end of our journey. The Royal Navy lay at anchor off the coast of Pointe d'Oest, which lay under the aegis of the Duc de Morhban.

I remembered the name. Quincel de Morhban was the host of the Longest Night masquerade to which Melisande had brought Phèdre. I'd never met the man, but that surely didn't endear him to me. And since Admiral Rousse had communicated solely by encrypted messages in the past year, odds were good that de Morhban was restricting his access. Tsingani went everywhere, though; renowned and respected for their horse-breeding skills as much as they were regarded with suspicion for their ability to gull the gullible.

The closer we drew to the Hippochamp, the more Tsingani we saw on the road, ranging from young couples on horseback with a single yearling to trade to large *kumpanias* consisting of numerous colorful wagons and strings of horses.

Hyacinthe was in his element.

I'd been wrong to take him for nothing more than a popinjay, sailing blithely through life on flashy charm and a smooth line of patter. Tainted by his mother's moral failing in the matter of her seduction, a sin compounded by teaching him to use the gift of the *dromonde*, he'd never been a fully accepted member of Tsingani society. He'd made a place for himself in the more risqué aspects of D'Angeline society peddling fortunes and gossip—and he'd started a thriving enterprise with his livery stable—but he would never be accepted as fully D'Angeline, either.

The Tsingani had a word for what Hyacinthe was: *Didikani*, half-breed. That was how we explained Phèdre's appearance. But here on the open road, no one knew Hyacinthe from the small community of Tsingani in the City of Elua. Seeing his cheerful enthusiasm, his brown skin and black hair, and the mirthful glint in his dark eyes, they thought him a dashing young Tsingano man; nothing more and nothing less. Unwed women, identifiable by their uncovered hair, flirted with him as we passed, laughing and teasing in their own dialect, which was a mixture of D'Angeline and Tsingani.

I received my share of covert sidelong glances, whispers, and titters. As a *gadje* without a drop of Tsingani blood in my veins, I was off-limits, but I was enough of a novelty to warrant curiosity. It was a piece of irony that amongst the three of us, it was Phèdre who drew the least attention. With an embroidered headscarf tied around her hair to indicate she was a wedded woman and the saffron hood of her cloak drawn to conceal her features, she appeared demure and unobtrusive as long as no one looked too closely—and no one did.

Spring had arrived while we journeyed through the Senescine; trees budding, pale sprouts of winter wheat emerging from the earth. In the evenings, we made camp and I continued to practice juggling my daggers. I was working out a tale better suited to entertain children, too; there was one my brother Luc used to act out for us in a delightfully terrifying manner.

The Hippochamp was a vast green field, lush with spring grass. There were hundreds of Tsingani present and thrice as many horses in all manner of breeds from dainty high-stepping palfreys to majestic drays with their thick waterfalls of mane and tail. We'd arrived in good time. The oldest and most powerful *kumpanias* had claimed the center of the field, circling their wagons around a vast campfire and setting up paddocks, but smaller troupes and even a few wagonless parties of individuals were claiming spaces around the outskirts. Hyacinthe set out stakes with bright green ribbons to mark ours, evoking a brief unpleasant memory of the holmgang for me.

After what I'd learned of Hyacinthe's history, it was touching to see him so joyous amidst a gathering of his own people. Phèdre had confided in me that he'd longed to find his family all his life. He had loved his mother and held her in the utmost regard for the sacrifices she'd made to raise him, but he couldn't help yearning to be a part of the community that was his birthright, and especially his grandfather Manoj.

Of course, it was possible that Hyacinthe's grandfather would reject him out of hand due to his half-breed status. So his mother had told him, for she had been outcast for the sin of having lost her virtue to a D'Angeline man—Hyacinthe was living proof of it. But he had long harbored a secret hope for acceptance.

In his usual easygoing manner, Hyacinthe befriended our nearest neighbors on the outskirts of the field, a small *kumpania* consisting of two couples and a half a dozen babes and young children among them. After trading them a wineskin for three bowls of a game meat stew, he introduced us.

He had concocted a more extensive history than I deemed necessary for Phèdre to explain her *Didikani* blood, and explained that she wore the headscarf of a wedded woman though her husband had died during the Bitterest Winter. Their head man Neci and his household accepted this without question and offered sympathy to her.

"And this . . ." Hyacinthe gestured at me. "This is a travelling companion who needs no introduction."

I rose, bowed, and swirled my cloak, spreading it like wings to reveal the rainbow hues lining its voluminous folds. Neci's family laughed and clapped, and the older children stared with wide-eyed delight.

At their invitation, we gathered around their campfire. Hyacinthe brought out his timbale and Neci's brother-in-law played the fiddle. I would have liked to stay for the ensuing discussion, but as soon as I set my bowl aside, all the children save the one yet a nursing babe surrounded me, clamoring for a story.

"Are you sure?" I asked them, feigning reluctance. "It might be scary!" All of them responded at once, yes, yes, yes, they were sure, they wanted to hear a scary story, high-pitched excited voices spiraling into the night sky. "All right, then!"

I made them clear a circle for me, then began juggling my daggers. Neci's wife and her sister came to watch, oohing and ahhing at the display. I staged a few near-misses just to make them gasp, then sheathed my daggers and began spinning a story for them. I couldn't remember the details of Luc's version, but it had to do with witches and bears. I set my version in Skaldia, wherein an exiled Cassiline Brother turned down the hand of a Skaldic princess, despite her declaration that no man could refuse her and live. The princess ordered her brother, who possessed a magic bearskin, to kill the Cassiline. In the gloriously terrifying—at least to a seven-year-old boy—culmination, the protagonist is attacked by a bear. Alone, with Cassiel's blessing on his sword, the Cassiline slays the bear . . . and when he skins its hide, he finds a man's body inside it.

Ideally, of course, the story would be told with a bear hide—Luc used an old bearskin rug from one of the attic rooms. But a Mendicant's robe is meant for storytelling. I dropped onto all fours, working the hidden rods to make the fabric hump and flare, giving my best approximation of a bear's growl. The children shrieked with fear and delight, their mothers laughing and clapping as I folded the wings of the cloak flat.

By the time I'd finished, Phèdre was sitting alone and untended, watching the Tsingani dance, Hyacinthe among them. Their dancing was as lively as their music, the women twirling their flounces and holding their shoulders just so, the men's feet a blur as they stamped out complex rhythms.

"What passes?" I asked.

She gave me an amused sidelong look. "Well, you make quite the Mendacant, messire Verreuil."

I laughed. "I spoke of our quest."

"Neci is eager to make a name for his *kumpania*," she said. "Hyacinthe promised him a considerable amount in gold coin to take us to Pointe d'Oest if he can't find a larger *kumpania* willing to escort us."

"Good," I said. The Queen had given us a generous purse for this undertaking. "When would we leave?"

"Three days hence, once the horse fair concludes," she said ruefully. "I would that it were sooner."

"It's worth the delay to travel in a safe disguise." I followed Phèdre's gaze. She was watching Hyacinthe dance with a young unwed woman. "What news of Hyacinthe's purported grandfather?"

"Manoj." She pointed toward the center of the vast field where the biggest and brightest of the carts were encamped. "They call him the Tsingan Kralis." I shook my head, not understanding. "King of the Tsingani."

I raised my brows. "So he really is . . . ?"

Phèdre nodded. "The Prince of Travellers."

CHAPTER THIRTY-NINE

I'd assumed that we would pay a visit on the Tsingan Kralis first thing in the morning, but Hyacinthe was unsure of his welcome. If it were true that his mother Anasztaizia was the King's daughter, her family would surely know he was *Didikani* and not a full-blooded Tsingano, so he chose a more indirect approach.

We strolled around Manoj's paddock, surveying and discussing his herd. Tsingani display their wealth in necklaces and headkerchiefs and earrings strung with coins, worn by the women. *Galb,* they were called; Hyacinthe had his mother's, three tiers of coins to which we'd added a goodly number of gold ducats from the Queen's treasury.

For safety's sake, it had been hidden in my care, but it had to be displayed to establish our credibility. Since the Tsingani would take offense at a man wearing *galb,* it fell to Phèdre to wear it. I placed it around her neck myself, arranging it over the fringed silk shawl she wore to conceal Melisande's diamond—the signet ring on its chain hung low enough that her bodice hid it. I arranged the *galb* to display it to its best advantage, lingering over the task. She touched my hands in acknowledgment, smiling up at me beneath her colorful headscarf. I wished we'd thought to sew the scarf with dangling coins just to add to the undeniable charm of Phèdre nó Delaunay in Tsingani attire.

With that amount of gold on display, it wasn't long before a member of Manoj's troupe—one of many nephews—came over to talk with us. Even then, Hyacinthe didn't reveal his heredity, only that we were in search of a *kumpania* willing to escort us to Pointe d'Oest in a highly lucrative venture. It was enough to garner an immediate audience with the Tsingan Kralis in his tent. Smaller *kumpanias* like Neci's camped on the outskirts, sleeping under the stars or in their wagons; the big ones had spacious tents erected in their encampments and the Tsingan Kralis' was the largest, brightly striped and appointed with carpets and various niceties.

Manoj was an imposing presence: fierce, staring dark eyes in a weather-beaten face, iron-grey hair, and a luxuriant mustache framing a mouth like a clenched fist. Half a dozen or so family members were in respectful attendance. Manoj looked us all over with an impassive gaze before addressing Hyacinthe in the Tsingani dialect.

"He wants to know why Hyacinthe wants to take his people and horses west," Phèdre murmured. "And what *kumpania* he hails from." She listened, concentrating hard. "Hyacinthe is telling him that the Royal Admiral is at Pointe d'Oest and requires horses for his ground troops."

Having said his piece, Hyacinthe bowed to the Tsingan Kralis; Phèdre and I followed suit. Manoj waved a hand in disdain, speaking again.

"He's asking where Hyacinthe heard such a rumor." Phèdre winced. "And asking about his *kumpania* again."

Hyacinthe straightened from his bow and looked the Tsingan Kralis in the eyes, speaking in D'Angeline. "I come from the City of Elua where I know many people and hear many things," he said. "I am Hyacinthe, son of Anasztaizia. I am born to your *kumpania*, Grandfather."

In the rear of the tent, a woman dropped an earthenware cup.

Manoj blinked. "Anasztaizia's son? Anasztaizia had a boy? A son?"

"I am her son," Hyacinthe said.

That was the last exchange I understood for quite some time. None of us had known what to expect of the old patriarch's response, but he began shouting for someone named Csavin, a Tsingano of middle years, who flung himself on his knees before Manoj, hands clasped in a plea for forgiveness. Manoj gave him a solid buffet on one ear, then rose weeping to embrace Hyacinthe, kissing his cheeks.

I swear, it was like being cast down from the great tower on the plains of Shinar in the Tanakh into the chaotic profusion of tongues Adonai gave unto humankind. Members of Hyacinthe's newfound family were talking all at once in their Tsingani dialect, which bore influences from a dozen tongues along the Long Road. Phèdre, who had a gift for language, understood just enough of their conversation to look horrified.

"What is it?" I murmured.

She pressed the heels of her hands against her closed eyes. "You know, I always believed Hyacinthe's mother was seduced by an unscrupulous D'Angeline lordling. That's what she told him."

"No?"

She shook her head. "No. The *kumpania* did visit the City of Elua long ago, but she wasn't seduced. She was tricked. This Csavin fellow was her cousin. He lost a big wager at Bryony House." Her mouth twisted. "He wagered her virtue and paid the debt with it."

I knew little of Bryony House save that it catered to patrons who loved wealth and craved the excitement of risking it, but this; this broke the sacred tenet of consensuality. "Is that even legal?"

"It oughtn't be," she said soberly. "But Guild laws only protect D'Angeline citizens. I don't know. Either way, Bryony House ought to be charged with heresy."

I agreed.

Tsingani culture bewildered me. Hyacinthe's mother—who'd been Manoj's only child and much adored by him—spent her life as an outcast exiled from her entire family. Her betrayer Csavin had forfeited all his possessions and rights, but he had been allowed to remain among his people. Now here was Hyacinthe, conceived in heresy and born into his mother's exile, being welcomed with open arms in his grandfather's tent. Nothing would do but that we hoist up our stakes and join Manoj's *kumpania* that very moment.

After determining that Phèdre was neither a blood relative nor Hyacinthe's wife, the myriad family members were content to ignore her, save for a few of the unwed girls who wanted to know if she planned to remarry. Me, they regarded with mild bemusement, but wandering Mendacants were familiar to the travelling Tsingani troupes, and my presence did not seem overly strange. They held a great fete that evening, which was much like the fete the first night only this time we were in the heart of the Hippochamp, amongst the great companies, at the insistence of the Tsingan Kralis. Hyacinthe danced and played his timbale, face flushed and eyes shining in the firelight.

My heart wasn't in storytelling that night, but as a Mendacant I was beholden to perform for the hospitality given me. I juggled my daggers. This time a number of men gathered around to watch. When one of them loudly challenged my demonstration, indicated that my daggers were dull props, I cast one then the other, planting them in the ground a few inches from the toes of his leather boots. He jumped back with a shout. I bowed and made a gesture inviting him to retrieve them. The Tsingano did so, ran his thumb over the edge of one, then nodded to the crowd and handed them back to me with a grin.

I accepted my daggers with another bow and spun them higher and higher, firelight glinting from the spinning steel. When I sheathed them after a final catch and flourish, the crowd clapped and stamped their feet.

At our new encampment, Phèdre was seated on a folding stool outside Manoj's tent. She had been watching the dancing when I began my performance, but now she was engaged in an intense-looking conversation with a very elderly Tsingani woman, wizened and bent-backed under the staggering amount of gold coinage in her *galb*.

I couldn't make out words, but the old woman jabbed a gnarled forefinger at Phèdre, cackling, then tottered away.

I joined Phèdre. "Trouble?"

She shrugged. "Who knows? It seems I'm fated to be targeted by Tsingani fortunetellers; only this one read my past. I'll be glad when we're on our way. Do you think Manoj will provide us the escort Hyacinthe asked of him?"

"I think Manoj will give him anything he asks for," I said. "Including Csavin's head on a platter."

"Manoj was boasting about his daughter's gift earlier." Phèdre looked troubled. "Hyacinthe didn't tell him he had inherited the *dromonde* and his mother taught him to use it."

"Does it matter?" I asked.

"I don't know." She watched the dancers. "It might."

At the Hippochamp the second day is for talking; and Elua have mercy, I've never heard so much discussion of horseflesh in my life. I had a good eye and Phèdre had become a rather skilled horsewoman in her own right, but there was only so long either of us could endure the endless analysis.

Manoj was willing to strike a deal. There were a handful of young men in his *kumpania* eager to make a name for themselves, and half a dozen three- and four-year-old horses of hunter stock he was willing to sell us. Since barter didn't officially begin until the third day, the Tsingan Kralis tested his newfound grandson's knowledge, challenging us to try the horses, puffing up with pride when Hyacinthe identified a colt with a slightly gamy leg.

There was a strain of unspoken tension between Phèdre and Hyacinthe that night, and I could guess why. He had undertaken this journey for her sake as well as for the realm, but finding his family and gaining their acceptance was the secret dream he'd held close in his heart for many years. Now he had found it—but he couldn't have the dream without losing any hope of a future with Phèdre. There was no place for her in Tsingani culture; if they knew her true history she would be declared *vrajna*, forbidden.

I might have broached the subject with him on our third and final day at the Hippochamp had matters fallen out differently. It was a fine day, pale blue skies with only a few wispy clouds high above.

Hyacinthe and I were doing a final stroll around the outskirts of the horse fair where Tsingani vendors were selling tack, clothing, footwear, and all manner of supplies. We were shopping for foodstuffs for the remainder of our journey to Pointe d'Oest. A few groups of savvy Kusheline peers had arrived to peruse the first horse fair of the season and purchase the cream of the crop.

"Look." Hyacinthe nodded at Manoj's encampment, where Phèdre was sitting amongst the wedded women, listening attentively. "They're teaching her a few tricks of the *Hokkano*, ways to part the *gadje* from their coin."

"Yes." Once again I remembered racing atop the garden walls in Rive-de-Lusande, chasing Toulouse in hot pursuit of the Tsingano lad. I watched a D'Angeline noblewoman surreptitiously hand a silk parcel to one of Hyacinthe's many great-aunts, knowing she would return to find it gone. "I've heard of it."

"Don't get sanctimonious on me," Hyacinthe said dryly. "I was only just beginning to tolerate . . . oh, holy *hell*!"

I spun. "*What?*"

"Put your hood up and draw your robe tight, you thick-skulled towering Adonis," he hissed, pointing with his chin. "It's House Shahrizai."

I spat out a curse.

There were five of them, three men and two women, and twice as many House Guards in attendance. All the peers had the distinctive stamp of House Shahrizai, whose bloodline descends from Kushiel himself and has been carefully maintained—blue-black hair that fell in ripples, ivory skin, and those bedamned sapphire eyes. I swear, if there are any babes born into House Shahrizai with blonde hair or brown skin, they lock them in a donjon and never let them see the light of day.

Of course, Melisande was among her kin.

Phèdre.

The thought of her panic was like a gong ringing inside my head, deafening me to everything else. Across the field I saw her see and stiffen in rigid fright. Rational or not, this was the thing she'd feared above all. I tensed to sprint to her side.

"No." Hyacinthe's hand clamped tight on my upper arm. "We go together. Hurry, but don't draw attention."

It took all the restraint I had not to run the last few paces. She was frozen in place, eyes wide with terror, face white and drained of blood. On the far side of the field, the Shahrizai were strolling idly, commenting on the horseflesh on display. They'd taken no notice of us yet, not even Melisande.

"Phèdre!" I grasped her shoulders and squeezed. She stared blindly past me, her pupils so dilated that her eyes looked like twin pits of blackness, a single crimson petal. Her heart was beating like a trapped rabbit's, her breath coming in short, shallow gasps. I shook her. "Phèdre, it's all right, you're safe! She hasn't seen you!"

There was no response, as though she couldn't hear me over the gong ringing inside her own skull.

"Move, Cassiline." Hyacinthe's voice was hoarse. Kneeling before Phèdre, he took his hands in hers and spoke the *dromonde*, gazing intently at her face and willing her to hear him. "Phèdre, listen. Listen to me. *She will pass, and see nothing.*"

There was no mistaking what he'd done. As short and simple a foretelling as it was, his words resounded with that eerie, hollow echo. They hung in the air between all of us and Phèdre came back to herself with a sharp indrawn breath, her gaze returning from a distance consumed by Melisande's presence.

Among the members of Manoj's *kumpania* present, silence built until it burst into an outcry. "*Vrajna!*" One voice took up the cry, then another and another, fingers pointing. "Anasztaizia's son speaks the *dromonde*! He brings a curse upon us all!"

All of them, every single one who had taken Hyacinthe to heart, great-aunts, aunts and uncles, cousins—all of them turned on him in a heartbeat, pointing fingers and shouting in outrage. I drew my daggers and crossed them low in unobtrusive warning.

They fell silent when Manoj stumped furiously over from the nearest encampment, parting at his approach. The old patriarch's mouth was working and there was a mixture of rage and anguish in his fierce stare. "Is it true?"

Hyacinthe bowed. "Yes, Grandpa-ji," he said quietly. "I have the gift of the *dromonde*. My mother taught me to use it."

"It is *vrajna*." There was utter certainty in Manoj's voice. "*Chavo*, my grandson, Anasztaizia's son, you must renounce it. The *dromonde* is no business for men."

Out of the corner of my eye, I could see the House Shahrizai party making their way slowly down the length of the field, Tsingani staring at the striking picture they made in their night-sky-black garments laced with gold embroidery. The Shahrizai hadn't noticed us yet—a group of Tsingani arguing at a horse fair was no novelty—but it was only a matter of time before they drew near.

Hyacinthe bowed to his grandfather again, tears of regret in his dark eyes. "Forgive me, Grandpa-ji. I cannot. You cast my mother from your *kumpania,* but I am her son. If it is *vrajna* to be what she made me, then I am *vrajna.*"

"So be it." The Tsingan Kralis turned away to face his people, squaring his slumped shoulders. "My daughter is dead," he announced. "I have no grandson."

They began to wail, mourning Hyacinthe as though he were dead. He stood in shock, ashen after speaking the *dromonde.* Phèdre looked dazed, like she'd awakened from a nightmare. The Shahrizai were rounding the near turn.

I took charge, shoving my daggers into my sheaths. "Tsingano!" I cuffed Hyacinthe's head hard enough to get his attention. Adding to the incongruity of the situation, he had a string of sausages that we'd purchased dangling from around his neck. "Take Phèdre, your mounts, whatever you can carry. Go back to Neci's camp. I'll follow."

Hyacinthe nodded, pulling Phèdre upright. She looked at him with dawning horror. "Ah, Elua! I'm sorry, I'm so, so sorry!"

"Don't be," he murmured. "You did me a favor."

"Talk later." I pointed. "Go!"

Members of Manoj's *kumpania* watched in silence as I gathered up our belongings; fortunately, we'd not unpacked anything but our bedrolls and a cooking pot. "You." I beckoned to one of the young men who would have travelled with us. "Fetch my horse and our pack-mules." He hesitated. I fished in the purse tied to my belt—not all of our wealth was on display in the *galb*—and fetched out a gold sovereign. I flicked it contemptuously on the ground. "For your *kumpania*'s hospitality."

Manoj met my eyes with a level gaze, then nodded to his great-nephew, who assisted me wordlessly.

In our original campsite, I approached Neci. "Are you still minded to make your name?"

The young Tsingano headman was startled. He looked to his wife, who shrugged and looked at her sister and brother-in-law. They nodded and it was decided.

"Good," I said. "Get your horses and your things. We're riding west."

It was impressive to see how swiftly a *kumpania* could pull up stakes and take to the road. By the time Neci had concluded a trade for the horses we'd requested, his wife Gisella had the wagon packed and ready to depart. For a moment, I feared he might change his mind after having heard the gossip regarding the Tsingan Kralis' grandson being outcast for speaking the *dromonde*, but when I offered him a considerable deposit for the journey, ambition won out over superstition.

Once again, we were on our way, leaving the Shahrizai unaware behind us.

The first day was awkward, all the easy camaraderie we'd shared with Neci's family given way to tense uncertainty. Both Phèdre and Hyacinthe were unwontedly quiet, leaving me to fill the void. Like most Tsingani, everyone in the *kumpania* spoke D'Angeline at will; they simply preferred their own dialect. I wheedled the children into teaching me more Tsingani words. In exchange, I taught them the rudiments of juggling using boiled eggs, which made everyone except Gisella smile, and showed them how to work the hidden rods in my Mendacant's cloak.

Bit by bit, the tension eased.

In the evening, Phèdre and Hyacinthe excused themselves to speak in private. I stayed well out of earshot and made sure everyone else did, too. Hyacinthe had given up his birthright for her sake. They deserved time alone.

"Are they wed in secret then?" Gisella asked in confusion. "She's not *Didikani*, is she?"

"No." I saw no point in lying. "They're not wed, but they have promised themselves to each other since they were children."

She frowned. "Is she even a widow?"

"No," I said. "But until now she was a debt-servant. *Vrajna*."

Neci touched one finger below his left eye. "That one is god-touched," he said. "Or cursed."

I nodded. "I know."

Blessed Elua have mercy, I knew it all too well; what I didn't know was whether I was god-touched, cursed, or just a fool for loving her. All three, mayhap.

Before I wrapped myself in my bedroll, I checked on them. They were asleep, worn out by strong emotion, Phèdre's head on Hyacinthe's shoulder, her hair drifting like a dark river of silk across his chest. Their legs were entwined, his arms around her.

I fetched a blanket and spread it gently over the both of them, ignoring the ache in my heart.

CHAPTER FORTY

Our *kumpania*'s progress was slow, but steady.

Spring was everywhere in the green fields and valleys of inland Kusheth. We did not speak of what had happened at the Hippochamp. I assumed that Phèdre and Hyacinthe had discussed the matter between them. She felt guilty at having created the crisis by panicking in the first place. If Hyacinthe regretted his decision, he surely didn't belabor it. Beyond that first night's conversation, it didn't appear that anything significant had changed between them.

Not, of course, that that ought to be any concern of mine.

When we reached the rockier terrain of western Kusheth, our pace slowed. The roads were steeper, so steep at times that we needed to push the wagon from behind. There were rockfalls to be cleared and the lack of grazing land meant we had to spend extra time doling out precious fodder.

Nonetheless, we crossed the province in safety. Any travellers we encountered actually gave a wide berth to our colorful Tsingani wagon filled with too many adults and half a dozen children.

We knew we were growing close when the air carried a salty hint of sea water in the distance. Phèdre and I climbed atop the highest hill at our campsite and compared landmarks to the map that Ysandre had provided, one drawn by a skilled cartographer.

"Pointe d'Oest." Phèdre pointed to a peninsula jutting into the shimmering swathe on the horizon where sea met sky. "Rousse's fleet is anchored a league or so to the north. If we strike out early, we might reach him by midday."

"Good." Squatting on my heels, I sifted a handful of dirt. Even in the rocky soil, seedlings were taking root. I showed Phèdre. "Spring's coming, even here. How long do you think Waldemar Selig will wait?"

"We're months from the first harvest," she said. "He can't possibly provision an army yet."

"It's not so far off," I murmured. "And we've a long way to go."

"Tomorrow," she said in a firm tone. "We'll reach Quintilius Rousse tomorrow."

She was wrong.

Like as not we'd been crossing lands belonging to the Duc de Morhban for the past day without any sign of border guards. Today, they found us. We were pushing the wagon up the crest of a hill when one of the children cried out a warning in Tsingani. *"Dordi-ma! Gaverotti!"*

On the downslope, twenty mounted guards awaited us clad in armory and livery marked with the insignia of House de Morhban, a raven and the sea. Hyacinthe took the lead as we'd agreed, putting a Tsingani face to our unlikely *kumpania*. He rode out to meet them, requesting passage to conclude a trade with Admiral Rousse. The captain of the guard turned his head to spit casually on the ground before replying. Hyacinthe responded with a shrug and a respectful bow before returning.

"He said we need the Duc's permission to cross his lands," he said. "And we must wait for his grace to plead our case."

"Do they suspect us?" I asked.

He shook his head. "I don't think they're looking for us, just a handsome bribe."

"If they were looking for us, we'd be in custody," Phèdre said. "But I've met Quincel de Morhban. I don't think he'd stoop to petty extortion. I think he's blocking access to the Royal Admiral."

I'd never met the Duc de Morhban, but I knew who he was; in addition to being the head of the sovereign duchy of Kusheth, he had hosted the Longest Night masquerade to which Melisande had brought Phèdre.

My skin prickled. "Phèdre . . ."

She looked sidelong at me, the crimson mote in her eye vivid in the weak sunlight. "What?"

I drew a slow breath. "Nothing. Just . . . let Hyacinthe handle this."

We spent an hour cooling our heels and waiting for the Duc de Morhban. The Tsingani were anxious. I couldn't blame them for it, and I couldn't help but think how unfair it was that folk like the Tsingani and the Habiru had no protection under D'Angeline law. Hyacinthe did his best to put them at ease. Meanwhile, the children had discovered a nest of baby rabbits and were wholly absorbed by it.

Quincel de Morhban arrived with an additional score of guards. He was a tall, lean man with a harsh, rugged beauty to his features that echoed the terrain over which he ruled, greying hair, and eyes the color of tarnished steel. "You seek passage through my lands," he said to Hyacinthe. "Why? What do the Tsingani want with a sailor?"

Hyacinthe bowed. "Your grace de Morhban, we have an agreement to trade with the Queen's Admiral."

"Since when does a sailor need a horse?" The Duc's hard gaze swept over the lot of us, settling on me. "What in Elua's name is *that*?"

I dismounted and bowed with a flourish, swirling my cloak. "I am but a humble Mendacant from Marsilikos. If you would be entertained, allow me to tell you—"

"Enough." He waved me to silence, thinking. "So Quintilius Rousse thinks to build himself a horse patrol, does he? Perhaps I might make a better offer for your stock, Tsingano. What do you say?"

There was a murmur of excitement among Neci's family; they had only embarked on this journey for a profit worthy of making a name for their *kumpania*. But Hyacinthe shook his head in regret, spreading his hands in a helpless gesture. "Alas, your grace, I gave my word to the Admiral. I swore it on my mother's own spirit, may she rest in peace."

"Did you?" de Morhban asked wryly. "Pray tell, what is a Tsingano's word worth? Double Rousse's offer, perhaps?"

"Perhaps we might offer a token for our passage," Hyacinthe countered. He indicated the mount he rode. "A fine steed, let us say?"

"Rousse must be offering you a great deal," de Morhban mused. "No, I don't think so, Tsingano. It's not in my interest to see the Admiral horsed. But I'll play you fair and pay his price and more."

"As your grace wishes." Hyacinthe put on a pitiable voice. "Only convey my regrets to the Admiral and beg his forgiveness, for if you do not, my mother's *mulo* will ride the night winds and plague my sleep forevermore."

Quincel de Morhban was unmoved. "No, I don't think so. Unless there's aught else you'd care to tell me?"

"My lord!" Nudging my mount forward, I drew my daggers in one smooth motion, proffering the hilts. "Genuine Cassiline daggers forged three hundred years ago. Allow me to tell you how—"

"No." The Duc raised one hand. "I've no need of priests' trinkets, Cassiline or Mendacant or whatever you are. So if the lot of you have no further business with the Admiral that you'd care to discuss with me and naught else to offer in trade, let us be done with it."

Blessed Elua, we were *so close.* If I squinted, I fancied I could see the Royal Fleet anchored only a few miles up the coast, tiny ships bobbing on the wrinkled grey sea. Mayhap we could make the trade, bid Neci's *kumpania* farewell, and circle around to gain the shore in a more covert manner.

The Duc de Morhban had the same thought. "The sooner it's done, the sooner you can be on your way," he said. "I'll give you an escort to the Kusheline border to ensure your safe passage."

I met his unwavering gaze. If he were loyal, we could simply show him Ysandre's signet. If he wasn't, we'd be dead. The Queen hadn't trusted him. But I rather thought he was playing his own game and I couldn't see any way out of it.

"My lord!" Phèdre lifted her head and drew back the saffron hood shadowing her features. She rode forward, pulling off her headscarf, lustrous hair spilling loose. "My lord, there is somewhat else we may offer in trade for passage."

"You!" The surprise in de Morhban's face was genuine. Whatever in the seven hells he'd thought of our company, he hadn't expected it to contain Phèdre nó Delaunay disguised as a young Tsingano widow. His iron-grey eyes narrowed. "Melisande's creature. But I heard you were condemned for the murder of Anafiel Delaunay."

"Phèdre." Leaning over in the saddle, I caught her arm. "No."

She shook my hand off, her gaze fixed on de Morhban's face. "You know what I am, your grace," she said evenly. "You know what I offer. One night. Free passage. And no questions."

He didn't so much as blink. "You couldn't dictate such terms in the City, *anguissette.* What makes you think you can do so here and now?"

Neci and the other Tsingani exchanged glances, confused by the proceedings. They knew Phèdre wasn't a half-breed and that she had been a debt-servant, but they'd had no idea what kind of service was entailed.

"I own my marque and I dictate the terms I choose," Phèdre said evenly. "I've named my price. From you, I will accept no other."

De Morhban's gaze flicked briefly over me. "I seem to recall there was a Cassiline involved in the matter," he said. "What would the Queen pay for such knowledge?" He gauged Phèdre's reaction. "Or House Shahrizai, perhaps? Melisande likes to know things."

Phèdre said nothing.

I could feel the tension between them. I didn't want her to have to make this choice; not like this, not under duress, presenting herself to the Duc de Morhban like a tender morsel to a hungry wolf.

The wolf smiled, a smile that made me shudder. "What business of mine is it if someone sends Tsingani horse traders, whores, and priests to the Queen's Admiral?" he said. "Very well. Your offer is accepted. I will extend hospitality to your party for one night. In the morning, I grant you passage to trade with Quintilius Rousse. Is it agreed?"

Hyacinthe and I protested at the same time.

"Yes." Phèdre overrode us. "We'll draw up the contract in your quarters, your grace. Do you have a priest to witness it?"

Quincel de Morhban inclined his head. "I will send for one."

We followed the Duc and his entourage. The de Morhban castle sat high above the sea, impregnable on three sides. It was an excellent strategic location for a stronghold, especially in a province ruled by strong passions, but it was a remote and bleak place.

My trust in human decency was worn thin enough that I halfway expected de Morhban to break his word, imprison Phèdre, and dispose of the rest of us, but I was wrong. The Duc was a scion of Kushiel and he regarded Phèdre's gift as sacred—a sacred gift he was entitled to possess for a night.

I hated that entitlement.

I knew Hyacinthe did, too. Phèdre made a point of avoiding the both of us as we rode to the castle, where de Morhban directed his men to escort the rest of us to low outbuildings used to quarter servants during harvest season.

Hyacinthe and I exchanged another look, and he nodded to me. I dismounted, pushing the folds of my robe back to offer a formal Cassiline bow. "Your grace, I am oath-sworn to protect my lady Phèdre nó Delaunay," I said to the Duc. "I beg of you, please do not ask me to be foresworn."

"So you say." He shrugged at me. "Then again, that's exactly the sort of mindless loyalty a Cassiline would voice. Do you actually perform as a Mendacant?"

I bowed again. "Yes, your grace."

"Fine. You may entertain my household this evening."

A number of his men-at-arms looked rather excited at the prospect. Flourishing the cape, I gave one last sweeping bow and smiled at the Duc. "Harm her and you will die," I said under my breath. "That I promise."

"Do you?" The wolf smiled back at me. "But she was meant to be harmed."

I grabbed Phèdre's arm as the Duc called for his chamberlain. "Don't do this. I'll find another way—"

"Joscelin, stop." She touched my cheek. "You made Cassiel's choice. You can't keep me from making Naamah's." She unlatched the Tsingani necklace then fished out Ysandre's signet, lifting the chain over her head. "Just keep this safe."

I felt lonely and a bit foolish performing for the Duc's household that night; first in a common chamber in the guards' barracks and later in one of the lesser salons inside the keep for the domestic servants. Either way they cheered, the guardsmen appreciating the dazzling knife tosses, the others cheerfully amused by the romance of my tale of the cursed Cassiline priest. I politely declined offers of bed fellowship from aficionados of both.

I'd settled in to pass my vigil propped in a chair beside the banked oven in the kitchen when two figures poked their heads around the door, one larger than the other. My hands flew unthinking to my daggers before I recognized Hyacinthe with Neci's youngest son, Dimiti. Gesturing me to silence, Hyacinthe raided the racks of yesterday's loaves, handing two to Dimiti and keeping one for himself.

"Take those back to the *kumpania*," he whispered to the boy, who obeyed.

I watched Hyacinthe make himself comfortable sitting cross-legged atop a wooden table. "What in the world are you doing?"

He tore off a hunk of bread. "Thought you might want company."

"I don't."

He chewed and swallowed. "Well, I do."

"All right." I fetched an earthenware tub of butter from the pantry and accepted a chunk of bread. "What's on your mind?"

Hyacinthe gave me a wry look; we both knew damned well what was on each other's minds. "I hate this part."

I tilted my chair back. "You'd have hated every moment of our time in Skaldia."

"How bad was it?" he asked.

"Bad."

"And yet here we are." He popped a piece of bread into his mouth.

"It's not the same." I let the legs of my chair drop. "Believe me."

"How do you reckon?" Hyacinthe regarded me. "This choice was forced on her, too."

"Tsingano . . ." I sighed. "I don't like it, either. You heard me try to stop her. But do you honestly believe for one second that Phèdre nó Delaunay isn't *exactly* where she wants to be?"

He opened and closed his mouth, surprised. "No," he admitted. "I suppose not. That's the problem, isn't it?"

I looked away first, not wanting to give away too much of myself. "I don't claim to understand what pleasure lies in forcing another to yield body, heart, and soul to you; and I surely don't understand the pleasure in doing so. But I recognize that it exists."

Hyacinthe gave a short, rueful laugh. "You know, whatever else happened in Skaldia, you gained some wisdom there, Cassiline."

There was a great deal more the onetime Prince of Travellers and I could have said to each other that night, but I wasn't ready to think about such things, let alone discuss them. He and Phèdre had a long history, I had no business coming between them. It was far easier to skirt the topic and switch to a more casual tone.

After finishing his bread, Hyacinthe rose and dusted his hands. "I'd best get back to the *kumpania* before de Morhban's guard changes shifts."

I nodded. "My thanks for the company."

He made to go, then hesitated. "Not her heart."

Mine fluttered strangely. "What?"

"You said 'yield body, heart, and soul,'" he said. "I know Phèdre has loved all of her patrons at least a bit—that's Naamah's grace in her. But she's never yielded her whole heart." He paused. "Not that I know of."

Oh.

I said nothing.

Hyacinthe saluted me. "I'll see you in a couple of hours."

I dozed fitfully after he departed. There were a myriad more pressing problems than one outcast Cassiline Brother's wayward heart, though I fear I was bristling more than necessary when at last I was summoned to the salon where Phèdre and the Duc de Morhban were breaking their fast over tea. I trusted her judgment, but we'd been betrayed before by a Kusheline noble and I wouldn't trust she was safe until I saw for myself.

"Are you disappointed, Cassiline?" de Morhban inquired with amusement. "I'm sorry. I confess, I'd be curious to try the mettle of one of your kind."

I shot him a look to say *anytime, anyplace,* before taking a knee at Phèdre's side. "You're all right?"

"His grace de Morhban honored his contract." She wore luxurious new

D'Angeline travelling clothing and a flawless ring of black pearls. Twisting the latter on one finger and avoiding my gaze, she looked at the Duc. "And are we free to go, then, your grace?"

Quincel de Morhban gave her a frustrated scowl, then gestured eloquently with one hand. "Our contract is complete," he said formally. "You have free passage throughout Morhban to the Royal Fleet and beyond."

Phèdre inclined her head. "My thanks, your grace."

He lifted a finger. "One day, Phèdre. I give you one day before I decide if it behooves me to question the Queen's Admiral."

She smiled at him. "You're very kind."

CHAPTER FORTY-ONE

I was walking too quickly through the stone corridors of the castle and had to pause for Phèdre to catch up. She was moving slowly and painfully. "Are you fit to ride?"

She gritted her teeth. "I'll manage."

Thinking of my conversation with Hyacinthe last night, I couldn't help but shake my head. "Blessed Elua have mercy, no matter how I try, I'll never understand how you find pleasure in what you do."

Phèdre laughed. "With your temper? You should."

That halted me in my tracks. "I do not have a temper! And what has that to do with it?"

"You have a terrible temper, Joscelin Verreuil," she said calmly. "You've just buried it in Cassiline discipline." She rotated her arm, rubbing her shoulder. "And not all that well. I've seen you lose your temper against the Skaldi, Joscelin. I've seen you fight like a cornered wolf when you had no chance of winning. Tell me, what does it feel like in that moment when you let everything go? When you lash out with everything in you, despite knowing you're going to be beaten to the ground? Is it a relief to surrender to it?"

I admitted it. "Yes."

"Well, then." Something snapped audibly in Phèdre's shoulder and she shook out her arm. "Imagine that relief compounded ten times, a hundred times, with every blow, through pain, through agony, to become a pleasure so great and awful it fixes you like a spear. Then you will understand, a little bit, what it is to serve Kushiel."

"Not among the Skaldi," I said. "That was different."

"No." Her voice hardened. "You know why. That, I think, is what it is like to be used by an immortal."

"Kushiel's Dart," I mused, then shivered inexplicably, eyeing Phèdre and wondering what in Elua's name de Morhban had done to partially dislocate her bedamned shoulder. Likely it had somewhat to do with the rope burn circling her wrists. And yet he'd given her everything she'd asked for and more. "All right. Will the Duc keep his word?"

"For a day, yes," she said. "I don't think he's disloyal to the Crown, but I don't think he's loyal, either. He'll see which way the wind blows."

I withdrew the Queen's signet on its chain and returned it to her. "Let's be off."

Neci's *kumpania* was eager to be done with the journey. I don't know what all Hyacinthe had told them about our purpose—surely not the whole truth—but none of the Tsingani were fooled into thinking this was an ordinary matter of trade anymore. They had a sense that grave stakes hung in the balance, and that one day they might either boast of having taken part in our enterprise, or rue having ever assisted us.

It was a fair day and the Kusheline cliffs looked less forbidding in sunlight, the blue-grey sea less bleak. We followed a winding coastal road for an hour before coming around a high outcropping to see a narrow bay where the entire Royal Fleet was anchored offshore, forty tall-masted ships flying the pennant of House Courcel. There was a large encampment on the sandy shore, the small figures of sailors scurrying to and fro.

We had reached the end of the Lungo Drom, the Long Road, as far as it reached upon D'Angeline soil. The children jumped up and down, shouting and laughing. In an excess of exhilaration, our entire company descended too hastily down the steep approach to the beach. Laughter turned to shouts of alarm as the wagon lurched off the path and nearly toppled before getting hung up on a ridge. At the base of the coastal road, a perplexed group of Admiral Rousse's men gathered to meet us.

"Go," Gisella said to the three of us, watching the Tsingani men wrestle the wagon. "They will free it and join you. Go make the trade, make a name for Neci's *kumpania,* who rode to the outermost west for gold."

By the time Phèdre, Hyacinthe, and I had picked our way to the base, a tall, burly figure was striding across the flat sand beach, bellowing fit to challenge the heavens. "Elua's Balls! What vagabonds do we have here?" he roared. "Have the Travellers decided to push their Long Road across the sea?"

"My lord Admiral!" Phèdre dismounted and curtseyed. "I bear a message from the Queen."

Royal Admiral Quintilius Rousse gaped at her. He was an imposing fellow, broad-shouldered and barrel-chested, with blue seafaring eyes in a scarred face. "By the ten thousand devils of Khebbel-im-Akkad!" he shouted so loudly nearby sailors grinned and covered their ears. "Delaunay's whelp!" With that, he seized Phèdre in a bone-cracking embrace, lifting her off her feet as he wrapped meaty arms around her so hard she wheezed. "What in the seven hells are you doing here, girl? I thought those idiots in the City convicted you of murder."

"Ow, ow!" Phèdre winced as he put her down. "They did. That's one of the reasons I'm here and not there."

The Admiral gave her a calculating look, taking in our presence and that of our stranded *kumpania*. "What's the other?"

She took a careful breath, testing her bruised ribs. "I speak Cruithne."

"Aahhh." A shrewd gleam lit his bright blue eyes. "Come along, then. We've got a great deal to discuss."

The fleet had been encamped there for some time and the Royal Admiral's tent was a sturdy semi-permanent structure appointed with carpeting, numerous stacked chests piled with an array of novelties and treasures, and a table with a set of low Tiberian chairs, where we were invited to take a seat.

"All right," Quintilius Rousse said once Hyacinthe and I were introduced. "Start at the beginning. Who killed Anafiel Delaunay?"

Phèdre told him what had befallen us, starting with his messenger's appearance at the marquist's atelier. He interrupted only once; after Phèdre named Duc Isidore d'Aiglemort the traitor, he listened in a silence so increasingly thunderous that I could swear storm clouds gathered around him.

When she finished, the storm broke in a hail of profanity. "Godsbedamned pig-fucking Skaldi!" Rousse roared, hurling a pitcher. "Elua's Balls, I swear I'll tear that slippery silver-haired goat-sucking d'Aiglemort in half with my bare hands!" A tray of uncut gemstones went flying. "Thrice-cursed honey-tongued asp of a Shahrizai, I knew Delaunay was too soft on that she-viper!" He squinted hopefully at Phèdre. "Any chance that you're lying?"

She shook her head with regret, withdrawing Ysandre's signet and laying it flat on her palm. "The Queen gave this to me. She bade me show it to you and give it to the Prince of the Cruithne."

"Rolande's ring." The Royal Admiral gave it a cursory look. "Oh, I know. I know the truth when I hear it. But I tell you, I'd sooner sail up the Rhenus and set us in place to crack Skaldi skulls than go chasing off on a fool's errand to Alba."

"What if it's not a fool's errand?" Phèdre asked.

Rousse gave her a shrewd look. "We tried it before. We launched from Siovale and went leagues out of our way to avoid the Straits and reach the far shores of Alba. Know what we found? A thousand lime-haired Dalriada shrieking curses and casting spears. We never even made landfall."

"How many ships did you send?" Hyacinthe asked unexpectedly.

"Fifteen," Rousse said. "Why?"

"One." Hyacinthe's voice was strained. "You only need one. That's what I saw when Ysandre asked me to speak the *dromonde*. One ship."

"The *dromonde*." Quintilius Rousse lifted his gaze to the heavens. "A night-blooming flower, a Tsingano fortuneteller, and an outcast Cassiline . . . this is what Ysandre sends me? I must be mad." He rumpled his hair, a half-braided tangle of ruddy locks that wouldn't look out of place among the Skaldi. "You've been quiet, Cassiline. What do you say?"

I bowed to him. "My lord Admiral, I say that whatever you choose, you must do so quickly. Because by noon tomorrow at the latest, the Duc de Morhban will be here asking questions."

"Morhban." He grimaced. "He's got me penned in like a fox with chickens. How'd you get past him? I could barely even get messengers out and he's gotten more suspicious since the King died."

Phèdre raised her eyebrows. "Naamah's way."

Quintilius Rousse chuckled. "Delaunay's pupil to the end! So I must decide, and quickly. Does the Queen have a plan for getting past Elder Brother?"

And therein lay the great flaw in our plan.

The three of us exchanged glances of dismay. "My lord Admiral . . . we thought you had gained passage from the Master of the Straits," Phèdre said. "You treated with him, you won an answer—when the Black Boar rules in Alba!"

"And nigh foundered to gain it." Rousse rubbed the thick cable of scar angling across his face. "I've no right of passage *there*, child; only the right of return if we succeed in returning the folk of the Cullach Gorrym to power. That answer was all I gained; that and the bare chance to cling to my life. Why do you think Delaunay and his boy Alcuin were working so hard to unravel the mystery of him?"

I felt empty.

It had been a foolish assumption on our part that Rousse's message meant the Master of the Straits had granted us passage to Alba. After all, it seemed quite enough that we were somehow to inspire the Dalriada to take part in a civil war to restore Drustan mab Necthana as the Cruarch before he would allow the Alban forces to cross the Straits.

Outside the tent, the Tsingani had begun passing the time by entertaining the sailors, who clapped along to the sound of the fiddle and tambor. Hyacinthe roused himself from the depths of our collective misery. "My lord Admiral, we promised this Tsingani *kumpania* a lucrative trade for the horses they brought. They've done us a good service to provide a safe disguise for our journey here."

"Might as well." Rousse rummaged in a chest he'd kicked over and came up with several long dangling strands of seed pearls and rubies. "This is like to rest on the bottom of the Straits ere I get a chance to spend it. We'll send 'em back on the Long Road with something to boast about, eh?"

It was a good deal more than Neci's family had expected; a good deal more than any of us expected, except mayhap Phèdre, who wore a veritable fortune etched onto her skin in addition to the diamond at her throat. Although the Tsingani would depart at daybreak, we said our farewells that evening. None of us knew for certain what the morning would bring—Quintilius Rousse had yet to make up his mind—except that our ways would be parting. I entertained the children quietly with one last Mendacant's tale—the tale of the Chevalier of the Rose, for which I'd plucked stolen roses from de Morhban's castle grounds and hidden them in the pockets of my cloak. Neci spoke at length to Hyacinthe, clasping his forearms in a solid salute. Afterward Hyacinthe spoke privately to Phèdre, and I let them be, tending to our horses staked in a picket line.

Dusk had fallen by the time they returned to Rousse's encampment, where I had set up our own modest site. A gibbous moon and the pinpricks of stars lit the night sky above us, scores of campfires burning along the shore. Quintilius Rousse was a dark silhouette pacing between them, periodically pausing to stare across the rippling expanse of black sea, the masts bobbing peacefully beneath the flickering stars.

"I'd best go speak with him," Phèdre said at length.

"What are you going to say?" Hyacinthe asked her quietly. "I mean . . . he's right. It might be a fool's errand."

"Do you believe that or the *dromonde*, Tsingano?" I asked him.

He laughed mirthlessly. "I wouldn't be here if I didn't believe the *dromonde*."

Phèdre rose. "Nor I."

Hyacinthe and I watched her cross the sand and approach the Royal Admiral, kneeling gracefully as she'd been trained to do from childhood, waiting patiently with her hands clasped in her lap while he stomped back and forth and ignored her. But if Quintilius Rousse thought he could outwait her, he had yet to encounter the vast reserves of profound and enduring stubbornness in the young woman he'd only known as Delaunay's pupil. A dart is a weapon small enough to pierce a chink in any armor in time.

And at length he spoke to her, squatting to speak on her level. On her knees in the sand, Phèdre lifted her head and replied to him. Admiral Rousse stood up, turned his back on her, and walked away.

She rose and returned.

"Is it over?" I felt as though the pit of my stomach were dropping into a bottomless hole.

"No." That unearthly gaze. "We sail at dawn."

CHAPTER FORTY-TWO

I was a wretched, wretched sailor.

There was no way I could have known. As a boy, I'd rowed a skiff on the placid waters of Lake Verre. During my years at the Prefectory I'd spent countless hours in the bywaters of the Lusande River.

But I'd never been to sea.

Until we arrived on the verge of Pointe d'Oest, I'd never even seen the sea; how it filled the horizon, how it was like a living thing unto itself. At its narrowest, it's said that one can see the cliffs of Alba, but that is farther north in Azzalle. Here, it appeared endless.

In accordance with Hyacinthe's prophecy, and the practical concern that it would be unwise to dissolve the Royal Fleet, we were venturing forth with a single vessel, the Admiral's flagship. Quintilius Rousse himself would command it. Oarsmen in their longboats ferried us to the ship, where we climbed rope ladders to meet the sailors aboard the spray-slickened decks. Rousse's second-in-command showed us to a cabin with hammocks where we might sleep and stow our gear. As soon as we had done the latter, the Admiral gave the command to raise the anchor and hoist the deep royal-blue sails with the silver swan insignia of House Courcel.

It was a heady business, this conjunction of engineering, the forces of nature, and the adventurous human spirit. I admired the design of the ship, the intricacies of the lines managing the tiers of sails on the two tallest masts, the way the shape of the prow cut through the waves, the system of gears and ropes and pulleys that allowed the great ship's wheel to guide the rudder. Once we were underway, Rousse breached a keg of wine for the traditional leave-taking toast. His sailors took turns lining up to fill mugs, and the Admiral himself insisted that we join in for luck. Everyone with a hand to spare gave a cheer and quaffed their rations as the ship gained momentum.

Alas, the wine hit my stomach at the exact moment when the ship took its first unexpected lurch.

No one warned me about the lurching.

I was sure-footed and I had excellent balance; I'd cut my eyeteeth fighting Selwyn on narrow beams with a bone-breaking drop beneath us; I'd scrambled up the face of an avalanche; I'd stayed afoot—mostly—being dragged behind Gunter's horse through fields of snow; I'd fought and defeated multiple opponents in the icy forests. There were Cassiline forms and patterns with so much swift rotation that cadets had been known to puke after practicing them, but I'd never felt any dizziness.

'Tis not boasting to speak the simple truth that nothing in my life's experience prepared me for my body's betrayal at sea.

It must have shown on my face when that first swallow sloshed sideways in my belly. Quintilius Rousse strolled past and clapped me on the shoulder. "Drink it down, lad," he said. "Just bend over the side and pay your toll to the Lord of the Deep if it comes back up."

It did.

"Looks like Cassilines aren't fit for the Long Road," Hyacinthe said cheerfully when I retched over the railing. "Not if it goes overseas."

Reckoning I was too miserable to tease, Phèdre shooed him away and fetched a waterskin so I could rinse my mouth, a kindness for which I thanked her. "Better?" she asked. I nodded, not yet daring to step away from the railing. She leaned against it beside me. "Keep your gaze on the horizon, I'm told it helps."

There was nothing to see save grey-blue wavelets meeting a hazy blue-grey sky in the distance, but my roiling stomach eased a bit. "How long do you reckon?"

"Less than a day's sail were it not for the Master of the Straits," Phèdre said ruefully. "I don't know. Tales vary in all the written accounts. Lord Rousse says he's encountered him halfway across the Straits. He thinks if we veer far enough around the southernmost point, we may steer clear of his reach, but Thelesis de Mornay was in sight of the Alban shore when he manifested. They say you'll know when the skies darken, the storm gathers, and the face of the waters appears."

"What *is* he, though?" I asked. "Were you able to determine?"

She shook her head. "An immortal, a sorcerer, a fallen angel, a barbarian god, an elemental avatar . . . no. Only possibilities."

The wind was beginning to pick up, but only slightly, kissing the tops of the wavelets with foam-white curls. "Do you suppose Delaunay knew?"

"I don't think so." Phèdre rubbed her temples. "He'd have sent word if he knew anything certain. But whatever he did learn in the course of his research, he and Alcuin, it died with them."

"He should have included you," I said.

"I wish he had," she murmured. "Blessed Elua knows, no one could have seen this day coming, but I wish he'd prepared me better."

The wind and weather held steady for a couple of hours, long enough for Admiral Rousse and his crew to begin making hopeful sounds. And mayhap it would have been different if the fleet had been anchored further south and we could have made for the wide-open sea and avoided the Straits altogether; or mayhap if we'd clung to the D'Angeline shore and inched our way down the coast for days.

In the end it didn't matter, for the die had been cast: We were one ship, sailing from Terre d'Ange to Alba.

And the Master of the Straits found us.

It happened fast. I was still hovering near a railing trying not to get in the sailors' way as they went about their tasks when the foam-kissed wavelets grew into peaks and troughs, setting the ship to pitching. Our ship had been running before a westerly wind. Now a strong crosswind began buffeting us from the south, rendering Admiral Rousse's planned indirect course of approach to Alba's shores untenable. In the depths, unseen currents that ran counter to nature roiled the waters. Phèdre had been speaking with Rousse as he manned the great ship's wheel. One moment he was swaying comfortably beneath the hazy blue sky; in the next, he cast his gaze upward as light leeched away. Storm clouds gathered like a vast flock of crows, blotting out the pale sun and turning day into night. Streaks of lightning played in the bruise-dark clouds like the swords of dueling angels.

With a crack of thunder that sounded like the world being split in twain, the skies unleashed a downpour. The wind howled and the sea howled in answer, rising to obliterate the horizon with towering crests and deep, sloping troughs. Quintilius Rousse was roaring commands the wind snatched from his lips, the sailors scrambling to lower the sails as the ship pitched. All of the Admiral's attention was on the wheel, the corded muscles of his arms bulging as he strained to keep the ship upright.

Phèdre . . .

She'd gotten out of Rousse's way, but not far; unable to reach safety, she clung to the nearest mast.

I inched my way along the rail, all thoughts of seasickness, all thoughts of anything save Phèdre forgotten. I waited until the ship listed hard to starboard to let go, allowing momentum to carry me across the rain-slick deck, skidding past sailors struggling to cling to the vessel. In a single wild rush, I managed to hook one arm around the mast, swinging my body around to shelter Phèdre from the buffeting winds. She gave me a grateful look through the sodden locks of hair plastered across her face.

"My lord Admiral!" I shouted above the din. "Do we turn back?"

He answered by pointing one trembling finger. "Too late! *Here he comes!*"

The waves rose, coalescing to form a dripping face so vast it obscured the sky. Its hair was wrought of storm clouds and lightning flickered in the deep well pits of its eyes. The face of the waters, the Master of the Straits. His voice thundered down upon us, uttering intelligible words. "WHO DARES CROSS?"

Lashed to the wheel, Quintilius Rousse replied in kind, roaring into the winds. "I do, you old bastard! And if you want your precious Black Boar to rule in Alba, you'll let us cross!"

The Master of the Straits laughed and grew three sizes taller, laughter so loud it felt as though my eardrums would burst. "THAT IS NOT *YOUR* DREAM, SEAFARER. WHAT TOLL WILL YOU PAY?"

A toll . . . the spark of a thought ignited inside me.

It couldn't be that simple, could it?

"Name your price!" Rousse shouted, wrestling the straining wheel. "Just name it, you bastard! I'll pay what it takes!"

It was the wrong answer. The Master of the Straits only laughed, and now there was a dark maw opening above the peak of the wave that the flagship was cresting, rising to balance teetering before we spilled into the maw and the waters drew us down and devoured us whole, our journey ended—

Peeling my body away from Phèdre's, I clung to the mast with one hand and leaned into the rain-whipped air. "A song!" I cried out. The ship pitched, forcing me to steady Phèdre, hauling her upright. "Listen, and she will sing you a song such as has never been heard sung upon these waters, my lord of the Straits!"

"What song?" she shouted at me, wide-eyed with terror. "Joscelin, *what song?*"

The gale around us keened, tearing the words from my lips. It didn't matter. Phèdre and I had learned to communicate in silence as slaves in Skaldia. I mouthed the words *Gunter's steading* at her.

She understood.

There are singers in Terre d'Ange with voices of unearthly purity, capable of scaling heights and plumbing depths of tone that make the listener weep for the sheer beauty of their gifts. Phèdre was not one of them; as a highly trained courtesan, she merely sang very well in an ordinary mortal range. And it was a very ordinary song that she sang to the Master of the Straits—a hearth-song sung by Skaldic women waiting for their men to return home from hunting and raiding, a remembrance of every handsome thane slain too young. It was a litany of the simple, homely chores performed by the women of the steading, spinning and weaving, sewing and mending, brewing and baking. It was a song that had never been sung on these seas. The waves grew calmer, and the enormous face of the waters began to subside. Phèdre looked uncertainly at me.

"Keep singing," I murmured.

And so she sang another hearth-song and another, all of them committed to memory at a scarred table in the great hall of Gunter's steading where she jotted down her own translations with a burnt twig. The seas became tranquil and the storm clouds overhead were thinning. I kept hold of the mast with one hand, the other supporting Phèdre. Her voice was growing hoarse from singing over the storm.

At the wheel, Quintilius Rousse stirred like a man rousing himself from a dream. "Elder Brother!" he cried. "Do you accept our toll?"

The sea shuddered and the face of the waters emerged with a benign countenance. "YES," it replied. "YOU MAY PASS."

And then it subsided and didn't reappear. There were only soft waves lapping at the sides of the ship, a westerly breeze, seagulls crying out in the misty blue skies. Phèdre stopped singing and drew a ragged breath. "Is it done?"

The Royal Admiral grimly surveyed the damage to his vessel and assessed casualties to his crew. "It is done." He turned his attention to Phèdre, squinting at her. "What in the world was that, child? Did Delaunay teach you a song to soothe Elder Brother's rage after all? You should have told me."

"Delaunay!" Her laughter cracked with exhaustion. "No, my lord. I'd no idea. Those were the hearth-songs of Skaldic women, whose husbands and brothers and sons may yet slaughter us all."

I felt her muscles go slack and caught her, scooping her into my arms. "I'll take her below to rest."

On my way, I found Hyacinthe and hailed him with relief. He'd lashed himself to a railing using a waist-scarf and was picking at the knot, abandoning it in a panic when he saw Phèdre's limp figure. "Is she—?"

"Fine," I said quickly. "She fainted. You?"

"In one piece." Unable to undo the knot, he slashed through the scarf with his belt knife. "That was Phèdre. Singing."

I nodded. "Skaldic hearth-songs."

"Skaldic hearth-songs," Hyacinthe echoed, then shuddered. "I saw two men swept overboard. It would have been all of us."

"I know."

Hyacinthe helped me ease Phèdre down the narrow stairs and halls to our cabin in the lower deck. I found a dry blanket in one of our half-soaked packs and wrapped her in it before nestling her into a hammock. I checked to make sure her breathing was still strong and steady, and her eyelids fluttered. The cabin felt too crowded. My throat was tight and my stomach was reverting to a state of discomfort. "Are you all right?" I whispered to her.

Phèdre nodded, eyes cracked open to reveal twin slashes of darkness and the ragged edge of a crimson starburst. "Need sleep."

I squeezed her hand. "You've earned it."

"Go upstairs," Hyacinthe said to me. "Get some fresh air. I'll keep an eye on her."

Since it would be far better to puke over the railing again than in the close, dank air of the cabin, I took him at his word. It was surreal to emerge into a world of calm seas and peaceful skies, almost as though the entire episode had been a vivid dream. But no; Rousse's sailors were busy untangling and splicing ropes, swabbing pools of water from the deck, setting the sails to raise once more. They were searching for survivors, a lookout in the crow's nest high atop the main mast calling out to spotters below.

"Any luck?" I asked Quintilius Rousse, knowing it was unlikely and more so as the ship got underway.

The Admiral shook his head curtly. "No. We'll hold a service at dawn for those lost in the crossing. How's our girl?"

"She'll be fine after sleeping," I said.

He was silent for a moment, concentrating on the wheel. "You know, I liked her well enough as a child. She had those charming little ways they teach 'em in the Night Court, all pretty manners and smiles."

"I'm sure," I said diplomatically, not volunteering the fact that my initial impression of Phèdre was far from charming.

"Never thought she had the makings of a spy," he mused. "Just a headful of baubles and fripperies."

Once upon a time, I'd believed the same thing; it felt like a lifetime ago. Now I was beginning to suspect I might not be the only man willing to follow Phèdre nó Delaunay into hell and back. I gave the Admiral a wry smile. "I thought that, too."

CHAPTER FORTY-THREE

Three days later our ship was becalmed and fogbound.

We had made good progress after the Master of the Straits granted us passage, rounding the southernmost tip of Alba and making our way along the vibrant spring-green coast toward the territory of the Dalriada. From time to time we saw inhabitants on the shores, but we didn't dare make landfall. If they supported Maelcon the Usurper we would be outnumbered in enemy territory. Even among the Dalriada, we were unsure what manner of reception awaited us. Since they'd driven Rousse's fleet away on a previous attempt, a warm welcome was unlikely. But that had been fifteen ships, enough to appear like an invasion, not a lone ship sailing as a diplomatic envoy.

On the day of our becalming, our progress had already slowed as we were forced to tack into a steady northern wind. It happened so gradually I didn't notice for some time. I'd finally gotten my sea legs and I took the opportunity to do a full and proper telling of the hours on the foredeck, sailors stamping and clapping as though I were a solitary dancer performing for their benefit. I was sweating in the crisp air when I finished, wisps of steam rising wherever my skin was exposed. The surface of the sea was steaming, too. The wind had gone utterly still, sails and lines sagging limply from the masts.

At the wheel, Admiral Rousse had begun bellowing orders, sailors scurrying to obey. Tendrils of mist twined and thickened, creeping like insubstantial vines up the sides of the ship. A dense bank of fog squatted above us, obscuring the pennants and crow's nests, sinking lower to meet the mist rising from the sea. The shoreline had been swallowed by mist and fog. Rousse called for the sailors to go to oars, a slow and cumbersome process generally used to maneuver in narrow bays and inlets, not in the open sea.

Every now and then, we caught a glimpse of green as the sailors hauled the long-shafted oars before it vanished once more.

Picking my way through the mist, I found that Rousse had turned the wheel over to his second-in-command and was engaged in earnest conversation with Phèdre. “What passes?” I asked. “I thought we were beyond the Master of the Straits’ reach.”

Scowling, Quintilius Rousse scratched at his ruddy mane of disheveled hair. “We are. This is somewhat else. A fluke of wind and water or ancient Alban magics, bedamned if I know which.”

“The lord Admiral hopes Hyacinthe may be able to guide us ashore using the *dromonde*,” Phèdre said.

“Can he?” I asked her.

She took a deep breath. “It appears we’re going to find out.”

I fetched Hyacinthe from a morning doze in our cabin, the color draining from his skin when I told him why. He followed me, unwontedly silent, to join Admiral Rousse and Phèdre in the prow. “All right, lad,” Rousse said gruffly. “Where do we make landfall in this bedamned fog? Point the way.”

Hyacinthe stepped away from me, angling his head this way and that, but he was as cloud-blind as the rest of us. “I can’t see it,” he whispered after a few moments. “Phèdre, I can’t see our road.”

She went to him, wrapping her fingers around his arm. “You can, Hyacinthe. I know you can! It’s only mist. What’s that to the veils of what-might-be?”

He shivered from fear or cold. Admiral Rousse had ordered the rowers to halt and there were no wavelets, no sounds of the sea save for the muffled, mocking cries of seagulls in the distance. Beads of condensation formed on Hyacinthe’s brow. “It’s *vrajna*,” he said in despair. “Manoj was right, this is no business for men.”

Phèdre sought his gaze. “Prince of Travellers, the Long Road will lead us home. Let it show the way.”

He turned away from her and there was the strange, blurred blackness in his eyes as when he’d spoken the *dromonde* before; but this time, there was fear behind it. “No. You don’t understand. The Long Road goes on and on for the Tsingani. There is no home for us, only the journey.”

“You’re half D’Angeline!” It was always startling when Phèdre raised her voice. She squeezed his arm. “Hyacinthe! You’ve Elua’s blood in your veins to ground you home and Tsingani to show the way. You can see it, you have to! Where do we find the Cullach Gorrym?”

His head turned back and forth again, searching in vain. "I can't see it!" He shuddered. "It is *vrajna*. They were right. I should never have looked, ever. Men were not meant to part the veils. Now this mist is sent to veil us all for my sins."

I gritted my teeth, half wishing I could try to shake the *dromonde* right out of him, fully aware that was the worst thing I could do. Phèdre lifted her gaze skyward, where the sun was a white disk in the shrouded sky. "If you can't see through it, then see *over* it," she said fiercely to Hyacinthe.

He looked at her as though returning from an absence. "Up there?" Lifting his chin, he stared at the bottom of the crow's nest atop the mainmast, the rest of it lost in the dense fog. "You want me to look from up there?"

Phèdre's response was unexpected. "Your great-grandmother gave me a riddle," she said. "What did Anasztaizia see through the veils of time to teach her son the *dromonde*? A horse-drawn wagon and a seat by the *kumpania*'s fire, or a mist-locked ship carrying a ring for the Queen's betrothed? It is yours to answer." Hyacinthe continued to stare upward in silence, then grasped the rope ladder stretching from the tall platform and began climbing. The ship's crew held their collective breath, waiting as the Tsingano clambered up the ladder, disappearing into the fog.

"What was that you said to him?" I murmured to Phèdre.

She watched the fog skirl in the wake of Hyacinthe's ascent. "Do you remember the old woman at the Hippochamp? She was his great-grandmother and those were her words."

It made sense that there was a reason that Hyacinthe's mother chose to teach him the *dromonde*, that there was a pressing need for it that she glimpsed beyond the veils of time. I wondered why that frightened him now. He'd already chosen it over taking his place among the Tsingani as Manoj's grandson.

What was more fearsome than losing one's deepest, most heartfelt desire?

"There!" It was Hyacinthe's voice high above us and it held the ring of surety.

Unfortunately, no one could see him, let alone determine where he was pointing. "What are you gawping at, you thrice-damned idiots?" Quintilius Rousse roared, stomping around the deck. "Get a relay going! You!" He pointed at the nearest crew members. "And you! Move! Get up that rigging! Marchand, get the oarsmen to put their backs into it! We follow the Tsingano's heading!"

At Rousse's orders, the sailors dispersed and took up their posts while their commander resumed the helm. "Two points to port!" someone shouted down from the mainmast. "And a lantern in the prow, Admiral!"

Phèdre and I stayed out of the way as the crew scrambled to obey. The big flagship turned slowly to align with the direction Hyacinthe was indicating from his fogbound perch. The second-in-command, Jean Marchand, had procured a large drum and was beating out time, the oarsmen chanting in response.

"That's it, lads!" Rousse shouted. "Now *row*!"

It was a slow, hard slog rendered tense by our inability to see. Hyacinthe's vision was pointing us in a straight line, but the coast was ragged. If we ran afoul of an unexpected outcropping, the ship could sustain grave damage. All we could do was wait and hope, hearts in our throats.

And indeed, after we'd been some hours inching through the fog, Hyacinthe called for Admiral Rousse to set the course for the unseen shore. The fog began to thin, giving us glimpses of green land through its rent veils. Out of nowhere, a brisk wind blew away the trailing mist-wraiths and filled our sails. We soared ahead of it, emerging into bright sunlight dazzling off the steely waters of a narrow, rocky bay straight ahead of us, with a swift river plunging over green slopes to a stony beach. A great cheer went up, and I felt a surge of renewed hope.

And then I saw the sword-waving reception party awaiting us.

"Drop anchor!" Quintilius Rousse shouted. "Now!"

Water churned as the oarsmen backpaddled. Others hurried to release the great anchor and lower the sails. Hyacinthe descended from the crow's nest on shaking legs, dark circles beneath his eyes. Secured, our vessel was anchored in deep waters, turned broadside to the shoreline. Reaching into his belt purse, Rousse drew out a golden coin and tossed it overboard. It turned end over end in the sunlit sky, landing with a splash; a tribute to the Lord of the Deep, an old sailor's superstition. I leaned on the railing, studying the party ashore. They hadn't assembled in force. There were only a dozen sword-bearing warriors, and two smaller figures that perplexed me.

Rousse joined us. "What do you make of that?" he asked Phèdre, nodding toward the landing beach.

She glanced at me, then ashore when I shrugged. The smallest figure was leaping about, brandishing a spear at . . . seabirds? The other was very still. "A child, lord Admiral; mayhap two."

He scowled. "All right. You're the Queen's emissary. What do we do?"

"We go to meet them," Phèdre said firmly. "Bring six men skilled at arms, my lord. I will bring Hyacinthe and Joscelin."

"We'll be outnumbered," the Royal Admiral observed.

"It will show good faith," she said. "My lord, if it's a trap and there are hundreds of troops waiting in hiding, all your men would not suffice. If it's not a trap"—she gave me an amused sidelong look—"we'll not be outnumbered with a Cassiline in our midst. And my lord, if you're willing, we ought to bring the Dalriada a worthy guest-gift from your hoard. The Queen will recompense your loss."

He gave a brusque nod. "So be it."

Hyacinthe reached the deck as Rousse vanished into the captain's cabin to rummage through his Akkadian treasure.

"Are you all right?" Phèdre whispered to him.

"Honestly?" He passed one hand over his face, his eyes still blurred and strange in their bruised-looking sockets. "I'm not sure. Are we going ashore?"

"Yes."

He sighed. "Good."

Admiral Rousse reappeared with a coffer filled with silks, gems, and spices, showing it to Phèdre. She nodded in approval. An oar-boat was lowered, a rope ladder secured over the side. The sailors assisted her and Hyacinthe with careful respect, eyeing both of them with a degree of awe—our sight-blessed guide and the woman who had appeased the Master of the Straits with a song. As a foresworn Cassiline Brother they knew best for puking at sea, I invoked no such sense of wonder, but all that mattered was that I was where I belonged, protecting my ward. Phèdre stood in the prow of the oar-boat, her head held high, doing her best to appear confident and regal. One thing was certain, she looked D'Angeline through and through with that cameo-perfect profile and luminous eyes.

The sailors set to at the oars and our small vessel slid forward through the shining waves. The men awaiting us were fair skinned and ruddy haired with brawny thews, reminding me of the Skaldi; and yes, that was a boy among them, a very young one with unruly red-gold hair and a golden torque around his neck. He was jumping up and down with excitement, shouting and waving his child-sized spear.

The other small figure was a young woman.

She was still and quiet, but she had an air of self-possession and the warriors gave her a respectful berth. Unlike the Dalriada, she had nut-brown skin and long, silken black hair parted in the center to frame her face.

"*Croisos!*" she cried out to us, extending one hand. The Dalriada shouted and hoisted their swords in salute before sheathing them and plunging into the shallow surf to grasp the sides of our boat and haul us ashore, our keel grinding on the rocky beach. "*Croisos*," the young woman repeated, smiling in warm greeting. There were twin lines of blue dots etched across her brown cheekbones.

Phèdre inclined her head. "I am Phèdre nó Delaunay," she said in careful Cruithne. Based on the names invoked, she proceeded to make her introduction and request for an audience with Drustan mab Necthana on behalf of Queen Ysandre. The warriors in their plaids stamped and cheered at Drustan's name, and the boy shouted with them. The young woman put her hands on his shoulders, stilling him, and gave what sounded like a very simple response. With a perplexed look, Phèdre turned to us. "It's all right. This is Drustan's sister, Moiread. It seems we were expected."

"How?" Rousse demanded.

Her brows drew together. "I've no idea."

The Dalriada helped her ashore, escorting her to meet Moiread while the rest of us fended for ourselves. I left the sailors to secure the oar-boat and took up my place a pace behind Phèdre's left side. Now Moiread took Phèdre's shoulders in her hands and spoke earnestly at length. She had wideset dark eyes and an air of grave calmness about her. There was somewhat altogether uncanny about this summit.

Whatever she said, Phèdre shivered before collecting herself and asking a question in response.

Moiread said somewhat in Cruithne, her gaze sweeping over our party and settling on Hyacinthe. She approached him, touching his face with her slender fingers. He stood stock-still under her touch, a strange expression on his face.

"She said she dreamed of the boy Brennan throwing his spear at a swan," Phèdre murmured to us. "While we followed a waking dreamer." Turning to Moiread, she repeated our request for an audience. The Cruarch's sister smiled as she replied, gesturing at the footpath winding through the rocky green hills. Phèdre translated. "Drustan will meet with us, but first we must be presented to the Twins, the Lords of the Dalriada."

We left a pair of sailors to man the landing boat and report to the others waiting on the flagship while the rest of us followed Moiread and the Dalriada up the path. The warriors were laughing and jesting, playing horse-a-back carrying the boy in the torque high on their shoulders. Our sailors looked confused and wary, while the Royal Admiral was scowling and stomping up the long incline, carrying the coffer with our guest-gift.

The royal seat of the Dalriada was called Innisclan. The settlement was dominated by a great stone hall, crevices filled with clay daub, and the whole of it painted gleaming white with lime. There were seven doors leading into it in accordance with the rank of those who entered it. Later, I learned that the thatch-roofed hall at Innisclan was built in emulation of the hall of Tea Muir across the sea where the High King of Eire rules.

Moiread bade us wait in an antechamber, vanishing into the main hall. We heard the sound of quarreling before and after her return, but all she reported to Phèdre was that the Twins would see us. Now it was only three of us accompanying the Queen's unlikely emissary: Quintilius Rousse, Hyacinthe, and me.

There were two thrones side by side in the great hall and the royal pair was seated in them. It transpired that the Twins were brother and sister, not a pair of brothers as I'd assumed. They were tall and strapping with a marked resemblance to each other and matching gold torques around their throats, but the sister was the more striking of the two. She had abundant red-gold hair the same hue as the boy on the beach's, scattered with jeweled hairpins that shone with amethyst and citrine and polished green malachite as she leaned forward with interest. Her brother leaned back with folded arms, his expression obstinate.

Admiral Rousse bowed and presented Phèdre with the coffer; Phèdre, in turn, with all the grace of a Night Court–raised courtesan knelt and proffered it with both hands, her head bowed and eyes downcast. The brother—Eamonn, Eamonn and Grainne, I later learned—accepted the coffer and set it aside, making a sharp query.

The Dalriada speak their own tongue which crossed the narrow seas from Eire with them. It bears some kinship with Cruithne, but not enough that Phèdre could understand it readily. Moiread conferred with her before replying.

Eamonn scowled; his sister Grainne rose with flashing eyes and made a proclamation. I was intrigued to see that she bore a sword at her waist. It wasn't some decorative ceremonial blade, either; the leather-wrapped hilt looked like it had seen a good amount of wear in the not-distant past. Phèdre spoke haltingly to them, then turned to us. "They are sending for the Cruarch."

Moments later, Drustan mab Necthana joined us, accompanied by his mother and three sisters and a handful of armed Cruithne guards. *Your blue boy,* L'Envers had called him dismissively, and he was blue; tattoos of blue woad bisected his brow, spiraled on his cheeks, framing the sockets of his eyes.

But he was no mere boy.

The Cruarch of Alba was a young man, but he possessed a gravity beyond his years. The Cruithne tended to be a quick, slender folk, brown-skinned and black-haired. Drustan moved with lithe strength and surety despite the impediment of a clubbed foot. Despite his age, he had a tremendous presence. The cloak of fine-combed red wool he wore swayed as he approached Phèdre, who was still kneeling patiently. She lifted her gaze to meet his.

He asked her a question.

Phèdre rose, withdrawing the chain with Prince Rolande's signet ring, and held it out between them, addressing him in near-fluent Cruithne, and I heard her invoke the name of Ysandre de la Courcel.

Drustan's hand closed around the ring, a spark of hope flaring in his eyes—and in the eyes of his mother and sisters, too. Then he quenched it ruthlessly, asking another question in a harsh tone.

I could guess it was some variant of "At what cost?"

Relinquishing the ring to him, Phèdre inclined her head. Her reply was quiet and firm as she explained the situation to the exiled Cruarch. It was enough to reignite the fire in his gaze, and Drustan approached the thrones to address the Twins in ringing tones. The Twins promptly began shouting at each other, and occasionally at Drustan, who raised his voice in reply, and was shouted down for it. The other Dalriada and Cruithne present listened attentively to the exchange, finding nothing untoward in the manner of it. At one point, Grainne shook her head so vehemently that hairpins went flying like dragonflies. At another, Eamonn nearly slammed his sister's hand in the lid of the coffer. And then it seemed Drustan's prowess had been challenged; he laughed and spread his arms wide, his cloak slipping to reveal corded muscle and whorls of blue woad on his shoulders and wrists. His right foot was twisted so that the side and not the sole struck earth, but he moved surely on it.

I knew that laugh, too. That was the laughter of a warrior genuinely amused by the notion of defeat. Waldemar Selig laughed the same way.

Now the quarrel *did* spill over into the hall, and suddenly Cruithne and Dalriada were shoving and arguing like their leaders. In our small party, Quintilius Rousse was gritting his teeth and looked on the verge of roaring and cracking heads. I moved unobtrusively to shield Phèdre, and Hyacinthe positioned himself beside me.

Lady Grainne waded into the midst of folk, shouting, her sword half-drawn in warning. I had to own, she was impressive, but it wasn't until Eamonn stomped after her that the pandemonium settled fully. Hyacinthe and I parted to let Phèdre step forward. Eamonn addressed her, and then Drustan, in formal-sounding language. Whatever he said, both inclined their heads in acknowledgment, but it was Necthana, sister to the slain Cruarch and mother of his heir Drustan, who spoke.

"Drustan is saying this notion of war is too great a matter to decide in haste," Phèdre murmured. "His mother Necthana agrees this is wise, and reminds him of the Twins' duty to provide hospitality. There will be a feast in our honor tomorrow night."

It seemed everyone was in agreement on that point. Clapping her hands imperiously, Grainne began issuing orders to their household staff. Eamonn wrapped his cloak around his injured dignity and departed with the Dalriadan warriors, while Drustan spoke in low tones to his attentive guard.

The Cruarch's mother and her daughters paused to speak with us—or at least to Phèdre, who listened intently and replied with an earnest inquiry, a pleading note in her voice. Necthana smiled and replied in brief, touching Phèdre's brow before departing.

"What was she saying to you?" I asked Phèdre, who wore her vaguely abstract pensive look.

"She said the Twins are like an ill-matched team pulling at the traces," she mused. "And I must balance them. Any ideas?"

I surveyed our surroundings. The threat of imminent violence had subsided into everyday chaos, with a great many people bustling about with more energy than purpose; except for the large, honking goose that ran unexpectedly through the hall, the bright-haired boy Brennan in hot pursuit. The Lady Grainne snatched up the boy as he passed, tucking him against her hip while a fellow in baggy cross-gartered breeches chased the goose. She continued her conversation unfazed by the squirming child, whom I was just realizing must be her son.

"Not a one," I admitted.

CHAPTER FORTY-FOUR

I found the Dalriada to be belligerent, boisterous, quarrelsome, fun-loving, and generous; quick to anger, quick to forgive.

Of a surety, they placed great value on hospitality. An empty visitors' longhouse was opened and scrubbed clean, the spring wind blowing away the sour dust of winter. Bed linens were shaken, water ewers filled. Half of Rousse's crew joined us, eager to spend time ashore and stretch their legs on solid ground; and, for those who fancied women, to romance the local girls, who were tickled by their mimed overtures. Phèdre was given a bed in Breidaia's room—she was Drustan's eldest sister, and would in time become the mother of his heir in accordance with the matrilineal tradition of the succession among the Cruithne.

It was strange to think that if our far-fetched plan succeeded, the heir to Terre d'Ange would be half Cruithne while the heir to Alba wouldn't possess a single drop of D'Angeline blood. It didn't trouble me, but there were surely peers of the realm that would balk at it.

That, however, was an obstacle that lay far in the distance. I'd count us fortunate were we ever to reach it.

Between Phèdre's translated summaries and bits and pieces I garnered talking to various folks using hand gestures and my smattering of Cruithne, I developed a more detailed understanding of the situation.

Maelcon the Usurper's insurrection was supported by his mother's people, the Tarbh Cró, or the folk of the Red Bull. The old Cruarch and his sister's son were of the Cullach Gorrym, the folk of the Black Boar. The crux of the matter lay between those folk. The folk of the Golden Hind in southern Alba had remained neutral. The Dalriada, the folk of the White Mare, had extended sanctuary to Drustan mab Necthana, his family, and what remained of the army of the Cullach Gorrym in honor of an old oath of mutual loyalty. But thus far, the Dalriada had refused Drustan's request for aid in taking back the throne.

I couldn't blame them. It was a grave thing to lay one's life on the line for someone else's cause. They were great believers in signs and portents, though; and from what I garnered, our appearance sufficed to ignite the Lady Grainne's passion. I had the sense she was ready to lead the Dalriada into battle in a heartbeat, while her more cautious brother grew increasingly stubborn and dug in his heels.

How did one balance such opposing forces?

That remained an unsolved puzzle.

The official welcoming feast was held the day after our arrival. As one might anticipate, it was a riotous affair. Alba is a fertile country rich with game, and there were endless platters of food; venison dripping in its own juice, crusty bread, spring greens, hunks of cheese aged until they were sharp on the tongue. There were impromptu arguments and songs, and children and dogs underfoot.

It felt safe here; or at least more safe than I'd felt for a very long time. We were on dry land. We weren't fleeing, no one was hunting us, we weren't falsely condemned murderers, we weren't hiding our identities. We were honored guests, not slaves. And most importantly, Phèdre was unharmed and in no immediate danger.

I didn't relinquish my vigilance, but I allowed myself to relax a measure. When there was nothing but bones and scraps left on the platters, the children were packed off to bed and the *uisghe* came out. It was a distilled spirit made from fermented barley mash, wildly potent and tasting faintly of smoky peat. One sip from the gilded drinking horn foisted upon me by the insistent Twins was enough.

For everyone else, the *uisghe* flowed freely. The Dalriada are great storytellers—they could teach a Mendacant a trick or two—and began reciting lengthy poems about the glorious battles of heroes of yore, which Phèdre did her best to convey to the rest of us. She was already glowing with drink and laughter describing an ancient Dalriadan hero who transformed from a handsome warrior to a bulging-eyed berserker in the midst of battle, and I had to question the accuracy of her understanding of Eiran. Quintilius Rousse took it upon himself to respond with a particularly bawdy D'Angeline sailor's song accompanied by a set of vulgar gestures that rendered moot the need for any verbal translation. I was quietly mortified, but the Dalriada and Cruithne were delighted, clapping to the beat and yelling out a phonetic version of the refrain.

During the performance, I noticed that a handful of Dalriadan warriors in Eamonn's guard were glancing in my direction and muttering amongst themselves. One of them, half a head taller than the others, offered me a mincing Cassiline bow.

I looked away. There was no point in engaging with him and stirring trouble we didn't need; or at least so I thought. The fellow—Carraig was his name—refused to be ignored. He cleared a space in the hall, drew his sword, and beckoned to me. I looked to the Twins, hoping one or the other would order him to stand down, but they were quaffing *uisghe* and shouting encouragement. No help there.

Not that I was loath to spar with the Dalriadan. Even as I debated how to proceed, he was mocking what he took to be the Cassiline fighting style after seeing me tell the hours that morning, prancing and spinning his blade in a clumsy figure eight. But I didn't want to humiliate him if it might further upset this elusive balance we were seeking to attain, and I surely wasn't going to be forced into a fight to the death.

So I gave Phèdre an inquiring look. Drunk or sober, she was Queen Ysandre's chosen ambassador. In turn, she looked to Drustan. Whatever silent exchange passed between them, Phèdre rose and announced our acceptance of the challenge, setting the terms of it. There were cheers, and I stood to offer a precise, properly executed Cassiline bow. "I told them no bloodshed," she said. "You'll fight to disarmament or surrender."

Admiral Rousse strolled over with a rolling gait that was part land-legs, part *uisghe*. "Thought Cassilines only fought to defend."

"The Prefect of the Cassiline Brotherhood abjured him," Phèdre informed Rousse. "Joscelin's blade is sworn to Ysandre."

"Ah." The Admiral's eyes crinkled. "I see."

I don't know what he thought he saw, but it wasn't that simple. *I* didn't know exactly who I was anymore. I was a fully fledged Cassiline Brother who had been declared anathema. My allegiance was to the Queen and that took precedence on this mission. My broken, beating heart belonged to Phèdre, but that was a complicated business. The one thing I was sure of was that anathema or not, I remained Cassiel's Servant. It was the Brotherhood that asked me to turn away from the path of the Perfect Companion.

Once the final wager was placed, Eamonn shouted out an order to begin—or so I assumed based on the fact that Carraig was bearing down on me with a roar, his broadsword cleaving the air on a downstroke. How he intended to deliver such a blow without splitting my skull, I couldn't say. It felt good to whip my crossed daggers free of their sheaths, catching and deflecting the Dalriadan's stroke with ease. He was damnably tall and strong, but he wasn't accustomed to having his own strength and momentum used against him. I spun away from him opposite his expectations, giving him a moment to gather himself.

Fight me.

I realized I was smiling.

I loved the sound of steel; the scrape of blade against leather, the clanging bell-tone of flats clashing, the higher keening of an edged strike. That was my music, this was my dance. Carraig essayed another blow. This one I deflected off my left vambrace, flipping the dagger in my right hand as he overreached. He had some bits of leather wrapped around his hands, but no gauntlets. When I smashed the pommel down onto his right hand, it opened involuntarily, his sword clattering. I jabbed my knee hard into the back of his leg. It crumpled and Carraig pitched forward. That was all I needed to pin him to the floor, one knee against his spine and my daggers at the sides of his throat. "Do you yield?"

Eamonn's champion understood the question, if not the words. He lifted one arm, turning his hand palm-upward in a gesture of surrender. I rose, sheathed my blades, and offered him another formal bow. In turn, he spread his arms wide and embraced me with a roar of laughter, pounding my back.

The other warriors, Dalriada and Cruithne alike, crowded around. Whether adeptly or not, we all danced to the song of steel, and the more curious among them were eager for me to demonstrate the Cassiline technique. It was an easy camaraderie, something I'd not experienced outside the Prefectory. From time to time, I surveyed the hall, finding no cause for concern. With assistance from Phèdre, the Lady Grainne was conversing with Quintilius Rousse, appraising him with the frank interest of a buyer eyeing a prize stud. Hyacinthe was speaking earnestly to Drustan's sister Moiread, who had garnered a bit of D'Angeline after Prince Drustan's secret engagement to then Princess Ysandre. They spoke in broken sentences, gestures, and glances as though it were a private language.

The intensity and immediacy of the attraction between them surprised me a bit. I'd always known him to be more than half in love with Phèdre. At the Hippochamp, he'd thrown away his birthright simply to reassure her;

but mayhap his fate had been steering him toward this moment all along. It wasn't the sort of thing one could ask about, or so I supposed. Was it? I didn't know how men and women interacted together if not as bodyguard and ward. *What am I, if not a Cassiline Brother,* I'd asked Phèdre during our flight from Skaldia. I remember her smiling up at me in the cold winter air and saying, *the* Cassiline.

But what was a Cassiline who wasn't a Cassiline, other than just a man? My predecessor Guy was trained as a Cassiline cadet, but he was expelled before taking his final oath, like Selwyn and Toulouse. When all was said and done, I was different from them. I'd completed my training, I was oath-sworn, I had walked the dagger's edge between earth and heaven.

I'd made my choice knowing full well what it meant.

Still, it was nice to be Joscelin for a night, plain and simple, a man at ease in the company of fellow warriors. I even took another swallow of *uisghe,* just enough to make the torches burn a little more merrily. I glanced around the hall—and name of Elua, *everyone* was drunk. Everyone who was left, anyway. Neither Hyacinthe nor Quintilius Rousse was still present. Drustan and his mother and sisters were gone, too. The Twins were in the midst of another squabble.

I encountered Fortun, one of Rousse's sailors. He was dark-haired and square-shouldered and he had a quiet steadiness that I appreciated. "What are they fighting over now?" I asked, nodding toward the Lords of the Dalriada. "Any idea?"

Fortun cleared his throat. "I, ah, believe it's our lady ambassadress."

No.

Oh, no, no!

Of course it was true; even as I watched, Eamonn grabbed Phèdre around the waist and hoisted her into the air. It evoked bad memories, but he set her firmly on her feet on the seat of his throne, stepped back, and folded his arms. His sister Grainne gave him an amused sidelong glance and tossed her mane of coppery hair. Like the torches, Phèdre shone a little brighter with drink, a flush along her cheekbones and a hectic gleam in her eyes. Standing atop Eamonn's throne, she presided over the hall like a young queen of mayhem. I debated whether or not to attempt to extricate her from the situation with a modicum of dignity. Meanwhile, Phèdre was tying a silk scarf over her eyes. She spun around three times, managing to keep her feet, then pointed blindly at the Lady Grainne.

Beside me, Fortun chuckled, falling silent when he saw my scowl. Blindly, my arse—Phèdre nó Delaunay had keenly honed observational skills and a sense of hearing like a bat's. Whatever she thought she was doing, she was doing it deliberately, and I hadn't drunk nearly enough *uisghe* to think it was a good idea.

CHAPTER FORTY-FIVE

Almost everyone was worse for the wear in the morning, including Phèdre, who looked rather like I felt aboard the ship. One marked exception was the Lady Grainne, breaking her fast at the head of the table, tearing off a generous hunk of crusty bread and looking altogether pleased with the world.

I had no sympathy for Phèdre.

"It's a disgrace," I said to her in a low tone. "Do you honestly think every problem can be solved by falling into someone's bed? Do you think *that's* what Ysandre de la Courcel chose you for?"

She gave me a wry look. "Forgive me. I've not your skill with a sword to resolve matters thusly. Anyway, I might not have fallen there if you hadn't all left me unattended. Mayhap you ought to try it. It might improve your mood."

"I have never—" I began. Phèdre's brows rose a fraction. "That was different."

"Yes." She sighed and rubbed her temples. "It was. And this is what happens when you send a Servant of Naamah to do a diplomat's job and ply them with strong drink."

I didn't want to smile at that, and yet I couldn't help it; one corner of my mouth twitched upward. "At least you had the choosing of it, or so it seemed."

"Oh, I chose, all right," she admitted.

I glanced at Grainne. "She does have a certain barbarian splendor."

Phèdre laughed uncontrollably, clutching her aching head. "Ow!"

Later that day, Drustan mab Necthana escorted Phèdre and me on a tour of Innisclan, accompanied by several of his Cruithne. Ostensibly, it was to admire the smithy and the mill, the village square, the vast herds of cattle for which the Dalriada were famed; in actuality, it was a chance to consult in privacy. He pointed eastward in the direction of Bryn Gorrydum. It had been the traditional seat of the Cruarch since the great Cullach Gorrym warrior Cinhil Ru united the four folk of Alba to drive out the Tiberian empire over a thousand years ago. Now Maelcon the Usurper sat upon the throne.

I caught a word here and there, enough to understand Drustan's teeth-baring snarl when he spoke Maelcon's name. Phèdre made an inquiry regarding Eamonn. Drustan shook his head, launching into a discussion of the Twins. As best I could make out, he thought Grainne was more than willing to lead the Dalriada into a war to reclaim the Cruarch's throne, but Eamonn was the sticking point, and for all her impulsive passion, Grainne wouldn't act unless the two of them were in agreement.

Ill-matched horses, indeed. I had an uneasy feeling that Phèdre thought she'd found a way to balance them.

Drustan was speaking in a different tone, quiet and wistful, of Ysandre and the dream they had shared of two kingdoms, Alba and Terre d'Ange, united by love. I'd seen the cool and composed young Queen blush when she spoke of Drustan, but she'd been a sixteen-year-old girl when they met and I confess, it had crossed my mind that this star-crossed romance with an exotic barbarian prince was born in part of a girlish fantasy.

But no, even if I could only understand one word in ten, the way Drustan's eyes lit up when he spoke of Ysandre said volumes. He laid out his thoughts and intentions, which Phèdre translated for me during our return to the hall. In essence, Drustan was determined to give the Lords of the Dalriada a week to make a decision. If the Dalriada wouldn't ride to war on his behalf, he would take his Cruithne and march on Bryn Gorrydum.

"Does he think he can succeed without the Dalriada?" I asked.

"No," Phèdre said ruefully. "Some tribes will rally to the banner of the Cullach Gorrym, but not enough. He wants us to sail back to Terre d'Ange and tell Ysandre that he'll come for her if he lives."

"And if he fails, our journey was for naught," I murmured. "No Alban army coming to our support, just a lot of Cullach Gorrym slain in a war we set in motion."

Phèdre nodded in somber agreement. "I'm going to do somewhat else you won't like," she warned me. "Just . . . abide it and hold your tongue. I swear to you, on Delaunay's name, I've a good reason for it."

Oh, I knew.

Over the course of the next few days, Dalriadan clan lords visited Innisclan. They cut imposing figures wrapped in multicolored woolen plaids and intricate goldwork. Those predisposed to war wore their hair in chalky lime-washed spikes, but they weren't a majority among their folk. I did pity Phèdre then. As the Queen's ambassador, it fell to her to discuss the situation with each new dignitary; as our only fluent Cruithne speaker, she had to carry the additional burden of translating for the rest of our party. It was work that became exhausting after a period of time—and atop that, she had to contend with Eamonn's insistent advances.

Every time Phèdre was in his vicinity, he fixed her with a hot gaze. She politely declined his overtures without deigning to explain why, which only added fuel to his fire. The Dalriadans took up factions supporting one or the other of the Twins and tensions grew higher between the exiled Cruithne and their Dalriadan hosts. At one point, swords were drawn in earnest, until Drustan waded bare-handed into the fray to put an end to it with lightning-fast reflexes and sheer force of will.

Watching Phèdre string the Lord of the Dalriada along, I realized it was a mistake to think that she was vain enough to believe her beauty and skills in the bedchamber alone would move Eamonn to send his people to war. It wasn't about *her*; it was about evening the score with his sister. Phèdre might as well be a fine dagger, a hound, a well-bred steed—what mattered was that she'd spent a night in Grainne's bed, and Eamonn couldn't rest until he'd received the same gift bestowed on his sister.

For six days, that string drew taut to breaking. That evening, Drustan mab Necthana addressed the Twins and their guests, standing before the fireplace in the great hall. I knew what he was saying as he bowed to Eamonn and Grainne, expressing gratitude for the sanctuary they had extended to his people. Then he held up his right hand, Prince Rolande's heavy gold signet ring gleaming in the firelight, reminding them that he had sworn an oath upon that ring. He announced his intention to take his Cruithne and depart for Bryn Gorrydum on the morrow.

On the heels of Prince Drustan's announcement, arguments erupted from every faction in the hall.

Ignoring them, Phèdre approached the Twins' thrones. She knelt gracefully and offered thanks for their hospitality, then rose with a deep curtsy, turned, and walked away.

Eamonn came after her and grabbed her shoulder, hot-eyed and intent enough that I eased through the crowd to take my place beside her, even as she shook off his hand with indignation.

"Stand fast," she murmured to me.

Eamonn snatched his hand back as though scalded. Glaring at her, he made an angry argument. Phèdre refuted it with a cool shrug; whatever she said, it sounded calmly dismissive, and it sent him over the edge. He began shouting, working himself into a fury. Others were pausing to watch. On her throne, Grainne wore a look of amusement she didn't bother to conceal.

Fists on hips, Eamonn demanded somewhat of Phèdre. She shrugged again, her features expressionless, and offered another cool response. Grainne followed it up with a mocking comment that drew laughter from the crowd.

That was it. Eamonn replied to Phèdre through gritted teeth, and then roared a furious declaration, thrusting one clenched fist into the air. Fierce cheers of approval followed his words, and one didn't need to speak Eiran to understand what had transpired.

The Dalriada were going to war.

Laughing and bright-eyed, Eamonn pumped his fist in the air. I nearly began to think he'd forgotten Phèdre entirely, then he turned to her with a grin and took her hands, asking a question with boyish glee.

Inclining her head, Phèdre responded in the affirmative with a genuine smile.

The Queen's ambassador had found a way to balance the Twins.

I sighed and watched them go, Eamonn wasting no time in escorting Phèdre out of the gathering hall. I felt . . . I didn't know what I felt. Jealousy, to be sure; I was a fool if I tried to convince myself otherwise. I'd been jealous when she offered herself to de Morhban in exchange for passage, but I'd told myself it was because I was uncomfortable with Naamah's service; because I hated to see Phèdre as a commodity, especially after Skaldia; because I wasn't reconciled to her dark, sharp-edged desires. With Grainne, I'd told myself there was no cause for jealousy, that it was a matter of Phèdre's hectic side and propensity for wild schemes merging with an excess of *uisghe*.

I had been jealous, though; and I was jealous now, even knowing that Phèdre had chosen this assignation for specific purposes—purposes on which the fate of at least two realms rested. I could tell myself I was concerned for her safety, that it was my duty. There was truth in that, but not the whole truth.

The truth was that I was jealous as a man is jealous of his beloved.

And that was unfair. I hadn't even declared my feelings. Insofar as Phèdre knew, I'd made my choice to turn my back on the Brotherhood out of pure intention, that I was called upon to serve Cassiel as the Perfect Companion. That was true; but again, it wasn't the whole of the truth, because I didn't know what it meant to be the Perfect Companion. All my life, I'd been taught that Cassiel's choice to remain at Blessed Elua's side was the purest possible expression of divine love—asking nothing, sacrificing everything.

Since the night in the cavern, an insidious question had crept into my thoughts: What if it *wasn't*? What if Cassiel chose to follow Blessed Elua to the Terre d'Ange-that-lies-beyond out of love, plain and simple?

Blessed Elua and his Companions left their stamp on every part of Terre d'Ange. Their blood runs in our veins, and a shepherd might have a lineage every bit as divine as a King or Queen. Every Companion save Cassiel claimed his or her province, and shared their gifts with their descendants. Only Cassiel trod lightly upon the soil of Terre d'Ange and left no footprint upon it. He claimed no territory, sired no children. He was the Perfect Companion, a chaste embodiment of Adonai's love for his wayward grandson Elua.

Or so we were taught.

But there was nothing in the earliest recorded histories regarding the nature of the relationship between Cassiel and Elua. To suggest that it was anything but chaste would be pure heresy in the eyes of the Cassiline Brotherhood. And yet . . . if it were true, it would be the greatest love story never told. What if our understanding of what it meant to be the Perfect Companion was wrong? It would be an extraordinary thing.

I didn't know that it was true, though. And if it were, was that the course I wanted to set upon? I didn't even know how Phèdre felt about me—or about Hyacinthe, for that matter, though he seemed unexpectedly taken with Moiread. All I knew for sure was that her intimate affections would never be reserved for one person alone. Pure fidelity among D'Angelines was rare in the first place; Phèdre was pledged to Naamah's service and pricked by Kushiel's Dart. Her desires were god-driven.

I didn't know if I could live with that.

I didn't know if I couldn't.

CHAPTER FORTY-SIX

In the aftermath of his assignation with Phèdre, Lord Eamonn of the Dalriada had a great beaming grin and an energetic sense of purpose.

The departure Drustan had announced was delayed by some days. With the support of the Dalriada, the quest to retake the throne was no longer a desperate attempt likely doomed to fail, it was a viable possibility. And if it were to succeed, passion needed to be supported by logistics and strategy. Planning was Eamonn's strong suit. Together, he and Drustan chose ten teams of warriors, each team a pair of Cruithne and Dalriada, to spread word of the coming counter-insurrection and call upon tribes to rally to the twin banners of the White Mare and the Black Boar. While his sister Grainne conducted training drills, Eamonn was securing supply lines for our advance.

The Lords of the Dalriada took to the battlefield in horse-drawn war-chariots, something that Phèdre and I agreed was like seeing an old Hellene tale sprung to life. I will own, Lady Grainne fascinated me. I'd never encountered a female warrior before—it simply wasn't a part of D'Angeline culture—but they featured largely in the history of Alba and Eire, and from what I saw, Grainne was a warrior of deserved renown.

Our departure may not have been immediate, but it was swift. The grass was growing thick and lush, flowers were blooming on the hillsides, the trees were in full leaf, and Alba was going to war. We would be accompanying them along with half of Rousse's crew. If we succeeded, we would continue onward across the Straits. If we failed, the sailors remaining with the ship would search for a southeastern passage to Marsilikos and carry word of our mission's fate.

Like Terre d'Ange, Alba was crisscrossed by old Tiberian roads. Although they were in a state of centuries' worth of neglect, they still provided a useful map of the swiftest routes through the Alban terrain. We set off from Innisclan in long straggling lines astride and on foot, the Twins in their war-chariots in the forefront. Our D'Angeline party took up the rear, along with Necthana and her daughters and a few other members of the household.

It was a strange time. Our early outriders were still at large, leaving us in the dark regarding what we might expect in terms of allies rising up to support the rightful Cruarch. And, too, there were different stakes for all of us. For Drustan and his people, the stakes were extraordinarily high. If he failed to retake the throne, there would be no second effort.

For the Dalriada, it was both an assertion of loyalty and a bloody lark. If we were to lose this battle, they would mourn their dead, then regroup what survivors remained and return to Innisclan, relatively safe from any reprisal in the shadow of their kinfolk in the Kingdom of Eire a short sail away.

The stakes were high for us. If Drustan's forces failed to defeat Maelcon's, our mission was a failure, too—and we would be left without recourse. We'd be left stranded in exile while either Isidore d'Aiglemort seized the throne under false pretenses or Waldemar Selig's forces defeated ours and he laid claim to Terre d'Ange.

What would become of us in either event, I couldn't begin to guess.

Our outriders had left embers of insurrection smoldering in their wake, and now our passage fanned the flames. Although it made our progress increasingly unwieldy, it was a relief to see the influx of warriors joining our army on a daily basis, the front line spreading north and south far beyond the delineations of the ancient Tiberian road.

The first to join us were from various tribes of the Cullach Gorrym, flocking to the banner of the Black Boar on its crimson background, vivid and defiant against the misty green Alban spring. Despite Eamonn's best efforts, supplies ran short within three days of our departure as our ranks swelled. Game was abundant in the wild and the Cruithne were excellent archers. The army foraged from farmsteads for fodder and the remnants of winter's stores, Drustan assuring disgruntled owners that he would repay them threefold when he reclaimed his birthright. At night, our campfires were spread out like a field of fireflies.

As we drew nearer to Bryn Gorrydum, more allies joined us. Phèdre rattled off the names of individual tribes within the Four Folk—Decanatii and Corvanicci, Sigovae and Votadae—with the excitement of someone seeing a history book come to life. I just counted the numbers and prayed.

And then the tide turned.

A handful of the tribes to join us were of the Tarbh Cró—the folk of the Red Bull, to which Maelcon the Usurper's mother was born. They wore woad tattoos like the Cullach Gorrym and dressed their hair for battle with lime like the Dalriada. They brought a hearty attitude of fierce defiance, and the unwelcome news that six of our outriders had been slain by Tarbh Cró tribes loyal to Maelcon.

Maelcon knew we were coming, and he was raising an army. And the next day worse news reached us. The south of Alba had declared for Maelcon, and those who weren't flocking to join his standing army at Bryn Gorrydum were planning to circle behind us, razing and burning the homesteads of any tribe supporting Drustan's cause.

That night mutiny hung in the balance, with half our forces tempted to turn back and protect their own homes. Drustan was tireless in his efforts to convince the troops to stay, riding from campfire to campfire, listening to their concerns and assuring them that it was nothing more than a false rumor used as a scare tactic.

"How can he be so sure?" Hyacinthe wondered aloud; we were seated around our own campfire, and he held Moiread's hand loosely clasped in his own. If it troubled Phèdre, she didn't show it.

"He's not *sure*," Phèdre said. "But it's what I told him I suspected when he asked for my counsel."

He blinked at her. "Why?"

She shrugged. "It would be a clever gambit with a clever mind behind it. From what I know, Maelcon's not that clever—but his mother is."

"Foclaidha." I remembered her name. "She was clever enough to conspire with the Lioness of Azzalle. They nearly put Prince Baudoin on the D'Angeline throne."

"Exactly," she said.

"I hope to hell you're right, lass," Quintilius Rousse said quietly. "But one way or the other, we're about to find out."

Truly spoken, and we didn't have to wait long. Come dawn, the morning mist cleared to reveal a sizeable force amassed on the horizon. Unprepared to engage so suddenly, our troops scrambled to assemble. Now that they were pulling steadily in tandem, the Twins were ready to lead a headlong charge.

Drustan bade them wait.

It was frustrating to be unable to see or hear what passed on the front lines. As much as he appeared to value Phèdre's counsel, it had no place on the battlefield. So we waited in an agony of uncertainty until a Cruithne rider came pelting to the rearguard to report that the forces amassed across from us were allies, folk of the Golden Hind, come to join the assault on Maelcon the Usurper. Cheers rippled across the fields as the news spread throughout our troops.

With these new forces enfolded into ours, the army had grown to an imposing size. It was as though an entire city was approaching Bryn Gorrydum—and approaching we were. When we made camp the following evening, word went around to expect a battle on the morrow.

Admiral Rousse was troubled. It had always been part of the plan that he and the score of sailors with him would take part in the battle—his men weren't just seafarers, they were fighters, too. Now, he was second-guessing that decision and speculating that it would be better if the D'Angeline company stayed behind the lines to protect the Queen's ambassador.

"If the battle breaks against us, you should at least have me and my lads to safeguard your retreat," he fretted.

It was Sibeal, Drustan's middle sister, who responded; Necthana and her daughters spoke interchangeably on behalf of the exiled Cruarch's family.

Phèdre translated for her, looking directly at Rousse. "If you will not die for us, you cannot ask us to die for you."

He scowled at Sibeal. "I don't want anyone to die; but least of all, her majesty the Queen's ambassador."

Inclining her head, Phèdre conveyed his response to Sibeal, then talked with all the women in the family, turning at last back to Quintilius Rousse. "My lord, if you're asking for the sake of your men, I say yes, for I've no desire to see D'Angeline blood shed on foreign soil. But if you're asking for my sake, I say no." She met his gaze squarely. "I cannot countenance it. Not with what we're asking of them."

"Blessed Elua's bulging balls!" The Royal Admiral clutched his hair. "Are you jesting? Do you have to choose *now* to be so thrice-damned high-minded, you bloody brilliant bed-hopping little spy? Elder Brother bugger me with a trident, Anafiel Delaunay would have had my guts for garters if he knew I'd abandoned you on the arsehole of a battlefield!"

It went on for a while.

Phèdre waited for Rousse's outrage to run its course. "We'll stay well behind the battle lines, my lord Admiral," she said calmly. "I will take no risk that Prince Drustan's own mother does not share. And I have Joscelin."

Rousse stooped to jab a thick forefinger at my face. "You'll stay with her? You swear it, Cassiline? You'll not leave her side?"

What a foolish question. I rose and executed a formal bow. "I *have* sworn it, my lord. To damnation and beyond."

And still he wasn't satisfied. "My men are itching to fight. They've seen no action since we fought the hellions of Khebbel-im-Akkad. But I swear to you, Phèdre nó Delaunay, if harm comes to you in this battle, your lord's shade will plague me beyond my dying day! Believe me, I've no wish to have your death on my head."

"*She will not die.*" Hyacinthe had been so quiet and inward-looking, it was a double shock to hear him speak in the hollow tones of the *dromonde*. He looked at Rousse, his eyes all night-black pupil, blurred and strange with the sight. "Her Long Road is not ended. Nor yours, Admiral."

"Do you say we will be victorious?" Rousse demanded. "Do you say so, Tsingano?"

Hyacinthe shook his head. "I see you returning to water, my lord Admiral, and Phèdre, too. More, I cannot see."

There was more cursing before Quintilius Rousse acceded. "So be it. We fight for Ysandre's blue boy, then, and let Alban blood taste D'Angeline steel." He bowed to Phèdre. "May Elua bless you, my lady, and your Tsingano witch-boy and Cassiline whatsit protect you. We'll meet again on the water or the true Terre d'Ange-that-lies-beyond."

"Blessed Elua be with you." She rose and embraced him, kissing his scarred cheek. "No King or Queen of Terre d'Ange ever had a truer servant, my lord Admiral."

He flushed visibly, returning her embrace with genuine affection. "Nor a stranger ambassador," he said. "Nor a better one, girl. You've brought them here, haven't you? Elua be with you."

I slept hard that night, falling back on my Cassiline training. On the edge of battle, we had sentries posted everywhere around the perimeter. We were as safe as we were going to be, and I had to be as well rested as possible.

Drustan roused the army before dawn. We'd made camp on the verge of a copse of young beech trees. Beyond the copse was a steep valley, and beyond that, a straight passage to Bryn Gorrydum.

In the histories we studied at the Prefectory, battles were always depicted with the benefit of hindsight. Historians described the strategic placement of infantry units, of the use of cavalry, lines of pikemen. Plans laid and mistakes made were analyzed on parchment by a critical eye. The reality, at least here in the fields of Alba, was a great deal messier. We had some six thousand foot-soldiers from a dozen different tribes, seven hundred horse, and fifty Dalriadan chariots. The conjoined forces of the Twins, Drustan's most loyal Cruithne, and our small D'Angeline company would lead the advance on Bryn Gorrydum in a show of allegiance. Beyond that, our troops were a formless horde with dense knots where the larger tribes had amassed.

There was a rocky outcropping yards from our campsite that afforded a vantage point for those of us behind troop lines. From atop it, we saw Drustan mab Necthana ride slowly back and forth before the copse, his head held high, unmistakable in the long scarlet cloak that was a badge of the Cruarch's status, proclaiming his identity for all the world to see. His voice rang out in the misty dawn. Cruithne and Dalriada responded with loud cheers, banging the flats of their blades against their bucklers.

"He is calling upon them to restore the Alban throne to its rightful heir," Phèdre murmured, her head cocked in concentration. "Reminding them that Maelcon killed his own father to seize the throne."

Drustan spoke again.

"He is naming them his brothers and sisters," Phèdre translated. "Calling them his kin—" Her voice faltered in the wake of his.

A hush fell over the gathered troops, a soft golden silence spreading with the dawn sun, rays streaming through the leaves of the beeches, tendrils of mist rising from the dark loam of the soil. It was a black boar; no, it was *the* black boar, vaster than any I'd seen. It emerged from the copse with the rising sun at its bristle-ridged back, throwing its shadow long before it. Its tusks were monstrous and huge. It raised its snout and snuffled the air, its fiery eyes glaring with ancient fury.

A shiver ran over my skin.

This was Alban magic, steeped in symbol and portent. The Cullach Gorrym had been invoked; the Cullach Gorrym had answered. I heard Phèdre catch her breath beside me, and it seemed the whole of the army was holding its breath until someone let loose a choked cry of wonder. Wheeling, the great boar trotted back into the copse—and it ran with a half-gaited limp that was nonetheless steady and assured.

Now a battle-cry went up from nearly seven thousand throats, and in the distance, Drustan mab Necthana drew his sword and gave a fierce shout, his blue-marqued face a warrior's mask, and every soul present understood his meaning.

"Follow the Cullach Gorrym!"

He heeled his mount in pursuit of the boar, and the entirety of our army followed.

It wasn't the attack that we'd intended. We'd thought to find Maelcon's forces arrayed in defense of Bryn Gorrydum, enabling a tactical approach and not this pell-mell chase after a mythical boar of epic size. But we heard the clash and roar of battle echoing from the valley beyond the copse within mere minutes. Later, we would learn that Maelcon had planned an ambush. His troops had crept into the valley overnight. Ten more minutes—and Drustan's speech had bade to go on at least that long—and they would have been waiting for us in the beech copse and circling round to flank our sides. Instead, their stealthy ascent was met by thousands of Cruithne and Dalriada pouring over the edge of the valley.

At the time, those of us left behind could only wonder and pray, straining to make sense of the sounds of battle. There was no seeing through the copse of trees that lay between us and the battlefield.

But there was one of us whose sight wasn't constrained by the boundaries of time. Until Phèdre turned to Hyacinthe in alarm, shaking him by the shoulders, I hadn't realized the *dromonde* had taken him.

"What do you see?" she asked him urgently. "Hyacinthe! What do you see?"

"Death," he whispered, sight-blind and terrified, looking behind us. "Death."

A score of mounted Tarbh Cró warriors were arrayed there. I cursed myself for not having kept a watch to the rear. We had been so focused on the distant battle, not even Phèdre had sensed their approach. One of them said something, drew his sword, and smiled, and they spread out in a semicircle. Our small party was exposed. Necthana and her daughters had left their hunting bows at the campsite. Now Maelcon's men were between us and the site.

There was only me.

My daggers were already drawn, the blood singing in my veins with righteous fury, the taste of steel in my mouth. I spared one quick glance for Phèdre, a spark of understanding passing between us. I dropped lightly onto a ledge halfway down the outcropping and bowed to the dumbfounded Tarbh Cró below with crossed vambraces.

"In Cassiel's name," I said. "I protect and serve."

On the ledge, I was out of reach of men on horseback. Putting faith in their superior numbers, all save their leader dismounted to assail the outcropping on foot. I stomped one heel hard on the first brawny hand within reach, breaking fingers, then cut the man's throat with a low lunging slice. A left-handed backward stab plunged my other dagger into the thigh of another attacker. Now they came in earnest, swarming the outcropping. I killed another with a solid upward thrust, yanking my right-hand dagger loose when it stuck in the bone of his breastplate. Too slow; over to my left one of the Tarbh Cró had gained the summit, where they managed to shove him back over the edge.

There were too many of them.

"Joscelin!" Phèdre's voice rang out. "Draw your sword!"

I should have drawn it at the outset, for I had every intention of killing anyone attempting to harm Phèdre or any member of our party. Shoving my daggers into their scabbards, I reached over my shoulder and drew my sword. The honed edges of my blade caught the light, flaming in the dawn. Time slowed down and I fought with deft precision. I dreamed a dream of fighting in which I saw every opponent's move before its execution, in which I stitched back and forth across the rocky face of the promontory, keeping them at bay. And then a figure darted past me from behind—swift and lithe, a minnow in a stream. Sleek black hair, wideset dark eyes.

Moiread, the youngest.

I checked myself to allow her passage; later, I wished I hadn't. She dashed past half a dozen men to gain the campsite, seized her bow and quiver, and began shooting at the Tarbh Cró with deadly accuracy. One fell, then two; and now it was raining rocks on our attackers as Hyacinthe returned from the distance of the *dromonde* to hurl stones at them.

Still mounted, their leader wheeled his mount and shouted somewhat, drawing a short throwing spear. I let out a shout of fury and denial as he cocked the spear and cast it; I heard heartbroken cries atop the outcropping as Moiread wrapped both hands around the spear haft blossoming from her chest.

Closing my eyes for the merest second, I whispered a prayer to Cassiel. "*Use me.*"

The final book of the Tanakh speaks of refiner's fire, that which burns away the dross and leaves only pure gold. It burned in me. My eyes were full of sunlight and death as I leapt from the ledge and descended into the midst of our attackers, launching a slashing attack in midair and spinning as I landed. There are fights I can remember blow by blow. This was not one of them. I only remember that the refiner's fire blazed through me and I fought and fought. Somewhere inside me there was a deep sense of regret, but no remorse. The Tarbh Cró's numbers dwindled. Hyacinthe joined the fray, finishing off the maimed and wounded with his boot dagger, his expression grim. Necthana and her two surviving daughters followed him, sharp belt knives drawn and plunging.

And then there were no more Tarbh Cró standing.

And Moiread mab Necthana, who had dreamed of swans and met us upon the farthest Alban shore, was dead.

But Phèdre was safe.

The refiner's fire that had blazed in me went out like a blown candle flame and the weight of all the killing I had done drove me to my knees. I should have been able to save Moiread, too. I tried to let go my sword, but my hands were stuck to the hilt with coagulating blood, more blood than anyone ought to shed.

"Joscelin." Phèdre stooped before me, holding a waterskin. I looked up at her. She poured clear water over my blood-sticky hands, then stoppered the skin and pried my fingers loose. "Tilt your head." I obeyed. She rose and sluiced more water over my head and face and it ran down in scarlet-tinged rivulets.

I bowed my head, and she kissed my bloodstained brow like a benediction.

It was an hour or more before Drustan returned victorious, his own woad-tattooed arms splashed with gore, his mount lathered. He wore a look of ferocious exultation that faded as soon as he beheld the scene before him; Moiread's slender, motionless form and the grief written on the faces of his mother and sisters, the rest of us somber.

"No," he said. "Ah, no."

Necthana rose to face her son, her expression grave, and posed a question to him.

Our warriors were straggling through the trees, returning from the battlefield, including the Twins in the war-chariots. Eamonn's was dragging a corpse behind it. Drustan gestured in response and spoke.

"Maelcon," Phèdre murmured.

It was impossible not to be shocked at the treatment of his body, but Maelcon the Usurper was very, very dead, his reddish hair clotted with blood and dirt, his eyes covered with a film of dust, and his face fixed in a grimace.

Eamonn let out a victorious shout, lashing the reins, then saw Moiread. "Dagda Mor! No!"

Necthana spoke again, tears shining in her dark eyes, and Phèdre translated quietly. "For every victory, there is a price."

CHAPTER FORTY-SEVEN

War takes a terrible toll.

I thought I knew somewhat about it after Skaldia, but nothing had prepared me for the scale of death unleashed on the battlefield. In a sense we'd been fortunate, for Maelcon and his forces, caught unexpected in the valley, had suffered casualties in the thousands. But we'd lost our share, too, including four of Rousse's sailors as well as hundreds of the Alban warriors who had rallied to Drustan's banner.

We didn't ride triumphant into Bryn Gorrydum on the heels of our victory, but spent the day tending to the wounded and gathering the dead. Drustan had ordered a great cairn built for our fallen. I helped haul stones from the hillsides, finding a certain grim solace in punishing my body with hard labor.

Phèdre worked with Necthana and her daughters bringing water to the battlefield, exchanging her waterskin for a bucket and dipper. I refused her offer, reckoning there were others who needed it more. She proffered it a second time. "You did what you had to, Joscelin. They drew to kill."

"I know." I hoisted another stone. "But I should have saved her, too."

She left me be, then, understanding that this was a penance I needed to perform. Blessed Elua knows, if there was one thing someone pricked by Kushiel's Dart understood, it was penance.

Despite the losses, there was a celebration among the majority of the campsites come nightfall. Eamonn revealed that an entire supply wagon at the rear of our train held casks of *uisghe*. Warriors drunk on victory, survival, and strong spirits sang and cheered and keened and mourned long into the Alban night, telling and retelling the stories of their individual experiences on the battlefield.

Our campsite, where Moiread lay covered upon a bier, was a somber one.

We did hear Quintilius Rousse's version of the battle when he limped over to our campsite, bandages wrapped around his calf and head, to describe the way Maelcon's forces panicked and scattered as if blown by a strong wind. He described the battle between Drustan and Maelcon, and how Grainne drove her chariot in circles around Eamonn to allow him time to lash the corpse behind his own conveyance. In time, he spoke of the D'Angeline dead.

"They knew, my lady," the Royal Admiral said to Phèdre, who had been silent throughout his tale. "You may believe it, all those who sign on with me know the risks. To die on land is a glorious thing. 'Tis death by water that we fear." He cleared his throat. "I promised them somewhat."

She inclined her head. "Yes, my lord Admiral?"

Rousse hemmed again and scratched his bandaged scalp. "I promised them they'd be knighted, those that lived. At your own hand."

Phèdre stared at him in startlement. "*My* hand?"

"You're the Queen's ambassador," he said with a gruffness that didn't belie his genuine pride. "They respect you. And you've the right to do it."

"They do? I do?"

I stirred. "You do, Phèdre."

She blinked at me. "If that's so, Joscelin, then no one is more deserving of being knighted than—"

"No." I shook my head. "I am Cassiel's Servant, not a Chevalier. But they deserve it."

"Let it be done, then, if they truly wish it," she said.

The Royal Admiral stuck two fingers in his mouth and gave a long, piercing whistle. A line of D'Angeline sailors assembled around the circle of light cast by our campfire, and I was glad to see my friend Fortun and several of his boon companions among the survivors. Rousse assisted Phèdre to her feet. Drawing his sword, he extended it to her hilt-first. Still looking bewildered, she accepted it. Rousse taught her the words to say, and she repeated them as sailors filed forward, one by one, to kneel before her. "In the name of Blessed Elua and Queen Ysandre de la Courcel, for your extraordinary valor in service of country and crown, I appoint you a Chevalier of the Realm."

It was no jest to these men, I could see it in their eyes. They had seen Phèdre nó Delaunay sing the face of the waters to stillness, they had watched her singlehandedly galvanize the Dalriada to war. Their pride in being knighted at her hand was deep and sincere. When it was finished, Quintilius Rousse retrieved his sword and clapped her on the shoulder. "Well done! I'll give this lot a fighting name, eh? Phèdre's Boys, I'll call them."

Phèdre laughed, though there was a touch of despair in it. "My lord, I wish you wouldn't."

"We're at war, little night-blooming flower." Rousse took a long pull on a wineskin. "Or so you tell me. What did you expect? If they will fight for you, well and good. If they take pride in dying for your name, so much the better. What did you think would happen when you bade me on this mission?"

"I don't know." She buried her face in her hands and sighed. "Call them what you will."

"I already have," he said.

Despite everything, I smiled a little at the absurdity of it. Quintilius Rousse and his lads took their leave, returning to their own campsite. Phèdre rose and touched my shoulder lightly in what might have been an apologetic gesture or merely a kind one, then approached Hyacinthe where he knelt motionless at Moiread's bier. I hadn't spoken to Hyacinthe since the battle. Our relationship had grown easier with familiarity, but there had always been a certain awkwardness between us. We were not quite friends, not quite rivals. I knew he was in pain, but I didn't know how to speak to it.

Phèdre did.

She'd known him since they were children. Hyacinthe was the most constant thing in her life. I'd taken their romance to be a frivolous thing not so very long ago, and although it seemed as though a decade had passed since that first encounter in Night's Doorstep, I'd failed to understand the bedrock on which it was built. The bond between them ran deep. Now I watched her raise him to his feet, watched him wrap his arms around her like a man drowning. I watched her kiss him, take his hand, and lead him into the darkness beyond the light of any campfire.

In the midst of thousands of allies, I was lonely.

I wished Selwyn were there. He was the only person with whom I could have borne to discuss my feelings for Phèdre. Then again, Selwyn hadn't trusted me enough to talk about the desires that drove him, probably because he knew it would be met with disapproval and a self-righteous lecture on Cassiline willpower and discipline.

I wasn't that person anymore, but he would never know it.

Watching Drustan's family in the bittersweet aftermath of triumph and tragedy, I thought of my own family. I wondered if they would be disappointed in me—for what I'd done, for what I hadn't done.

I hoped they were alive and well. I hoped that I'd be able to see them again one day, so they might know the man I'd become.

Overhead the stars turned slowly. Other Cruithne came to pay their respects at Moiread's bier. Necthana lifted up her voice in a soft, lyrical song of mourning. One after the other, Breidaia and Sibeal joined in, their three voices forming a twining refrain. Other voices came and went, adding strands until the song grew like a great braid reaching toward the heavens; and then Drustan added his voice, a deep chanting note rooting the song in the Alban soil where her blood had been spilled.

The song went on and on into the night, other voices raised around other campfires to praise and mourn the fallen. I knelt quietly and listened, letting the river of grief flow over and encompass me.

At some point, Drustan mab Necthana approached me. Phèdre and Hyacinthe must have returned from finding solace in each other, for she was attending the young Cruarch. I'd forgotten that the latter spoke some Caerdicci until he crouched at my side to address me. "You fight for family." He extended his hand. "Brother."

Gazing at the small figure on the bier, I shook my head. "Your sister is dead, my lord King," I said. "Do me no honor. I failed you."

He beckoned to Phèdre, who translated for him. "Thousands died this day, and I could not save them. Not even I, born Cruarch to give my life for my people. But if I had not fought, they would not have died. Do you say right was not done this day, Prince of Swords?"

Drustan's gaze was intent in his blue-whorled face, features framed by sleek black hair like his mother's and sisters'. Trusting Phèdre to translate, I spoke directly to him. "My lord King, it is your birthright you've taken and the death of your own father that you avenged. It was rightfully done. It was I who failed in my trust."

He frowned in thought, rubbing at cramped muscles in his bad leg. "You swore no vow to the Cullach Gorrym. We risked our lives to regain Alba. Do not lessen the worth of Moiread's death."

The words took me aback, for I had intended no such thing, but he was right. Moiread was a fierce fighter in her own right. She fought for all of us; fought and killed. To blame myself for her death demeaned her sacrifice. Drustan held out his hand again, and this time I took it. "Brother," I said to him. "If you will have me."

He smiled and pulled me into a hard embrace, and I was glad for it.

On the morrow, we entered Bryn Gorrydum, not entirely sure what we would find. Maelcon was dead and his army had surrendered in the field, but the city and fortress that had served as the Cruarch's seat since Drustan's long-ago ancestor drove the Tiberians out of Alba had yet to formally declare fealty. We marched along the shores of a wide, flat river where, despite everything, crofters were hauling spring crops and bales of fleece from the first shearing in the hope of finding the market square open for trade.

Bryn Gorrydum was located on the shores of the Straits. Although it had been largely blocked from outside engagement for the past thousand years, the ancient Tiberian walls still surrounded it. But the walls were empty and unmanned, and as we entered the city by the westernmost gate, the commonfolk turned out to cheer us.

Not all of them cheered, of course; there were plenty who had hitched their wagons to Maelcon's star and stood to lose status and privilege. And too, there were men and women whose opposition to the Cruithne matrilineal tradition of inheritance was genuine. Most, however, were fiercely happy to see the betrayal and murder of the old Cruarch avenged and his sister-son ascending triumphantly to the throne.

The Tarbh Cró issued a formal surrender and gave Maelcon's mother Foclaidha over into the custody of Drustan's forces.

Drustan moved swiftly to secure his power and was sworn in by the highest-ranking members of the Four Folk of Alba. The banners flying the Red Bull came down from the towers of Bryn Gorrydum, to be replaced by the great Black Boar. Lest anyone forget the cost of treason, Maelcon's head was nailed above the central gate.

It was a shocking thing to see, a reminder that some Cruithne customs were barbaric to a D'Angeline eye. Drustan's first official ruling as Cruarch was to hear his father's wife Foclaidha plead for clemency. As the Queen's ambassadress, Phèdre was present—and not just merely as an observer, for Terre d'Ange had reason to accuse Foclaidha of plotting to undermine the D'Angeline crown.

The audience went on for some time while Foclaidha delivered an impassioned speech before the Crown. Phèdre loosely translated the parts I wasn't able to follow. The slain Cruarch's wife cut an imposing figure, tall with flashing eyes, a warrior like Lady Grainne of the Dalriada with a Cruithne warrior's facial markings. It was rumored that she'd killed several men when the garrison came for her. I cannot imagine she was an easy person to have for a mother. Her speech may have been a rousing one, but it swayed no one, least of all the Cruarch and his family, listening with their dark eyes as polished and unreadable as black pebbles in a river. Drustan turned to the Twins to ask if the Dalriada pled for clemency on her behalf; Eamonn and Grainne adamantly refused.

Then he posed the same inquiry to Phèdre, taking her by surprise. She squared her shoulders and answered in a cool tone. “My lord, Foclaidha of the Brugantii conspired against the Crown of Terre d’Ange. It has been proven. We do not bid for clemency.”

“You will die for your treachery,” Drustan said to Foclaidha. “For the blood ties between us, I grant it will be swift.”

He beckoned to two of his most trusted warriors, who seized Foclaidha by the arms and drove her to her knees. Without a second’s hesitation, Drustan mab Necthana drew his sword and beheaded her.

It would be disingenuous to claim that our methods of punishment for one convicted of high crimes against the realm were morally superior. Faced with the same sentence, the Lioness of Azzalle was given the choice of dying by poison. She was no less dead than the body slumped on the floor of the throne room of Bryn Gorrydum, and depending on the effects of the poison, she likely suffered longer and worse in her death throes.

Still, the immediate and brutal nature of her death, like Maelcon’s head above the gate, was unexpected. Phèdre barely managed to contain a squeak of shock when Foclaidha’s head bounced on the flagstones. I squeezed her elbow in a tight grip to steady her and she shot me a grateful look.

And then it was done.

The Black Boar ruled in Alba.

CHAPTER FORTY-EIGHT

Our journey was far from over.

First we had to wait while Drustan shouldered the more tiresome burdens of being Cruarch, hearing petitions from lesser lords across the realm to settle old quarrels and new, for many issues created by Maelcon's uprising had gone unresolved during Drustan's time in exile. And too, he felt a need to ensure that his rulership in Alba was built upon a very solid base before departing for Terre d'Ange. His mother Necthana would rule in his stead, but he needed to leave enough troops behind to enforce her will. To that end, it was impossible that the entire Alban army would be dispatched to assist us, but the force Drustan pledged was a sizeable one. Three thousand foot-soldiers and four hundred horse would make the crossing.

"You know that's nothing compared to Selig's forces," Phèdre said to me in private. "He's ten times as many men, plus the Allies of Camlach, too."

"I know." Days after the battle, I was still working traces of blood out of the detailed bits of my arms and armor. "At least until the moment Waldemar Selig turns on d'Aiglemort. And unfortunately, we have no idea how that's going to play out."

"Nor what manner of loyal forces Ysandre has raised," Phèdre added, voicing a concern on everyone's mind.

The plan was for our Alban forces to march south, to one of the narrowest parts of the Straits, and from thence attempt the crossing that the Master of the Straits had promised to allow us. It would be a dangerous undertaking even with his permission, for Alba lacked a navy and our transport would be a piecemeal assemblage of any vessel that would float, especially flat-bottomed sailing scows sturdy enough to accommodate horses. A full half of our numbers proceeded the remainder to the beaches of Dobria to prepare for the crossing.

If everything went smoothly, we'd make landfall in northern Azzalle, where we would liaise with the Royal Commander's son Ghislain de Somerville. If we were lucky, Admiral Rousse's fleet would have slipped away from de Morhban's duchy to join them. If we were exceedingly lucky, the Skaldic invasion would not yet have begun. Given the odds, I'd be grateful for one out of three.

This time, Drustan mab Necthana sent outriders to spread the word that the Black Boar ruled in Alba. Having regained control of the treasury, he made good on reparations to those farmers and crofters whose supplies our army had conscripted—and he sent his outriders with generous purses offering gold coin for the usage of all manner of boats, as well as stores to restock our supplies.

In the midst of the whirl of activity, I found a moment to seek out Hyacinthe, who had been quiet and removed since Moiread's death. As a pretext, I asked his advice on the mounts that had been allocated to us; in truth, I was worried about him. He came down to the paddocks with me to examine the horses, and found them sound. After recommending oil for dry hooves that could become brittle if untreated, he straightened. "You didn't really ask me here to look at the horses, did you?"

"No." I leaned against the slats of the paddock fence, which stretched extensively into the distant green hills. The grass was a rich emerald blanket, and there was no denying that we were past spring and into summer. "I just wanted to ask how you were."

"I'm fine," Hyacinthe said.

I raised my brows at him.

He sighed and ran a hand through his messy black curls. "What do you want me to say, Cassiline? I'm sad. I don't know how to put a name to what there was between Moiread and me. Whatever it was, it died stillborn."

"I know," I murmured. "I'm sorry."

"I know." Hyacinthe patted a broad-backed chestnut gelding on the shoulder. "I'd like to tell you I'm fine, Cassiline; that I'll be fine and so will you and Phèdre and all of us. But I'm not fine and I can't see the future. The *dromonde* has narrowed to a single point. A ship and the sea."

"Nothing more?" I asked him.

"No," he said. "Not since we landed on Alban shores. Moiread . . . she and her sisters, their mother, too—they all have a kind of sight, but it comes to them in dreams and symbols. The eldest, Breidaia, said she dreamt I was on an island." He shrugged. "But she couldn't say what it meant."

I didn't know what to say beyond reiterating my sympathies. I believed in the *dromonde* because I'd seen it at work, but I'd no wisdom to offer in a discussion of sight and portents and dreams. And I'd managed to not think about Phèdre taking Hyacinthe by the hand and leading him into the night, but now that I was having a private conversation with him, it grew harder to avoid the thought. I was spared by the arrival of one of Rousse's sailors, Remy, who'd become friendly with Hyacinthe during our crossing. "Hey, Tsingano!" he called out cheerfully. "Any luck getting your hands on some gold thread?"

Hyacinthe grinned, his whole demeanor brightening. "I had to track down Foclaidha's looted wardrobe, but believe it or not, yes."

I looked from one to the other. "What in the world are you up to?"

Remy's green eyes sparkled. "Come see, messire! You can tell us whether or not her ladyship will take it amiss."

Bryn Gorrydum's barracks were full to overflowing, but Drustan had made space for our men, who were accustomed to travelling light and bunking in tight quarters. Hyacinthe and I accompanied Remy to the long room they shared, bedrolls lining an aisle where a pair of sailors were stitching a scarlet starburst onto an expanse of black fabric. Hyacinthe pulled a short wooden rod wound with gold thread from an inner pocket and tossed it to one of the men sewing, who whistled in approval and unwound a length, stretching it across the ragged burst.

Remy clapped a hand on my shoulder. "What do you think, Cassiline? It's going to be the standard for Phèdre's Boys."

Now I saw it: the crimson mote on the sable field, pierced by the gold of Kushiel's Dart. "Oh, Elua!" An involuntary laugh escaped me. "It's . . . striking."

"Do you think she'll like it?" he asked earnestly; in fact, all of them were looking earnestly at me.

I had absolutely no idea, and based on the half smile tucked into the corner of Hyacinthe's mouth, he didn't, either. "There are chants," he informed me. "Marching chants."

"I'm sure she'll love it," I assured them.

The march to Dobria, the coastal settlement at the narrowest point of the Straits, only took three days once we were underway at last. It seemed to me that Phèdre was uncharacteristically reserved from the outset, brooding as we rode under clear skies toward the next phase of our endless quest. And mayhap it was just the endless nature of it, for neither of us had had a place to call home since the brutal murder of Delaunay and our entire household, but I thought there was somewhat more in it, too—somewhat I recognized.

After conferring with Rousse's cadre of sailors on the second day, I returned to my place at Phèdre's side in our long column. She acknowledged me with a quick smile before returning to her thoughts.

"Will you take it all on your shoulders, Phèdre?" I asked in a gentle tone. "Can you slow time or shorten our road? I was reminded not long ago not to take upon myself that which is not mine to carry."

She sighed. "I know, I do. I just can't help but worry. The Skaldi . . . we've spoken of their numbers. If the Cruithne are riding toward death, they're doing it at my word, Joscelin."

"No," I said firmly. "Not your word, Ysandre's. You did but carry it for her. They made their choice freely."

Phèdre wasn't assuaged. "It may have been the Queen's word, but I spoke it," she murmured. "And I did everything in my power to sway them. The Dalriada wouldn't be here if I hadn't. None of them would."

"I know." I wasn't going to lie to her. "But Drustan rides for love, and a pledge. *Love as thou wilt.* You can't gainsay it."

It was true and Phèdre knew it; she was silent for a moment before whispering her own truth so no one else might hear. "I'm afraid of this war, Joscelin. What we saw in Alba . . . I never want to see the like again, and what awaits us in Terre d'Ange may be worse." She lifted her gaze to meet mine, and it was fearful in a way I'd not seen before. "I don't have the strength to face that much death."

"It scares me, too," I said. "There'd be somewhat wrong with us if it didn't, Phèdre."

"Do you remember waking up in that cart after Melisande betrayed us?" she asked me, and I nodded. Of course I did. "I could have died, and I wouldn't have cared." She touched the diamond at her throat. "Hating her was the only reason I had to live for a while. But I don't feel the same, now. I'm afraid of dying."

My heart ached at her words. Phèdre nó Delaunay had been forced to put on a brave front for a very, very long time. "Do you remember Gunter's kennels? When I thought you'd betrayed me, hating you kept me alive. If you'd asked me before, I'd have sworn I'd kill myself before I endured such humiliation. And Selig's steading? You shamed me into living."

She flushed at the memory. "I was desperate. Are you going to do the same to me?"

"No." I turned in the saddle, pointing behind us. "They are."

Quintilius Rousse's men had fallen into a wedge formation behind us with Remy marching at the head with a furled standard, while the Admiral himself rode alongside them on the big chestnut, chuckling. Remy unfurled the flag with a series of sweeping gestures to reveal the splash of scarlet vivid in the center of the sable field, pierced through with a shining dart embroidered with gold thread, barbed at one end of the shaft and fletched at the other.

Phèdre stared, wide-eyed and open-mouthed. "Oh, Blessed Elua!"

In the lead, Remy gave a sharp whistle and stamped the butt of his standard on the crumbled paving stones of the old Tiberian road. *"Whip us till we're on the floor, we'll turn around and ask for more, we're Phèdre's Boys!"*

I truly wasn't sure until that moment how Phèdre would react, but when Quintilius Rousse began roaring the refrain along with his men, she laughed at the sheer outrageousness of it. "Oh no! Elua!" There were tears of helpless mirth in her eyes. "Joscelin, did you know about this?"

"I might have," I admitted. "They need to believe, Phèdre. They need to fight for somewhat they know; a name, a familiar face. Rousse told me as much. These men have never seen Ysandre de la Courcel. You, they know."

"We like to hurt, we like to bleed, daily floggings do we need, we're Phèdre's Boys!"

"But . . ." She gestured, still laughing. "Like *this*?"

I grinned at her. "You sang the seas calm and you drove the Dalriada to war, whatever it took. They know that. That's why they adore you. But everyone needs to laugh in the face of death. They're following an *anguissette* into battle. Give them credit for seeing the absurdity of it. *You've* been dwelling on it long enough."

Once, Phèdre might have taken umbrage at my words; now, she merely gave me a sidelong glance with a glint in her eye. "Oh, I'll do better than give them credit." Wheeling her horse, she dismounted. Remy halted his marching chant and looked apprehensive. Reaching up, Phèdre grabbed his auburn sailor's queue and yanked his head down to kiss him soundly on the mouth. The D'Angeline company yelled and cheered as she released a stunned-looking Remy and swung gracefully astride her mount, arranging her skirts. "To any man that survives," she announced, "I swear to you, I will throw open the doors of the Thirteen Houses of the Court of Night-Blooming Flowers!"

They cheered long and hard for that proclamation.

I cocked an eyebrow when she rejoined me. "How do you propose to do that?"

"I'll find a way." She laughed. "If I have to take an assignation with the Khalif of Khebbel-im-Akkad, I will!"

That, I didn't doubt.

I only wish she wouldn't have enjoyed it so.

CHAPTER FORTY-NINE

I could see Terre d'Ange; or at least I could see a low smudge on the eastern horizon that Quintilius Rousse assured us was our homeland. It was visible from atop the high white cliffs of Dobria, where an unmanned fortress and a crumbling lighthouse were all that was left of Tiberium's long-ago occupation.

There were hundreds of vessels assembled on the beaches and in the shallows of the bays below us. There were a few one-masted ships, but the Albans had not taken to the deep seas since the Master of the Straits had manifested in these waters over a thousand years ago, and their vessels were fishing boats and scows, portage barges, even rafts steered with long-handled paddles. The Straits were narrow, but they weren't *that* narrow—seven leagues across according to the Admiral. I'd learned in Skaldia that distance tricked the mind and eye. A destination that appeared to lie within a morning's brisk walk would inevitably require an entire day's hard slog. I was no seafarer, but it didn't take one to see that crossing the Straits with this motley flotilla was going to be dangerous.

It took two days to organize the attempt. Rousse divided up his men amongst the vessels, spreading their expertise as far as possible. The Dalriada, who had more seafaring experience than the Cruithne, did the same. Supplies were stored, stashed, and lashed. Lengths of cloth were cut for blindfolds for those horses that would be transported on unsteady, unsecure vessels, with the caution that were a mount to panic, it was better to lose one to the sea than capsize and lose all. There were a hundred causes for concern, but there was only one that raised my hackles in an eerie manner.

It was an old Alban fisherman. There was nothing remarkable about him—rough-spun clothing, a deeply wrinkled face with squint-lines at the corners of his eyes, wispy grey hair poking out from the hood of his tunic. I saw him slipping through the busy throngs to approach Drustan, which was nothing out of the ordinary. Plenty of folks wanted a word with the young Cruarch. This fellow, though . . . he was fully present when I looked directly at him, right down to gnarled hands with swollen knuckles, a bulbous tip to his nose. Yet when I looked at him sideways, he seemed to trickle out of my field of vision like rivulets of water vanishing into dry soil.

The old fisherman tugged on Drustan mab Necthana's scarlet cloak and addressed him insistently.

Drustan replied politely.

I looked away, then looked back. The old man had vanished back into our mingled forces, nondescript and unremarkable. I caught Phèdre returning from the exchange. "What was that about?"

She frowned. "It was odd. He said the deep waters were the Sea-Lord's hunting ground and warned Drustan not to let his men fish within three spear-casts of shore. He was adamant about it."

I scanned the beach and found no sign of the fellow. "Well, we're not setting out on a fishing excursion."

Still, it unnerved me. There was somewhat uncanny about the old man's appearance, the insistence of his warning, the way he seemed to disappear from the corners of my eyesight. But mayhap in a land of portents and dreams, it didn't seem strange.

Drustan took it seriously enough to include it in the speech that he delivered to our troops as we prepared to embark. He kept his speech short, for the seas were calm and the breeze light. The sooner we were underway, the better. Over the weeks, I'd garnered enough Cruithne to follow the gist of it, and Phèdre translated for the benefit of our entire party.

"We cross now to follow a dream of two kingdoms united," Drustan said in ringing tones. "We cross now to honor a pledge that I made long ago to Ysandre de la Courcel, who is now Queen of Terre d'Ange, that lies across the Straits. Does any man or woman among you wish to turn back, do so now, and do it with my blessing. I ask no one to risk death for this dream, this pledge. But do you seek honor and glory beyond countless bards' telling, follow now and find it!"

The army cheered, and I cheered, too.

Drustan's face glowed, his heart uplifted. "This I tell you! The Lord of the Waters has sworn us safe passage. We shall reach the other side. I have done it before, and I know! But these deep waters are his territories. Respect his sovereignty and harm no creature. What do you say? Will you dare this crossing?"

This time, the shouts of agreement, the stamping, and the clattering of arms rose skyward, vying with the noisy seagulls circling overhead. Further cheers echoed across the harbor from a late-arriving party of Tarbh Cró. Drustan overlooked their tardy arrival and announced our departure.

"Let us go!" he cried.

Rousse had predicted that our watery exodus would be ugly, and it was. The horses were problematic, and it took another hour to get every vessel in our wretched armada manned and launched. But the weather held, the seas remained calm and the skies clear, and at last we were underway. In the port of Rive-de-Lusande, they hold a contest in midsummer in which villagers race between the north and south piers of the harbor in anything that floats—laundry tubs, bassinets, bed frames, wine barrels. If the stakes here hadn't been so very high, this would have been nigh as comical.

We had one of the finest ships, a single-masted sailing ship that had made the passage before, bringing the old Cruarch and his entourage across the Straits. Now it carried Drustan again, along with Phèdre and me and Hyacinthe, and Royal Admiral Quintilius Rousse commanded the ship. Our armada straggled into a ragged line almost immediately, the swiftest and most capable ships taking the lead save for ours. Rousse held us back to shout orders and encouragement to other vessels. As sparse as our numbers were relative to the Albans', one could hear D'Angeline voices lifting up across the water, adapting the marching song of Phèdre's Boys to a sailor's rowing chant.

"*Man or woman, we don't care; give us twins, we'll take the pair!*" they called out, making Phèdre laugh and cover her face with her hands. "*Just because we let you beat us, doesn't mean you can defeat us!*"

Others took up the song, Cruithne and Eiran voices chanting along by ear. Quintilius Rousse chuckled and shook his head. "Never been anything like it, I tell you! This crossing will go down in history, I promise! And Elder Brother bids fair to keep his word." He shouted to Hyacinthe, standing alone in the prow. "What do you say now, Tsingano? Care to point our way to landfall?"

Wrapped in his travel-worn saffron cloak, Hyacinthe made no response.

Phèdre made her way to his side and I followed her. "What is it?" she asked him. "What do you see?"

"Nothing." He turned his gaze on us, blurred and blind with the *dromonde*. "That's just it. I don't. I can't see our landing."

"What does it mean?" I asked.

Hyacinthe cast his unseeing gaze across the wavelets. "It means that somewhere between here and the far shore lies a crossroads. And I cannot see beyond it."

A loud commotion arose off the port bow. Looking over the side, we saw a raft full of Tarbh Cró latecomers laughing and shouting and flailing. Without enough oars to go around, one of their warriors had put his time to use by dangling his arm in the water as though he were fishing for brook trout. He shouldn't have caught anything—and yet there it was, a large, apparently very curious saltwater eel. It must have been disturbed by our flotilla as it passed over. The warrior had managed to get the creature on the raft, wresting it with both hands, but it was as long as he was tall, thrashing and slime-sided, which didn't help the nausea rising from the pit of my belly. The other men on the raft were yelling and pounding at the eel with their oars.

I looked at the white cliffs of Alba rising behind us; a mile away or more.

More than three spear-casts.

At last the battered eel gave a final shudder and died, the slick, dark length of it gleaming against the worn wood of the raft.

And the seas *erupted*.

On our first crossing, there had been warning—signs of a storm, of the wrath of the Master of the Straits descending upon us. The wind-driven face of the waters had come toward us, had approached us.

Now it was simply here. It was beneath us, it was around us, a great maelstrom that boiled into being, vessels pitching down the sides of its steep, swirling slopes toward its maw. Our ship was nigh standing on its prow. I lost my footing in a wash of water and only caught myself by hooking a cleat with one hand. Figures slid past me. Men and horses were screaming, a terrible sound. Rousse was roaring orders. I looked frantically for Phèdre and saw her clinging to the railing like a tumbler's monkey.

I hauled myself upright as the face of the Master of the Straits arose from the sea, thrice as tall as the abandoned lighthouse atop the cliffs of Dobria, seaweed waving and fish swimming in the translucent water of his features. He let the maelstrom go and our fleet fell crashing onto the surface of the waters. The impact flung Phèdre halfway over the railing and I lunged for her, grabbing her wet, salt-stiff cloak and hauling her to the relative safety of the deck.

The Master of the Straits loomed above us, as high as the distant cliff tops. The face of the waters formed a mouth that opened and spoke with that thundering voice. "WHO HUNTS MY SEAS?"

Drustan mab Necthana stepped forward fearlessly to address him. "They are my men, Sea-Lord! I failed to warn them! I am to blame!"

The face bent forward, water streaming. "*YOU* LEAD . . . ALBAN?"

"Oh, bloody hell!" Quintilius Rousse abandoned the helm, shouting up at the Master of the Straits. "What buggery is this? You're breaking your word, you mad old bastard! 'Tis my ship and I command it. If you've come to take a toll, take it from me!"

I was clinging to the railing with one hand, my other arm wrapped firmly around Phèdre's waist, anchoring her in place. A few yards away, Hyacinthe was collecting himself, unsteady but unharmed. I felt Phèdre shiver inside the circle of my arm and tightened my grip. She pulled away reluctantly. "Let be."

Bowing my head, I released her.

She stepped away from the railing, lifting her face skyward. Her voice wasn't fearless like Drustan's or furious like Rousse's, but it was clear and sure. "My lord, *I* am the emissary of Ysandre de la Courcel, Queen of Terre d'Ange!"

The looming face of the waters turned her way, the dripping cavern of its mouth opening, lightning flickering in the sockets of its eyes. There would be no promise kept for a war waged and won, no passage for a song. "I WILL TAKE YOU ALLL!"

And then it sank, but did not vanish, for a wave rose beneath our ship—and only ours—in a great, glassy hump and lifted it, carrying it far away, far toward the south, into the wider part of the Straits, away from the white cliffs of Dobria and the dim promise of Terre d'Ange on the horizon. It was an endless wave that rolled across the seas as sure and directly as a hawk in flight, counter to currents and tides and winds, and none of us, not even the Royal Admiral himself, could do aught but watch the water rush past us. We had no idea where we were bound, nor if the Master of the Straits had left any survivors behind us. The thought of thousands of men, hundreds of horses, struggling and drowning amidst the debris of our makeshift flotilla was like a leaden weight in my gut.

Just as terror and uncertainty eroded into listless despair, an island appeared directly in the path of our unbreaking wave—a barren, stony isle with sheer grey cliffs. We were travelling so swiftly atop the wave it seemed we would be dashed upon the isle's shores in the space of a few heartbeats.

I was calculating how best to shield Phèdre from the worst of the impact when she let out a cry and pointed. "There!"

There was a narrow harbor, a long-ago fissure in the cliffs that had pried open a channel between the rocks. The wave slowed and carried us into the passageway. Deep in shadow, it opened into a small, still bay where the wave deposited us as gently as a mother laying her babe to sleep and withdrew. We stared at each other, then stared at our surroundings. Smooth terraced steps led to a ledge above the bay, then ascended the cliff before us in tiers that grew broader as they rose. Far above us at the top, marble columns of a temple were silhouetted against the sky.

Nearer, we weren't alone.

Two figures in long grey robes with hooded cowls awaited us on the ledge, so still and colorless they blended into the very rock.

Despite the unnerving nature of their presence, they were unarmed and didn't appear inclined to threaten us. The taller of the two stepped forward to address Quintilius Rousse, who was attempting to gauge the depth of the waters and the distance from shore. Pushing back his cowl, the figure revealed himself to be an ordinary-looking young man. "The waters are deep, sirrah," he said in archaic, formal-sounding D'Angeline. "Bring thy ship in close and thou mayest lower a plank."

"Do it!" Rousse said abruptly to a bewildered-looking Cruithne warrior. "Go on, to oars!" He turned to Phèdre. "Tell these wild blue lads to bend their backs, Queen's emissary, and let's see what game Elder Brother's playing at."

She obeyed, translating his orders into Cruithne and explaining for their benefit that we'd no more idea what passed than they did. Drustan added a word of agreement, though he was mostly silent, staring from the stern in the direction from which we'd come. Although there was nothing to see but the crack in the sheer cliffs, a slice of sky above and sea below, I knew he was thinking of everyone we'd left behind, everyone who had set forth to follow him across the Straits to fight in a war that wasn't theirs. Hyacinthe was quiet, too, in that same inward-turned way he'd been since Moiread was killed.

"What do you see?" Phèdre asked him when her translating duties were done. Drustan's men were using our long-shafted oars to maneuver the ship alongside the promontory.

Hyacinthe looked at her with the strangest smile. "I see an island. What do you see, Phèdre nó Delaunay?"

She frowned at him, perplexed. Quintilius Rousse ordered anchor dropped and the gangplank set in place.

The second robed figure drew back his cowl; he was an older man with hair gone white. "There are those among thee that the Master wishes to see," he announced, indicating us with a gnarled forefinger. "Thou, thou, thou . . . and thou."

Drustan, Rousse, Hyacinthe . . . and Phèdre.

I offered a bow with daggers crossed, the formal on-guard bow of the Brotherhood. "Where she goes, I go," I said politely. "I have sworn it in Cassiel's name."

"Violence will not avail thee," said the younger of the robed acolytes or priests or whatever they were. His voice was mild, but the sea behind us rippled like the skin of a cat readying itself to pounce at his words. "Thy companions are safe on the shores of First Sister. Whilst thou jeopardize their safety?"

The Master of the Straits had dealt unfairly with us and I was weighing my angry response when Drustan grabbed my arm. "My folk, my people. He says they have them safe, my brother. I beg you, do nothing to harm them."

I looked at Phèdre as she translated his words. "I've sworn it, Phèdre," I said in despair. "To damnation and beyond."

She kept her voice to a taut whisper, but there was an adamant fury in her eyes that I hadn't seen since she shamed me into choosing life in a filthy Skaldic woodshed. "Joscelin, I will kill you myself before I let anyone die for your vow. I swear it."

I believed her. By the fierceness of her tone, I wondered if mayhap she thought I cared more for my vow than for *her*. After the choice I'd made she ought to know better, but both of us had too much death on our consciences to be wholly reasonable.

Elua knows how I would have responded if the older acolyte hadn't raised one hand, forestalling the younger. "He is Companion-sworn," he said. "Let him come."

The younger inclined his head. "Gildas will take thee to the Master of the Straits. I will offer rest and succor to the others."

The five of us disembarked, steps echoing on the rough-hewn gangplank.

We began climbing after the white-haired acolyte Gildas. Drustan and Rousse went first, the former's pace ragged on the stairs—and there were a lot of stairs. I was a step behind Phèdre, who held her skirts raised so as not to trip on them, and climbed with grim determination. Hyacinthe followed us. Behind our party, the younger acolyte led the rest of our men and the horses boarded in our hold down a side path.

Our destination was the temple looking out over the sea. A massive base of white marble perched atop the cliff, the narrow stairs smooth and polished and nigh vertical. But heights have never troubled me overmuch, nor exertion, and I would sooner have made the climb three times over than spend that much time aboard a ship. By the labored breathing I heard, not everyone else felt the same way, although the old acolyte wasn't even winded. He was a mortal human man, though . . . or at least I thought so. We had seen the face of the waters that named itself the Master of the Straits, and it was *not* a mortal being. This man's flesh was ordinary flesh, creased with age. The hems of his robe and sleeves were dingy and thread-worn, his leather sandals were worn and salt-stained.

So what awaited us in the temple?

I spared a glance at Phèdre. Saving her breath, she shook her head. There was nothing in her research that lent insight into our dilemma. Whatever Anafiel and Alcuin had learned, it died with them. Who or what was the Master of the Straits? Mortal or immortal? God or demigod? An elemental spirit of the sea or a sorcerous force?

It felt as though we'd climbed so high the air was thin as it was in the mountains of Siovale. I wondered if I'd ever see home again—my father and mother, my brothers and sisters. I missed them, but only uncertainty lay before me. Whatever we were facing, it was the first time I'd be entering a perilous situation in which all my warrior's skills would be useless, because whatever in the world the Master of the Straits truly was, it wasn't anything that could be defeated by a sword any more than one could turn back the tide.

There was no gate from the sea cliff to the temple, just an opening in the low parapet that encircled the temple. One by one, we climbed through it. Phèdre allowed me to assist her up the last few steps, then doubled over at the top, gasping for breath.

It had been a very, very long climb.

The base of the temple's platform was a smooth marble disk some fifty paces in diameter, laid so finely not a single groove was visible. It was perfectly symmetrical. Four perfectly placed white columns stretched into the sky. In the very center of the temple stood a massive bronze vessel in the shape of a shallow bowl, set into a footed bronze tripod.

A lone figure stood motionless before it with a face as stark and white as bleached bones and eyes like the sea.

The Master of the Straits.

CHAPTER FIFTY

I had a wild urge to draw my sword.

I didn't do it, of course; it would have been a useless gesture. This place was fraught with the Master of the Straits' power, for not only did the seas rise at his command, but the winds and clouds and lightning answered to him.

"Come," Gildas said.

The Master of the Straits was a tall figure, an unearthly being in human form wrought from the sea's elements themselves. He was robed in grey like his acolytes, but it was the grey of granite under clear water; and then a cloud passed across the sun and his robes darkened as though a shark's shadow slid across the granite. Despite the breeze, neither the folds of his robes or his long iron-grey hair stirred.

Phèdre knelt. "My lord."

Drustan mab Necthana was angry, and fearless with it. Taking a halt-gaited step forward, he clenched his fists and met the Master of the Straits' gaze. "Lord of the Waters, you gave us your pledge. When the Cullach Gorrym ruled in Alba, you would grant us passage. Why are we here?"

The Master of the Straits' bone-white face smiled and the eyes I'd taken for sea-green shifted to a wraith-like misty hue. "You were warned, young Cruarch." His words echoed around the temple and it seemed as though he heard and spoke all languages of the world at once in a single voice. "You were warned, Alban."

"Lord of the Waters," Drustan said with an edge to his tone. "You gave your warning like a hunter laying bait. Why have you brought us here?"

"Why?" The Master of the Straits repeated the word and the waves far below curled their foamy caps in question. "Why." Turning away from us, he clasped his hands behind his back and gazed at the sea. When he looked back, his changeable eyes were as dark and turbulent as thunder clouds. "Eight hundred years I have ruled, chained to this rock, claimed by neither earth nor sky." Raising his voice, he summoned eddies of wind that lashed around us like bullwhips, the sea churning below. "Eight hundred years! And you ask me *why*?"

I took a knee beside Phèdre, bracing her against the wind. She squinted through the roar, trying to follow their exchange.

"*Why?*" Drustan shouted the word. He'd laid his life and the lives of his people on the line, and he wasn't about to back down. "Lord of the Waters, you hold my people hostage? *Why?*"

The winds died as unexpectedly as they'd risen. The Master of the Straits pointed with one pale forefinger at the gold House Courcel signet ring Drustan wore. "You have the courage to live the dream that will free me, Alban," he said. "Your mother saw it in the dark behind her eyes. The swan and the boar. Alban and D'Angeline, love defiant. But it is only half."

Half of what, exactly?

Phèdre squeezed my hand and I helped her rise. She took a slow, careful breath before addressing the Master of the Straits. "My lord, this I understand to be true. You are bound here, to this isle, against your will. You wish to break this binding. Two things are needful. One is the union of Alban and D'Angeline present in the betrothal of Drustan and Ysandre. What is the other?" I stared at her, trying to figure out how in the world she'd threaded through the wild cacophony of wind and wave, fear and fury to reach such a very specific and concise conclusion.

"Ah." The Master of the Straits approached. I tensed and felt Phèdre shudder as he lifted one alabaster hand to caress her face. "One who listens, hears, and thinks. That is well. You have named the riddle. Answer it in full and you may leave."

I gritted my teeth, despising him. The Master of the Straits might command sea and storm, but he was nothing more to me than another man laying his hands on Phèdre nó Delaunay's flesh without her consent. And I was so far beneath his notice, I might as well be a piece of furniture. I wondered if seawater would spout from the stump of his neck if I cut his head off. I imagined it might, just before the seas rose up to crush us all and the face of the waters towered high enough to blot out the sun.

I held my tongue and temper.

The Master of the Straits swept his arm across the shallow bronze cauldron. Its waters rippled to reflect not sky, but the image of Ysandre de la

Courcel. She sat on a makeshift throne listening intently, and there were the accoutrements of a war camp in her surroundings. Her youth and weary mien made my heart sore for her. It seemed the burden of war we'd feared had settled on her slender shoulders. Drustan let out a sharp cry of longing, and Quintilius Rousse pressed his fist to his brow in an unthinking pledge of loyalty.

"Answer the riddle in full and you shall have my aid in full." The Master of the Straits' eyes paled like wintry moons. "Fail and the sea shall claim you." He pointed at the sun setting red in the west. "I give you tonight. When the sun stands overhead in the sky tomorrow, you will answer or die."

Thus was the promise of a safe crossing, one for which so much blood had already been spilled, dangled farther out of reach.

Although one couldn't see it from the bay where our ship was anchored, there was a stone tower on a summit beyond the temple. Gildas led us down another series of broad marble steps and along a paved pathway. The setting sun's rays gilded the grey stone and set alight a series of oriel windows on the uppermost story set with colored glass that glowed like gemstones. It was an unexpectedly lovely and lonely sight. Inside the reception hall was a homelier and more welcoming sight—a polite household staff, ordinary isle folk clad in unassuming linen attire.

"Thy shipmates are well tended, thy horses stabled," Gildas said to us. "No harm will come to thee in this place. By thy leave, we offer the Master's hospitality—warm baths, dry clothes, wine and supper."

"And the rest of my folk?" Drustan demanded. "Phèdre, ask this priest if he stands surety for their safety."

Gildas bowed in response to her translated question. "The isle of First Sister lies some three leagues thence," he said, nodding toward the south. "She is rich in kine and fowl and cider, and thy folk have been brought safe to her shore. Do thou no harm here and they shall be well. On my head, I swear it."

It wasn't as though we had a choice in the matter, but I'd be more reassured if I knew how much the man valued his head.

"Will the Master of the Straits dine with us?" Phèdre asked him.

He shook his head. "Nay, my lady. Thou wilt share thine own company."

"You serve him," she observed in that deceptively mild manner that meant she was hot on the trail of somewhat. "Are you his priest?"

Gildas hesitated before replying. "'Tis true that we fill the bronze mirror with seawater, Tilian and I; once at sunrise, once at sundown. And betimes we may speak as his voice when it is needful. Thus are we privileged to serve. But those of us who are born to the Three Sisters cannot break the *geis*."

Phèdre eyed him. "So the binding upon him can't be broken by one born to the isles?"

Another pause. "As thou sayest. Wilt thou and thy company honor us by accepting our hospitality?"

"Yes." Unexpectedly, she smiled. "Thank you."

A winding stairway encircled the tower's interior. Members of the household staff led us to chambers where we might bathe and don clean attire. Phèdre was given her own suite and servants to attend her. Drustan and Hyacinthe would share another, while I shared one with Admiral Rousse. I wasn't keen on the notion of leaving Phèdre unguarded in these strange circumstances, but she was comfortable in the assurance that so long as we played his game, the Master of the Straits intended no harm beyond that he'd already wreaked upon us.

It felt like we had stepped into the past. The tower's chambers were appointed with ornate furniture. There was a marble bathing tub with clawed feet, there were four-posted beds in the sleeping chambers draped with dusty velvet canopies. The linens on the beds were clean and smelled of soap and sunlight, but the array of men's finery in the clothing chests retained a faint, musty odor.

"Drowned men's clothes," Rousse said, tossing me an austere doublet of black velvet. "Here."

I set the doublet aside. "Does that trouble you?"

The Admiral squinted at a brocade vest. "Not overly much. It's this damned business of a riddle that troubles me. That, and the fact that we're prisoners with our entire army held hostage. Any thoughts?"

"Plenty," I said. "None useful."

"Our girl's got somewhat brewing in that pretty head of hers." He paused, raising thick auburn brows. "Blessed Elua, you don't suppose she's thinking she can bed-hop her way out of this, do you?"

I began to laugh, then stopped, remembering how she'd shuddered when the Master of the Straits had touched her. "No. Not this time."

After we'd bathed and donned sea-salvaged finery, a footman escorted us to a dining hall where a long table polished until it gleamed by candlelight was laid with silver platters and goblets. All the men had preceded Phèdre's arrival, and we rose at her entrance. She wore a shimmering gown of bronze satin worked with seed pearls, and her hair had been brushed until it gleamed, and braided into an elaborate pearl-adorned coiffure. It had been a long time since I'd seen Phèdre in the attire of a courtesan worthy of Kings and Queens. In many ways, I found her beauty at its most transcendent when it was unadorned, but there was no denying the impact of art and artifice combined to enhance it.

"My lady Phèdre." Quintilius Rousse bowed deep and extended his arm for her to take, Royal Admiral to Queen's ambassadress.

"My lord Rousse." She gave him a sparkling look; by his blush, he hadn't been on the receiving end of one before. "You all look so very fine."

It was a strange meal, to be sure. We were served a generous repast by servants with downcast gazes. Based on what Phèdre had gleaned from the servants who attended her, they took pride in their work and in serving the Master of the Straits. Whatever binding lay over the isles known as the Three Sisters, it bound them, too. Few had ever ventured past the isles and none had returned. They were insular and unaccustomed to strangers. Their manner of speech sounded archaic to the modern ear simply because without outside influence, it hadn't changed over many generations.

Altogether, it made for uneasy hospitality and I was grateful when the servants left us with a decanter of cordial and five glasses.

"So." Admiral Rousse poured out a glass for each of us, quaffing his in a single gulp. "We've a riddle to solve. Shall we pool our wits and put to it, then?"

No one spoke. I remained silent because I had nothing to contribute. We had among us a master sailor, a seer, a spy, the Cruarch of Alba . . . as a warrior, I would give my life for any one of my companions, but I had no insight into mysterious curses, and I could not speak for the others. All I could do was sit amidst a rising tide of unease, the fine hairs at the nape of my neck prickling like hackles.

Phèdre rose, glass in hand, and drifted to one of the windows. She gazed out at the night, then closed her eyes and leant her brow against the glass.

"You know." Soft words, spoken in Cruithne. It was Drustan who had spoken. Not leaving the window, Phèdre nodded. "And there is a price."

"There is always a price, my lord Cruarch." She splayed her fingers against the glass. "This one happens to be worth it."

Drustan rose and waited for her to turn and face him, bowing as she did so. "I will see you on the morrow. Know that I will pay it if I can."

"What did he say?" Quintilius Rousse sounded as bewildered as I felt. "By the ten thousand devils . . . I thought we were here to resolve a mystery!"

"Ask Phèdre." It was the first Hyacinthe had spoken since we'd set foot on the isle. He lifted his gaze from his cordial glass and it was shadow-haunted. He ran his hands blindly over his face. "She thinks she *has* solved it. Ask her, and see if she'll speak."

She responded unasked, her voice soft and gentle. "If this riddle is mine to answer in full, I will. Don't begrudge me that, Hyacinthe."

Hyacinthe laughed and it was a harsh sound, jagged and full of pain. "Would that Delaunay left you where he found you!" He stood unsteadily, as though he'd overindulged in drink. "I rue the day he taught you to think." She winced, but said nothing; he offered a mocking flourish of a bow and followed in Drustan's wake.

Quintilius Rousse scowled after him. "I dislike this. If you've found an answer, share it, lass! Let us put our heads together."

"My lord Admiral," she said. "Forgive me, but no. If Anafiel Delaunay found this answer, he would not share it. Nor will I. If you come to it on your own, so be it."

I rose and went to stand beside Phèdre at the window, clasping my hands behind my back. Rousse muttered darkly about Delaunay's folly, then bade us a curt goodnight and stomped away. Beside me, I could feel a measure of tension drain from her. "I'm not going to like this, am I?"

"No," Phèdre murmured. Side by side, we gazed out at the night. There were just enough stars in the sky that the sea was visible as a moving expanse of blackness, only the occasional glint separating water from air. "Joscelin." She laid one hand on my upper arm. "I've been a trial to you since the day you were assigned to ward me. I've strained your vows in so many ways your own Brotherhood declared you anathema. I swear to you, I'll only do it once more." Her throat worked as she swallowed hard, gazing at me. "If we . . . if we must part, you must abide it. You were trained to serve royalty, Joscelin, not the ill-conceived offspring of Night Court adepts. You swore your sword to Ysandre's service. If you would serve her, protect Drustan. Promise me as much."

I looked away.

I wanted to grab Phèdre by the shoulders and shake whatever secret she was keeping out of her. I wanted to kiss her until we were both too dizzy to stand. I wanted to wrap my arms around her and hold her safe while the world fell to pieces around us. But one thing I couldn't do was promise to abandon her.

"I can't," I said.

Her fingers dug hard into my arm. "Promise me!"

I raised my voice. "I do Cassiel's will! Beyond it I cannot swear."

Phèdre sighed and released me, accepting my answer reluctantly. "Even Cassiel bent his will to Blessed Elua. Remember it."

I eyed her. "Remember you are not Elua."

CHAPTER FIFTY-ONE

The sun was climbing toward its apex when the robed acolytes came to escort us to the temple. All five of us had gone our separate ways that morning, Drustan and Rousse to check on the well-being of those men and horses aboard our vessel and convey what little information we possessed to them. Phèdre had discovered the tower's true treasure, a library filled with tomes including some believed lost to the ages. I'd gladly have passed the time there with her, but I'd a strong sense she wanted to be left alone.

As for Hyacinthe, he'd simply made himself scarce. So I found a lonely plateau where I could tell the hours in peace, on dry land, with no curious onlookers. When I'd finished, I felt centered within myself and as braced as I could be for what was to come.

Wherever we had spent the morning, the acolytes found us all and brought us together under the open-skied temple where the Master of the Straits awaited us. There was no ceremony. There was only the riddle.

"Have you an answer?" he asked in a voice that rolled like waves all around the temple.

There was a long, taut silence.

"Yes, my lord." Phèdre's voice sounded very small breaking it, breaking my heart along with it. "One of us must take your place."

The Master of the Straits bent his fearsome gaze upon her. "Are you prepared to answer in full?"

"Yes," she whispered. "Yes, my lord."

I caught my breath in a sharp hiss. Phèdre *had* found the key to his riddle. She meant to take on his curse and be bound to this fate. My palms itched pointlessly for my hilts. No. But there was a way, another way. I could take her place, I could make this sacrifice.

I could—

"*No.*" Hyacinthe sounded so unlike himself, for a moment, I wasn't sure it was he who'd spoken the word on the tip of my own tongue. He gave a short, despairing laugh, raking a hand through his black ringlets, all his mirth and merriment gone. "You summoned me, my lord," he said to the Master of the Straits. "I am here. I will stay."

"No!" Phèdre reached for him, cupping his face. "Hyacinthe, no!"

He caught her wrists and removed her hands. "Breidaia dreamed me on an island, Phèdre; do you remember? I couldn't see the shore. The Long Road ends here for me. You may have unraveled the riddle, but I'm meant to stay."

"No." She whirled on the Master of the Straits. "You seek one to take your place; you posed this riddle, and I have answered it. It's mine to answer in full!"

"It is not the only riddle on these shores." There were shadows moving in the depths of his changeable eyes and old, old sorrow in the depth of his voice. "There is this. Who takes my shackles inherits my power. Name its source if you would be worthy to serve."

I swore.

Dealt this one last and unexpected riddle, Phèdre lifted her face and stared at the sun until I was afraid she would lose her sight, then lowered it, blinking. "It is the Book of Raziel, my lord."

And I swore again with a sinking sense in my gut, because I *knew* Phèdre was guessing based on a combination of research and instinct—and it was a good guess, probably the right guess, a guess I might have made myself if I'd remained a scholarly minded Siovalese nobleman's son and not a thrice-damned disgraced and love-addled Cassiline Brother. Adonai and Blessed Elua have mercy, I could even see myself in now-bitter memory, gazing at Anafiel Delaunay's archives and saying, *He's got everything here but the Lost Book of Raziel.*

The Master of the Straits inclined his head in acknowledgment and began turning toward Phèdre.

"Only pages." Hyacinthe's voice was raspy and hollow. "Pages from the Lost Book of Raziel that the One God gave to Edom the First Man to grant him dominance over earth and sea and sky. When Edom disobeyed him, the One God took away the book and cast it into the depths."

The Master of the Straits paused, considering him. "Continue."

I could see the *dromonde* in Hyacinthe's dark eyes now, it was spilling out of him, only he was not looking forward but backward, hurtling from a distant past through centuries of vision. "The pages were a gift from your father, yes? The Admiral calls him the Lord of the Deep and tosses him gold coins. But the Yeshuites name him Prince of the Sea; the angel Rahab, they call him, Pride, and Insolence. He fell from grace but not to become a Companion." He shook his head. "He begot you, my lord, on a D'Angeline girl who loved another, who loved an Alban. A mortal, a son of the Cullach Gorrym. Is it not so?"

"It is."

"The Straits were still open then," Hyacinthe said, seeing what none of us could. "Your father took her here, to this isle yet untouched by the scions of Elua. She bore you here . . . and although she loved you, she sang in her sorrow and captivity like a bird in a cage until her song carried across the waters, and the Alban who loved her sailed the Straits to free her . . ." He fell silent.

"They died." The Master of the Straits gazed at the sea. "The waters rose, their boat overturned, and the deep water took them. I know where their bones lie."

"The One God punished Rahab for his disobedience and banished him to the depths," Hyacinthe murmured. "And for the heart of a woman he could not sway and his own lost freedom, Rahab took revenge and laid a *geis* upon you, my lord. He brought up scattered pages from the deep to give you mastery over the seas and he bound you here, that Alba and Terre d'Ange would ever be separated by the waters you ruled—until love daring enough to cross the breach was born once more, and one came willing to take your place."

The Master of the Straits placed the palms of his bone-white hands together and bowed his head. "It is so."

I wanted to weep.

Hyacinthe, Prince of Travellers; merry, high-spirited, and shrewd, loyal to the marrow. He was the last person deserving of such a fate, bound to this lonely isle for the rest of his days.

Shaking off the thrall of the *dromonde,* Hyacinthe laughed; a wild laugh with a hectic gaiety to it. "Well then, my lord, will I serve?"

"You will serve." The hue of the Master of the Straits' eyes shifted to a deep, sympathetic blue. "A long and lonely apprenticeship, until you are ready to take on the chains of my *geis*, freeing me to leave this earth and follow Elua's path to where Heaven's bastard sons are welcome."

It had happened so fast, it seemed the sun had scarce moved from its apex. In that time one man's life had changed forever, and our quest bade fair to resume. Phèdre was pale with shock, eyes wide in disbelief as she took in the fact that Hyacinthe had well and truly taken upon himself the sacrifice she'd been planning to make the instant she'd figured out the riddle.

Only she hadn't counted on the *dromonde*, nor the riddle having such very deep roots.

"You've used us harshly, Elder Brother." Quintilius Rousse's tone was dark. "What's to become of the lad?"

"I've used you less harshly than fate has used me," the Master of the Straits said implacably. "The sea has loved you, friend sailor; count it a blessing. A full half your folk would have died in this crossing had I not intervened. My successor will be bound to this isle as I was. That curse will not be broken until the One God repents of my father's punishment, and His memory is long."

"What of the Straits?" Drustan demanded in Cruithne. "Will the crossing remain forbidden?"

The Master of the Straits pointed at his gold signet ring. "You hold the key. Wed, and open the lock."

"Naught but twenty thousand howling Skaldi and the traitors of Camlach stand in the way," Rouse observed with bitter irony. "While we languish on a forsaken rock in the middle of the sea with no army in sight."

The Master of the Straits was impervious to the sting of sarcasm. "I promised my aid and you shall have it." As he'd done yesterday, he swept his arm over the great bronze bowl, the surface of its waters rippling. "Here in my sea-mirror, I will show you all that has passed in Terre d'Ange in your absence. I will bring your men, horses, and arms safe to land. No more can I do. Will you see?"

Drustan began to reply, but Phèdre cut him off. "No," she said unsteadily. "My lord, if it please you . . . I would ask a little time, mayhap an hour. Might we have that long?"

"I will send for you an hour before sundown." He bowed, then addressed Hyacinthe. "This day I give you. Only know that your feet will never again leave this soil."

It was done.

The five of us reassembled in a sitting room with unshuttered bay windows open to sea and wind, where tower servants brought us wine and bread and cheese. My emotions were in a welter, as I daresay were everyone's. I'd had a flash of impatience when Phèdre asked for more time, but now I was glad for the space to let my thoughts unfold. There was a part of me that was deeply, profoundly relieved that the Master of the Straits' fate hadn't fallen upon Phèdre. At the same time, I mourned the fact that it had fallen to Hyacinthe. But even if I'd figured out the riddle myself, nothing could compete with the depth of the backward-looking *dromonde*.

Hyacinthe and Phèdre withdrew to one of the bay window seats where they sat with fingers intertwined, speaking in low, intent tones.

It is an awkward thing to involuntarily eavesdrop on others' private thoughts and feelings, so the three of us—Drustan, Rousse, and I—spent the afternoon speculating about what the Master of the Straits' sea-mirror might reveal to us. Rousse used bits of cutlery and crockery to outline a crude map of Terre d'Ange and the possible strategies that may have been employed if the Skaldi had already begun their incursion. It was a pointless exercise in some ways, but it occupied our minds.

When it came time to return to the temple, Hyacinthe declined to accompany us. He offered no reason and no one pressed him; I daresay Phèdre knew.

Now the sun stood handspans above the horizon, casting the long, gilded glow of a summer evening over the temple. The Master of the Straits beckoned us to gaze into the bronze bowl in the very center, passing his hand and sweeping sleeve above the still waters. "Behold," he said. "War."

The surface of the water stirred, images forming upon it—not simple images such as the lingering image of Queen Ysandre's weary face, but a vast, moving tapestry of images that came in a patchwork flurry.

Skaldi.

Tens of thousands of Skaldi, pouring through the Northern Pass to ride along the Rhenus River, ambushing D'Angeline ships with volleys of spears and whirling in retreat. Skaldi seizing the lower two of the Great Passes, gaining and holding ground on D'Angeline soil. In the inner mountains of the province, Isidore d'Aiglemort held the Allies of Camlach, five thousand men strong, in reserve. None of us had known the details of d'Aiglemort's plan, but it grew more obvious as events unfurled. The Skaldi in the north regrouped and now there he was, there was Waldemar Selig leading them, a larger-than-life warrior on a great-necked charger, his thanes flying white wolf pelts lashed to poles as his standard.

For a few moments, it appeared as though the Queen's Council's attempt to convey our warning had fallen on deaf ears—but no, the official

D'Angeline Royal Army and allies had been marching to defend the lower passes. Now they turned back westward to Namarre to intercept the Skaldic army, and we saw Percy de Somerville's apple tree banner flying beneath the Courcel swan.

Did Isidore d'Aiglemort know himself betrayed by Waldemar Selig at that moment? There were already too many Skaldi amassing. Nonetheless, d'Aiglemort gathered his own private army. We watched him raise his arm and utter a command.

Obedient to his command, the Allies of Camlach began their charge, then halted in confusion, milling about and turning. There was a rebellion in the back where crude banners with the insignia of House Trevalion, three ships and the Navigator's Star, had been lofted on spear hafts. Chanting a single word, the furthest ranks of the rearguard fell on their own comrades from behind.

"Baudoin," Phèdre murmured without raising her gaze from the surface of the waters. "Those are his Glory-Seekers."

It had been a part of the Queen's Council's plan to send Prince Baudoin de Trevalion's former cadre to feign loyalty to Duc Isidore. I was surprised he fell for the ruse since members of the Glory-Seekers had been loyal to Baudoin, and I said as much aloud.

"'Tis vanity." Quintilius Rousse watched d'Aiglemort wheel his mount, his sword red with blood as he charged through the ranks of his own men toward the treacherous rearguard. "He believes he's destined for greatness and the throne. He *wants* to believe that Baudoin's men were eager to offer him their loyalty because he's the most brilliant, fearless leader they've ever seen in their lives."

Selwyn had thought so.

Selwyn had died at the hands of Camaeline warriors attempting to overthrow d'Aiglemort and thwart his ambitions. It was a thought my mind shied away from—if Selwyn had lived, we would be on opposite sides in this battle.

Although it was enough to shatter d'Aiglemort's charge, the Glory-Seekers paid a heavy price. Most were slain in the melee. A handful escaped to beat a swift retreat through the mountains, and a few were captured alive. We watched one of the captured men kneeling before the Duc laugh and spit on his boots. A terrible look dawned on d'Aiglemort's face. He hadn't yet realized that Waldemar Selig had betrayed him and meant to conquer the realm. He knew it now. He had opened the paddock gate and now the wolf was at our door.

Isidore d'Aiglemort killed the messenger with a single stroke of his sword.

Too late.

The sea-mirror followed the fleeing survivors down a winding trail through the mountains . . . straight into the path of a party of Skaldi warriors scouting the terrain. Phèdre looked away.

"Watch," the Master of the Straits said to all of us.

We watched.

The last of Prince Baudoin de Trevalion's Glory-Seekers were slaughtered by the Skaldi, putting an end to that chapter of D'Angeline intrigue. Our view expanded; we watched the battle unfold as though we were birds on the wing, soaring high above the steel clamor, blood, and filth of war. Queen Ysandre had assembled a strong array of forces. There were dozens of banners from almost every province aloft in our battalion. I looked in vain for House Verreuil's banner, but there were too many to discern if it was among them. A company of a thousand spearmen flew the gold lion of the royal House of Aragon. There was Barquiel L'Envers leading a small company of Akkadian-trained archers on horseback, harrying the Skaldi right flank.

It wasn't enough. There were simply too many Skaldi and they were coming from too many directions. When Waldemar Selig, roaring soundlessly, led an attack from the left, the D'Angeline army was routed and forced to retreat.

I couldn't count the slain. It was a great many, even though the retreat was an orderly one thanks to de Somerville's command of strategy. A line of L'Agnacite archers with longbows knelt and delivered a steady hail of arrows, spending the currency of their lives to safeguard the army's withdrawal. We followed the retreating army across Camlach to the foothills of northern Namarre to a walled fortress where stocks and supplies to last throughout a long siege awaited them—as did the Queen.

Ysandre's face, weary with the weight of grief, was the last image we saw before the waters went still. A map of Terre d'Ange rose to replace the shifting images, motionless and detailed with every river, every mountain, every city.

"Do you understand?" The Master of the Straits' pointing finger hovered over the map. "Here is Troyes-le-Mont where the D'Angeline army is besieged and surrounded by the Skaldi. Other Skaldi forces are arrayed along the Rhenus River and harry the northern border of Azzalle." His finger moved. "Fighting is at a standstill in the lower passes. The allied city-states of Caerdicca Unitas sent a force to hold the southern border."

It was a weak response. If Waldemar Selig's army made it to Eisande, most of Terre d'Ange would already have fallen.

"My lord, can you tell me where my fleet lies?" Admiral Rousse asked in what passed for a polite tone.

"They fly the swan." The bone-white finger moved along the course of the Rhenus. "Here. They hold the northern border with the Azzallese."

"So the Duc de Morhban let them go." Phèdre pored over the sea-mirror. "But I didn't see his banner on the battlefield." She looked up. "Where are Isidore d'Aiglemort and his army now, my lord?"

"The silver-haired hawk of the north. Here, today." The Master of the Straits touched one fingertip to an area that bordered Camlach and northern Namarre. Gentle circles rippled outward. "Tomorrow, near. He has trapped himself in his folly."

"Good." Phèdre's tone was bitter; we had only just begun to reckon the cost of d'Aiglemort's vainglorious treachery. "Where is Melisande Shahrizai?"

The Master of the Straits hesitated, the slanting rays of the setting sun filling his eyes with flames. He shook his head. "Great events, I see reflected; small, I cannot see unless the face is known to me."

"History hinges on small events," Quintilius Rousse said darkly. Blessed Elua knew that was true; there had been so very many small turning points that had brought all of us together in this eerie place.

Ignoring everyone, Drustan tapped the surface of the water himself, right atop the fortress of Troyes-le-Mont. "There. There is where we will go."

The Master of the Straits inclined his head. "Cruarch of Alba, you spoke truly when you said I did not play you fair. I will set your fleet where you will, wherever the sea touches shore. No more can I do. I have no mastery over land."

"My lord Admiral?" Phèdre inquired.

Rousse squinted in thought. "To the mouth of the Rhenus, Elder Brother, and as far up her shores as your wind may drive us." He scratched the old cable of scar that slashed across his cheek and brow. "We'll rendezvous with my fleet and Ghislain de Somerville's forces and secure the northern border. Once we've combined forces, we'll lay plans to break the siege in Troyes-le-Mont."

All this while, the sun had been sinking below the horizon, going swifter and swifter past the halfway mark. Now only a red-gold sliver glowed in the distance while darkness settled from above. The Master of the Straits' shadow stretched over all of us, his face white as the rising moon, iron-grey hair and robes as still as stone. "Tomorrow at dawn the seas will carry you where you wish. Be ready."

Beside me, Phèdre repressed a shiver and curtsied. "Thank you, my lord. We will be."

All save one.

In the tower, Hyacinthe was waiting for us. We gathered in the library, where Phèdre called for a pen and paper and immediately began sketching a detailed map of Terre d'Ange that included all the strategic locations, placement, and movements of troops we'd witnessed. It was the very exercise Admiral Rousse had undertaken as a distraction earlier in the day, only now we actually *knew* where matters stood; and Phèdre's map was a considerable improvement over a tabletop strewn with cutlery and salt cellars.

Hyacinthe listened with shadowed eyes as we spoke of the visions the sea-mirror had shown us, and I could tell it pained him. I'd have guessed he would spend his last evening making the most of our companionship, but after a working repast of cheeses and cured meats that the servants brought to the library, he promised to see us off in the morning and took his leave.

I looked at Phèdre.

She was gazing after Hyacinthe, brow furrowed. I remembered the two of them bright-eyed and laughing at the Cockerel, teasing and exchanging kisses. The streetwise Prince of Travellers and a rising star in Naamah's service, a little bit in love with each other, a great deal in love with life.

It seemed like a very, very long time ago.

I felt Phèdre's glance fall upon me, uncertain and questioning. It was our old wordless communication, the deep-rooted bond forged of necessity. I knew she would go to him tonight. I could still read her expression like the weather when she let me. Betimes I wondered what she read in mine. Now I only smiled wryly and opened my hands.

"My lord Admiral," she said to Quintilius Rousse. "You do not need me, I think, to plan a war."

"You trace a fine line . . ." he began, then saw Phèdre's expression. "No, my lady. We don't need you tonight."

After her departure, we worked in relative silence for a time. Rousse had found a folio of illustrations of Tiberian siege weapons and was explaining their various uses to Drustan and speculating about their employment. I listened with half an ear and added input when I was able. Cassilines study the history and stratagems of war, but our angle of interest is different. We do not seek to win wars, but to protect our wards. And at least I would be spared that concern, for while Phèdre nó Delaunay had proved to be much more than a plaything for the wealthy, she would most assuredly not be taking to the battlefield. When I considered our plan, I was looking for points of danger along the way.

If Phèdre were sensible, she'd resign her role as the Queen's emissary to Admiral Rousse and allow me to escort her as far as possible from the warfront. And mayhap there would have been the slightest possible chance of that happening if we hadn't seen Ysandre in the Master of the Straits' mirror. They were of an age, the two of them; pampered young women raised in invisible cages of debt-servitude and royal duty, thrust by the vagaries of fate into shouldering weighty burdens. Phèdre had brought this terrible responsibility home to Ysandre, who had in turn entrusted her with an impossible undertaking. And Ysandre . . . name of Elua, she wasn't a soldier, she could have dispatched the army under Percy de Somerville's command and awaited his reports, but she had chosen to take a stand with her loyal folk in the besieged fortress.

Of course, Phèdre meant to see this through or die trying. It was my job to ensure it wasn't the latter.

"Does it ever bother you?" Quintilius Rousse asked, tilting his head in the direction Phèdre and Hyacinthe had gone.

"Why would it?" I said. "They've been fond of one another since I was a boy in Verreuil playing hide-and-hunt with my brothers and sisters. And I'm a Cassiline."

Rousse looked dubious. "Hmm."

I had a good deal of respect for Admiral Rousse, but it wasn't a conversation I wanted to have with him, or anyone. Excusing myself, I traversed the winding stair and retired to my bedchamber in the suite I shared with Rousse. Sitting cross-legged beneath the dusty velvet canopy of my opulent bed, dressed in a drowned man's clothes, I whetted and polished my blades, letting my hands do the work while my mind grew still, soothed by the familiar rhythm and the scent of steel.

It was a pity I couldn't smooth the jagged edges of my heart.

CHAPTER FIFTY-TWO

Our ship bobbed in the narrow harbor at the bottom of the marble steps that descended the cliff face. The dawn light came from behind us and the bay was in shadow, the sea glistening darkly.

I didn't relish the idea of getting back on a ship.

I didn't relish the idea of saying farewell, either. Every time I looked at Hyacinthe's somber face, I felt a twisting pang in my guts. But in that steep harbor, the acolytes Gildas and Tilian were overseeing the loading of our crew and supplies, taking extra care with the half-spooked horses.

It was time.

"My lord Cruarch," Hyacinthe said to Drustan. "I will be watching." He gripped Drustan's arms. "Blessed Elua keep you safe."

The Cruarch of Alba nodded. "The Cullach Gorrym will sing of your sacrifice."

Not standing on formality, Quintilius Rousse enfolded Hyacinthe in a heartfelt, rib-crushing embrace. "Ah, lad! You guided us through the mists to a safe landing. I'll not forget it, and I'll curse the name of the Master of the Straits no longer, Younger Brother. If there's aught you've need sail for, send the wind to whisper in my ear."

"Bring them safe to shore," Hyacinthe said. "I ask no more than that, my lord Admiral."

And then there were only the three of us, Phèdre, Hyacinthe, and me, who had been sent forth on this impossible quest across land and sea. "Tsingano." I reached out to clasp his wrists. "I have no words."

Hyacinthe smiled; a wry smile, but a true one. "Funny. There's plenty I could say to you, Cassiline. You've come a long way since I first saw you, looking like you'd swallowed vinegar. Now you've even made the beginnings of a fair Mendacant."

"I owe that to you," I said. "And a lesson in courage, too." I tightened my grip on his wrists, feeling the human warmth of his flesh, mortal and vulnerable, and remembered hearing the traditional Tsingani farewell. "I will speak your name and remember it."

"And yours." Hyacinthe pulled me close, black curls tumbling in the sea breeze, and murmured in my ear. "If you let any harm come to Phèdre, I swear to Blessed Elua and all his Companions, I will raise the very seas to crush you." Now it was he who returned my hard squeeze. "Do you understand?"

I gave him a look. "What do you think?"

"Well, I wasn't sure," he said. "Since you're too dense to figure out that she's in love with you."

I jerked away from him. "*What?*"

"Go." Hyacinthe pointed. "Leave, Joscelin Verreuil. You've got a job to do and a life to live. Go."

I went, stumbling slightly on the smooth marble stairs, his parting words echoing in my ears. Phèdre in love with me? No, I didn't think so. I didn't doubt that she loved me, but *in love* was another matter, *in love* was scrabbling in chains on the filthy floor of a Skaldic woodshed with my heart bursting into shards. Was there a powerful bond between us? Yes, of course. We owed our lives to each other. I was Cassiel's Servant and she was my ward, now and until I died. That was the bond that Hyacinthe sensed without fully understanding it. How could he? Phèdre and I didn't fully understand it ourselves.

Anyway, we had a war to win.

On the first landing, I paused to wait for Phèdre, descending from saying her final farewell to Hyacinthe. She was crying silently, half-blind with tears. "I'm here," I murmured. "In case you slip."

She nodded with gratitude. At the bottom of the stairs, the gangplank was in place. On the far end, Drustan stood waiting to assist Phèdre into the vessel itself. I followed, and no sooner had my boots hit the deck than our makeshift crew was stowing the gangplank and Quintilius Rousse was shouting for the anchor to be raised and the sails to be hoisted. A wind sprang up behind us like a gentle but firm hand pushing us out of the narrow bay, past the sheer grey walls, into open water.

There was a reckless wildness in me, somewhat that had been clamoring in protest since I first laid eyes on the Master of the Straits. This time I heeded it, scrambling up the rigging of our single mast. The ship surged into open water and heeled hard right, sails bellying. The mast to which I clung swayed and tilted perilously, but I could see the small figure of Hyacinthe on the clifftop temple receding in the distance. Clinging to the mast with one arm as it came back to vertical, I drew my sword and raised it in salute, the blade shining in the rising dawn. Atop the cliff, Hyacinthe returned my salute, one hand outstretched in a gesture of farewell as the sea widened between us.

The Cruithne were pointing and shouting at me, and Quintilius Rousse bellowed at me to get the hell out of his lines. I sheathed my sword and clambered down the rigging with alacrity. I was as adept at sea as the next man, until the seasickness caught up with me. Dropping to the deck, I found Phèdre still in tears, and laughing through them. "Are you all right?"

"Yes." Gasping with laughter, she dashed at her eyes. "No. Ah, Elua, Joscelin! What did he say to you there at the end?"

Leaning on the railing, I gave her a sidelong look. There was no way I was telling her the whole of it. "He told me not to tell you. He said not knowing would drive you mad."

"He did not!" she retorted indignantly. "Did he?"

"No," I admitted. "He said if I let harm come to you, he'll raise the very seas to fall upon and crush me."

She smiled despite her lingering tears. "That sounds like Hyacinthe."

There was no great surging wave this time, just a strong, swift wind that carried us due north. We hewed near enough to the D'Angeline coastline to search for our missing fleet. The Master of the Straits had promised to deliver them safe to our chosen landing spot at the mouth of the Rhenus, but he had twisted one promise out of true already and the Admiral was loath to trust him. But no; the Straits narrowed and we sailed past the white cliffs of Dobria, leagues away on Alba's distant shores, heading for the northern tip of Azzalle.

The Rhenus is one of the largest, and it crosses the whole of Terre d'Ange, bordering the peaceable Flatlands to the north, to spill into the Straits where a broad wake of rich brown river water trails behind it like the train of a woman's gown. When we rounded the tip, we found a wide harbor and our motley fleet beached there.

After that, it was all waving and shouting, all the Alban forces and Rousse's stalwart sailors lining the shore to welcome us in exultation. Drustan stood in the bow, his gold torque and crimson cloak announcing him the Cruarch, but there were tears of gratitude in his eyes at seeing so many of his people safe. It was a day for tears; tears for a loved one lost, tears for loved ones found.

We were hauled ashore by many eager hands. Our army's presence was deceptive, for the port would have been bustling with traders and its harbor filled with proper ships were there not profound unrest in the land. It was the Twins who welcomed us, Grainne and Eamonn, bursting with gladness and pride, and as we exchanged tales of what had befallen us, we learned it was the Twins who had kept the entire enterprise together. When the Master of the Straits deposited our flotilla on the shores of First Sister, there had been widespread despair and terror. Grainne had rallied them with her own indomitable high spirits, igniting a spark of hope. Eamonn had turned his orderly mind to the task of survival, keeping the forces busy doing useful work—gathering and sorting our supplies, setting up an encampment.

Indeed, they'd done such a fine job of it that when the face of the waters returned to bid them return to their vessels, much of the Alban crew was minded to cling to the isle rather than risk the seas again. It had taken Eamonn and Grainne's combined powers of persuasion to prevent a mutiny.

"She cut off a man's ear," my friend Fortun told me.

The Lady of the Dalriada greeted Phèdre by lifting her several feet in the air before setting her down. Phèdre was laughing; not in tears, just laughing, and I was glad to see it. "Wait. She did what?"

"That fellow." Fortun pointed discreetly in the direction of an Alban warrior with an abashed look and a bandage wrapped around his head. "She just lopped it right off. Said since he was a coward, he'd carry the mark of it for everyone to see. Then she asked, who's next?"

"Well, he'll have a tale to tell if he makes it home alive," I said. "None of you doubted?"

"Us?" Overhearing our conversation, his comrade Remy slung an arm around Fortun's neck. "Never! We're Phèdre's Boys." His expression turned somber. "Sorry to hear we lost the Tsingano, though."

I will speak your name and remember it.

"Hyacinthe," I said softly. "Hyacinthe, Anasztaizia's son."

"Is it true?" Fortun shuddered. "He's taken the place of the Master of the Straits? *Forever?*"

"Unless we find a way to break the curse," I said. "Though I fear it will be an apprenticeship of many years before he has mastery over wind and sea."

"And to think I taught him to fish," Remy said half to himself.

"We'll all miss him," Fortun said. "He was good company when the sight wasn't on him. Come on, time to saddle up." To me, he said, "We're off scouting upriver for the Royal Fleet and Ghislain de Somerville's army. You met his father the Comte. Is it true he smells like apples?"

The belief that those of Anael's lineage smelt of apples was a common one; I tried to remember if Percy de Somerville had. "I didn't notice."

Remy gazed in Phèdre's direction. "What does *she* smell like? Our royal ambassadress?"

"How should I know?" I said. "Seawater with a trace of woodsmoke, most likely."

They scoffed. "Come on, man," Remy said. "Give us somewhat to comfort our lonely souls in wartime."

I looked at Phèdre. She was expressing her gratitude to Eamonn, gazing into his eyes, one hand on his arm. Ingenuous, sincere. Damned if he didn't have that schoolboy blush again. Seawater and woodsmoke was unfair, she'd been bathed and pampered and burnished in that strange tower, and probably smelt of lye soap, age-cracked unguents, and a night of lovemaking with Hyacinthe, which I'd prefer not to think about. And anyway, that wasn't what they were asking.

"Jasmine," I said abruptly. "But not a posy under your nose or a whole field in bloom. Jasmine in the distance, carried on the breeze so far that you wonder how a scent can be so delicate and strong at the same time."

"Intoxicating?" Remy suggested.

I folded my vambraced arms. "That's enough for Phèdre's Boys to know and more than I ought to have told you. Now get out of here and find us an army."

They grinned and saluted. A scouting party of five of Rousse's men on the soundest, swiftest mounts to cross the Straits set out before sunset to canvas the Rhenus. A part of me was impatient and wished the whole army had set out in their wake, but our troops were unsettled and unrested, hungry and out of sorts, and there were several hundred head of horses that needed tending.

We spent the day restoring order and camped for the night, setting out at dawn. There were only a handful of seaworthy vessels with sufficient oar-power to buck the current, so for the most part we rode or marched. I was assigned a tall, good-tempered grey gelding, while Phèdre was given a place of honor riding beside the Lady Grainne in her war-chariot. The western segment of the Rhenus is a broad, placid river that winds in great, slow curves through the flat green land. With our wicker war-chariots, lime-crested Dalriada, and woad-tattooed Cruithne, we must have looked a sight marching along its bank. It was sparsely populated on both the D'Angeline and Flatlandish shores, mostly small fishing villages or farmsteads, which was good since a number of people fled in terror from our approach.

But those who stood their ground welcomed us with wary gladness upon learning that the Alban army was here to fight for Queen Ysandre. Admiral Rousse's presence reassured them, and Drustan and the Twins certainly made an impact. What the Azzallese fishers and farmers thought of Phèdre, I couldn't say. I did my best to attend her with Cassiline formality. I didn't have the proper attire, but I had my unmistakable weapons.

"How can you maintain a vaguely menacing scowl for that long?" Phèdre asked me the second night of the march, rubbing her own jaw.

I laughed. "'Tis second nature. Do you hurt in sympathy?"

"No, it's that bedamned chariot," she said. "I know it's an honor, but name of Elua, it's a teeth-rattling ride."

It felt good to take a moment's pause and speak of inconsequential matters. I folded my arms behind my head. "*I* think you enjoy the Twins' attention."

She smiled under her lashes at me. "*I* think you know me too well."

I wished it were true. There were times I wished we were an ordinary man and woman, living ordinary lives. I wanted to take her in my arms for comfort's sake as we'd done to survive in Skaldia; I wanted to hold her safe against me and keep the pain at bay. But that was my own yearning speaking. A sterner voice inside me warned that I ought to keep my distance out of respect for her grief at Hyacinthe's fate.

Following the path of the Perfect Companion, I opted for the latter and wished her a good night's sleep.

Midday on the morrow, we spotted a couple of Rousse's riders pelting back along the wide, curving river, letting out loud whoops as they approached us. True to form, they carried a House Courcel standard and the frayed banner of Phèdre's Boys, waving it in salute.

Quintilius Rouse made his way to the forefront of our troops to greet them. "What news, lads?"

"Lord Admiral!" the first rider shouted. "The fleet comes!"

"When?"

He pointed. "Now!"

Sure enough, there was the entire D'Angeline Royal Navy rounding a broad bend some hundred yards ahead, every mast flying the silver swan on an azure field declaring their fealty to Queen Ysandre de la Courcel.

CHAPTER FIFTY-THREE

Our reunion with the Royal Fleet and the remarkable presence of the combined Alban and Dalriadan army were cause for raucous cheers—and that was all the time we had to celebrate, for Rousse's second-in-command, Jean Marchand, bore urgent news. He apprised us of the situation while our foot-soldiers were dispersed amongst the vessels for swifter conveyance.

Selig had dispatched a sizeable number of his warriors to attempt to take and hold the Rhenus. If they succeeded, it would give them control of the whole length of the Azzallese border. Thus far, they hadn't done so, but their efforts had tied up the Azzallese forces. Now, Jean told us, the Skaldi were attacking the easternmost bridge across the Rhenus to secure a foothold on both shores. The fleet had amassed there to support Ghislain de Somerville, the Royal Commander's son, who was in charge of half the Azzallese army; the other half of their forces were farther westward along the Rhenus under the command of Marc de Trevalion, successfully recalled from exile.

"There's some fifteen hundred Skaldi ready to cross that thrice-damned bridge," Marchand said. "We destroyed the midsection, but they're trying to repair it. And I tell you what's worrisome, they're using some tricks of Tiberian engineering. This is a great deal more than a barbarian raiding party writ large."

I remembered Phèdre in Gunter's steading whispering against my chest as we lay on my straw bed by the hearth, *The Skaldi have found a leader who thinks.*

Quintilius Rousse grinned. "But if we sail upriver with three thousand wild Cruithne warriors . . ."

"The Skaldi will shit their breeches," his second-in-command said, adding, "Apologies, my lady."

"I've heard worse," Phèdre said mildly. "Let's get underway."

Our fair wind stayed with us, the last trailing gasp of the Master of the Straits' promise fulfilled. Between the wind and the oarsmen, we made good time despite travelling against the current. We were a mere day and a half on the broad face of the Rhenus before we heard the roar and clash of battle around the next bend.

"We'll drop anchor on the flagship at fifty yards. You'll remain belowdecks," he said to Phèdre, and then pointed at half a dozen of his sailors. "You lot will stay behind with the Cassiline. If the battle goes against us, turn the ship and flee. Understood?" We acknowledged his orders, although I was reasonably certain Phèdre didn't have the slightest intention of remaining belowdecks.

"I'm not going below," Phèdre informed me the moment Rousse stepped away.

I grinned at her. "I know. I'd actually rather you didn't, it cuts off an escape route if we do get boarded."

"Which we won't," Fortun said, testing the edge of his cutlass with his thumb; the others agreed.

The Skaldi had been diligent in the absence of Rousse's fleet, mounting a full-scale effort to rebuild the broken gap in the bridge. They'd dug fortifications on the far side of the Rhenus and constructed narrow walls that slid on wheels to protect the builders. Discipline was not their strong suit, for the moment the breach had been tenuously covered with rough-hewn planks, hundreds of Skaldi warriors surged across it. Outnumbered, his contingent of archers having spent their arsenal, Ghislain de Somerville had been forced to fall back before the growing onslaught.

If we'd arrived any later, it would have been a resounding defeat. Instead, it turned into a rout. The Skaldi had been prepared for the return of the Royal Fleet. They had not been prepared for the army that accompanied it. Their forces broke ranks, scattering as our ships ran aground in the shallows and the Alban army surged forth down gangplanks and ramps. Drustan's deadly Cruithne archers laid down a hail of cover for our mounted warriors charging upriver to plunge into the fray.

It was a damned good thing that Rousse's riders had alerted the Azzallese forces, else they might have taken us for invaders from across the sea. For several long, confused moments after breaking ranks, the Skaldi weren't sure what to make of these newcomers with their blue faces and wild manes, as barbaric to the eye as any doughty thane. Nigh out of nowhere they found themselves pinned against the very bridge they sought to repair and seize, and the Albans fell upon them like a hammer and tongs.

I do not think we would have won so handily if Waldemar Selig were in command, but he was leading the attack on Troyes-le-Mont. Or mayhap not, since Selig's plans for conquest surely didn't factor in the restored Cruarch of Alba marching to the aid of Terre d'Ange. When his plans were laid, there was no reason to even consider such a possibility.

At any rate, the battle was a rout—and it became a slaughter, for the Skaldi refused any offer of quarter and fought to the death.

Before the end of the day, it was over. There were Skaldi dead and dying on both sides of the Rhenus, on the partially destroyed bridge, on the decks of our ships, and in the river itself, the long, slow train of its current dragging a bloody hem.

We were lucky. Between the advantage of numbers and the element of surprise, our losses were light. The Cruithne set about scouring the countryside for stones to build a cairn for the Alban dead and the Azzallese tended to their own and began digging an immense ditch in which to dispose of the Skaldi dead. We found Ghislain de Somerville supervising the endeavor. He was a pragmatic and down-to-earth fellow, wearing a simple steel cuirass and an unadorned helmet and looking a bit poleaxed by the turn of events. "Lord Admiral," he greeted Quintilius Rousse. "I didn't believe it when my men told me."

The Royal Admiral bowed. "My lord de Somerville, I present to you Drustan mab Necthana, the Cruarch of Alba, as well as Eamonn and Grainne mac Conor, Lords of the Dalriada."

"Your majesties." Ghislain offered a belated bow to the threefold personage of Alba's rulers. "You did it," he said to Rousse. Removing his helmet, he ran a hand through sweat-damp golden hair. "You really did it."

"Not I." Rousse presented Phèdre, who curtsied. "Phèdre nó Delaunay, Ysandre's emissary."

Ghislain's light blue eyes widened. "*You're* Delaunay's whore?"

Whatever response he expected, it was not the one he got. My daggers flashed out of their sheaths as I stepped before Phèdre and shifted into a defensive pose. Rousse's men booed and hissed their disapproval. Drustan gave one sharp order and half a dozen Cruithne and Dalriada drew steel, leveling points at Ghislain.

"My lord," Phèdre said calmly to him. "I was born to an adept of the Night Court, trained by Cecilie Laveau-Perrin of Cereus House, and completed my marque in bond-service to Anafiel Delaunay de Montrève. Is my lineage in question, or the merits of Naamah's service?"

"Not at all." Ghislain flushed, and damned if there wasn't a faint scent of apples in the air. I stood down and sheathed my daggers. "But the Servants of Naamah do not generally serve the Palace in, um, such a capacity."

Quintilius Rousse coughed.

Drustan gave me an inquiring look and I explained in a patois of D'Angeline, Cruithne, and Caerdicci. "He says Servants of Naamah, who are trained to deal in pleasure, are not usually royal ambassadors."

Smiling, Drustan translated the comment for the benefit of the Twins. Eamonn grinned. Grainne laughed aloud and slung a friendly arm around Ghislain de Somerville's shoulders. "You should," she said to him in Eiran. "Why else do you think the Dalriada came to fight for you?"

"My lord." Taking pity on Ghislain, Phèdre steered us back to matters at hand. "We have a very long story to tell you, but the short truth of it is we have brought Alba's army in accordance with the wishes of the Queen of Terre d'Ange, and we are in grave need of your guidance. We know the Royal Army is besieged at Troyes-le-Mont, and little more. Will you grant us your hospitality and share your news? We bear foodstuff of our own, I give my word we'll not strip your camp."

"Do you jest?" Ghislain gave himself a little shake and removed Grainne's arm from his shoulders as politely as possible. "You saved our hides, you're welcome to aught we have. Gather your folk and I'll bid my men make them welcome."

He strode off shouting. After conferring, Drustan and the Twins departed to establish an encampment along the eastern shore, while Rousse retired to his fleet's current flagship to speak with his second-in-command, Jean. I dispatched Fortun and a few of Phèdre's Boys to commandeer the best tent they could find, barring Ghislain's.

"It's fine," Phèdre protested. "Joscelin, it's not as though I haven't slept on the ground more often than not for nigh onto a year."

I folded my arms. "You're not a runaway slave or an envoy in disguise, my lady. You're Ysandre's ambassadress and you should be shown respect accordingly. If Ghislain hadn't been so discomfited, I'm sure he would have seen to it."

Phèdre's Boys were in wholehearted agreement and the matter was settled. They scoured the Azzallese camp for a tent and other niceties. By the time we'd gathered our belongings and returned to the site of our encampment, the dart-pierced scarlet mote flew below the House Courcel standard atop our tentpole.

Ghislain de Somerville's tent served as a command station as well as a sleeping space. He had a worktable spread with an array of detailed maps. After listening in amazement to the tale of our journey, he gave us his version of the Skaldic invasion, the D'Angeline resistance, and the current status of the war. It accorded with what we had seen in the Master of the Straits' sea-mirror, with updates on enemy troop positions along the Rhenus and insight into the strategy of the Royal Commander, Percy de Somerville.

"My father did his best to prepare," Ghislain said. "But it took so damnably long to get the pieces in place and rally loyal forces without tipping our hand to d'Aiglemort. It was always likely to result in a siege." He indicated the fortress of Troyes-le-Mont on a map. "There's a good deep well, no chance of losing water, and it's well stocked in preparation. But still, their food can only last so long, and Selig's got the whole damned country at his disposal. As long as his discipline holds . . ." He shrugged. "It's only a matter of time."

Drustan conferred with Phèdre. "How many Skaldi?" she asked for him.

The response was grim. "Thirty-odd thousand."

I whistled softly through my teeth; it was more than even Phèdre and I had reckoned. "And our forces?" she asked.

"Eight thousand at the start." Ghislain slid out a diagram of Troyes-le-Mont. "I don't know how many are left to hold the fortress. No word's going in or out. But most, I think; this was a planned retreat." He pointed at the parchment. "There is an outer wall here, trenches and stake-pits here and here, with a second wall of fortifications here." Drustan leaned over the worktable while Phèdre translated for clarity's sake. "So far, they've held this belt of ground, but my news is no fresher than yours if the Master of the Straits' sea-mirror told true. After that, they've naught but the fortress itself."

"And after that?" Quintilius Rousse asked.

Ghislain's gaze was somber. "Prince Benedicte is doing all he can to rally a larger force amongst the Caerdicci city-states, but the Caerdicci look to their own. There's no more help coming from that quarter."

I stared at the maps and struggled against a wave of despair; all of us did, all of us thinking the same thing, which was that there were simply too many Skaldi to defeat. "Then they fall," I said. "And Terre d'Ange falls with them."

"We have one chance." It was Phèdre, thinking aloud with that infuriatingly vague look that set all my senses on edge. I knew that look. It presaged somewhat dangerous. Her focus sharpened. "Joscelin, do you remember how fractious the tribes were at the Allthing?" I nodded. "Waldemar Selig united blood enemies. If we can stir them up, mayhap it will break Selig's discipline . . . it's somewhat, at least."

Rousse looked skeptical. "And how do we do that?"

I hadn't expected Ghislain de Somerville to give merit to Phèdre's suggestion, but he took it seriously. "Blessed Elua knows, the Skaldi don't scare easily, but the Cruithne unnerved them. They're a superstitious lot, you know." He drew a circle around the outermost fortifications. "If we could harry their flanks, small strikes and swift retreats, that might sow discord in their ranks. We'd need a secure retreat, somewhere in the mountains, here. Somewhere hidden."

"How many of us would be like to survive?" Phèdre asked Ghislain, not yet translating his words.

He took a deep breath. "In the end? None. We'd live as long as we were lucky, and no longer. And it may be that we'd die for naught. It's the only course I see, but our chances are slim at best."

She inclined her head, then spoke at length to Drustan and the Twins in Cruithne. Drustan walked away without a word, gazing out the open tent flap. Eamonn and Grainne exchanged glances.

"Tell him I'll see his folk returned to Alba's shores," Quintilius Rousse said gruffly. "Every last blue-stained, clay-haired one of them. We didn't ask 'em here to commit suicide."

Drustan responded without waiting for Phèdre to translate, his voice impassioned, speaking in Cruithne too swiftly for me to follow. He turned to fix his deep gaze on her, intent and demanding, holding up his right hand with the D'Angeline royal signet flashing gold in the dim light of the tent.

"I don't know," Phèdre whispered in Cruithne, tears welling in her eyes. "My lord, I am so sorry."

He spoke again, then called sharply to Grainne and Eamonn. They fell in beside him and made an abrupt exit.

"What passes?" Ghislain de Somerville asked gently.

Phèdre rubbed her face, gathering herself. "The Cruarch reminds me that our companion Hyacinthe chose a terrible fate that this mission might succeed, and that if it yet fails, the Master of the Straits' curse remains unbroken. There will be no safe return to Alba's shores. Drustan's mind is fixed," she added. "This course is his destiny. But he will not force an unwinnable war upon his people. He is going to offer them the choice."

"Fair enough," Ghislain said. "Whatever you told them, they couldn't have understood the odds they'd face. None of us did. But if your forces go, I'm going with them. My father's in there." He slammed one hand on the map-strewn table, then gave me a hard, long look. "And if I'm not mistaken, so is yours, Cassiline."

CHAPTER FIFTY-FOUR

It shouldn't have come as a surprise, and yet it did.

In the moment, I merely thanked Ghislain de Somerville for the information; he nodded and continued. Although I was a middle son of a Minor House and he the first son of a Major House, we recognized each other as the sons of D'Angeline noblemen with keen senses of honor and propriety.

As night fell, I found myself desiring solitude to ponder the news. There was no real privacy in a war camp, but after asking Fortun to keep an eye on Phèdre, I found a little space under an elm tree. I sat on a grassy hillock and watched the bright pinpricks of stars emerge in the darkling blue twilight overhead while all around me hundreds of orange cooking fires blossomed over acres of blood-soaked ground.

In time, Phèdre found me. She sat beside me in silence for a time. "Did you know?"

I shook my head. "I wasn't sure. I looked for our banner on the isle, but I didn't see it."

"I'm sorry." Her voice was soft.

"Don't be," I said. "House Verreuil has always served. Did you know my father fought in the Battle of the Three Princes? That's when he won the title Chevalier." I smiled a little. "You know, the one you bestowed on Rousse's men."

"I've no right to grant lands, though," she said.

"No, I know." I regarded the twinkling stars. "Verreuil's a small estate, but it's been in the family for six hundred years. We're of Shemhazai's lineage, we kept a proper library like all faithful Siovalese, sent one son a generation to the Cassiline Brotherhood, and served the throne of Terre d'Ange as need required."

"Is it just your father representing your House?" she asked.

"No," I said. "Luc would have gone with him."

"Luc?"

"My elder brother." I'd spoken little of my family. The Cassiline Brotherhood frowned upon such familiarity. "He was named for our uncle Luc, who was pledged to Cassiel's service. I've a younger brother, too," I added. "Mahieu. But they would have made him stay. Mother's comfort, the youngest; father's strength, the eldest. And the middle son to Cassiel. My sisters used to tease me." I smiled with rueful fondness at the memories of my childhood. "I've three of those, too."

Phèdre took my arm and squeezed it in wordless sympathy.

"I thought I'd have a chance to see them again," I said. "Before . . . well, before the end, I suppose. In the Brotherhood, they let us visit home at age twenty-five if we've served well. But I'm anathema now." A shudder ran over my skin as I said the thing I feared aloud. "Does my family know, do you think? Did the letter I sent arrive? Or do they know only that I'm a condemned murderer convicted of killing Anafiel Delaunay?"

"No one who knew you would believe it, Joscelin," she said with certainty.

"What do they know?" There was a harsh note in my voice. "I was ten years old, Phèdre! How do they know what I became?" I turned my hands upward, gazing at my empty palms. "I hardly even know myself anymore. Blessed Elua, did we come all this way for nothing more than this?"

"I don't know," she murmured.

I wished we had all the time in the world to speak of such matters and more. Phèdre hadn't entered the world as a highly trained courtesan anymore than I had as a Cassiline warrior-priest. I knew next to nothing of her early childhood save what I'd learned from Alcuin. And mayhap there would come such a time if we lived to see it, but now was not it. Reluctantly, I returned my thoughts to the here and now. "Well, whatever the Albans decide, we'll make ready to ride for Trevalion on the morrow. It's well garrisoned. Ghislain's extended his hospitality and Rousse will spare us half a dozen of your boys to serve as your personal cadre."

Phèdre looked at me.

"No." My temper flared. "Oh, no. Don't even think it."

"They came at my word," she said.

"They came at the Queen's word!" I retorted. "You did but carry it!"

"Ysandre de la Courcel did not play on the Twins' jealousy to spur the Dalriada to war," she said. "Or leave her oldest friend in the world bound to a lonely rock to win passage toward a doomed battle. I can't abandon them, Joscelin."

"What in Rousse's seven hells do you think you can do?" I was shouting. "It's a *war*!"

"I can translate." Her expression was set with that subtle obstinance. "And I can put a face on what they're fighting and dying for. That's what you told me, isn't it?"

"And if the Cruithne and Dalriada vote to retreat?"

"I'll go to Caerdicca Unitas and offer my services as a royal ambassadress to Prince Benedicte," Phèdre said, surprising me. "What other course is there? Drustan will stay no matter what his folk decide. Mayhap if the Caerdicci hear of the Cruarch of Alba's sacrifice, it will sway them."

"The Caerdicci won't fight for Terre d'Ange." I tried to gentle my words, knowing she was grasping at straws. "The city-states are more fractious than the Skaldi and more jealous than the Twins. Not even Naamah's wiles can bind them together, Phèdre."

"I know," she said. "But it's better than waiting to fall into Selig's hands." Kissing my cheek, she rose. "I'm sorry about your family, Joscelin. I'll pray for them."

"Pray for us all," I murmured.

Before long, I returned to our campsite. One of the youngest and brashest of Phèdre's Boys—Ti-Philippe, his comrades called him—was on watch outside Phèdre's tent. I thanked him and took his place, laying my bedroll across the threshold.

In the camps of the Cruithne and the Dalriada, the fires burned long into the night as they debated the matter. Come morning, we reconvened and Drustan mab Necthana gave his people's answer, speaking in Caerdicci that his answer might be clear to all.

"We will stay and fight."

It wasn't the answer Ghislain had expected. "All of you?"

Drustan gave a brusque nod, turned to Phèdre, and spoke in Cruithne. "If you will swear us this. If we fall, someone must carry word to Alba. Our families and friends must know how we died. The poets must sing of our deeds."

After translating his words, she replied unhesitatingly. "I promise it. I swear it will be so, my lord Cruarch." She turned to Ghislain. "I swear it. In the Queen's name."

A sigh escaped me.

"Joscelin, think about it," Phèdre said in the reasonable tone she used when proposing somewhat unreasonable. "If we do fail . . . if *I* cannot cross the Straits, who can?"

"She has a point, Cassiline," Quintilius Rousse observed.

It was true, actually; with Hyacinthe the heir to the Master of the Straits, Phèdre was the one person on earth like to be granted passage at will. "It was Caerdicca Unitas last night," I muttered. "Tomorrow she'll want to sail to Khebbel-im-Akkad. If you ask me, my lord Admiral, we ought to lock her in a dungeon and throw away the key."

Phèdre smiled sweetly at me, knowing I didn't mean a word of it; or possibly at fond memories the word "dungeon" evoked. One couldn't be sure.

"Then it is decided," Ghislain de Somerville said firmly. "I've sent word to Marc de Trevalion asking to meet." He indicated an area farther east along the Rhenus on one of his maps. "We'll conference here. Lord Admiral, by your leave, I'd have you stay with your fleet and command the defense of the western bank."

Rousse inclined his head. "As you bid, my lord."

"Good." Ghislain began rolling his maps and placing them in leather carrying cases. "Strike camp. We're moving out."

We spent the remainder of that day cleaning and mending weapons, gear, and clothing; tending horses; and consolidating our supplies. On the morrow, it was another day and another leave-taking.

I daresay Admiral Quintilius Rousse would have left his fleet under his second's command and ridden with us if de Somerville hadn't asked him to stay. As it was, he dispatched all thirty-one surviving Phèdre's Boys to ride in his stead. I could tell Phèdre was minded to protest, but I gave her a look and she accepted their service with grace.

For all his bluff manner, Rousse had become more than passing fond of her. After exchanging firm handclasps with Drustan and me, he enfolded Phèdre in a great smothering embrace, which was rather like seeing a bear embrace a doe. "Elua keep you, girl," he said to her. "You've courage enough for ten in your own perverse way, and your lord's bedeviled sense of honor to boot. If you need to cross the Straits again, you know I'm the man to do it."

She hugged him in return. "Thank you, my lord Admiral."

It was a mere day's march to the meeting place, where Marc de Trevalion awaited us with the rest of Azzalle's forces. The former Duc's presence marked the success of the Queen's Council's solution to the thorny problem of House Trevalion. The loyalty of the whole province had been questionable since Marc's wife Lyonette and their son Baudoin were executed for treason, and the duchy placed under Ghislain de Somerville's authority. But Marc and his daughter Bernadette had been recalled from exile in our absence. Now Ghislain and Bernadette were wedded and their first child heir to the duchy; in the meanwhile, the loyalty of Azzalle was secure.

It was all very complicated, but such were the necessities of building stable alliances in a civilized society.

Marc de Trevalion maintained an air of polite reserve, even when confronted with the welcome but admittedly startling appearance of the Cruarch of Alba, the Lords of the Dalriada, and three thousand warriors ready to fight for Terre d'Ange. "My kinsman Gaspar spoke well of your lord Delaunay," he said to Phèdre upon being introduced. "He held him in the highest regard."

She inclined her head, eyes bright with tears. "Thank you, my lord."

In her role of the Queen's emissary, Phèdre presented Drustan mab Necthana as the Cruarch of Alba—Eamonn and Grainne had grown bored of so much foreign conversation. I was pleased to see the former Duc acknowledge him with a respectful bow.

Ghislain laid out our plans in a succinct, unemotional manner. Marc de Trevalion heard him out, pacing in thought. "You know the odds of your survival?"

"I do," Ghislain said, while Phèdre translated the exchange in a low murmur for the Albans. "We all do."

"Then you must try," de Trevalion said somberly. "Never fear, we'll hold the Rhenus for as long as Troyes-le-Mont stands."

They clasped wrists in a declaration of solidarity, the former Duc and his son by marriage. Ghislain unfurled his maps and they began pondering the best route to circumvent Troyes-le-Mont. Ceding the discussion of the realm's terrain and roadways to the commanders, Phèdre obtained writing materials from one of de Trevalion's attendants and withdrew to her modest tent to compose a letter.

I watched her write in a quick, graceful hand, the nib of her pen skimming over the paper like a damselfly along a creek. "What are you about?"

Phèdre sanded the wet ink and showed me the letter. "It's to Thelesis de Mornay. If . . . if neither of us live through these next weeks, she'll be able to carry word to Alba. Rousse would take her. The Master of the Straits has granted her passage before and Hyacinthe knows her." I raised my brows and she smiled wryly at me. "Did you think I was counting on doing it myself? I know the risk my choice entails."

So she did know. "I'm not sure whether to be glad or frightened that you grasp the extent of it."

She blew on the sanded ink. "Be glad for the sake of Alba and its poets."

Once the letter was finished and sealed, we found Remy. Two or three of Phèdre's Boys were almost always within shouting distance, ready and at hand for whatever might be needful. She held up the letter, rolled in a leather tube. "I've a mission for the boldest and shrewdest among you," she said to Remy. "I need this letter carried across hostile terrain to the City of Elua and delivered into the hands of the Queen's Poet. Are there men among you willing to undertake this mission?"

"Do you jest?" Remy grinned and stuck out his hand to take it. "Give it here, my lady, and we'll see it reaches berth as sure as any ship I've ever sailed!"

After some discussion, Rousse's lads decided to send a party of four riders and drew straws for the honor. I was sorry to see that a spot didn't fall to either Remy or Fortun. With the precise locations of Skaldi scouts and outlying patrols unknown, it was a risky quest, but not as risky as the sure death awaiting us on the battlefield surrounding Troyes-le-Mont. The chosen riders wasted no time in gathering their things and saddling their mounts. Freshly provisioned and armed with Marc de Trevalion's latest intelligence, they bade us and their companions farewell and set forth for the City.

I watched them go. "You're not quite as foolhardy as you seem."

"Not quite," Phèdre said. "Only just almost. I wish you'd go with them, Joscelin."

One might as well ask the sun to rise in the west, and she damned well knew it. I gave her a wry smile. "Will you never be done testing my vow?"

"No." Her voice changed; there was an unexpected note of raw honesty in it. "Not if I have my choice in the matter, Cassiline."

I wasn't sure I'd heard her aright, if she was saying what I thought it meant. Her words sounded in my chest like a beaten gong, resonating throughout the whole of my being. I bowed, forearms crossed. "Elua grant you the chance," I said. "I'm willing to live with it if it means your survival."

Smiling a bit, Phèdre looked up at me, her long-lashed eyes wide and lustrous, that crimson petal floating on the dark surface of her left iris, offering her heart on the point of a spear.

I began to say—

"My lady!" Ti-Philippe approached us at a quick jog. "The Cruarch asked me to fetch you, they've need of their translator."

The moment passed; it was foolish to speak of such matters with the world in chaos. There was no merit in making plans for a future that likely didn't exist. Nonetheless, I could not help but think of Hyacinthe's parting words and wonder, what if it *were* true? The thought of it squeezed my heart like a fist. If it were true, the gods themselves must be laughing, for there surely couldn't be a more unlikely pairing than an *anguissette* and a Cassiline.

"Ah, good." Marc de Trevalion glanced up at our return. "I was just attempting to explain the significance of Isidore d'Aiglemort's whereabouts. He's still in command of the Allies of Camlach."

"Do you know where they are?" I asked while Phèdre spoke with Drustan.

The former Duc shook his head. "Holed up in the Camaelines. You might as well beard a badger in its den as track him there." He pointed at the map. "There's your likeliest avenue of retreat," he said to Ghislain. "I've one piece of advice for you. Take out Selig." He nodded at Phèdre and me. "If their information is good, and it has been thus far, Waldemar Selig is the key. If he falls, the Skaldi are leaderless."

Waldemar Selig; Waldemar the Blessed, proof against weapons, a leader who thought. I suppressed a humorless laugh at the notion that removing him from the battlefield would be a simple solution to effect. Knowing Selig, he would be at the forefront of the siege, nowhere near the rearguard and flanks.

"We will try," Ghislain said. "That much I can promise."

"My lord de Trevalion," Phèdre said. "What befell Melisande Shahrizai while we've been gone?"

There were times when I questioned the extent of Melisande Shahrizai's significance in this complicated conspiracy. I would never, ever forget seeing her mercilessly beautiful face blur in my vision as I slid into unconsciousness and awoke in a wagon bound for Skaldia, but I wondered if Phèdre gave her too much credit for her role in the unfolding game. That bedamned diamond hanging from her throat was a testament to the incomprehensible bond between them. Though it would have been a deadly error to have kept the missive she had sent to Waldemar Selig and tipped our hand, I wished it had been possible. I'd only had a glimpse of the letter and I couldn't claim to recognize her handwriting.

But Marc de Trevalion didn't have any doubts. His expression darkened at the mere mention of Melisande's name. He had lost his wife and son, had lost his title and been sent into exile due to Melisande Shahrizai's betrayal of House Trevalion. "The last I knew, the Cassiline Brotherhood was looking for members of House Shahrizai at the Queen's behest to bring them in for questioning. But I never heard they succeeded."

There was nothing save our word to prove the extent of Melisande's culpability. D'Aiglemort didn't know that she had conspired to use him for her own purposes. Were he to somehow emerge victorious, she would remain in good standing with him for having removed Prince Baudoin de Trevalion from the path to the throne. If Selig prevailed, presumably he would make good on whatever reward he had promised her.

Yet if it all fell apart, her role would vanish like wax in a bronze casting, melted away in the forge of battle and leaving only absence in its place.

It was something I thought about as our blended company set forth on yet another march. We struck out toward the south, planning to give Troyes-le-Mont a wide berth and gain the foothills to the east.

It wasn't the matter uppermost in my mind, though.

Phèdre had come very near to a declaration of love—and I had, too.

Did one need to say the words? If I did, was it the final betrayal of everything I had believed?

I was anathema, I had no right to such concerns. But I had them nonetheless. I had taken the vows of water, fire, and steel. I had walked the blade's edge and made my final pledge. Cassiline Brother or not, as long as I drew breath, I would remain Cassiel's Servant. As Phèdre would remain Naamah's Servant and bear the beautiful blood-prick that marked her as chosen by Kushiel.

One thing I knew for a surety, she would never pledge herself solely to one person. Not to Hyacinthe, not to me—Melisande might have thought it once upon a time, but that possibility died in a welter of bloodshed. And even before then, I don't believe it. Melisande thought after that first assignation that she knew how far she could push Phèdre to break her.

She was wrong. Neither of them knew the depth of endurance that Kushiel's Chosen possessed. Phèdre would walk barefoot over broken glass before she'd cross the threshold of Melisande's bedchamber again. But that part of her that belonged to the gods would never be faithful to one single mortal.

I knew it.

And I was the opposite side of the same coin. I had never envisioned being with anyone; like the good Cassiline Brother that I was, I'd never let my thoughts so much as wander. Love had driven me to my knees before I would acknowledge it, and I simply couldn't imagine feeling that way about anyone save Phèdre nó Delaunay in all her deep-rooted complexity. I couldn't conceive breaking my vow for anyone but her. Cassiel was the Perfect Companion, and it mattered not a whit to him how many lovers Blessed Elua took nor how many children he sired. How could I attempt to follow in his footsteps and do otherwise?

But Cassiel was the divine essence of the Lord's love. Whether his love for Elua was as pure and chaste as the Brotherhood believed, or a romance of the heart the depth of which lay behind mortal understanding, Cassiel was not human. He was flaming steel and the stuff of Heaven incarnate. He was not subject to human foibles and frailties.

I was.

When it came to it, we knew how to be Cassiel's Servant and Kushiel's Chosen, Phèdre and I. What we might be together as an ordinary mortal man and woman, I didn't know yet. The possibility filled me with delirious excitement and a measure of trepidation. I turned the thought over and over in my mind as though it were an engineering puzzle, a delicate thing wrought of cogs and wheels that could only mesh just so.

It was a puzzle I set aside as we marched south into Namarre—Naamah's province, filled with rolling green hills, springs and rivers and quick silvery waterfalls. Summer was in full bloom as we passed fields of wildflowers, poppies and bellflower and vetch.

Blessed Elua have mercy, Terre d'Ange was a beautiful country.

We looped south of Troyes-le-Mont and then back northeast toward the foothills bordering the plain on which the fortress was situated. Thanks to the Cruithne warriors' skill at woodcraft, our march was less eventful than it would otherwise have been. Scouting in parties of four or five, the Cruithne located several outlying companies of Skaldi. One by one, our Cruithne archers took them out with their deadly shortbows. It was Drustan who ordered the killings, with the full support of Ghislain de Somerville.

As a strategic maneuver, it was only pragmatic, but I could see that these fatal ambushes weighed on Phèdre's conscience.

"Do not let it trouble you," Drustan said to her when he noticed. "Their deaths are fairly earned."

"You needn't mince words with me," Phèdre said somberly. "I survived slavery in Skaldia and the Battle of Bryn Gorrydum, and I've seen what violence humankind is capable of wreaking. They're not taking any survivors, are they?"

"No." The Cruarch's black eyes were as hard as stone. "But these are not honorable warriors. They are scouts and raiders, and they are stealing and killing as they go. It is not enough to strip a simple farmer of his hard-worked crops, but to slay him and anyone that might raise a shovel in defense, from stripling boys to grandmothers. Sometimes they keep a pretty girl to pass around for a while."

Phèdre gave a grim nod of understanding. It was no more than either of us had expected, but now it was confirmed.

We marched onward.

CHAPTER FIFTY-FIVE

The low Namarrese mountains surrounding the plain of Troyes-le-Mont were challenging terrain. Although nowhere near as high or vast as the Camaelines that formed a natural border against the Skaldi, they were riddled with narrow passageways like giant worm-trails and plunging gullies with crags jutting from every cliff face and casting jagged shadows over every crease in the rock. The scant number of Skaldi guards posted in the mountains was a measure of Waldemar Selig's confidence in his command of tactics and his mastery of the territory his army had conquered. One of Rousse's men was familiar with the region and led the Cruithne scouting parties while the army wended its way through backtrails. Selig had assigned lookouts with furled red banners on long poles at every likely vantage point to relay an alarm if D'Angeline forces were spotted in the mountains.

Not a single banner was hoisted and unfurled.

The Cruithne were too surefooted and silent; even their shortbows loosed with a humming sound, not the resonant thrum of a L'Agnacite longbow. It was thanks to their stealth and skill that we entered the mountains along the western edge of the plain of Troyes-le-Mont without tipping our hand.

It wasn't until Ghislain, Drustan, and the Twins deemed our position secure that we dared peer over the crest of the mountain at the distant battlefield.

"Blessed Elua have mercy on us," I whispered at the sight. Lying on her belly beside me, Phèdre swallowed hard.

There were *so many* Skaldi. We had known, the two of us, better than anyone in our company. We had seen the clans gather at the Allthing, knowing that those vast numbers of tribesmen only represented a fraction of their tribes. We'd seen their army overrun the D'Angeline army in the Master of the Straits' sea-mirror. None of it prepared us for the actual sight of the forces gathered on the plain of the besieged fortress. The outermost defensive wall had been breached. The inner bulwarks yet stood, but even at this distance, we could see the defenders were spread thin. Once the Skaldi won through, the remnants of the D'Angeline army would be forced into the fortress itself. After that it was only a matter of time before our supplies ran out and the Queen was forced to concede the realm.

And the Skaldi were prepared; the Skaldi were employing further Tiberian tactics and building siege towers, constructing them on the plain beyond the reach of any catapult or trebuchet mounted on the ramparts of the fortress.

"That's where we ought to attack." Ghislain jerked his chin at the nearest construction, being built with scavenged materials. "They won't be looking for it, their attention's on the tower. Agreed?"

It was agreed.

"Good." Ghislain glanced behind him. "We'll plan our retreat in stages. We need to make a clean break of it to survive."

I took one last look at the fortress and its surrounding wall. Ghislain's father was behind those crumbling bulwarks; if he were right, so was mine and my brother Luc, too. Guessing at my thoughts, Phèdre brushed her shoulder against mine in sympathy. I gave her a grateful glance before turning to study the terrain a retreat would cover, thinking about the game I'd devised for the Second Cohort when I'd been their mentor. There were plenty of opportunities to lay traps and pitfalls amongst these crags.

Grainne demanded somewhat of me in Eiran, her copper-bright hair escaping its jeweled pins and unfurling like a Skaldi warning banner in the breeze.

"Lady Grainne wishes to know what you're plotting," Phèdre informed me. "She can see it in your face."

I smiled grimly. "We're going to play a game with the Skaldi."

Ghislain de Somerville embraced the idea as though it were his own. He noted blind-ended trails, switchbacks, twists, and turns along our route as we melted deeper into the mountains, farther from the sound of battle. We established a sprawling campsite near a spring-fed creek under the cover of tall pine trees.

Our foray was two days in the planning, and we would have taken longer were it not for the sense of urgency driving us. If our plan were to have any impact whatsoever, it needed to be implemented while the Skaldi were still spread out over the plain, different tribes in their own encampments. When they broke through the inner ring of fortifications, they would be united with a fresh sense of immediacy and less vulnerable to any tactics intended to distract and divide them.

The plan was to conceal the bulk of our numbers and send a small, swift party of archers to attack the nearest siege tower at first light, setting it ablaze with oil-soaked wadding and pitch-dipped arrows while the invaders were still wrapped in their bedrolls on the churned soil of the plain. The key to its success was a long, steep gully with precarious overhangs. We trimmed saplings into levers, hewed logs into fulcrums, and hauled them into place. We drove wedges into faultlines and heaved boulders into unstable piles, preparing to release an avalanche to secure our retreat. Depending on how determined the Skaldi were to eradicate the threat we posed, it would only hold for so long. Our scouts began combing through the mountains to lay the groundwork for further withdrawal in the instance of a dogged retaliation.

It was quiet the night before the raid, or at least as quiet as an army of several thousand armed warriors and hundreds of horses could be. We were dirty and weary, but we had fresh water. Thanks to Eamonn's practical, organized approach from the very outset, we were reasonably well supplied with foodstuff and fodder. On Ghislain's orders, campfires were kept to a minimum and laid in pits—small, low-burning fires no larger than it took to cook a pot of barley pottage nestled in the embers.

A league away, campfires were spread in profusion over the war-torn fields surrounding Troyes-le-Mont.

"What happens if we fail?" Phèdre asked in a low voice.

I picked engrained grit from the calluses on my palms. "We fall back. We make another plan."

"Not just tomorrow." She gestured at the faraway plain. "What if we fail altogether, Joscelin? What if the Skaldi take Troyes-le-Mont? What happens to your father, your brother? To Ghislain's father . . . to the whole Queen's Council. The *Queen* is there. What will Waldemar Selig do to Ysandre?"

I dusted my hands. "Selig's cunning. If my father and brother are taken alive, he'll likely kill them along with a number of liege lords from Minor Houses to set an example. He'll keep higher-ranking peers like the Comte de Somerville and the Duc L'Envers as hostages. And he will either execute Queen Ysandre de la Courcel in a very public manner or—"

"Forcibly wed her and declare himself King of Terre d'Ange by right of conquest and marriage," she murmured. "I know. I don't know why I asked."

"Ysandre shouldn't be here," I said. "She should have stayed in the City of Elua with a plan to fall back to Eisande and a seaport that affords a means of escape. She should never have put herself in this position."

Phèdre raised her brows in the starlight. "Are you speaking of the Queen or me?"

"Both," I said. "What do you think Waldemar Selig would do to *you* if you were captured?"

"Me?" She looked away with a shudder. "I don't know, but it would be bad. Very bad. I'd rather die than find out."

During the hours of sullen predawn darkness, our troops moved into position, filing down the gullies through the crags. Drustan was leading a mounted sortie of fifty archers. Their mounts' hooves were wrapped in rags to muffle the sound of their descent, only a single shuttered oil lantern to light their way. Ghislain's L'Agnacite longbow archers sought strategic perches atop high outcroppings while Dalriada and D'Angeline warriors stood shoulder to shoulder, ready to lean on levers and release an avalanche.

Once again, we would be too far from the action to see what transpired, but this time, over a thousand troops were held in reserve between us and the course of battle. Phèdre's Boys would stay behind as an honor guard. I wasn't taking a chance on a raiding party stumbling across us, and if matters went badly, we had to be prepared to lead the retreat. Remy chose the tallest pine for a lookout, hacking branches away here and there to make better hand- and footholds. He clambered up the trunk a good thrice the height of the mainmast of the Royal Fleet's flagship.

Phèdre caught me contemplating doing the same. "Please don't."

"I won't," I promised.

It was difficult to be in that situation again, useless and unaware. Remy relayed what he saw unfold in the distance to those of us on the ground. Against all counsel, Drustan mab Necthana had insisted on leading the charge himself. Drustan wasn't driven by a sense of false pride or a hunger for glory, but his sense of honor demanded this of him. Now, half a league away, the party of mounted Cruithne emerged from the mountains, a trail of ants seen from far above. Remy called down that they were ready to attack.

The Skaldi guards on duty around the perimeter of the battlefield were too astonished to shout out a warning as fifty Cruithne warriors loomed out of the fading dregs of the night, riding hell for leather, dark eyes glittering in blue-whorled faces. Under Drustan's leadership, they struck swiftly and ruthlessly, setting the base of the siege tower alight and firing arrows into the sleeping Skaldi before turning back for the foothills at a flat-out gallop.

"They're coming!" Remy called out, leaning from the trunk and craning to see.

Even in the heights, we heard the roar of Waldemar Selig's army rousing and setting out in pursuit. Hundreds of them were racing to intercept Drustan's small band of archers, thousands more on their heels. Ghislain's longbowmen laid down a covering rain of arrows as our men gained the main pathway between the crags until a dwindling arsenal and Skaldi spearmen drove them back.

Too many.

There were just too many Skaldi.

They came in waves, clearing the corpses of their own comrades to create a passage. They caught Drustan's rearguard before the Dalriada pelted them from above using sling-stones heavy enough to crack a man's skull.

And still the Skaldi kept coming.

There was a series of thunderous cracks and rolling peals as Ghislain's men released the traps we'd laid. Slabs of granite split and tumbled as hammers pounded wedges into cracks, levers toppled stacked boulders.

A cloud of dust arose, our men and horses stumbling out of it. Our position here was the first fallback. They had gained a respite, but it wouldn't last. "How does it look from up there, sailor?" Ghislain de Somerville shouted to Remy.

The latter saluted with one hand. "The paths are blocked, but they're already working on it. I give it an hour." Calling for a fresh horse, Ghislain rode back for a closer look, Drustan and several of his Cruithne riding alongside him.

"Get the supply train ready to go," Eamonn said to the nearest Dalriada in Eiran, wrapping a leather strap around a grazed forearm. "*Now.*"

It wasn't long before Ghislain and his party returned with grim looks. "We retreat," the Royal Commander's son said to us. He raised his voice to issue the order. "Retreat!"

We fell back toward the east, heading deeper into the mountains. Dozens of scouts set forth in twos and threes, ranging in a semicircle to spy out the terrain before us, while a larger party followed in our wake, unleashing additional blockades to deter pursuit and erase the signs of our passage. The mood among our troops was subdued. The raid had succeeded without great losses on our side, but every one of Drustan's men caught in the rear-guard had been slain on foreign soil, never to lie buried in the land of his ancestors.

And it had slapped us in the face with the undeniable truth. No matter how many raids we attempted, we were a swarm of gnats buzzing around their perimeter, too easily swatted away. If we had more time to harry them, more time to spread rumor and superstition, to target different tribes' camps . . . it mattered naught. We *didn't* have time, and the problem was as it had ever been. With the military factions of Terre d'Ange divided, there simply wasn't a large enough force to resist the Skaldic invasion. At least we'd managed to conceal the extent of our numbers. Insofar as the Skaldi would have seen, there were only a few hundred of us. Hopefully it was enough to convince them that with Troyes-le-Mont on the verge of collapse, it wasn't worth the cost of chasing down a small rebel force.

But it left us with no avenue of attack save to continue pestering their flanks, a course of diminishing returns.

And Troyes-le-Mont would fall, and Terre d'Ange with it.

We pushed ourselves, our mounts, and our pack-mules hard that day and into the twilight, collapsing at last when Ghislain called a halt after several of Drustan's scouts returned from tracking their pursuit to report that the Skaldi had stopped to regroup and camp for the night, and appeared to be debating turning back.

Phèdre was nigh limp with exhaustion as she dismounted. We'd known worse sheer physical exhaustion fleeing across Skaldia—this was a result of living in or near mortal fear for a prolonged period of time. I was tethering our mounts for the night when one last outlying scout returned from the south, his report to the Cruarch of Alba producing a loud outburst and a volley of conversation.

"I've need of your services, my lady," Ghislain de Somerville called to his translator. "What passes?"

Leaving our small campsite, we approached Drustan's fire where he was questioning the returning scout, who was speaking in a quick, breathless tone and pointing toward the south. Frowning, Phèdre listened, then spoke with Drustan before turning back to us. Her face had gone pale. "He says there's an army, my lord. A D'Angeline army encamped in a valley not a mile from here."

There could only be one D'Angeline army hidden in these mountains.

Ghislain de Somerville said his name like a curse. "Isidore d'Aiglemort."

After debate, we decided not to strike camp that night. Our forces were equal in number, and though all our troops were weary from the long journey and the battles they had fought, we had the advantage of surprise. There was time enough to rest overnight and decide on the morrow. Or so I thought until the soft rustle of fabric awoke me to find Phèdre stepping carefully over me where I lay across the threshold. Worst of all, I realized she was returning; and shivering in a manner that had naught to do with any chill.

Nonetheless, I grabbed the warmest item at hand—my Mendacant's cloak—and wrapped her in it. "Where were you?" Her expression was strange and frozen. "What is it? Is aught amiss?"

"No." She huddled into my many-colored cloak, voice catching with a slight hysterical edge. "Not yet."

I sighed. "Phèdre."

"I couldn't sleep," she murmured. "And I had a thought. I went to speak with Ghislain about it."

"You should have—"

"I didn't want to wake you." She cut me off. "I didn't want you to talk me out of it. And yes, you *are* a light sleeper, but not for the first twenty minutes."

"All right." I waited.

Phèdre wrapped her arms around her knees. "I mean to convince Isidore d'Aiglemort to join us."

I hesitated. "Not by—"

"No!" She lifted her chin and glared at me. "Name of Elua, I'm hardly that vain nor foolish! But I do understand the levers of desire, Joscelin. And we can offer Isidore d'Aiglemort his heart's greatest desire."

"The throne?" I asked drily.

She shook her head. "He's already lost the throne. That dream is dead. I suspect he doesn't know how yet. What do you suppose he'll want when he does?"

A whisper of the chill she'd caught brushed against my skin, giving me an involuntary shudder. "Vengeance."

"Vengeance," Phèdre echoed.

CHAPTER FIFTY-SIX

A day later, a thousand of our number were positioned in the mountains surrounding the deep valley where d'Aiglemort's army was encamped, waiting for Ghislain de Somerville to give the signal.

The traitor Duc's forces included the remnants of the Allies of Camlach. They were well hidden in the valley; it was due to sheer happenstance and the skill of our Cruithne scouts that we'd come across them. But there was nowhere for them to go. At least we could continue to fall back. There were places in Caerdicca Unitas or Aragonia where we might seek asylum. There would be rebellions plotted in less central provinces like Siovale, Kusheth, and Eisande. There was the Royal Fleet, or what remained of it, and the whole of Alba lying beyond the Straits praying for its leaders' return.

But there was nowhere for an army loyal to Duc Isidore d'Aiglemort to turn.

The valley lay in shadow when the slanting rays of dawn illuminated the peaks where we were concealed. D'Aiglemort's men were just beginning to stir below when Ghislain de Somerville's standard-bearer hoisted the banner of House Courcel, and a trumpeter on either side of the valley sounded a long, ringing blast as we stepped forward to reveal ourselves ringing the rim of the valley; and along with the silver swan flew the de Somerville apple tree, the Navigator's Star and ships of House Trevalion, and the four folk of Alba: the Black Boar and the White Mare, the Red Bull and the Golden Hind.

Along with them, there flew a ragged red starburst pierced by a threadbare golden dart, the white parley flag flying beneath it.

In the valley far below, men gathered in clusters, shading their eyes and staring at the peaks. Only one stood alone, one hand resting on the hilt of his sword. Even in shade, his silver-blond hair shone like his armor.

Kilberhaar, the Skaldi called him; silver hair. The traitor Duc Isidore d'Aiglemort.

Ghislain de Somerville stepped up to the precipice, cupped his hands around his mouth, and shouted. "Isidore d'Aiglemort! We wish to parley! We send our heralds unarmed in good faith! Will you honor the concords of war?"

Rather than attempt to shout to the mountaintops, the shining figure offered an exaggerated bow.

"Go," Phèdre murmured to Remy. Her three favorite Chevaliers had insisted on serving as heralds. "Elua keep you."

"You promised to throw open the doors to the Night Court," he reminded her with a grin.

She laughed through tears. "All that you desire and more. Come back and claim it, Chevaliers."

Spurring their mounts, they set forward, descending a narrow goat-track while d'Aiglemort conferred with his lieutenants to select a receiving party to meet our heralds partway down the mountain. Atop the peaks, we watched and waited while the parties met on a rocky escarpment. If d'Aiglemort wasn't acting in good faith, his men would likely send the message by killing our heralds outright.

Instead, they listened; hands on hilts, but they listened. They rode down and relayed our request to d'Aiglemort while our heralds waited unmoving on the escarpment, and then Duc Isidore assembled a score of his own hand-picked warriors to ascend the trail and meet with our forces.

Isidore d'Aiglemort was armed and armor-clad but helmetless, his long hair glittering in the sunlight. He had black eyes that narrowed like a hunting cat's. Despite the L'Agnacite longbows nocked and leveled at him, he strode fearlessly to confront Ghislain de Somerville. "I'm here, *cousin*," he said with mocking courtesy. All the Major Houses are linked somewhere in their history by blood or marriage. "You wished to speak with me?"

Ghislain's square, handsome face was impassive, but I do believe he enjoyed delivering his response. "The emissary of Ysandre de la Courcel, Queen of Terre d'Ange, wishes to speak with you," he corrected him. "Your grace."

Raising his brows, d'Aiglemort scanned the arrayed faces. Looking past mine and ignoring Phèdre altogether, he checked in startlement at the sight of the blue-marqued Cruithne warriors led by Drustan mab Necthana in his Cruarch's crimson cape and heavy gold torque, the promise of death in his steady gaze.

"What—" d'Aiglemort began.

Inclining his head to Phèdre, Drustan stepped aside.

"My lord," she said to d'Aiglemort.

"You." He looked down, seeing her at last. A different kind of surprise widened his eyes. "I know you."

"Yes, my lord." Phèdre's tone was deceptively polite. "I gave *joie* to you at the Midwinter Masque where Baudoin played the Sun Prince. I was nine years old. You remembered when last we met." Somewhat shifted in his expression. "You were fostered among the Shahrizai," she said. "They should have taught you to recognize the mark of Kushiel's Dart, my lord."

Though a muscle in d'Aiglemort's jaw twitched, he maintained his composure. "Delaunay's *anguissette*. I remember. I had you sent to Skaldia as a favor to Melisande in reparation for a plan gone awry. I didn't expect you to survive. But your lord's death was not of my will, *anguissette*."

"So I'm given to understand," she acknowledged. "That's not why we're here."

Isidore d'Aiglemort frowned at our gathered forces. "So you're not here for revenge against me? What, then? You brought the Picti . . . how? Why?" Pausing, he saw the answer to his own question. "Anafiel Delaunay. That's what he and Quintilius Rousse were about all along, isn't it?"

"My lord." Phèdre's voice was calm, her gaze unflinching. "This is the army of the Cruarch of Alba and Ghislain de Somerville. And we are here to offer you the choice of your manner of death."

Despite the numbers arrayed against them, d'Aiglemort's escort reached for their hilts. He raised one hand to halt them. "How do you say?"

"You're a dead man, Kilberhaar." Phèdre spoke his Skaldic name and the blood drained from his face. "Terre d'Ange knows you for a traitor and Waldemar Selig used you for a fool. He'll not let you live if he defeats us. You're a fool, but a dangerous one. Selig's too smart to leave a weapon like you poised at his back. I know, I spent considerable time in his bed thanks to you. You're dead no matter who wins. We can offer you a chance to die with honor."

Isidore d'Aiglemort showed his teeth in a deadly smile, his nostrils flaring. "What possible reason would I have to take it, *anguissette*?"

I swear to Blessed Elua, if he uttered the word with that dripping disdain one more time, I was going to take his head off.

"I am Phèdre nó Delaunay," she said, soft and merciless and impervious to his tone. "And I will give you a reason, my lord. Because if you do not, and Selig prevails, Melisande Shahrizai will dance upon your grave."

She had gambled on the fact that d'Aiglemort didn't know. She was right. Betimes on the battlefield, one sees a man take his death-wound and continue to fight, unaware in that moment before the body fails that he is already dead.

Not the Duc d'Aiglemort. He knew his death-wound the instant Phèdre dealt it. His eyes burned in his sockets like embers in his stricken white face. "Melisande was in league with Selig?"

"Yes, my lord." Phèdre held his terrible gaze. "I found a letter she'd written him in her own hand. I know it well. You would be well advised to do her no more favors."

Isidore d'Aiglemort turned away to stare into the valley. No one else moved; not his men nor ours. The only sounds save the creak of leather and stomp of a hoof came from across the peaks. Somewhere a new chorus of Phèdre's Boys' marching song was being recited with bawdy laughter. On the western rim, the Twins were shouting louder than the impatient Dalriadan warriors they were trying to hush.

I touched Phèdre's elbow and she gave me a quick, grateful look.

"So I am the sword you would plunge into Waldemar Selig's heart," d'Aiglemort mused aloud.

"Yes, your grace," Ghislain said. "Camael's sword."

"The betrayer of the nation turned its savior." Isidore d'Aiglemort's laugh was a bark of irony. With the silence broken, his men and our heralds were talking in hushed whispers, neither allies nor enemies, just ordinary D'Angeline soldiers exchanging news in wartime. "Will you feed them?" he asked abruptly. "Ysandre cut off our supply train and sealed every door in Camlach against us."

"We will," Ghislain promised.

D'Aiglemort turned to face the Royal Commander's son and field marshal. "What do you propose?"

"I propose that we unite our forces and mount an attack on Selig's army," Ghislain de Somerville said. "And strike as hard as we can for Waldemar Selig." He paused. "No one is asking you to die alone, cousin."

"Selig is mine," d'Aiglemort said in a tone of absolute finality. "Swear it, and I will grant what you ask."

It was to be expected; and yet a pang went through me at the knowledge that revenge against Waldemar Selig wasn't mine to take. But it was fitting. Revenge was not Cassiel's province.

"I swear it," Ghislain said. "Do you, Duc Isidore d'Aiglemort, pledge your loyalty to her royal highness Queen Ysandre de la Courcel, on Camael's honor and in the name of Blessed Elua?"

It didn't sit well with d'Aiglemort. "I'll pledge my loyalty to the destruction of Melisande Shahrizai."

Ghislain gave Phèdre a querying glance; touching the diamond at her throat, she nodded.

It would do.

We combined our forces in the valley, sending our supply train in the first wave to ensure that the half-starved Camaelines were absorbed in the process of dividing and distributing the foodstuff we carried. Even so, it was a tense moment when our troops divided into multiple streams to descend after the pack animals, our lines strung out and exposed to projectile weapons from below.

But d'Aiglemort's men kept his word and the Duc rode alongside us as surety, sitting easy in the saddle. "I remember you," he said to me, bringing his mount alongside us where the path widened. "You were the Cassiline, weren't you? Melisande's favor."

The Cassiline.

But I wasn't the only Cassiline the Duc d'Aiglemort had known. It galled me to think that Selwyn had died for this man.

"Yes, my lord," I said in a flat tone. "Joscelin Verreuil, formerly of the Cassiline Brotherhood."

"You're better off," d'Aiglemort said drily. "Cold faith and hot steel are an unnatural mix. I'm impressed, though. I'd have thought slavery would kill a Cassiline. I'll want to hear all you know of Waldemar Selig later," he added, spurring his mount past us as the trail ahead narrowed.

"If we didn't need him, I swear I'd put a dagger in his heart," I muttered to Phèdre through gritted teeth. "How can you trust him?"

"He was a hero once." Her voice held soft regret; she had been a nine-year-old adept-in-training at Cereus House offering *joie* in a crystal glass to a dashing prince and the hero of the Allies of Camlach as their stars were on the rise. "Whatever else he may have been, he was that. If we succeed—or even if we die trying—he'll be remembered as a hero in the end. Without this, his name will ring throughout history as Waldemar Selig's dupe. And he dies knowing Melisande used him to do it."

"*Why*, though?" I asked. "She could have gained the nation with him."

Phèdre shook her head. "The Skaldi would still have invaded. Selig was using him, too. Who knows what *he* promised Melisande? At his side, she stands to gain two nations. She played a deep game. If Selig wins, you can count the number of survivors who know her role on one hand. He'll have an empire. Even if he weds Ysandre, sooner or later he'll need an empress he can trust."

It had never occurred to me that Melisande Shahrizai was playing for the rulership of not one, but two kingdoms. "Is that what you think?"

"What else?" she said. "Melisande plays for high stakes. I can't think of any higher. Ysandre's the only loose thread, and those are easily trimmed." She frowned in thought. "Unless she means to eliminate Selig himself once he's gained the D'Angeline throne and full mastery of both realms."

"Elua have mercy." I gazed at the armies spreading across the valley floor below us, already wracked by casualties. "How could she bear so much blood on her hands? How could anyone?"

"I don't know," Phèdre said quietly. "It's the game that compels her. I don't think she ever reckoned the cost in human lives, not truly."

"Nonetheless," I said. "It's monstrous."

"I know."

Torches burned long into the night after our army was encamped and our combined commanders met to discuss an attack on Troyes-le-Mont. For all that I wished I'd been able to coerce Phèdre to shelter at House Trevalion after we'd defeated the Skaldi at the Rhenus, these discussions would have been a great deal more difficult without a translator. Drustan's D'Angeline had improved, but not to the point where he could translate fluidly for the understanding of the Lords of the Dalriada, who had no particular interest in mastering any foreign tongue. By dint of necessity, Phèdre had acquired the knack of nigh simultaneous translation, the words flowing through her like water through an aqueduct.

Isidore d'Aiglemort and the Allies of Camlach were ready for a battle, readier than they'd known. They were hungry and gaunt, but there was fire in their bellies. At this point, they were supposed to be the saviors of the realm with the Skaldi in retreat, enjoying the prospect of whatever d'Aiglemort had promised Waldemar Selig in exchange for posing as a threat to the realm—wealth, political alliance, a seat at the civilized world's table. Instead, they were the laughingstock of the Skaldi and pariahs in their own country.

Not every man would jump at the chance to risk death to restore their honor; but the scions of Camael's lineage would.

Plans were debated and analyzed, laid and sketched onto pieces of foolscap. The Camaeline infantry would lead the attack. Once the Skaldi realized they were under attack from behind their lines and began to rally, Drustan and the Twins would unloose attacks on the northern and southern flanks of the Skaldi. In the ensuing chaos, the first wave of infantry would part to force an opening into which Isidore d'Aiglemort would lead the Allies of Camlach's cavalry like a spear thrown at Waldemar Selig's heart.

The strategy assumed that Selig would turn to meet this new threat head-on and lead the counterattack in person, which Phèdre and I both thought was nigh certain. "Waldemar Selig is a warlord, not a head of state," she reminded the others. "If he's going to keep Skaldia's loyalty, he needs to keep the myth alive."

Waldemar the Blessed, proof against steel.

"How good is he?" d'Aiglemort asked me abruptly. "Do you know?"

"He disarmed me in the heat of battle." It was a bitter memory. "He is that good, my lord."

D'Aiglemort understood. I loathed him with reason, but we were both fluent in the language of steel. "Then I shall have to be better."

I hesitated, then gave him honest advice. "Don't wait to engage him. He'll move inside your guard while you do. He fights without thinking, the way you or I breathe. Don't be fooled by his size. He's faster than you think."

The traitor Duc nodded and gazed at the map of his fate. "Thank you."

Despise him or no, I hoped my counsel would serve him well. It wasn't a battle we could afford to lose.

CHAPTER FIFTY-SEVEN

The last defensive wall surrounding Troyes-le-Mont had fallen.

That was the news we received on the morrow when the latest teams of scouts returned. The Skaldi pursuing us had retreated. All eyes were on the fortress now, and we didn't have long before it fell, too.

It was strange once again being in the war party, yet not of it. Mayhap it was the inescapable awareness that my father and brother were behind those fortress walls and there was nothing I could do to save them.

If I weren't a Cassiline . . .

I wasn't, though; I was anathema. But I felt Cassiel's presence abiding in my soul. I believed, truly believed that I had upheld the one vow that mattered most, the only vow that mattered in the end.

Protect and serve.

I could no more leave Phèdre's side in wartime than Elua's Oak could tear its roots from the earth and walk the streets of the City. It was the job of the oak to protect. This was the course that fate had cast me upon when I was born a middle son to a family that observed the old noble traditions. This was the fate I had chosen of my own accord when it took a turn no one but poets and playwrights could have anticipated.

Nonetheless, the sight of the fortress of Troyes-le-Mont with a sea of Skaldi warriors breaking like waves against its foundation made my heart ache. It took two days' march to relocate our army without detection. With the sun setting blood-red over the plain, the fortress walls were still standing, the Courcel swan still flying from atop the ramparts. The defenders were repelling the Skaldi with arrows and trebuchets. The Cruithne had succeeded in destroying the outermost siege tower and the half-burned skeleton of another crumbled alarmingly near the moat. The Skaldi had constructed two more that were nearly in position and they were dismantling the other to build a battering ram.

Once those were in place, it was only a matter of time.

There were more guards posted around the perimeter of the battlefield, but discipline in the sprawling encampment was lax. They were prepared for another attack by a small group of nimble raiders, not a full-blown assault from a sizeable army.

"We'll wait for daybreak," Ghislain de Somerville murmured as we surveyed the scene. "Pray those in the fortress know us for allies. The sooner they counterattack the Skaldi rear, the better our chances."

"Do you think they'll flock to the d'Aiglemort eagle?" Isidore d'Aiglemort asked. "Don't count on it, cousin. Better we fly no standard."

"My father's no fool," Ghislain said curtly. "Drustan's men are flying the Cullach Gorrym. He'll know."

"If he can even see the Black Pig over thirty thousand howling Skaldi." D'Aiglemort shrugged. "Listen, man. We'll do as much damage as we can and pray it's enough to break the siege. But for every minute your father hesitates, and for every minute it takes them to marshal a counterattack, we'll die by the hundreds. That's just the truth of it."

One of Rousse's long-sighted sailors atop the vantage point with us caught his breath in a hiss, pointing.

I wished he hadn't. Far below, Skaldi warriors were leading a line of prisoners along the northern verge of the plain, shoving them when they stumbled. Women. The prisoners were D'Angeline women, their stained and torn gowns yet bright against the muddy field of the war camp. They clustered in brief knots like flowers blooming, petals dropping as men vied for bedmates and hauled them away. Phèdre froze, unable to look away. I drew her back and she turned in my arms, shuddering and hiding her face against my chest.

Isidore d'Aiglemort's expression was somber. "I am sorry," he said quietly. "For what was done to you both. For what it's worth, I am sorry."

It wasn't worth a damned thing, but I suppose he didn't need to die hearing it. I nodded in acknowledgment.

"Daybreak," Ghislain said.

Our own encampment was as secure as we could make it. Between the Cruithne and the addition of d'Aiglemort's men we had ample sentries. At Ghislain's insistence, the company of Phèdre's Boys had been assigned until further notice to serve as the dedicated honor guard of the Queen's emissary. If this gambit failed, they would escort us in a retreat. Once there was no one left to resist them, the Skaldi were likely to take the City of Elua. We would retreat to Marsilikos. Thanks to its strategic location as the realm's largest seaport, it would be one of the last strongholds to surrender.

For what it was worth, as d'Aiglemort had said, which was next to nothing. Pockets of resistance would exist, but the realm would be gutted and transformed into a Skaldic fiefdom. It was hard to contemplate plans for a future in which everything I held dear had been destroyed. I daresay Phèdre was feeling much the same way. She had been quiet since we'd seen the Skaldi thanes taking bed-slaves. It was a long journey and we'd come around full circle to confront the fate from which she'd escaped.

"Try to sleep," I said to her in the little tent that Remy had commandeered for her weeks ago. "Do you want me to stay?"

She paused, then shook her head. "I need to be alone with my thoughts tonight. But will you do me a favor?"

I sat back on my heels. "What?"

Phèdre wrapped her arms around her knees. Her eyes were soft and warm and shining. "Let down your hair for me."

Hey, boy, pretty boy, let down your long fair hair, oh.

It was a request as intimate as a touch, almost shocking; the jolt of a spear hidden behind the brush of a silken hem. I felt unaccountably shy lifting my hands, unknotting the leather thong, untwining the plaits of my long single braid. It was foolish; Phèdre nó Delaunay and I had been together in all the naked glory with which Adonai the Creator imbued humankind, she had seen me, seen this, combed out the full length of my bath-damp hair with her own hands . . . and yet.

I let it spill over my shoulders, hanging straight and pale gold down my back. "Better?"

"Yes." There were tears in her eyes, welling without spilling until she sniffled involuntarily, and both of us laughed. "Thank you."

I hesitated. "You're sure . . . ?"

Her voice was firm. "I'm sure."

I took up my usual post wrapped in a bedroll outside the tent's threshold. Lying with my arms folded behind my head, I stared at the stars spangling the summer night. It was warm; it would be hot as hell on the battlefield tomorrow. Dusty, too. It hadn't rained for days. I couldn't remember if it had rained since we'd made landfall. I wasn't even sure if we were before or past the midsummer solstice. Here on the eve of a battle for the fate of the realm,

I ought to be thinking profound thoughts. Instead, I watched the stars and listened to the rustling, creaking, shuffling, muttering sounds of the camp until I drifted into a fitful doze . . .

. . . and awoke to silence.

No.

Nothing had changed in the camp, it was quieter, but there were the same normal sounds of an army at rest, sentries on duty moving as little as possible to avoid awakening their sleeping comrades in arms.

Not silence.

Not stillness.

Absence.

I knew before I looked, but of course, I looked anyway. The tent was empty. I had a sense of a lingering blessing, a brush of sorrowful grace upon my brow. Gone. Phèdre was gone. And I knew exactly where and why she'd gone. I really ought to have seen it coming. She'd even bade me farewell.

I stepped outside of the tent. It was mayhap an hour or two past moonrise. She would have waited until I fell asleep, waited for those twenty minutes when I slept hardest to creep past me. Betimes I forgot that Delaunay had trained her in the arts of covertcy and stealth.

I lifted my face to the night sky and spoke a prayer to Cassiel. "*Use me.*"

It wasn't the refiner's fire I'd felt in the hills outside Bryn Gorrydum; only a spark tingling in my palms, in the soles of my feet. It would come. I had passed through water and fire and over steel to reach this moment. My hands moved unbidden, binding my loose hair in haphazard Skaldic braids that I twined together and knotted. It was a pity I didn't have my hooded wolfskin cloak anymore. It had probably been burned with the rest of our filthy garments months ago. I checked my weapons and tested the edges one last time.

Phèdre's campsite had a few yards' worth of privacy for her tent. Elsewhere, men were sleeping cheek by jowl, crowded as we were while trying to keep an entire army from detection. I stepped around slumbering figures when I could and over a few I couldn't avoid otherwise. There were sentries and messengers delivering quiet reports and soldiers with full bladders stumbling toward the latrine ditches.

I got past the first ring of sentries before a voice stopped me. "You're going after her, aren't you?"

"Yes."

Isidore d'Aiglemort rose from the boulder on which he'd been seated. "She awakened me to tell me the fortress would be awaiting our attack."

I nodded. "And you let her go."

"I was going to," d'Aiglemort said. "She slipped away while I was speaking to a sentry. You don't actually think you can save her, do you?"

I ignored the question. "Don't worry, I won't give us away."

He bared his teeth in a bitter moonlit smile. "I'd kill you myself if I thought otherwise."

"You could try." I tested a buckle-strap on my baldric. "We're seldom given a chance to spend the coin of our death as we choose. I had a friend at the Prefectory, Selwyn de Gaunt. Do you remember him? He gave his life to save yours."

D'Aiglemort's face was spare and pitiless in its stark hard-edged beauty. Cousin, kinsman, peers called each other; but we were all kin, highborn and low. All of us were descended from the offspring of gods and angels, all of us had traces of ichor whispering in the red mortal blood of our veins.

But I was Cassiel's Servant, and that was a different thing altogether.

"Yes," d'Aiglemort said. "I remember."

"Good." I flexed my hands in their chainmail-backed gauntlets. "Make your death count, your grace. For all of us."

To that Isidore d'Aiglemort said nothing.

I walked away from him, away from the army, away from the encampment. Away from Ghislain de Somerville, the Royal Commander's loyal son. Away from Drustan mab Necthana, the Cruarch of Alba, who had come here following a dream and the promise of love and two kingdoms shared in peace; away from the Lords of the Dalriada, Eamonn and Grainne, who had come out of loyalty to an old oath of alliance, out of high spirits and adventure, each one spurring the other. Away from all the Cruithne and Dalriada who followed them to fight on foreign soil for glory and deeds worthy of poets' tales; away from Phèdre's Boys, bawdy, brave, and irrepressible.

It was a path strewn with loss and leave-taking, from Delaunay's murder to Hyacinthe's lonely fate, and all the casualties along the way—all those sailors and soldiers lost to the Master of the Straits' fury, to the battlefield. Moonlight cast the world in stark blacks and ambiguous greys. I moved swiftly but carefully, using clouds crossing the moon's surface to blend my movements with the shifting night as I ventured past our perimeter into the miles of no-man's-land that lay between the mountains and Troyes-le-Monte.

It would have gone faster if I'd taken a horse, but with the sentries on alert, a rider was far too likely to be spotted. At my best guess, Phèdre had at least an hour on me, but I was faster than her on foot. I didn't know how she planned to get past the ruined walls of the outer bulwarks. The breaches were heavily guarded. Flirt, mayhap; it would be easy enough for her to pose as a prisoner of war, although I couldn't conceive what excuse she'd make for being outside the walls. And of course if she were seized, she might never reach the fortress.

I should have known that would be her goal the moment d'Aiglemort said somewhat about those who would lose their lives because we were unable to give the fortress advance warning. I knew she felt responsible for carrying Ysandre's word across the seas and sending brave warriors to die for it.

Was it a worthy risk?

No.

Was she going to do it anyway? Yes, absolutely; because she was gods-driven, and having conceived this thing, no matter how long the odds against its success, she was bound to attempt it or die trying.

Or both.

At fifty yards away from the bulwarks, the stench of the battlefield struck me; ordure and piss, men, horses, woodsmoke and charred flesh, with a faint underlying note of rot. The Skaldi burn their dead, but I had a feeling there were hundreds of D'Angeline bodies in shallow trenches nearby.

There was a sentry posted at every breach, silhouettes visible in darkness alleviated by the campfires and torches beyond the outer walls, and mounted patrols circulating inside the perimeter every quarter hour. I scouted some ways around the bulwarks in either direction, walls undermined by sappers and eventually burst by rams, possibly the great one they were hauling toward the gates. To the north I found a gap in the timbers and broken masonry just large enough for a slender-shouldered person to wriggle into the structure. Too small for me, but I'd wager ducats to ducks Phèdre had squeezed through this narrow aperture.

Since I couldn't go through it, I went over it. It was a long, tricky climb up a tumbling slope of granite blocks that threatened to slide underfoot, and one slip left me dangling from one handhold and frantically searching for another, gritting my teeth to keep silent when my scrabbling fingernails tore.

Atop the wall, I lay flat on my belly and considered my options. Tens of thousands of dozing Skaldi warriors lay between me and the fortress; presumably, the eternal love and bane of my life was picking her way through them on foot, trying to avoid being captured and violated before warning the defenders of Troyes-le-Monte. I strained my eyes trying to see one small figure walking a sword's edge between life and death across the plain, but it was a useless venture—I couldn't have identified my own father at twenty paces in the muddy flame-streaked darkness.

My father . . . Elua, that was one of the reasons Phèdre was doing this, too.

Did she truly imagine I could face my family after letting her die at Waldemar Selig's hands?

It didn't matter; I'm not sure Phèdre *did* think when the gods' prompting was upon her, any more than I did during a battle. I understood it. Somewhere inside she had to know that I would awaken, that I would come for her. That I would always come for her. As I had to acknowledge that if she'd told me, I wouldn't have let her go, I would have done everything to thwart her and keep her safe.

So she hadn't told me.

And here I was.

It wouldn't be easy to reach the fortress itself. Since the siege began, Selig had succeeded in keeping the defenders contained, unable to send or receive word. Now every window within the fortress would be shuttered, every door barred, every possible ingress fortified. The Skaldi had had days to study the battlements. There was no unguarded approach, no secret passage, no hidden postern gate for Phèdre to essay.

But there was a half-burnt siege tower. At this distance, in this darkness, the four-story-high structure wasn't even visible. When I closed my eyes, I could see it positioned at the northeastern corner of the keep. According to Ghislain, there were trebuchets on the ramparts, and a stockpile of barrels of *feu d'Hellas,* if it hadn't run out. There was a good wide moat around the keep and the Skaldi hadn't managed to bridge it yet. We hadn't seen the defenders' war machines in action, but something had taken off the top of that siege tower and set it ablaze. Assuming Phèdre was able to reach it under cover of darkness and climb to the top of the brittle, sooty structure without it collapsing beneath her, there was a slight chance she might be seen from the ramparts and manage to deliver a warning.

If I were able to help her, it would double our chances of success. The moon was riding lower in the sky. Time to steal a disguise and a horse.

I swear, the plains of Troyes-le-Mont were worse than the Allthing. At least the cold had frozen the mire of thousands of Skaldi tribesmen. In the D'Angeline summer, they'd not bothered with shelter, but mostly slept where they lay in proximity to their tribe's cooking fires. After emerging from the shadow of the bulwarks I walked soft-footed among them, avoiding the glint of eyes partially open beneath slitted lids to find an outlying thane deep in slumber. He wore a filthy woolen cowl that I plucked from around his neck, pulling the hood over my head. I grabbed a round wooden buckler from beside another sleeping fellow and made for the nearest picket line.

All quiet, still.

Luck was with me; the horses were the short, stocky Skaldic breed, good-natured and docile, left tacked and half tended in the crude hackamores and saddles the Skaldi use. I whispered softly in its whiskery ear as I untied the reins and eased it away from the picket line. There was a tall staff mounted with a pair of elk horns leaning against the sapling trestle. I took that for good measure, hoping to pass as a tribal standard-bearer.

I turned my mount's head toward the fortress and set forth at a quick jog-trot, reckoning the distance over level ground to be about half a mile.

I got halfway there before all hell broke loose.

CHAPTER FIFTY-EIGHT

There were Skaldi voices raising a hue and cry near the fortress.

I was too far away to make out the words, but it was obvious from the tenor that somewhat had transpired. It had begun, and the odd sense of calm and unrealness I'd felt gave way to a cold, heavy surge of dread, my heart dropping like a lead plumb weight into the pit of my stomach.

The voices rose and the watchfires nearest the fortress blazed higher. Torches were dipped and lit, streaking trails of flame as Skaldi warriors ran for the damaged siege tower. They clustered at the base of the tower, yelling to each other, then began climbing the splintering, crumbling lattice of charred beams.

I dug my heels into my mount's flanks and whacked its haunches with the flat of one hand, plunging forward.

The shouting came toward me like waves as word passed from mouth to mouth, the news travelling through the Skaldi forces in a series of ripples. I understood enough of their tongue that I needed no translation. It was nothing according to the first wave, only a reluctant bed-slave putting up a fight; no, it was one of the defenders trying to escape the fortress; no, it was a spy trying to warn the defenders.

Yes, it was a spy.

Yes, it was a spy; it was a woman and she had been captured; yes, it was a woman, Selig's runaway bed-slave.

Yes, she was alone.

And then as the waves spread outward, the tide against which I was beating shifted, and everyone's attention turned toward the fortress where the watch-fires were being stoked higher and the torches forming a great ring like an arena before the main gates of the fortress of Troyes-le-Mont where the defenders watched on the ramparts and Skaldi thanes held the small figure they'd captured on the scaffolding of the burned tower because Waldemar Selig was coming for her.

In the wake of that rumor was a hush that scared me more than the shouting. The vast scattered patchwork of Skaldi soldiers were assembling in loose formation, crowding together and straining to see, blocking my passage. I'd thought to save space cutting across the battlefield on horseback and I was caught in a mass of foot-soldiers. "Move!" I hissed in my best Skaldic. "Now!"

They shifted somewhat in response to my command, to the pressure of nigh a ton of equine flesh, to the antlered tribal standard I'd stolen, but not enough to allow me to make consistent progress toward the fortress. At least my horse was stubborn and game, tossing its head impatiently and shoving forward through every gap in the crowd while I prayed none of the Skaldi took too close a look at me in passing.

Atop the ramparts of Troyes-le-Mont, more torches were kindling, shadows wavering on the faces of the parapets as the besieged defenders ringed the ramparts, trying to determine what passed in the small hours of the night. They found out soon enough. Still caught mid-army, I couldn't see the torchlit square before the gated fortress moat where Phèdre's captors forced her to kneel. I didn't see Waldemar Selig dismount and strike her across the face, holding her head upright by a fistful of hair.

I did hear that the spy had managed to convey a message to the fortress, that the archers manning the meurtrières, the arrow-slits, had heard it. I heard the words of that message delivered in D'Angeline repeated in phonetic form and laughed inside with an admiration almost absurd in its purity.

Tell the Queen that Delaunay's other pupil has done her bidding.

Even here, even now, Phèdre had conceived a way to deliver the message in a manner that meant absolutely nothing to anyone save the Queen's loyalists. Waldemar Selig could trumpet his suspicions all night long, but there was nothing he could prove. Somehow, against all likelihood, the D'Angeline bed-slave fit for Kings had found a way to deliver a warning to the Queen.

I didn't hear the threats Selig uttered for Phèdre alone. It didn't matter. Whatever he threatened, she refused. But I did hear him raise his voice loud enough for the watchers on the ramparts to hear. "Ysandre de la Courcel!" he shouted to the fortress. "See what becomes of spies and traitors!"

Phèdre's scream set the night on fire.

It was a raw, throat-shredding scream of pure physical agony that lifted the hair on the nape of my neck and strung my nerves to breaking. I don't recall lashing my mount or trampling foot-soldiers, only that my entire world was ringing like a struck gong and there was a gyre of pure fury building inside me. The muttering Skaldi soldiers packed onto the battlefield began falling silent around me. No one touched me. I rode through the aisle as they parted, yanking off the hooded cowl.

The fortress hulked in the background like a sheer dark face crowned with tips of fire. Two White Brethren held Phèdre's arms stretched wide as she knelt between them, her head hung low. The back of her gown had been sliced open and Waldemar Selig stood behind her with a hunting knife, the edge set against a thick, meaty slab of skin he was methodically cutting and peeling from her shoulder blade. The wet flesh glistened in the torchlight, a sheet of blood spilling down her back.

Waldemar Selig was skinning her alive.

He began to cut and she screamed again, an ear-splitting scream that rang and rang inside my skull.

I raised my voice like it was Cassiel's own bedamned flaming sword. "Waldemar Selig, I challenge you to the holmgang!"

Selig paused; his thanes loosed their grip on Phèdre, who crumpled bleeding into the dirt. Selig stared at me in disbelief. At last he believed and laughed with joyous hatred, opening his arms wide. Blood dripped from his hunting knife. "You? You, too? It would have been too much to ask! Ah, All-Father Odhinn is generous! Yes, Josslin Verai, let us dance upon the hides, and let Terre d'Ange see how Waldemar Selig deals with her champions!"

A dozen spears were leveled at me. Skaldi thanes hauled me from the saddle and divested me of my purloined buckler and the elk-horn staff, but they dealt me no injuries.

That privilege awaited Waldemar Selig.

The White Brethren had dragged Phèdre back to her knees. Sagging between them, she looked at me through agonized tears with a mixture of bewilderment and fury, not understanding yet what I meant to do. It was the one thing, the only thing, left to do. But I needed to distract Selig to do it.

Waldemar the Blessed, proof against steel. It wasn't mere ego, it was part of his mythos. He was a leader who thought, but the Skaldi would never have united behind him if they hadn't believed in the myth. I think Selig had begun to believe it, too. The Skaldi were roaring, eager for the holmgang. The tidal wave of news rippled and reverberated—it wasn't just a mad D'Angeline with a death wish who had challenged Selig, it was Gunter's kennel-slave, the other runaway slave.

Selig's eyes were keen with anticipation. "You know this is just for show," he said to me as the hide was staked in place. He had sensual lips, his auburn beard trimmed around them. I would have liked to split my knuckles against his teeth. "You're a dead man."

I said nothing. He was right. The rods anchoring the hide were pounded into the packed soil. The pounding continued as the spearmen drummed their butts and the swordsmen began smacking the flats of their blades against their bucklers, raising a steady din.

Waldemar Selig and I took our places. I bowed to him with Cassiline precision and kept my features schooled to inexpressiveness. He bowed to the fortress with a sweeping, mocking flourish, echoing his words in gesture: *Behold, see how I deal with Terre d'Ange's spies and champions.*

Selig was as I remembered him, tall and broad-shouldered, moving with the spare, purposeful grace of a man whose body was doing exactly what it was born to do. He thought he had my measure and he had, once; but I wasn't the same man he had faced in the snowy depth of a Skaldic winter.

And I didn't care about winning. I wasn't going to survive this encounter. All I needed was enough space and a heartbeat's worth of time to do what must be done. I had space, more space than I needed. Waldemar Selig himself had ordered it cleared for the holmgang so that the defenders on the ramparts and Phèdre kneeling in blood-streaked agony could watch him defeat and kill me.

The rhythmic pounding grew louder. In accordance with the rules of the holmgang, as the challenger, I'd ceded the first blow to Selig. He set his shield, hefted his blade, and grinned at me before he struck. Name of Elua, he was fast; faster than I remembered. I was glad that I'd warned d'Aiglemort. I parried and spun, then reversed my motion and cracked his buckler with a backhanded blow. I felt his blade etch a shallow slice in my flesh as it glanced off the top of my right vambrace and rent my sleeve.

Damn.

First blood; the beating of spears and blades halted while the Skaldi watched to see if my blood would fall and stain the hide. Without taking his gaze from mine, Waldemar Selig reached behind him for another shield. I tugged on the buckles of my vambrace with my teeth, shifting it to stanch the blood.

Selig didn't wait for me to set my stance before attacking, he simply came at me with that overwhelming combination of strength and speed and innate skill—but my feet were already in motion, tracing steps I'd traced thousands upon thousands of times before, the very first quarter-turn pivot in the very first Cassiline form accompanied by a high, sweeping blow, the point of my sword scoring a line the length of Waldemar Selig's jaw.

It happened fast. A red rivulet of blood spilled into the gold-wrapped points of Selig's forked beard. Fat drops of blood gathered, swelled, and fell to splatter on the worn hide like rain.

I bowed and sheathed my sword.

I was Cassiel's weapon now.

Slowly and deliberately, Waldemar Selig wiped one palm along his bleeding jaw. He shook it contemptuously, spattering more blood. I had won the holmgang, but I had lost the battle before I set foot on the hide. That was all right. The victory I was fighting for wasn't what Selig thought it was. Raising his sword, he pointed it at my unprotected heart. "For that," he said softly, "I will let you live long enough to see what's left of her when I'm done, and have given what remains to my men."

I drew my daggers. "In Cassiel's name, I protect and serve."

With those words, the world dwindled to a single point. I was in motion before Selig had any idea what I was doing, and I don't think he would have conceived it regardless. The *terminus* has no place in Skaldi culture.

The *terminus* has no place in the world, save for that place where the perfect whiteness of utter despair meets the blazing glory of absolute faith. Through the smoke and firelight and tears that streaked my vision, I saw Phèdre understand at last. A look of relief and unspeakable gratitude settled over her like a mantle. Hanging between the White Brethren, she lifted her chin, the torn neckline of her gown exposing the bare skin of her white throat, Melisande's diamond shining above her heart like a beacon to the blade.

Love flooded her gaze and her lips moved . . .

Do it.

My right-hand dagger gleamed in the air as I tossed it end over end. I had all the time in the world. Across the square, Phèdre's eyes closed softly, her pulse throbbing in the hollow of her throat. I set the point of my left-hand dagger below my right ear, my gauntleted fist wrapped tight around the hilt, ready to slit my throat as I caught the tip of the airborne dagger and cocked my arm for the final throw—

Horns.

Those were battle horns sounding from the ramparts, and across the moat, the creak of chains as the portcullis gate inched upward. Elua have mercy, they were risking opening the entire bedamned fortress to give us a chance to escape. I flung my right-hand dagger, taking out the White Brother on Phèdre's left while I crossed the space between us at a dead run. The second thane barely had time to release Phèdre and fumble for his blade before I retrieved my thrown dagger and took him out with a quick double strike.

"Run." I grabbed Phèdre's arm and hauled her to her feet and it was like taking the blade's edge to my own skin, I could see she was strained to breaking with teeth-clenching agony, but I couldn't carry her fast enough. "Run!"

I hauled her stumbling in my wake, the Skaldi army rousing with outrage behind us; and then trebuchets thumped atop the ramparts and the skies lit up as gouts of flaming pitch were hurled at the Skaldi. Behind us, men screamed and hit the ground rolling, desperate to extinguish the clinging flames.

"Advance!" Waldemar Selig was roaring at his troops. "Advance and get ahead of it, you fools!"

I didn't dare look, but I heard their shouting surge closing in on our heels—and then the horns sounded again and four Siovalese cataphracts came pounding across the drawbridge, horses and warriors encompassed in gleaming armor. Wielding longswords and battle-axes, they pushed back the Skaldi line. A company of lightly armed Akkadian horsemen with turbaned helmets followed them, half of them loosing arrows into the tightly packed mass of the Skaldi front line.

One leaned over in the saddle as he swooped past, extending one arm like a hook. "Cassiline!" he shouted. "I'll take her!" I half threw, half shoved Phèdre over the pommel of his saddle. Another rider stuck out a hand without looking and I grabbed it and swung astride behind him.

"Back!"

"Back, fall back!"

One more bucket-load of *feu d'Hellas* arched flaming from the ramparts, sparks raining down on the battlefield as the cataphracts split off and thundered back into the keep, followed by the light cavalry.

I glanced over my jouncing shoulder as we made our escape, seeing the last two riders forced to leap the dwindling distance to gain the drawbridge as it slanted upward, defenders frantically hauling on the chains. The drawbridge slammed into place, the counterweights were loosed to close the portcullis with a bone-shuddering thud, and the gates were barred.

Phèdre and I were inside Troyes-le-Mont.

And we were alive.

CHAPTER FIFTY-NINE

The torchlit courtyard of the keep was crowded with horses and men. I slid over the crupper of my rescuer's horse, scrambling to reach Phèdre as her own rescuer—whom I realized to my surprise was Duc Barquiel L'Envers—lifted her carefully down.

She hit the flagstones and kept going, her eyes rolling back in her head. Figures on foot pressed close around.

"Let her be!" I took a knee beside her. "Send for a doctor. Now!"

Phèdre gripped my hand with bone-grinding strength, her expression incandescent. "Blessed buggering Elua!" she hissed. *"It hurts!"*

"Make way for the Queen!" a herald's voice shouted over the din, and there was Ysandre de la Courcel and her entourage, including a pair of grim-looking Cassiline Brothers some twenty years my senior and an Eisandine chirurgeon with a calm demeanor who shooed away everyone to examine Phèdre.

"Messire Verreuil. It *is* you." The Queen's face was pale and haunted, her eyes set in violet-smudged hollows. She looked like she scarce dared breathe, let alone hope. "Tell me what passes! Is it possible?"

"Yes, your majesty." I hovered over the chirugeon's shoulder as she gently sponged away the blood and called for her assistant to thread a sturdy needle. "But the honor of telling you should fall to Phèdre."

"It looks worse than it is," the chirurgeon added helpfully, pressing the strip of raw skin and exposed flesh in place on Phèdre's shoulder blade. "It appears he was aiming for pain and not death."

Phèdre scarce waited for the last knot to be tied and bandaging secured before she was on her feet, curtseying to the Queen with her blood-soaked gown hanging half-loose from her shoulders. "Your majesty."

To her credit, Ysandre de la Courcel, Queen of Terre d'Ange, gathered her composure and inclined her head to acknowledge her emissary. "Phèdre nó Delaunay. Have we understood your message aright?"

"Well?" Barquiel L'Envers echoed her query, and the Royal Commander Percy de Somerville was pushing through the throng, his broad L'Agnacite farmer's face streaked with pitch soot.

I winced as Phèdre drew a breath so deep it strained her bandages. "An army of seven thousand stands ready to attack Selig's rearguard at daybreak," she announced, the news carrying across the courtyard.

A spark kindled in the Royal Commander's gaze. "Seven thousand Albans!"

"No, my lord," Phèdre said. "Half the force is Alban. The other half is Isidore d'Aiglemort's army."

I hadn't expected cheers at the mention of d'Aiglemort's name, but I hadn't expected the uproar of protest in the wake of Phèdre's announcement, and I felt her taken aback by the strength of it. I gave her my arm to steady herself, her fingers curling hard around the rim of my left vambrace.

"D'Aiglemort!" Duc Barquiel had wrenched off his conical Akkadian helmet and thrown it in annoyance. "Whose fool idea was that?"

"Mine, my lord," Phèdre said in an even tone. "It was implemented by my lord de Somerville's son."

"Ghislain?" Percy de Somerville demanded. "Ghislain is with them? Alive and well?"

"Yes, my lord, along with a few hundred of his men," she confirmed. "He left Marc de Trevalion in command in Azzalle along with Admiral Rousse. And then they planned the attack together—Ghislain, I mean, with d'Aiglemort and Drustan. And the Twins."

"The Lords of the Dalriada," I added, seeing the blank faces. "Their army rides with the Cruarch's."

"Why would Isidore d'Aiglemort aid us?" the Siovalese Comte de Toluard inquired as he joined the impromptu conference.

"Because he is D'Angeline, my lord, and he is dead no matter what happens," Phèdre said grimly. "I gave him the choice of a hero's death."

Barquiel L'Envers fixed her with a hard stare. "Are you that sure of him, Delaunay's pupil, that you'd risk our lives on it?"

"Yes, my lord. I am." She returned his gaze measure for measure. "Why did you risk your life for mine when you despised my lord Delaunay?"

"Because as you say, we are D'Angeline, Phèdre nó Delaunay," L'Envers said wryly. "And because young Verreuil here afforded Selig's men a distraction. Good thing we got there before you played out your Cassiline endgame, eh?" he added, ignoring my incredulous look to clap me on the shoulder. "But d'Aiglemort is a traitor. What does he care who sits the throne if he's dead either way? We played him false sending Baudoin's Glory-Seekers. Why wouldn't he take the chance to return the favor?"

It was a fair question, even if his delivery made me grit my teeth. Phèdre squeezed my steel-clad forearm, asking me silently to stand down. Ysandre had made no comment since we had delivered our news. Now she looked to Phèdre for her answer, listening and deliberating her own response.

"Oh, Isidore d'Aiglemort cares." Phèdre let go of my arm, her hand closing around the diamond that hung from her throat. "He is not playing for you, your majesty," she said to Ysandre de la Courcel. "He is playing against Melisande Shahrizai."

No one spoke for a moment.

"That would do it," admitted Barquiel L'Envers, who appeared to have no intention of standing on ceremony with his niece the Queen.

"My lord de Somerville!" Ysandre's voice was crisp as she asserted control of the situation. "We will support our allies and mount a counterattack on the Skaldi army. Will you lead it?"

Percy de Somerville bowed. "Your majesty, I will."

Outside the thick walls of the fortress came the sound of a renewed assault. A messenger from the gatehouse came at a run to announce that the Skaldi were making another attempt to dismantle the remnants of the siege tower and bridge the moat, setting off a round of debate amongst the commanders.

"Your pardon, my lord." I caught Tibault de Toluard's attention. "Can you tell me if my father is here? Chevalier Millard Verreuil of Siovale? He'd have come with my brother Luc and a few men-at-arms."

The Comte shook his head with regret. "I'm sorry, messire, there are some sixteen hundred Siovalese. They're under the Duc de Perigeux's direct command."

"His grace de Perigeux is on the battlements," a passing soldier offered. "The trebuchet on the north wall's jammed."

"Go find them," Phèdre said to me; I hadn't realized that the Queen was waiting to speak with her in privacy. "I'm fine."

I gave her an incredulous look, realizing that she was actually unaware that she was shivering like a plucked wire. "You're a long way from fine." I scooped her into my arms, careful to protect her wounded shoulder. "Your majesty."

The crude battleground hospitality of Troyes-le-Mont was a long way from the luxury of the Royal Palace. Ysandre led us to a suite of rooms she shared with three of her ladies-in-waiting, sending a lone servant to fetch bread and cheese and wine while the chirurgeon—Lelahiah Valais—wrapped a bit of clean bandaging around the gash in my forearm. The Queen's companions withdrew to the adjacent chamber, one returning with a gown to replace the blood-soaked garment Phèdre could scarce hold together.

Ysandre sat very upright in a high-backed chair. "We don't have much time," she said formally. "But I wish both of you to know that no matter what happens today, I issued a pardon before we left the City proclaiming your innocence in the death of Anafiel Delaunay. History will record it."

It was a small thing in the grand scheme of things, but it meant a great deal to me. I bowed deeply as Phèdre offered our thanks, tears in her eyes.

Ysandre waved a dismissive hand. "I would have done it sooner, but we didn't dare alert d'Aiglemort or Melisande Shahrizai. Even to the very end, we weren't entirely sure who could be trusted."

"You didn't find Melisande?" Phèdre asked, even though she already knew the answer.

"No." The Queen was blunt. "The Cassiline Brotherhood sought word of her as they rode courier service, but they had to be discreet for the same reason I couldn't pardon you publicly."

"Of course."

Ysandre took a deep breath, then rose restlessly, pacing the floor. "So it is true, then, that Drustan mab Necthana rules as Cruarch in Alba?" She paused, her fair brows drawing together in a consternation she didn't quite know how to voice. "Did he send any word for me?"

Ah, Elua!

I ducked my head to hide a smile; of course. Despite everything that Ysandre de la Courcel had taken on her slender royal shoulders—the weight of a crown, an impending invasion, a nation beset by treachery—she was a young woman with a dream of love in her heart, too. I saw the realization strike Phèdre at the same moment, and there was a gentle note in her tone as she gave her answer.

"Your majesty, I saw him crowned before we left Alba's shore," she said to the young Queen. "He sent no word to you tonight because he didn't know what I intended. Forgive me. I didn't tell him because I didn't expect to survive it. He wouldn't have allowed me to make this attempt if he'd known, his honor wouldn't have let him. It grieves him to put his people at risk, my lady. But this I can tell you. Alone among our allies, Drustan mab Necthana rides toward Troyes-le-Mont with his head held high and a joyful heart, because he rides toward you. The dream that you shared together of two mighty nations ruled side by side lives on in him. If his people had not risen up to follow him, he would have set out to retake his throne alone; and had he fallen in the attempt, his last thought would have been of you."

It was an unabashedly romantic speech, and it brought a flush to Ysandre's cheeks. "Thank you."

"Your majesty," I said to her. "One of the great honors of my life is Drustan mab Necthana calling me brother. He is a courageous and good leader, and I think in his quiet Cruithne way, he is very madly in love with you."

The Queen was not too flustered to give me a pointed look. "I didn't think Cassilines were supposed to notice such things."

"No," I agreed. "We're not."

There was a soldier outside the door bawling out an urgent request from Percy de Somerville. A good deal of formality had gone by the wayside in the embattled fortress; Ysandre merely rose with alacrity, her guards falling in beside her. "I expect you'll want a moment alone," she said to us. "Sunrise is nigh. I'll see you on the battlements."

Phèdre looked at me.

I looked at my hands.

What in the name of Blessed Elua and all of his Companions does one say at such a time? Neither of us knew. It was too big for words.

"How did you know?" Phèdre asked me at length.

"I don't know." I shook my head. "I awoke and knew somewhat was amiss. When I saw you gone, I just knew. And I knew what Selig would do if he caught you."

"I thought—" she began, then stopped for a heartbeat. Regarding me steadily with an apology in those dark, lustrous eyes, she finished. "I thought at first that you'd betrayed us all for your vow. I'm sorry."

A choked sound caught in my throat, half a laugh. No one else on the face of this green and thriving earth but Phèdre nó Delaunay would apologize for mistaking a mercy killing for an attempt to save her life. I understood it, though.

"I don't blame you," I said quietly. "It's something we're taught. Every Cassiline Brother learns the *terminus*. But no one in living memory has performed it." I thought about my uncle, who had died rather than violate the gravity of that utmost sacrament. I looked away again. "I nearly killed us both."

"Joscelin." Phèdre cupped my cheek with one hand, waiting until I made myself meet her gaze. "I know." Her fingers trailed down the side of my face, lightly touching the gouge the tip of my dagger had made below my right ear, the point where I'd set my blade to slit my throat. Taking my hand, she pressed it to her breast, to the tender flesh in which I would have planted the dagger I'd flung. "And until the day I die, I will be grateful for it."

I covered her hand with mine and squeezed it as hard as I dared. There was a great deal more to be said, but not now. Already we could hear a rising chorus of relayed news and orders, feet pounding in the hallways. "Well, if I'd let Selig have you, it would have saved Hyacinthe the trouble of drowning me," I said with gallows humor. "Can you walk?"

"I'd have walked here if you'd have let me." Phèdre's carriage was rigid with pain, but determination, too. "Go. Find your father."

If my father and brother were among the defenders of Troyes-le-Mont, by now they would already be in position and prepared to take part in the counterattack. Even if I were willing to abandon Phèdre's side at the onset of battle, attempting to locate them now would merely be disruptive and self-serving. "It's too late at this point. Blessed Elua willing, I'll find them alive." I smiled ruefully. "And if fate is unkind, at least my father will have known I was no murderer before the end."

Phèdre was still holding my hand. We had done everything humanly possible and more to prevent the conquest of Terre d'Ange, but the odds remained against us.

There were just *so many* Skaldi.

She didn't offer me any words of false hope or encouragement, only returned my squeeze. "Come on."

CHAPTER SIXTY

Atop the battlements it was a scene out of a nightmare. It was one thing to have witnessed from afar, but even crossing the slumbering battleground hadn't prepared me for what it was like to be in the eye at the center of the maelstrom. The fortress of Troyes-le-Mont was the size of a city block and built to withstand a siege, but it was as isolated as the Master of the Straits' lonely tower jutting above the vast, roiling sea of the Skaldi army.

Dawn hadn't yet broken and Waldemar Selig had already redoubled his attack on the fortress. There were trebuchets mounted on all four walls of the outermost battlements and arrow-slits in the walls manned by crossbowmen, but the defenders were doing their damnedest to hold ammunition in reserve for one last push.

Ysandre stood conferring with her commanders in the shadow of a tall merlon of the crenellated wall. Percy de Somerville waved us over. "Selig just sent out scouting parties in six directions," he informed us. "What's Ghislain's angle of approach?"

Phèdre pointed toward the horizon where the distant foothills had yet to emerge from the darkness. "Due east."

"How long until they arrive if they move at first light?" he asked.

"Two hours?"

"Less," I said. "They'll be moving in a hurry. I wouldn't worry about Skaldi scouts, our Cruithne will spot them first. But once they reach level ground, there's no concealing an entire army. An hour, mayhap."

"If Selig divides his forces, we're in trouble," Barquiel L'Envers mused. "He could leave ten thousand men to pen us in and still outnumber the Albans two to one."

"They'll follow Selig." Phèdre rose on her toes to peer through the nearest arrow-slit. Just out of projectile range, Waldemar Selig rode back and forth on a tall courser. "It's the one order they're like to disobey—if he turns, they'll go, too. And Isidore d'Aiglemort is aiming for him."

No one liked the fact that the plan rested on the Duc d'Aiglemort, and I didn't blame them. I didn't like it, either.

"So be it." Comte Percy de Somerville heaved a sigh in the smoke-streaked air. "Cousin, I leave the battlements in your command," he said to Gaspar Trevalion. "Hold your fire to the east when we attack the Skaldi rearguard."

Gaspar clasped his forearm. "Elua be with you."

"And you." De Somerville turned to Ysandre and bowed. "Your majesty, I served under your grandfather for many years. But if I die today, I die proud to have served under you."

Standing tall and regal on the ramparts of the besieged fortress, Ysandre de la Courcel inclined her head. "And I to have been served by you, Comte de Somerville," she said to him. "Elua's blessing upon you."

"Take care of yourself, Ysandre, you make a damned good Queen." Barquiel L'Envers kissed his niece on the forehead. "We'll do our best to make sure you stay one." He nodded at Phèdre and me. "Keep these two with you, will you? They seem to be damnably hard to kill."

It nearly startled a laugh from me. The Queen's Cassiline attendants didn't seem as amused by the comment. I wouldn't have appreciated it were I in their situation, either; yet oddly, it made me like L'Envers better. Well, that and the fact that he'd saved our lives.

Gaspar Trevalion was attempting to convince Ysandre to shelter indoors rather than observe the battle from the ramparts. I had an idea how well that insistence was going to be received.

"No." Ysandre's voice was firm, her chin held high. She wore a simple gold filigree crown. Silhouetted against the encroaching dawn, a cloak of deep Courcel blue embroidered with silver swirling around her, she looked like a painter's allegory of a beleaguered monarch's fidelity to country. "I will stay here, my lord. Terre d'Ange stands or falls with us this day, and so do I."

The waiting dragged on for a small eternity. I kept my eye to the arrow-slit while Ysandre and Phèdre passed the time speaking of the Queen's father's diary, that volume which related the ill-fated love between Rolande de la Courcel and Anafiel Delaunay de Montrève.

You, and you alone.

That was the oath Delaunay had sworn, and he'd kept it for the entirety of Prince Rolande's life. Insofar as I knew, there was no such equivalent oath of the Perfect Companion to bind one's heart and soul to another's in perpetual fidelity. But mayhap that was not done with words. I rubbed the nick under my right ear. Mayhap it was written in blood at the point of a dagger.

". . . became of your Tsingano friend?" Ysandre was inquiring. "Did he remain with Ghislain?"

"Hyacinthe," Phèdre said softly. "No. 'Tis a long tale, my lady."

"A Mendacant's tale," I agreed.

The Queen glanced toward the eastern horizon. A line of crimson dawn was breaking above the distant foothills and there was no sign of our army. "I do believe we could all benefit from passing the time with a Mendacant's tale at the moment."

I told it myself and I hope I did justice to it. If the truth of the story of Hyacinthe, son of Anasztaizia, chosen heir of the immortal Master of the Straits, were to die with us that day, at least it was told well once. When Gaspar Trevalion returned to report, he found Ysandre wide-eyed with wonder, uncertain whether or not to credit our tale. If naught else, it had afforded her a brief distraction, for Gaspar brought nothing but unwelcome news.

"Pray they don't fail us," he said grimly. "The Skaldi are filling the moat with rubble at the barbican and there are sappers digging under the northwestern tower. We've let them get too close. If help doesn't come, we won't last the day."

"They'll come," Phèdre said with dogged assuredness. I prayed she was right. I didn't doubt Drustan or the Twins or even Ghislain for a second, but I didn't have the same faith in the traitor Duc d'Aiglemort that she did.

Except . . .

The rising sun was striking glints of steel in the foothills. There were no settlements on those crags, there was no ore in those gulleys—that was the distant trickle of the combined forces of Ghislain, Drustan, and the Twins beginning their descent. I pressed my hands flat against the stone blocks, staring until I was certain. "They *are* coming!" I manhandled Gaspar Trevalion into place. "Look, my lord!"

He took a long look, then stepped back and bowed, ceding the space to the Queen. "Your majesty."

Ysandre pressed her face to the arrow-slit and looked. She took a deep, shaking breath. "Phèdre. You brought them. You should see."

She looked, lips parted in awe. "Name of Elua!"

On level ground, the Skaldi forces hadn't spotted the threat approaching from the rear yet. Our height atop the ramparts gave us an advantage, and it seemed that our sentries in the field had proved a foil for Selig's scouts. Trusting to their reconnaissance and concentrating on the fortress, the Skaldi on the plain failed to spot the telltale glimpses of the long line of armed soldiers snaking down from the foothills.

"How long do we wait to attack, my lord?" Ysandre asked Gaspar Trevalion. His herald was standing at the ready.

Gaspar hadn't taken his gaze from the horizon. "As long as it takes for Selig's troops to break ranks."

At the arrow-slit, Ysandre resumed her vigil. Unable to bear not knowing, Phèdre slid cautiously from behind the tall merlon. She gave a quick furtive glance to see if I'd try to stop her, but I simply wrapped my vambraces in a protective shield around her. In the shadow of the fortress, Waldemar Selig was riding back and forth on his tall horse, exhorting his thanes to redouble their efforts. A mile away across the plain, the vanguard of our army broke from its remaining concealment. The first company of L'Agnacite longbowmen and Camaeline infantry emerged from the slopes. Under the command of Ghislain de Somerville, they began moving in a solid line to take control of the breached bulwarks.

The endgame had begun.

There were no cowards among the Skaldi, that much I will own. The first among them to spot this fresh threat responded quick as thought. Mounted sentries from the rear of the perimeter peeled away to pelt toward Waldemar Selig on the front lines at a flat-out gallop. Without a moment's hesitation, the tribesmen in the rearguard of the siege turned as smoothly as schools of fish banking midstream, moving in unison to block the breaches in the barricade. Last night, I had felt the ripple of news passing through the Skaldi camps as a physical presence; today, we could actually see it happen as the sentries rode for the front shouting a frantic warning, ripples cresting before them, trailing in a V-shaped wake after them.

I saw Waldemar Selig's head come up sharply as the news reached him. His body reared back in the saddle, hands wrenching at the reins hard enough that his big destrier sank on its haunches in protest.

His troops milled around him. Half a mile away, the shining line of our forces was advancing—Camaeline infantry covering the archers as they knelt and loosed their longbows, volleys of arrows sowing chaos in the Skaldi rearguard. Rallying, the Skaldic tribesmen rushed en masse to engage them. And the Skaldi had the numbers. They spilled north and southward to flank our advance line. Our forces in the field began taking heavy casualties while the D'Angeline Royal Army remained pinned in the fortress.

Selig was uncertain, his attention divided between the near-victory before him and the new threat behind him. He exhorted his sappers and engineers to keep working, he interrogated couriers running frantic messages from the new front of attack. Across the plain, great plumes of dust arose as the Albans took to the field, surging from behind the Camaeline infantry to drive the Skaldi back from the flanks.

Whatever the Skaldi expected, it wasn't thousands of Alban warriors in plaids and woolens and hardened leather armor, with swords and slings and bows, tattooed and lime-crested, on foot, horseback, and in battered war-chariots hauled for hundreds of leagues and across stone and sea. All of the long effort, the battles endured, the leagues crossed, and dreams dreamt went into the wild charge of the Four Folk of Alba.

And still, Waldemar Selig's discipline held. Too many; there were too many. Our distant lines buckled, crumbling around the edges.

Gaspar Trevalion withheld his orders, even as the screams of the dying reached our ears.

"Please, my lord!" Phèdre begged him.

He gave her a haunted look. "We must be able to clear the gate, my lady. Otherwise, the Skaldi will pick us off one by one."

I was watching. "Look!"

In the far reaches of the battlefield, the silvery line of Camaeline infantry firmed and straightened, making one last convulsive push forward to claim ground before parting ranks and opening like the doors of a vast gate.

In the gap, a single horn sounded a note of pure defiance.

On the face of it, there's no way that Waldemar Selig could have known it was the sound of Isidore d'Aiglemort coming for him. And yet I do believe Selig heard his destiny calling in that single note. He would have to deal with d'Aiglemort sooner or later—he just hadn't expected that confrontation to take place here and now in the form of this desperate challenge. Back and forth he rode, furious at the unexpected disruption of his well-laid plans, while the hard-driving wedge of the Allies of Camlach plunged into the Skaldic forces with Duc Isidore d'Aiglemort shining like the tip of a spear at the forefront of the charge.

Now the cries arose. "Kilberhaar!" Skaldic voices shouted, and feet and hooves trampled the soil as some sought to fight, some to flee. "Kilberhaar!"

It was a warning and a call to arms alike. Waldemar Selig was a warlord who thought, but he was also a warlord who had united this army by dint of skill at arms and sheer charisma.

Waldemar the Blessed, proof against steel.

Let Terre d'Ange see how Waldemar Selig deals with her champions, he had said last night when I'd challenged him to the holmgang.

And he had lost.

Phèdre and I owed our lives to the mad dash of Barquiel L'Envers and his riders, but not before I'd spilled a drop of Selig's blood on the hide. By the letter of the law, he had lost the holmgang. It fed into the fury that drove him, into that deadly pride that led him to believe Terre d'Ange ought to be his simply because he willed it so. This new challenge to his mythos was untenable.

Wheeling his mount, Selig shouted to the men around him and drew his sword. "Kilberhaar!" he roared, plunging into the center of the unraveling fray and heading for the central plain. "Kilberhaar!"

"Now!" Gaspar Trevalion said to his herald, who raised a trumpet to his lips.

"Battlements, attack!" the herald bawled, then blew four long, resounding blasts on his trumpet. Other trumpets answered in quick succession from all the towers. Bowstrings hummed with the release of the dwindling reserves of our arsenal. The trebuchets were primed and loaded with a smoldering pitch mixture, the *feu d'Hellas* that burned with blue fire when ignited by flaming torches. One by one, the catapults were loosed with cacophonous thuds. Burning pitch spattered through the air in deadly gouts, clinging to the skin and clothing of attackers on the ground.

The Skaldic army was turning like some vast wheel, but no one was in command of the rearguard. Caught with no avenue of retreat, men and horses screamed in agony, rolling on the earth in attempts to douse the flames.

In the courtyard of Troyes-le-Mont, Percy de Somerville issued a single command. In the barbican towers, crossbowmen laid down a hail of bolts, driving back attackers seeking to broach the moat. Once again, the great portcullis was raised—and this time, an endless river of D'Angeline soldiers flooded across the lowered drawbridge, riding four abreast.

Atop the ramparts, with the screams and stench of dying men and beasts ringing in our ears and assaulting our nostrils, above the midst of all the blood, smoke, and ordure of the battlefield, we cheered.

That was war.

And in the center of the field, Waldemar Selig and Isidore d'Aiglemort rode toward each other.

Let the poets sing of that battle if they wish; I will not do it. It was an epic feat—Isidore d'Aiglemort's body was found to have endured seventeen wounds before he met his death, and I've no idea how many Selig bore. They fought on horseback until their mounts were slain beneath them, and then they fought on foot to the bitter end. They were two very gifted swordsmen and leaders who believed themselves anointed by their respective gods to perform extraordinary deeds.

But in the final tally, the only extraordinary deed they performed was killing each other on the plains of Troyes-le-Mont.

Upon the death of Waldemar Selig, the Skaldic army's discipline unraveled with a thoroughness that was startling even to those of us who expected it. Few of them fully shared Selig's vision of conquest. They'd been promised the mother of all raids on an unsuspecting realm; instead, they'd encountered prepared resistance and the rise of enemies from unexpected quarters. Most of them had no more lofty political ambition than the average thane in Gunter's steading.

Meanwhile, the Allies of Camlach were fighting for the last shreds of their tattered honor while the Royal Army and our allies were fighting for love of Queen and country. Cutting their losses or securing any small loot they'd already seized, the Skaldi began to retreat. At first they peeled off in smaller groups of a dozen, and then entire companies of warriors streamed toward the foothills, breaking down along the tribal lines that Phèdre had observed.

"Your majesty!" It was Phèdre who pointed, although even Ysandre was no longer taking shelter behind the crenellations now that the tide of battle was turning. In the northeast, a band of riders led by the Cruarch of Alba were cutting a swath across the roiling field to assist the Allies of Camlach.

"Drustan!" The Queen gazed at the small figure, the red cape swirling around him. "Is it truly him?"

"Oh, it is!" I assured her. "That's Drustan mab Necthana."

"I wish we could—" Phèdre began, pausing at the sound of a fresh commotion arising within the walls of the fortress itself. Her expression changed. "There's fighting in the courtyard."

"Your majesty!" Gaspar Trevalion came at a run, trailing half a dozen crossbowmen. "Stay atop the battlements! There are Skaldi inside the gates!"

I was only half a step behind Phèdre as she darted across the flagstones to peer over the interior walls at the melee in the courtyard below. A considerable force of Skaldi had seized the drawbridge in the wake of Percy de Somerville's foray onto the field and fought their way through to the inner quadrangle. Members of the departing ranks of de Somerville's infantry had turned back in hot pursuit and were now outnumbered and fighting for their lives. It was all close combat, and Gaspar's archers on the ramparts didn't dare loose into the throng for fear of striking one of our own.

My palms began to prickle, itching for the solid heft of a hilt.

"Blessed buggering Elua," Gaspar muttered, then addressed his herald. "Signal for reinforcements."

One of the D'Angeline warriors was making a hell of a stand. He was tall, taller than any of his opponents. There was somewhat familiar about the set of his shoulders, the way the long blond braid snaking from beneath his helm whipped as he fought—

"Luc!" I loosed my older brother's name in a shout, my hands clenching. I gauged the obstacles and distance between us. "Luc!"

"Your brother?" Phèdre's voice was urgent; all I could do was give her an agonized nod. "Can you get to him?" Seeing the answer in my eyes, she shook me. "Then go! Name of Elua, Joscelin, go!"

I wanted to, by all that was holy and sacred, I wanted to. "If ever there was a time when I dared not—"

Phèdre grabbed my hair with both hands, yanked my face down to hers, and kissed me hard. "I love you," she said fiercely. "And if you ever want to hear those words from my lips again, you will *not* choose this idiotic vow over your brother's life!"

I stared at her for a split second, then turned on my heel and set out at a dead run, soldiers ducking from my path. I half slid, half clattered down two stories of winding tower stairs, emerging on the narrow parapet that led to the gatehouse. Not only was that my brother Luc fighting grimly in the courtyard, he and several others were providing cover for my father. I knew him by his profile, by the same broad, angular shoulders; but his were hunched, protecting some grave injury.

My *father.*

I was Joscelin Verreuil, Cassiel's Servant, and my daggers shone like stars as I drew them at a run and launched from the parapet, offering up the name of my ancestral house in a battle-cry. "Verreuil! Verreuil!"

It was probably the most foolhardy thing I'd ever done, and I would have done it a thousand times over because my brother Luc was fighting, my father was in danger, and Phèdre nó Delaunay had just told me that she loved me. I dropped from the sky on wings of steel, twelve feet tall and invincible.

The Skaldi scattered like drops from a puddle as I landed amongst them in a crouch. I came up spinning and dispatched two, clearing enough space to hurdle a fallen thane and draw my sword.

"*Joscelin?*" Luc's incredulous gaze met mine across the heads of Skaldi warriors.

I flashed him a ferocious grin. "In Cassiel's name, brother!"

CHAPTER SIXTY-ONE

My father had lost his left hand.

An immense ballroom in Troyes-le-Mont was serving as the main hospital ward. Once the tide turned in the courtyard and the surviving Skaldi invaders laid down their weapons in surrender, Luc and I, accompanied by two of Verreuil's men-at-arms, escorted our father there as quickly as possible.

If there were no heroes in the epic battle that put an end to this war, there were heroes aplenty in the hospital ward—chirurgeons, doctors, and apprentices, as well as dozens of assistants and volunteers. One of the latter saw to my father almost immediately, although there was naught he could do but bid us keep the maimed limb elevated and stanch the bleeding until a chirurgeon was available. Only then did my father allow himself to look at me with bemused wonder. "Joscelin? What in the world?"

It encompassed a host of questions; they had departed Verreuil without receiving my last correspondence. I crossed my forearms and bowed in reflex, trying to frame a succinct response.

"We know a bit of it," Luc added. "Brother Jacobe sent a letter."

I blinked in surprise. "He did?"

My father braced his elbow on his knee and winced. "He said you broke your vows, refused penance, and were declared anathema in the Cassiline Brotherhood. All for a woman's sake."

There was a great deal more to it, but in the end, there was nothing false in the statement. I met my father's gaze squarely. "I did."

He tightened his lips and nodded, absorbing my confirmation. "Brother Jacobe also said he believed in his heart that you must have had reason for it. And that Terre d'Ange itself might have cause to be grateful for it. Is that so?"

"Also, why do you look like you've been living in the woods and brushing your hair with pinecones?" Luc added.

Blessed Elua, I'd forgotten I still looked ready to step onto the hide for the holmgang. I pushed my hair back, still feeling Phèdre's hands yanking my face down to hers. Her kiss. The words, she'd said the words—

—and she was completely out of my guard on a crowded, unsecured, highly dangerous battle site.

"I believe so," I said respectfully to my father. "And I will tell you the tale in full. But I must excuse myself at the moment. I'll return as soon as I can, I know they'll give you good care."

"I'll make sure of it," Luc said. "You know Father, he'll be acting as though one hand's all he ever needed in no time. Is it the woman?"

"She's my ward," I said.

"Right." Luc took my arm, guiding me away. "Is it true that she's a Servant of Naamah?"

On the opposite side of the ballroom-turned-infirmary, a ragged voice began singing a familiar marching tune, a second voice joining the chorus with the defiant bawdy humor of the battlefield.

I sighed.

Luc raised his eyebrows. "That's about her?"

"That," I said, "is the marching chant of Phèdre's Boys, an elite company of soldier-sailors in the Royal Navy who followed a Servant of Naamah across the Straits, through civil war in a foreign land, and home to victory at the besieged fortress of Troyes-le-Mont. Yes. It's about her."

"Elua's Balls!" Luc regarded me. "You really are in love."

"Look after Father," I said. "I'll be back."

I'd already lost track of Phèdre. Atop the battlements, Gaspar Trevalion informed me that over the Queen's protests, Phèdre was among those bringing water to the wounded and dying on the plains. "Of course she is," I said wearily. "And I suppose she found a sturdy wooden yoke so she could carry *two* pails across her shoulders like Yeshua ben Yosef carrying his wooden cross on the road to Golgotha."

"What?" Gaspar stared at me. "No, I don't think . . . Oh. You're jesting."

I was, mostly.

Like war, loving a god's chosen was something that required a certain sense of absurdity to survive with one's sanity intact. And I did indeed love Phèdre nó Delaunay with every part of my battered heart, body, and soul, but she had an undeniably overdeveloped sense of melodrama and an affinity for martyrdom. It would have been a pleasant change if for once she had chosen a sensible course of action over the most excruciating one.

By the time I borrowed a mount and tracked her down on the battlefield, however, I'd no heart in me for anything but grief. Phèdre was kneeling in the mud beside the fallen figure of Eamonn mac Conor where the Albans were honoring his sacrifice. Ah, Elua! I hadn't known we'd lost Eamonn. The Dalriada had laid his body reverently beside his war-chariot. The Lady Grainne was there, blood-spattered but unharmed, her eyes bright with the endless tears streaking her face. Drustan knelt on one knee. As I watched, he gave his belt knife to Phèdre, who hacked loose a curl of her hair and placed it under Eamonn's still hands. Shoulders hitching, she wept, too.

"Phèdre." My voice sounded raw and scraped. She looked up at me, eyes raw-rimmed with pain and exhaustion. "You're in no shape to do this."

She rubbed her brow with the heel of one hand, leaving a smear of dirt. "Your brother? And your father?"

"They're well enough." I hoped it was true. "They survived." I turned in the saddle to bow deeply to Grainne mac Conor. "I grieve for your loss, my lady."

She acknowledged my words with a grave nod.

I extended my hand to Phèdre, who rose to mount behind me. My weary horse didn't even spook at the empty clattering bucket she carried as we plodded back to the safety of the fortress walls.

In the brutal aftermath of war, especially after the harrowing torture Phèdre had endured, I was grateful that we enjoyed a place of privilege within the Queen's entourage at Troyes-le-Mont. There was precious little space to be found in the fortress, every square inch having been occupied by its defenders. While drawing rooms were converted into additional hospital quarters and exhausted soldiers taking shifts to rest in barracks packed as tight as salt cod in a barrel, we'd been allotted a servant's bedchamber in the Queen's suite. It was a piece of luxury. A bath was out of the question, but I found a bit of soap and a clean rag. The chirurgeon had cleaned Phèdre's wound thoroughly before tending to it and I left those bandages in place, but I washed the gore and dirt and soot from her face and hands, pouring a ewer of water over her head, the ends of her hair stiff and clotted with her own dried blood.

"You, too," she murmured after I settled her on the servant's pallet, careful to keep pressure from her injured shoulder. Her eyelashes were already fluttering closed; like a soldier, Phèdre had learned to sleep at a moment's notice. "I need you."

I need you.

The words "I love you" were like a starburst in my heart. This feeling was just as vast, but deeper and heavier. I unbuckled my vambraces. There was blood in the joints and detail work, blood stiffening the leather and clotting the buckles. I'd given my sword and daggers a cursory cleaning, but they were in a disgraceful state. For the first time in my life since Brother Jacobe came to Verreuil to claim me for the Cassiline Brotherhood, I left my gear in an untended pile. Stripping down to an undershirt and breeches, I scoured my hands and face and my arms to the elbow, then clambered into the pallet beside Phèdre.

She cracked her eyes open just enough to smile at me, and slid into my arms with that easy housecat's grace. I wrapped my arms around her waist, careful not to graze her shoulder. "I love you," I whispered into the perfect grimy shell of her ear. "And I need you, too. I'm just not good at saying words."

"I know." Phèdre propped her chin on both hands on my collarbone. "Neither am I. Not aloud, not when it matters."

I moved my hands to her hips. "And I matter?"

A complicated expression crossed her face like a shadow: mirth, sorrow, desire, joy, and helplessness. "Joscelin . . . you're my home. I mean . . ." A rueful note colored her tone. "If you'll have me."

My hands tightened. "Are you insane?"

Her dark eyes gleamed, the crimson mote floating above the surface of her left iris. "Is that what you think?"

"Yes," I said to her. "No. I think you're brave and beautiful and vain, kind and wise and impulsive. And I would rather show you than tell you, because I have no gift of words to give you and no home to offer you save the place where you dwell within my heart."

Phèdre cupped my cheek. "That's a remarkably poetic way of reminding me that we have nowhere to live."

I smiled. "That, too."

It was true and strange to consider in its way. Neither of us had given thought to what a homecoming meant. My sword was pledged to Queen Ysandre's service, but I'd no idea what that meant in practical terms. Surely she understood that I had only vowed to serve her as Phèdre's guard; nonetheless, I was hers to command by the oath that bound me to Cassiel's service. And Phèdre would be a free woman for the first time in her life, but she had no home to which to return. Aside from Melisande's diamond—which admittedly might suffice to pay the cost of renting a small villa for a year—

and the ink on her back, everything Phèdre might have called her own had been seized along with Anafiel Delaunay's townhouse and the rest of his possessions.

At the moment, though, it was enough that we had spoken of making a life together; where and how that would take place was the least of our concerns. The battle of Troyes-le-Mont may have ended the war, but it hadn't settled the peace.

Ysandre's first official act as Queen of a victorious and united Terre d'Ange was to welcome Drustan mab Necthana at the gates of the fortress as the Cruarch of Alba, her equal among rulers, and her betrothed. Their union was celebrated with uproarious cheers from D'Angeline, Cruithne, and Dalriadan soldiers, though I regret to say that there were a number of officers drawn from the ranks of royal houses who looked askance at the prospect. None of them were foolish enough to give voice to concerns at a time when Terre d'Ange owed its sovereignty to the small island nation of Alba.

By the same token, Ysandre received Grainne mac Conor—now solely the Lady of the Dalriada—with profound respect, extending to her the Crown's deepest gratitude and sympathy for the loss of her brother Eamonn.

Although Thelesis de Mornay had taught the Alban tongue to a half a dozen scholars since we set out on our mission, her majesty preferred to rely on Phèdre to serve as her translator. Months of immersion in the spoken tongue had given Phèdre a level of fluency unmatched by classroom studies; and, quite simply, Ysandre trusted her. Since my duties consisted of paying attention and looking menacing, I spent a great deal of time standing with crossed forearms and glowering.

The Queen's Cassiline Guards regarded me with tight-lipped disapproval. There were four pairs of brothers working in shifts to guard Ysandre around the clock. It wasn't even two years since King Ganelon de la Courcel had added his granddaughter to the Cassiline Brotherhood's royal duty roster. Blessed Elua, I hadn't even dared envy them—I'd envied those full-fledged brothers only a few years older than me who might hope to be granted a post from which one of the more senior brothers had been promoted.

Instead I'd been granted what I'd thought must surely be the most frivolous posting in the history of Cassiel's service.

And now I was anathema, a living affront to the entire Cassiline Brotherhood and every member who surrendered the greater part of his identity upon passing through the Prefectory gates at ten years of age and kept every vow that followed. Looking at the stern features of the guards who would have been my brethren as surely as Luc, I felt the weight of that betrayal and the ensuing disapproval.

That would always be with me, but I had made my choice.

Nonetheless, I will own to being apprehensive upon introducing Phèdre to my brother and father.

It was a hurried business. Ysandre had granted clemency to the Allies of Camlach. At the request of what leaders remained among the forces Isidore d'Aiglemort had commanded, she granted them leave to pursue fleeing bands of Skaldi. Ghislain de Somerville, who had ably led us since we departed from the banks of the Rhenus River, was reunited with his father, the Royal Commander. Dispatches from Marc Trevalion assured us that with Admiral Rousse's fleet patrolling the Rhenus, his forces continued to push the straggling Skaldi invaders eastward toward the border.

The resources of the besieged fortress were strained before the arrival of our army. In consultation with her military commanders, Queen Ysandre gave orders to dismiss the households of those soldiers and their staff not enlisted as standing members of the Royal Army, from bakers and cartwrights to the scions of Major and Minor Houses. It was done with gracious haste, and Queen Ysandre's profound and sincere gratitude stood as surety for a promise of commendations to come.

As one such household, House Verreuil took its leave amidst a contingent of Siovalese volunteers.

I'd spent as much time as possible visiting my father in the hospital ward. Although I was loath to leave Phèdre unattended at any time, a dozen of her Boys had survived the battle without critical injuries. I was willing to entrust her safety to them long enough to check on my father's condition. The chirurgeons had done a remarkable job of using ligatures to seal and sew the injury, and it looked to be healing cleanly. It must have hurt like seven hells, though as Luc predicted, our father endured it with stoic disregard.

If it took more than the loss of a hand to ruffle his lordship the Chevalier Millard Verreuil's feathers, my tale did the trick. It had spread by now. Outside of the Queen's Council, knowledge of my and Phèdre's role was limited—it had been deemed wiser to attribute the information we brought out of Skaldia to a covert program of diplomatic espionage than to let the realm know that the conspiracy was uncovered quite by accident by one Servant of Naamah and a Cassiline Brother who emerged from the wilderness to bear witness to it.

Our role in the quest to Alba was likewise withheld from general awareness. Again, it had been rightly deemed more reassuring to announce that the Royal Admiral Quintilius Rousse had undertaken a mission at the behest of the Queen's Council to seek aid from our Alban allies. But there were enough survivors who knew the full truth—Phèdre's Boys, eager to tell their own unlikely tale of how the Royal Admiral crossed the Straits at the behest of a pain-loving courtesan, a Tsingano fortuneteller, and a disgraced Cassiline Brother.

The stories were already circulating by the time I was able to tell Luc and my father.

A part of me wished it weren't so, for soldiers in the infirmary related the Taming of the Twins with as much relish as the Calming of the Waters.

"So it's all true?" Luc asked when I'd finally managed to tell them in my own manner. "All of it?"

"Everything I told you." I gestured around the pallet-filled chamber. "Elua knows what you've heard in here."

"I wish you'd found a way to tell us," my father said quietly. "If it hadn't been for Brother Jacobe . . . Joscelin, we were told you were convicted of murder."

My hands went cold. "Did you believe it?"

"Of course not." My father gave me a bemused look. "But we'd no idea what had befallen you."

"Forgive me," I said. "I should have found a way. Brother Jacobe wasn't there. I never thought to find aid within the Cassiline Brotherhood."

"And yet you did." My father hesitated, his brow furrowed. "Joscelin . . . are you willing to reconsider a path to atonement? I will write to the Prefect when matters are settled and beg a boon of him."

I shook my head and made my voice as gentle as possible. "No."

"I could—"

I crossed my vambraces and offered my father a silent bow; a silent refusal. I would not dishonor my father by arguing with him, but I had held my ward's life and my own in the palm of my hand. I had come within a hair's breadth of performing the *terminus*, and no one, not even the Prefect of the Cassiline Brotherhood himself, could tell me how to walk the path of the Perfect Companion.

It had been my hope to arrange a private meeting prior to their departure, but Phèdre's translation skills remained much in demand. As a result, her introduction to House Verreuil was both hail and farewell.

"I understand you're somewhat of a scholar," my father observed after I'd made a formal introduction. Luc mouthed disbelief at me over his shoulder.

It wasn't exactly atop the list of qualities for which Phèdre was known, but it wasn't untrue, either. She responded as if she were perfectly accustomed to being described first and foremost as a scholar, quoting a Caerdicci orator my father admired. "'I do but sample from the feast-table of my forefathers.'"

My stern father smiled, his eyes crinkling at the corners. "Naamah's Servants are seldom so learned in Siovale," he said. "Perhaps it is a rebellion against the teachings of Shemhazai."

"Shemhazai has his passions, my lord." Phèdre smiled back at him. "And Naamah her store of wisdom."

He laughed—my father the Chevalier Millard Verreuil, Lord of House Verreuil, laughed—then laid his hand on her arm. "I have heard what you did. Terre d'Ange owes you a great debt for your service."

She inclined her head to me. "If not for your son, I would be dead many times over, my lord."

"I know." My father adjusted the sling supporting his maimed arm, then met my gaze squarely. There was a deep, quiet pride in his expression that made me feel solid and centered within myself. "Whether or not I agree with the path you've chosen, I cannot say. But you have acquitted yourself upon it with honor."

It was enough. I bowed to my father again, this time in silent gratitude and acknowledgment.

"Well, I can't disagree, seeing the cause!" Luc grinned at Phèdre with a candid appreciation that would have been offensive if it weren't so sincere. "Elua! Will you come visit us, Phèdre? At the least, you ought to give me a fair chance before you decide on Joscelin."

Phèdre opted for a diplomatic response. "Neither of us have decided anything, my lord, but I would be honored to see Verreuil."

Luc punched me in the shoulder as though we were boys again. "You can come, too, I suppose."

"I will," I promised. "Someday."

"You would be welcome," our father said firmly. "Any day. Your mother longs to see you." He turned his gaze to Phèdre. "And you will always be welcome in our home, Phèdre nó Delaunay. I knew the Comte de Montrève. I believe in the end, he would have been proud of his son Anafiel and what he has wrought in you."

The unexpected tribute brought tears to Phèdre's eyes, and she swallowed hard. "Thank you, my lord."

It was a gift that my father gave her that day, and one I daresay few might have offered, for there weren't many who could speak to the heart of a Siovalese nobleman whose son had made an unwelcome choice in love. I was blessed to have a father whose heart was large enough to encompass it. And then the Siovalese contingent was underway and there was no time for aught but a final goodbye. After offering her wishes for a safe and swift journey, Phèdre withdrew to allow us a private moment.

"Tell Mother that I love her," I said to them. "And Mahieu and the girls."

Luc clasped my forearms, anchoring us in place for one brief moment. "Of course. Take care of yourself."

I slung an arm around his neck and embraced him. "You, too."

When last I'd been parted from my family, I was the one leaving, bound for a future circumscribed with certitude. After a decade of training, I would take my final vow and become a Cassiline Brother, disciplined, chaste, and pure. I would be part of the great tradition of Cassiel's Servants, keeping the light of faith burning for the Misguided that they might one day return to their rightful home.

The man I had become was very different from the one my ten-year-old self had imagined.

As the outlying provinces drew down their forces, Queen Ysandre kept her court at Troyes-le-Mont. Entourages of D'Angeline nobility came daily to the fortress. Some delivered tribute in the form of much-needed supplies, renewing the pledges of loyalty they'd sworn when Ysandre was crowned. Others who had withheld troops or been stingy with material support came to plead for clemency; and still others made the pilgrimage to the seat of power with accusations of disloyalty against the Crown.

The Duc de Morhban was one of the latter—and he came with a prisoner in tow.

I fetched Phèdre as soon as I saw his entourage approaching the plain. She was at the smithy helping settle a misunderstanding regarding repairs to several of the Dalriadan war-chariots.

"What is it?" she asked.

"Come and see." It was easier than explaining, and her gaze would be surer than mine. Phèdre issued a sharp edict to the disgruntled smith and followed me back to the inner keep and up the winding tower stairs to the ramparts. I pointed westward. "There."

Quincel de Morhban rode at the forefront of a square formation. Banners with the raven and sea insignia of House Morhban flew at every corner. The Duc and his men-at-arms were clad in the gleaming, undented armor of soldiers who had traversed the breadth of a realm at war without seeing battle.

A solitary figure rode in the center of the formation. Even if she hadn't been the only woman in the company, it would have been impossible to miss her. I heard Phèdre catch her breath, and steadied her.

"Melisande," she whispered. "Ah, Elua!"

CHAPTER SIXTY-TWO

It was her own kin who betrayed her.

Betimes I wonder what it must be like to spend one's childhood in a family of peers at once as tightknit and cutthroat as House Shahrizai. All the members of the Shahrizai have a reputation for being clannish, hedonistic, and dangerous clever. They're as thick as thieves, and the only sin in House Shahrizai worse than being crossed by an outsider is one of their own getting caught plotting against the family's interest.

If Melisande's plan had succeeded—and it bade fair to do so whether Selig or d'Aiglemort prevailed—her House would have been the first to laud her, albeit behind closed doors. But our unlikely trio had aroused the Duc de Morhban's suspicions when we showed up on his doorstep seeking access to the Royal Admiral. As he had warned us, he questioned Rousse's men after our departure. After that encounter, the subtle observations of those Cassiline Brothers serving as couriers had been less discreet in their inquiries than we'd reckoned, at least to the Duc de Morhban's eye. Whatever else is true of Kushiel's scions, they have unparalleled insight into the deepest impulses driving humankind—the darkest desires and hidden weaknesses.

When Quincel de Morhban realized that the Cassiline Brotherhood was quietly searching for Melisande, he put enough pieces of the puzzle together to continue hedging his bets. While we fought against the dire magic of the Master of the Straits, the occupying force of Tarbh Cró usurpers in Alba, and the invading forces of Skaldia in Terre d'Ange, de Morhban cultivated ties with a pair of ambitious young members of House Shahrizai and waited to see which way the tide would turn. If it hadn't turned in Ysandre's favor, I don't believe for an instant that de Morhban would have succeeded in betraying the Lady Melisande Shahrizai.

But it did.

Under normal circumstances, there would have been a formal trial with Parliament providing oversight, but wartime rules prevailed in the field and the Queen was within her authority to entertain cases and issue judgments. For this trial, however, Phèdre's and my attendance would be required.

Especially Phèdre's. I could attest to Melisande's role in our abduction, but only Phèdre had seen the letter written to Waldemar Selig in Melisande's own hand; handwriting she knew by sight. Only she had read its damning contents. For that and for all the reasons that lay between them, this battle was hers to wage.

"I'm sorry," Ysandre said to her with genuine compassion. "I would have spared you if I could."

"I know, my lady," Phèdre murmured.

Troyes-le-Mont was built as a defensive fortress, not a soaring tribute to D'Angeline architecture. The throne room was small and dank with thick stone walls that kept out the worst of the summer's heat. Queen Ysandre was seated on the heavy gilt-trimmed oak throne, flanked by a pair of Cassilines and half a dozen members of the former Dauphine's Guard who were implicitly loyal to her.

Phèdre and I stood behind them, awaiting the Queen's signal. The Duc de Morhban approached the throne and dropped to one knee, pressing his fist to his brow in a declaration of fealty. "Your majesty," he said without rising. "The Allies of Camlach have paid a reckoning for their betrayal, but it comes to House Morhban's attention that there is one conspirator who has thus far evaded justice."

"You speak of the Lady Melisande Shahrizai." The Queen was not minded to mince words with him.

"I do." Straightening, Quincel de Morhban stood aside. His men parted behind him, allowing Melisande to approach the throne.

I looked down at Phèdre. She was utterly without expression and so motionless that I almost feared she wasn't breathing, but the diamond that hung from her throat was vibrating ever so slightly.

"Lady Melisande Shahrizai." Ysandre's voice was flat and implacable; anyone who had not realized there was steel in this young Queen's spine was making a grave mistake. "You stand before us accused of treason. How do you plead?"

"Your majesty." Melisande curtsied gracefully. Her face was calm and lovely, her expression one of respect. "I am your loyal servant, and innocent of the charge."

Ysandre leaned forward in the throne. "You are charged with conspiring with Isidore d'Aiglemort to betray the nation and seize the throne. Do you deny this?"

Lamplight shimmered on the rippling curtain of Melisande's blue-black hair, highlighting the alabaster symmetry of her face. No one had ever denied Melisande Shahrizai's beauty. "For a thousand years, House Shahrizai has served the throne." Her voice was as rich as ever, but it was somber. "His grace de Morhban makes charges, but he offers no proof and has much to gain if his loyalty and my estates are at stake." She gestured at the Duc with restrained eloquence, letting a deliberate note of anger edge into her tone. "Where was he when the battle for D'Angeline sovereignty was waged? Yes, your majesty. I refute the charge. If he has proof, let him offer it."

She didn't know.

I hadn't been sure until that moment. Melisande Shahrizai had played a very long, deep game, but de Morhban had played a canny one with the unexpected hand he'd been dealt. The damnable thing of it was that between the two, I'd have believed Melisande if I didn't know better.

Queen Ysandre was watching her intently. "You are also charged with conspiring with Waldemar Selig of the Skaldi."

Until that moment, I do believe Melisande thought she still had the game in hand; even now, she laughed. "Does the Duc claim as much?" The words came easily, the notion scarce worthy of consideration. "Well might I say it of him, or anyone, your majesty. It is easy to make a charge that cannot be gainsaid by the dead."

"No," Ysandre said. "Not de Morhban."

Melisande grew very still; when she spoke, her voice was low and dangerous. "Do I not have the right, your majesty, to know who accuses me?"

Turning, the Queen made a slight gesture of command to the guards behind her. They parted ranks for us.

"I do." Phèdre stepped forward. There was a tremor in her voice, but she met Melisande's gaze and held it. One hand rose to grasp the diamond; with a single definitive yank, she jerked it from her throat and broke the cord. "That is yours, my lady." She held the diamond on one palm, the frayed ends of the cord trailing like a hawk's jesses, then flung it at Melisande's feet. "I am not."

The diamond settled with a series of faint chinking sounds. In the silence that followed, Melisande Shahrizai turned a bloodless white.

I swear on Cassiel's dagger, I saw that woman taken by surprise twice in her life, and she was more unnerved by Anafiel Delaunay's death than the immanence of her own demise. She gave a short laugh, gazing into the past. "My lord Delaunay, you play a considerable endgame," she murmured, then looked back at Phèdre. Her sapphire-blue eyes held genuine curiosity. "That was the one thing I couldn't fathom. Percy de Somerville was prepared for Selig's invasion. You?"

"I saw a letter you wrote to Selig in your own hand." Phèdre's voice was shaking, but determined. "You should have killed me when you had the chance."

If Melisande hadn't spared me a glance, one would have thought they were the only two people in the room. Stooping, she picked up the cord of the fallen necklace, regarding the diamond as it hung from her fist, scintillating in the surly lamplight of the throne room. "Leaving you the Cassiline was a bit excessive," she acknowledged. "Although it seems to have agreed with him."

Ysandre was in no mood for games. "Do you dispute this charge?"

Considering the diamond dangling from one hand, Melisande raised her brows. "I assume you have proof of their story?"

"I have Palace Guards who will swear they saw Phèdre nó Delaunay and her Cassiline guard with you the night of Anafiel Delaunay's murder," Ysandre said calmly. "And I believe, my lady Shahrizai, that thirty thousand invading Skaldi attest to the truth of their tale."

Melisande closed her hand around the diamond, lowered it, and shrugged. "Then I have no more to say."

"So be it." Queen Ysandre beckoned to her guards. "You will be executed at dawn."

No one else spoke; no one was willing to speak on a condemned traitor's behalf. The Queen had issued a sentence that was wholly deserved and there was nothing else to say. I felt the weight of the silence in the throne room as members of the Royal Guard escorted Melisande to confinement.

"It's over," I murmured in Phèdre's ear. "It's over, Phèdre."

She touched the naked hollow at the base of her throat, not looking at me. "I know."

Although it went against the grain, I sent for Fortun after the meeting and requested a boon. Amongst all of Phèdre's Boys, I placed the most trust in him. I bade him take extra care to ensure that he or one of the others he trusted kept a discreet guard on her at all times until the Lady Melisande Shahrizai's execution at dawn tomorrow.

"Of course. We always do, even when you don't ask." Fortun frowned at me. "What's different?"

I considered my answer. "Melisande was a patron."

"Oh."

It didn't begin to explain. "Not just any patron. The patron who paid her debt-bond and gave Phèdre her freedom. Before trading her to the Skaldi rather than killing her."

"*Oh.*"

I glanced toward Phèdre, who was facilitating a conversation between Ysandre and Drustan. "She'll want to be left alone today, as much as possible, anyway. And today of all days, I think it's best if I do so."

Fortune nodded. "I understand. Joscelin . . . will she want to attend the execution tomorrow?"

Blessed Elua have mercy, it hadn't occurred to me. "I'll be there if she does."

It troubled me throughout the day, never far from my thoughts. I wished the business were over and done so that we might truly put it behind us—or at least as far behind us as the passage of time would allow. None of this could be undone. Melisande Shahrizai's death wouldn't restore Alcuin and Anafiel Delaunay or their household. It wouldn't change Hyacinthe's lonely fate. There was an obscene trail of innocent lives lost in the wake of Melisande's machinations.

Not hers alone, to be sure. Isidore d'Aiglemort and Waldemar Selig sought to seize the realm for their own purposes. But they had meted out their bitter justice on each other, and it was a fitting fate.

Now it was Melisande's turn. I would take no joy in the manner of her death, but I couldn't pretend I wasn't grateful that her existence was ended.

I left Phèdre in the hospital wards that night. Although she had no formal training in medicine, one of the chirurgeon's assistants had taught her a few simple skills. Most importantly, she was good at listening to others. The Cruithne and the Dalriada among the gravely injured were especially grateful, often unable to communicate with those trying to aid them. And for those who feared they might never leave the plains of Troyes-le-Mont, Phèdre transcribed letters for their loved ones on whatever bits of paper she could scavenge. It brought them comfort, and her, too. Anything we were able to do to alleviate the suffering created by this war brought a measure of solace.

By the time the moon was high overhead, Phèdre was still wide awake, sitting with a feverish young Dalriadan who was clutching her hand and muttering as he went in and out of sleep. I found a quiet corner to catch a few hours' sleep of my own.

I was awakened by Ti-Philippe in the darkness before the dawn, on my feet and reaching for my daggers in a heartbeat. "What is it?"

"That woman sent for her," he said. "I didn't think it was my place to stop her. But our lady's been on the battlements since."

It took a moment to tease out his meaning: Melisande had asked to see Phèdre. Phèdre had gone to see her, then retired to the ramparts.

I sighed and went to her.

Another long night, another bloody dawn. A pair of the Queen's Guard greeted me and pointed me toward Phèdre, standing alone at the parapet and watching the stars fade in the east. I stood for a moment simply watching her until I saw the slight shift in the angle of her head that meant she knew I was there.

"You went to see her," I said. "Why?"

"I don't know." Phèdre turned to face me. "I suppose I owed her that much. Joscelin . . ." She searched my eyes, trying to find a way to explain it. "There are things I will never be able to forget. And there will be times when I need to try."

"I know." I stood beside her, not touching her. A god's chosen, marked by the prick of Kushiel's Dart. That scarlet mote was the seal on a puzzle box of dark and thorny desire that only Melisande Shahrizai had ever fully opened. It would always be there, as much a part of her as blood and bone. It was not for me to open. "You know that I could never hurt you, even if you asked it of me?"

"I know." Taking my arm, she squeezed it hard against her. "We've survived thirty thousand Skaldi and the wrath of the Master of the Straits. We ought to be able to survive each other."

I laughed because it was true. Phèdre pressed her face against my chest and I held her. It didn't matter what the puzzle box contained because her heart was mine. I held the whole of her in my arms and awaited the laden approach of dawn. As difficult as it would be, I felt a measure of ease in her body as the first hazy fingers of gold began spidering over the crests of the distant foothills.

It was then that we heard shouting.

A company of the Queen's Guard spilled out of the towers and onto the ramparts, questioning the guards on night watch with hands on hilts. Recognizing their captain by the insignia on his tunic, I caught him in passing. "What's happened?"

"They were to execute the Lady Melisande Shahrizai at dawn," the captain said in a grim tone. "She's gone."

CHAPTER SIXTY-THREE

It would prove a mystery in the end. Sometime between moonrise and dawn, Melisande Shahrizai sent for Phèdre. They spoke for no more than a quarter of an hour, after which Phèdre retired to the battlements. She remained there until Ti-Philippe woke me. When the guards came to escort Melisande to her execution, they found an empty cell. Two guardsmen and the keeper of the postern gate were dead.

There were no clues. Someone had assisted the traitoress Melisande Shahrizai in her escape. No one was immune from suspicion.

Ysandre was furious, and rightfully so. She had the fortress searched from cellar to rooftop and nigh overturned every broken stone of the much-abused outer fortifications. She sent out scouting parties. She had everyone who was at liberty that night in the fortress itself interrogated—including Phèdre and me, the very witnesses whose testimony had condemned Melisande in the first place.

For that, the Queen did apologize.

I was glad, though, that I'd made sure Fortun and the lads had kept an eye on Phèdre and were able to corroborate her story, especially as days passed and it became increasingly evident that Melisande Shahrizai had well and truly vanished on the eve of her execution. I was glad, too, that Ysandre didn't know that Phèdre's initial response to the news of Melisande's disappearance was hysterical laughter.

I didn't ask until days later when the search had officially been declared futile. "What did she say to you that night?"

"Not much." Phèdre's mouth twisted. "I think she just wanted me to know that even after everything, I still answer to her call."

"Do you?" I asked.

She didn't answer. "I asked her *why*. I wanted to know why she did it, all of it. Do you know what she said, Joscelin? She said, 'Because I could.'"

"Were you expecting a better answer?" I inquired wryly. "An answer that would make sense to you?"

"Truly?" Phèdre thought about it. "No."

It is a hard thing to see a woman put to the sword; I'd been shocked by Drustan mab Necthana's unexpectedly swift and violent dispatch of his father's wife upon her condemnation. Nonetheless, I'd have sooner seen Melisande Shahrizai meet a brutal death than to vanish and live to plot another day, especially since she couldn't have managed this without aid. Someone else in the fortress that night was a traitor.

Whoever it was, they had blood on their hands; but whoever it was, they'd covered their tracks well. She was gone.

With reluctance, the Queen's Council was forced to confront the fact that there were far more pressing matters at hand than tracking one fugitive noblewoman. For now, the only punishment Melisande would be forced to endure was whatever exile she had established in the event that her plans to found an empire went awry.

In the meanwhile I prayed this put an end to Melisande Shahrizai's machinations, because I don't think anyone but Phèdre truly understood how instrumental she'd been in setting the wheels of war in motion.

What had Selwyn said so long ago? *After all, she's just a woman.*

The Cassiline Brotherhood had a lot to learn about women.

In late summer, when the grapes were ripening on the vine and the air was full of the scent of lavender and the sound of honeybees, Queen Ysandre held a formal ceremony of gratitude in preparation for relocating the throne to its proper seat in the Royal Palace of the City of Elua. She restored sovereignty of the fortress and its holdings to the Duchese de Troyes-le-Mont, who had taken sanctuary in Marsilikos for the duration of the war. She arranged for reparations to the families of the fallen and for all the villagers and crofters who had seen their lands trampled and goods seized by Skaldi invaders and Terre d'Ange's defenders alike, and for the restoration of Naamah's temples.

With the most urgent business settled, Ysandre de la Courcel's wartime court and its noble allies made an official victory procession to the City.

A week's journey took two, for word of our deeds had spread while we were at Troyes-le-Mont. At every village we passed through, folk lined the roads and threw flowers in tribute, offering their blessings to the victorious young Queen. And they came, too, to see the Cruarch of Alba, the heroic foreign ruler pledged to wed Ysandre. They came to see Drustan and the woad-tattooed Cruithne in their fierce barbarian majesty, the proud warriors of the Dalriada with their tall crests of hair and war-chariots out of an ancient legend. Phèdre and I often rode alongside Grainne's chariot, offering what solace and companionship we might.

Both of us forbore to tell Ysandre that the bloodstained sack hanging from the Lady of the Dalriada's chariot contained her brother Eamonn's head preserved in lime so that she might bring it home to Innisclan.

In the City of Elua, our progress slowed to a crawl as the citizens of the entire city turned out to greet us. It was a far more sparsely populated city than the one I'd entered a year ago. Sickness and war had taken their toll. But for the first time, entering the City of Elua felt like a homecoming.

And it was a joyful one.

The first order of business in the aftermath of the victory of our united realms would be Ysandre and Drustan's wedding. To that end, the Queen kept Phèdre in her service as her ambassadress and translator. We were provided with our own suite of rooms in the Palace, which resolved the matter of a place to live for now. I was fitted for livery in Courcel midnight blue in a style that hewed close to the familiar cut of Cassiline greys.

A steady stream of couturières and maquillage artists tended to Phèdre's wardrobe and appearance. I'm fairly sure she bathed at least twice a day during our first week of enjoying royal largesse.

Thelesis de Mornay, the Queen's Poet, was the first guest to call upon us. With her she brought Cecilie Laveau-Perrin, a legendary courtesan. She had retired from the Night Court many years ago, but even as a child in the mountains of Siovale, I remembered hearing her name. A friend of Delaunay's, she had served as Phèdre and Alcuin's mentor in Naamah's arts. There was a tremendous kindness and grace to Cecilie, and I had grown enough in my understanding of human nature to know that it was those qualities far more than physical beauty or skills in the bedchamber that made a great courtesan.

It was her gentle presence and the reminder of less troubled times that undid Phèdre for the first time since the leaderless Skaldi had fled the battlefield. She flung her arms around Cecilie's neck and wept unashamed; the latter stroked her back and murmured meaningless reassurances.

"Forgive me, my lady." Composing herself, Phèdre wiped her eyes. "It's been a long journey."

"Phèdre, child." Cecilie took her face in her hands, kissed her brow. "Few of Naamah's Servants ever truly know what it is like to walk in her footsteps." I was uncertain how to behave in the face of such a naked display of emotion, but Cecilie put me at ease. "Such a beautiful young man, Joscelin Verreuil," she said, taking my hands. "And a true hero, too." Smiling, she tapped one of my vambraces. "Never let it be said Naamah lacks a sense of humor."

I could feel myself blush, but I laughed and bowed to her. "I'll accept such a compliment from the Queen of Night-Blooming Flowers."

"Truly, Elua's blessing is on this day," Thelesis de Mornay said in her melodious poet's voice. "For all that is lost, so much is won."

It was a simple, eloquent truth.

Terre d'Ange was ready for a celebration. There was mourning to be done, but there was rejoicing, too. Nobles whose Houses had proved their loyalty to the Queen flaunted their invitations to the royal wedding; others vied with each other to curry favor. Ateliers began creating attire that did homage to our new Alban allies, incorporating accents of Dalriadan plaid and embroidery that echoed the intricate lines of Cruithne tattoos.

Queen Ysandre sought Phèdre's counsel on all of these matters and others; most of which, Phèdre confided to me, had naught to do with facilitating communications. Ysandre de la Courcel was a crowned monarch presiding over the greatest military victory in a generation, but she was also a young woman facing her impending wedding day. She intended to enjoy every ounce of ceremony, and she needed someone to share the pleasure of planning the intimate details of the event.

"I don't think she's ever had a girlfriend near her own age before," Phèdre mused, then paused. "Nor have I."

I understood. I'd never had a friendship quite like the one I'd had with Selwyn. I didn't imagine I ever would.

In honor of the one longstanding friendship that had sustained her since childhood, Phèdre made good on a promise to Hyacinthe. Facing an eternity of exile, Hyacinthe had still thought to write out a deed to his mother's house and his livery stable business to give to Emile, the second-in-command of his crew. It was on a bit of scraped vellum Phèdre had kept ever since the Straits. Emile kissed her hands and wept with gratitude and sorrow, and I was embarrassed to think how quick I'd been to judge Hyacinthe as a shallow popinjay.

Though Blessed Elua knows, he'd been just as quick to gauge me a Cassiline prig. And neither of us were wholly wrong.

It wasn't easy to find time for such personal matters with Phèdre at the Queen's beck and call, but she kept another promise, too. After some persuasion and Cecilie Laveau-Perrin's influence, the Dowayne of Cereus House, First among the Thirteen Houses, agreed to open the doors of the Night Court to the survivors of Phèdre's Boys. Since there were only fifteen of them, I rather thought the Night Court got a bargain for the goodwill it created.

There was one last promise that Phèdre had made to Hyacinthe. We made an offering in his mother's name at the great temple of Elua.

It was the first time I'd set foot in a temple since that fateful Longest Night. A pair of acolytes greeted us in the vestibule. They bade us sit upon one of the ancient carved benches and knelt to remove our boots and shoes and stockings that we might approach the altar unshod. The Great Temple of Elua in the City is the oldest temple in the whole of the realm. As with other temples, it lay open to the skies. A tall pillar stood at every corner, though there were oak trees that had grown taller than the marble pillars, their leafy crowns breaching the roofless space.

Phèdre presented the acolytes with a pouch of coin. Elua's blessing was given freely, but gifts were traditional and this was a generous one. In return, we were given posies of scarlet anemone for our offering.

Together, Phèdre and I crossed the grounds of the sanctum. Wildflowers and weeds grew rambling among the oaks. The air smelled of damp soil, oak wood, the sweet, delicate fragrance of the anemone.

I had expected Elua's effigy to be a more ornate depiction, in keeping with the City's elegance and sophistication, but it was simply wrought. The lines were as old and elemental as the effigy in the Prefectory, the scale more vast. Elua stood three times larger than life, the moss-streaked lines of his face calm and serene. His arms were open, palms outward, fingers spread in blessing. His effigy stood upon a low plinth, and the marble of Elua's carved feet was smooth and shiny where generation upon generation of D'Angelines had pressed their lips in prayer.

I did so now, laying my posy of anemone on the plinth. I knelt and bowed, kissing the worn stone.

Like hope, Elua's love endured.

Dampness seeped through the knees of my breeches as I knelt and sat on my heels. Beside me, Phèdre placed her offering on the plinth. Scarlet petals spilled across the veined white marble stone. She murmured a prayer in honor of Hyacinthe's mother, then bowed her head, kneeling in silence.

Together, we prayed for all of those lost to us along the way—and I prayed, too, for those who survived, that we might make every sacrifice worthwhile. We stayed there until a robed priest came smiling toward us, his hem softly brushing the long grasses, a flutter of dusty-winged moths rising in his wake. I rose to greet him with alacrity.

"Cassiel's child, do not rush," the priest said, hands in the sleeves of his robe. Beneath the murmuring green shade of the trees, his gaze was filled with secrets hiding like speckled trout in a deep forest pool. "You have stood at the crossroads and chosen, and like Cassiel, you will ever stand at the crossroads and choose, choose again and again, the path of the Companion. The choice lies ever within you, the crossroads and the way, and Elua's commandment to point you on it."

Love as thou wilt.

I looked at Phèdre's bowed profile. She rose and the priest smiled, oak leaf shadows casting a pattern on his brow as he touched her cheek. "Kushiel's Dart and Naamah's Servant. Love as thou wilt, and Elua will ever guide your steps."

Bowing to us both, the priest took his leave.

Phèdre laughed softly when he'd gone. "It seems my time for dire prophecy has passed."

"You can have mine," I said to her. "It seems *I'm* doomed to make the same choice a thousand times over."

She looked up at me with vulnerability. "Are you sorry?"

"No." I shook my head, feeling my hair loose. "No," I whispered a second time, taking Phèdre's face in my hands and kissing her. I felt her catch her breath, her lips parting as she slid her hands beneath my hair, around my neck. I pulled her against me. "But there will likely be times that I am."

"Likely there will," she agreed, a sparkle in her eyes. "As long as it's not now."

"No." I smiled at her. "Not now."

Not then and not later. That night, Phèdre and I made love for the first time since the gods had flung us together and given shelter to our half-frozen wounded bodies and let us knit our shattered selves together.

This was different.

It was as the priest had said: I had chosen this path. I'd stood at the crossroads and chosen my fate. I'd chosen the path of the Perfect Companion. I stood at the crossroads and Cassiel was the sun setting at my back, casting my shadow before me; I stood at the crossroads and Cassiel was the rising sun at my face. I turned to my right and my left, and Cassiel's presence was as real as the hilts of my daggers.

I chose.

I chose Phèdre nó Delaunay, and for all that she was Kushiel's Chosen, for all that she was Naamah's Servant with a marque of thorny splendor echoing the crimson prick of the mark of a god's sign, for all that she had endured slavery in Skaldia, sung the Master of the Straits to calm, and led a foreign army across the sea to victory, she was still a girl. She was a girl with fair skin, dark hair, and delicate features, with lips that always looked ready for kissing and eyes that dared almost anyone to try it. And there were many who had and likely more who would do so. We were who we were and served the gods we did. But there was one thing Phèdre would never be to anyone else.

Our bodies sang like harpstrings tuned to the same note. Buried deep inside her, I whispered the word in her ear. "Mine."

She opened her eyes, and whispered it back. "Yours."

EPILOGUE

It would have been enough.

After our visit to the temple, I was in as calm a state as circumstances allowed. There were questions that would need to be resolved at some point, but for now, Ysandre considered Phèdre's services indispensable and our tenure as denizens of the Palace was open-ended. "I'd no idea there were so many monumental decisions involved in a royal wedding," I said to Phèdre when a frantic page summoned her. "What is it today?"

"There's pressing diplomatic business at hand. It's somewhat to do with Grainne's wedding attire." She stooped to kiss me in passing. "After all, we want to do justice to the Lady of the Dalriada."

I had some business at the smithy that day—my weapons hadn't been given a proper edge for far too long. With Phèdre attending the Queen, for the first time in long months I had no urgent concerns for her safety. There was a high degree of watchfulness among the guard with Melisande Shahrizai's disappearance an unsolved mystery and one or more traitors in our midst, which boded well for security. And, oddly, I doubted Melisande had any intention of taking revenge on Phèdre for giving the testimony that condemned her. Melisande was gracious in defeat.

Anything else would have been . . . petty.

Mayhap it lulled me into a false sense of reassurance, for I was startled when Phèdre stumbled into our chambers in search of me later that day, looking wide-eyed and feverish. "What is it?" I caught her arm. "Are you all right?"

"No!" She swallowed hard. "I'm a peer of the realm."

I stared at her. "What?"

It was true.

It took some time for Phèdre to get the words out to explain properly, but once the issue with Lady Grainne's tailoring was settled, Ysandre had summoned the Chancellor of the Exchequer to speak to Phèdre regarding Anafiel Delaunay's estate as casually as though she'd invited them to enjoy an afternoon cordial.

"Alcuin and I were formally adopted into his household," she said. "But I didn't realize Delaunay had named us his heirs."

I frowned in thought. "But he wasn't—"

"Montrève." She interrupted me, rubbing her face. "Delaunay never held the title, it went to his cousin after his father disinherited him. But his mother added a codicil. If the cousin died without issue, Montrève was to revert to Delaunay or his heirs. And . . . and that's what happened."

Montrève; Elua have mercy, it was in Siovale. My father had known the Comte de Montrève, he'd said as much to Phèdre. "Delaunay's kinsman died without issue?" I asked carefully to make sure I understood aright.

Phèdre nodded. "He was killed in the fighting at Troyes-le-Mont."

I opened my mouth, then closed it. "And you're telling me that you're the Comtesse de Montrève."

"Yes."

I offered a deep Cassiline bow. "Well met, my lady. How may I serve you?"

So it was as the Comtesse de Montrève and her escort that Phèdre and I attended the royal wedding of Ysandre de la Courcel, Queen of Terre d'Ange, and Drustan mab Necthana, the Cruarch of Alba.

The ceremony took place in the vast Palace gardens beneath a bower of intertwining roses that included the fragrant, sprawling roses of Terre d'Ange with the more delicate Alban variety. Ysandre was a D'Angeline vision in periwinkle silk with blue forget-me-nots lending a dainty note to her elaborate coiffure; and yes, I took care to notice and appreciate these small niceties on such a momentous occasion. Drustan's red cloak of state had been re-created in sumptuous velvet with a satin lining and his gold torque shone against the brown skin of his throat.

An elderly priestess of Elua with beautiful silver-grey hair that fell like a river down her back performed the ritual. When she had done, Drustan and Ysandre clasped hands and stood together before the realm as Cruarch and Queen; but they kissed as lover and beloved. Everyone in attendance cheered, and in the streets of the City beyond the Palace, they took up the cry from the meanest docks to the heights of the Night Court; bells rang out carrying the news beyond the white walls of the City of Elua, and all across the land, D'Angelines celebrated love.

There was a lengthy state dinner upon the greensward with wine and song and dancing and toasts. When Grainne delivered one of the latter in memory of her brother Eamonn, Phèdre leaned over half-drunk with mirth and spirits to confide that the problem with the Lady of the Dalriada's attire was that she was with child and her measurements were changing almost daily.

I eyed Grainne with awe. "Did she know?"

"She wasn't sure at the time," Phèdre whispered, laughing in my ear. "She's quite sure it's Admiral Rousse's!"

"That," I said, "will be a very boisterous child."

By the end of the night, I was more than a little bit drunk, too, my mouth ablaze with the icy sweetness of *joie*. It was a magical night, and everything seemed brighter and brimming with life and love. I danced with Phèdre, drawing on long-ago childhood lessons, and watched her dance and flirt with men and women alike. I danced with Cecilie Laveau-Perrin, who taught me more about flirting in the time it took for the musicians to play a single tune than I'd learned in my whole life. I politely refused a number of advances, some of which were merely gambits to see if the Cassiline apostate was fair game.

I was not.

But it gave me a quiet hum of pleasure nonetheless, and it tickled me to see Phèdre's eyes glint with jealousy and amusement.

I think there must have been no one asleep for the whole of that night in the City of Elua. Somewhere in the small hours Ysandre and Drustan made their retreat and the great throng of revelers followed them as far as the doors of her chambers, singing songs, shouting well wishes, and throwing rose petals until her Cassiline Guards turned us grimly away.

"Shame on you, Brother," one of them muttered at me.

I paused. "I beg your pardon?"

"Joscelin!" Phèdre turned back, tugging my arm, rose petals in her hair. "Oh." Her voice changed. "I see."

I bowed. "They were merely bidding us a good evening. Isn't that so, messires?"

After a few heartbeats, both bowed stiffly in response. I recognized the tenor of the gesture all too well. It was the rigid bow one offers when pride makes it hard to bend one's neck. But neither of them were minded to argue with me, which was good since the last thing I wanted to do was fight a Cassiline Brother. It was the only sour note, but it was one I would think about another day. Cassiel in his inhuman compassion had gifted his servant with a great many things to consider. For now, I was content to watch the sun rise over the City of Elua with the world's least likely heroine wrapped in my arms.

I had a secret.

I *knew* Phèdre nó Delaunay. For now, she was content to watch the sunrise in my arms. Tomorrow, our world would shift as Queen and Cruarch set their faces toward the future and the governance of our realms. There were legal, financial, and practical details to be sorted before Phèdre took official possession of the estate of Montrève. There was the matter of Phèdre's Boys, three of whom had made formal requests to serve as men-at-arms for the newly appointed Comtesse de Montrève.

There was a great deal to be done.

But once it was done, Phèdre's thoughts would turn toward the riddle-within-a-riddle that the Master of the Straits posed. Hyacinthe had solved the riddle of his existence, but the *dromonde* couldn't see what came before. Who was the angel Rahab, so punished for pride and disobedience that Adonai cast him into the watery depths of this mortal world and bound him there? Could the curse be broken?

If there was an answer, it would lie in the lore of the Habiru, the Yeshuite folk to whom Adonai sent his son, who in turn begot Blessed Elua—I had studied it a bit at the Prefectory. Delaunay's library had been sold when his properties were seized, but it might contain valuable research that could be retrieved. It would be a starting place.

And if it ended with Phèdre nó Delaunay knocking on Heaven's gates or picking the lock and stealing through them, I'd be there beside her.

Phèdre craned her head, trying to see my face in the golden light of dawn. "What are you smiling at?"

I smiled down at her. "You."